P9-BZZ-507

# *Praise for the novels of JoAnn Ross*

## *THE CALLAHAN BROTHERS TRILOGY*

***BLUE BAYOU***
***RIVER ROAD***
***MAGNOLIA MOON***

"The talent for storytelling is obviously embedded deep in Ms. Ross's bones."
—*Romantic Times*, Top Pick

"[I]rresistible. . . . A delicious read with a vast array of zany characters to keep you glued to the pages."
—*Rendezvous*

"The touching love stor[ies] . . . and unforgettable characters create a marvelous read you can't put down."
—*Old Book Barn Gazette*

"Sexual sparks fly. . . . Covering terrain similar to that of Nora Roberts's Irish trilogies, Ross spins a warm romance amid a setting loaded with charm."
—*Publishers Weekly*

## *OUT OF THE MIST*

"The story's robust momentum and lively characters make this a fun, energetic read."

—*Publishers Weekly*

"A great afternoon read. . . . I'm looking forward to the remaining sisters' stories!"

—*Old Book Barn Gazette*

"Ross weaves the search for the missing family treasure and the growing attraction between two creative spirits with aplomb in this charming romance."

—*BookPage*

## *FAIR HAVEN*

"Not only does JoAnn Ross provide her usual impressive blend of tender warmth and fascinating characters, but she also adds a colorful dash of the supernatural."

—*Romantic Times*

"As magical as Ireland itself. . . . A masterpiece of writing from the heart. Storytelling at its all-time best."

—*The Belles and Beaux of Romance*

## *FAR HARBOR*

"A profoundly moving story of intense emotional depth, satisfying on every level. You won't want to leave this family."

—CompuServe Romance Reviews

"A wonderful relationship drama in which JoAnn Ross splendidly describes love the second time around."

—Barnesandnoble.com

## *HOMEPLACE*

"This engrossing story of love's healing power will draw you in from the first. . . . A great read."

—*Old Book Barn Gazette*

"Like cherished silver, *Homeplace* just shines!"

—*Romantic Times*, Barnes and Noble Top Pick

**Books by JoAnn Ross**

Blaze
Homeplace
Far Harbor
Fair Haven
Legends Lake
Blue Bayou
River Road
Magnolia Moon
Out of the Mist
Out of the Blue
Out of the Storm

Available from POCKET BOOKS

# JoAnn Ross

# The Callahan Brothers Trilogy

POCKET BOOKS
New York London Toronto Sydney

The sale of this book without its cover is unauthorized. If you purchased this book without a cover, you should be aware that it was reported to the publisher as "unsold and destroyed." Neither the author nor the publisher has received payment for the sale of this "stripped book."

POCKET BOOKS, a division of Simon & Schuster, Inc.
1230 Avenue of the Americas, New York, NY 10020

This book is a work of fiction. Names, characters, places and incidents are products of the author's imagination or are used fictitiously. Any resemblance to actual events or locales or persons, living or dead, is entirely coincidental.

*Blue Bayou* copyright © 2002 by The Ross Family Trust
*River Road* copyright © 2002 by The Ross Family Trust
*Magnolia Moon* copyright © 2003 by The Ross Family Trust

All rights reserved, including the right to reproduce this book or portions thereof in any form whatsoever.
For information address Pocket Books, 1230 Avenue of the Americas, New York, NY 10020

ISBN: 1-4165-0735-3

This Pocket Books trade paperback edition January 2005

10 9 8 7 6 5 4 3

POCKET and colophon are registered trademarks of Simon & Schuster, Inc.

Manufactured in the United States of America

For information regarding special discounts for bulk purchases, please contact Simon & Schuster Special Sales at 1-800-456-6798 or business@simonandschuster.com

These titles were previously published individually by Pocket Books.

# Contents

# Blue Bayou

*To Christy Marchand, who took me to Nottaway,*
*and my guys, Jay and Patrick, with whom I've*
*passed many a good time,*
*and last, but never least, Marisa and Parker Ryan Ross,*
*the* lagniappe *in my life.*

# 1

*The moon hung full* and low and bloodred over the bayou as Jack Callahan sat out on the *gallerie* of the crumbling plantation house, working on a bottle of whiskey that wasn't working on him. It had been a sweltering day, and even at midnight the air, which smelled of damp brick and night-blooming jasmine, dripped with moisture.

The old swing squeaked as he slowly swayed; an alligator glided silently across water the color of burgundy wine, its eyes gleaming in the dark like yellow headlights.

A mist that wasn't quite rain began to fall as he watched the storm gather out over the Gulf and thought back to the night when Beau Soleil had resembled a huge white wedding cake. A night when music floated on the sultry summer air, fairy lights strung through the limbs of the chinaberry trees twinkled like fireflies, and white candles anchored in fake water lilies glowed invitingly on the smooth turquoise surface of the pool water.

White jacketed waiters had circulated with trays of mint juleps and flutes of French champagne while belles in tulle and taffeta danced magnolia-scented nights away. The girls had been mouth-wateringly pretty in airy flowered dresses that showed off their tanned shoulders and long slender legs. And Danielle Dupree had outshone them all.

*Danielle*. He lifted the bottle to his lips; flames slid down his throat. You'd think, after all these years, he'd be immune to the closest thing Blue Bayou had ever had to a princess. But the memory of that night created a rush of molten heat hotter than any the Jack Daniel's could stoke. He'd known, of course, that he had no business wanting her.

"Never have been any good at taking your own counsel, you," he muttered, slipping back into the Cajun patois he'd spoken growing up among his mother's people.

Celibacy was not an easy virtue at any age. For a testosterone-driven eighteen-year-old kid coming off nine long months banished to a last-chance, hard-time military-styled lockup for delinquents, it was damn near impossible. Especially when the girl in question had recklessly, for that brief, shining time, wanted him, too.

Those crazy days and hot nights were, as his daddy used to say, yesterday's ball score. He might not have ended up on Angola's death row, like Judge Dupree had warned, but he'd definitely gone to hell like so many in Blue Bayou had predicted.

"Gone to hell and lived to remember it."

He was no longer viewed as the devil of Blue Bayou. Even *The Cajun Clarion* had picked up a quote from *The New York Times Book Review* declaring him a new generation's Joseph Wambaugh. Thanks to all those folks in Hollywood, who threw money around like confetti, he now owned the crown jewel of Louisianan antebellum homes. Not that it was much of a jewel at the moment, but he, more than most, knew outward appearances could be deceiving.

During his years as an undercover drug agent, he'd become a chameleon, able to move among the movers and shakers at a Beverly Hills dinner party one night, while the next night would find him working the street scene in Tijuana, then with only a change of clothes and syntax, he'd be hanging out at the beach, listening to surfer songs and making deals and subsequent busts beneath the Huntington Beach pier.

Outwardly his appearance hadn't changed all that much since his undercover days. He still tied his thick black hair in the same ponytail at the nape of his neck and the gold earring served as a daily reminder that trying to outrun your past was an exercise in futility. But even these leftovers from his former life didn't tell the entire story.

A casual observer would never suspect that his mind was a seething cauldron of drug dealers, strung-out hookers chasing their next high, crooked cops, and hard-eyed kids who lost their innocence before their baby teeth.

Scenes flashed through his mind like movie trailers set to fast forward: the wasted body of a Guadalajara whore, her nose still wet from sniffing cocaine; a nine-month-old baby killed in his crib by a drive-by shooting in El Paso; a fourteen-year-old girl in Las Vegas traded by her mother to a biker gang for a weekend's worth of methamphetamine and black tar heroin.

And if those Technicolor memories didn't cause mental black clouds to gather overhead, there was always Jack's personal golden oldie: blood blossoming like a garden of scarlet poppies across the front of a lace-trimmed, white silk nightgown.

Even now, guilt slashed at him like a razor. *Don't get personally involved.* That had been rule one of the job. A rule he'd broken once in his life, with fatal consequences.

The fact that he'd nearly died as well did nothing to soothe his conscience or wash the blood from his hands.

"You didn't have any choice," Jack tried telling himself what the investigators who'd been waiting for him when he'd come out of surgery the next day had told him. He hadn't been in any mood to listen. Not then. Not now. The fact was, he'd screwed up. Big time.

During the years away from Louisiana, Jack had developed the ability to live in the moment, which was handy when your life could come to a sudden, violent end at any time. The covert activities he'd carried out all over the world had been as dangerous as they were secretive, and when they were completed, he shed the more unsavory aspects of his career along with whatever identity he'd taken on, leaving them behind in his dark and murky past.

And then, as always, he moved on.

Some of those who'd worked with him had called him crazy. Others proclaimed him a reckless cowboy. Still others accused him of having a death wish and refused to work with him again.

Jack hadn't much cared what anyone thought. Until he'd held up his former partner's trembling, black-clad widow while she stoically accepted the American flag that had been draped over her husband's mahogany casket.

Back from the dead, he'd turned in his snazzy government badge and his Glock semiautomatic, then walked away from a guaranteed salary, health benefits, and a pension he hadn't believed he'd live long enough to collect, retreating to the isolation of the moss-draped, foggy Louisiana bayou, where he didn't have to worry about being blown away if his Louisiana Cajun accent suddenly came out, blowing his cover story, whatever the hell it was that day.

It was only then that Jack realized he'd been playing at roles for so many years, he'd not only lost his soul, but any sense of who he was.

The first three months, spent in alcohol-sodden oblivion, passed by in a blur. Jack's only vivid memory of those early days after his homecoming was the night he'd hit rock bottom and ended up floating aimlessly through the swamp in his pirogue, stewed to the gills, the barrel of a .38 pressed against the roof of his mouth.

It would have been so damn easy to pull the trigger. *Too* easy, he'd decided, hurling the revolver into the water. The idealistic altar boy who'd confessed his childish digressions every Saturday afternoon at Blue Bayou's Church of the Holy Assumption Jack had been amazed to discover still lurking somewhere deep inside him required penance for adult sins.

Shortly after choosing life over suicide, he'd awakened from a three-day binge, pulled an old legal pad from its long-ago hiding place beneath a floorboard, and begun to write. A week later he'd discovered that while he couldn't exorcise all his old ghosts, he could hold them somewhat at bay by putting them down on paper.

Still working on instinct, when he ran out of clean pages, he went into town, bought an old Smith Corona manual typewriter at a secondhand store—electricity tended to go out a lot in the swamp—and reams of paper. After returning to the camp, he settled down to work, and with words flooding out from too-long-ignored emotional wounds, he wrote like a man possessed.

Things probably would have stopped there if an old friend, who, concerned about his welfare, hadn't ventured out into the swamp to check on him. When he found him sleeping like the dead he'd once longed to be and read the pages piled up on every flat surface, he'd convinced Jack to send them to a New York agent he knew.

Three months later Jack had received the life-altering call offering to buy his first—and decidedly uneven—novel about an alcoholic, burned-out, suicidal DEA agent. Eighteen months after that he'd hit the publishing jackpot when *The Death Dealer* soared to the top of every best-seller list in the country.

Now wealthier than he'd ever dreamed, he spent his days working up a sweat wielding crowbars, claw hammers, and axes, clearing away the kudzu that was threatening to consume the house, tearing apart crumbling foundations, ripping off rotted shingles.

When it grew too dark to work, he passed sleepless nights pounding computer keys, reliving those dark and violent memories that had amazingly also found a huge international audience.

He should have been in tall cotton, but since moving into Beau Soleil's *garconnière*, originally constructed as quarters for the young men of the plantation house, Jack had been haunted by memories which lingered like bits of Spanish moss clinging to a long-dead cypress.

He cursed viciously, then heard an answering whine. Glancing down, he viewed a mutt standing beneath one of the ancient oaks. She was a mess, her frame, long legs, and huge feet and head suggesting that she'd be about the size of a small horse if she hadn't been starved down to skin and bones. Ribs protruded from her sunken sides, her filthy fur was the color of dirty straw, and a nasty wound oozed across her muzzle.

"You and me, we got something in common, *chien femelle*. Two messed-up bayou strays."

She whined again but, seemingly encouraged by him talking to her, started slinking up the steps, her tail between her legs, limpid chocolate brown eyes hopeful.

"Christ, you're a sorry sight. Flea-bitten, too, I'll bet."

She dropped down on her haunches at his feet but was still able to look him in the eye.

"I suppose you want a handout."

She whined. Thumped her tail.

"Somethin' to eat?"

He'd obviously said the secret word. The tail began wagging to beat the band, revealing a remarkably optimistic nature for an animal who'd obviously had a helluva tough time.

"You can crash for the night. But I'm not looking for any long-term relationship here."

She barked. Once, twice, a third time. The expressive tail went into warp wag.

Shaking his head, Jack pushed himself to his feet and crunched across the oyster-shell drive to the *garconnière*, the dog so close on his heels she was nudging the back of his legs.

The contents of his refrigerator were not encouraging. "We've got two six-packs, a half-empty carton of milk I'm not gonna vouch for, and a brick of something green I think used to be cheese."

It was always this way when he was deep in a book. Worse when he was fighting with uncooperative characters as he'd been the past days. He'd forego sleep. Forget to eat, shower, shave. Hell, the entire planet could blow itself to smithereens, but if he was writing, he probably wouldn't notice until he lost power to his laptop.

Despite his warning, the dog's sharp bark suggested she was willing to take her chances.

"Wait a minute." He unearthed a dish from behind the beer, sniffed it, and tried to remember how many days it had been sitting in there.

"You like crawfish jambalaya?"

She barked again. Pranced, her nails clicking on the heart-of-cypress floor.

"Guess that's a yes."

After she'd wolfed the seasoned rice and crawfish down, Jack retrieved a bottle of hydrogen peroxide from the bathroom and cleaned the dog's wound. It had to have stung like the devil, but she sat perfectly still, staring at him with those big brown trusting eyes.

"Don't get used to it. Because tomorrow you and I are takin' a visit to the animal shelter."

The dog taken care of, he took the six-pack over to the old wooden kitchen table that had been handcrafted with trees milled from Beau Soleil's back woods. Those earlier thoughts of Danielle's birthday ball had stirred his balky muse, throwing up a series of *what-ifs* that seemed promising.

What if, he asked himself as he popped the top on one of the bottles, the aging drug kingpin had a daughter? A young woman as distant and unreachable as a star. A woman the alcoholic DEA agent—who was trying to bring her father down—was inexorably drawn to, even knowing it was suicide?

By the time a soft lavender predawn light was shimmering on the horizon, he'd worked his way through the six-pack, and the ceramic crawfish ashtray was piled high with cigarette butts, but the computer screen was filled with new scenes. Jack saved them onto his hard drive, pushed back from the table, staggered into the adjoining room, and crashed on the unmade bed.

As the dog sprawled onto the floor at the foot of the bed with a long satisfied sigh, Jack fell like a stone into sleep.

* * *

Danielle Dupree had always believed in fairy tales. And why not? After all, she'd grown up a princess in a storybook white-pillared plantation home, and even after bayou bad boy Jack Callahan broke her heart, she'd continued to believe in happily-ever-afters.

The only problem with fairy tales, she thought now as she lugged a heavy box of books out to her Volvo station wagon, was they didn't warn impressionable little girls that a few years down that Yellow Brick Road Prince Charming might decide to move into a new castle with a Vassar-educated princess who could better assist his career climb to king, subsequently die in a freak accident, and it'd be back to the ashes for Cinderella.

It had been a month since Lowell's death, yet it still was so strange to think of herself as a widow when she'd expected to be a divorcée.

Dani wasn't certain anyone deserved to have a piano drop on his head. Still, there was some irony in the fact that it happened to be Lowell's fiancée's gleaming white Steinway that had snapped its cable while the deliverymen were attempting to bring it in through the balcony French doors of their fifth-floor apartment.

Dani was, of course, sorry the man she'd married right out of college was dead. After all, he was her son's father. But still, she hadn't experienced any sense of grave personal loss. It certainly hadn't been as devastating as that fateful day nineteen months ago when a reporter from *The Washington Post* had called her and told her to turn on the six o'clock news.

Watching Congressman Lowell Dupree's press conference—held in the Watergate, where apparently he'd leased a cozy little love nest with his brunette barracuda chief of staff—Dani had been stunned to hear her husband tell the world that he was divorcing his wife.

Divorcing her.

Since he was the one who'd been so hot to set up housekeeping with another woman, Dani hadn't understood why he'd dragged their divorce out for eighteen long, contentious months during which time he'd raided their joint bank accounts, held back child support for the flimsiest of grounds that never held up in court, and refused to grant her lawyer access to financial records.

It was only after his death that Dani discovered her husband's high-flying venture into tech and Internet stocks had gone south, leaving him to die deeply in debt.

"Mom, I can't find my Hot Wheels."

"I packed them with your Hogwarts figures in the box with the orange stickers."

Her eight-old-son, Matt, was a die-hard Baltimore Orioles fan, which was why she'd assigned him orange in her moving-box color-coding system. She'd chosen red for herself, since it was supposed to be a power color, and she figured right now she needed all the help she could get.

"I forgot. Thanks, Mom."

"You're very welcome, darling." She drew a line through the box of books on her packing list.

Pleased to have averted a potential crisis, Dani returned to the house to strip the sheets off the king-size bed, which surprisingly hadn't proven at all lonely during the nineteen months she'd been sleeping by herself.

Three hours later the house was emptied, and her son was buckled into the backseat of the wagon with its READ vanity license plate.

"It feels funny not to be going to school," Matt said.

"I know, but you'll be in your new school in just a few days." Dani turned a corner and left the red brick Federal house—along with her former life—behind in the Volvo's rearview mirror. "Today we're going home."

# 2

*The day dawned hot* and drenched with humidity. Outside the open window a jay raucously scolded the rising sun, and the distant thrum of an outboard motor echoed from somewhere on the water. When a soft breath fanned against the back of his neck, every nerve in Jack's body went on alert.

There'd been a time when he would have been out of bed like a shot, weapon in hand, adrenaline racing through his veins. Now he forced his mind to calm and thought back to last night.

How much had he drunk? While there had admittedly been mornings in the past when he'd wake up in bed with some strange woman, unable to recall the events that had gotten them there, Jack knew this wasn't one of those times.

He'd been fighting his new book for a week. He remembered telling the construction crew not to interrupt him unless it had to do with blood—and a helluva lot of it—or fire. Then, shutting off the outside world, he'd waded back into battle with his rebellious characters.

He recalled taking a break last night, emerging from the isolation of his writer's cave to check out the work that had been done on the house. Satisfied at the progress, he'd been sitting on the *gallerie* when he'd started thinking about Danielle. Which was always a mistake, though probably inevitable since he was, after all, living in her house.

He remembered the bloodred moon. . . . The flashes of lightning out on the Gulf. . . . The croak of hidden bullfrogs. . . . The dog.

He turned his head, which some fiendish intruder had obviously split in half with a ragged ax while he'd been sleeping, and found himself staring straight into huge, adoring, crusted dark-rimmed eyes.

"I know damn well I didn't invite you up here."

Undeterred by his gritty tone, the mutt stretched her lanky frame. Then licked his face—a long wet slurp.

He wiped the back of his hand over his mouth, which tasted as if he'd sucked up all the mud in the entire Mississippi delta. "Didn't your *maman* ever warn you about climbing into a strange man's bed?"

As her tail thudded against the mattress, Jack wondered how many fleas she'd deposited in his sheets.

He crawled out of bed, allowing himself the indulgence of a few ragged groans that stopped just short of being whimpers. Bracing one hand against the wall, he dragged himself into the bathroom.

He blearily regarded the face in the mirror through eyes as red-veined as a Louisiana road map. He rubbed his hand over the heavy stubble of dark beard. "You should be writin' horror, you. 'Cause you're a dead ringer for *Loup Garou.*" The legendary shapeshifter was the bayou's answer to the Abominable snowman.

Whiskey, beer, and stale nicotine were seeping from his pores. Since it was a tossup which of them smelled worse, he debated dragging the dog into the shower with him, then decided not to bother. She'd get a bath along with her tick-dip at the shelter.

He steamed up the small bathroom, willing the pounding water to beat the poisons out of his aching body and continued to think back on last night. By the time he'd staggered to bed, the drug kingpin's daughter had begun spinning her deadly web for the DEA agent, and he'd unearthed his story's conflict. From here on in, it should be easy sailing.

Too bad he'd probably never finish it. Because odds were he'd be dead by noon.

The crew had already arrived and was at work on the roof of the big house, the drumming of hammers echoing the pounding in his head. Jack let the dog out the screen door, cringing against the squeak of the hinges he'd been meaning to oil for weeks, and watched her sniff around the base of one of the old oaks.

"That's good you're housebroken. It'll make it easier to find you a new family."

After drawing a glass of water from the tap, Jack swallowed three aspirins, then made coffee. He was waiting for what seemed like an interminably long time for the damn water to drip through the dark grounds when a high-pitched barking struck like an ice pick into the most delicate part of his brain.

"Hey, Jack," a male voice called. "Want to call off your mangy guard horse?"

"She's not mine." He pushed open the screen door again and vowed that if he lived another five minutes, he'd find the WD-40 and oil the damn thing.

"Hey, you," he said to the mutt. "Knock it off. Nate's on our side. He's one of the good guys."

She immediately stopped barking. With back fur still bristling, she sat down beside Jack, pressing against his leg.

"Remember when I was building an addition onto Pete Marchand's Tack-in-the-Box store a couple months back?" Nate Callahan, Jack's younger brother and the contractor in charge of Beau Soleil's renovation, asked.

"Yeah, I recall something about that. Why?"

" 'Cause I saw a real nice hand-tooled saddle in the window that'd probably fit your new pal just fine."

"Boy, you're such a comedian I'm surprised no one's given you your own TV show." Jack rubbed his throbbing temples.

"Hangover?"

"Thanks, anyway. But I've already got one of my own."

"Hope it was worth it. So, the dog gotta name?"

"Hell if I know." She wouldn't, if she was depending on him. "She's a stray." Jack leaned a shoulder against the door frame, folded his arms, and braced for bad news. "What's today's problem?"

He'd been warned, before buying Beau Soleil, that restoring the plantation house to its former glory would be a challenge. That had proven an understatement. The truth was, the place was not only a money pit, it was turning out to be one damn thing after another.

The first day he'd discovered he was going to have to replace most of the rotting foundation walls. Things had gone downhill from there.

"No problem. At least not yet. But hell, the day's still young."

Nate held out a foam cup. Jack pried off the lid and appreciatively inhaled the fragrant steam. Risking a scorched tongue, he took a drink of the black chicory-flavored coffee and decided he just may live after all.

"Too bad you're my brother. Otherwise, I could just turn gay and marry you so you could bring me coffee every morning."

"Sorry, even if we weren't related, you're not my type. I've got this personal thing about not locking lips with someone with a heavier beard than mine."

"Picky, picky."

"Though," Nate considered, "it might solve my recent problem with Suzanne."

"Marriage bug bite again?"

"I don' know what's gotten into women lately." Nate whipped off his billed cap and plowed a hand through his sun-streaked hair. "They're fabulous creatures. They smell damn good, too. You know I've always enjoyed everything about them."

"That's no exaggeration." From the moment he'd hit puberty and stumbled across their older brother Finn's stash of *Playboy* magazines, Nate had acquired a genuine appreciation for seemingly the entire female gender. From what Jack had been able to tell, the majority of those females had appreciated him right back.

"Used to be you could hit it off with a woman and the two of you'd pass a good time. Everyone had a little fun, nobody got hurt. Or mad. But no more. Hell, you go out a few times, share a few laughs . . ."

"A few rolls in the hay." Amused, Jack lit a cigarette.

"A gentleman never rolls and tells. But, Christ," Nate continued, "even when both parties agree goin' in to keep things light, the next thing you know, she's askin' whether you like Chrysanthemum or Buttercup better."

Jack shrugged. "Most women like flowers."

"That's what I thought when she first brought it up. But turns out they're not flowers. They're goddamned silverware patterns."

"I'm no expert on the subject, but my guess would be it's best just to go along with whatever the lady likes."

"Easy for you to say. She happens to like Chrysanthemum because it's the same pattern her momma has, is from Tiffany's, and a single damn iced-tea spoon would probably pay my subcontractor bills for a month. But my problem isn't about any damn flatware."

"Just the fact that you know the term *flatware* suggests you're in trouble, little brother."

"My point," Nathan plowed on through gritted teeth, "is that the female pattern is always the same. Have a few dates, share a few kisses, okay, maybe go to bed, and suddenly copies of *Bride* magazine start mysteriously showin' up on the bedside table and you're giving up NASCAR to watch *Sense and Sensibility* on the chick channel."

Jack blew out a surprised cloud of smoke. "You're kidding."

"I wish I were. A guy could die of estrogen overdose watching that movie. Last night it was *Sleepless in Seattle*. And this morning she brought me breakfast in bed."

"Well, that's certainly a hangin' offense. Are we talkin' fresh fruit in dainty crystal bowls and croissants on flowered plates with white doilies? Or a decent manly meal with buckets of grease and cholesterol?"

"This morning it was boudin, cush cush, three fried eggs, and cottage fries."

"Gotta hate a woman who'd fry you up a mess of sausage and eggs." Jack's mouth watered. "Maybe when Suzanne gets tired of cookin' for an unappreciative yahoo, you can send her out here."

"You'd run her off in a day. Besides, it's not the cooking that's my problem, it's the reason a woman who probably grew up not even knowin' the way to the kitchen has gotten all domestic in the first place. Dammit, Jack, I feel like a tournament bass trying to hide out in the shallows, and she's on the bank baitin' the damn hook."

"So, don't bite."

"Easy for you to say," Nate grumbled as they watched the new roof going on. "Good to see you finally coming out of hibernation, even if you look like death warmed over," he said, switching gears. "Does this mean the book's finally starting to go well?"

"Depends on your meaning of *well*."

"I sure don't understand, given all that happened to you, why you'd want to write about murder."

"It's called makin' a living."

"You can't sit at that computer twenty-four hours a day. Ever think about running for sheriff when you get this place all fixed up? Lord knows this parish could use a new one. Jimbo Lott gets more corrupt every year."

"I notice he keeps getting elected."

"Only 'cause nobody runs against him."

"In case you haven't noticed, the reason I came back here is because I'm out of the crime-fighting business."

"Nah. You may be a hot shot novelist now, but you've got our daddy's blood running through your veins. You and Finn always were the most like him, always wantin' to play cops and robbers."

"While you were off dragging lumber in from the swamp."

"Somebody had to build the jail to put the robbers in after you two captured them. I don't believe you can ignore nature, Jack."

"Believe it. I turned in my badge because I finally realized that tilting at windmills just gets you ripped to fuckin' pieces."

"So you're going to spend the rest of your life hiding out here, trying to find redemption by writing your depressing books?"

"Unlike some people who haven't learned how to mind their own business, I don't believe in redemption. And a helluva lot of readers must like depressing, because I sell damn well."

Jack had never been able to figure out why readers the world over would actually pay to share his nightmares, but as his agent and editor kept assuring him, his thinly veiled true crime stories about a divorced, alcoholic narcotics agent who lived on the fringes of society had found a huge audience.

"There's probably an audience for televised executions," Nate said mildly. "But that doesn't necessarily mean the networks should supply it."

"Hell, if they ever figure out a way to get by the government censors, Old Sparky will become a Saturday night blockbuster."

"You know, I'm beginnin' to worry you may just be nearly as cynical as you're trying to convince me you are."

"Not cynical. I'm just a realist. I decided after holding up my dead partner's widow at his gravesite that I'd leave saving the world to people like our older brother."

"You've always had a knack for tellin' stories," Nate allowed. "But ever think 'bout writing more uplifting ones?"

"I just write the world like I see it."

"Well, I sure don't envy you your view."

Jack merely shrugged.

"Speaking of views, the scenery around Blue Bayou's about to get a whole lot prettier."

An intuition Jack had learned to trust, the same one that had saved his life on more than one occasion, had the hair at the back of his neck prickling. As the sun burned off the morning mist, he curled his hand around the cup and waited.

"Danielle's coming back home."

Ignoring the sideways look directed his way, Jack polished off the rest of the cooling coffee and wished to hell it was something stronger.

* * *

Heat shimmered on the empty roadway, a glistening black ribbon that twined its way around laconic waters and through root-laced swamps, unrolling before Dani like a welcome mat. Despite all her problems, the deeper into the bayou she drove, the more her tangled nerves began to unwind. There was something calming about this land that time had forgot. Calming and infinitely reassuring, despite the rumbling from storm clouds gathering on the horizon.

Fields of sugar cane were occasionally broken by an oak tree, or a sleepy strip town, often little more than one house deep, the valuable land being needed more for crops than commerce. Lush green fields were laid out in a near-surgical precision at odds with the personalities of the Cajun farmers who lived there. Here in southern Louisiana the mighty Mississippi hadn't carved valleys as it had upriver. Instead, it had carried rich topsoil washed away from northern states and deposited it across the soggy terrain to create valuable fertile land. Water and bog warred continually, with water winning more battles over the eons.

Pretty Victorian homes stood next door to brightly painted Creole West Indies cottages, which neighbored antebellum plantation homes, many of which were crumbling, reclaimed by time and water. Every so often Dani would pass a sugar mill, whose sweet odor, come winter grinding season, would make the eyes water.

It was a long way from Fairfax, Virginia, to Blue Bayou, Louisiana. An even longer way from the hustle and bustle of the nation's capital to this secret, hidden corner of the world. Dani had missed it without knowing it'd been missed. Trying to keep a demanding life on track, while juggling the roles of congressional wife, student, mother, and librarian, running from a painful past she tried not to think about, had kept her nearly too busy to breathe. Let alone stop and think. Or feel.

Which is why, she thought sadly, she hadn't realized that Lowell had emotionally left their marriage—and her—before they'd returned from their St. Thomas honeymoon.

Matt, who normally passed long drives with his nose in a library book, wasn't saying much about the change of scenery, but whenever Dani would glance in the rearview mirror, she'd see him drinking everything in.

"Some of the kids didn't believe me when I said we were going to be living in a library," he offered from the backseat.

"We're not going to be living *in* the library. We'll be living *above* it."

Dani had been more than a little relieved when an on-line search of the *Cajun Clarion*'s classified pages had revealed an opening for parish librarian. She'd immediately called the number, which turned out to be the mayor's office, and had, in the space of that single phone call, been hired by Nate Callahan, Blue Bayou's newly elected mayor. The pay might not be up to big-city standards, but Dani would have been willing to clean tables and wash dishes in Cajun Cal's Country Café if that's what it took to feed her son.

"Since the library's been closed for the past two months, ever since the former librarian moved to Alexandria to live with her granddaughter, the parish commissioners were so relieved to hear they were going to be able to open it, they threw in the apartment as a *lagniappe*." Which was fortunate, since the salary would have made paying rent difficult.

"*Lagniappe* means 'something extra.' "

"That's exactly what it means." She smiled at him in the mirror. "You're so smart."

His brow furrowed. "What if I was only smart at Fox Run? What if the kids in my new school know more than I do?"

"Your test scores were great, darling." Hadn't she, on the school counselor's advice, allowed him to skip third grade? "You'll do fine here."

"What if they don't like me?"

"Of course they'll like you. And you'll have your cars to break the ice."

"Yeah. I will," he said, seemingly relieved. "Grandpa's really going to live with us, too?"

"Absolutely." Dani refused to consider the prospect of her father rejecting the home she intended to make for them all.

Judge Victor Dupree had always wanted to control everything and everyone around him, which is probably partly why he became a judge in the first place. She'd often thought it was also one of the reasons her mama had run away when Dani had still been in diapers. If there was anything Lowell's untimely death had taught her, it was that life was too short to hold grudges. She and her father had already lost enough years they could have been a family. Her son was going to know who and where he'd come from if it was the last thing Dani did.

*And if Daddy doesn't like it, tough.*

Thunder rumbled a low warning in the distance. A flash of lightning forked out of darkening clouds, and the wind picked up, rustling the cane stalks.

"Is a hurricane coming?"

"Oh, I'm sure we don't have to worry about that." Dani flipped on the windshield wipers.

"Are you sure? I saw the signs," Matt said over the drumming rain on the station wagon's metal roof. "The evacuation route for when there's a hurricane." Even being more than a year younger than most of his classmates, he was the best reader in his fourth grade. There were times, and this was one of them, that wasn't necessarily a good thing.

"It's just a little afternoon rain, sweetie."

"Too bad." He pressed his nose against the window. "It'd be cool to call Tommy and tell him we were in a hurricane." Tommy had been his neighbor and best friend in Virginia.

"I think I'd prefer we pass on that excitement."

"It'd still be neat."

A siren screamed over the crash of another thunderclap. The flashing lights in the rearview mirror yanked Dani's attention from her dreary thoughts as she glanced down at the speedometer, which revealed that she was going well within the speed limit.

"Are we getting a ticket?"

"I don't think so." She certainly hoped not. The last thing her checkbook needed was a traffic fine and an increase in her insurance premium. She pulled over to the shoulder, breathing a sigh of relief as the red car belonging to the parish fire chief tore past.

Unlike so many of the strip towns which had sprung up to serve the farming and shrimping south Louisiana population, Blue Bayou had been painstakingly designed by a wealthy planter who'd visited Savannah for a wedding and had so admired that city's lush green squares and gracious architecture, he'd returned home and formed a partnership with one of the *gens de couleur libres*—free men of color—an architect who shared his artistic vision.

Together they changed the rustic fishing town named for the blue herons which nested on the banks of the bayou into a planned hamlet which, although the town's name of *Bayou Bleu* had been anglicized over the years, remained an example of the short-lived period of booming antebellum prosperity.

As Dani crossed the old steel bridge leading into town, the gaslights along oak-lined Gramercy Boulevard—which was actually a narrow cobblestone street—flickered on, yellow shimmers through the falling rain, which she was glad to see was letting up as the storm passed on toward New Orleans and Mississippi.

Returning to this hidden corner of Louisiana was like going back in time. Not just to Dani's more recent personal past, but to a romantic era far more distant. It took no imagination at all to hear the clatter of horses' hooves on the cobblestones or the rustle of petticoats skimming the brick sidewalk lined with leafy trees and planters overflowing with color.

Some things had changed since the last time she'd been home, which had been for her father's trial seven long years ago. Lafitte's Landing, the old restaurant, dance hall, and gathering place, was closed; the drugstore where she and her girlfriends would perch on vinyl-seated swivel stools and moon over Johnny Breaux as he'd build hot fudge sundaes was now an Espresso Express, and Arlene's Doll Hospital had become a video rental store.

But Cajun Cal's Country Café still advertised the Friday night fried-fish special; they were still perming hair at Belle's Shear Pleasures, though according to the white script painted on the window, Belle had added pedicures, and the Bijoux Theater still dominated the corner of Maringouin and Heron. They also still had live entertainment on Sunday nights. According to the marquee, this week's singer was billed as *The Chanteuse Acadienne, Christy Marchand.*

Blue Bayou was a pretty, peaceful town where children rode bikes down quiet, tree-canopied streets, where mothers pushed baby carriages, and the residents sat on front galleries beneath lazily circling ceiling fans to sip sweet tea in the afternoons and watch their neighbors.

It was the kind of small rural southern town where Andy Griffith could have been elected sheriff, if Andy had only spoken French. Dani hadn't realized how much she'd missed it until she'd come home.

The lush green town square was flanked on one end by the Church of the Holy Assumption, its twin Gothic spires lancing high into the sky. The silver rain clouds had gathered around the stone towers like pigeons flocking together for the night.

The opposite side of the park was anchored by the majestic

Italianate courthouse, boasting tall stone steps, gracefully arched windows, and lacy cast-iron pilasters. It had served as a hospital during the War Between the States, and if one knew where to look, it was possible to find minie balls still lodged in the woodwork.

A red, white, and blue Acadian flag hung below the U.S. and state flags on a towering pole, and a bronze statue of Captain Jackson Callahan—a local boy who'd risen above his Irish immigrant status by joining the mostly Irish 6th Louisiana Volunteer Infantry known as the Confederate Tigers—graced the lawn.

The soldier who'd begun the war as Private Callahan had fought in virtually every Eastern front battle from the Shenandoah Valley Campaign of 1862 under Stonewall Jackson to the hand-to-hand warfare at Fort Stedman, amazingly returning home in one piece after Lee's surrender at Appomattox Court House in 1865.

The fact that the former ragtag orphan, who'd grown up wild and barefoot in Blue Bayou's Irish swamp, had, by means of battlefield promotions, returned a captain, had been considered by many to be a miracle.

"That's a cool horse," Matt said.

"I always thought so. A lot of people believe that touching his nose before entering the courthouse brings good luck."

"Can we try it?"

"After we get moved into the apartment, we'll come back," Dani promised. Unfortunately, the horse she'd so loved to sit on as a child hadn't worked its lucky magic for her father.

It was in this courthouse that Judge Victor Dupree had sat on the bench for decades, earning a reputation as a hard-line law-and-order advocate whose tendency to throw the book at those convicted in his courtroom had earned him the nickname of Maximum Dupree. It was also in this courthouse he'd been convicted of bribery and perjury and sentenced to seven years in Angola prison.

Dani couldn't resist glancing up at her father's courtroom window. Her heart hitched; tears misted her vision. Blinking to clear her gaze, she reminded herself of the list she'd made while sitting in her kitchen in Fairfax. Her first priorities were to get settled into their new home and enroll Matt in school. Next she'd reopen the library. Then, once those items had been crossed off, she'd tackle the problem with her father.

Fortunately, the storm had passed quickly. Only the occasional drop of rain splattered on the windshield. She turned off the wipers, deciding to take the fact that she wouldn't have to be lugging things into the apartment in a downpour as a portent of more good luck.

The library was two blocks away, on Magnolia Avenue. Dani could have driven there blindfolded. She turned the corner, only to find the street blocked by barricades and the patrol car she'd feared earlier, its emergency lights casting the scene in a surrealistic blur.

This couldn't be happening! She stared in disbelief as she watched the arcs of water spraying from shiny brass nozzles onto the top floor of the three-story redbrick building with the wood and brass Blue Bayou Library sign on the lawn. Men in helmets and heavy yellow jackets dragged heavy hoses, wielded axes, and shouted out orders.

"Wow. Is that our apartment?" Matt asked.

Dani didn't immediately answer. She could barely breathe.

"Wait here," she said. "I'll be right back."

"But, Mom . . ."

"I said, wait here and do not get out of this car," she instructed in the no-nonsense I'm-your-mother-and-you-will-obey-me tone she hardly ever had to use with her normally obedient son. "Do you understand me?"

"Geez, yeah. You don't have to yell."

"I'm sorry." She leaned back and cupped his freckled face between her palms. "I'm sorry I snapped at you."

"Don't worry, Mom." His defensive mood passed, as swiftly as the earlier storm, and he gave her a reassuring smile. "Everything'll be okay."

It was the same thing he'd said the day the moving men had taken his father's things from their house. Her husband had always chosen his career over his family. And in doing so had inadvertently created an intensely strong bond between his wife and son.

"I know, darling." Dani gave him a quick kiss, ruffled his hair, reminded him once again to stay put, then waded into the breach.

# 3

*The fire had drawn* a crowd, the spectators watching her dreams go up in smoke with the same fascination they might gather at a train wreck. Dani's feet crunched on the broken glass strewn over the slickly wet pavement like shards of ice. A sooty-faced fireman sat on the wide running board of the fire truck, drinking in hits of oxygen.

"What happened?"

He lifted the mask. "Dunno. Probably a lighting strike." His red-rimmed eyes swept the scene as he stood up and fastened his yellow helmet. "Or electrical." They both looked up at the flames licking from the shattered windows. "That's up to the fire marshal to determine."

Sparks wheeled like orange stars in the darkening sky as he clapped down his face shield and walked away.

Dani's hammering heart sank to her wet sneakers. Just when she didn't think she could feel any worse, she viewed a man wearing the brown uniform and shiny badge of authority swaggering toward her and imagined she heard the warning rattle of a snake's tail over the roar of water. Which was ridiculous. Blue Bayou's sheriff had never been a man to give his adversary any warning.

"Well, if it ain't little Danielle Dupree." His belly strained against the front of his khaki uniform, spilling over his belt. There were dark circles of sweat beneath his arms and red hot sauce stains on his brown tie. He was, Dani thought, the antithesis of Andy Griffith. "Fancy meetin' you here."

The smile beneath his shaggy black mustache held more smirk than warmth. If an alligator could smile, it'd look like exactly like Sheriff Jimbo Lott.

"Sheriff Lott." Voice mild, she resisted rubbing the tension knotted at the back of her neck.

"Any special reason you're at my fire scene?"

The flat-lidded reptilian gaze crawling over her managed to be both sexual and detached at the same time. He'd looked at her the same way years ago, when he'd caught her with Jack out at the Callahans' camp and forced her to get dressed in the glare of his patrol car's spotlight.

When she couldn't quite restrain an involuntary shiver at both the memory and the intimidation in those hooded eyes, his thick lips curved in another sly innuendo of a smile.

"It happens to be my fire scene, as well." Her eyes stung from the smoke. "I was supposed to be moving into that apartment tonight."

"That a fact?" He didn't sound surprised. "Guess that apartment wasn't as bad as some of them shacks out in the swamp, but it sure don't seem much like a place a U.S. congressman's widow would wanna live, either." The flashing lights from the fire trucks shadowed, then highlighted a cruel, self-indulgent face and weak double chins. "Looks like its gonna end up one helluva mess. Lucky you hadn't moved your stuff in yet. Would've been tragic if that fire'd started later tonight, when you and your boy were sleepin'. Y'all would've been lucky to escape alive."

She'd never fainted in her life, but as she imagined Matt trapped in the third floor apartment with those hungry flames and that suffocating, stinging smoke, Dani's head began to spin.

"Yep," he continued as she braced a hand against the side of the fire truck and fought against the swirling vertigo, "too bad you've come all this way, only to have to turn right around and go home."

She drew in a breath that burned. "This *is* my home, Sheriff."

"You've been gone from Blue Bayou for a lotta years, Missy. And it's not like you've got family here, with your daddy locked away up in Angola. Things change, even in these backwaters. Power shifts. Ever hear the old sayin' 'bout folks not bein' able to go home again?"

"Yes." The challenge was a like a cold wet slap in the face. Dani welcomed the anger that steamrollered over her earlier shock. She tossed up her chin. "I've just never believed it."

She was about to cut this unsatisfactory conversation short when someone called her name. Turning around, she saw Nate Callahan leap the black-and-white police barricade. He could not have been more welcome if he'd been wearing a suit of shining armor and riding astride a white stallion.

"Are you okay?" He took both her hands in his, comforting her the way he once had so many years ago, after his brother had broken her heart.

"I'm fine," she lied. "But I should get back to Matt." Another window exploded; shards of glass rained down.

"More'n likely your boy's having himself a high old time," Lott drawled. "Never did meet a kid who didn't get off on fires."

Dani speared the sheriff with a disgusted look, then turned her back on him.

"Why don't you introduce me to your son?" Nate suggested mildly, ignoring Lott as well.

Her throat was raw from smoke and pent-up emotion. As he put a steadying hand around her waist, walking back with her to the wagon, Dani tried not to weep.

*What on earth was she going to do now?*

The first thing was get hold of herself. This wasn't the end of the world. She'd think of something. After all, hadn't she'd surprised a lot of people, including herself, by not crumbling when Lowell had left her?

She'd picked herself up, turned her part-time library work into a fulfilling career, and had been in the process of building a new life for herself and Matt when that damn piano had changed things yet again.

Dani stiffened her resolve and pasted a reassuring look on her face for her son. This fire was admittedly a setback, but nothing she couldn't overcome. She would not allow herself to think otherwise.

Watching the genuine warmth with which Nate greeted Matt, Dani wasn't surprised he'd grown up to be mayor. He'd always been the boy everyone gravitated to at parties, the one all eyes automatically went to when he was out on a ball field, either tossing spiral passes or diving off third base to steal a home run from an opposing team's batter. By the time he was nominated for senior class president, not a student in the school considered running against him.

All the girls had harbored crushes on him. All but her. Dani only had eyes for his brother, Bad Jack.

"Looks like we've got ourselves more company," Nate observed as a pink Cadillac with mile-long tailfins harkening back to Detroit's glory days pulled up, Elvis's *Blue Suede Shoes* blasting from the radio.

A woman in her sixties, sporting a towering birdnest of orange hair, climbed out of the driver's seat. A cartoon drawing of a fighting crawdad standing on its tail, claws outstretched in a boxer's stance, adorned the front of her purple caftan. Red plastic crawdad earrings flashed with hidden battery-operated lights. Orèlia Vallois was a retired nurse who'd worked in her physician husband's office; Dani could not remember ever seeing her in traditional nurse's white.

"Why, if it isn't pretty little Danielle Dupree, come back home where she belongs," the deep contralto boomed out.

Orèlia had always been one of Dani's favorite people. Warmhearted and outspoken, she'd gone out of her way to treat Judge Dupree's motherless daughter special. She was also one of a handful of people who knew Dani's deepest, darkest secret.

"It's so good to see you," Dani said, grateful for a gift in the midst of disaster.

"It's grand to have you back home again. *Comment c'est?*"

"It's not exactly a banner day."

Behind the rose-tinted lenses of rhinestone-framed cat's-eye glasses, dark eyes, enhanced with a bold streak of purple color that matched the caftan, offered a warm welcome. "*Viens ici, bébé*, an' give Orèlia a hug."

After nearly squeezing the breath out of Dani, Orèlia gave her a quick once-over, then studied Matt, who was observing the gregarious nurse as if she were some sort of wondrous alien from a Saturday morning cartoon. Dani knew he'd never seen anything like Orèlia Vallois in Fairfax County.

"An' this must be your darling *fil*."

"This is Matt." Dani placed a hand atop his head, absently smoothing the cowlick. "Matt, this is Mrs. Vallois."

"Hello, Ma'am" he answered with his best Fox Run manners.

"Aren't you the mos' handsome young man Blue Bayou's seen in a long time." She pinched Matt's cheek. "You have your *maman*'s mouth, Monsieur Matthew."

"I do?" Dani gave him huge points for not squirming.

"*Oui*. You'll break more than a few girls' hearts, you. Why, I bet you already have yourself a special girlfriend."

A flush as bright as the fighting cartoon crawfish rose in his face. He rubbed the darkening red spot where she'd pinched him. "Not really."

"Well, isn't there plenty of time for that? Anyway, it's best to play the field at your age. Besides, now I won't have to worry 'bout female competition while you're living with me."

"Living with you?" He shot Dani a confused look.

"Oh, Orèlia, as much as I appreciate the offer—"

"Now, Danielle, darlin', there's no point in arguing. Besides, I've just been rattlin' around in that big house since my Leon passed on. It'll be good to have some company." She chucked Matt beneath his chin. "Follow me home, and I'll feed this man of yours."

"I really don't want to impose—"

"Stop talking foolishness," the older woman cut her off again. "You need a place to stay and your boy needs food." The gregarious redhead had morphed into the bustling office nurse who'd jabbed more than a few needles into patients' bare butts over a forty-year career. "At least for tonight, then we can talk about your future in the morning, when things are lookin' brighter."

The orange birdnest teetered a bit as she tilted her head and studied Matt. "You look like a chicken-fried-steak man to me. That sound good?"

"I guess so."

"Of course it does. Nobody in this parish makes a better chicken fried steak than Orèlia. We'll get you some dirty rice and buttered snap beans, too."

"Dirty rice?"

"Oh, it's wonderful, darlin'. You'll love it. I can't believe your *maman*'s never cooked it for you."

Deciding this was not the time to try to explain that the only time Lowell had wanted any reminders of his Louisiana constituents, whom he'd always considered beneath him, was when he was hosting his annual Mardi Gras fund-raising party for well-heeled lobbyists and wealthy corporate types, Dani didn't respond to the friendly gibe.

"And some hot-milk cake for dessert," Orèlia decided. "I'll bet you like that good enough."

"I don't know. I've never had it."

"You haven't?" A beringed hand flew to her breast. "*Bon Dieu!* What on earth happened to your *maman* while she was away living with the Americans?"

Knowing that old-time Cajuns considered the rest of the country as something apart from themselves, Dani didn't bother to point out that Blue Bayou was technically as American as Virginia.

Orèlia flicked a measuring gaze over Dani. "Your handsome boy isn't the only one who needs supper. Don't they feed you good in the city, *chère?* You're nothin' but skin and bones. But don't you worry, Orèlia will take care of getting you some curves."

She wagged her hand toward the station wagon. "Now shoo. I'll meet you at the house and flirt with Matty and fix him some supper while you and Nate take care of business."

Events decided, at least in her own mind, she swept back through the crowd like a ship steaming out of harbor to the Caddy.

"The sign says No Parking," Matt pointed out.

"She was probably in such a hurry she didn't notice it." Dani ignored Nate's smothered laugh. They both knew that Orèlia was no fan of rules.

"Are we really going to live with her?" Matt asked.

Dani watched the steam rising from the charred building that was to have been her new home, considered her options, and reluctantly decided that she didn't have all that many.

"Just for a little while," she decided. "Until we can get the apartment repaired."

Fortunately, the lower floors didn't look as if they'd been too badly damaged. She hoped the books would be salvageable.

"When the apartment's fixed up, it'll be better than new," she said optimistically. "I'll start looking for carpenters first thing in the morning."

Already forming her plan to literally rise from the ashes, Dani didn't notice Nate wince.

The dying sun bled red in the water as Jack poled the pirouge up to the dock. The No Name wasn't a place where you could take a pretty girl dancing on Saturday night, or where a family might show up for dinner after Sunday mass.

Neither was it known for its rustic charms, a waterfront tavern where you'd romance a woman over glasses of wine, or where a guy could play a few convivial rounds of pool with pals, listen to some zydeco on the juke, and shoot the bull.

The No Name—the original name had been forgotten after the sign had blown down in a hurricane in the 1940s—was a specialty shop: a bar where you could feed the spiders crawling around in your head and get quickly, ruthlessly, and efficiently drunk enough that you could no longer remember anything about your life. Not even your own name.

And Jack had a shitload of stuff he wanted—needed—to forget.

The thick plank front door had been painted a bright lipstick red by a previous owner, but had faded over the decades to a dirty rust. There were a few muttered complaints from the shadows when he opened the door and let in the bleeding red light. Jack figured the growled curses were probably the most words any of the regulars had managed to string together all day.

The interior was even worse than the outside. It was dark and cheerless, smelling of sawdust and despair. It suited his mood perfectly.

"Give me a double Jack Black, straight up, no water on the side," he said as he slid onto a barstool. There were bowls of sliced lemons, limes, and cherries on the bar and behind it, dark bottles, dim lamps, and dusty bottles of wine.

The bartender, a tall, whippet-lean man with the look of a long-distance runner, which he'd been in high school, splashed the Jack Daniel's into a short glass. "Bad day at Black Rock?"

"You could say that." Jack tossed down the whiskey, enjoying the burn down the length of his throat as it seared its way to his gut and sent smoke upward into his brain.

He shoved the empty glass back toward the bartender, who arched a black brow but refilled it without a word.

Alcèe Bonaparte was in his early thirties, same as Jack. They'd gone to school together, and both their mothers had worked for the Dupree family—Marie Callahan as a housekeeper, Dora Bonaparte as a cook—and they'd grown up together. Despite the fact that Alcèe was African-American and Jack was white, they'd been as close as brothers, with Alcèe playing the role of the good twin, Jack the bad.

Whenever Jack filched beer from the back of the Dixie delivery truck, often as not it was Alcèe who left behind the change to cover the theft.

When Jack got drunk, went on a tear, and bashed in mailboxes with a baseball bat not unlike the Louisville Slugger currently hanging on the wall beneath the bottles, it had been Alcèe who'd convinced him to confess to the judge, who'd sentenced Jack to replacing every one of the vandalized boxes, and working off the cost cutting cane on the Dupree farm.

What the judge never knew, and they sure as hell didn't tell him, was that not only had Alcèe dug the posts for the new mailboxes, he'd passed up a long awaited church trip to the New Orleans cemeteries to labor besides his best friend in the staggering, breath-stealing heat of the cane fields.

With the easy understanding of lifelong friends, neither man spoke. Alcèe continued to pour drinks, washed glasses in the metal sink, and wiped off the bar that was permanently stained, pale white circles left by wet glasses telling the years like the rings of ancient trees.

After ten minutes he disappeared through the swinging doors into the back, returning with a huge po'boy, which he stuck in front of Jack.

"I don't remember ordering that." Unfortunately, Jack could still remember more than he wanted.

"You need somet'ing in your stomach besides whiskey, you. Befo' you go fallin' off that there stool and break your stiff coon-ass neck."

"Don't give me that bayou black boy jive. I happen to know you received a Jesuit education."

Alcèe folded his arms across the front of the gaudy blue-and-white flowered Hawaiian shirt.

"You so smart, you should also know that the Jesuits are Catholicism's kick-butt hardasses. So why don't you eat that sandwich before I have to, in the name of Christian charity, stuff it down your throat."

Jack's curse was short and pungent and bounced right off Alcèe like BBs off a Kevlar vest. Knowing from experience that arguing was useless, he bit into the dripping sandwich and nearly moaned as the flavors of shrimp and sauce piquante exploded on his tongue.

"So," Alcèe asked casually as he took away the empty highball glass and, without being asked, spritzed Coke into a new, taller one filled with ice, "do I owe this visit to the fact that a certain *jolie blonde* is coming back to town?" He tossed some cherries into the Coke and placed the glass down in front of Jack.

"I don't know what you're talking about." Jack took a long swallow, feeling the sugar hit like a firecracker in his head, which he would have preferred muddied.

Alcèe looked inclined to argue when he noticed a grizzled old guy get up from a table in the far corner. He was out from around the bar and as Jack watched, he bent down and talked quietly but intensely to the man who'd opened his mouth to argue, then obviously realized the futility and sagged back down onto the chair. Alcèe sat down at the table and continued to talk to him.

It was common knowledge in Blue Bayou that Alcèe was a former priest who'd temporarily lost his faith and his bearings in a fog of alcoholism. One fateful night on the way back to his New Orleans rectory after a drinking binge in a blues club with an alkie pal, who'd just happened to be a monsignor, he'd driven off the road into the river. He'd survived—just barely—and, after countless dives, had managed to get his passenger out of the car.

Unfortunately, the other man, whose blood later tested at a level nearly three times the legal limit, hadn't been wearing his seat belt. He'd spent a month in a coma and another two years in rehab before being spirited away by the Church to wherever they put their problem clergymen.

Alcèe didn't even try to fight the drunk-driving and reckless-endangerment charges. He dried out and did both his time and his penance while running a prison ministry. When he was released, he left the priesthood and returned home to the bayou. Now the No Name was his parish, the hard-core drunks and strung-out druggies who frequented it, his flock.

Last New Year's Eve he'd gotten himself engaged to a nurse in the maternity ward at St. Mary's hospital, a former beauty queen from Mississippi who was every bit as warmhearted as Alcèe himself was. Jack had agreed to be best man at their wedding next month, something he was looking forward to, even though he felt that in the case of him and Alcèe the title was definitely a misnomer.

The fact was, Jack owed Alcèe Bonaparte big time. He'd been on a fast slide right into hell and might not have lived long enough to see his old friend get married if Alcèe hadn't shown up at the camp that day and convinced him to send his manuscript to a lit grad who'd spent a year in the same seminary Alcèe had attended. The guy had subsequently decided he wasn't cut out for a life of celibacy and had gone on to become a New York literary agent, but he and Alcèe had kept in touch over the years.

The door opened onto a gathering well of darkness. Heads swiveled toward the woman backlit by the neon blue parking-lot light. Even the old drunk seemed to sit up a little straighter as Desiree Champagne glided across the sawdust-covered floor. Her hair was a riot of dark gypsy curls, her eyes the color of wood smoke in autumn.

She was wearing a red silk dress slashed nearly to the navel that hugged her curves like a lover's caress and spindly heels so high Jack marveled that she could walk without breaking both ankles.

When Alcèe started to get up from the table, she waved him off, a diamond the size of Texas flashing like lasers in the smoky light.

"You stay where you are, hon," she said in a throaty voice designed to tug masculine chords. "I can get my own drink." She went around the bar and began mixing a martini. "Hey, Jack." Every male eye in the place was riveted on her as she shook the drink, poured it into a glass, and added a trio of olives. "What are you drinking, darlin'?"

Jack heard Alcèe clear his throat. Ignoring the veiled warning, he answered, "Jack Black."

She poured a shot of whiskey into a glass and held it out to him. *Come and get it*, those flashing dark eyes were saying. *Come and get me*.

After he'd taken the drink, and thanked her for it, she came around the bar, perched on the stool next to him, and crossed her legs, revealing a mouthwatering length of thigh. "It's been a long time." Her lips curved into a sultry seductive smile. Even knowing it was practiced, did not lessen its appeal. "I've missed you."

"I've missed you, too."

It was true enough, Jack decided. He might not have thought about her during the weeks he'd been working on Beau Soleil and slogging away on his book, but a part of him would probably always miss their easy camaraderie dating back to the days when two outsiders found a bit of escape and comfort in each other's arms.

"Did you hear Dani's coming back?" She plucked the olive from the plastic pick with full, glossy lips.

"Nate mentioned it."

"I wonder why."

He shrugged. "I guess 'cause her husband died, so she's coming home."

"The only trouble with that scenario is that *you're* in her home."

He didn't respond, since that thought had been going round and round in his mind ever since Nate had dropped his little bombshell this morning.

The scarlet silk slid off one shoulder when she shrugged. "I guess she'll have to find herself another one."

"No offense, sugar. But I really don't feel much like conversation tonight."

"Fine." She crossed her legs again with a seductive swish of silk. "Then we won't." She sipped the martini, eyeing him over the rim of the glass. "I can't stay long, anyway. Since I think I'm expecting company tonight."

"You don't know?"

"I'm not quite sure." Her fingers stroked the thin stem of the glass in a blatantly erotic way. "Yet."

The gilt-rimmed feminine invitation was lingering in the smoke-filled bar between them. Jack polished off the whiskey and threw a twenty-dollar bill on the bar. "Let's go."

She smiled. "I thought you'd never ask." She blew a kiss toward Alcèe, who was on the black pay phone. Jack knew, from having watched similar discussions over the past months, that he was probably arranging for someone to drive the old guy home.

As he left with Desiree, he waved goodbye to his old friend, who waved back. But there was no mistaking the concern in Alcèe's Bambi-brown eyes.

"Alcèe doesn't approve," Desiree said.

"Once a priest always a priest," Jack muttered as they went out into the steamy night.

"He thinks I'm not good enough for you."

"Alcèe's never been one to judge. Even when he was wearing the collar."

"Perhaps." She thought about that as they made their way across the parking lot, her arm around his waist, his hand on her hip. "I suppose he's used to hookers. Even his old boss forgave Mary Magdalene."

"You're not a hooker."

"Not anymore." She leaned against the shiny red fender of a late model Porsche and looked up at him. "But even if I was, *chère*, you wouldn't be having to pay. Not with our history." She'd been the first girl he'd ever had sex with, and they'd passed some good times in the backseat of his candy-apple red GTO back in high school. She dangled the keys in front of him the same way he supposed Eve had offered that shiny red apple to Adam. "Why don't you drive?"

He hesitated just a moment too long.

"Hey, darlin', if you don't want to, it's no big deal."

He saw the flash of hurt in her eyes. "Sure I want to. It's just that I've got this damn dog."

"A dog?"

"Tied up over by the pirogue."

"I don't believe it." She stared at him as if he'd just told her that he'd returned from a little jaunt to Mars.

"Something wrong with a guy getting himself a dog?"

"Nothing at all." She patted his cheek and with hips swaying, walked over to where he'd left the mutt, who began wildly wagging her tail.

"Oh, she's darling!"

"She's a mess, is what she is."

Desiree bent down to pat the dog, giving Jack an appealing view of her shapely ass. "She just needs a bath. Don't you, darlin'?"

The dog, thrilled to pieces to be noticed, did what Jack figured just about every guy in the No Name would give his left nut to do: She licked the lush swell of Desiree's fragrant breasts.

Desiree laughed merrily, scratched the mutt's ears and, if the wild metronome swing of the dog's tail was any indication, sent her into ecstasy. Desiree kissed the end of the brown nose, then turned back to Jack. "What's her name?" she asked as she returned to the Porsche with the dog.

"I haven't a clue. And I'm not about to give her one 'cause she isn't going to be staying with me."

"Sure, darlin'. That's why you're taking her for boat rides."

"I was gonna take her to the shelter, but got caught up with work and didn't get into town in time to drop her off 'fore it closed."

"Whatever you say." She patted his cheek. "You know, it's good you found her. After all, a dog's supposed to be a man's best friend."

"I'm not in the market for any new friends."

She shook her head. "You can pretend all you want, Jack, but we go back too far for you to be fooling me with that heart-of-stone bullshit." She clicked the remote, standing back as Jack opened her door. "You rescued that dog the same way you rescued me from my son-of-a-bitch stepdaddy back when I was still a girl."

She slid into the driver's seat, turned the key, and brought the powerful engine to roaring life. "Climb on in, darlin'. There's not a lot of room, but your doggie can squeeze in back."

She was speeding out of the lot before Jack had a chance to tell her yet again that the mudball mutt was not *his* dog.

# 4

*Less than twenty minutes* after arriving in town, with her son in Orèlia's competent care, Dani was sitting with Nate in a room that had served as the late Dr. Vallois's office. Like the rest of the rooms she'd glanced into coming down the hallway, it reminded her of Aladdin's magic cave.

There was barely enough room to move around in and seemingly less room to breathe. Pretty, delicate little English porcelain boxes shared crowded tabletops with plastic tourist alligators, candles of various shapes, and tacky souvenirs from all over the world.

The cypress-paneled walls were lined with shelves boasting an eclectic collection of books that ranged from worn leather-bound classics to the latest true-crime paperback. It was, she thought, skimming a glance over the spines, a marvelous collection. It was also in desperate need of cataloging.

Dani loved order. Ordinal order, cardinal order, alphabetical order, the world just made more sense when it was logically arranged. Lowell had often accused her of using the Dewey decimal system to organize her underwear. It was an exaggeration. But not by much.

"It's really great to have you back home again, Dani. Motherhood obviously agrees with you."

Nate earned Dani's gratitude for not appearing to notice that she undoubtedly looked like a bedraggled stray cat. She could smell the stench of smoke in her hair and clothes.

"It does. It's the most fulfilling thing I've ever done."

"Since I know you're temporarily strapped for cash, I want to assure you that the parish council will pay your salary even though you probably won't be able to open the library for a while."

"That's very generous."

"Hey, you left your home to come to work here. That fire puttin' a crimp in the timing certainly isn't your fault."

"I appreciate the salary, because, quite honestly, as I told you on the phone, I need it." She absently shifted a carved wooden giraffe across the table next to the matching lion. "But surely it won't take very long to repair the apartment. Since you're a contractor, you must know all the workmen around here. If you'll give me some names, I can start calling around first thing in the morning."

Silence descended, like a stone falling into a deep dark well. "Nate?"

"It might be a problem finding someone to do the work, *chère*. Since nearly every carpenter, painter, electrician, and plumber in the parish is working on Beau Soleil."

"Beau Soleil?"

Dani had assured herself that she'd gotten over the loss of her family home. If the way her mouth had gone dry was any indication, she'd been fooling herself.

"Hell, Dani, I'm sorry. I figured you knew. After all, you signed the sales contract."

"Sales contract?" Needing something to do with her hands, she began straightening the magazines spread across the old mariner's chest in front of her. "Beau Soleil wasn't sold. My father lost it to taxes after he went to prison."

The idea of her father as a common felon was still hard to contemplate and even more difficult to say out loud.

Nate tilted his head and narrowed his eyes, clearly puzzled. "It looked as if he was going to lose it to back taxes. Then he deeded it over to you and Lowell."

"He did what?"

Seeming to read the shock Dani suspected must be written across her face, he poured a glass of tea from a ceramic rooster pitcher Orèlia had brought in when they'd first arrived, and held it out to her.

"I don't understand." She took a sip of the tea and tried to steady her mind, which was spinning like the old Tilt-A-Whirl she used to ride on the midway during the annual Cajun Days festival. "How could Lowell own Beau Soleil without me knowing about it?"

"Beats me." Dani hated the pity she thought she saw in his eyes.

"My guess would be he didn't believe you'd be wild about him sellin' it to the Maggione family."

"The same people my father went to prison for taking bribes from?"

Despite his hard-line legal stands, her father had always been an advocate of legalized gambling. After all, Andre Dupree had won Beau Soleil in a *bourré* game before the War Between the States. Still, Dani would never believe that her father had taken money to cast his parish council vote in favor of a casino run by one of New Orleans's most infamous mobsters.

"That's them. Though, for the record, I never believed your daddy took that bribe."

"Obviously the grand jury that indicted him didn't see it that way," Dani said dryly. It still hurt. Even after all these years. "Why would the Maggione family want Beau Soleil?"

"They figured it'd make a good centerpiece for their casino project."

"Are you telling me that it's been turned into a casino?"

Dani hated imagining the home she'd grown up in filled with roulette tables with clouds of cigarette and cigar smoke staining the ceiling murals. The idea of the discordant jangle of slot machines drowning out the angel fountain in the courtyard was a nightmare.

"No. Before the sale closed, the family got busted by the Justice Department for some money-laundering scheme. Then Papa Joe died, and the family splintered into different factions. By the time they were ready to try to set up shop here, someone else outbid them."

"When was that?"

"Last year."

"Last year?" Grateful she was sitting down, Dani took another, longer drink of tea.

"People around here figured, when your husband showed up with that quit-claim deed you'd signed and put the place on the market, that it must've been part of a property settlement deal the two of you had agreed upon."

"It certainly wasn't anything of the sort. And I never signed a thing."

Dani had suspected Lowell had skimmed the legal boundaries of campaign financing laws. She'd known he was an adulterer and, unfortunately, had possessed all the paternal instincts of a tom cat.

But to discover that he'd stolen her home out from under her was staggering!

"Who bought it?"

Obviously uncomfortable, he frowned down at his hands. "Nate?" She placed a hand on his arm. "Who bought Beau Soleil?"

"Aw, hell, Dani. I hate being the one to tell you this." He hitched in a noticeable breath. "Jack bought it."

"Jack?" The blood drained from her face. Drop by drop.

*My Jack?* she thought but did not say.

"Yeah." His eyes narrowed. "Are you okay? You've gone dead white."

"I'm fine." That was a lie. She drew in a deep breath that was meant to calm. But didn't. "It's just that . . ." Her voice broke, forcing her to try again. "Well, it's certainly a surprise."

"He's doin' some great work on the restoration." He was studying her carefully. As if, Dani thought, he feared she might shatter into pieces at any moment.

"Isn't that nice?" If she didn't get out of here now, this horrible smile was going to freeze onto her face. "As much as I'd love to hear all about them, I really do need to see how Matt's getting along. It's been a long trip and an eventful day."

"Sure. I really am glad you've come back, Dani. You've been missed."

"I missed you, too." That much, at least, was the truth. Ordering her legs to support her, Dani stood up. "More than I can say. You've no idea how much I appreciate you giving me this job. You saved my life."

"It's you who've saved mine. To tell you the truth, Mrs. Weaver didn't exactly retire. I fired her." He shook his head. "It wasn't that she didn't work damn hard, 'cause she did, but she just didn't have the people skills necessary to run a library."

Dani wasn't particularly surprised Agate Weaver had been fired. The woman who'd been as hard as her name, had stomped around in heavy, sensible shoes, had pulled her hair back into a face-tightening bun, and was constantly shushing anyone who dared speak in the hallowed halls of the library. She was the quintessential stereotypical librarian, the only one Dani had ever actually encountered.

"Well, I'll try to do better."

"A gator on a bad day could do better than that woman. Drove me nuts how she was all the time telling the young readers' groups about me losing that Horatio Hornblower book back in sixth grade. Which wouldn't have been so bad, since at least it showed the kids that we can all screw up, and go on to live productive lives, but she was becomin' more and more difficult to deal with professionally.

"The parish council had a knock-down, drag-out battle with her when she initially refused to have the Harry Potter books in the library because she said they were nothing more than pagan propaganda designed to lead innocent children into witchcraft. I also hated the way she'd decide whether or not to waive late fees depending on how she personally felt about a person, but the last straw was when she decided not to let Haley Villard take any books home because of the cockamamie idea that since the Villards grew peppers, the books might get pepper residue on the pages and blind some other kid who might pick up the dried pepper from the paper, then rub his eyes."

"Well, that's certainly a unique concern." Despite all her problems, Dani was beginning to feel better. Nate had always had that effect on her, which had her wishing, just for a moment, that she could have fallen in love with him instead of his brother.

"How about having dinner tomorrow night? We can catch up."

Was he asking her out on a date? This was definitely not the time to go jumping into the dating pool, especially with a man who'd charmed most of south Louisiana's women between the ages of eight and eighty. Before he was out of his teens.

No, when it came to men and relationships, Nate Callahan, as nice as he was, was definitely out of her league.

"Oh, Nate, I've love to, but I'm going to be so busy, what with this problem with the library, then there's Matt to worry about—"

"Bring him along."

*Relief*. He wasn't talking about a date. "Can I have a raincheck until I get Dad settled in with us?"

"Sure. The judge can come, too. It'll do him good to get out and around again after all this time away. You know, it's a real nice thing you're doing, movin' him in with you."

"He's my father," she said simply. "I hope the apartment will be finished by the time he's released. You'll have to come visit."

"It'll be great to see him. Jack says he's looking forward to gettin' sprung."

"Jack?"

"Damn. This seems to be my day for screwing up."

"Don't worry about it," she murmured through her hurt. "Obviously it's my day for surprises."

Jack was living in Beau Soleil. Jack had been visiting her father, the same man who'd sentenced the son of his housekeeper to a boot camp for delinquents and forbidden Dani to have anything to do with him after he'd been released.

What on earth did they find to talk about? Did they ever talk about that summer Jack had returned home? And more important, if so, what had her father told him about those months after he'd taken off again?

There was a roaring in her head like the sound of the sea, making it difficult to concentrate. She wrapped her arms around herself and tried to believe the icy air blowing through the wall vents was the reason she was chilled to the bone.

Nate gave her a quick peck on the cheek. "I'll set up a meeting with the fire marshal for tomorrow so we can see what we're going to need to do to get the library up and running again and the apartment fixed."

"I'd appreciate that," she heard herself say.

"I'm spendin' most of my time lately out at Beau Soleil, but how about we shoot for afternoon? About two?"

"That'll be fine. It'll allow me to enroll Matt in his new school in the morning."

Dani managed one final smile and walked him out to his SUV, then returned to the house. She closed the heavy oak and etched-glass door, leaned back against it, shut her eyes, and assured herself that Jack being back in Blue Bayou, even living in her old home, had nothing to do with her.

She told herself that again as she entered the homey kitchen. But when she sat down at the table beside Matt and dutifully expressed delight over the bounty Orèlia had prepared, Dani wondered miserably when she'd become such a liar.

"Don't worry, sugar," Desiree soothed as she ran a hand down Jack's bare chest. "It happens to every guy sooner or later."

"Not to me." Christ. What the hell was the matter with him? He hadn't had that much to drink. Yet. And God knows, Desiree had certainly done her part.

She hadn't bothered with preliminaries. They knew each other too well to need them. As soon as he'd entered her house, she'd pressed herself against him, her nipples diamond hard against his chest, and kissed him with the smooth and clever tongue action she'd always been so good at.

Enjoying the slap of lust, Jack had swept her up and carried her up the Caroline staircase.

The bedroom, which, rather than the stereotypical velvet and gaudy gilt one might think a former New Orleans call girl might favor, was a sea of soothing white. As soon as they entered the room, she'd turned to face him and with her eyes on his, slowly untied the silk sash at the waist of the dress and let it slide down her lush body to where it pooled at her feet on the snowy carpet.

Beneath the robe she'd been wearing a skimpy bra and a matching pair of thong bikini panties so brief Jack had wondered why she even bothered with them. The scarlet lace added another splash of hot color to the cool white decor.

He'd watched, appreciating the view, as she went around, lighting a collection of fragrant beeswax candles.

"I truly have missed you, Jack," she'd murmured once the room was glowing with a warm light.

She'd slipped out of the lace bra, revealing lush, round breasts he knew from their teenage days to be her own.

"Let me show you how much." Engulfing him in a fragrant cloud of the white roses she had specially blended at a shop in New Orleans's French Quarter, she'd run her palm down the front of his jeans, stroking his rock-hard erection.

His entire nervous system had been aroused. Expectant.

"Oh, yes," she'd murmured. Her smiling eyes had echoed the licentious approval in her throaty tone. "This is going to be a very good night."

She'd drawn back the satin comforter and turned on the stereo. But before she could switch it to CD mode, a newsflash broke into the country radio station.

Jack's blood had instantly chilled at the news of a fire at the library where Nate had told him Dani would be living with her son. His erection had deflated like a three-day-old balloon and remained that way, even after he'd learned no one had been in the building when the fire had broken out.

Desiree had certainly done her part to turn things around. Pretending not to notice, she'd unzipped his jeans, pulled them down his legs, then retraced the path with sharp, stinging kisses designed to make any man rock hard.

She'd nibbled at his thighs; blown a warm breath against the front of his white cotton briefs. Then, with a clever practiced touch, she'd released his still-flaccid cock from the placket of the briefs.

They'd fallen onto the bed, rolled around on Egyptian cotton sheets that felt like silk and probably cost as much as Jack's first car. She'd murmured hot sexual suggestions. Things she wanted him to do to her, things she planned to do to him.

But even when her ripe red lips replaced her stroking touch, his mutinous body had refused to cooperate.

"Don't worry about it," she repeated now.

She touched her lips to his, this kiss meant to soothe rather than arouse, then climbed out of bed and walked across the sea of white carpet. Her tousled hair fell halfway down her back; her bare ass was high and firm and appealing. But Jack didn't need to lift the sheet to know that even that seductive sight wasn't working tonight.

She didn't bother closing the bathroom door. When he heard the sound of water running into the tub, Jack dragged his hands down his face. The unpalatable fact was that he was a lost cause and the more she tried, the worse things were going to get.

"Jack, darlin'?"

"Yeah?" He sighed. Glared down at the offending body part, which continued to defy him.

She returned wearing a short white robe that clung in all the right places. "Why don't you get your dog?"

"The dog?" This was the last damn thing he'd been expecting. "Why?"

"Because we're going to give the sweet thing a bubble bath."

Two hours later, with the mutt smelling like a high-class brothel, Jack was sitting in the kitchen, eating his way through a steak Desiree had grilled and ignoring the bits of meat she kept slipping the dog beneath the table.

The mood was relaxed, even comfortable, and as he filled her in on Beau Soleil's progress, and his new book, Jack almost managed to convince himself that tonight's problem had everything to do with overwork and nothing to do with Danielle.

# 5

*She couldn't sleep.* Somewhere before dawn, after tossing and turning all night, Dani crawled from her rumpled bed and slipped out of the house. She sat out on the porch, looked out over the still, darkened bayou in the direction of Beau Soleil and wondered if she'd made a mistake coming home to Blue Bayou after all these years.

She'd thought she'd put the past behind her, believed she'd moved beyond the feelings of pain and loss. Oh, granted, every April when she'd write another birthday letter to the daughter who'd never read any of them, she'd sink into a depression that could last the entire month, but she'd always been able to hide it from her husband, her child, and the other librarians she worked with, and eventually it would pass.

But while she'd been lying alone in that single bed in Orèlia's guest room, staring out the window, she'd found herself thinking back to other nights spent looking out another window, hoping against hope that Jack would come and take her away. Bygone scenes had flashed through Dani's mind, forcing her to consider the idea that she may have been fooling herself all these years.

She'd certainly been in deep denial after Jack had disappeared from her life. Despite the fact that the only sex education she'd ever received had been a short vague film about menstruation shown in her seventh grade all-girls gym class, Dani had done enough research on her own at the library to know exactly how unprotected sex could lead to pregnancy. But Jack had been so careful to protect her, always using a condom, she'd never thought it could happen to her.

"Famous last words," she murmured now with a touch of bittersweet affection toward that naive and foolish seventeen-year-old girl she'd once been. Even after the condom had broken the last time they'd made love together the night before he'd left town, she'd been quick to assure Jack that it was a safe time of the month for her, even though she'd known otherwise. But surely you couldn't get pregnant from just one slip, and besides, a secret part of herself actually hoped she *would* get pregnant. Then she could move out of her father's house, and she and Jack could get married.

Then she began to throw up, not just in the mornings, but all during the day and evening as well, but having begun to realize that Jack really wasn't coming back, she'd pretended to herself that it would all go away.

One Saturday afternoon, three months to the day after Jack had last made love to her, Dani had taken the bus to New Orleans, where, with a dry mouth and sweaty hands, she'd bought a self-test pregnancy kit at a French Quarter drugstore. Since the instructions had said the test had to be taken in the morning, she'd had to sneak the white paper pharmacy bag into the house, hiding it in the closet behind her shoe rack, as if her father might actually suddenly decide to search her room.

The sad truth had been he would have been more likely to have flown to the moon on gossamer wings than enter her bedroom for any reason. As far as she could tell, most of the time she was invisible to her father, and on those rare occasions when he *would* acknowledge her presence, she seemed more annoyance than daughter.

Time had crawled with nerve-racking slowness while she'd waited for the test results, which, as she'd begun to fear, had proven positive. She'd known she wasn't going to be able to hide her pregnancy forever, but that didn't stop her from being paralyzed by the fear of what would happen when the judge discovered her shameful secret.

Dani had continued to live her lie for another two agonizing weeks, pretending everything was normal, while she felt as if she was dying inside, until finally Marie Callahan, of all people, guessed the truth and dragged her into kindly Dr. Vallois's office, where he'd confirmed what she'd already determined for herself. She was going to have a baby. Jack's baby.

With the clarity of hindsight, Dani realized that Marie must have been as stricken as she herself had been, but the Dupree housekeeper and grandmother of Dani's unborn child had nevertheless literally stood beside her as, with sweating palms and pounding heart, she'd haltingly confessed the truth to an icily cold father.

The night before she'd broken the news of her pregnancy, instead of Jack returning on his own, she'd dreamed that her father would immediately leap to her aid and track Jack down, wherever he was, and insist he married her. He would, of course, belatedly realize exactly how much he loved her, apologize for having caused her so much pain, then, just like her earlier rosy scenario, they'd live happily ever after.

The reality proved far different from the fantasy.

With the same efficiency he'd always demonstrated in his courtroom, Judge Dupree made a series of phone calls and within minutes had found Dani a place to live for the remainder of her pregnancy. Devastated and emotionally overwrought from months of bottling up so much stress, she'd tearfully begged to be allowed to stay at home.

But her father had remained adamant, and two days after her decidedly unwelcome revelation, Marie had driven her to Atlanta and helped her move into a Catholic home for unwed mothers, where the homily at Sunday mass inevitably focused on the biblical story of King Solomon, where the real mother was willing to surrender her child rather than see it cut in two.

A soft shimmering light began to glow on the horizon. Somewhere in the bayou morning birds began to trill, and across the street Chief Petty Officer Daniel Cahouet greeted the new day by standing on his front lawn and playing an off-key rendition of Reveille on his trumpet as he'd been doing every morning since returning home from the Pacific at the end of World War II.

Brushing the tears from her cheeks, Dani stood up and went back into the house to get ready to face what she feared was going to be a very trying day.

"So how bad is the library?" Jack asked as he hammered a piece of crown molding onto the newly plastered wall.

The molding Nate had hand-tooled looked good. Better than good, it had turned out goddamn great. You couldn't tell where the original stuff left off and the new began. It was times like this when Jack allowed himself to feel optimistic about ever restoring the plantation house to its former glory.

"Not as bad as it looked last night." Nate lifted another strip of molding onto a pair of sawhorses. "I couldn't do a full walk-through because the windows were boarded up and a lot of the third floor was blocked off, but from what the fire marshal told me, if we can free up a couple guys from here, and I split my week between the two projects, we could probably get the place livable in a couple months. Less the time it takes for permits."

From his perch atop the sixteen-foot-tall ladder, Jack could see across the bayou where the mist was beginning to rise. His head was clear this morning. Too clear for comfort. It had him remembering things he didn't want to remember. Thinking thoughts he didn't want to think.

"She looks good," Nate volunteered. "A little on the slender side, perhaps, which could just be some female fashion thing. And tired, which is to be expected, after driving down from Virginia. But she still looks damn fine."

Jack drove in another nail. "I don't remember asking how she looked."

"I know. I figured I'd save you the trouble of tryin' to figure out how to slide it into the conversation while pretending you didn't care."

Jack swore, then swung the hammer with more force than necessary, risking denting the millwork. "Her husband was a damn fool."

"It gets worse." The saw screeched as it sliced through the wood, sending sawdust flying. "Turns out she didn't know you'd bought this place."

Jack looked down at him. "You're fuckin' kidding."

"Nope. Hell, she didn't even know they'd owned it all these past years. The guy must've forged her signature on the papers."

"He wasn't just a fool, he was a goddamn son of a bitch."

The force of Jack's voice had the dog, who'd been sprawled in a morning sunbeam, glance up, her expression wary.

*Terrific.* Now he was scaring dogs. Maybe when he finished up here for the day he could drive into town, drop by the kindergarten, and terrorize little kids.

He climbed down the ladder, reached into an orange bag, and tossed the mutt a Frito. She snatched the corn chip from the air and swallowed it without bothering to chew. Her anxiety sufficiently eased, she sighed, stretched, and settled back to sleep.

"Too bad we didn't know about this before," Jack muttered. "Finn's in D.C. We could have him shoot the bastard."

"Yeah, that's a real good idea. The Mounties might have Dudley Do-Right, but the FBI has Finn Callahan. Not only does our big brother probably not jaywalk, I'd be willin' to bet he doesn't even piss in the shower."

"Good point." Of the three Callahan brothers, Finn was the most like their father. Although only a few years older, he'd also served as their surrogate father after Jake Callahan had been killed in the line of duty.

Nate moved the molding to the miter saw. "Dani's lucky to be rid of the guy even if she does have to keep a lot of plates spinning these days, what with the new job, getting her son settled into a new place, and bringing the judge home from Angola."

"Unfortunately, that isn't the half of it."

"You know something I don't?"

"Other than the fact that fire could have been arson, which could put her and her kid at risk if the arsonist decides to try again?"

"What makes you think it was arson? It's an old building. I made sure the electrical was up to code before I invited her to stay there, but there's always a chance something external, like lightning, sparked that fire."

"Sure, there's a chance," Jack allowed. "But don't you find it a little interesting that the place the judge will be coming home to in a couple weeks just happened to nearly burn to the ground?"

"He's done his time. Why would anyone want to keep him from coming home?"

"If you were the guy who framed him, would you want him livin' in your backyard?"

"You still think he didn't do it?"

"I know he didn't."

"Because he told you."

"Yeah. The judge may be one hard-assed son of a bitch, who's undoubtedly earned his share of enemies during his lifetime, but he's honest to the core. He wouldn't have taken a bribe to save his soul."

"Well, the jury didn't see it that way. And he sure didn't contribute anything to his own defense."

"So I heard." Jack wondered if things might have gone down differently if he'd been living in Blue Bayou seven years ago.

"And now there's another problem?"

"Yeah."

"If you and the judge are thinkin' about playing detective and gettin' involved with the mob to try to prove his innocence, I need to know. As mayor, it's my job to keep the peace."

"Technically that's the sheriff's job."

"Then run for sheriff and we'll have someone who'll do that."

"I told you, I've gotten out of the crime-busting business."

And Jack wasn't one to break a confidence, not even to one of the three people in the world he trusted, his brother Finn and Alcèe being the other two. Unfortunately, the judge had specifically instructed him to keep their conversation to himself.

"Look, I can't talk about why, and it doesn't have anything to do with that old case, but stalling work on that apartment so Danielle will have to stay with Orèlia instead of movin' right into the apartment with the judge would be the best thing you could do for her right now."

"That's not gonna be easy. She's a smart lady; she might accept some initial delays, but I'll need some reason to drag it out."

"Blame me." Jack pounded in two more nails, then jammed the hammer through the leather loop of his tool belt. "Tell her I'm a hard-driving son of a bitch who's holding you to a legally binding schedule and you can't afford any late fees."

"She'd never believe that. You're my brother."

"Trust me. She'll believe the worst."

Nate exhaled a slow, soft whistle. "That won't win you any points, Jack."

"I'm not looking for points." Jack pulled a cigarette from his pocket and jammed it between his lips. "I'm also not looking to get involved in her life. Which, as you pointed out, is already messy enough."

"She's gonna to be furious," Nate warned.

Jack's only response was a negligent shrug, even as the idea of causing Danielle any more pain scraped him raw.

"It must be one helluva secret."

"Yeah." Jack blew out a stream of smoke. "It goddamn is."

He hadn't been quite honest with his brother. The fact was that years fighting the bad guys had made him suspicious of any coincidences. Such as the apartment over the library suddenly catching fire on the very day Danielle Dupree arrived to set up housekeeping for herself, her kid, and her father, Maximum Dupree, who'd certainly sent more than his share of criminals up the river.

But even if Jack's internal radar hadn't gone off the screen when he'd heard about the fire, there was another problem lurking in the wings. One Danielle couldn't be expecting.

He damned the judge for not being up front with her about his health problems from the beginning. Hell, refusing to have any contact with her all these years while he'd been in prison had been unnecessarily cruel, but keeping a secret like this, when who knew how much time they might have together, was even worse.

Oh, he'd claimed he'd been avoiding any contact with her all these years to protect her and her kid from the pain of scandal, but since she'd already suffered enough of that from her lying, cheating husband, Jack suspected it was more a case of the judge's damn stiff pride. And shame. Not only for whatever had landed him in prison, but possibly just perhaps he was feeling guilty about having run his daughter's lover out of town so many years ago.

Jack had already put that in the past. And even if he hadn't, if those prison doctors had gotten the diagnosis right, the judge should be concentrating on forging some sort of paternal relationship with Danielle before it was too late.

Jack had long ago decided that if he'd had a teenage daughter, he damn well wouldn't have wanted her running around with the wild kid he'd been back then. But if the judge had truly cared about what happened to Danielle, he wouldn't have pushed her into marrying that slick politician who, until the breakup of his outwardly perfect marriage and death, had seemed to be on a fast track to the White House.

She'd deserved better than Louisiana congressman Lowell Dupree.

And she sure as hell deserved better than him.

# 6

*What do you mean* I can't open the library until the work's completed on the apartment?" Dani asked the Blue Bayou fire marshal.

It had been three days since she'd arrived to find her new home in flames. Three very long and frustrating days spent waiting for this man to complete his inspection.

"The third floor is admittedly a mess," she conceded. "But the only thing wrong with the lower floors is some water damage I can take care of myself."

"The other floors appear okay," he allowed. "But the thing is, what you've got yourself here, Miz Dupree, is a hazardous situation. You're gonna have construction crews working with dangerous equipment, carrying ladders around, there'll be hot electrical wires hangin' loose, all sorts of stuff that could endanger innocent citizens."

He chewed on a short, fat unlit cigar and looked around the building, as if picturing the possible chaos. "Nope. Can't risk it."

Since she'd eventually need this frustratingly little man's signature on the final inspection report, Dani managed, just barely, to rein in her building temper.

"It's not as bad as it sounds." He appeared almost sympathetic for the first time since he'd climbed out of his red pickup truck. "Once you get your construction permits, it shouldn't take long to get things fixed up just fine. Better than ever, in fact, since you'll be upgrading the electrical, which should save you from any more unpleasant surprises."

Dani only wished life were that simple. "When will the permits be ready?"

"Oh, I wouldn't know 'bout that." He shrugged and closed his metal clipboard, his work here obviously finished. "You and your contractor—"

"My contractor is Nate Callahan. The *mayor* of Blue Bayou." Surely stressing Nate's position in the town hierarchy might help all those stacks of paperwork she'd had to fill out move through the grindingly slow parish governmental system a bit faster?

"So I heard. Well, anyway, you'll both need to appear at the monthly zoning commission meeting and request a variance if you're planing to live above the library."

"But the apartment's been part of the building for decades."

"Not anymore. It burned up," he reminded her. "Which makes it uninhabitable. A former commission grandfathered the original apartment in, allowing a dwelling in a commercial structure. But as it stands now, you're not zoned residential."

Dani fought the urge to grind her teeth. "Do you expect that to be a problem?"

He shrugged. Adjusted his red-billed cap. "It's not my job to say one way or the other. But, if I were a gambling man, I'd say you should get your permits. Sooner or later."

"When is this meeting?"

"Just had one last week. Settled a little dispute about some private boat docks and allowed Miss Bea's Tea House to serve lunch outside on the building's *gallerie*.

"So"— he chomped on the cigar as he checked a calendar on his clipboard—"that'd put the next one three weeks from yesterday."

"Three weeks?"

"Sorry. It's not—"

"Your job," Dani said dryly.

"No, ma'am. I'm afraid it's not."

Wishing her good luck, he pasted a fluorescent-yellow notice warning that her library was Hazardous and Unsafe for Occupation on the front door, then ambled back to his truck.

"I will get the permits," Dani muttered to herself as she drove to the parish offices in order to attempt to coax the planning and zoning commission secretary into scheduling a special meeting so she wouldn't have to wait another three weeks.

She was on a mission, and although it might be stretching comparisons, she was beginning to understand Scarlett O'Hara's determination when she'd yanked up those turnips.

"She had to save Tara." Thanks to her husband and father, Dani no longer had a huge antebellum plantation house to worry about. "All you have to do is fix up a two-bedroom apartment for your family."

How difficult could that be? This might be the New South, but some things never changed. The ability of a southern woman to survive was as strong in her as it had been in her great-grandmother Lurleen, who'd worked her fingers to bleeding as a dressmaker in order to pay off her husband's gambling debts and save Beau Soleil from those New York Yankee bankers.

Dani refused to complain or whine. She'd win her case before the zoning board. But first, she decided, as she parked in front of Paula's Pralines, she'd pick up a pretty gilt-wrapped box of candy for the zoning commissioner's secretary.

Three days later Dani's vow not to complain had flown out the window.

"I don't understand why the man can't pick up the damn phone," she muttered as she slammed the telephone receiver back in its cradle. "It's not like I'm going to insist he return my home. I just want a carpenter."

After blatantly bribing the secretary with those pralines, two tickets to the Dixie Chicks Baton Rouge concert, and a promise to put the woman's name at the top of the reserve list for the next Jack Callahan novel, Dani had gotten her permits. Which wouldn't do her a bit of good unless she could find someone to do the work.

Oh, Nate had been apologetic. Sympathetic. Even remorseful. But the fact remained that not only was Jack Callahan living in her house, he was standing in the way of her making a new home for her son.

"Perhaps he's all caught up in writing his new book," Orèlia suggested.

"Well, he's got to stop to eat." Dani threw her body onto a chair and snatched a piece of raisin toast from the plate in the center of the table. "Why can't he check his messages, then?"

It stung that Jack was ignoring her. But she'd worn down his defenses that summer. She'd just have to keep trying. After all, the stakes were so much higher this time. Back then she'd only risked her heart. Now the future of her family was at stake.

Dani liked Orèlia a great deal, and enjoyed the older woman's company. And it was, admittedly, a huge help not to have to worry about finding someone to stay with Matt after school while she was fighting her battles with the town bureaucrats and dealing with the million and one moving details. But they needed their own space. Space where Matt could be a normal little boy, free to run through the rooms without worrying about knocking some valued collectible off a table.

The apartment was a good stop-gap measure, until she got her debts paid off, but eventually Dani intended to buy her own home, with a big backyard for a swing set and a tree house.

With a renewed burst of optimism, as she absently centered the napkin holder and salt and pepper shakers, Dani thought that once they were permanently settled, perhaps she'd buy a few plants and take up gardening.

The series of storied terraces surrounding the swimming pool at her former Fairfax house may have won a prestigious national landscape design award and been featured in *Southern Living* magazine, but Dani hadn't been allowed to work in the garden for fear she might disturb the intricately planned design.

As for the lovely furniture that had been in her family for generations, furniture she'd taken from Beau Soleil when she'd married, she'd ending up selling that at a staggering loss to help pay off the enormous attorney bills the divorce had racked up.

Galling was the fact that she'd had to end up paying a major portion of Lowell's lawyer's fees as well as her own.

"*T'en fais pas, chérie,*" Orèlia said when Dani sighed again.

"I'm not worried." She would not allow herself to be. "Just frustrated."

As she rinsed off the empty plate and put it in the dishwasher, Dani wondered, yet again, where the hell Jack was hiding.

The phone was ringing, as it had been for the past two days. The dog quirked an ear that had been torn in some previous fight and looked questioningly up at Jack. When he didn't appear inclined to do anything about it, she lowered her head to her front paws and went back to sleep.

Jack turned off the belt sander he'd been using on the wainscoting and waited for the machine to pick up.

"Jack?"

Her voice, which as hard as he'd tried, he'd never been able to get out of his mind—or, dammit, his dreams—hadn't changed. It was cultured and touched with the soft cadence of the bayou South.

The first three times she'd called, he'd thought he'd detected a bit of nervousness; this time it was definitely irritation lacing those smooth magnolia tones.

"Dammit, Jack, are you there?"

Silence.

He heard a muttered, brief, pungent curse. The receiver on the other end of the line was slammed down. Jack hit the switch on the sander and went back to work.

# 7

*The sky was darkening,* the only visible light a band of purple clouds low on the western horizon. Dani had forgotten how quickly night came to the bayou. As she steered the rented boat through the maze-like labyrinth of waterways, fireflies lit up the waning twilight while nutria and muskrats paddled along, furry shadows in waters as dark and murky as Cajun coffee.

Bullfrogs began to croak; cicadas buzzed; blue herons glided among the ancient cypress which stood like silent, moss-bearded sentinels over their watery world.

The boat's light barely cut through the warm mist falling from low-hanging clouds; when the ridged and knobby head of an alligator appeared in the stuttering glow, looking like a wet brown rock amidst the lily pads, Dani's nerves, which were already as tattered as a Confederate soldier's gray uniform, screeched.

"This is nuts."

If she had any sense at all, she'd cut her losses now and return to town. But she'd already come this far, and unless both her internal homing device and the boat's GPS system had gone entirely on the blink, she couldn't be that far from Beau Soleil.

She checked her watch. Despite the way the isolation and deepening shadows had seemed to slow time, she'd been out on the water for less than half an hour.

"Five more minutes," she decided. If she hadn't reached Beau Soleil by then, she'd turn back.

A moment later she came around a corner, and there, right in front of her, was the Greek Revival antebellum mansion. Dani was glad she'd undertaken the nerve-racking trip tonight; as bad as the plantation house appeared, it would have been far worse to first see it again after all these years in the hard, unforgiving glare of southern sunlight.

The double front entrance harkened back to a time when if a suitor happened to catch a glimpse of a girl's ankles, he was duty bound to marry her. In a typically southern blend of practicality and romance, the house had been designed with dual sets of front steps—one for hoop-skirted belles, the other for their gentlemen escorts. The ladies' staircase had crumbled nearly to dust; the other was scarcely better, held up as it was with a complex design of erector-set-style metal braces.

Beau Soleil had survived being set on fire by the British in the War of 1812, cannonballed, then occupied by Yankee soldiers—and their horses—during the War Between the States. It had also stalwartly stood up to numerous hurricanes over its more than two centuries. Seeing the once noble plantation house looking like an aging whore from some seedy south Louisiana brothel made Dani want to weep.

It had belatedly dawned on her, after she'd left town, that her plan to catch Jack unaware could backfire if she came all the way out here only to find the house dark and deserted. But she'd been so frustrated that she'd acted without really thinking things through.

The light in the upstairs windows of the once stately house was an encouraging sign as she eased the boat up to the dock that was still, thankfully, standing. It appeared to be the same dock her father had paid Jack to build the summer of her seventeenth birthday, the summer her carefree, youthful world had spun out of control.

With a long-ago learned skill some distant part of her mind had retained, she tied up the boat behind an old pirogue and then studied the house. Amazingly, most of the centuries-old oak trees had survived time and the ravages of storms; silvery Spanish moss draped over their limbs like discarded feather boas left behind by ghostly belles.

She lifted her gaze to a darkened window on the second floor and envisioned the reckless teenager she'd once been, climbing out that window to meet her lover. Her skin, beneath her white T-shirt, burned with the memory of Jack's dark, work-roughened fingers encircling her waist to lift her down from that last low-hanging limb.

"A smart *fille* like yourself should know better than to sneak up on someone at night in this part of the country," a deep, painfully familiar voice offered from the blackness surrounding her.

Dani yelped. Then hated herself for displaying any weakness. Splaying a palm against her chest to slow her tripping heart, she turned slowly toward the *gallerie*.

He was hidden in the shadows, like a ghost from the past, with only the red flare of a cigarette revealing his location.

"You could have said something. Instead of scaring me to half to death."

"If I figured you and I had anything to say to each other, I would have returned your calls." His voice was even huskier than Dani remembered. Huskier and decidedly uninviting.

"So you did get my messages."

"Yeah. I got 'em." Although night had dropped over the bayou, there was enough light shining from the windows of Beau Soleil for her to see him. He was wearing a gray Ragin' Cajun T-shirt with the sleeves cut off, a pair of jeans worn nearly to the point of indecency and cowboy boots. He was rugged, rangy, and, dammit, still as sexy as hell.

"But you chose to ignore them."

He took a swig from a longneck bottle of Dixie beer. "Yeah."

Well, this was going well. "I happen to know your mother taught you better manners."

"I was never known for my manners. Drove *Maman* nuts."

That was certainly true. He'd been known throughout the bayou as Bad Jack Callahan. A devil in blue jeans with the face of a fallen angel.

"I was sorry when she died."

Unlike so many of the large sprawling Catholic families who made the bayou their home, Dani had no brothers or sisters, nieces or nephews, aunts, uncles, or cousins. After her mother had abandoned them before Dani's second birthday (subsequently dying two years later), there had only been her and her father, and while single fathers may have been a staple on television, her own had left her upbringing to a revolving parade of housekeepers.

And then had come that fateful day when, after the shooting that had tragically claimed her husband's life, Marie Callahan had shown up at the house, her three teenage sons in tow. Marie had quickly stepped into the role of surrogate mother; she'd baked Dani birthday cakes, taken her shopping for her first box of tampons, and soothed her wounded pride when an attack of nerves had her failing her driver's test the first time.

Of course, Marie had also sided with her employer against the two teenagers that bittersweet summer that still, after all these years, lingered in Dani's mind like a dream remembered upon awakening.

When she'd died, too young, of breast cancer, Dani had swallowed her pride and sent Jack a handwritten note of sympathy. He never responded. Nor did he return home for his mother's funeral, something that surprised even his most stalwart detractors, who'd reluctantly admitted that despite his wild devilish ways, Jack Callahan had always been good to his *maman*.

"Yeah. I was damn sorry, too." He sighed heavily as he flicked away the cigarette, which flared in a sparkling orange arc that sizzled, then snuffed out when it hit the water.

After polishing off the beer, he tossed the bottle aside, pushed himself to his feet, and came down the stairs, crunching across the gleaming oyster-shell walk on the loose-hipped, masculine stride that had always reminded Dani of a swamp panther.

Now, as he loomed out of the blackened shadows, his tawny gold predator's eyes gleaming, the resemblance was a bit too close for comfort.

He'd always been outrageously handsome, and the years hadn't changed that. But time had carved away whatever bit of softness he'd kept hidden away deep in his heart. His full sensual lips were drawn into a forbidding line, and a savage slash of cheekbones cut their way across features far more harshly hewn than they'd been when he was younger.

His hair appeared nearly as long as hers and glistened darkly with moisture. It flowed back from his strong forehead and was tied at the nape of his neck in a way that made her think of the pirates who used to escape to Blue Bayou after raiding Spanish merchant ships in the Gulf. Taking in the surprising gold earring he hadn't owned when she'd known him last, Dani decided that all he was missing was the cutlass.

*Dangerous* was the first word that sprang to mind. Maybe Bad Jack Callahan himself didn't present any danger to her, but the unbidden feelings he'd always been able to stir in her certainly could be.

"You shouldn't have come here, Danielle," he said bluntly.

He'd said those same words to her once before. Warning her off. Dani hadn't listened then, nor could she now.

"You didn't give me any choice, hiding away out here in the swamp like some mad hermit trapper."

He didn't respond to her accusation. Just gave her a long, deep look. Then grazed his knuckles up her cheek. "You're bleeding."

Her skin heated, as if he'd skimmed a candle flame up it. Dani took a cautious step back, lifted her own fingers to the cheek she belatedly realized was stinging and had to remind herself how to breathe.

In.

"It's undoubtedly just a scratch from a tree limb."

Out.

"This isn't the easiest place to get to, with the road gone."

In again.

"Flooding from last season's hurricane wiped out the road," he revealed "Since the place was already crumblin', the parish commissioners didn't see any reason to spend public funds to rebuild a road to make it easier to get to some place no one wanted to go anyway."

"Which, from what I hear, suits you just fine. I suppose you would have been happier if I'd gotten lost coming out here."

"Hell, no, I wouldn't have wanted you to get lost." He blew a frustrated breath between his teeth. "I'm paying to have the road graded, since I've decided it's got to be cheaper than continuing to bring things in by water. If you'd only waited another week, you could have avoided the boat trip."

"I couldn't wait that long."

*"Sa c'est fou."*

"I've done crazier things."

A rough, humorless sound rumbled out of his broad chest. "I sure as hell won't be arguin' with that, *chérie*."

Dani was not foolish enough to take the endearment to heart. Hadn't she heard him call his old bluetick hound the very same thing?

"We were both damn crazy that summer," he mused aloud, with something that surprisingly sounded a bit like regret.

*Jack* was the one who'd deserted *her*. If he'd regretted his behavior, he could have called. Or written. Instead, he'd disappeared off the face of the earth, leaving her to face the consequences of their reckless romance alone.

"I'm not here to talk about that summer."

His eyes, which had seemed to soften a bit with remembered affection, shuttered, like hurricane shutters slammed tight before a storm. "Then why are you here?"

Good question. If it'd been only herself, she would have slept on the street rather than come crawling to Jack for anything. But she had Matt to think of. An innocent little boy who needed a roof over his head.

There was nothing Dani would not do for her son, including winding her way through inky-black bayou waters risking gators and heaven knows how many different kinds of snakes to beg this man for help.

"You seem to have hired every available construction worker from here to Baton Rouge."

"As impossible as it may be for you to fathom, sugar, this place is even worse structurally than it looks. It's a smorgasbord for termites, half the roof blew away in the last storm, the plumbing's flat rusted through, and what the inspector laughingly referred to as an electrical system is a bonfire waiting to happen.

"I could hire every damn construction worker from Lafayette to New Orleans and probably still not have a large enough crew to finish the work in this lifetime."

"Perhaps you ought to just build a new house that won't give you so many problems," she suggested with openly false sweetness.

"And let the bayou reclaim Beau Soleil? Not on your life."

The force in his tone surprised Dani. "I never realized you felt so strongly about it."

He rocked back on his heels as he looked up at the once magnificent house draped in deep purple shadows. For a fleeting second his tawny eyes looked a hundred years old. "Neither did I."

"Well." That unexpected bit of honesty left Dani at a momentary loss for words. She reminded herself of her mission. "I need a carpenter, Jack. And I need him now."

He gave her another of those long unfathomable, brooding looks. Then shrugged again. "I don' know about you, but I skipped lunch today to meet with a pirate who calls himself a septic tank engineer and I'm starvin'.

"There's some chicken in the smoker, and after we take care of that scratch on your face, you can peel the shrimp while I make the roux.

Then we can pass ourselves a good time over some gumbo and jambalaya and see if we can come up with a way for both of us to get what we want."

Determined to settle her business, Dani forced down her concern about getting back to town. Marie Callahan had once told her that the way to a man's heart was through his stomach. At the time, since she'd been sleeping with Marie's son, Dani had known—and kept to herself—the fact that Jack's other hungers had held first priority.

Still, perhaps he might be more amenable to negotiation after a good meal. Even one he'd cooked himself.

"That sounds like a reasonable enough solution."

A waning white moon was rising in the sky as they walked in silence toward the house, the bayou water lapping against the raised narrow pathway. Dani had just about decided that the rumors she'd heard of Jack as a dark and crazy swamp devil, living out here like the fabled *Loup Garou,* were merely gossip, when he suddenly crouched down and plunged his hand into the inky water.

The violent splash sent a flock of ducks who'd been sleeping in the nearby reeds exploding into the sky, firing the night with a dazzling shower of falling stars.

"*Bon Dieu,*" he murmured. "I've never seen the ghost fire so bright." He brought up a broad, long-fingered hand that glowed with phosphorescence in the purple velvet dark surrounding them. Sparks seemed to fall back into the water as he stood up again. "You still set this bayou on fire, *mon ange*."

His feral gold eyes drifted down to her lips and lingered wickedly for what seemed like an eternity, as if he were remembering the taste and feel of them.

He moved closer. Too close. But if she tried to back away, she'd risk falling into the water.

"I'm not your angel," she insisted, even as erotic pictures of them rolling around on a moss-stuffed mattress flashed through her mind, making her breasts feel heavy beneath the white T-shirt that had been pristine when she'd begun her long, frustrating day but was now clinging damply to her body.

Although it had to be at least ninety degrees, with a humidity equally high, her nipples pebbled as if she'd dived naked into the Arctic Ocean. She dearly hoped it was dark enough for him not to notice.

It wasn't. "You can lie to me, sugar. You can try to lie to yourself. But your pretty angel's body is saying something else. It remembers, she. The same way mine does."

Dani managed, with herculean effort, to drag her gaze from his, but couldn't resist skimming a look over his broad chest and still-flat stomach, down to where his erection was swelling against the faded placket of his jeans.

"See something you like, *chère?*"

Heat flooded into her face. "You know how it is," she said breezily. "You've seen one, you've seen them all. It is comforting to discover that not everything around Blue Bayou has changed. You still have sex on the mind."

"*Mais* yeah," he countered without an iota of apology. His wicked eyes glittered with predatory intent as they took a blatantly male appraisal from the top of her head down to her sneaker-clad feet. Then just as leisurely roamed back up to her face. "The day I stop reacting to a desirable female is the day I tie some weights around my neck and throw myself in the bayou as gator bait."

Dani was no longer a virginal Catholic girl experiencing sexual desire for the first time. She was a grown woman who, in the years since she'd left home, had overcome a broken heart, married, given birth to a son she adored, and, if it hadn't been for that wayward piano, would have been the first divorcée in Dupree family history.

This bayou bad boy leering at her should not make her stomach flutter and her pulse skip.

It shouldn't.

But, heaven help her, it did.

As they resumed walking toward Beau Soleil, she vowed not to let Jack's still powerful sexual magnetism turn her into some fluttery, vapid southern belle who'd swoon at his feet. Or any other part of his anatomy.

But when he put a casual, damp hand on her hip to steady her as she climbed up the braced stairway to the *gallerie*, Dani feared that if she wasn't very, very careful, she could discover exactly how dangerous supping with Blue Bayou's very own home-grown devil could be.

# 8

*Jack had taken* an immediate inventory the minute she'd stepped out of the boat. Five-five, a hundred-ten pounds, blond hair, and although he hadn't been able to see them from the *gallerie*, he knew her eyes were a bluish green hazel with gold flecks. Other than that scratch on her cheek, she had no distinguishing marks or scars. There were probably millions of women in the world who'd fit that physical profile. Yet in none of those women would the physical details have been put together in a more appealing package.

He'd managed to convince himself that just as he'd changed over the years, Dani would have, too. It was true she'd changed. For the better.

There were the expected outer differences: hair that had once flowed to her waist was now woven into a loose braid that fell a bit past her shoulders. Despite the slenderness Nate had reported, her body was more curvaceous than it'd been when he'd last seen her. Touched her. Tasted her.

When they entered the house, the light streaming from the chandelier in the grand entry hall revealed bruise-like shadows beneath her eyes. Long-dormant protective instincts stirred.

Dangerous thinking, that. Bad enough the way those wide, hit-you-in-the-gut expressive eyes still dominated her oval face, bad enough that he could remember, with aching clarity, the taste of her unpainted lips, and God help him, it was fuckin' damn deadly dangerous the way whatever sunshine scent she'd splashed on before leaving town smelled like heaven and drew him like a silver lure.

She'd been forbidden fruit thirteen years ago. Jack was trying to recall all the reasons she still was when he heard a familiar clattering sound.

"Oh, shit. Brace yourself." He managed to jump in front of Dani just as the huge ball of yellow fur came barreling into the hall, tore past him like a running back evading a blocker, stood on its hind legs, braced both huge paws on her shoulders, and began licking her face.

"Well, hello," she greeted the dog, with amazing aplomb for a woman who'd just been attacked by a beast that weighed nearly as much as she did.

He grabbed the leather collar and yanked the stray to the marble floor. The dog wagged its tail and continued dancing around Dani. There was a muddy pawprint the size of Jack's spread hand above her left breast.

"Sorry about that," he muttered. "She tends to be standoffish with strangers."

"So I see." She scratched the enormous head that thrust itself beneath her palm. "I had no idea you had a dog."

"She's not really mine." If he owned a dog, it'd damn well be better trained, like the obedient German shepherds he'd worked with on various drug-smuggling investigations. It sure as hell wouldn't jump up and slobber all over people the minute they walked in the door. "I'm just letting her crash here for a while till I get around to taking her to the shelter in town."

"I see." It was clear she didn't believe him. Which wasn't all that surprising, since he was starting not to believe it himself. "What kind of dog is she?"

"My guess would be a Great Dane-yellow Lab-Buick mix."

Her answering laugh slipped beneath his skin and over his nerve endings like quicksilver. "I always wanted a dog."

"I never knew that."

"There was a lot you didn't know about me," she said mildly. "Why are you locked up inside on such a lovely night, sweetheart?" she asked the dog.

"Because last night she decided to go nine rounds with a skunk, and I don't have enough tomato juice left for a rematch," he answered for the mutt.

"Poor baby." Dani smiled at the dog, who appeared to grin right back. "What's her name?"

"Turnip. Because she just turned up," he elaborated when she quirked a brow.

"Well, it's certainly original."

Her smile faded as her gaze drifted to the mural that covered the walls of the two-story hall, rose to the plaster ceiling medallions he'd repainted, then up the curved sweeping staircase that had shown up in more than one movie.

"That's odd."

"What?"

"I'd always heard that when you come back home as an adult, things are supposed to look smaller, less grand than you remembered them."

"Hard for Beau Soleil not to look grand. Even in the sorry state it's in."

"True." The mural depicted Acadian forced deportation from Nova Scotia and the deportee's subsequent arrival in Louisiana, continuing up the stairs with the story of the star-crossed lovers Evangeline and Gabriel, immortalized by Longfellow. "It's different," she murmured. "But the same."

"I had it cleaned and touched up. It was a bit tricky because in the nineteenth century murals were painted right onto the plaster, which aged as the plaster aged. These days they're done on canvas that's glued to the wall, so the owners can take them with them when they move to a new house."

"Well, isn't that handy." She turned toward him, her expression bland, but the quick, intense flair of passion in her eyes warned that she wasn't as calm as outward appearances might suggest. "I'm going to be honest with you, Jack. I hate the idea of you living in my home."

"Fair enough," he allowed. "But you hatin' it isn't going to change a thing."

"Of all the houses, in all the world, why did you buy this one?"

"Would you have preferred I let the bayou claim it?"

"Of course not."

"How about the mob? Would you have enjoyed coming home to tourists playing blackjack in the summer parlor to a background music of slot machines?"

"You're supposed to be an intelligent man," she said through set teeth. "You should be able to figure out the answer to that yourself."

She moved along the wall, from where the men, women, and children were being herded by British troops onto the ships of exile during *Le Grand Derangement*—The Great Madness—out of Nova Scotia, eventually to the Evangeline oak where the long-suffering, tragic heroine awaited her beloved Gabriel.

"It has such a tragic ending," she murmured, seeming to momentarily put aside her pique. "For a love story."

"Most love stories are tragedies."

"Do you honestly believe that?"

"Sure." He shrugged, wishing he'd kept his big mouth shut. "Look at you and me."

She paled, then quickly recovered. "I didn't come here to talk about us," she repeated, giving him a haughty-princess-to-serf look that didn't exactly have him quaking in his boots. It hadn't worked on him back then, and sure as hell wouldn't now. "And that summer didn't have anything to do with love."

"Maybe not. But it sure was hot." He leaned closer. Skimmed a palm over her shoulder. "And a lot of fun while it lasted."

"Definitive point. It didn't last that long." She batted away his light caress and headed toward the kitchen. "And don't touch me."

"I remember when you liked me touching you." Begged him to, actually, but Jack decided she wouldn't appreciate him reminding her of that.

"That was then. This is now."

"*Oui*. But like you said, some things, they don't change."

"Dammit, Jack—"

This time when she slapped at his touch, he caught hold of her hand. "I still want you, *'tite ange*." God help him, it was the truth. Understanding all too well the dark, drowning sense of inevitability his fictional drug agent felt when he was in the same room with the gorgeous, lethal drug dealer's daughter, Jack drew her closer, until they were touching, thigh to thigh, chest to chest. She was like the Evangeline and Gabriel mural, he considered. Different, but the same. "And you still want me."

"You need a little help with your dialogue." Jack got a perverse kick at the way she lifted her chin. The out-of-reach bayou princess was definitely back. All that was missing was a satin ballgown and sparkly tiara. "The only thing I want from you is a carpenter." She pulled away.

Though it wasn't his first choice, he let her. "And supper," he reminded her.

"Not even that. Just tell me what it'll take to get your cooperation, short of taking my clothes off," she tacked on quickly when his mouth twitched. "Then I'll be on my way."

"You've been livin' in the city too long, you." To please himself, he played with a silky strand of hair that had escaped the braid. "Where people don' know how to take time to enjoy themselves." He wanted his hands on her. His mouth. And that was just for starters. "Things move a little slower here in the swamp."

"Tell me about it. I could have built the damn Taj Mahal in the length of time it took to maneuver my way through the byzantine maze the zoning bureau refers to as policy and procedures to get a permit to get repairs done on the library."

"You could have gone back home." It'd be better—safer—for both of them if she did.

"I did." She tossed up her chin in a way that made Jack want to kiss her silly. "Blue Bayou is my home."

Jack sighed. Skimmed his thumb up her cheekbone. "Let's clean this scratch. Have ourselves a little gumbo. Then we'll talk."

Dani didn't want to stay. For a multitude of reasons. The first being that it hurt, really hurt, to see someone else, even this man she'd once loved, living in the home that had belonged to her family for so many generations. The home she'd always envisioned raising her own babies in.

She also didn't want to stay because Jack made her uneasy. He may be a hotshot writer now, he may have worn a tux when he mingled with Russell Crowe and Jennifer Lopez at the premiere of the movie made from his first book, he may have been interviewed by a breathless Mary Hart on the famed red carpet at the Academy Awards, but beneath the polish he'd picked up since she'd known him—loved him—were those same rough, workingman's hands that had once caused such pleasurable havoc to her body, the flowing black pirate's hair, the unyielding jaw, the lush, sensuous mouth that suggested all sorts of sins and might have appeared feminine had it not been for the contrast of his ruggedly hewn face that had been compared to a young Clint Eastwood. Put it all together and you got a combination more dangerous than mixing TNT and nitroglycerin and setting a match to them. A danger a prudent woman would avoid.

"Sit down on that bar stool and I'll get the medicine kit." His take-charge attitude grated, even as his roughened voice curled through her like dark smoke.

"I'm perfectly capable of taking care of a little scrape by myself."

"You're a guest," he said mildly, as if living in Beau Soleil for a few months made him damn lord of the manor.

Acting as if it were his perfect right to touch her, he put his hands on either side of her waist, lifted her onto a bar stool at a curved granite counter that hadn't been there when she lived in the house. When he left the room, Dani slid off the stool, seriously considered pulling the plug on this fool's effort and escaping back to town. Where it seemed she belonged, since there was no longer any place for her here at Beau Soleil.

"Going somewhere?" he asked casually when he returned with a brown bottle.

"I've decided I'm not hungry after all."

"Then you just watch me eat while we talk about your problem. Meanwhile, let's get this clean."

"Ow!" She drew her head back at the sting when he touched the dampened cotton ball to her cheek.

"Hold still." He caught her chin in the fingers of his left hand and continued to clean the scratch.

"Dammit, you're doing this on purpose."

"Doing what?"

"Using that instead of some nice modern antibiotic cream."

"This happens to be all I've got in the place. Besides, I'm an old-fashioned kind of guy. And I don't remember you being such a whiner."

"I'm not."

"Good. Then why don't you shut that pretty little mouth up and think of something pleasant."

"Such as the sheriff throwing you out of Beau Soleil?"

His damnably sexy lips quirked, just a little, revealing that her barb hadn't stung. "Never happen. Old Jimbo Lott'd have to get off his fat butt first."

"He was at the library fire."

"That's not such a surprise. Mos' everyone likes to see the results of a job well done."

This time it was surprise, rather than pain, that had her pulling away. "Surely you're not suggesting Sheriff Lott set that fire?"

"I'm not saying he did. But I'm not sayin' he didn't, either. The man's definitely got motive and opportunity."

"What motive would he have to burn a library?"

"Maybe he doesn't want you setting up housekeepin' in Blue Bayou. Maybe he doesn't want you makin' some nice cozy place for the judge to come home to."

"I don't understand."

"You don't need to, you." He tossed the cotton ball into a wastebasket and capped the hydrogen peroxide. "All you have to do is just stay at Orèlia's till the judge is sprung. Then go back home to D.C. or Virginia, or wherever you came from."

"I came from here. Washington was never my home. Nor was Virginia. It was only where I had to live because my husband was a member of Congress. *This* is my home," she repeated. And she wasn't going to let Jack or Jimbo Lott or anyone else chase her away.

"Maybe it was once upon a time ago, but as you pointed out, I'm livin' in it now. So, looks like there's nothin' to keep you here in Blue Bayou."

"Only Dupree roots going back generations. Roots I want to pass on to my child."

A guilt she was never very far away from stirred as Dani recalled another child she'd once longed to bring home to Beau Soleil. She took a took a deep breath and decided this was the time to bring up a thought that had been spinning around in her mind ever since Nate first told her that Jack had bought Beau Soleil.

"What if I were to make you an offer? Would you leave?"

He arched a black brow. "You always have been one for surprises, *chère*. Didn't realize you had that much money stashed away."

"I don't," she admitted. "But maybe we could work something out."

"For old time's sake?"

She wouldn't have thought, since he'd been the one to run away, that Jack would want to bring up old times. "Not exactly. But as you pointed out, Beau Soleil needs a lot of work. Surely the renovation must interfere with your writing."

He shrugged and lit a cigarette. "Not that much. I'm pretty much in a zone when I'm working. 'Sides, I sorta like bein' a man of property."

"Why can't you be a man of someone else's property?"

"Because I want Beau Soleil."

"And the great and mighty Jack Callahan gets everything he wants, right?"

His eyes shadowed, just for an instant, then hardened. "Not always." The cigarette dangled from his lips as he skimmed a long, intimate look over her. "But if you were to sweet-talk me real nice, sugar, you and I might just be able to work out some sort of arrangement."

He'd proven himself untrustworthy at eighteen. Dani didn't trust him now. "What kind of arrangement?"

She knew she'd made a mistake asking the question when his eyes glinted and his smile turned from sexually seductive to downright feral. "I could always take it out in trade."

Heat as red as the glowing end of his cigarette shot into her cheeks. "Isn't it strange how time dims memory? I certainly don't remember you being so disgusting."

That was it. If she didn't leave now, she'd give into impulse and start throwing the knives from the nearby oak rack at his head. She'd just have to take her search for workmen a bit farther, to Baton Rouge or New Orleans, perhaps.

"You don't wanna leave now." He caught her by the waist again as she began to march away. "Just when things are beginnin' to get interesting."

"Obviously we have a different definition of interesting." She managed to keep her tone cool even as those long fingers digging into her skin beneath her T-shirt made her feel shaky. Edgy. And, heaven help her, needy.

The only time Lowell had ever touched her was in bed. Then finally, nearly two years ago, he'd stopped touching her all together. She thought that the fact it had been six months before she'd noticed the absence of any sex said a great deal about her marriage.

"The place isn't exactly ready for company. But how about I give you the grand tour? Show you how things are progressin'."

Damn. Trust him to dangle the one bit of bait she found almost impossible to refuse. Dani hesitated, curiosity warring with the primal, survivalist urge to run. She didn't trust him. Didn't like him. Her head knew that. Her heart knew it, as well. But for some unfathomable reason, her body hadn't seemed to get the message. *It* wanted him. It didn't care how obnoxiously arrogant he'd become, or even that he'd stolen her birthright. Her son's birthright. All it wanted—

desperately—was to feel his hands moving over her body, taking that same slow path his dangerously tawny eyes were currently traveling.

She stomped the hot unbidden sexual desire down and reminded her rebellious body that she'd sworn off men after her husband had gone on television and made her the most publicly pitied woman in America. And she'd definitely sworn off *this* particular man after he'd taken off for parts unknown, leaving her to face the worst days of her life alone.

Dani sighed, realizing that although she'd grown up a lot since that summer, the memories still hurt.

Jack waited, giving her time to sort out her feelings. It had to be tough, he allowed, returning home widowed from a bad marriage to find the man who'd taken her virginity, then deserted her without a word, living in her childhood home.

She blew out a breath. Briefly closed her eyes, which had shadowed while he was watching the range of expressions move across her face. Then shrugged. "I suppose it might be interesting to see what changes you've made to my family's home."

His eyes narrowed, but for some reason—a faint leftover shred of southern chivalry, perhaps?—he refrained from reminding her again that it was *his* home now.

# 9

*They began with* the English jury paneled library that looked out onto the garden, which had gone to seed. Since flowers were the least of his problems, Jack hadn't worried about that.

"The books are all gone," she murmured, looking up at the built-in shelves that had once held leather-bound first editions.

"The judge put them in storage before his sentencing. Said he didn't want the vultures getting them."

"Well, that's certainly flattering."

"He wasn't talking about you, *chère*. Some of them are a little moldy from bein' in a warehouse in Baton Rouge all these past years he's been away, but I found a place in New Orleans that specializes in restoring old books. Looks like we'll probably be able to salvage most of them."

She stopped running her fingers over the fluted pilasters around the bookcases and looked up at him. "So you now own *them*, too?"

"Yeah." Jack heard the stiff accusation in her voice but refused to apologize. "I'd just come back to town when Earl Jenkins, the guy who owned the warehouse where the judge had stashed the books died, and his kids sold the moving and storage business to some company based in New York City.

"Turns out Earl hadn't bothered collecting any rent, 'cause he figured he owed the judge, who'd gotten his second cousin, Tommy Lee, into an alcohol-treatment program instead of jail after a DUI.

"But the damn Yankee, he didn't care about paying off moral debts, he just wanted the paper one taken care of. The judge had to either come up with the bucks for all those years of back storage, or the books were going to be sold at auction. So he called me."

"Why you?"

"Hell if I know. Maybe he'd read about those Hollywood folks making that movie out of my book and figured I might have enough dough to bail the books out of hock. Maybe he thought that since I owned the house, I might want somethin' to fill the shelves. Or it could be he remembered how I was always sneakin' in here to read them."

What Jack didn't share with Dani was that the judge had eventually turned out to have an entirely different agenda, like wanting the same guy he'd once run out of town, if not on a rail, at least in a candy apple red GTO, to use his—and his FBI brother's—connections in the law-enforcement community to prove that he'd been framed seven years ago. And by whom.

"I never knew you did that."

"That was kinda the point of sneaking. *Maman* was always scared the judge was going to discover me in here and fire her."

There'd been a time, back in his teens, when Jack had thought his *maman* had been overly concerned about losing a job she'd never wanted in the first place. A job she'd been forced to take in order to support her three sons after her husband was killed. It was only later, after the debacle in Colombia—which Jack continued to think of as Callahan's major fuckup—had taken away his own confidence in his ability to do his job, that he'd finally understood how the gunman who'd taken his father's life that day in the Blue Bayou courthouse had not only cost his mother her husband, but robbed her of any sense of security.

Which was why, when the judge had threatened to fire Marie Callahan if her middle son didn't leave Blue Bayou—and Danielle—Jack had thrown some stuff into a duffel bag, headed off across the country to San Diego, and hadn't looked back. Until his world blew up in his face, leaving him nowhere else to go.

"Turns out the judge had known about me reading his books all the time," he revealed. There hadn't been much that old bastard missed. Which was why Jack was surprised he'd let himself get caught up in such an obvious frame.

They continued the tour through the long double parlors which opened up onto a private courtyard designed for steamy hot summers. Then moved on to the formal dining room with the ceiling frescoes which were, like the grand hall mural, being restored. Since it was the largest room in the house, the ballroom was currently being used as an indoor shop, allowing work to continue even on the wettest of days.

As they went upstairs, Jack realized that having been surrounded by construction for so long, he hadn't realized how much he'd actually accomplished. Beau Soleil would be a lifetime project, not just to restore, but to keep up. The funny thing was, he, who'd always sworn to escape Blue Bayou, didn't mind that idea at all.

It was so hard, Dani thought. Seeing all that Jack had done to her home, then having to constantly remind herself it was *his* home now. But even as difficult as she found the rest of his impromptu tour, she was battered by emotions when she walked into her former bedroom.

Once upon a time ago this room had been scented by the potpourri Jack's mother made from Beau Soleil's antique roses. Now the odors of dust and mold assaulted her senses.

"The roof leaked and the moisture went through the attic floor to here," he said as she lifted her gaze to the ceiling, where a brown spot shaped like an amoeba darkened the plaster. "I've got a guy coming in to fix it as soon as I replace the rotted wood on the floor above next week."

"That's good," she murmured absently. She skirted the two sawhorses and went over to the window where an industrious spider had spun a web in the upper-left corner.

"The tree's still there," he said.

"I know." She did not volunteer how, when she'd first arrived, before she'd known he was sitting on the *gallerie*, she'd imagined herself climbing down it. Imagined his hands on her hips, helping her to the ground.

"I had to saw off a limb that kept scrapin' against the window, 'cause I was afraid it'd break the glass."

"I imagine it'd be difficult to find replacement glass this old."

"Not around here. There are one helluva lot of fine old places crumbling away all through the bayou."

But Beau Soleil would not be lost. Thanks to him. Dani tried to be grateful for that.

As she looked around the room, instead of the yellowed wallpaper, crumbling plaster ceiling, and missing baseboards, she saw it as it had once been, when white rosebuds had blossomed on a field of palest green, when creamy molding had run across the top of the wall and a lacy white iron bed, which had belonged to her great-great-grandmother, covered with tea-dyed crocheted lace had dominated the room.

"The bed's out in the carriage house," he said, as if he'd plucked the question right out of her mind.

"It's nice something survived."

"I heard the judge had a lot of the furniture shipped to your house in D.C. after your marriage."

"It was Virginia. He insisted he wanted to close off some rooms since he was the only one living here."

"You gonna have it shipped back?"

"No. I ended up selling it to pay bills."

"What kind of bills?"

"You know." Her shrug didn't come off nearly as negligent as she'd hoped. "The normal day-to-day stuff. Along with lawyer fees from the divorce, and of course there was the funeral."

"Your husband didn't have insurance?"

"Lowell had his legislative insurance, but he'd changed the beneficiary on the policy to his fiancée."

Who'd cut her losses, hadn't bothered to chip in to bury the man she'd stolen from his family, and was currently working for an up-and-coming young congressman from Rhode Island. Dani hoped the politician's pregnant wife kept a closer watch on her husband and her marriage than she had.

"He had some other policies we'd bought together over the years, but he'd cashed them out to cover margin calls on his stocks."

"No offense, but you went off and married yourself one helluva louse."

"I'm afraid you're right. But the furniture wouldn't have fit in the apartment over the library, anyway." A pain she'd thought she put behind her flared, scorching her nerves. When she felt her hands begin to tremble, she shoved them into the back pockets of her shorts.

"Wasn't it Thoreau who said our life is frittered away by details? I should know because I'm a reference librarian and we're supposed to know everything. . . .

"Yes, I'm sure it was Thoreau. He was so before his time, wasn't he? With his *simplify, simplify* message."

Lord, she was on the verge of babbling. Dani never babbled. Not ever. "Those are such inspirational words to live by, aren't they? The world would be ever so much better off if everyone followed his advice."

"Walden Pond might get a little crowded."

Because it hurt, really hurt, to be in this room, where they'd once, during a wonderful, reckless night, made love in that lovely antique iron bed now being stored in the carriage house, Dani flashed him a bright, utterly false smile.

"You're undoubtedly right. But it's Thoreau's idea that's important, isn't it? Not the reality. People don't spend enough time thinking about the impact they have on the world. After all, our environment is so fragile . . .

"Hell." She drew in a ragged breath. When Jack moved toward her, his face showing concern for the crazy lady, Dani backed away and lifted her hands, palms out. "I'm okay. Really. It's just been a long day and the trip out here did a number on my nerves. But I'll be fine. I just need a moment." Thoroughly disgusted with herself, she turned toward the door, seeking to escape with some small shred of dignity intact.

"It got to me, too, *chère*."

His quiet statement had her pausing. She turned back toward him and read the truth in his eyes. "What?" she asked, even as she knew the answer.

"Remembering. You and me, together in here." He tilted his head toward where her bed had once been but didn't take his gaze from hers. "First time I walked into this room I felt as if someone had hit me in the gut with a fist."

He crossed the room to her and leaned close. Too close. "I figured it was just bein' back here again. Told myself that I'd get used to it." Closer still.

"Did you?"

"Not yet. Sometimes, late at night, I come in here, sit on the floor and get a little drunk while I look out at the moon and remember how good you looked—how good you felt—in that pretty white bed."

He braced a hand on the doorframe above her head. "You ever think about that? While you were lying alone in that marriage bed you made, waiting for your husband to come home from his girlfriend and make love to you the way a woman like you should be made love to?"

"No. I didn't," she lied. He couldn't have known. It was only a lucky guess. Ducking beneath his arm, she headed for the back stairs.

"You'll think about it tonight," he predicted.

Dani thought about arguing, but knew that he was right.

As desperately as she wanted to leave, Dani needed carpenters worse. And it seemed the only way she was going to get them was to humor Jack by staying for supper.

"Do you know, I doubt if my father was in this kitchen more than half a dozen times in his life," she murmured, peeling the shrimp while he heated the oil in the old iron skillet for the roux.

Turnip was standing on her hind legs, oversize paws on the counter, licking her muzzle with canine appreciation.

"My uncle started teachin' us boys how to cook about the same time he and my dad taught us to bait our first hook." He yanked the dog down by the collar. "Lie down, you."

Obviously uninjured by his firm tone, Turnip turned around three times, lay down, curled herself into a tight ball, put her head on her back legs, and continued to watch Jack's every move.

He added flour to the oil. The way he whisked the browning mixture with deft, easy strokes suggested he did it often. "It's a Cajun rite of passage, like your first game of *bourré* back from when men had to feed themselves during all those lonely months out at their camps, fishing and trapping."

"Do you still have the camp?" Damn. Bringing up the place where he'd taken her so they could be alone, especially after having been together in the bedroom, was definitely a tactical error.

One Jack thankfully let lie. "The three of us inherited it when *Maman* died. Nate uses it a few times a year, Finn's probably been back twice. I stayed out there when I first came back."

The whisk stilled for a moment. He glanced over at her. "Nate told me you didn't know I'd bought Beau Soleil."

"No." She began peeling a little faster. The pile of shrimp shells grew higher. "That came as a surprise." Her voice was calm, her hands were not.

He turned down the heat. "I'm sorry."

"Sorry that you bought my home? Or sorry that my husband let me think it'd been lost to taxes after my father was sentenced to prison?"

"Helluva thing, your daddy gettin' convicted like that."

"Yes," she said. "It was." She took a sip of the smooth California Chardonnay he'd poured her when they'd first returned to the kitchen.

Jack blew out a breath. "Look, Danielle, we may not be friends, but I'm not exactly your enemy, either."

"Then what, exactly, are you?" Other than the man who'd broken her heart, nearly destroyed her life, then stolen her home.

"I'm the guy who bought Beau Soleil, and if it weren't for me comin' up with a higher bid, your no-good, screw-around husband would have sold her to the Maggione family. You may not like the idea of me living in your fine old Louisiana plantation home, which, may I point out, the Dupree family didn't exactly come into by the sweat of their brow in the first place, since everyone knows old Andre won it on that riverboat by stacking the cards, but the fact is, I *am* living here. And I'm not goin' anywhere anytime soon.

"I'm also not going to apologize for buying her, because she was crumbling back into the bayou from years of neglect, and I'm exactly what she needs to make her beautiful again. But I am sorry that your husband was such a prick."

She hated that he had a point. About everything. "Well, that makes two of us."

"What the hell made you do it? Marry a guy like that?"

"I don't suppose you'd believe I liked the idea of not having to change my last name?"

"Try again. The Dupree name's on mailboxes and tombstones all throughout this parish. It didn't have to be him. Hell, if that was all you were lookin' to do, you probably would've been better off marrying old Arlan down at the Bijoux."

Arlan Dupree, who washed windows and changed the posters at the theater, was in his sixties and slow-witted from being hit in the head during all his years in the boxing ring. Despite having made a living with his fists, he was as gentle as a lamb.

"I suppose, in retrospect, I mostly married Lowell because my father wanted me to."

"That's one helluva piss-poor reason to get married."

"Tell me about it." Dani sighed and began sweeping up the shells as the air in the kitchen grew steamy with spices.

When she'd first met the congressional candidate who'd moved to Louisiana from coastal Texas, his smooth, cultivated Ashley Wilkes charm had proven a balm to the wounded heart she'd been nursing for too long. The fact that Judge Dupree had endorsed both of Lowell's campaigns—the one for the U.S. Congress, and the one for his daughter—had been another plus in his favor.

As distant as her father had been all her life, he'd barely spoken to her since those days of her summer love. She'd been so desperate for his approval, as well as wanting to make up for past sins, that she didn't hesitate accepting Lowell's proposal within weeks after they'd first met. Besides, if she were to be perfectly honest, marrying such a classically handsome, popular man seemed no hardship at the time.

Despite being uncomfortable in the media spotlight that was part and parcel of a tightly contested political campaign, Dani had enjoyed the attention Lowell lavished on her during their whirlwind courtship.

When they married, two weeks before the election, his poll numbers took a huge post-wedding bounce. After all, while the judge might not be the most liked man in the parish, he was highly respected; if the young politician was good enough for Judge Dupree's only daughter, then he was good enough for the voters of south Louisiana. By marrying Danielle, candidate Lowell Dupree rid his campaign of any lingering charges of carpetbagging and went on to win the congressional seat in a landslide.

The night before her wedding, she'd confessed to misgivings. That was when her father told her that Lowell had promised him a federal court appointment—maybe even the Supreme Court *when*, not if, he got to the White House. Both men had been so full of ambitious plans, she thought on a soft sigh. Plans that had nothing to do with her.

"It's hard to explain, but marriage seemed like a good idea at the time. Daddy thought Lowell had a brilliant future, and while being a judge might have made him important down here, looking back on it, I think he liked the prospect of playing on a national stage."

Surprising herself by giving Jack even that much personal insight into her life, Dani wasn't about to tell him that she'd also hoped that marriage would stop her from thinking about him. And those painful, lonely months after he'd left.

"You can't make anyone love you. Not even by trying to live up to expectations and tossin' away your life."

Dani ripped apart another shrimp. "Not that it's any of your business, but I don't consider the years I spent married to Lowell wasted."

"Because of your boy."

"Yes. Because of Matthew."

"He's lucky to have you, Matthew is."

The simple honesty in his deep voice took a little of the wind from her sails. "I'm the lucky one."

She'd never uttered a truer statement. During the nine months of her pregnancy, she'd been concerned, in the secret-most corner of her heart, that perhaps, subconsciously, she was trying to replace the child she'd lost. If that were so, it'd be a terrible burden to place on any infant. But the first time she'd held her son in her arms, she'd loved him with a power that had almost frightened her, it was so strong.

Which was why, even considering how things had turned out, she could never regret having married her husband. Because if she hadn't walked down Beau Soleil's *Gone With the Wind* staircase that fateful day of her wedding, her precious child, the sun around which Dani's entire world revolved, wouldn't exist.

As the conversation shifted to her son, Dani realized they'd slipped into playing roles. For a brief time, it was almost as if they were merely old friends getting together to catch up on life. Which, she supposed, if she had to stay, was better than focusing on the reality of their situation.

She told him about Matt's generosity, his intelligence, his collection of Hot Wheels, and his love of books, which in turn led to Jack's novels, which he seemed surprised to learn she'd actually read.

"I don't know why you'd be surprised. I am, after all, a librarian."

"Bet you don't read every book in the Dewey decimal system."

"No, but if the displays in the front of the bookstores and the library waiting lists are any indication, most of America must be reading yours."

The timer she'd set for the rice dinged. She took the lid off the pot. "Of course I knew, back in high school, that you'd become a famous writer," she allowed, giving him that much, since she knew how hard he'd worked to overcome his father's belief that writing stories was "sissy work."

Having grown up with a larger-than-life father herself, Dani suspected Jack might not have found it all that easy to escape Jake Callahan's broad shadow. She wondered idly if he might still be trying to prove himself to the father he'd lost, then reminded herself that she didn't care.

"You and *Maman* were sure as hell the only people in town who thought so."

"That's because no one else had read your writing."

She'd found the pages out at the camp while he'd been catching fish for their supper and had wept when she'd read the coming-of-age story of a boy whose Confederate father had been killed in the War Between the States by his Yankee uncle.

"*Writing* is a relative term. What I did back then was scribble clichéd, sentimental claptrap."

"I liked it."

"You were easy." He paused in the act of spooning gumbo into bowls. "Hell." He blew out a breath. "I didn't mean it the way it sounded, Danille."

Dani shrugged as she carried the plates of shrimp jambalaya to the table. "I suppose I was, back then." At least where he was concerned. "But I was young. And foolish." And desperately in love.

"And a lousy judge of literature."

She let out a short laugh, relaxing for the first time since she'd pulled the boat up to the dock. "So, what made you turn from historical drama to thrillers?" she asked as they sat down at the table.

"They say write what you know." His tone turned distant as he topped off her wine. "So, want to discuss our carpenter situation?"

Able to recognize when a door had just been slammed in her face, Dani reminded herself of her reason for being here, in this kitchen that was both familiar and new all at the same time and launched into her carefully prepared argument.

# 10

*Thank you for dinner,"* Dani said later as Jack walked her to the dock where she'd tied up the rental boat. "I can't remember the last time I had gumbo."

"You've been deprived, you."

"So Orèlia keeps telling me. Now that I'm back here, I'm going to have to learn how to cook the food I grew up eating."

She could not have said anything that better reminded him of the vast social chasm that had once separated them. Danielle had lived in luxury, while his widowed mother had slaved away over a hot stove making sure the judge and his pretty daughter never knew hunger.

"Gumbo's not that hard. Jus' a combination of African and Indian recipes, some Spanish seasoning, and my own Cajun culinary genius."

"He said modestly."

"It's not braggin' if it's true."

"Good point. . . . I appreciate you sharing your carpenters."

He'd promised her two men. Which, Nate had already told him, would allow her to open the library in a few days, while still keeping her from moving into the more-damaged upstairs apartment. At least until after the judge's release. "Ready to go?"

She ignored his outstretched hand. "It's very nice of you to offer to take me back to town, but it's not necessary."

"The hell it isn't. In case you've forgotten, the bayou can be a damn dangerous place at any time. But 'specially at night. You could get lost."

"I have a GPS."

"Which isn't gonna be worth squat if some gator decides to flip that little boat of yours and lands you and your fancy tracking device in the water. I'll bet *M'su Cocodrile* would find your sweet little female body one helluva tasty change of pace."

She shivered a bit at that. But held her ground. "It may surprise you to learn that I've grown up, Jack. I'm quite capable of taking care of myself. And my son."

"I've not a doubt in the world that's true. Any man with eyes in his head can tell that you've grown up just fine. Better than fine," he decided, skimming a glance over her. "But I'm still taking you back to Orèlia's."

He flashed her a deliberately provocative grin. "Unless you want to spend the night here."

Because she feared arguing any further would only stir emotions that could lead to others far more dangerous, she threw up her hands. "All right. But I'm only agreeing because we're wasting time arguing."

"We'll take mine," he said, when she started to climb into the rental boat.

"I have to return this to Pete's Marine tonight or it's going to cost me a small fortune."

"Don't worry about it. I'll call Pete and tell him it's my fault, and I'll have one of the guys take it back in the morning."

Dani looked with misgivings at the shallow, narrow boat he intended to take her back to Blue Bayou in. "I would have thought, with all your money, you would have at least bought yourself some fancy bass boat with a big engine."

"Why would I want to dump more gas and oil into the bayou when I've got this?" He ran a hand over the narrow rub rail in a slow sweep that could have been a caress. "My daddy and I built this pirogue the summer before he got killed. She may be old, but she still rides on the dew."

"I've no doubt she does. But *my* boat rides on the water."

He folded his arms. "I never figured you for a coward."

"Good." She tossed her head. "Because I'm not."

"Then prove it."

Blowing out a frustrated breath, she turned on him, hands splayed on her hips. "That's not only a ridiculously juvenile dare, it's an entirely unfounded accusation. If you knew even half of what I've been through, what I've had to help my son get through, you'd never dare suggest such a thing.

"Oh, it's easy enough for you," she said, on a roll now, "coming back to town like some kind of conquering hero, buying respectability—and my home—with all those damn buckets of best-seller money—"

"*Dieu.*" He caught hold of the hand that she'd slapped against his chest. "Don't remember you havin' such a temper."

"I still don't," she shot back. "Usually."

"It's good I provoke you." He uncurled her tightly fisted fingers, one by one. "Shows you have feelings for me."

"Murderous ones." She tugged on her hand. Without overt force, he refused to release it. "Dammit, Jack, if you're going to insist on taking me home, can we just get going?"

"Sure enough, sugar." When he trailed a fingertip over her surprisingly sensitive palm, unwilling desire spiked. Dani ruthlessly squashed it. "You know, you'd probably enjoy the trip better in the daylight," he said. "Are you sure you wouldn't rather stay here tonight?"

"In your dreams."

"Well, you know, I've already tried that. And while it's not bad, in its way, it's nothin' like back when you and I used to get hot and bothered and fuck ourselves blind every chance we got."

She tossed her head. "And to think I used to consider you reasonably sophisticated."

He irritated her further by laughing. "What did you know 'bout sophistication, *chère?* You were just a little girl."

"Apparently you didn't consider me too little to sleep with."

She knew she'd pushed too far when she felt him tense. "Let me give you a hand. Sometimes she's a bit tippy till you get settled in." A razor-sharp warning edged his reasonable tone.

Dani couldn't get a handle on the man. It was obvious he was no longer the bad boy of Blue Bayou. He did, after all, have a respectable occupation, which was not what most people in town had predicted. Despite having bought Beau Soleil, he certainly hadn't surrounded himself with the usual trappings of wealth she might have expected from a best-selling writer whose third book had sold to Hollywood before it was even written.

He was still sinfully sexy, still sultry temptation personified. But there was a quiet strength surrounding him. Plus, although he refused to admit it, a genuine affection toward that big yellow mongrel he'd rescued and named and who so obviously adored him.

Underlying everything else was an edgy, dangerous darkness she couldn't remember having been there before.

She wasn't a coward. But neither was she eager to go back into that dark swamp alone. Assuring herself that all he represented was a ride back to town, Dani gingerly climbed into the pirogue she'd once been so eager to ride in back when they'd race across dark waters to his camp.

For a while neither of them spoke as he poled the boat across the bayou, apparently navigating by instinct and memory. He'd always seemed at home here in the swamp. Which, she supposed, was why he'd chosen to return to Blue Bayou rather than buy a house in some trendy playground of the rich and famous.

"You should be proud of yourself, Jack," she said, finally breaking the silence. "You've done so very well."

"You haven't done half bad either. For a girl who was still a baby when her daddy married her off."

She thought, but wasn't about to say, that having a child alone, without any emotional support or love, tended to make a girl grow up real fast. Unfortunately, that didn't mean that she hadn't jumped from one bad relationship right into another worse one. "I'd graduated from college."

"Hell, that doesn't mean anything. You'd been so sheltered by the judge you didn't know a damn thing about the world. Wasn't a boy in town who'd dare as much as cop a feel with you for fear of the judge puttin' him in the slammer and tossing away the key."

"You weren't afraid."

He laughed, the sound echoing around them. "Hell, I was crazy back then."

"We both were."

"*Mais* yeah. That's sure true enough. But as soon as he found out you'd gotten yourself a taste of sex, the judge put you in a convent."

"I wasn't in any convent. It happens to have been a boarding school in Atlanta."

"Any guys livin' there?"

"Of course not." During the months at the home for unwed mothers, her mail had been censored, telephone calls monitored, and boys had been prohibited from even stepping foot on campus. But that hadn't stopped her from hoping Jack would arrive, like some knight in shining armor to rescue her. "Then after graduation I went to a Catholic women's college."

"Might as well have been convents, then." He took a pack of cigarettes from his shirt pocket, shook one loose, and lit it.

"There may not have been any male students. But I had dates. And sex." All right, that may have been a lie, but Dani excused it as being none of his business.

Jack exhaled a plume of smoke as he battled back the spike of jealousy. "Good for you. *Maman* wrote to me about your wedding."

He didn't reveal that he'd always suspected his mother had waited until after the ceremony for fear he'd try to return home and stop it.

Would he have? *Could* he have? The two questions had bedeviled him for more than a decade. It had also caused him to get drunk on her anniversary for years.

"She said it was like somethin' out of a fairy tale."

"Unfortunately it didn't have the requisite fairy-tale happily-ever-after ending."

"Must have been hard, moving in such powerful circles when you were still just a small-town bayou girl." Jack suspected being rich back home in Blue Bayou, Louisiana, didn't mean squat in the nation's capital.

"I didn't have much time for socializing. I was going to Catholic University in D.C. for my MLS, doing volunteer work, becoming a mother . . ."

Her voice drifted off. She shook herself a little, reminding Jack a bit of how Turnip had tried to shake off last night's skunk stink.

"There seemed to be a dinner or party or reception nearly every night, so I was honestly relieved when Lowell preferred attending most of them—except those hosted by constituent groups from home—with one of his aides or his chief of staff. It made sense, too, in a way, since they weren't really social occasions but political ones."

Jack thought about the photographs he'd seen of the woman her husband had left her for and suspected most women's internal alarms would have triggered at the idea of their husband spending his evenings with a woman whose glossy sophistication bespoke her Main Line Philadelphia heritage.

In contrast, he had to smile when he remembered the day she'd talked him into taking her fishing with him in this very pirogue. In her neatly pressed navy shorts, white designer T-shirt, and a billed cap advertising Bernard's bait shop he'd plunked on her head to protect her face from the sun, she'd looked like a pretty girl on a Louisiana tourist poster. Her feet had been bare, her hair loose, her smile dazzling.

As dusk had settled over the bayou, brightened by the flitting fluorescent green glow of fireflies, he'd taught her how to fry catfish in a beer batter, then they'd eaten them with grilled corn on the cob and shrimp cornbread he'd filched from his mother's kitchen.

After supper they'd sat out on the screened-in porch of his camp and watched the molten sun dip into the water, giving way to a perfumed night lush with promise.

The sex had been different that night. Slower. Sweeter. And infinitely more satisfying. It was only later, as he'd stared up at the canopy of stars while she'd dozed in his arms, Jack had realized, that somehow, when he hadn't been paying close enough attention, he'd fallen head over heels in love with pretty little rich girl Danielle Dupree.

*Yesterday's ball score*, he reminded himself.

"You were naive, keeping your husband on such a long leash."

She sighed. "If a man needs a leash, the odds of keeping him probably aren't all that high, anyway."

Thinking back on that fateful day when the judge had succeeded in changing both their lives, Jack felt like sighing as well.

"But I've thought about it a lot during these past months," she said. "And I'm actually glad I was never jealous, because then I'd be a different person than I am. I don't want to have to use jealousy to keep my husband faithful.

"I didn't suspect Lowell was committing adultery with Robin because I believed—and still do—that a solid marriage can only be built on a foundation of trust."

"That's probably a more effective theory if both people are deserving of the trust."

"Good point."

"I'd think you would have been an asset with the Louisiana campaign contributors. By marrying you, which pegged him statewide as Judge Victor Dupree's hand-picked son-in-law, the guy overcame his working-class roots." Jack remembered reading that the congressman had been the son of an alcoholic Gulf oil rig worker.

"I suppose I was an asset. Until the scandal." She looked away, out over the still black water. He studied the delicate profile that was etched on every one of his memory cells. "Then it was as if he'd never heard of Daddy."

"He sure took advantage of the judge's problems and bought Beau Soleil at a bargain tax-sale price fast enough."

"I'm trying not to think about that. Because if he wasn't already dead, I'd want to kill him."

"Sounds reasonable."

"It sounds terrible." She shook her head. "I didn't really mean it."

"Didn't you? I'm not sayin' you really would have done murder. But didn't you at least imagine striking back after he humiliated you on television in front of millions of nightly news viewers?"

"All right, I'll admit to a fleeting fantasy involving him driving a flaming Lexus of Death off the Francis Scott Key bridge into the Potomac River filled with politician-eating sharks."

"There's hope for you yet."

Once he'd gotten to know Danielle, Jack had been surprised to discover that what he'd always taken as regal self-assurance, was actually innate shyness and a critical case of the Melanie Wilkes Curse, which seemed to result in certain female children growing up unflaggingly sweet, malleable, self-effacing comforters of the emotionally wounded.

It was, Jack, suspected, a distinctly southern affliction. He'd sure as hell never run across it anywhere else.

"Nate told me you've been going up to the prison."

He heard the question in her voice and chose to dodge it. "From time to time." As the water deepened, he switched on the electric motor and sat down across from her, close enough that their knees were touching.

"I'm surprised. Since my father was the one responsible for you spending that year in the detention work camp."

She didn't know the half of what the judge had done to him. To them both. But Jack wasn't prepared to share the truth. At least not right now. "Hell, he probably saved my life. I was on a pretty slippery slope in those days."

"You weren't nearly as bad as everyone thought you were."

"That was a matter of opinion." When now familiar ghosts rattled their rusty chains, Jack wished for a whiskey. Or better yet . . .

She was definitely curious. Tempted. He saw it in her moon-spangled eyes, in the way her lips parted, ever so slightly as she looked at him.

When a jagged, white-hot bolt of hunger seared through him, Jack fought back the brutal urge to plunder, to crush his mouth down on hers, to tear off her clothes and taste her perfumed skin.

He wanted her bucking beneath him as she'd done that summer out on that moss-filled mattress at the camp, wanted to watch her eyes go blind as he drove her up, then feel her shatter as he filled her, reclaiming what had been stolen from him.

Deciding her taste would definitely be preferable to burning tobacco, he flicked the cigarette away.

"This would be a mistake." Her wide fascinated eyes darkened as they stared at his mouth, belying her soft denial.

"Maybe yes. Maybe no." He slowly leaned forward and felt her shiver when he touched the tip of his tongue to the sexy little indentation between her chin and her bottom lip. "But so what? You've never made a mistake in your life, *chère?*"

"That's the point. I've made too many."

"It's just a kiss, Danielle." He soothed her tense shoulders with his palms. Moved his hands down her arms until his fingers braceleted her slender wrists. Her pulse, beneath his thumbs, skittered. "I won't hurt you."

But he once had. And they both knew it.

"Jack . . ."

Hearing the plea rather than the protest, he took her mouth.

# 11

Heat, *thick and sweet* as boiled sugar cane, surged through Dani's veins. Her breath choked up in her lungs as Jack leisurely, thoroughly kissed her.

Somewhere in the bayou, a hound howled at the rising moon. An owl hooted. A jumping fish splashed. But Dani ignored them as the outside world telescoped in, narrowing down to the almost painfully exquisite sensation of Jack's mouth claiming hers.

How could she have forgotten this? How could she have failed to remember how her mind clouded with only the touch of his firm masculine lips on hers? How could she have forgotten *him?*

The truth, she admitted, for the first time in more than a decade as he tilted his head, changing the angle, deepening the kiss, degree by breath-stealing degree, was that she hadn't.

In nine years of marriage she'd never had an orgasm with her husband. She'd never trembled at his touch, never wanted him to rip her clothes off and bury himself deep inside her with a force that would make her scream.

Lowell had certainly never made her scream.

The thought of how her husband might have reacted if she actually screamed during lovemaking caused a little gurgle of laughter against Jack's mouth.

"I must be losin' my touch if this is makin' you laugh."

"That's not it. A thought just crossed my mind."

"Why don't you think later?"

Before she could answer, his mouth was on hers again, sending her swirling back into the mists.

This kiss was harder. Hotter. Deeper. Dani moaned beneath the pressure of his mouth as it fed on hers. Her heart thundered in her ears as he dragged that ravenous mouth down her throat, teeth raking against her heated skin.

When he released his hold on her wrists, and cupped her breasts, she arched against his hand and feared they could both end up in the water when the pirogue rocked.

"I knew it." His deep voice was rife with satisfaction. The pressure lessened, as his mouth cruised up to nibble on her earlobe.

"What?"

"That you'd taste good." He teased her nipples into aroused, aching points. "Feel good." A small, needy sound escaped from between her ravished lips as anticipation wound like a tightened spring. "That some things never change." Proving that he still knew his way around women's clothing, he unfastened the back of her bra with a single deft motion, freeing her breasts to his touch.

"It's only chemistry." She moaned as his kneading caress grew increasingly rough and caused a low, throbbing ache that seemed to vibrate all the way into her bones.

"Don't knock chemistry." His touch gentled again; but the feel of his fingers trailing slowly down her torso was no less seductive as they left a weakening trail of sparks on her flesh beneath the cotton T-shirt. "It's what turns dinosaurs into gasoline, carbon into diamonds, and hops into beer."

He palmed her, the heel of his hand pressing against the placket of her shorts, sending time spinning backward, tempting her nearly beyond reason. When she felt those same wickedly clever fingers that had unhooked her bra move to the button at her waistband, Dani drew back.

"As much as I appreciate the science lesson, Professor Callahan, if it's all the same to you, I'd just as soon not tip the boat over." Even as she struggled for some semblance of composure, the ragged need in her voice gave her away.

"We'd have to be a helluva lot more sedate than I intend to be with you, that's for sure," he agreed easily. "Anytime you want a refresher course, just whistle."

Dani knocked away his hand when he moved to refasten her bra, wanting—needing—to do it herself and gain some control over the situation. "You really can be horrendously insufferable."

He flashed her a wicked, cocky smile. "It's one of my many charms."

"Insufferable," she muttered, folding her arms across breasts that could still feel the erotic touch of his hands as the pirogue drifted back into the reeds.

Jack stood up and began using the pole again, pushing against the mud to navigate. They could have been the only two people in the world as they continued through the inky black darkness, the boat's yellow headlight cutting a swathe through the rising fog on the way back to Blue Bayou.

The scent that had blossomed from Dani's pearly white skin lingered in Jack's mind as he returned to Beau Soleil. He'd said good night to her at her car, which she'd left in Pete's Marine's parking lot.

She was right about having changed. She was no longer that nubile teenage princess who could crook her little finger and bring every male in the parish to his knees. Every male but him, he'd once vowed.

Before that fateful summer, Jack had prided himself on his ability to avoid her silken snares. He'd initially considered Danielle Dupree a pampered, spoiled girl who flirted, flattered, and charmed as only a pretty southern belle could. It was only when he'd discovered that beneath the polished veneer was a very vulnerable, very lonely young woman, he'd fallen. Hard.

After tying the pirogue to the dock, he spent a long time sitting on the *gallerie*, staring out over the inky water. And remembering.

At seventeen Jack had believed himself to be the toughest guy in the bayou, and there'd been few who'd argue his self-appraisal. He'd been hell on wheels, driving his *maman* crazy, bringing her to frustrated tears more than once, but there had been so goddamn much anger driving him, he couldn't stop. Not even for her.

Not even when his older brother Finn had come home from college and broken his nose after he'd been caught siphoning gas from Judge Victor Dupree's caddy.

Whenever Jack viewed his life, which he tried like hell not to do all that often, it seemed to be divided into chapters.

The first consisted of those years when his dad had been alive and his mother had done whatever mothers did to create a warm and comfortable home.

Then had come the flash point, that sweltering summer day a wild-eyed, pissed-off swamp dweller had burst into the courtroom determined to kill Judge Dupree for signing the restraining order aimed at keeping an abusive husband from continuing to beat his soon-to-be ex-wife black and blue. Jack's father, Blue Bayou's sheriff, had been on the stand, testifying in a DUI case. When he saw the revolver, he did what came naturally. He dived onto the judge, pushed him down, and got himself mortally wounded in the process.

Jake Callahan hadn't been wearing a bulletproof vest. It was too hot, and besides, Blue Bayou was a peaceful place. A good place to raise a family, his dad had always told his *maman*, who'd smile and agree. Of course, she'd agreed with just about everything her husband said. And he'd agreed with her right back.

They'd been, even after two decades of marriage, flat out crazy about each other, which had embarrassed the hell out of Jack on more than one occasion.

Like the night before the shooting, when they'd slow danced a lot closer than parents were supposed to at his father's surprise fortieth birthday party. The night his father had eaten smoked boudin and chicken, laughed with his many friends, and kissed his wife as they'd danced to a sad Cajun song about love gone wrong.

Fourteen hours later Jake Callahan was lying in his middle son's arms, blood spurting out of a wound in his broad chest, turning the black-and-white marble floor into something like a Jackson Pollock painting.

Jack had come to the courthouse with the po'boy his mother had fixed for his father's lunch. He'd arrived just in time to catch the action. But hadn't been able to do a damn thing to save his father's life.

And had never quite forgiven himself for that failure.

"Fuck." He rubbed his forehead. Squeezed his eyes shut and welcomed the swirling white dots that replaced the scene that was frozen, like a fly in amber, in his mind.

Chapter Two consisted of those years when he no longer gave a shit about anything. Or anyone. Least of all himself.

The judge, perhaps out of a feeling of guilt, obligation, or kindness, Jack had never figured out which, hired the widow Callahan on as Beau Soleil's housekeeper. While Jack began his downward slide into delinquency. He ditched school, drank too much, smoked too much—pot and Marlboros—and if trouble was anywhere within a three-parish radius, he'd find it.

When he was seventeen he stole Sheriff Jimbo Lott's cruiser to go drinking and racing the backroads with a trio of badass buddies who probably hadn't had a working brain between them. There'd been a new moon. The night was pitch, the fog was rising off the water, and Jack had been plowed when he spun around a corner too fast and went sailing into the bayou.

They'd all gotten out with only a few cuts and bruises. It had taken a salvage team from nearby Lafourche parish to pull the wrecked cruiser out of the mire.

And the judge finally lost patience with his housekeeper's son.

Since the parish was too small to have a juvenile court system, Judge Dupree claimed jurisdiction. Justice may have been blindfolded, but she was swift.

The judge made a few phone calls, and within an hour Jack had been interviewed by an intake case worker, referred to the D.A, who'd immediately pressed charges, landing Jack before the bench, where the judge sentenced him in less time than it had taken him to hotwire that patrol car and he was sitting, handcuffed, behind the grill in the back of a DPS cruiser headed to the Juvenile Detention boot camp before the sun had risen.

At the time he'd been too drunk to be fully aware of the events of that night, but later, when he sobered up and remembered the stone-cold hatred in Sheriff Jimbo Lott's eyes glaring at him across the courtroom, Jack realized that the judge could well have saved his life.

By lights out that first night, Jack had also come to the conclusion that compared to most of the other delinquents in the camp, he was a wet-behind-the-ears baby when it came to hard crime. He stopped swaggering and actually listened to the Scared Straight lectures given by the Angola lifers who were bussed to the youth camp each month.

It didn't take long to figure out that as much as he might hate his life, a future behind prison bars was no future at all.

He made goals. The first was to get out of this place alive. Understanding that education was his way out of Blue Bayou, his second was to graduate on time from high school, join the navy, spend some time seeing the big wide world outside the swamp, then let Uncle Sam pay for college.

His third goal was somehow, someday, to make his mother proud of him.

For twelve excruciatingly long weeks he wasn't allowed any interaction with the outside world. Even phone calls were off limits.

When Marie Callahan finally arrived with Nate at the camp for her first visit, Jack would have had to have been blind not to see the hurt in her moist green eyes. She never laid a guilt trip on him. She didn't have to because always hovering unspoken between them was the shame Jack would have caused his father if Jake Callahan had still been alive.

He did his time, building up his body with intense physical training and building his mind in the library, where he read every book in the place. Twice. On the day before his eighteenth birthday, Jack walked out of the camp gates a free man.

A party had been in full swing when he arrived at Beau Soleil. Surrounded by a gaggle of adoring boys, Danielle could have been Scarlett O'Hara at the barbecue at Twelve Oaks.

He was headed to the kitchen when she spotted him.

"Jack! You're home!" Before he could escape, she'd run around the end of the sparkling blue pool and taken hold of his hand. "Come dance with me."

Wanting to save the bus fare, he'd hitched his way home, leaving him hot, dusty, and sweaty. He figured he fit into this scene about as well as a skunk at a garden party.

"I don't think that's such a good idea."

"Oh, pooh, don't be a spoilsport." Her remarkable eyes danced, her moist, too-tempting cherry pink lips coaxed. "It's my seventeenth birthday and I refuse to take no for an answer."

He couldn't help laughing at her persistence. She's always been a sweet, pretty little girl, who'd, his brothers had ragged him, obviously idolized him as she followed him around Beau Soleil like a little blond puppy. Then, when she turned fourteen and began being battered by female hormones, she turned as dogged as one of his daddy's old tracking hounds.

There'd been no escaping her. If he was working in her daddy's fields, she'd show up with a thermos of icy sweet tea that tasted, beneath the sweltering summer sun, like ambrosia. If he was lying beneath his car, cussing up a blue storm while fixing yet another damn oil leak, the enticing scent of flowers would waft into the garage over the smell of grease and there she'd be, pretending to be in desperate need of a screwdriver for some alleged household chore.

And Jack had definitely learned to stay away from the swimming pool, where she'd lie in wait, a wild child in a skimpy bikini she didn't begin to fill out, too young to know what kind of danger she could be courting.

He'd done everything he could at the time to convince Danielle that he wasn't interested, even while he tried not to break her innocent heart. Finally, after attempts to hide from her had failed and reasoning only fell on deaf ears, he'd had no choice but to tell her straight out that he already had a real woman, someone who knew how to please a man, a woman who didn't have to sneak out of the house to be with him and leave his bed before dawn because it was a school day.

She'd surprised him with her remarkably calm reaction, but it was obvious from the pain in her expressive eyes that she was crushed. Before he could try to smooth things over, he'd gotten drunk, stolen Jimbo Lott's cruiser, and ended up in juvie camp.

Danielle hadn't visited him. Her father certainly wouldn't ever have permitted that and neither would Jack. But not a week went by that he didn't receive a letter from her, telling him all about the goings on at Beau Soliel and at school, how his *maman* was, and his brothers. The tone was always light and chatty, in no way revealing either her crush or his curt treatment of her.

"Please, Jack?" she'd wheedled prettily that fateful night. "Surely you're not going to cause me crushing humiliation by rejecting me while the entire parish is watching?"

No. He may have been known around these parts as Bad Jack Callahan, but even he wasn't that cruel.

"Just one dance," he'd said. "Then I've gotta go tell *maman* I'm home."

"She'll be so thrilled. She wasn't expecting you until tomorrow." There was honest warmth in her smile.

"They needed my cot, so they sprang me a day early."

"I'm glad." She went up on her toes and twined her slender white arms around his neck. Her young firm breasts softened against his chest.

As he'd drunk in the scents of shampoo and lingering sunshine and everything that was sweet and lovely and innocent and female, Jack had smelled the snare the same way a wild animal could sense a trap buried in the swamp.

He'd reminded himself of his plan to escape this small town, warned himself that the southern belle who felt too damn good in his arms represented a helluva lot more trouble than he'd already managed to get involved with over his admittedly rocky eighteen years. Then hadn't listened to a word.

"*Dieu*, when you're right, you're right," he muttered now.

There were still times when he thought back on it and was amazed at the risks they'd taken. Crazy. That's what they'd both been that summer.

He wasn't going to think about Chapter Three, Jack decided. Those days returned to haunt him enough while he was sleeping; there was no point in reliving them when he was awake.

And now, here he was at Chapter Four. Right back where he'd started.

Same house.

Same girl.

"Proving," he said to Turnip, who burst out of the door the moment he opened it and began sniffing the night air as if searching out skunk, "that fate has one goddamn screwed-up sense of humor."

# 12

*True to his word* and more trustworthy than when he'd promised to meet her out at his daddy's camp and had never shown up, Jack arrived at the library the next day while Dani was going through the ruins, sorting out anything that was salvageable. If her heart lifted a little as she watched him climb out of the truck and walk toward her on that lazy, loose-limbed stride, she told herself that it was only because of the two carpenters he'd brought with him.

As they'd walked through the apartment, which still smelled of smoke and looked as if a horde of vandals had sacked it, both men demonstrated a reassuring knowledge of the work needed to be done to make the apartment livable.

"Won't be long before it'll be better than new," the younger man, Derek McCarthy, assured her. "And you and your boy can settle in."

"Could you give me a ballpark figure how long that might be?"

"Probably a month," John Reneaux, the older of the two men said as his gray eyes swept the scene. "Maybe two."

"That long?"

"We'll work fast," Derek promised. "And you'll be able to open your library up a lot sooner than that."

Which was, Dani thought, trying to look on the bright side as they went right to work, better than nothing. She watched Derek moving with catlike agility and confidence along the top of a rafter, and thought about how much difference a day could make. What a difference Jack had made.

"Thank you," she said after she'd walked him back to the truck, which, she noted with veiled amusement, boasted a bumper sticker proclaiming him to be *Coonass and Proud.* "I honestly do appreciate your generosity."

"It's no big deal." He rubbed his thumb up her cheek.

The light caress sent her pulse skittering.

Across the street Ernie Egan was sitting out on the bench in front of his barbershop, smoking his pipe between haircuts as he'd done for as long as Dani could remember.

Max Pitre was sitting beside him and from the way Ernie was jabbing his pipe in Max's direction, Dani guessed they were arguing about something. As they'd done for as long as she could remember.

Mrs. Mercier was arranging plump chickens, pork chops, and various sausages in the chilled display cases in the front window of the Acadian Butcher Shop while her husband unfurled the cheery striped green-and-white awning.

Arlan was changing movie posters at the Bijoux, and in the little park across the street a dark-haired woman was teaching her little girl, who appeared to be about a year old, how to toss bread to the ducks floating on the bayou water.

All around her, life seemed to be continuing on as normal. But for Dani, the world stopped spinning.

Jack combed her hair behind her ear.

A familiar thrill danced up her spine.

His lips quirked, but his gaze grew thoughtful as he looked down into her face. Unwilling desire percolated. Dani could feel it, bubbling up from some deep well of emotion inside her. Everything took on a slow-motion feel as he lowered his head.

A mistake, she warned herself. But did not, could not, move.

He brushed a quick, friendly kiss atop the crown of her head. "See you around, *chère*."

Caught off guard yet again, Dani blew out a surprised, frustrated breath, then shook her head to clear the fog as he drove away.

"What did you expect?" She rubbed at her cheek, which felt unreasonably hot, and was chagrined at the soot that came off on her fingers. "You undoubtedly look like a ragpicker."

And a far, far cry from the way she'd looked that night of her birthday party, when he'd finally granted her the wish she'd been wishing on the first star of the night for five years, ever since his mother had come to work at Beau Soleil.

The birthday night he'd held her in his arms. That moon-spangled, magical night when she'd been poised on the brink of womanhood, dancing with the man she firmly believed she was destined to spend the rest of her life with.

"You don't want to get involved with him," she warned herself firmly. After all, if his brother, Nate, was in another league, Jack was in an entirely different universe. As his truck turned the corner, she vowed to keep reminding herself of that fact.

"Dani?"

When she recognized the woman calling from the park, she laughed, welcoming the distraction. "Marisa? Is that you?"

Marisa Parker had been her best friend all through school. As little girls, they'd shared Barbies; in high school they'd exchanged confidences about boys and crushes. Then Dani had been sent to Atlanta for most of her senior year, Marisa's father, an oil engineer, had gotten transferred to Saudi Arabia, and they'd lost track of each other.

Dani hadn't realized how much she'd missed her friend until she watched her running across the street, pushing the stroller in front of her.

"I can't believe it!" Like the two teenagers they'd both once been, they hugged each other and rocked back and forth. "I heard you were coming home, but you didn't call—"

"I didn't know *you'd* come back," Dani said.

"Dennis teaches sixth-grade math at Assumption."

"Dennis? Are you talking about Dennis McGee?" He'd driven Marisa crazy; they'd fought nearly nonstop from the fifth grade on.

"Yep." Marisa flashed a gold band. "We got married three years ago. Tammy's our first." She pressed a hand against her flat stomach. "And Tyler or Kelli is on the way."

"How wonderful." Dani looked down at the baby, who was looking up at her, studying her with solemn blue eyes, and felt a prick in her heart. "Hello, Tammy. Aren't you a pretty girl?"

The baby's copper-penny-red brow puckered and she looked ready to cry. "She's at that stranger-danger age," Marisa said, plucking her daughter from the stroller and bracing her on her hip.

"She's precious," Dani said. "I'd heard you were living in New York." Dani bent down and picked up the stuffed dalmatian the baby dropped. When she held it out to her, Tammy continued to regard her suspiciously but snatched it away.

"I was. Living in SoHo and working on Madison Avenue cranking out advertising art."

"Did you like advertising?" All through high school Marisa had talked about going to Paris, having wild hedonistic affairs with crazed painters, and becoming a famous artist.

"It was okay." She shrugged. "Art's art, right? Even if it's telling the world about a new panty hose."

"Absolutely," Dani agreed loyally, secretly wondering how many kinds of panty hose the world really needed. Tammy looked Dani straight in the eye, then threw the dalmatian again.

"Hell, who am I kidding? I was miserable. Then, since my dad retired here, and Mom went back to teaching music at Assumption, I came to visit for the holidays. I went to the Christmas pageant, and to make a long story short, Dennis was there, we bumped into each other over the punch bowl at the cast party, and I was blindsided by a chemical brainbath that just about knocked me off my feet. I went home with him that night." She dimpled merrily. "And never left."

"I'm so happy for you."

"I'm happy for me, too," Marisa said as Dani bent down and retrieved the dog yet again. She glanced over at the building. "I hear you're going to reopen the library."

"That's my plan."

"I'm so glad. As bad as Mrs. Weaver was when we were growing up, she'd become an absolute terror in her old age."

"So I heard. I'm really looking forward to it; I have some ideas I wanted to try in Fairfax, but since I wasn't branch manager, and the last hired, I was pretty much relegated to reference work."

"And now you're in charge. Must be a nice feeling."

"It is nice to have the freedom to be innovative. Of course I'm also in charge of date stamping and reshelving. And if I hate my boss, I have only myself to blame."

They shared a laugh, and for a moment it felt like old times.

"I'm really sorry about all you've gone through," Marisa said. A shadow crossed her face. "I wanted to call. Or write, but your number was unlisted."

"Matt and I are surviving. I wouldn't wish the past two years on my worst enemy, but there have been some advantages. I've gotten tougher and I've definitely gained a better sense of who I am and what I want from life. And I actually speak my mind."

"Hallelujah, this calls for a celebration. I always wondered if you were going to spend your entire life playing the role of the quintessential Goody Two-shoes southern girl."

If the accusation had come from anyone else, Dani might have been offended, even if she was reluctantly coming to the conclusion it was true.

"Not always," she countered, thinking of Jack.

"That's right, you did have your little rebellion that summer before your senior year. I can't say I blame you. If I wasn't a happily married woman, I might have had an attack of rampant lust while I was working on Beau Soleil."

"You worked on Beau Soleil?"

"Yeah. I've gotten into painting again. I got my master's in art restoration and have landed a few jobs working on murals. I'm also teaching art classes two days a week at Assumption and an adult class at the community center on Wednesday nights."

"So it was you who touched up the mural?"

"It surely was. What did you think?"

"I think it's wonderful. And a much better showcase for your work than panty hose."

"Well, it was certainly a challenge. But fun. And thanks to Jack giving me the chance, I've picked up a few more jobs in Baton Rouge and New Orleans." When Tammy reached her arm back to send the dalmatian flying yet again, Marisa deftly plucked it from her daughter's pudgy hand. Which set off an ear-piercing scream.

"It's past her nap-time. I'm afraid she inherited my temper, which Mom says is payback for all the trouble I gave her." She plunked the wailing baby into the stroller. "We'll have to have lunch soon, reminisce about old times, and catch up. I'm dying to know what's going on between you and Bad Jack."

"Absolutely nothing."

"Yeah, it looked like nothing." She fanned her face as Tammy slapped her pudgy hands onto the stroller tray. "I got hot and bothered just watching the two of you."

"You're pregnant. Rampant hormones go with the territory."

"Well, that's certainly true enough." She hugged Dani again. "I'll call as soon as you get settled into your new job and we'll set a date for lunch. I can't wait to tell you about Luanne Jackson's supposed affair with some married state senator."

Luanne Jackson had been two years ahead of them in school, with curves that would put Kim Basinger to shame, a mass of long dark hair, and smoky eyes that offered sensual favors. She'd left Blue Bayou right after high school for New Orleans, where rumor had her changing her name to Desiree Champagne as soon as she'd stepped off the Greyhound bus. The stories went that she'd worked for a few years as one of the Big Easy's highest paid call girls before marrying Jimmy Ray Boone, a wealthy south Louisiana car dealer. Since Boone had been a big contributor to Lowell's campaigns over the years, Dani had occasionally hosted the couple at fund-raising parties and had always felt uncomfortable around his wife.

It hadn't been because of the prostitute thing; not being one to judge others, Dani figured that was between Luanne and her husband. No, this had been something entirely different. It had been almost, Dani had considered on more than one occasion, as if Luanne had some reason to resent her. Once, a few years ago, after another of those strangely strained dinners, Dani had wondered if the other woman might be having an affair with Lowell, but then he'd gone on television proclaiming his love for his chief of staff, and she'd immediately put the question out of her mind.

After Jimmy Ray had died—making love, the stories went—Luanne had surprised everyone by returning home and building a huge home on the outskirts of town. She may be, with the possible exception of Jack, the wealthiest person in the parish, but it appeared the widow was still Blue Bayou's Scarlet Woman.

As she watched her former best friend cross the street and load Tammy and her stroller into the minivan, Dani experienced a low tug of something that felt like envy.

She didn't begrudge Marisa her happiness. But it did strike Dani that her friend was living the life she'd once thought *she* would be living. Marisa had always been the one with the career plans, while all Dani had ever wanted was a husband and a houseful of children.

Reminding herself that she was no longer the lovesick teenager who'd once dreamed of making an idyllic life with Jack, the girl who'd envisioned having make-believe tea parties with daughters in pink tutus and attending Little League games for sons who'd wrestle in the backyard and put frogs in their sisters' sock drawers, Dani shook off the uncharacteristic self-pity, put aside her gilded, unrealistic romantic fantasies, and returned to work.

# 13

*Like a child* before the first day of school, Dani had a hard time sleeping the night before the library opened. She told herself she had nothing to be nervous about. After all, she was well prepared. The new books she'd ordered had arrived, been unboxed, cataloged, and were sitting on the special *New Release* shelves Derek had built for her, waiting for residents of Blue Bayou to take them home.

She'd had additional lighting installed to brighten up the interior and had covered the bulletin board that had held an outdated jumble of memos and notices dating back years with a bright, eye-catching sunshine yellow burlap and had tacked up glossy covers of suggested novels for the upcoming summer vacation season. She also posted notices announcing the formation of a book discussion group, a weekly children's story hour, and a reading competition for the middle school children, the weekly prize being free passes she'd cajoled Delbert Dejune, owner of the Bijoux Theater, into donating.

She'd spent the day before the opening cleaning until the windows sparkled like crystal and the old-fashioned oak catalogue cases, which Derek and John had moved from the storage room for her, gleamed with a lemon-oil sheen. As much as Dani appreciated her computer, which had every book in the library catalogued and was connected to other libraries throughout the state, she suspected that here, where time moved a little more slowly, some patrons might prefer the old-fashioned cards. As she secretly did.

The little pieces of paper were cut and ready for note taking, short yellow pencils sharpened. She'd designated the children's reading center by painting a corner of the room a welcoming sunshine yellow and had found a rug woven in crayon colors at an antique store in Houma.

A woman on a mission with a limited budget, she'd talked the owner into cutting the price by half, then throwing in a sturdy pine table for another five dollars. Derek had cut the legs down for her, making the table, which she'd painted a bright crawfish red, the perfect height for little readers.

Knowing when a valuable resource had dropped into her lap, she recruited Marisa to add her talents to the project, and by the night before the reopening, a parade of beloved book characters danced across the yellow wall.

At precisely ten o'clock on the morning of her first day on the job, she unlocked the door, a welcoming smile on her face, ready to greet the first patron. When five minutes passed, then ten, then ten more, she began to worry that perhaps the people of Blue Bayou had gotten so accustomed to not having a library, they'd just decided they could do without one.

Then, at ten twenty-eight, Marisa walked in the door with a half dozen other women she introduced as mothers of children in Tammy's playgroup.

"We're in desperate need of escapism," she announced. After asserting that the reopening of the library had saved their collective sanity, they made a beeline for the romance novels Dani had finally finished cataloging late last night.

From then on it was as if the floodgates had opened. Dani wondered if there was anyone in town who hadn't had a sudden need to check out a book. She knew that a great many of the people came out of curiosity but didn't care. So long as they came.

Finally, after lunchtime—which she'd skipped in order to find a book on boat building for Wilbur Rogers and another about dog training for Annie Jessup, whose fiancé, Jimmy Doyle, had surprised her with a cocker spaniel puppy for her birthday—the crowd cleared out, leaving Dani to catch her breath.

As soon as she solved this one last problem, she could duck into her office and eat the sandwich she'd brought with her.

"It's a red book," the woman repeated impatiently.

"A red book," Dani agreed with a smile that had begun to fade after five minutes. "About sex."

"Not sex," the woman corrected. Her silk dress, diamond earrings, and matching brooch were definitely overkill for a weekday. "Fantasies."

"Fantasies of a sexual nature," Dani clarified. Right now her own fantasies were centered more around a Big Mac and fries.

"Do you have a problem with that?" The woman's eyes frosted.

"Of course not." Dani wished she was wearing her *I Read Banned Books* pin.

Did she look like a stereotypical prude librarian who kept any books with a remotely sexual content hidden away beneath the counter? The kind she'd seen while watching *Citizen Kane* with Orèlia the other night on the classics movie channel—that bun-wearing, pursed-lip glaring dragon lady who ruthlessly guarded the gates of knowledge from perceived infidels?

The idea was too depressing to contemplate.

"I was just trying to narrow things down," she said mildly. "There are quite a lot of titles on fantasies."

"This one has a red cover."

"Red. Right." Dani decided that if she ever had the opportunity to build a library from scratch, she'd cross-catalogue all the books by color, since that's how so many people seemed to remember them.

The woman glanced around, combed a self-conscious hand through her sleek, expertly streaked blond hair, then leaned across the desk and whispered a single word.

Without so much as blinking an eye, Dani nodded and searched the computer database for *whips*.

Success! She plucked a stubby yellow pencil from its clothespin can holder Matt had made her for Mother's Day last year in Cub Scouts and wrote *Whips and Kisses*, along with the catalogue number onto a piece of paper.

"It's on the second floor. I can show you."

"That's all right. I can find it." As if uncomfortable having shared even that possible glimpse into her private life, the patron snatched the paper from Dani's hand and headed off toward the elevators, four-hundred-dollar high heels click-clacking on the pine floor.

"You're welcome," Dani murmured.

Since the Blue Bayou library was a great deal smaller than the Fairfax County branch she was accustomed to, Dani was exceedingly grateful for the inter-library loan system. She was filling out ILL requests when the door opened and in Jack strolled, looking outrageously sexy in jeans, a black T-shirt, and those wedge-heeled cowboy boots that gave even more of a swagger to his walk.

"Anyone ever tell you that you look too damn sexy to be a librarian?"

"Perhaps you should join the twenty-first century," she said sweetly. "Things have changed. Why, I can't remember the last time I wore my hair in a bun."

He tilted his head and studied her. "Wouldn't make any difference if you did. Any male with blood still stirring in his veins would just fantasize taking out the pins and running his fingers through it."

When a too vivid, long-ago memory of him arranging her waist-length hair over her bare breasts flashed through her mind, Dani began straightening the reservation requests, tapping the edges together. A good many of them were for Jack's latest.

"Tell me you're not here to take your carpenters back."

He briefly glanced up at the hammering coming from the third floor as if he'd forgotten that the men were working up there. "No. Actually, I came to check out the librarian."

"You really ought to find a collaborator to help write your dialogue. Because that pickup line probably goes back to a time when books were carved in stone."

"Next time I'll do better." He toyed with the ends of her hair. "What I really need is to get myself a library card."

"A library card?" Dani knocked his hand away. Jack had always been one to touch easily and often. Having grown up in a house where casual affection was an unknown, alien thing, with the exception of her child, Dani was not.

"This is a library, isn't it?"

"Of course it is."

He tucked his thumbs in his pockets, the gesture drawing her attention to the front of those outlaw black jeans that intimately cupped his sex. "Then I guess I've come to the right place."

She forced her gaze back to his face, which wasn't all that much of a help due to the devilish, knowing look in his eyes. "Why do you want a library card?"

" 'Cause I agree with Groucho Marx. 'Outside of a dog, a book's a man's best friend. Inside of a dog, it's too dark to read.' "

She absolutely refused to smile. Letting her guard down for even a minute with this man was just too dangerous. "Don't you have a book of your own to write? Or some paint to scrape?"

"The book's in the mulling stage. My heroine is temperamental." His smile was slow and rakishly seductive. "Like most beautiful females I know."

He made himself comfortable on the edge of her desk. "As for the paint, it'll be there tomorrow. Maybe I'll even check out a book on solvents." He trailed a lazy finger down the back of her hand and set her nerves to humming. "See if I can find somethin' to replace elbow grease."

"I'll need a photo ID." The trick, Dani told herself firmly, was to keep everything businesslike.

His lips quirked a bit, as if he privately thought she was being a bit petty demanding identification, which she admittedly was, but stood up again and whipped his driver's license out of the back pocket of his jeans, which, when he handed it to her, Dani took as yet more proof that life wasn't fair. Wasn't there some law against taking a terrific picture at the DMV?

She typed the information into the computer, then printed out the card.

"Just remember," she warned as she handed it to him. "I know where you live. Plus I can look up lots of ways to get back at people who don't return library books."

"Sounds kinky."

As if on cue, the blond chose that moment to return with her red *Whips and Kisses* and two other thick books of erotica.

"Go ahead." Jack moved out of her way. "I'm going to be a while."

"If you're sure." She gazed up at him as if she were a chocoholic and he'd been dipped in Hershey's syrup, causing Dani to wonder if that particular scenario was in any of those sex books she was checking out.

He flashed her an all-too-appealing smile, appearing worlds different from the grim-faced man on the jacket photo of his books. "My *maman* taught me to always let pretty ladies go first."

It was all Dani could do not to roll her eyes as the patron squeezed in front of him. The sexuality she radiated was turning the artificially cooled air in the library so steamy Dani could barely breathe.

Jack glanced over the woman's shoulder, then lifted his eyebrows at the titles as Dani date-stamped the books.

After slanting him one last-ditch come-hither look, the woman left the library.

"I'd sure as hell love to have myself a little glimpse into her fantasy life," he mused.

"If you leave right now, you can probably catch up with her." How fast could a woman walk in those ridiculous ice-pick heels anyway? "I've no doubt she'd be delighted to share a few of the more kinky ones with you."

"*Non*," he decided. "She's pretty enough. But not my type."

Dani would not demean herself by asking what his type was these days.

He placed both hands on her desk and leaned toward her. "Wanna know what kind of lady I like?"

He was close. Too close. "Not particularly."

Needing space, Dani swept up a stack of books from the return bin and headed off to reshelve them.

"Too bad. Because me, I'm gonna tell you." He took the books from her.

"What do you think you're doing?"

"Makin' up for an oversight."

"What oversight is that?" She shelved the book on animal husbandry he handed her and moved on to the next row.

"I never carried your books to school like a proper boyfriend."

"It was summer. There wasn't any school." She slipped a how-to book on building your own deck between one on construction materials and another on roofing. "Besides, you were hardly a proper boyfriend."

"That's true enough." His chuckle was warm and wicked. "Nothing proper about me. Which I seem to recall was just the way you liked it."

He handed her another book and followed her around the corner. "You ever do it in the stacks, *chère?*"

"Of course not."

"Me neither." Dani suspected the smile he flashed was undoubtedly much like the one Lucifer had pulled out to convince all those heavenly angels into joining him in hell. "It'll give us something to look forward to."

"I wouldn't hold your breath." Though she'd go to her grave before admitting it, his sexual arrogance fit him as well as those snug black jeans.

"You're a tough nut to crack. Good thing for both of us I've always enjoyed a challenge."

He took the last two books from her hands, tossed them onto the rolling cart nearby, then shifted her so that her back was against the book-filled shelves.

Dani drew in a sharp breath. "Don't."

"Don't what?"

"Whatever it is you think you're going to do." Her voice hitched. "This is a public library, Jack."

"And I'm the public." He moved in, pressing his body against hers. His fully aroused body. "You're trembling."

The husky note in his voice felt like a caress. "I am not," she lied.

"You don' have to worry, Danielle. I'm not gonna hurt you."

"I'm a librarian." Her pulse quickened and her bones began to melt as he lowered his head and brushed his lips against hers.

He nibbled on her bottom lip and drew a shudder from deep inside her. "A very tasty one."

"We can't do this," she complained, her body belying her protest as it molded compliantly against his. It took every ounce of restraint she possessed not to start rubbing against him.

"Don't look now, but we're doin' it pretty damn well. So far."

"That's my point." She managed to get her hands between them before she did something that would land her on the front page of the *Clarion.* And perhaps even on Jimbo Lott's police blotter. "We've already gone too far." She pushed against his chest. "Are you trying to get me fired?"

She felt him tense. Then back away. "Not today." He was looking at her not with lust, but an odd, unreadable sort of curiosity that had her more nervous than the sex thing. "Thank you."

"For what?" She scrambled to tuck her blouse back into her skirt before someone came looking for her.

He kissed her fingers, which seemed to have established a direct connection to other, more vital body parts. The bad-boy grin returned. "For giving me a new fantasy to contemplate while I'm getting all hot and sweaty pounding nails this afternoon."

Danielle knew she was in deep, deep trouble when the thought of Jack Callahan all hot and sweaty was almost enough to make her go running after him.

# 14

*The day of Dani's trip* to Angola prison dawned dark and rainy. Not a very propitious sign, she thought as she watched the water streaking down the kitchen window. She knew Matt was picking up on her nervousness. His eyes followed her, concern easily readable in them.

"Don't worry, sweetie, it's going to be okay." She ruffled his hair. "Better than okay. It's going to be great." She wondered which of them she was encouraging, her son or herself.

"Do you think he'll like me?"

"I *know* he'll *love* you. How could he not? He's your grandfather. And you're a very special boy."

There was a knock at the front door. A moment later Orèlia entered the kitchen with Jack. "Look what the cat dragged in," she said with robust cheer.

"Morning," he greeted them.

Dani's nerves were already tangled enough. She didn't need Jack making them worse. "What are you doing here?"

"It's lovely to see you, too, *chère*." He skimmed a look over her. "Don't you look pretty as a speckled pup. You remind me of Audrey Hepburn in that movie. You know, the one about eatin' breakfast in a jewelry store."

Having no clue what the appropriate attire to wear to a prison might be, she'd changed clothes three times before finally settling on the simple sleeveless black dress. She'd twisted her hair into a smooth French roll she hoped would withstand today's humidity.

It was foolish to be dressing up for her father, but although she'd assured herself that she'd grown up, that she no longer yearned for his approval, Dani had also decided there was nothing wrong with looking her best when he saw her for the first time in more than seven years.

"A jewelry store's a funny place to eat breakfast," Matt said.

"Perhaps. But it's a very nice movie nonetheless." Dani snatched up his cereal bowl and headed toward the dishwasher.

"Mom, I'm not finished yet."

"Oh." She felt Jack's amused look as she plunked it back down in front of him. "Sorry."

"You must be Matt," Jack said. "I'm Jack Callahan."

Matt eyed Jack's hair and earring. "You're not a pirate, are you?"

" 'Fraid not."

"I didn't think so," he said a little wistfully. "But mom told me about the pirates who used to live here, so I thought just maybe a few might still be around."

"None that I know of," Jack answered. "Except for a couple subcontractors I've been dealing with lately," he added on afterthought. "And I'm not real certain, but I suppose, since my *maman*'s people have lived here just about forever, there's a chance I might have a pirate lurking somewhere in my family tree."

"That'd be cool."

"I guess it would, at that." Jack grinned. "I'm an old friend of your *maman*."

"From when she lived here?"

"Sure thing. We went to school together."

"Mom said she went to the same school I'm going to. Holy Assumption."

"That's the one. So, what's your favorite class?"

"Reading."

"Hey, mine was, too. Looks like we got somethin' in common, you and me."

"Did you like made-up stories?" Matt asked. "Or real ones?"

"Both. They each have their appeal."

"I like made-up ones," Matt said. "Sometimes I think up stories, but I've never written any down."

"You should." Jack tugged the Orioles cap lower over Matt's eyes. "An imagination is a great thing. You wouldn't want to waste it. . . . What else do you like to do? I liked recess a lot."

"Me, too."

"Is the baseball diamond still there?" Jack asked.

"Yeah. But I don't play baseball."

"Guess you're a hoops man." Jack rubbed his jaw and studied Matt. "Or maybe football. You look like a running back to me. I'll bet you can slip through the line like greased lightning."

"Not really. I don't play because nobody picks me for their team."

"I didn't know that." Dani was surprised. He'd always been one of the more popular boys at Fox Run. "It's probably because you're the new boy in class," she said consolingly.

"That's not it. They don't pick me because I don't know how to play."

Oh, Lord. She didn't need this. Not now. Not with a possible confrontation with her father looming and Jack seeming to take up most of the cozy kitchen.

"I wish you'd said something before now. But don't worry, we'll get a book and learn together."

"It's okay, Mom," he assured her quickly, looking as if he wished he hadn't brought the subject up. "The guys let me keep score, 'cause I'm real good with numbers and have all the rules memorized. Besides, you can't learn to play baseball from a book."

"Of course you can," the librarian in her rose to the occasion. "You can learn to do anything from a book."

"Your *maman*'s right," Jack said. "Books are powerful tools. But sometimes it's easier to learn things by doin' them. Me, I'm no Barry Bonds, but I used to play with my brothers, one who was good enough to get himself a scholarship playing third base at Tulane. How 'bout I give you a few pointers?"

"Really?"

When the wild hope in his eyes lit up enough to banish all the clouds from here to Mississippi, Dani enjoyed seeing her son so excited. She was also disturbed that Jack was the cause.

"Sure. It'll be fun. Maybe we can talk your *maman* into shagging fly balls."

"That'd be way cool. Did you used to play with her? When you were in school together?"

"*Mais* yeah." Dani heard the choked laughter in his voice and didn't dare look at him. "Your *maman* and me, we played some mighty fine games once upon a time ago."

Matt looked up at Dani, as if seeking confirmation. When she didn't immediately respond, his gaze shifted out the screen door. "Mom, look." He pointed toward the lawn where a six-foot-long alligator lay, seeking warmth from a narrow ray of sun that had broken through the dark pewter clouds. "The alligator's back."

"Bet you never saw any gators at your old house," Jack guessed.

Dani admired the subtle way he'd managed to point out a benefit to their move, a positive counterpoint to balance her son's less-than-positive playground problems.

"The most we ever had in Fairfax was squirrels."

"Squirrels are okay. But a gator's somethin' special. When I was a boy, just 'bout your age, we had one who lived at our house. My daddy tried like heck to get it to move on down the road. But *M'su Cocodrile*, which is another name we Cajuns sometimes call our gators, he liked it right where he was. So Daddy had to figure out some other way to deal with him."

"Did he shoot it?"

"Nah. That wouldn't have been fair. Since the gator was jus' lying there soaking up the sunshine, minding his own business. *Mon Dieu*, he'd stay out there all day, so long his shiny black skin would turn all gray and ashy lookin'."

"So what did he do?" Matt asked. "Your dad, not *M'su Cocodrile*."

"He tamed him."

"No way."

"Way. My hand to God." Jack lifted his right hand. "Now, it's not easy, trainin' gators, but my daddy, he was a patient man. The first thing he did was get down on his belly, flat out on the ground, so he was lyin' eyeball to eyeball with *M'su Cocodrile*."

"Really?"

"Absolutely. And then they had themselves a staring contest, that ole gator and my daddy."

Matt's eyes had widened to huge blue saucers. Dani tried to remember the last time she'd seen him so engaged in anything, and came up blank.

"Who won?"

"My daddy, of course. Wasn't a man nor beast in the state could stare him down. And I know, having tried it a time or two myself."

"Did *M'su Cocodrile* go away after he lost the staring contest?"

"*Non*. Oh, he wasn't happy about bein' bested that way, he. So he up and slapped his tail onto the water so hard—*wham!*"—Jack slammed his palm onto the table and made Matt jump—"water went sprayin' so high in the air, the weather guy on KXKC over in New Iberia reported that it was rainin' *crevi* over three parishes. That's a little teeny crawfish," he explained.

Clearly skeptical, Matt rubbed his nose. "Crawfish were coming down from the sky?"

"They sure were. Oh, it was somethin' to behold, let me tell you. But M'*su Cocodrile*, even as mad as he was to be bested by a man, still wasn't about to leave, because he liked our front yard so much. But we didn't have to worry any longer."

"Why not?"

"Because, you see, my daddy had already proven who the better man—or gator—was. So they came to an understandin', my daddy and M'*su Cocodrile*, that they'd just leave each other to his own business. Later my daddy taught him to bellow."

"I seem to recall alligators knowing how to do that without any special training," Dani interjected dryly.

The story was all lies, of course. But it was certainly entertaining her son.

"Sure enough they do," Jack agreed without missing a beat. "But I'll bet you never heard of one who'd do it on command."

He turned back to Matt. "All my daddy had to do was whistle." He pursed his lips and let out an earsplitting sound that had the alligator out on the lawn lifting his wide, corrugated head. "And M'*su Cocodrile*'d come from wherever he was in the swamp and pull himself up onto our lawn.

"Then he'd arch his back, which was as wide as this table, just like this"—he demonstrated again—"and let out a huge roar people could hear all the way across Blue Bayou, even down to the Gulf, where shrimpers would say that roar was the spookiest thing they ever did hear."

"He roared? Like a lion?"

"Not exactly. More like if you were to cross a lion with a locomotive. This was a roar that warned folks that they'd better not make the mistake of foolin' around with M'*su Cocodrile*. That sound shimmied itself right up your backbone and down again, rattlin' all your bones.

"Why, the family who lived down the road a ways swore that gator just roared their house right off its foundation."

"Wow." Matt let out a huge breath. "That's amazing."

"I thought so, too." Jack winked at Dani. "I sure did like that old reptile. He was an ugly fella, but likable, in his own way. Every day, round noontime, he'd come up to the boat dock, beggin' handouts. Got so my *maman* would make an extra po'boy just for him."

"I never heard of an alligator eating sandwiches."

"Oh, they're not choosy. They'll eat most anything you toss their way."

"What happened to him?"

Jack rubbed his jaw. "I don't know. One day he just up and went away. When I got a little older and learned about girls, how pretty they are and how good they smell, I sorta figured he met up with a lady gator and decided to set up housekeeping in *her* bayou."

"Alligators don't smell good."

"They do to other gators." The grin he flashed earned one back in return from Matt. Story finished, he turned to Dani. "You ready?"

"For what?"

"To drive on up to Angola and pick up the judge."

"I was intending to do that myself."

"Well, now, I can see why you might want a little privacy the first time you see your daddy after all these years, but the thing is, I sorta promised the judge I'd be the one to come fetch him."

"I see." An entirely different type of jealousy than the one caused by the erotica-reading blonde stirred. "I was planning to surprise him."

"Oh, you'll be doin' that, sure enough. Even with me doing the driving."

"Won't it be a little crowded in your truck?"

"Would be, if I'd brought it. But I've got the GTO today."

"Do you really have a GTO?" Matt breathed the name of the car with awe. Dani knew that in her son's personal hierarchy, this outranked even a pirate.

"Sure do. Three deuces, a four-speed, and a three-eighty-nine. That big ol' engine can suck birds from the sky. Have to be careful whenever I drive past mamas taking their newborns for walks, so I won't accidentally suck their little babies right out of their carriages."

"Mr. Callahan has always been fond of exaggeration," Dani informed her son.

"Why don't you call me Jack," he suggested to Matt. "Since Mr. Callahan sounds awful formal for friends. And to tell the truth, I haven't sucked any babies up, but like I said, that's because I'm real careful whenever I drive by 'em.

"My aunt Marielle found the car out in her barn over in New Iberia after her husband passed on and gave it to me way back when I was in high school. It needed the rust ground off it and a new paint job, but the minute I lifted that old tarp and saw what Uncle Leon had been hidin' under there all those years, I thought I'd died and gone to heaven."

"Wow." Matt exhaled a long breath, enthralled by the thought of such a wondrous event. "You were really lucky."

"Yeah. I've had to store it for a lot of years, since I was sorta moving around the world, but the first thing I did when I got back here was get her detailed and lookin' as fine as ever. So you like cars, huh?"

"Yessir!"

"I doubt if there's a Hot Wheels car my son doesn't own," Dani said.

"Mom doesn't understand it's a guy thing," Matt explained to Jack.

The remark was so out of character, Dani could only stare at him.

"Your mom's a terrific lady, but what can you expect from someone who drives a station wagon?"

"That car just happens to be the safest vehicle on the road," Dani informed him. She'd studied all the crash tests before buying it five years ago to ensure Matt's security.

"Probably is. But it's still a chick car. A mom chick car," he tacked on.

She folded her arms. "Perhaps that's because I *am* a mother. Who wants to keep my child safe. It also happens to be a grown-up car. Unlike some others."

"The GTO sure isn't for grown-ups," Jack agreed easily. "That's what's fun about it." He grinned at Matt again. "There's a car show in Baton Rouge next month. Wanna go check out the new concept cars?"

"Wow! Can I, Mom?"

"*May* I. And we'll see."

"You can come, too," Jack offered magnanimously. "Maybe find yourself a nice new minivan."

"Thank you." Her answering smile was sweetly false. "I'm quite happy with the vehicle I have."

"Please may I go, Mom?" Matt asked again on something perilously close to a whine.

"I said, we'll see."

"Give your mom some space, Matt," Jack suggested. Then he winked, guy to guy. "I'll work on her on the way to the prison."

Dani folded her arms, preparing to stand her ground. "I still don't need you to drive me—"

"I think it's a grand idea," Orèlia entered the argument. "You wouldn't want to risk making a wrong turn along the way, gettin' lost in the storm, and keeping your papa waiting."

Dani refrained from pointing out that since her father had, by his own choice, by ignoring all her letters and phone calls and refusing to let her visit the prison, waited seven long years to see her and his only grandson, a few minutes one way or the other wasn't going to make that much difference.

But it would. The idea of her father being in prison was horrible enough. The mental image of him walking out with no one there to meet him was unthinkable.

Jack was standing there, leaning against the refrigerator door, legs crossed, hands in his pockets, appearing deceptively easygoing. But the steely look in his eyes assured Dani that she didn't stand a chance to win this one.

Knowing when she was licked, she relented on a huff of breath. "All right. It appears I don't have any choice."

"Oh, you always have a choice, *chère*," he responded easily. "And this is a good one you're makin'."

She kissed Matt, said goodbye to Orèlia, who'd watched the little drama being played out in her kitchen with undisguised interest, then made a dash through the rain to the car, which he'd painted the same candy apple red it had been that summer.

"You really didn't have any right to do this," she muttered when they were both in the car.

"Far be it from me to start a day out by arguing with a pretty woman, but you're wrong. I told you, sugar, I made a promise."

"I don't know why *that* should bother you. Since you've certainly broken promises before."

"Be careful what buttons you push, Danielle." He twisted the key in the ignition. "Because sometimes a person can get into trouble when they don't know what they're talking about."

The engine came alive with a mighty roar that vibrated through her bones, reminding Dani of those reckless drag races that could have gotten him killed, even though he'd always won. "I know what happened," she countered. As soon as she'd shared the innermost secret of her heart—that she loved him—he'd taken off.

He shot her a look. "You're dead wrong."

The easygoing man who'd offered to teach her son how to play baseball, who'd invited him to a car show, and concocted that ridiculous tall tale about Sheriff Callahan taming an alligator was gone. In his place was a rough, dangerous man who looked every bit the devil people had once claimed him to be.

Not having any idea what to say to this intimidating stranger, Dani held her tongue on the drive out of town.

Perhaps it was because the rain streaming down the window and the dark, lowered sky heightened the intimacy of their situation, perhaps it was because he'd been thinking of her continually these days as his heroine took on more and more of Dani's traits.

Perhaps it was because whenever he did finally fall into bed after a long day of working on the house and an equally long night of writing, his dreams were filled with her.

Or it could be, Jack considered, because she was back in the same car where they'd passed so many hot summer nights. More than likely it was all of the above, but the woman was driving him crazy.

The scent blooming from her skin was like green meadows after a summer rain, reminding him all too vividly of the day they'd gotten drenched going out to his camp in the pirogue. They hadn't bothered to dry off. He'd dragged her to his bed as soon as they'd gotten in the cabin door, and they'd rolled around on the moss stuffed mattress, ripping at each other's clothes, her soft white hands as desperate as his, her mouth as hungry, her slender body as fluid as water, as soft as silk, as hot as hellfire.

He wondered if she'd taste the same.

Wondered if she'd still make those sexy little noises when he took her breasts into his mouth and sucked so hard he could feel her tightening around him.

Wondered if she'd still scream when she came?

"I don't understand why you're doing this," Dani said, breaking the silence.

"I told you, I promised the judge."

"I wasn't talking about driving to the prison. I'm referring to the way you've been treating me. It was obvious you didn't want to see me when I first came home. You wouldn't return my calls, you made me come all the way out into the swamp at night to track you down at Beau Soleil, and when I did, you said the same thing you told me that summer, that I should stay away from you."

"You probably should."

"Then why did you show up at the library and talk about carrying my books? Why did you go out of your way to be nice to Matt? Was all that talk about baseball and cars just a way to sleep with me?"

"*Bon Dieu*, I'd never use a boy to get sex from his *maman*." Since it grated that she'd actually believe he was capable of something that low, he decided if she was going to think the worst, he might as well help her out. He twisted his mouth into a mocking leer of a smile. Then winked. "I can handle that all on my own."

"You're doing it again." Jack liked the heat in her voice. Liked that he could still get beneath her skin and tap the passion he knew flowed there.

"Doin' what?" he asked, knowing exactly what she was talking about.

"Swinging back and forth between treating me like you'd just as soon I pack Matt in the car and drive back to Virginia, then acting as if you want me in your bed—"

"Oh, there's no acting goin' on there. I definitely want you in my bed. Or *your* bed. Or the backseat, like in the good old days, and on top of your tidy little library desk.

"The truth of the matter is that I want you just about every place and every way there is to do it, sugar. And a few that haven't been invented yet."

"That's just sex."

"Hell yes, it's sex. And it'd be damn good. The best you've ever had."

"When you get around to using that library card, Jack, you might want to check out a dictionary."

"Why?"

"So you can look up your picture under *arrogance*."

"It's not braggin' if it's true," he repeated what he'd said when she'd complimented him on his gumbo.

Jack gave her points for trying, but he wasn't buying that cool act. Her hair was already escaping the neat French roll, little tendrils of it trailing down her cheek. She could pull her lips into as tight a line as she wanted, but any man still alive below the waist could see that full, luscious mouth had been created to satisfy male fantasies.

In her little black dress and pearls she could have been on her way to some uptown lady's tea. But Jack could see beneath the almost prim exterior to the woman who, ever since she'd landed back in town, had him thinking too damn much about dark rooms, hot nights, and tangled sheets.

He reached across the space between them and caressed her leg.

"We didn't have all that much in common back then." He slipped a finger beneath the short hem of her skirt, traced a slow, figure eight on the silky skin at the back of her knee, and was rewarded by her sharp intake of breath.

"Jack—"

"The princess and the jailbird," he murmured, ignoring her intended protest. Not quite sure which of them he was tormenting more, he kept his eyes on the rain-slick road while moving his hand higher. "But we were sure damn good at driving each other crazy."

She didn't even attempt to answer that. Her breath turned choppy as his fingers skimmed up the inside of her thigh to play with the elastic band at the leg of her French-cut panties. He had the hard-on of his life and heaven was just a few inches away.

"Dammit, Jack, would you just knock it off?"

It was like turning off a lightbulb. One minute she'd been lifting her hips, like a fluffy marmalade *'tite chatte* begging to be petted. The next she was jerking away as if he'd replaced his finger with a red-hot poker.

Which, Jack thought with grim amusement as he returned his hand to the steering wheel, was damn close to what he wanted to do.

She massaged her temples. "I don't know what gets into me whenever I'm with you."

"Same thing gets into me, sugar. Lust, pure and simple."

"It's not simple." She leaned her head against the back of her seat and pressed her fingers against her eyelids. "Nothing about you has ever been simple."

"Me?" He lifted a hand to his chest. "I've always been an open book."

It was, admittedly, a lie. But Jack had gotten so used to lying, it sure wasn't going to keep him up at night worrying about it.

"The kind of book that comes in a brown paper wrapper."

She shot him a bleak, confused look that if his groin wasn't throbbing so damn hard would have probably strummed any lingering chords of conscience he might have buried somewhere deep inside himself.

"How do you do it? Five minutes with you and I'm seventeen years old again."

He shrugged. "You're not a teenager anymore, Danielle. You're a woman. A beautiful, desirable woman with a strong sex drive. You should be celebrating, you. Instead of fretting that pretty head over somethin' that's as natural as breathing."

"For you, perhaps."

"*Mais* yeah." Just as he'd refused to deny it the other night, he would not now.

"I'm not made that way."

"Coulda fooled me." As often happened in this lowland country, the rain ceased as quickly as it had begun. When the sun broke blindingly through a break in the clouds, he pulled a pair of sunglasses from his shirt pocket and shoved them onto his face. "Another couple minutes with my hand up your skirt, and you would have been jumping right into my lap."

"That was a mistake." She pretended a sudden interest in the stands of cypress outside the GTO's passenger window. "One that won't be happening again."

"You go ahead and tell yourself that if it makes you feel better. But I remember having to wear a shirt all that long hot summer because your fingernails kept stripping skin off my back. And don't think I've forgotten how you went off like a Mardi Gras firecracker the first time I put my mouth between your legs. And—"

"I get the point," she cut him off. "But for your information, I was only that way with—"

She slammed her mouth shut, but it was too late.

"With me." Hell, perverse as he was, Jack was even enjoying the way she was glaring at him.

"Arrogant," she muttered.

"And good," he reminded her. "The best you've ever had, I believe you were going to say."

She arched a blond brow. "Now you're a mind reader?"

"*Non*. I don't have to. Not when your pretty face and curvy little body is saying, 'I want to fuck Jack Callahan.' "

"I've never used that word in my life."

"Don't have to say it to do it, angel."

She cursed. It wasn't the *F* word. But it was damn close. Jack grinned.

"Good as I was, I've gotten a whole lot better. Jus' you wait and see."

"Why don't I take your word for it, and we'll leave it at that," she suggested on a huff that did appealing things to her breasts.

Of course, everything about Danielle Dupree was proving appealing. Which, if he had any sense, would scare the shit out of him. But oddly enough, as successful as he'd become these past years, for the first time in a very long while Jack was enjoying himself immensely. Enjoying her.

# 15

*If it weren't* for the seriousness of her mission, if they were only out for a Sunday drive, Dani would have appreciated the stunning scenery. Towering oak trees draped in silver Spanish moss lined the road, pecan trees stood in straight rows in rolling fields and towered over houses in small yards. The azaleas were in bloom, dazzling the eye with riots of color.

"You know," she murmured as the scenery flashed by the passenger window, "you won't be able to keep your promise to meet my father at the prison if you end up getting us both killed."

He slanted her a sideways look. "Wanna know one major difference between men and women?"

"Not particularly. But I've no doubt you're going to tell me."

"A man can actually quietly enjoy a car ride from the passenger seat."

"And women don't necessarily feel the need to drive faster than the speed of sound."

"This car, she wasn't meant to go slow." As if to prove his point, he stepped on the gas causing the car to shoot forward as if shot out of a cannon. "I remember a time when you liked to go fast."

"I was seventeen. There should be a general amnesty for any stupid, reckless things people do in their teens."

"You're not gonna get any argument from me on that, sugar."

Although he was still breaking the speed limit, he eased up on the gas. Just a little. Silence settled over them, broken only by the sound of Steve Riley and the Mamou Playboys doing the *Creole Stomp* on the radio.

"How much farther?"

Dani had been to the prison once, when a friend's parents had taken both girls to the rodeo put on by the inmates every Sunday in October. But that had been a very long time ago, and needless to say, she'd never had a reason to return. Until now.

"About fifteen more minutes."

Another milepost blurred by. Jack muttered a rough French word Dani didn't recognize, but didn't need a translator to know it was a curse.

"What's wrong?"

He blew out a breath. "Look, I made a promise to the judge."

"I know. To pick him up today."

"There's more." He shook his head. His smile was rife with a grim humor she couldn't decipher. "Who would have thought I'd have any conscience left, me?" he murmured, more, Dani thought, to himself, than to her.

At a loss, she wished she could see his eyes and realized, as she never had before, how much Jack kept hidden.

He'd always been so outrageously outspoken, seeming to enjoy scandalizing people by ignoring the polite and complex rules of southern society, that if you didn't look carefully, as she was doing now, you'd never notice how much he actually held back.

"I've been trying like hell to keep my word, but this isn't fair to you," he was saying when she shook off the sudden insight, deciding to think about it later. "If the judge ends up living with you—"

"He will be living with me." Dani would not allow herself to think otherwise.

"Then you have the right to know he's not well."

Icy fingers twisted at her stomach. Dani stared hard at a trio of Lycra-clad cyclists who were framed in the window for an instant as she and Jack sped past. "Exactly *how* not well? What's wrong with him?"

"In a nutshell? He says he's dying."

She shifted in her seat, turning not just her head, but her entire body—which throbbed as if it had been hammered with a two-by-four—toward him.

"I don't believe that." It couldn't be true. Surely her father would have broken down and written to her about that?

"Hell, Danielle, I'm sorry." His expression echoed his words. "I tried to talk him into at least lettin' the prison doctors get in touch with you, but, well"—he shrugged—"you know how mule-headed he can be."

"He doesn't want anything to do with me," she said flatly. "Even when he's dying." Of all the things her father had done to hurt her over the years, this was the worst.

"He didn't want to burden you."

"Burden me?" Dani's voice cracked. "He's my father, dammit!" She looked out the window again, the rolling green hills blurred by a veil of unshed tears. "We're supposed to be a family."

"I figure he feels he let you down when he broke the law."

"I refuse to believe he broke the law. But even if he had, he would only have done it to save his home. The same way Annabel Dupree did when the Yankee army marched upon Beau Soleil."

The former New Orleans socialite had killed every chicken on the place and roasted them for the invading Northern troops to keep them from looting and burning the plantation home.

Desperate times called for desperate measures. Dani had grown up on grand tales of the various sacrifices that had been made by her ancestors to keep the house in the family for generations.

"The judge always set some pretty high standards. As hard as he was on others, he was even harder on himself. Which, I suppose, is why he refused that plea bargain people say the D.A. practically got down on his knees beggin' him to accept."

"My father, unfortunately, can be incredibly rigid."

He certainly hadn't given into her tears when she'd begged to be allowed to continue dating Jack. He'd called him a delinquent, and perhaps he had been. But these days people would see an angry boy who'd been emotionally wounded that horrific day he'd held his dying father in his arms. The day Jake Callahan had given his own life to save Dani's father.

Fate, Dani thought on a soft, sad sigh, often seemed like a web, all the people and events being complexly connected, destined, no matter how they might struggle against its silken threads, to meet at the center.

Nor had he relented when she'd wanted to stay in Blue Bayou during her pregnancy. Or that memorable day, a week before her daughter had been born, when she'd used her single weekly allotted telephone call, pleading to be allowed to keep her child.

"You say he's dying. What's the diagnosis?"

"Congestive heart disease."

Hope instantly fluttered delicate wings in Dani's heart. "That's not necessarily fatal. Has he gotten a second opinion? A third? Or is the only medical care he's had the past seven years a prison doctor?"

"Hell, I don't know. It was like pulling teeth to get him to tell me as much as he did."

"Which was?"

"Apparently he signed up to be part of some medical test group five years ago after his first heart attack."

"First?"

"He's had two, that I know of. The second one got him kicked out of the test group, since instead of gettin' better, he's worse than he was."

"Which means for five years his heart problems were getting worse because he wasn't getting appropriate treatment?"

"That's how those tests work. You can't go combining regimes or no one would ever know which drug was working and which wasn't."

That earlier valiant hope took a nosedive. Dani managed to pull it up again.

"Surely there's something that can be done. Bypasses, transplants, shunts, that roto-rooter procedure I saw on some television news magazine, new drugs, defibrillators, all sorts of things."

"Like I said, I don't know the details. But I do know it was his choice to take part in the study. Nobody held a gun to his head."

"Why would he do such a thing?"

"Beats me. But knowing the judge, I'd guess he was trying to give back to society. Maybe make amends for what he did."

"Even if he did those crimes, which I'll never believe he did, that's what going to prison is supposed to be about. You do your time, pay your debt, and resume your life."

Damn the man! How could he be so egocentric? Didn't he realize he wasn't the only person affected by such a life-and-death decision? He might not want to acknowledge them, but he had a family. A daughter and a grandson he should have been thinking about.

She'd just begun the climb out of despair into irritation rising quickly to a healthy, cleansing temper when the prison came into view. If Jack's GTO was like a time machine back to the 1960s neither of them had ever personally known, this was like going back a hundred and fifty years.

Formerly a plantation farmed by slaves who'd been forcefully uprooted from their homeland in Angola, Africa, the Angola State Penitentiary was the largest—and one of the toughest—in the United States. Bordered by the levee of the Mississippi River on three sides, the eighteen thousand acres were now tended by a convict workforce.

When two straight lines of prisoners carrying hoes and shovels marched along the levee into the cotton fields, guarded by armed men on horseback, the harsh reality of her father's life these past years hit home.

Her stomach, which had been tied up in knots, lurched. "Could you please pull over?"

He didn't hesitate. Then got out of the car and waited calmly at the side of the road while she threw up.

"I'm sorry." The tears she'd been fighting broke free, trailing down her cheeks. She dashed at them with the back of her hands. "It's just that I'm beginning to feel like those balloon clowns they used to sell at Cajun Days. Every time I think I'm managing to stand on my feet, I get knocked down again."

He took out a square white handkerchief and silently handed it to her.

"Thanks." Dani blew her nose. "I didn't realize there was anyone anywhere in the world who still used these things."

"I'm an old-fashioned kinda guy," he said mildly as he retrieved a stick of gum from his shirt pocket.

Nervous about today, Dani hadn't slept well last night, and the sugar from the Juicy Fruit hit like a jolt in her bloodstream.

"And you may feel like one of those balloons, sugar, but the important thing is, you keep gettin' back up again."

She sniffled. "It's not that I have much of a choice. A single mother can't afford the luxury of a nervous breakdown."

"Maybe you just need someone to take a bit of the burden off your shoulders for a while."

He skimmed his palms over the shoulders in question. Then, as if it were the most natural thing in the world to do, drew her into his arms.

"Why, what a dandy idea." As if it were the most natural thing in the world for her to do, she rested her head against his shoulder. Just for a moment, Dani assured herself. "So, are you going to call my fairy godmother, or should I?"

He chuckled, but when he tipped her face up with a finger beneath her chin, lifting her gaze to his, his warm eyes were more serious than she'd ever seen them.

"You're spinning a helluva lot of plates right now. What with trying to get the apartment livable again after the fire, a new job, settling your boy in a new school, taking your father in."

"I'm handling things."

"Sure you are."

Jack liked the little sparks of temper and resolve he kept witnessing. The Danielle he'd known back then had been frustratingly acquiescent. In fact, the only time he'd ever seen her go after something was when she'd wanted him. And then it had been damn the torpedoes, full speed ahead.

Jack had long ago come to the conclusion that there was nothing more powerful than a teenage girl determined to snare herself a boyfriend.

"You're handling everything damn well, from what I can tell," he said. "But all of us could use a little help now and then. So how 'bout you let me be in charge of makin' you feel good?"

"I suppose feeling good would involve sex?"

"That's one of the most fun ways."

She looked up at him through moisture-brightened eyes. "Jack. Write this down. I am not going to have sex with you."

"Sure you are." He lifted her knuckles and grazed them with his smiling lips. "But me, I'm a patient man. Meanwhile, we'd better get movin'. Before one of those guards with the rifle in his lap decides to check out what we're doing here hangin' out on the side of this road."

"I hate thinking of my father working on a prison gang," she said when they were headed toward the prison.

"Then don't. Because he never so much as lifted a hoe."

"Because of his illness?"

"That might've had something to do with it. If he'd been in the general population. Which he wasn't."

"He wasn't?"

"Dani, the guy's a judge," he reminded her. "A hardliner who spent most of his adult life sending people to prison. *This* prison. Do you think the warden's actually going to risk having him spend his days and nights with grudge-carrying felons who are more than likely armed with some lethal homemade weapon?"

Dani had thought of that, early on. Then forced it out of her mind, when her father refused to have any contact with her and the worry became too difficult to handle. Heaven knows Lowell had been no help. He'd refused to even speak about his former mentor, the man who'd gotten him elected.

Nor had he done a single thing to attempt to get his father-in-law's sentence commuted or win a pardon for the man everyone, including the sentencing judge, acknowledged had, despite how people may have felt about him personally, been a pillar of integrity.

"He's been in solitary confinement for seven years?"

"Pretty much. But the past year they've let him volunteer in the hospice program, which I think has been good for him."

Dani drew in a deep, shaky breath. "I hate this."

"You could've stayed home."

"Not coming out here. I hate all this."

She waved a hand, taking in the fields, the workers bent over their hoes like some painting of slaves in the 1800s, the guards on their horses, the swamps on the fourth side of the penitentiary, the high fences, towers, the compound of buildings they were approaching.

"I hate thinking of my father wasting so many years behind bars with common criminals."

"Nothing common about the judge," Jack agreed.

Dani was grateful that he didn't point out, as he could have, that her father may not be common, but what he'd been convicted of, no matter the reason, had indeed been a criminal act.

And while she wasn't about to admit it, she was also grateful that she wasn't going to have to face her father for the first time after all these years alone.

As it turned out, things didn't go as badly as Dani had feared. They went worse.

To begin with, her father looked nothing like the larger-than-life figure she remembered. Despite Jack having warned her he was gravely ill, the first sight of him came as a terrible shock.

His formerly thick black hair was now a wispy bit of white, his complexion, beneath its prison pallor, the sickly hue of library paste. The white suit he'd always worn with the confident panache of Tom Wolfe strained at the seams.

"I thought he'd be thinner," she murmured.

"I checked with a doc in town about heart disease," Jack surprised her by revealing. "She said that when the heart isn't pumping right, fluids tend to build up, making a person look heavier, even when he isn't eating very much."

Rather than marching through the prison gate on his former robust stride, her father's stooped shuffle nearly broke Dani's heart.

"You gonna be all right?" Jack asked quietly when she sucked in a harsh painful breath.

He was leaning against the red fender of the car, arms folded over his chest.

"Yes." Dani set her face into a fixed half smile. She would not allow her horror to show.

Her father lifted a hand, as if to greet Jack. Then, as he viewed Dani standing beside him, his face darkened. "What are you doing here, Danielle?"

"Hello to you, too, Daddy." She kissed his cheek and steeled herself against the coldness that was even more painful than she remembered. "I came to bring you home."

"Don't have a home anymore." He shot a look toward Jack, whose expression remained inscrutable. "Callahan's livin' in it now."

"So I recently discovered."

His eyes, which were still as bright and avid as an eagle's, bored into hers. "You saying that husband of yours never told you he picked it up for back taxes?"

"No. I'd been under the impression that we'd lost it years ago."

He looked at Jack, who nodded. "Well," the judge decided on a shrug, "guess it doesn't matter all that much. What's done is done. Might as well get this show on the road."

Dani climbed into the backseat, leaving the passenger seat for her father, who did not seem inclined to speak as they headed back to Blue Bayou. A strained silence filled the car.

"Matt's really looking forward to meeting his grandfather," she volunteered after they'd gone about ten miles.

"I told you to tell the boy I was dead."

"The *boy's* name is Matthew and since I don't lie to my child, that wasn't an option."

"Better he think his grandfather dead than find out he's a jailbird."

"Matt knows you made a mistake you were punished for."

"So you told him his grandfather was put in time-out for seven years?"

"Something like that," she said evenly as Jack shot her an encouraging look in the rearview mirror. Not wanting to get into an argument that might make her father angry and cause him to have a heart attack before she could even get him home, Dani took a deep breath and tried again.

"Matt's a very special boy, Daddy. He's warm-hearted and extremely tolerant. He's always the first to make friends with the new children in his class. And he reads way above his grade level."

"So did you. Didn't you win the reading certificate every year?"

"I never realized you were aware of that."

"Just because I didn't come to the school awards assemblies didn't mean I didn't know what was going on. After all, who do you think wrote the checks to pay for those fancy frames Mrs. Callahan kept buying?"

Dani's spirits took a little dive at the idea that the only reason her achievements stuck in her father's mind was that they'd cost him money. For not the first time, she also realized how fortunate she'd been to have Marie Callahan as a surrogate mother during those turbulent teen years.

"Jack says you volunteered in the hospice program."

"Jack talks too much." The judge glowered Jack's way.

Jack shrugged, obviously unwounded.

Reminding herself that part of her reason for returning home had been to try to establish a sense of family for her son, Dani refused to allow her father's negative attitude to ruin their long-awaited reunion. "I hadn't realized they had hospice programs in prison."

"Eighty-five percent of the inmates in Angola are going to die in there. You think they all get shived in the shower? Most die of old age. Like they say inside, life's a bitch, then you die."

"What a lovely thought." Perhaps the prisoners ought to start printing it onto the license plates.

Dani wondered why she was even trying. She'd never been able to get through to the man. What on earth had made her think time would have changed the chasm between them that had often seemed as wide and deep as the Grand Canyon?

"I hope you're not going to talk this way to Matt."

"Should've told the boy I was dead."

Dani exchanged another glance with Jack in the mirror, hating the pity she viewed in his eyes.

"His name is Matthew," she repeated firmly. "Whether you like it or not, Daddy, we've come back home to Blue Bayou and you're going to live with us and get to know your only grandson, because if you really *are* terminally ill, the least you can do is make the most of your time.

"So, you may as well just get used to the idea and quit being so damn negative because I refuse to let Matt feel as shut out of your life as I always did."

He turned around and looked at her with blatant surprise. "When did you get that smart mouth?"

"When I discovered that nobody was giving out plaques to good, acquiescent southern girls."

He shot a look at Jack. "I suppose you've got something to do with this."

"Not me." Jack shrugged. "Though personally, I think it suits her."

"Figures you'd be all for her sassing her daddy. You also didn't have any right to go tellin' her about my heart condition."

"And have you keel over one morning and have her not at least know enough about your medical history to tell the EMTs? Besides, she's your daughter. She obviously, for some reason I sure as hell can't fathom, loves you. And she's damn well entitled to know the truth."

"Would you two stop talking about me as if I weren't in the car," Dani complained. "I'm horribly sorry you're ill, Daddy, and I don't want to unduly upset you, but if something bothers me, I'm going to speak my mind and you're both just going to have to damn well deal with it."

Her father folded his arms, glared out the window, and cursed beneath his breath. Dani met Jack's gaze in the mirror again. When he winked, she managed a faint, reluctant smile in return.

# 16

*Jack kept telling himself* that he shouldn't care that the judge was acting like a first-class prick to his daughter. After all, Danielle was a grown woman, capable of making her own choices. Her father might have wanted her to marry Lowell Dupree, but from what he'd heard, no one had held a shotgun on her, or dragged her kicking and screaming down the aisle.

No one had asked her to come back to Blue Bayou, either, and he knew the judge sure as hell hadn't invited her out to Angola today. It was obvious the old man wasn't turning cartwheels about her coming back home.

Hell, truth be told, Jack didn't want her here in Blue Bayou. He didn't want her, with her big hazel eyes and sweet lips and sexy little female body messing with his mind, making him think of things and times he'd done his best to forget.

He didn't want her *here*. But, *mon Dieu*, he sure as hell wanted *her*. It was just sex, Jack assured himself. That's all it was. That's all he'd let it be.

A woman like Danielle Dupree would take too much out of a man. Hell, he was already being sucked into emotional quicksand. When he'd found himself having to curl his fingers tighter around the steering wheel, to keep from punching the judge in his frighteningly puffy gray face for having made her look on the verge of crying again, Jack knew he was getting in even deeper.

Worse yet was the increasingly strong desire to take her back to Beau Soleil and make love to her in that once pretty room where they'd spent so many stolen nights, and promise to protect her.

Now that, Jack thought, was a fucking damn dangerous thought.

He'd stopped believing he could protect anyone that day in a Colombian warehouse when because of him, a helluva lot of people had died and a good woman had been widowed.

"What on earth?" Dani stared in disbelief at her son. His darling freckled face was bruised and battered, his bottom lip was swollen, his eye—surrounded by ugly purplish blue flesh—was nearly swollen shut, and his knuckles were bleeding.

"I didn't have any choice, Mom. I had to fight."

"There's always another choice besides fighting. You never fought at your old school."

"I didn't have to back there."

"I don't understand. Assumption is a Catholic school."

"Not all kids at Catholic schools are altar boys," Jack pointed out, reminding Dani that he certainly hadn't been.

"So, did you manage to get some licks in?" he asked Matt.

"Yeah." His split lip curved into a cocky grin. Dani didn't know whether to laugh or cry when her son's masculine pride revealed a bit of the man he would someday become.

"Good for you." Jack ruffled his hair.

"If you don't mind," Dani said, her voice frost, "I'd just as soon my son not believe problems are solved with his fists."

"Spoken just like a damn female," the judge scoffed. He shot a considering look down at the filthy boy Dani had dressed in his best T-shirt and jeans this morning for the meeting with his grandfather. "Sometimes men have to make a stand."

Matt nodded. "Like Gary Cooper did in *High Noon*. When he had to face down the bad guys." Dani decided that was the last time she'd let him stay up on a school night to watch old movies with her on the Western Channel.

"Precisely. Just don't go making a habit of it or you'll end up in trouble." The judge held out a blue-veined hand. "I'm your grandfather."

"Yessir, I know." Matt stuck his filthy hand into the judge's larger one. "That's what I was . . ." He slammed his mouth shut.

The judge arched a frosty brow. "So you were fighting about me, were you?" He may be ill, but there was definitely nothing wrong with his mind.

"Yessir." Dani was a bit surprised when Matt didn't appear all that intimidated by a man who'd been known to cause hardened criminals to quake in their shoes. "Some of the kids on the bus said you were a jailbird."

"They were right."

"I'm reading a book about this kid who got sent to this camp for bad boys for stealing sneakers. But he didn't really steal them, he was just in the wrong place at the wrong time when they fell on his head because of the curse put on his family by a one-legged gypsy after his great-great-grandfather stole a pig. So, it was really just a mistake." He sucked in a deep, noisy breath. "Just like Mom said you got sent to prison by mistake."

"It was a mistake of my own making. And I paid the price."

"Whenever I make mistakes Mom says she still loves me. Even when she has to punish me. So, you don't have to worry, Grandpa, because she'll still love you, too."

Dani wondered if it was moisture or a trick of the overhead light that made her father's eyes shine.

"I need some fresh air," he said gruffly. "That fool car was too damn stuffy." He shuffled out, leaning heavily on his cane.

"Well, that was interesting," Dani murmured.

"It's okay, Mom. Grandpa probably just has to adjust. Like me at school." Matt's forehead furrowed. "Mrs. Deveraux, the bus driver, said she was going to tell the principal about the fight. So, I guess you'll be getting a call to come to the school for a conference."

Dani sighed. It would be just one more in a recent long list of first-time experiences. "I suppose so."

Then, because she was feeling guilty for having put her child in a situation where he was forced to defend his grandfather with his fists, she smoothed the hair Jack had ruffled.

"Why don't you go upstairs and take a bath. Then I'll put some antibacterial cream on your knuckles, and we'll discuss alternative problem-solving methods."

"Okay. But I really didn't have any choice, Mom."

She watched him go up the stairs. "I can't believe he actually got in a fistfight," she murmured.

"He wouldn't be the first kid to have to stand up to bullies," Jack said mildly. "Won't be the last."

Dani rubbed her temples where the headache she'd had all day was escalating to jackhammer proportions. "He's just a baby."

"He's eight years old. That's no baby. You can't keep him in bubble wrap. It's no good for him."

"Excuse me." She folded her arms. Her voice and her gaze frosted over. "I should have realized you were an expert on child-rearing. Having so many children of your own." Even as she'd tossed that sarcastic comment at him, her conscience twinged and a familiar ache spread across her chest.

Instead of appearing offended, his deep, answering laugh rumbled through her. "*Mon dieu*, I do love it when you get up on that high horse, sugar."

Jack ducked his head and kissed her, a quick hard kiss that sent her head spinning and ended much too soon, then skimmed a finger down her nose. "Why don't you go play nurse to your son while I visit with the judge."

"So, how's it feel to be back home?" Jack handed the judge one of the bottles of RC cola he'd snagged out of the refrigerator.

"I wouldn't know. Since this isn't my home," the judge reminded him.

Jack refused to apologize for having saved Beau Soleil from those mobster gamblers and the ravages of the bayou environment.

"You know what they say." The sun was beginning to set, but the heat and moisture continued to hover over the bayou like a wet blanket. Another thirty minutes and squadrons of mosquitos would begin dive-bombing anyone foolish enough to still be outside. "Home's where the heart is."

"Then I still don't have a home. Since my heart's pretty much shot."

"So you keep saying." Jack sat down on the top step of the porch, spread his legs out, and took a long swallow of cola, enjoying the cool flow down his throat. "You know, Danielle's right. From what I've seen, she's sure as hell not the same little girl who let other folks decide what was good for her. She's gotten some steel beneath that pretty cotton-candy exterior, and she's not gonna just sit by and let you die on her without a fight."

"It's not her place to tell me what to do. I'm her father."

"Then perhaps it's time you started actin' like one, you."

"Perhaps you're forgetting who you're talking to, you," the judge countered with acid sarcasm.

"Last I looked, you weren't a sitting judge anymore. So you can't sentence me back to jail." Jack tilted the neck of the bottle toward him. "Besides, DEA agents don't intimidate real easy."

"I may no longer be on the bench, but you're no DEA agent, either." He swept a critical look over Jack's long hair and earring. "Sure don't look much like one, either."

"Well, you know, I tried goin' undercover in my Brooks Brothers suit, but for some reason the cartel got suspicious. And I may no longer be on the government payroll, but I could probably find a pair of cuffs around the house somewhere. In case Danielle needs help gettin' you to the doctor."

"There's no point. I'm dying. And that's that."

"Never thought I'd see the day you'd be actin' the coward."

"I'm not a coward. I'm a realist."

Jack shook his head even as he wondered why he was bothering to have this conversation. Getting involved in the complex, tortuous relationship between Danielle and her father was like invading a nest of water moccasins. It was definitely not something a sensible man would do.

The problem was, he'd never been known for his good sense. Especially not where pretty, sweet-smelling Danielle Dupree was concerned.

"If you really are dying, what would it hurt to go through a few tests? Just to satisfy her?"

"Easy for you to say."

"Okay, maybe it'd be a real pain. Maybe you'd just as soon spend your last days on earth sitting here on this porch, scratching your butt, and watchin' the sun rise and set than putting on a paper hospital gown with no backside and having people you don' know poking and probin' at you. But the thing is, Judge, you owe her."

"How do you figure that?"

"It was you who talked her into marrying Dupree."

"Hell, I didn't have to talk all that hard. Lowell Dupree was a charming, intelligent man who knew how to treat a woman."

"Yeah, he treated his wife real well, runnin' 'round on her, then leaving her to take care of her boy all by herself. As for the charm, I always thought the guy was more slick than charmin'. Like snot on a doorknob."

"If that's any example of your descriptive powers, I find it hard to believe you're a writer."

"It's hard for me, too, most times. And it was a long and crooked path gettin' where I am."

Jack frowned as he thought about the argument he'd had with his larger-than-life father back in the seventh grade when he'd announced his decision to become a writer instead of a cop. Three days later Jake Callahan had been killed. Jack often wondered if his daddy could see the success he'd achieved. And, more important, if he was proud of him.

"But we're not talkin' about me."

He shook off the sudden and unsettling realization that there was a chance he and Danielle had something more in common than just lust. If he were writing them as two characters in one of his novels, he'd have them both sharing a subconscious need for paternal approval from fathers who couldn't—for different reasons—ever give it to them.

"We're talking about you and your daughter. About you settin' things right before you kick the bucket. About acting like a father for once in your life."

"Don't you tell me I wasn't a good father. The girl never wanted for anything."

"Except love. Hell, the only reason she chased after me that summer was because she was so damn emotionally needy she was willin' to convince herself that she was in love. That's the only way a good girl like her could allow herself to get any comfort from havin' sex."

"I don't want to talk about you having sex with my daughter."

"That makes two of us. But you know, it seems real funny to me that you'd go to prison, even though we both know you were framed—"

"You didn't tell Danielle that?"

"No." But he'd sure as hell had wanted to.

"Good. I don't want her anywhere near that crime family."

Jack hadn't been real sure about that the first time the judge had insisted he keep quiet about what he'd learned about the Maggione family wanting to get the incorruptible law-and-order judge off the bench prior to the trial of one of Papa Joe Maggione's grandsons. Having spent time with Danielle and witnessed the woman she'd become, he suspected she might actually start rocking some potentially dangerous boats.

"I'm still havin' trouble figuring out why you'd be willing to spend seven years in prison, perhaps even ruin your health, to protect your daughter from getting mixed up with mobsters."

"It wasn't just that. There was her husband's career to think of."

"There is no way in hell I'm gonna believe that you'd let yourself get convicted just to further some politician's career. Especially if you were betting on him getting elected president some day and giving you an executive pardon. Hell, you'd get better odds with Armand Trusseau."

Trusseau was bookmaker of choice for southern Louisiana gamblers, taking bets on everything from horse races to pro and college sports to whatever the market wanted. Jack had even heard stories about him making book on the cake-baking contest at the parish fair, and which high school could get its football team all the way through the season without having one of its players arrested for underage drinking. Since most of the cops, and a number of the judges, were clients, it was only when the press started getting up in arms about all the offtrack betting, that the law would put any heat on Trusseau.

And even then, all he'd throw into their net would be some middle-school kid who was being used as a runner. Since no one had the stomach to jail a little kid for trying to make a few extra bucks, the case was usually dropped.

"So you're contending that you spent seven years trying to keep Danielle from having anything to do with the Maggiones, but you won't go the extra distance and try to make up for treating your only child like a stranger all of her life? Sorry, but that just doesn't wash."

"The girl never wanted for anything." The judge's garrulous voice gained strength, sounding, for the first time, more like it had when he'd been making rulings from the bench. He did not, Jack noticed, answer the question he'd been trying to pry out of him for months. Why the hell he hadn't fought what was obviously a frame in the first place.

"Now that's where you're wrong. She didn't have the one thing she wanted. Needed. She didn't have her daddy's love."

The judge opened his mouth. Shut it. Then drilled Jack with a razor-sharp look that had gone a long way to keeping order in his courtroom.

"What's going on between you and my daughter?"

"I wish to hell I knew," Jack muttered as he polished off the cola. "But I'm not sleepin' with her, if that's what you're worried about."

"None of my business if you were." The judge took a long swallow of his own. "The hell it isn't."

His eyes were hard, his mouth a grim warning. "You take advantage of my little girl again, Callahan, and you'll have to answer to me. Even if I have to crawl off my deathbed to rip your damn heart out."

"I'll keep that in mind," Jack drawled. "And while we're on the subject of your daughter, it's past time you told her why I left thirteen years ago. Because if you don't, I will."

The judge speared him with a lethal look that would have cowered a lesser man. "You've no damn business getting between me and my child."

"I'm tired of playing your scapegoat. I wasn't lyin' when I said I don't know what's going on 'tween Danielle and me, but I do know that I want to start out with a clean slate. Which means she's gotta know the truth."

"I'll take the matter under advisement." The judge didn't appear all that surprised by Jack's ultimatum. "How much time do I have?"

Jack shrugged. "I'll let you get settled in, but if you haven't told her in a week, I'm telling Finn to quit digging around in your case files."

The judge shot him another dark, killing look from beneath beetled white brows that seven years ago had been as black as Louisiana crude. "That's blackmail."

"I prefer to think of it as an incentive." There was a tight white ring around the judge's mouth that worried Jack, just a little, but he decided that having gone this far, he wasn't about to back off.

"If I were still on the bench, I'd toss your ass in jail and throw away the key."

"Good thing you're not on the bench."

"Fuck." The judge shook his head. "All right, I'll tell her. But there's something you ought to know, Callahan."

"What's that?"

"One of the most useful things they taught us in law school was to never wade out into unknown waters; never ask a question you didn't know the answer for ahead of time. Once you open this particular can of worms, you're not going to be able to get them back in. And you might be damn surprised what crawls out."

"I think you're mixing your metaphors a bit, Judge," Jack said mildly. "But I get your meaning. And I'm willing to take my chances."

The judge shrugged. Having reluctantly accepted the ultimatum, he now seemed bored with the conversation. "Don't say I didn't warn you."

* * *

Having expected World War III, Dani had been amazed when her father had actually agreed, without being held at gunpoint, to undergo a series of medical tests. She would have been happier if he'd been willing to go to a doctor in the city, but hadn't wanted to push her luck by insisting.

The dates on the medical degrees tastefully framed on Dr. Eve Ancelet's office wall revealed her to be in her early thirties. She was a slender woman with warm eyes and a bit brisk, but friendly attitude. After shaking hands, she folded hers atop a thick manila folder. Dani was grateful when she didn't waste time with small talk but got right to the point.

"I've already discussed all this with the judge after we'd gotten the results back yesterday," she said. "He gave me permission to share the details with you."

"Which is handy, since he refuses to discuss anything about his condition with me."

"It's hard for a man accustomed to control to surrender it."

"You'd think he would have grown used to that in prison," Dani said dryly.

"He undoubtedly learned to deal with it. In his own way. But I doubt he liked it." The doctor opened the folder. "First of all, the diagnosis by the prison doctor was correct: your father does have congestive heart failure."

The word *failure* carried with it a frightening finality. Dani's heart sank.

She tried to listen carefully, but the dreadful idea of her father dying before she found a way into his heart splintered Dani's concentration and many of the words became merely a buzz in her head.

"We're not sure how he contracted it, but my educated guess is that he suffered a virus which settled in his heart muscle," Dr. Ancelet was saying when Dani dragged her mind back from wondering how emotionally harmed Matt would be if his grandfather happened to die days after he'd finally met him. "Going back through the records, and what he told me about a time shortly before his arrest, it appears he'd suffered a case of flu. It's particularly memorable since apparently it kept him off the bench for nearly two weeks and all his cases had to be reassigned."

"I remember. He was furious." At himself, Dani recalled. "In fact, it was the first time in my life I could remember him being ill, so I was going to come take care of him, but I'd just discovered I was pregnant with Matt, and he insisted I stay home rather than risk catching something that might hurt my baby."

Dani rubbed a hand against her chest, where her own heart had begun to ache. If she had insisted on returning to Blue Bayou, would her father have recovered sooner? Could she have prevented his potentially fatal heart disease?

"He was right to be cautious. The fetus is far more vulnerable in the first trimester. However," the doctor said briskly, "there's no point in wasting time on *what-ifs*. Right now we need to concentrate on managing your father's illness so he can regain a better quality of life."

"Is that possible?" Hope returned to once again flutter delicate wings in Dani's breast.

"Actually, it is. While we can't beat the disease, at least not yet, we can help people live with it. The good news is that it's reversible. Of course, any success in treatment depends on a patient's age, condition, and goals, and needless to say, a younger person is going to have different goals than someone your father's age. They'd probably want to return to work, play with their children, make love, all those physical things that are important to them. An older person tends to have less ambitious objectives. Such as being less dependent on family and friends."

"My father hates being dependent on anyone."

"That's a universal feeling," the doctor agreed. "Heart function doesn't stay static once a person gets heart failure. It's always getting worse or better. Unfortunately, for the past seven years your father has been getting worse. I'm hoping we can turn things around and buy him some valuable time with you and your son."

"What about surgery?"

"That's not currently an option in your father's case. At least not at this time while he's so weak. I'll be frank with you, Ms. Dupree—"

"Dani."

"Dani." She smiled. "And I'm Eve. As I told the judge, at this point, I'd like to try treating him with medication and a change in attitude."

*Good luck getting that attitude adjustment*, Dani thought, but did not say.

"Your father is very obviously depressed."

"Who wouldn't be if they'd spent seven years in prison? Most of that time in isolation?"

"Granted, imprisonment could only make things worse. But his records suggest that he may have already been clinically depressed when he arrived at Angola. From talking with him, I suspect he's suffered several depressive episodes during his life."

"I don't remember him ever being depressed."

"How about angry? Or remote?"

"Well, yes. But I always figured that was just his personality. He's always demanded perfection of everyone around him, including himself, and he's an unrelenting control freak."

"Well, whether or not he was depressed in the past, he definitely is now," Eve Ancelet said. "Which isn't surprising since depression happens to be a very common side effect of heart failure. We're just beginning to get a handle on the connection between the two."

"Could depression have kept him from fighting back when he was wrongly accused of taking that bribe?"

Eve Ancelet nodded. "It might have. As a rule, when we diagnose depression, we warn patients against making any critical decisions until their medications begin working. Choosing not to participate in your own defense could certainly qualify as a critical decision."

"Why didn't his attorney tell the court?"

"There's a good possibility he never realized what he was dealing with. After all, your father isn't the most forthcoming patient I've ever had."

"Tell me about it," Dani muttered.

"I gave him several prescriptions. One's an antidepressant. Of course, whether or not he chooses to have them filled is up to him."

"He will." If she had to sit on his chest and stuff the pills down his throat.

"Good. You've undoubtedly heard about the studies being done that link mood and physical condition of patients. Empirical evidence points to the fact, which I've witnessed myself during my practice, that optimistic, positive-minded patients feel better and tend to live longer than pessimistic, negative-minded ones.

"Perhaps it has something to do with stress being a major factor in heart disease, or perhaps the folklore about our heart being tuned to our emotions is, indeed, fact. But the sooner we can turn your father's mood around, the better off he'll be. Also we'll want to start him on an exercise regime."

"Is that safe with a weak heart?"

"Certainly. While in the past, patients were admonished not to exercise to reduce the burden on their hearts, we've since learned that such restriction on lifestyle actually produces a severe deconditioning of the heart. More recent studies have shown the beneficial effects of exercise and with that in mind, I've worked out a daily routine with your father."

Dani was still skeptical. "I'm all for physical fitness, but he could barely walk out of the prison."

"Which is why we're going to begin slowly. I've recommended he begin taking short walks, just to the corner in the morning and evening. Needless to say, after having been so severely limited in his activity these past years, any cardiac conditioning is going to take longer than it would with a younger, more active patient. Still, if he sticks to the schedule I've outlined, your father could expect some improvement within a few weeks."

While Dani was a bit more optimistic than when she'd first arrived at the office, she couldn't help still being concerned. After all, Eve Ancelet was only a family physician in a small rural town. And barely older than Dani herself was.

"I'm considering taking him to Tulane." She didn't want to insult the doctor, but also felt a responsibility to her father.

"That's not a bad idea," the doctor responded easily. "Second opinions are always helpful, and I'll be happy to recommend cardiologists with whom you might want to confer. In the meantime, the medication I'm putting the judge on can't hurt him and working to change his attitude will only make things better.

"And if it helps to ease your mind, I've shared your father's tests with cardiologists at both Tulane and Johns Hopkins. And they agree with my diagnosis."

"That's reassuring. Not that I don't trust you—"

"I understand your concern." Eve smiled. "It's difficult, but although he might not see it that way right now, your father has a great deal going for him. Plus, he has a secret weapon not all patients are fortunate to have."

"What's that?"

"His family."

As she left the office, Dani could only hope they would be enough.

# 17

*A week later,* while Dani was sitting at the kitchen table, helping Matt with his homework and Orèlia was in the front parlor, watching *America's Most Wanted* on television, the judge returned from his evening walk.

When he'd first started he'd barely been able to make it down the steps. Tonight he'd managed to make it all the way to the corner and back. Without his cane. And while that doctor, who seemed to know what she was doing, even if she was young and a woman, had told him that it could take at least two weeks for those antidepressants Danielle was forcing down his throat every day to kick in, this morning had been the first time in a very long while he'd actually been glad to wake up.

During his days on the bench, he'd sent hundreds—tens of hundreds—of men and women to prison and had understood, intellectually, the life to which he was sentencing them. But even while he'd been kept from the general population, and thus, reasonably safe from harm, he'd quickly realized that there was no way for anyone who hadn't experienced that inimitable sound of a cell door sliding closed to realize how hard it was to lose the simple day-to-day freedom people on the outside took for granted.

His legs were a little shaky; he sat down on the top step of the porch and relished the ability to actually look up at a sky. As the first star winked on, he thought about Jack's threat and realized that he was running out of time.

After giving it a lot of thought, he still believed that he'd been right, although with hindsight he might admit that perhaps his methodology had been a little heavy-handed. Still, if he'd ordered

Danielle to stop seeing Marie Callahan's middle son, would she have?

"Not a chance in hell," he muttered.

Running his housekeeper's son out of town was one thing. The events that followed quite another. The judge knew that he wasn't exactly beloved in Blue Bayou; however, until he'd been framed on those bribery and subjugation of perjury charges, he'd always been considered a fair magistrate. He'd also never let a personal acquaintance with a defendant influence his decisions. Which is why he couldn't overlook the fact that he'd been guilty of a crime against his daughter.

Dani seemed to have forgiven him for not having been a warm and loving parent while she'd been growing up. But he'd already been a crusty bachelor of forty-eight when he'd made what at the time had been the worst mistake of his life by marrying her gold-digging slut of a mother.

If he'd been seeing clearly at the time, he would have realized that a twenty-two-year-old court stenographer would be unlikely to fall in love with a man more than twice her age. But he'd been blinded by her dazzling blond beauty.

Even after Savannah Bodine had trapped him the old-fashioned way—by getting pregnant—his ego had enjoyed her feminine flattery. Which, unsurprisingly, had come to a screeching halt the moment she'd gotten that five-carat pear-shaped diamond ring on her finger. In fact, while he had no real proof, he'd been bedeviled by suspicions that she'd had a fling with a streaked-blond, tanned beach boy who worked the cabana at the Caribbean resort where they spent their honeymoon. And that had been just the beginning.

By their first anniversary he'd paid for breast implants and a nose job, only to have her move into her own bedroom. By the second, she'd stopped any pretense of interest in sex with him, while making him a laughingstock by spending her evenings drinking vodka gimlets and flirting down at the No Name, as well as blatantly sleeping around with seemingly every single man in the parish. And not a few married ones, as well.

He would have divorced her. Should have. But back when he'd been thinking with his seemingly born-again penis, he'd foolishly signed a prenuptial agreement—ostensibly to protect their unborn child—and refused to reward her bad behavior by handing her a substantial chunk of his estate. But he'd miscalculated yet again, when, rather than allow herself to suffer by being trapped into a marriage she no longer pretended to care about, Savannah simply continued to ignore the little fact that she had a husband and a daughter at home.

The final straw was when a shrimp boat captain's wronged wife named her as correspondent in their divorce. When it looked as if his errant wife would actually have to appear in his own courtroom—the one place he was still admired and even feared—he'd thrown in the towel.

Two weeks before the third anniversary of their marriage made in hell, she'd taken off for Los Angeles with a hefty check in hand. Having already demonstrated that she had the maternal instincts of a black widow spider, the judge wasn't all that surprised when she left behind the blond toddler she'd once told him, in a furious flare of temper before Danielle was born, wasn't even his child.

After arriving in Tinseltown, Savannah Dupree née Bodine, had parlayed the voluptuous, albeit in hindsight, common beauty and a seemingly natural-born skill for blow jobs into a career in porno films. Once, at a judicial conference in Manhattan, he'd seen her picture on a flyer in his hotel room, advertising the pay-for-view adult movies.

Assuring himself that it was only natural curiosity, he'd paid nine dollars and ninety-five cents to watch his former bride have sex in more imaginative ways than she'd ever had with him.

Her career had turned out to be a meteor, rising fast, burning brightly, only to quickly flame out. She died on what would have been their fifth anniversary, when, high on drugs and alcohol, she'd driven her car off the Pacific Coast Highway.

The judge had been surprised to learn that he was still listed on all her legal documents as her next of kin. Until he discovered that she'd burned through the money she'd gotten from him as well as whatever she'd been earning for her X-rated films and had been in debt up to her bleached-blond roots. He'd paid to have her cremated, but decided to let MasterCard, Visa, and AMEX take care of themselves.

Given her outrageous behavior, there were bound to be those in Blue Bayou who'd wondered about Danielle's parentage. But no one had ever whispered so much as a word in front of him, and he'd taken some measure of pride in the fact that he'd clothed, housed, and fed the abandoned child who looked exactly like her mother and nothing like him.

For the first few weeks after she'd been brought to Beau Soleil from the hospital, the judge had ignored the infant, turning her care over to the same black nanny he'd always felt closer to than his own parents. But then one day, when she'd been nine months old, she'd caught a summer cold that had escalated into pneumonia.

Faced with the possibility of her actually dying, he'd belatedly realized how much he'd grown accustomed to having the well-behaved baby around the house.

After clearing his court calendar, he'd spent the next five days in the pediatric intensive care wing at St. Mary's Hospital, hovering over her crib as if his presence might protect her. Her mother, who'd taken off for a supposed trip to buy clothes in Dallas, was nowhere to be found, but even if she'd been in Blue Bayou, she'd never displayed any interest in her daughter when Danielle was well, so she certainly wouldn't want anything to do with this ill, cranky, croupy baby.

When Dani turned the corner and the fever that had created hectic red flags in her satiny smooth cheeks for too many nerve-racking days subsided, she'd smiled up at him, with her pretty rosebud lips and happy eyes that hadn't yet decided whether they were going to be green or blue, and stolen his heart.

He'd been afraid during his cribside vigil. After Savannah's departure, Victor Dupree came to understand the true meaning of terror. The more he bonded with the child which, if he hadn't given life, at least had given his name to, the more he grew to fear that someday his former wife might return to Blue Bayou and decide to claim maternal rights.

Oh, she wouldn't have a chance in hell, especially in his parish, but knowing how mercurial Savannah could be, he wouldn't have put it past her to hire some thug from her seamy underworld to kidnap their daughter just for spite. Or worse yet, for ransom.

Without being aware of doing so, little by little, the judge began to protect himself—and his heart—by distancing himself from Danielle again, even after her mother had died and the threat of Savannah taking her away was no longer valid.

Never a demonstrative man, he began to build an emotional wall around himself. Not for the reasons he had during those early months, when he'd viewed Danielle as a burden he'd never asked for, but because he couldn't bear the idea of losing the one person who meant the world to him. The only problem with that behavior, he'd come to realize, was that by protecting his own heart, he'd gravely wounded Dani's over the course of her life.

Judge Victor Dupree had been brought up surrounded by the mysteries of the Roman Catholic Church. He knew he was supposed to believe in one God, the forgiveness of sins, and life everlasting. Even having witnessed the aftermath of some of the worst things man could inflict upon his fellow man, he'd never bought into the idea of heaven and hell, having come to the conclusion in law school that it was nothing more than a fanciful concept humans had created in response to an inner need for reassurance that something existed beyond the here and now.

But seven years in near solitary confinement had given Victor Dupree a lot of time for introspection. Now, approaching death, possibly facing a judicial review far more crucial than any over which he'd ever presided, he feared he might be called upon to defend the actions of a lifetime.

He'd spent years being on guard for echoes of Danielle's mother in her, signs that he was losing control of his daughter (if she even *was* his daughter) as he'd lost control of his wife. Yet he had to admit, except for that reckless Romeo and Juliet teenage love affair with Jack Callahan, she'd never given him a lick of trouble. She'd been a model child, pretty, amiable, and obedient, even when he could tell it was hard on her. Even when he'd sent her away to Atlanta to give birth to Callahan's child, assuring her that he was protecting her reputation, when he realized now that it had been his own he'd been more concerned about.

Surprisingly, without having had any maternal role model to follow, other than Marie Callahan for those few years during her teens, Danielle had turned out to be a good mother. Her son—his grandson, the judge reminded himself—was a bright, inquisitive, interesting little boy who, along with possessing much of the attributes of his mother, in some ways reminded the judge of himself when he was Matthew's age.

*Hell.* Victor Dupree dragged a hand down his face. He had some fences to mend. Some ties to bind. Which is why, the judge decided, he wasn't going to die. At least not just yet.

Of course, staying alive had its own problems, now that Bad Jack was back in Blue Bayou, stirring things up again. The judge had never thought of himself as a coward, but he didn't want to think what might happen if the entire truth of what had happened that past summer came out.

Jack snagged the white plastic ball that came sailing off the yellow bat. "You're gettin' better."

"I know." Matt's face could have lit up Blue Bayou for a month of Sundays with wattage left over. "Huh, Grandpa?"

"You sure are," the judge agreed robustly, unable to recall when he'd enjoyed himself more. "Keep it up and you'll be in the majors before you know it."

"I'm too young," Matt said with the literal mindedness of an eight-year-old. "I just want to be picked at recess."

"You keep working on the fundamentals, and you'll be the star of the sandlot." Jack threw a slow looping, underhand pitch, which floated under the wild swing. "That was close."

"I still missed."

"Hey, even the greatest hitters of all time strike out twice as often as they hit."

"Really?" Matt tossed the ball back with surprising accuracy for a kid who hadn't even known how to properly hold it an hour ago.

"Sure." He really was a great kid, and the fact that his father hadn't realized that was more proof of what Jack had already figured out. That the congressman had been swamp scum and the world, particularly Danielle's little corner of it, was a helluva lot better off without him. "Ever hear of anyone battin' a thousand?"

"I never thought of it that way." Matt resumed his stance, standing a lot closer to the plate than he had when they'd first begun.

"It's something to keep in mind."

Jack threw another pitch, which was clipped and went rolling across the lawn. Turnip, lying nearby, watched it, as if trying to decide whether to go chasing after it, ultimately opting to remain where she was.

"That was closer. Hard to believe you've never played before."

"Dad was too busy." This time the return throw went wild, but Jack managed to catch it before it rolled into the water. "Making up laws."

"That's real important work." Jack only gave Danielle's ex that small credit for the kid's sake.

"That's what Mom always said." He frowned. But, Jack suspected, not in concentration. "But Dad was mostly interested in politics. Which was the only reason he wanted me."

"I think you may be a bit confused, sport."

"No, I'm not. It was because of the polls. Mom said more people vote for you if you're a family man."

"Loosen your grip," Jack suggested mildly as he unclenched his own hands, which had fisted. "You've got that gorilla hold thing goin' again."

When they'd first begun, Matt had a death grip on the bat. He'd begun to loosen up. Until the conversation had shifted to his father.

"Okay." Matt flexed his fingers. Drew in a breath.

"I can't believe your mother told you that about your father," the judge said.

"She didn't say it to me." He swung, managing to connect again for a nice little squibbed bunt up the imaginary third base line that might have earned him a single if they'd been playing a real game. "I heard her say it to dad. On the phone before he died. It was the day after I had to go to the Watergate to visit them because of the lawyers and accidently ran my scooter into Robin's new car.

"She's the lady Dad was going to marry. She called me a rotten little brat, but I never told Mom about that, because I didn't want to make her cry."

"I don't think that would have made her cry." Jack could, however, imagine Danielle marching over to the Watergate and ensuring no one ever dared talk to her son that way again.

"Dad made her cry a lot. When she was talking to him on the phone, she said that the devil would be making snowballs in hell before she let me go live with him and Robin."

Jack scooped up the rolling ball and exchanged a look with the judge.

"You shouldn't be eavesdropping on your mother's phone calls," the judge scolded without heat.

"I didn't mean to. I just had to get up to go to the bathroom and I heard her say that. Then she hung up. Then she cried."

"Well, this is certainly a surprise." All three males looked up as they heard the voice of the woman in question.

"Hi, Mom," Matt greeted her. "Did you see me hit the ball?"

"I did. It was quite impressive." Her voice was calm, her eyes were not.

"I hit it harder earlier." Excited about his accomplishments, he appeared oblivious to the tension swirling around the adults. "Didn't I, Jack?"

"You sure enough did, *cher*. Slammed it nearly out of the park."

"Kid's a natural," the judge said helpfully.

"Isn't that lovely." Dani's gaze settled on Jack. "Could I talk to you inside, please?"

"Mom, me and Jack were just getting good."

"Jack and I," she corrected.

"Jack and I," he repeated obediently. "Did you know that when Barry Bonds was just a little kid, he could hit a whiffle ball hard enough to break windows?"

"Mrs. Bonds was undoubtedly thrilled by that achievement." Dani knew she should be showing more interest, but it was difficult to keep her mind on a conversation about baseball when hornets were buzzing around in her head and she was shaking from the inside out. "I'm sorry to break up the inning, but it's important."

"Sure." Jack tossed the ball to Matt, who amazed Dani by dropping the yellow plastic bat and catching it with a one-handed snag that did, indeed, appear almost natural.

"Why don't you play some catch with your grandfather," Jack suggested. "Then, after your mom and I have ourselves a little chat, we can pick up some pizzas and take 'em out to Beau Soleil for supper."

"Really?"

" 'Bout time you see where your *maman* grew up. And now that the road's finally in, we can drive there in half the time as winding through the bayou in a boat."

"That's an excellent idea," the judge said heartily. "I haven't had pizza in a coon's age."

"And you won't be having it tonight, either," Dani said. "I have your dinner in here." She lifted the white plastic bag from the Cajun Market.

"If I have to eat any more egg whites I'm going to start clucking."

Dani had to admit that she'd perhaps been overly strict since her meeting with the doctor. But she was determined to turn her father's heart disease around so he could live long enough to get to know his grandson.

"No need." Orèlia came out the kitchen door to weigh in on the discussion. "I'm cookin' my special spaghetti that I invented for my

Leon's high blood pressure. I've got a whole cookbook full of recipes so good you'll be askin' me to marry you in no time."

Dani's father narrowed his eyes. "Never realized you were such a forward woman."

"Lot you didn't realize about me, you," she retorted, her hands on her hips.

Dani left them to the bickering they'd been doing since her father's arrival at the house.

Jack took the grocery bags from her hands and carried them into the kitchen. "You're pissed at me," he diagnosed as he put them on the wooden butcher-block counter.

"You're very observant." She took an onion out of the bag.

"I like looking at you, so I don't miss much. . . . Why don't you give me these." He took the cans of salt-free tomato sauce she'd pulled from the sack away. "Jus' in case you decide to throw 'em at my handsome head."

"I should." Her hands clenched into unconscious fists at her side. "You had no right . . ." Her voice choked. She could only toss her head in the direction of the backyard. "With Matt."

"Teach him to play ball? Hell, I'm only tryin' to help the kid get along better in a new school."

"I also heard at the market that he'd been telling the other boys that you were teaching him how to brawl."

"It was boxing." He reached down, took hold of her hand, and unfolded the tightly curled fingers, one by one. "I was only showin' him how to keep his guard up."

Like she should do, Dani thought, remembering the gossip she'd overheard at the market about a long-going affair between Jack and Desiree Champagne. She'd been insisting, not just to Jack, but to herself, that she didn't want to get involved with him. But the hurt she'd felt hearing about him with another woman, especially one built like a *Penthouse* centerfold, definitely suggested that she was, on some level, already involved.

"Whatever you want to call it, the result is the same. I don't want my son viewing violence as a solution to any problem. And I'm definitely not happy the way you've been insinuating yourself into his life in order to pump him for information about my marriage."

"I'd never do such a thing." Appearing honestly shocked, Jack dropped her hand. "He volunteered the information. When he told me that the reason he didn't know how to play ball was because his daddy didn't like him."

"Hell." She let out a ragged breath, briefly closed her eyes, and shook her head. "It was never him personally. Lowell never cared about anyone—or anything—who couldn't help his career."

"Then it's true? About him wanting a kid because he thought it might win him a few votes?"

It sounded even worse hearing it from someone else, Dani considered. Seeing the dark disapproval on Jack's face. How had she been so foolish?

Because, she answered her own rhetorical question, she'd been desperate to get over this man standing so close she could smell the scent of leather balm from his baseball glove on the hand that was skimming over her shoulder.

Close enough she could feel the warmth of his sun-warmed body and catch the tang of male sweat that was strangely, in its own way, appealing.

She'd never known Lowell to perspire. Not even in the heat of a Washington summer. Not even when making love.

She could live with knowing that her husband had never loved her. But how could she have married a man who wouldn't love her son? How could she have stayed with him without realizing the damage living with such a man might do to the one person she loved most in the world?

With the twenty-twenty vision of hindsight, Dani realized that she should have cut her losses when Matthew had been born the day of Lowell's second-term election.

Steeped in her southern upbringing of putting others first, she hadn't thought to utter a single word of complaint when he'd refused to cut his final day's campaigning short to be by her side as she labored to bring their son into the world.

And despite having felt as alone and abandoned as the first time she'd given birth, the very next day, between feeding her newborn and writing out thank-you notes for the mountain of infant gifts that had arrived at the hospital, she'd dutifully telephoned the wives of each and every one of Lowell's major financial contributors, personally thanking them for their political support.

"It's not that simple." She turned away.

"Few things in life are simple." Jack came up behind her, pulled her against him, rested his chin on the top of her head. "Look at you and me."

"I try not to."

"Doesn't do much good, does it? Because whether you want to admit it or not, you keep thinkin' about me. The same way I keep thinkin' about you." He rubbed his cheek against her hair. She could feel his breath on her neck. "During the day when I'm pounding nails."

He turned her in his arms and skimmed work-roughened fingertips up the side of her face. "During the evening, when I should be workin' on my book." He circled her lips with his thumb. "At night, when I should be sleeping."

"Sleeping with Desiree Champagne?" She could have bitten off her tongue when she heard that thought escape.

"Desiree and I are friends, sure enough. And I'm not gonna lie and say that we haven't passed some good times together, since you've undoubtedly heard some gossip. But I haven't been with her since you came out to Beau Soleil."

"Why not? She's certainly a beautiful woman and isn't exactly wearing widow's weeds, mourning her dear departed late husband."

"Desiree's a survivor," Jack said mildly. "She's had to be. But as appealing as she admittedly is, I'm not interested in her that way, because I don't want to be with anyone else but you, *chère*."

His eyes held hers as he cupped the nape of her neck in his hand. "I promise I'll answer any question you have about Desiree or any other woman in my past later. Right now there's something we need to get out of the way."

# 18

*Jack lowered his head* and kissed her. There was heat, burning through every cell of her body; smoke clouded thoughts she was struggling to form in her mind. The scent of Confederate jasmine and honeysuckle floated on the soft warm air. Somewhere in the chinaberry tree, a bird warbled a sad song while sweet desire sang in Dani's blood.

His clever, wonderfully wicked mouth beguiled. Seduced. His stunningly tender hands caressed. Persuaded.

When his lips left hers, and journeyed along her jaw, up her neck, to create a blissful havoc behind her ear, Dani's breath caught in her lungs.

"I thought you were a pretty girl before," he murmured as he glided his fingers down her throat, lingering in the hollow where her blood was wildly pulsing. "But you definitely blossomed into a beauty, *mon ange*."

The skimming caress continued downward, creating sparks of heat in the triangle of skin framed by the neckline of her blouse. Dani trembled as his fingertips brushed against the aching tip of her breast, a faint rasp of calluses against ivory silk.

The male scrape of afternoon beard against her cheek as his lips trailed back to hers sent her nerves skittering. "We still fit," he murmured.

"I'm on my toes." Linking her fingers together behind his neck, she sank into the deepening kiss. Into him.

"Height don' got a thing to do with it." His hands settled at her waist, drew her closer, fitting softness to strength. "We fit together in all the ways that count."

She drew in a surprised breath when he lifted her up onto the counter, then began to move between her legs. He stopped when he got a close look at her thighs, revealed by her hitched-up skirt.

"Nice." He skimmed a light touch along the lace top of her summer sheer stocking. "You wear these for me, sugar?"

"Hardly. Since I didn't expect you to be here when I got home." She sucked in a sharp breath as he slipped a treacherous finger between the elasticized lace and her too hot flesh. "They're cooler than panty hose. And more practical."

"I can see how that'd be." The hot desire that had simmered in his eyes only a moment earlier changed to a devilish laughter that nearly was her undoing. "Nothin' more frustrating than tryin' to unwrap your woman from a pair of damn panty hose."

"I happen to be my own woman." She batted at his hand. "And stop that before someone comes in."

She'd no sooner spoken when the screen door opened with a bang. "Hey, Jack," Matt asked, "who do you think's the best shortstop? Grandpa thinks it's Nomar Garciaparra, but I say Alexander Rodriguez."

"That's a no-brainer." Jack shifted gears with an alacrity Dani, who was busily tugging down her skirt, had to admire. "A-Rod, he's second behind Cal Ripken in home runs by active shortstops and isn't just the best shortstop in the game, he's the best offensive player money can buy.

"Nomar's averages are great, but the guy's injury prone. Then you gotta factor in Jeter, who's a notch behind the other two in offense, but he's more durable over a long season."

"Grandpa called Jeter a damn Yankee."

"Well, there is that," Jack allowed.

"Watch your language," Dani gently warned her son.

"Okay. But I didn't really say it. I was only saying what Grandpa said. . . . Thanks, Jack." He was almost out the door when he glanced back over his shoulder.

"Mom?"

"Yes, dear?"

"How come you're sitting up on the counter?"

"Your mama got herself a little scrape," Jack responded before Dani could think of any valid reason. "I was just checkin' it out for her. Maybe put a little lotion on it."

"Oh. Maybe Orèlia could help. Since she's a nurse."

"Oh, that's not necessary," Dani insisted, ignoring Jack's wicked grin. "I'll be fine."

"Okay." He was out the door. "Hey, Grandpa!" he hollered with more enthusiasm than Dani had heard in months. "Jack says you're wrong and it's a no-brainer."

"Great kid," Jack murmured as the door slammed behind him. He cupped her calf in his palm. "Now where were we?"

"We were discussing why I don't want you getting too involved with my son."

"Too late. I'm already involved. With the boy and his pretty *maman*."

"That's the point." She jerked her leg away and slid off the counter back onto the floor. "I've already been married once and it didn't work out."

"You hear me proposin' *chère?*"

Heat flooded into her face. "I didn't mean . . . Goddammit, Jack—"

"Better watch your language, Danielle."

His cocky smile left her not able to decide whether to hit him or smile back. In the end she did neither. "I realize you don't take anything seriously—"

"Now, there's where you're wrong." He caught her hand as she was combing it through her hair and laced their fingers together. "There's a helluva lot I take seriously, including a certain gorgeous lady who'd obviously walk through fire for her child."

"Matt's the most important thing in the world to me."

"It shows. And you don't have to worry. I'm not gonna do anything to jeopardize that."

She shook her head. In her expressive eyes he read both temptation and a wariness she hadn't possessed when he'd last known her.

"You have to understand that my decision to return to Blue Bayou wasn't an impulsive one," she stressed. "I'd thought about it so many times, but I stayed in Virginia because I kept foolishly hoping Lowell would realize how important Matt was. And how he needed a father in his life."

"If he didn't appreciate Matt's pretty *maman*, I doubt that would have happened."

"I know." She sighed. "Then, even after he died, I still weighed my options carefully."

"Made lists."

"Yes." Her eyes narrowed. "Are you laughing at me?"

"Never." He lifted their hands, brushed his lips across her knuckles. "Lists can be a good thing. I've been known to make a few myself from time to time."

"My point is, I never expected you to be back here in Blue Bayou."

"Well, that makes us even. Because I sure as hell hadn't expected to be, either. And I definitely hadn't expected you to come home."

"I don't know where whatever this is, is going."

"Why don't we just go with the flow and see where we end up? I won't lie to you. I want to touch your curvy little body. Everywhere and often. I want to taste your sweet flesh. All over. But you want to take it slow, then that's what we'll do."

His eyes on hers, he skimmed his thumb over her lips again, then backed away, giving them both some space. "Meanwhile, I need you to help me pick out some wallpaper."

"Why don't you get yourself a decorator?"

"Because a decorator wouldn't know Beau Soleil like you do. Come on, sugar. We'll look at some samples, share a pizza, and pass a good time. Besides, don't you want Matt to see the house his *maman* grew up in?"

From the bold confidence in those bedroom eyes, Dani knew that he realized he'd found the one lure impossible for her to resist.

"You really are terrible," she complained as she threw up her hands.

"I don't like arguing with a *jolie fille*, but I'm not terrible. I'm good. Hell, better than good, I'm—"

"The best I've ever had," she repeated the claim he'd made on the way to Angola.

He laughed and put a friendly arm around her shoulder. "Now you're getting the idea, you."

They went back out to the yard, where Matt was playing fetch with Turnip, who, apparently having decided to get into the game, would scoop up the ball he'd toss her way, then run around the yard in frenzied circles before returning to drop it in front of his sneakers.

"Isn't Turnip a great dog?" Matt called out to her.

"She certainly seems to be."

"Can we get a dog, Mom?"

"We'll see," Dani said. "It'd be a bit difficult to keep a dog in the apartment." Crowded, too, she considered.

"I'd walk it every day. I promise."

"I suppose we could take a trip to the shelter. After we get settled in the apartment," she qualified. "Just to check things out."

"Really?" Dani was amazed at how such a seemingly small thing could create such a look of stunned joy on his face.

"I'm not promising anything," she warned. There were other breeds, she reminded herself. Smaller, apartment-size dogs that wouldn't take up so much room and eat as much as a horse. "But I suppose it wouldn't hurt to look."

"Thanks, Mom!"

As he threw his arms around her, Dani's eyes met Jack's over the top of her son's head. He gave her a thumbs-up, and in that brief, suspended moment Dani remembered, after a very long time, how it felt to be truly happy.

"Wow!" Matt's gaze swept over Beau Soleil's circular, pillared entry hall. "Did you really live here, Mom?"

"I certainly did." Looking at her former home through her son's eyes, Dani saw not the work still to be done, but the glory that the house once possessed. And would again, thanks to Jack. "With your grandfather. And Jack's mother."

"Wow. It's as cool as the White House." He looked up at Jack. "So you lived here, too? With my mom?"

"No. My *maman* was the judge's housekeeper. We lived in town when my dad was alive."

"Your dad died, too?"

"Yep. When I was a bit older than you."

"Did you miss him?"

"A bunch," Jack answered. "Still do, from time to time."

"Jack's father was a very special person," Dani said. "He was sheriff of Blue Bayou."

"Really? Did he have a gun?"

"Yeah," Jack answered. "But he kept the peace well enough he never had to use it." Watching him carefully, Dani saw the dark shadows move across his eyes and suspected he was remembering that day his father had died to save hers.

"Then, after he passed on, my *maman* and brothers and I moved into one of the houses here at Beau Soleil."

"Was it as nice as this?"

"Not as fancy. But we liked it well enough. Even with it bein' haunted."

"It wasn't really. Was it?" Matt's eyes grew even wider.

"Sure was. Maybe still is. The ghost's supposed to be a Confederate officer who got lost in the bayou after the battle of New Orleans and showed up here. Since a bunch of soldiers from the Union army were camped out in this house, your *maman*'s ancestor hid him in one of the little houses out back.

"She sent her own personal maid to take care of him during the day, then every night after dinner, she'd dispatch the soldiers—"

"What does that mean? Dispatch? Like she killed them?"

"Fortunately, she didn't have to go to those extremes. The way I heard the story, she was pretty liberal with the port and would get them all drunk so they'd pass out.

"Then she'd sneak out of the house and take the night shift trying to nurse that Confederate boy back to health, which was a dangerous thing to do, since harboring the enemy was a hangin' offense."

"She must've been brave."

"Must have been. But then, the women in your *maman*'s family have always been pretty special. They've always been real good about gettin' around in the dark, too." His wicked grin was designed to remind Dani of her own midnight excursions from this house.

"Unfortunately, the soldier ended up dying, and it's his ghost who supposedly haunts the place. There were stories about the lady of the house telling people that he used to come visit her at night, but since she was an old woman, people just figured she wasn't quite right in the mind."

"What do you think?"

"I wouldn't know for sure. But I guess I sorta like the idea of the two of them finding some sort of happiness together in a troubled time. They're supposed to dance in the ballroom in this house, but I've never seen them. Though sometimes," he said with a wink Dani's way, "if I listen real close, I think I can kinda hear the music."

"That's so cool. Do you think we'll hear it tonight?"

"Never know what's gonna happen. After supper I'll show you around the rest of the place, then, perhaps, if you'd like and your *maman* says it's okay, we can check out the little house before taking you back to town."

"Can we, Mom?"

"If it's not too late."

"Cool," he said again as the mural drew his attention. "This is the biggest painting I've ever seen. Bigger even than the one the teacher showed us when my class took that field trip to the National Gallery."

"It tells a story about Evangeline and Gabriel, two people who were in love, but got separated when the Acadians first came to Louisiana."

"On those ships?" He pointed at the tall-masted vessels depicted on the mural.

"That's right."

"Did they ever get back together?"

"No. I'm afraid not."

"That's too bad. Can we have the pizza now? Baseball must make a guy hungry, because I'm starving."

"Excuse me?"

Two days later, pulled from a daydream in which Jack had played a sexy starring role, Dani looked up from where she'd been doodling lopsided stars all over the list of new books she was ordering and saw the man standing in front of her desk.

"I'm sorry. I didn't notice you."

"Don't worry," he said easily. "I tend to get a lot of that."

And no wonder, Dani thought as she skimmed a quick judicial look over him. He could have been anywhere from twenty-five to forty; his body was youthfully trim, but the lines extending outward from friendly eyes that were neither blue nor gray but an indistinguishable hue in-between, suggested he'd at least hit thirty.

His medium short brown hair was neatly trimmed; he was wearing a blue chambray shirt rolled up at the sleeves, bark brown Dockers, and loafers—without the tassels, which would've been sure to get him ragged by shrimpers or oilriggers if he made the mistake of dropping into a local bar. He was neither attractive nor unattractive; merely the most ordinary man she'd ever seen. She honestly doubted he'd be noticeable in a crowd of three.

"I could use some information." His voice lacked any accent; it could have been designated Standard American.

"Well, you've come to the right place," she said with a smile.

His answering smile deepened those lines around his face, and while he didn't turn into Brad Pitt before her eyes, suddenly he wasn't quite so ordinary. "I'm seeking information on a home around here. You may have heard of it. Beau Soleil?"

Her fingers tightened on her pen. "Of course I have. It's one of the parish's last standing antebellum homes."

"So I hear." He rocked back on the heels of his cordovan loafers. "I also hear it's haunted."

Reaching into a brown billfold, he pulled out a card which read *Dr. Dallas Chapman, Parapsychologist.* Along with listing him as a consultant to the American Society for Psychological Research, there were nearly enough other letters after his name to complete an entire series of Sue Grafton alphabet mysteries.

Dani lifted a brow and tapped the edge of the card with her fingernail. "Does this mean you're a ghostbuster?"

"Oh, I don't bust them," he said quickly, with another engaging smile. "I just study them. Chronicle their environment, their behavior, examine stories of various hauntings around the country in an attempt to better understand the phenomenon.

"Although people are often disappointed to hear it, I don't spend my time blasting hotels trying to catch nasty little green ghosts, I've never worn a jumpsuit, and unfortunately, my funding doesn't come close to allowing me to build a portable nuclear-powered particle accelerator like the ones they carried in that movie. And I've never been slimed."

"I imagine that's a bit of a relief."

"Absolutely." His expression turned a bit more serious. "Certain of my colleagues disliked that film because they felt it made light of our profession. But I enjoyed it as an entertaining piece of fiction, and discovered that rather than demean my work, it actually made it easier."

"Oh?" The movie may have been fiction, but try telling that to her son, who must have seen it a dozen times and had gone through a phase, when he'd been in the first grade, of wanting to become a ghostbuster when he grew up. Dani couldn't wait to see the look on Matt's face when she took this business card home and told him she'd actually met a real live ghostbuster, right here in her library.

"Now, at least, people have some concept of what I do for a living, albeit a skewed one, and when they bring up the idea of ghostbusting, I can set them straight as to what a parapsychologist actually does. Before that film came out, despite the field being more than a hundred years old, the public simply didn't have a clue."

Dani didn't admit she wasn't all that up on the subject, either.

He shook his head with a bit of what she took to be mute frustration. "I'd introduce myself at a cocktail party or on an airplane and people would just give me sort of a blank stare. Or perhaps they'd mistake me for a psychologist. Or even a psychologist's assistant, like a paralegal. You know, *para*-psychologist," he explained at her blank look.

"Ah." Dani nodded. "I can see how that might be a problem," she agreed, fighting back a smile. He appeared to take his career very seriously, and she didn't want to risk offending him.

"Oh, it was a terrible problem. Of course you, as a librarian, undoubtedly know that the word parapsychologist refers to the study of psi, which stems from the twenty-third letter of the Greek alphabet, denoting the unknown."

"Actually, I didn't know that."

"Well then, now you do. The worst problem is when I'm confused with someone who practices witchcraft." He leaned toward her. "In fact," he said conspiratorially, "there was this one memorable time, when I was flying to London from Rome, where I'd been speaking at a joint conference of the ASPR and our European counterpart. The pilot nearly had to do an emergency landing in Milan, after I made the mistake of trying to explain the concept of life after death, or as we professionals prefer to call it, the survival of bodily death, to a little old lady who was sitting beside me.

"I no sooner mentioned the words *apparition* and *hauntings* when she started screaming bloody murder in Italian and began hitting me on top of the head with her rosary. It seems she was certain I was in league with the devil and giving her the evil eye." He sighed. "It took three flight attendants and half the bottle of a very nice Chianti I was carrying home in my carry-on from the duty-free shop to calm her down."

Dani laughed. "Well, at least it doesn't sound as if your work is boring."

"Oh, it's never boring," he agreed. "A bit wearying from time to time. Since spirits are not always the most cooperative entities, the work can often entail spending a lot of time in abandoned, unheated buildings waiting for an apparitional haunting, but it's quite satisfying.

"As a matter of fact, I met my wife at a castle on the moors in the

Scots Highlands. I was there exploring stories concerning a former laird of the castle, who'd died in the sixteen-hundreds and was allegedly slipping into women's beds at night and making mad, passionate love to them while their husbands were sleeping right beside them."

Dani wondered how it could have been all that passionate if the husbands slept through it, but didn't want to sound as if she were challenging his claim. "So your wife's a parapsychologist, too?"

"Oh, no. At least she wasn't then. She was actually there as part of a team to debunk the ghost theory."

"Who won?"

His eyes lit up. "We both did."

"That's sweet." Despite her own failed romantic relationships, Dani remained a sucker for a happy ending.

"We've been married ten years next month," he revealed. "And collaborators for eight of those years. You may be familiar with our work. We wrote a quite well-received in-depth study of the infamous Bell Witch published two years ago by the University of Tennessee Press."

"I believe I must have missed that one," Dani said mildly.

"It's another house haunting and one of our better studies, if I do say so myself. It's my hope to have the same success with the ghost or ghosts of Beau Soleil. Why, if things work out as well as I hope, that Confederate soldier could put Blue Bayou on the map."

Knowing Jack's penchant for privacy, and wanting to protect her former home from sensationalism and her hometown from hoards of tourists seeking tacky glow-in-the-dark plastic ghosts to hang from their rearview mirrors, and Lord knows what else, Dani certainly wasn't going to tell the man how to get to Beau Soleil. Of course he could get directions easily enough from the myriad local guidebooks on the shelves, but there was no point in making things easier for him.

"I imagine you know of the house," he said, his voice going up on the end of the statement, turning it into a question.

"It would be hard to live in the parish and not know of Beau Soleil," she hedged. Dani decided the fact that she'd grown up there was none of his business. Nor was she going to share any of the haunting tales that had been handed down from each succeeding generation of Duprees, or those random occasions when she'd heard weeping, or music, or some undistinguishable sound that was, undoubtedly, nothing more dramatic than an old house settling into the swamp.

Still, her library was a place of knowledge and it was her responsibility to see that patrons received the illumination they were seeking.

"I can suggest a few books." She pulled out a piece of paper, turned to her computer screen and wrote some titles down. "Not just about Beau Soleil, but other houses and supposed hauntings." She hoped she could throw him off the track.

No such luck. "Thanks. But it's Beau Soleil I'm interested in," he said, taking the paper nonetheless. "That *is* where Jack Callahan's hanging out these days, isn't it?"

The distaste of lying warred with Dani's belief that Jack deserved his privacy. Plus, she felt a twinge of something she just couldn't quite put her finger on.

He chuckled when she hesitated answering. "Don't worry about betraying a confidence. I'm pretty good at digging out information; I'll just start with these books and go from there. It's been a delight chatting with you, Ms. Dupree. Hopefully we'll be able to repeat the experience again soon." He winked. "Meanwhile, keep your spirits up.

"I'm sorry," he said with another of those friendly smiles that she decided must have helped win over his wife to his side of the ghost argument. "I can never resist saying that."

Dani watched as he took the books from the shelves over to a study table by the window. Then Mrs. Rullier came in looking for the latest true-crime murder, Sally Olivier needed help with her Internet search for wedding-cake recipes for her niece's upcoming nuptials, and Jean Babin wanted a book on fiberglassing a pirogue. The next time Dani looked up, Dallas Chapman, ghostbuster, was gone.

# 19

*She liked it.* Although he'd told himself that it shouldn't make such a difference, he'd hoped she would. Which was why Jack found himself holding his breath while Danielle waxed enthusiastic over the progress he'd made on her former bedroom since she'd last seen it, a mere week ago when they'd brought Matt out to Beau Soleil.

He'd kept two crews working nearly around the clock to complete the work; the walls were now a misty green that echoed the view outside the window, the trim was a creamy white again, the floor had been sanded and stained to a lighter finish than it had been when she'd lived here. He'd hand-sanded the rust from the lacy white bed himself, and had, with Desiree's help, located a crocheted spread at an antique store in Lafourche Crossing, which could have been the same one he remembered being on this same bed so many years ago. And while he definitely hadn't understood Desiree's contention that a woman could never have too many pillows, he'd piled a dizzying array of ruffled pillows in various shapes and sizes atop the spread.

They'd moved on to the adjoining bathroom, where he was showing off the blatantly hedonistic round whirlpool tub that was nearly large enough to swim laps in when his cell phone rang.

"I've been thinking about your ultimatum," the judge said without preamble.

"Oh?" Jack had been watching Dani run her hand up the swan's neck of the tub's faucet, indulging a hot fantasy of her stroking him with such open pleasure when her father's curt words brought him crashing back to reality.

"I've decided you're right. She deserves to know the truth."

Having admittedly been concerned about what he'd do if the judge challenged his ultimatum, Jack felt a cooling rush of relief. "I see," he said mildly, waiting to hear when, exactly, Dupree planned to admit what he'd done.

"The thing is, I'm a dying man; I don't have the strength for confrontation. If you're so hot for her to know why you left town, then you can damn well be the one to tell her."

"I understand." Jack smiled reassuringly at Dani, who'd glanced over at him, obviously curious about his curt responses.

"Well, then. That's settled." The judge hung up, ending the call as brusquely as he'd begun it.

"I suppose so," Jack murmured to dead air.

"Jack?" Dani's expression was concerned. "Is something wrong?"

He rubbed his jaw, reminding himself of the old prohibition about being careful what you wished for. Now that the old man had dumped the problem in his lap, he wasn't quite sure how to broach the subject.

"No. At least I don't think so."

How in the hell did you tell a woman that the father with whom she was struggling so hard to establish a relationship during the brief time he may have left was a common blackmailer who'd played with both their lives as if they were no more than pawns he'd moved around a chess board if for no other reason than to prove he could?

"It wasn't my father calling, was it?" A little frown drew her eyebrows together.

Jack was a world-class liar. It was a talent he'd honed to perfection, a skill that had allowed him to continue working deep undercover far longer than was safe or wise. Street junkie to Median cartel leader, it hadn't mattered, and while he'd admittedly had his detractors, everyone he'd ever worked with had proclaimed him to be the best prevaricator in the drug-enforcement business. Hands down.

But Danielle was an entirely different story. There'd always been something about her, perhaps her own unwavering sense of goodness and honesty, that made it damn near impossible to lie. Which was why he hadn't dared say goodbye to her. There would have been no way he could have looked into those soft hazel eyes and not told her the truth about why he was leaving. So, to his everlasting shame, he'd taken the coward's way out, leaving Blue Bayou, and her, without a word of explanation.

"What makes you think it was the judge?" he asked.

Her frown deepened at his slight hesitation. "I don't know. There was just something about the way you were talking. . . ." Her cheeks, which had been touched by the sun during the picnic lunch he'd picked up at Cajun Cal's for them to share in the park on her lunch hour, paled. "It's not Matt, is it? Daddy wasn't calling to say anything had happened to him?"

"*Non*. You know I'd never keep any news of your boy from you."

"Then he's all right?" Her slender hand was on his sleeve, her short, neatly buffed nails digging into his arm.

"So far as I know he's still in the kitchen makin' pralines with Orèlia, same as when we left the house."

"And my father? Nothing's happened to him?"

"Hell, Dani, I know the judge thinks he's gonna kick the bucket at any moment and since the doc thinks there's an outside chance of that happening, it makes sense you've bought into the idea, too." He couldn't quite pull off what he'd wanted to be an encouraging smile, proving yet again how difficult it was to lie to a woman who wore her heart in her eyes. "But the way I figure it, he may just outlast all of us, being how the old bastard's too tough to die."

"Everyone dies."

"Yeah, you'd think that was the case. Your mother, my *maman*, my dad, even that prick you made the mistake of marrying are all gone. But you know what the judge tol' me when he caught me vandalizing those mailboxes back when I was fifteen?"

"No."

"I made some smart-ass crack about him being an old man who wasn't always gonna be sitting up on that bench, hinting, in my less than subtle teenage juvenile delinquent wannabe fashion, that I'd outlive him and continue doing whatever I damn well pleased." Jack smiled faintly at the memory. "He pulled me out of that chair like I weighed no more than Matt and told me I shouldn't count on outlivin' him, since he was damn near invincible, and when the world finally burned itself out, the only things gonna be left were him and a bunch of cockroaches."

"Isn't that a lovely thought." She sighed, making him want to put his arms around her and reassure her that everything was going to be all right. Which was a bit difficult to do since he wasn't so sure of that himself.

Christ. He'd been working toward this moment since he'd realized that finishing what they'd begun that summer was inevitable. It was time to get things out in the open, to finally put the past behind them. Jack knew he should tell her now. But the part of him that was about to explode was arguing with equal vigor that the potentially difficult subject could be broached more easily when he wasn't so distracted by a driving need to get naked.

She went over to the window she used to climb out of to meet him and leaned her forehead against the glass. "Do you remember those balls that used to tell the future?" she asked softly.

"Sure. Nate had one." He'd also claimed it had told him he was going to lose his virginity with Misty Montgomery, which turned out to be true enough, but Jack had always put that incident down to Misty's reputation more than any psychic powers found in some dimestore black plastic ball.

"I did, too. I used to stand here, watching out the window, and ask it if you'd come to make love to me."

"That was a pretty easy one since signs definitely pointed to yes," he said.

With her back to him, he felt the smile more than saw it. "I used to ask it everything. Would I get an A on my history test, would I get elected to Homecoming Court, would I grow up to be as pretty as people say my mama was—"

"That's an easy one. You're a lot prettier."

"How would you know? Our families didn't even know each other when my mother was alive."

"Maybe not. But I saw a picture of her once." He didn't say that it'd actually been a porn flick he and Nate had rented on a clandestine trip to an adult book store across the parish line. He'd been fourteen, Nate a year younger. For the next two weeks he'd had such hot dreams that every time he'd look at Danielle, he'd see her mother in her face, and his dick, which had already begun to torture him at the slightest provocation, would get as stiff as his old hunting dog Evangeline's tail when she'd point out quail.

"She was pretty enough in a flashy sort of way," he said. Flash and trash, he realized now, deciding there was nothing to be gained by admitting that she'd also been damn hot, especially for someone's mom, for Chrissakes, in her role as the nympho nurse who'd brought a whole new meaning to bedside manner. Hell, Nate had been so impressed, he'd given up that week's idea of becoming a pro baseball player and decided to go to medical school instead.

"But yours is a deep-down beauty. The kind that lasts."

She glanced back over her shoulder, her faint smile not quite reaching her eyes. "That's nice of you to say."

"It's the truth."

"I know it sounds silly now," she murmured. "But I really believed that silly ball."

Jack shrugged, wondering where, exactly they were going with this. "Don't feel like the Lone Ranger. So did Nate."

She laughed, just a little at that. Then sobered. "Wouldn't it be nice if there really was some way to tell the future?"

"I don't know. I suppose it depends on whether it'd be possible to change the outcome of events."

If he'd known his dad was going to die the next day, he sure as hell would have gotten to the court house earlier, before that wigged-out yahoo with the gun, so he could have at least tried to prevent his father's murder. But would he have wanted to know ahead of time if he'd also known that his father's fate was inescapable? Jack didn't think so.

He came up behind her. "I won't claim to be able to read the future, *chère*, but I do know what's going to happen here for the next little while." His lips brushed her neck.

"What?" Her breath shuddered out as his teeth nipped her earlobe.

"I'm going to do things to you, Danielle." He glided his fingers over her collarbone. "With you. Wicked, impossible, exquisite things." Watching their reflections in the night-darkened glass, he skimmed a fingertip down her throat. "I'm going to take you places you've only ever dreamed of. . . .

"Then I'm going to take you." He slipped his hands beneath the hem of her blouse and cupped her breasts in his palms, embracing the warm weight of them. "And you, *mon coeur*, are going to love it."

My *heart*. Dani might not have spoken nearly as much French as Jack had growing up, but she definitely recognized that endearment. It had been such a very long time since a man had wanted her. Longer still since she'd wanted a man the way she wanted *this* man.

"I've been wanting to do this since that night you first came to Beau Soleil." He began to unbutton her blouse, folding back the silk with extreme care, as if he were unwrapping the most exquisite of gifts. Just the sight of his dark hands on her body created a hormonal jolt. "Pretending you were looking for carpenters."

"I *was* looking for carpenters."

"Perhaps." He bit down gently on the sensitive place where neck and shoulder joined, sending a rippling thrill of anticipation racing through her. "But your sweet little body, and your lonely heart, they wanted me to do this."

He turned her in his arms, his hand fisted in her hair, pulling her head back to allow his mouth full access to her throat while his fingers tightened on her breast. When the wanting had her trembling, Jack smiled a slow, satisfied rogue's smile.

He didn't take his eyes from her face as he slowly unfastened her bra. Then, still watching, drew the straps with infinite slowness down her arms. There was a tenderness in his gaze Dani couldn't remember ever witnessing that long-ago summer. Of course then, with the exception of their last night together, the sex had been fast and hot, like an August whirlwind. How could she have reached adulthood without ever having known this slow, glorious torment?

"Lovely," he murmured. His fingers brushed over her like whispers on silk. He lowered his head, his tongue dampening her warming flesh as it sketched concentric circles outward to her nipple.

Lowell had always preferred silence during their lovemaking, and while her former husband was the last person she wanted to be thinking about right now, old habits died hard, and Dani bit her lip to keep from whimpering.

"Don't do that." He returned his mouth to hers. "I don't want you to hold anything back. I want to know what you like." His hands tempted, his mouth seduced, his tongue as it slipped between her parted lips, promised. "I want to know what gives you pleasure."

"You do," she whispered on a ragged thread of sound.

Dani felt his smile.

He continued undressing her with agonizing slowness, treating each new bit of flesh to the same prolonged exploration.

He watched her face again as the desire rose in her, watched her innermost feelings, witnessed firsthand how weak and needy he could make her feel.

She'd been surprised to discover since returning home that she and her father actually shared something in common: They both felt a need for control. The judge had found it by wielding power while she'd chosen instead a life of tidy, predictable order.

But now, with Jack, she was discovering that there was something alluring about surrendering control, of letting a man you trusted push you to the outer limits of your sexuality.

Imagined fantasies of what he might be planning flashed in her mind—erotic, vivid, demanding. Every nerve ending reached for his touch; every pore sought relief from a passion too long denied. It was frightening. And it was wonderful.

"*Bon Dieu*, you're the most responsive woman I've ever known."

Dani refused to think about the other women he'd known. They belonged in his past; she was the woman with him now.

"Only with you," she admitted on a ragged moan as he pulled her down onto the bed. Her melting, liquid thighs fell open.

"*I know*."

His lips tugged on her other nipple while he responded to the silent, unconscious invitation of her body by pressing the heel of his hand against her mound.

"Arrogant beast," she muttered even as desire sang its clear high notes in her blood.

"It's not arrogance."

"Because it's true?" The way he was looking at her, like a man about to feast on forbidden fruit after a long fast, warmed Dani from the inside out. No man had ever looked at her like Jack did. With such vivid, focused intensity.

"No point in lyin', sugar, when we both know it's true." He continued to caress her body from her shoulders to her knees. "Because you've always had the same effect on me. Do you have any idea how many women I had to sleep with before I got over you?"

"No." Her head was spinning, making it difficult to think. To speak. Heat spread beneath her skin, across her breasts, her stomach. Moisture pooled between her lax thighs.

"I don' know, either. 'Cause I never did." His tongue made a wet hot swathe down her stomach. "We're damn good together, *chère*. You and me."

"Jack . . ." As the pressure built inside her, Dani's hips moved restlessly, wanting, needing more. "Please."

"Not yet." He lifted her hands above her head, holding them with one hand as he lowered his body onto hers, pressing her deep into the mattress.

There was something unbearably erotic about being physically restrained while his fully dressed, fully aroused body moved against her naked one. Dani felt the prick of buttons against her breasts, the sharpness of a belt buckle at her belly, the rasp of the zipper, the roughness of denim. The stony hardness of his erection.

Once again, he reminded her of a pirate. One with ravishment on his mind.

"What did you say?" he asked against her mouth.

She hadn't realized she'd spoken out loud. But imprisoned by a hunger a great deal stronger than the strong fingers which continued to hold her hands above her head, Dani could deny him nothing. So she told him the truth.

"Ever since I first saw you on the *gallerie* that night, you've reminded me of Jean Laffite."

"Was that a good thing?" He kissed her again. Deeper, this time. "Or bad?" He continued to move against her, forward, then back.

"Bad. In a good way." The friction of their bodies sparked every nerve ending in Dani's body.

"Good." His tongue slid between her lips at the same time he brought her hand down and pressed it against her mound of golden hair.

"Jack . . . no . . . I can't." This was something done in private. With the bedroom door locked and the shades pulled.

"Sure you can. I'll help you." Ignoring her halfhearted protest, he began to move their joined hands, slowly at first, increasing the pressure, escalating the tempo, until breathless, Dani came in a long, slow, rolling wave that rose, crested, then settled.

"Oh, yes." The sigh shuddered out of her. "That was wonderful." And a great deal more satisfying than doing it all by herself.

"Hell, that was just to take the edge off so we can enjoy the rest of the night." He grinned wickedly, like the pirate he could have been. Then kissed her again. Longer. Deeper.

She murmured a soft sound of protest as he left the bed. Then began to watch, enthralled as he pulled his shirt from his jeans and began unbuttoning it.

He was as she'd remembered him, but different. Heavier, but without an ounce of fat from what she could tell. His shoulders were wide, his chest broad, skin tanned to the color of walnuts stretched tight over smooth muscle and sinew.

His eyes didn't move from hers as he stripped off the shirt and tossed it onto a nearby chair. Next he unbuckled his belt, pulling it through each loop with such aching slowness, Dani had to restrain herself from leaping up and finishing the job herself.

After he'd discarded the belt onto the chair with his shirt, he opened the metal button at his waist with a quick flick of his wrist. The hiss of the metal zipper was unnaturally loud in the absolute silence broken only by the sound of their breathing.

Dressed, Jack Callahan was remarkably handsome. Nude he was magnificent. Standing naked and rampant before her, he certainly didn't look like a man who earned his living at a computer keyboard. Male power radiated from every pore as he trailed his splayed wide hand down his chest, following the arrowing of dark hair.

"You do this." His voice roughened with hunger as he curled his long fingers around his beautifully formed erection. "All I have to do is think of you and I'm hard."

If the world had been coming to an end, if meteors had begun crashing into the Earth outside the window, if the bayou was rocked with earthquakes, engulfed in flames, Dani could not have moved from this bed. Could not have dragged her gaze away from the arousing sight of that rigid flesh thrusting from a thicket of tight jet curls. A single drop of moisture shimmered on the knobbed, plum-hued tip; struck with an overwhelming urge to lick it off, she heard herself moan.

Need welled up inside her. Years of emptiness waiting to be filled. Rising to her knees, she opened her arms, held them out to him as he returned to the bed on that loose-hipped, predatory stride which never failed to thrill her. The mattress sank beneath his weight. They knelt together, face to face, soft feminine curves pressed against hard male angles.

He tunneled his hand beneath her hair, cupped the nape of her neck, and kissed her while Dani moved her hands up his back, reveling in the play of long hard muscle beneath her touch, neat short nails nipping into his skin. She closed her eyes against the sweet agony of desire and urged him even closer, wishing she could absorb him into her burning flesh.

When her mind began to shut down, Dani allowed her body—and Jack—to take over, discovering that sexual surrender to the right man could be glorious.

He explored the terrain of her body with hands and lips and teeth and tongue, discovering thrilling points of pain and pleasure she'd never known existed. He touched wherever he liked, tasted what he wanted. Murmured words against her lips, her throat, her quivering stomach, silken cords twining around her heart, binding her to him.

The more control Dani relinquished, the more pleasure she received. There was nothing Jack could have asked for that she would not have willingly given.

Her fingers curled in his hair as his lips nibbled their way up the inside of first one thigh, then the other. Her body arched and she sucked in a deep, shuddering breath when he slid first one, then two fingers into the moist giving folds of her body and began to move them in and out of her with a wet, silky, ease.

"*Mon Dieu*, you're hot," he marveled. Drawing his head back so he could watch her face, he thrust his fingers higher, stroking, caressing, adoring the very heat of her while the erotic sucking sound make her crave him all the more.

Dani gasped as the orgasm flared, but before she could recover, he'd dragged her back down to the mattress and wrapped her fingers around the white iron bed frame. She thought she heard him tell her to hang on tight, but wasn't quite sure, with the blood pounding in her ears, whether it was his voice, or her own need that had her tightening her hold.

His dark head was between her thighs, stimulating already ultrasensitive flesh by alternately nipping and licking. Her stomach tensed, her thighs tightened in expectation, she arched her pelvis against his mouth, every atom in her body concentrated on the hooded tangle of tingling nerves hidden in her slick wet lips.

White hot stars wheeled behind her closed lids. Just when Dani feared she was in danger of shattering into a million pieces, a ruthless stroke of his tongue had her pouring over his hand.

Her body went limp, but once again Jack refused to give her time to regain her senses.

"Again." His rough voice was a primal growl as he sent her up once more. Higher this time, hotter. Dani's breath was coming in short sharp pants, her eyes fluttered closed again, the better to concentrate on these exquisite, terrifying sensations. She tossed her head on the pillow while her body, desperate to feel him inside her, bowed.

"Look at me, Danielle." Jack took hold of her chin and held her gaze to his. "I want to watch your eyes when I take you."

Unable to deny him anything, Dani opened her eyes, meeting his for a thrilling, suspended moment. Then he plunged into her with a force that left them both equally stunned and breathless.

Jack recovered first. He began rocking against her, thigh to thigh, chest to chest, mouth to mouth.

He was long and thick and rock hard. Dani's body stretched, then tightened around him; her nails dug into his back and she wrapped her legs high around his hips to take him into her, deeply, fully, arching up to meet each rough stroke, hot flesh slapping against hot flesh, her soft cries muffled by his ravenous mouth, his tongue thrusting between her parted lips in rhythm with his bucking hips.

He was, as he'd promised, taking her, claiming her. Consuming her. Dani could not have been more branded if he'd burned his name into her hot slick flesh. And all the time his intense, gleaming gold eyes never left hers.

Hearts pounded, jackhammer hard, jackhammer fast. His movements quickened. Deepened. His back arched, his head was thrown back, every muscle in his body in taut relief.

This time they came together. Dani wept as a seemingly never-ending series of orgasms racked her body while Jack moaned a string of gloriously naughty sounding French words she couldn't understand against her ravaged mouth.

She had no idea how long they lay there on the tangled sheets, arms and legs entwined, but she was still shuddering from the aftershocks when he brushed a kiss against her lips and began to lever himself off her.

She made a small murmur of complaint, tightening her arms around him, holding him close. The ceiling fan was slowly spinning overhead with a faint *click, click, click* sound, the moving air cooling bare, moist flesh. "Don't go."

"I won't."

Dani wondered if Jack was talking about not leaving the bed. Or her life. But wanting to enjoy this stolen time together, she didn't ask. Instead, she cuddled against him and basked in the afterglow of passion.

"That was even better than I remembered," she said on a soft, utterly satiated sigh. Until this evening she'd always believed the G-spot was yet another myth designed to make women feel insecure about their sexuality.

"So you did think of me from time to time." He did not sound at all surprised by that revelation. In fact, she thought he sounded downright smug.

"Every once in a while," she said with exaggerated casualness. "Whenever they showed *Rebel Without a Cause* on the Movie Channel."

"I suppose bein' compared to James Dean isn't bad," he decided. "But his character in that movie was kinda a whiney wuss."

"He wasn't whiney. He was sensitive."

"*Sensitive*'s just another word for *wuss*. The guy wouldn't have lasted forty-eight hours here in the swamp."

Unfortunately, he was probably right. Bayou males had a lot of appealing traits, but sensitivity, as a rule, wasn't exactly one of them. "So, how would you describe yourself?"

"If we're talkin' fifties flicks, I guess I'd have to go with a cross between Brando in *The Wild One* and Newman in *Hud*."

It fit, Dani admitted. Brando's smolderingly dangerous force with Newman's wickedly blue-eyed, smirking sexuality that clung to him like sweat to a bottle of Dixie beer in August. "I believe *Hud* was out in the sixties. And I find it interesting that you'd choose two Neanderthal misogynists as role models."

"Hell, those guys weren't misogynists. They were men's men."

"How refreshing to find a man in the twentieth-first century whose oversize ego allows him to not even pretend to be the slightest bit politically correct," she countered dryly.

"If I wasn't in such a good mood, I might argue that misogynist label, though I will admit to having never been a real fan of political correctness. As for my oversize ego"—he skimmed a lazy finger up the inside of her thigh—"just give it a couple minutes to recuperate, and this swamp-dwelling Neanderthal will be more than happy to supersize your sweet little pussy all night long."

She couldn't help herself. She snorted. "You really are incorrigible."

He touched his lips to her temple. "I didn't hear you complainin' when you were screaming my name in my ear like a wild woman, sugar."

She flinched, just a bit, when he skimmed that treacherous fingertip over the still tingling flesh between her thighs.

"Did I hurt you?"

"It's still just a little sensitive. And I did not scream."

"Sure sounded like screaming to me. But that's okay; I didn't need that eardrum, anyway. One'll probably do me just fine." He slid down the sheets, scattering kisses down her torso. When he dipped the tip of his tongue in her navel, Dani could feel her body heating up all over again. "Jack—"

"Don't worry, darlin'," he murmured against her stomach. "I'm just gonna kiss it and make it better."

When he lifted her against his oh, so clever mouth, Dani didn't have the strength to protest. Nor did she want to as he proceeded to use his hands and lips and supersized ego to take her far beyond better all the way to sublime.

Sometime, much, much later, Dani awoke in Jack's arms, unable to remember when, exactly she'd drifted off. The soft steady breathing on the back of her neck revealed that she wasn't the only one who'd fallen asleep. She glanced over at the bedside clock.

"Oh, my God," she said, trying to extricate herself from the tangle of sheets. "It's late. I've got to get home."

He pushed himself onto his elbows and blearily eyed the fluorescent green numbers. "It's not that late."

"Easy for you to say. You're not the one who has to get an eight-year-old off to school and show up at work on time." If she left now, she just may manage to squeeze in four hours' sleep before her clock radio went off.

He snagged her wrist when she would have left the bed. "Don't go."

"I can't have Matt waking up and finding me gone."

"I'll get you back to Orèlia's before he wakes up. But before you go, we need to talk."

"Really, Jack, that's not necessary. I don't need the pretty words I did when I was seventeen. After all, I may not be the most experienced woman in the world, but I'm adult enough to know that what we did was just sex. Terrific, dynamite, world-class sex, but—"

"That's not it." He thrust a hand through his loosened hair, which earlier had felt like black silk against her breasts, stomach, her back, as he'd seemed determined to make love to every inch of her body. "There's something I need to tell you." His voice deepened with an emotion she couldn't quite decipher, rumbling like the warning of thunder on the horizon. Goose bumps rose on chilled flesh that had, just a short time ago, felt as if it was burning up.

Looking into the handsome face that appeared uncharacteristically grim, Dani suddenly realized she'd seen that expression before. Earlier, when he'd been showing off the bathroom.

"It's about that call you got earlier, isn't it?" Dani braced herself for bad news.

"In a way." He sighed heavily. "It's about that summer. About why I left Blue Bayou."

# 20

Dani *couldn't speak* as Jack related the story. Couldn't think. She could merely lie in his arms, numbed, chilled, listening in disbelief as Jack related the sordid tale.

"My father was the reason you disappeared in the middle of the night without a word?" The judge might not have been Ward Cleaver; he'd been distant and sometimes out-and-out cold. But until this moment Dani had never thought him to be viciously cruel.

"Yeah. I wanted to talk to you, to try to explain, but he refused to let me say goodbye. Said if I didn't get packed and out within the hour, *Maman* would lose her job and I'd be tossed in jail on a statutory rape charge."

His words slashed through her like a razor. "That's so hard to believe." How could her father have done such a dreadful thing?

His lips pulled into a hard tight line. "I'm not lying."

"I didn't mean it that way."

Myriad emotions bombarded Dani, so many she thought she might be crushed from the weight of them. Pushing aside her own personal pain for a moment, she lifted a trembling hand to Jack's face, felt the sensual roughness of his beard against her palm and was amazed that even as she fought against the drowning feelings of betrayal and loss, she could still feel a distant, renewed stir of desire.

"It was so horribly unfair to you. To me." To our unborn child, she thought but did not say. A sob rose in her throat, nearly choking her. "And to your mother, who kept her job, but lost one of her sons that night."

Jack hadn't deserted her. Not really. The knowledge, after believing otherwise for so many years, was staggering. Reeling, unable to remain still, Dani abandoned the warmth of the bed, the comfort of his arms, and began to pace.

"All these years." She fought against the rising pain, struggled to keep it from engulfing her. "Ever since that night, my entire life has been built on a foundation of my father's betrayal."

She'd never tried to find Jack. Never attempted to contact him. Not even after she'd learned she was pregnant. Because—oh, God—she'd believed he'd left because he'd no longer wanted her.

Memories flooded back in a torrent of painful images, the worst of them being that autumn afternoon when her father had calmly, cooly, calculatingly convinced her Jack's desertion proved he hadn't loved her, so there was no reason to believe he'd want to learn he was going to be a father.

Oh, he'd been so logical, she thought, as she whipped back and forth across the newly sanded floor, painful memories filling her head like smoke. So clear-headed when she was not, calmly ticking off all the reasons why her gilded visions of a life with Jack Callahan were merely romantic schoolgirl fantasies.

Did she have any idea the emotional costs of a shotgun wedding? he'd asked. He'd seen the results, again and again: angry, bitter men who'd take out their frustration at having been trapped into a marriage on the women they blamed for ruining their lives. Even worse, he'd seen the damage done to innocent children unfortunate to have been born into such marital war zones.

In tears Dani had argued that Jack wasn't that way. That she knew he'd never, ever lift a hand to a woman or a child. To which her father had, in the same deep, self-assured voice he'd issued edicts from the bench, asked if she could have ever suspected he'd take her virginity, use her for his own summer amusement, then abandon her.

She could not challenge that point, because it was true that she'd never, in a million years, expected such behavior from Jack. But also true was the fact that somewhere, deep down inside her, she'd known that the boy she loved was nothing like the self-indulgent portrait her father was painting.

Unfortunately, at the time, alone, afraid, pregnant at seventeen, battered by confusion and hormones, she hadn't been able to think clearly.

Oh, God. She rested her brow against the rippled glass and pressed a hand against her stomach, which heaved in her throat the same way it had that day, when, unable to hide her morning sickness any longer, she'd been forced to tell her father she was pregnant with Bad Jack Callahan's child.

"There's no denying that the judge changed both our futures that day." Lost in her own whirling thoughts, Dani hadn't heard Jack come up behind her. He wrapped his arms around her waist, leaned her back against him and rested his chin atop her pounding head. "But it didn't all turn out so bad. It's obvious you adore Matt."

"Of course I do." She felt the hot traitorous tears begin to overfill her eyes. Tears of anger and betrayal. Of regrets too numerous to calculate. "He's the most important thing to me."

Jack held her tight when she would have pulled away. "He's a beautiful, bright child, Danielle. A blessing and you've no idea how many times in the past weeks I've wished he were mine."

He turned her in his arms, and to soothe himself, as well as Dani, he brushed away the glittering moisture trailing down her face with his fingertips. Her eyes were haunted and dark with something close to desperation he couldn't quite understand. Then again, he remembered feeling as if the judge had pulled the rug out from under him. It wasn't all that surprising that Dani would feel much the same way despite the passage of time.

"As you've already pointed out, Matt wouldn't exist if you hadn't married the man you did. Which you might not have done, if your father hadn't run me out of Blue Bayou."

He watched the storm of emotions rage and knew the exact moment when she accepted that reasoning. "You're right, of course. But I think I hate how you can be so calm, when I'm not."

"I've had more time to live with it. Come to grips with it." He combed a hand through the love-tousled silk of her hair.

"Thirteen years," she murmured. She was silent for a moment. Pensive. "I thought of you. I didn't want to, but I did. I didn't want to *want* you, either. But I did. Even after what I believed you'd done."

"I thought about you." He caught her chin in his fingers, brushed his thumb over her soft, love-swollen lips. "Too much and too often. Walking away from you, was one of the few regrets of my life." Jack had never spoken truer words.

She pressed her fingers to her eyes. "I would have hated you going to jail on my account."

"Hell, that's not why I left," he said on a surge of heated resentment he'd believed he'd left behind in the past. "Whatever it was we had together back then, did together, was worth risking a jail sentence. But the decision about *Maman* was tougher.

"The only job she'd ever had in her life was being a wife and mother. She didn't have any career skills. Finn was in college, and Nate was just turning seventeen; neither one of them was in a position to take care of her.

"I didn't really believe your father would actually follow through on his threat to fire her, but I couldn't take the chance. Can you understand that?"

"Of course I can." She was steadier, her eyes clearer. "My father understood it, too. So damn well." When she bit her bottom lip, Jack could see the wheels turning in her head and sensed what was coming next. "But you could have always come back, when I was of legal age, and my father wouldn't have had any say about what I did. Or with whom. I didn't marry Lowell for another five years."

"By then I was in the navy. Working shore patrol, which was damn ironic for a kid who'd spent a good part of his teens getting busted himself. You still had another year of high school. There was no way I was going to drag you around the country to wait stateside with the other wives in military housing or even worse, some tacky little trailer while I was off on cruises. You needed to get your education and grow up a little and I needed to become a man who could offer you something worthwhile."

"I always thought *you* were worthwhile."

"Bet you didn't think that after I took off. Bet you thought I was a real SOB then."

"Perhaps," she allowed. "But after a while I realized that you reacted like a lot of eighteen-year-old boys would when a girl told him that she loved him and wanted to have his babies." Tears began swimming in her eyes again. Jack couldn't remember a time when she'd appeared more fragile.

"Babies definitely weren't in my plans back then." But, while it was surprising the hell out of him, since he'd never envisioned himself as a father, Jack was finding the mental image of Danielle ripe and round with his child more than a little appealing. Just as appealing was the idea of being a daddy to her son.

*One step at a time.*

"That summer was a long time ago." Wanting to get past this, so they could get on with a future the judge had denied them, Jack lifted their joined hands and touched his lips to her knuckles. "It's all water under the bridge, and as sorry as I am about having to hurt you, with all that's happened, it just doesn't seem real important in the big scheme of things. So, how about I make you a proposition? We'll just consider it kid stuff and move on."

If only it were that simple, Dani agonized. *Tell him*, a little voice of conscience urged. *You'll probably never get a better chance*.

There was so much more to say, more secrets to reveal, more truths to confess. But it was so much easier to allow herself to be lifted into his arms and carried back to bed, lovers long ago lost, but found again.

Giving herself up to the glorious feelings, to Jack, Dani tried not to think about what he'd do when she told him everything that had happened after her father had driven him out of Blue Bayou that summer.

A slow, steady anger was still simmering in Dani as she made Matt French toast for breakfast the next morning. She pretended interest as he read her last night's sports scores from the paper, forced a smile at the latest *Get Fuzzy* comic strip which usually made her laugh out loud, and managed to wave him off on the yellow bus without either bursting into tears or imploding.

Then she returned to the kitchen where her father was drinking a cup of coffee.

"You're not supposed to be drinking that," she reminded him of Dr. Ancelet's instructions.

"One cup isn't going to kill me."

"True enough. But I may."

"Ah." He glanced at her over the rim of the mug, his expression revealing not a bit of guilt that she could see. "Can I infer by that comment that you've been talking to Callahan?"

"You don't sound surprised."

"I'm not. He gave me a deadline to tell you myself, but I decided to let him handle the matter in his own way."

"Too bad you didn't use such restraint that summer. When you ran Jack out of town."

"He didn't have to leave. I gave the boy a choice," the judge said, somewhat defensively.

"Between me or his widowed mother losing her job. What the hell kind of choice is that?"

"Watch your language, Danielle. There's no reason to talk like a sailor."

"After all you've done, you're actually worried about my language?" Her voice rose up the scale; she stared at him and shoved her hair back from her face with both hands. "I'm just getting started, Father. What on earth made you think you could play God with our lives that way?"

"I had to do something to protect you after Jimbo Lott came and told me he'd found the two of you screwing out at the camp."

"The person I'd needed protection from just happened to be Lott. Did the horrid perverted man tell you that he kept his patrol car's spotlight on me the entire time I was getting dressed?"

"No." His voice stayed steady, but a muscle jerked in his cheek.

"How about the fact that he knocked Jack out with the butt of his service revolver when he tried to defend me?"

"No. But I'm not surprised at either behavior. Lott redefines slime. It's a crime he's still sheriff. And Jack always has been too impetuous for his own good."

"*He* was protecting me."

"Which wouldn't have been necessary if he hadn't taken you out there in the first place," the judge said on the same reasonable tone he'd used to convince her to give up her child. Having disliked it then, Dani hated it now.

"I was trying to protect you, too. Besides, Callahan's mother wasn't any more happy about the two of you together than I was."

That hurt. "I thought Marie liked me."

"She did. But she was concerned about her son's future. She didn't want him to pay for foolish mistakes, become a daddy at eighteen, and ruin his chances to make something of his life."

He'd *been* a father. And had never known it. Guilt settled heavily on Dani's shoulders. Guilt and a sorrow that had become so much a part of her it had seeped deep in her bones.

"Think how you'd feel if Matthew came home some day when he was still a teenager and told you he'd gotten some girl in trouble. I'll bet you won't be so sanguine then."

"I'd be concerned. Probably even upset," she allowed, saying a small mental prayer that they'd be spared that experience. "But I sure wouldn't sweep it under the rug and pretend it never happened. And I'd never, ever be ashamed of him."

*As you were me*. She didn't need to say the words out loud; they hovered in the still morning air between them.

Dani wanted to rant. To rave. To throw things. For the sake of her father's health—for that reason only—she forced her temper down.

"Even if you thought you were doing what was best for me, you still had no right to threaten Jack."

"I didn't have any choice. The boy wouldn't take money to leave."

She drew in a sharp breath that burned. "You offered him a bribe?" This just kept getting worse and worse.

"Not a bribe. An incentive. You were too young to know your own mind."

His gray eyes turned to steel. Despite the way his heart disease had physically weakened him, Dani had no problem envisioning him back on the bench, literally wielding the power of life and death.

"You still had a year of high school," he reminded her. "Your entire life was ahead of you, and I damn well didn't want you throwing it away on a juvenile delinquent like Jack Callahan."

"He wasn't really a delinquent. He was just angry. If his father hadn't died—"

"I would have been the one lying dead on the courthouse floor. Is that what you would have wanted?"

It was an impossible choice. Just like the one he'd given Jack. She shook her head and stared unseeingly out the window. "I don't believe you would have followed through on your threat. I cannot accept the idea that the man I've respected my entire life would have tossed the woman whose husband saved *his* life out onto the street."

"I didn't believe it would come to that." The judge shrugged. "After all, for all Callahan's faults, no one could say he didn't love his mama. Especially since even if I didn't fire her, we both knew it'd break her heart if he'd been jailed on a statutory rape charge."

"That's one of the more disgusting aspects of this." Her stomach twisted at the idea of having something as beautiful as what she and Jack had shared turned into a public disgrace. "Did Marie know what you did?"

"Not the specifics. But she must've figured I'd done something because afterward she came and thanked me for helping her boy stay on the straight and narrow. The Navy was good for him, made a man out of him.

"If he'd stayed here in Blue Bayou, he would have been just one more troublemaker, mad at the world and taking it out on everyone around him. Even those who loved him. Most especially those who loved him."

"That's not true. That boot camp you'd sent him to had changed him. It made him realize that anger never solves anything."

"So you say. But that wasn't a chance I was prepared to take."

"It wasn't *your* chance to take."

"You were underage," he reminded her. "And he sure as hell wasn't showing a lot of sense—or honor—sneaking around with you in the first place. If he'd wanted to date my daughter, he should have come to me and asked my permission like a man."

"Your permission? We weren't living in the Middle Ages, Father. And for your information, Jack wanted our relationship out in the open. I was the one who begged him to keep it a secret. Because I knew you wouldn't approve."

She shook her head, shuddered out a painful breath. "But I never, in my wildest imagination, believed you'd stoop so low."

"Don't be so fast to judge, little girl. You're a mother. The day will come when you'll understand I did what I had to do to protect you."

"No." About this, Dani was very clear. "I'll always be concerned about Matt's future. And that of any other children, if I'm fortunate enough to have them. But I would never, ever, manipulate them the way you did Jack and me."

"It never would have worked out between the two of you anyway."

"Wasn't that for me to find out? Besides, *your* choice of a husband for me wasn't exactly stellar."

"Point taken. But you did end up with a wonderful little boy."

It was the same thing Jack had said.

As emotions welled up inside her, choking her, Dani reminded herself that it was control she needed now. Cool, calming control. It would not do either of them any good if she started screeching at her ill father, no matter now much he may deserve it. No matter how badly *she* needed to do it.

"As much as I love Matt, that still doesn't excuse what you did, Father. It could never make it right."

She turned to walk away.

"I'm not the only one with secrets," he called after her. "If you're such a stickler for honesty, why don't you tell Jack where you spent your senior year of high school? And why?"

Refusing to admit that about this, at least, he had a point, Dani walked out of the room without responding.

Like many bad days, this one just got worse. Needing a chocolate boost after her confrontation with her father, Dani stopped off at the market on her way to the library, where a clutch of women were gathered around the cash register, blocking her access to the Hershey's bars.

"Did you see this, Dani, dear?" Bessie Ardoin, an eccentric, octogenarian spinster who'd claimed to have been beamed aboard a spaceship that had landed outside Blue Bayou one night back in the sixties, waved a supermarket tabloid. "It's so exciting."

"Let me guess. Elvis has been found on an ice floe with a survivor from the *Titanic*."

"It's not nice to jest about the King, dear," Edith Ardoin, Bessie's twin sister, chided. While Edith hadn't experienced her sister's alien adventure, she *had* worked as an extra in Elvis Presley's movie *King Creole* when location shooting had been done in New Orleans. The way she'd continued to talk about it for more than forty years suggested it remained the high point of her life.

"I'm sorry, Miss Ardoin," Dani said.

"That's all right, dear," Bessie answered for her sister. "No harm done. Edith knows you didn't mean any disrespect. After all, how would you have any way of knowing that Beau Soleil's ghost is now famous all over the country?"

"What?" Dani snatched the paper from Bessie's outstretched hand. "Oh, no," she groaned as she read the screaming double headline: *Things that go bump in the Bayou. Thriller writer haunted by Confederate ghosts.*

"Oh, my God," she murmured as she skimmed the outrageously exaggerated story, then looked at the byline. "I can't believe this. It's that man who came into the library looking for information about Beau Soleil." He'd lied to her, she thought furiously. Dallas Chapman was no more a parapsychologist than she was a rock star.

"Well, he certainly went to the right place," Edith said. "How nice you were able to help him with his story."

"I didn't help him. I merely pointed him to some books." To

think he'd sucked her in with that story about he and his wife falling in love at some haunted Scots castle!

"It's a lovely picture of the house," Edith said.

"And you can see the ghost," Bessie said.

"Where?" Charlotte Cassidy, the day checkout clerk, leaned over the counter and peered at the paper over the top of her glasses.

"Right here." Bessie tapped her finger against a blurry white spot that at first glance did appear to be hovering above the house.

Dani looked closer. "That's no ghost. It's only the camera's flash."

"I can understand how one could think that," Bessie said. "But it's obvious to those of us who've experienced a paranormal event that it's an apparition. That white light is an obvious energy source, and everyone knows that spirits refuse to allow themselves to be photographed."

Ever since returning from the Mothership, Bessie had alleged to have the "Sight." She'd been supplementing her Social Security checks by doing tarot card readings down at the Shear Pleasures beauty parlor every first Saturday of the month for as long as Dani could remember.

"I've heard ghosts tend to be camera shy," Charlotte allowed.

She should have checked him out, Dani thought. At least done a database search for that Tennessee witch story he'd alleged to have written with his probably fictional wife. "He said he was a parapsychologist."

"One can be a parapsychologist *and* a reporter, dear," Bessie pointed out.

"I wonder if Jack's seen this yet," Edith mused.

"Won't he be pleased?" Bessie pointed to a paragraph toward the end of the story. "Look, it even lists the titles of his books and mentions the movies."

"I bet he won't be all that happy about the suggestion that the books are being ghostwritten by a dead Confederate soldier," Charlotte offered warily.

Dani briefly closed her eyes upon hearing that ridiculous piece of tabloid journalese. Not only would Jack be less than pleased at the story that was far more fiction than fact, she feared he was going to blow sky high.

# 21

*Are you going to marry* Jack?" Matt asked later that afternoon.

Dani looked up from dropping chocolate-chip dough onto a cookie sheet. Not sure she could trust her voice, she spooned up more dough, tried to decide how to handle the question that had come from out of the blue, and decided to hedge. "Where did that come from?"

He shrugged and snitched a scoop of dough from the blue mixing bowl. "You go on dates with him."

"They're not exactly dates. I'm merely helping him decorate Beau Soleil."

"You're going to that wedding. The one you bought a new dress for."

It had been an extravagance, bought on a whim, and she couldn't really afford the expense. It was also made of silk spun as soft as a whisper that rustled when she walked, with a garden of tropical flowers blooming on the short, flirty skirt. She'd tried it on for Orèlia, who'd taken one look at it, whistled and said, "That Jack's gonna be a goner for sure, he."

The older woman had also insisted on taking her into the city where she'd located what she'd declared to be the perfect shoes to match. The bright poppy color was highly impractical, since it wouldn't go with a single other thing in Dani's closet, the heels were so high she feared getting a nosebleed, and pencil thin, which was just asking for a broken ankle, she'd complained to Orèlia while the salesman was in the back of the store, looking for her size.

They were an impossible hue, ridiculously high, and dangerously thin. But as she'd taken the strappy, glove-soft leather sandals out of the box, Dani had also known that once again Orèlia was right. They were absolutely, positively perfect.

"It's not really a date," she said, dragging her mind back to the conversation. "An old friend of Jack's is getting married, and he didn't want to go to the wedding alone, so he asked me."

"Oh." He reached for one of the cookies already cooling on a nearby rack. "I'm glad you're not getting married."

That surprised Dani, since it was obvious that her son thought Jack Callahan hung the moon. "Well then, I guess it's good I'm not."

"Yeah. Because I like Jack a lot," he said around a mouth of chocolate chips. "But if you two got married, then he'd be my dad."

"I suppose he would," she said carefully. "If we were to get married. Which I'm not planning to do with anyone anytime soon."

"Okay." He shrugged thin shoulders beneath the league baseball jersey he was so proud of. Unsurprisingly, when they'd gone to the tryouts this afternoon, he hadn't earned a spot in the starting lineup, but the coach had assured him he wouldn't be spending the summer on the bench, either. *Thanks to Jack.*

He scooped another scoop of cookie dough from the bowl with his finger. "Jack's a lot of fun, but if you got married to him, he'd become my dad, then maybe he wouldn't hang out with me or talk about baseball and stuff anymore. Or come to any of my games like he says he promised to do."

Failure rose to grab her by the throat. She'd married a man she'd come to realize she hadn't loved, in a foolish attempt to get over the one she *did,* and in doing so had set a series of events into play that ultimately had hurt her child.

"Oh, sweetie." Needing to touch him, to reassure him, Dani smoothed down his cowlick with fingers that weren't nearly as steady as she would have liked. "You don't have to worry. If Jack told you he'd come to some of your games, he will. You can count on him to keep his word."

The roar of the GTO's engine had them both looking up. "He's here!"

Practically knocking the chair over in his enthusiasm, Matt jumped down from the table and raced out of the kitchen as Jack pulled into the drive. Wiping her hands on the white chef's apron she'd donned over the T-shirt and jeans she'd worn to the tryouts today, wondering if she still had any lipstick on, and suspecting she didn't, Dani followed her son out the door.

"Hey, Jack," Matt shouted, "look!" He thrust out his chest with masculine pride, showing off the pinstriped jersey. "I made the team."

"I never had a single doubt in the world you would," Jack said, with a wink toward Dani, who was surreptitiously tucking the hair that had escaped her braid behind her ears. "Didn't I tell you that you're a natural?"

"I'm not in the starting lineup. But Coach Pitre says that it's important to be able to come off the bench, too."

"It surely is. It takes a real talent to rev up your engines on a moment's notice."

"Yeah, that's the same thing Coach Pitre said. We're the Blue Bayou Panthers. Did you know that black panthers used to live around here?"

"Seems I heard somethin' about that. Though I never saw one myself."

"That's 'cause they're all extinct now, but it's still a cool name for a team, don't you think?"

"Sounds good to me."

"Mr. Egan, who owns the barbershop, is our sponsor. We're gonna have team pictures made and everything. And we're going to go away to a special camp so we can work on fundamentals and start feeling like a real team."

"Imagine that. This calls for a celebration. Why don't you and your mom and I go out to the Cajun Café, have ourselves a nice dinner, then take in a movie down at the Emporium. I saw on the marquee that *Gone in 60 Seconds* is playin' tonight. And it's not the remake, but the original one from 'seventy-four."

"Really?" Matt turned to Dani, eyes bright and begging. "Can we, Mom?"

"I've already made spaghetti sauce." It might not be anything as mouthwatering as the Cajun fare Jack could whip up from whatever ingredients he had on hand, but it was nourishing and something Matt would eat every night of the week if she let him.

"It'll keep," Jack said. "You can serve it up tomorrow night."

"Yeah, Mom, it'll keep," Matt repeated. "We can have it tomorrow."

Excitement blazed on his face. Dani knew she'd end up feeling like the Wicked Witch of the West if she denied him this special night out.

"Isn't that the movie about stealing cars?"

"Yeah. Remember I wanted to rent it."

"I also seem to remember that it's rated PG-13, and I told you I thought it set a bad example."

"Geez, Mom. It's not like I'm gonna go out and become a car thief or anything dumb like that. It's just a make-believe story about this guy who gives up a life of crime but has to steal a bunch of cars to save his brother's life. There's this neato police chase at the end where they wreck ninety-three cars!"

"Stealing *and* wrecking cars," Dani murmured. "How encouraging."

"It's just a movie, Danielle," Jack said. "And the seventy-four version's bound to be tamer than the remake. If it'll make you feel better about things, I'll explain about the downside of drivin' cars that don't belong to you."

"You don't have to do that." Still, car theft was a serious matter. It had certainly gotten Jack in trouble. So why were her lips curving even as she fought to keep them firm?

"I suppose this *is* a special occasion." She could feel herself caving in. "After all, while I couldn't swear to it, I do believe you're the first baseball player in our family. It seems that's something to celebrate."

"Yes!" Matt pumped a small fist into the air.

"We'd better quick take her up on the offer before she changes her mind, sport," Jack suggested. "You got someone you'd like to take along?"

Matt's small brow furrowed. "You mean like a friend?"

"I mean exactly like a friend."

"There's Danny Pitre. He's the coach's son and the best player on the team. I traded him my Dodge Viper GTS for his DeTomaso Pantera at lunch recess yesterday."

"Why don't you go give him a call? I'll wait out here with your *maman*."

" 'Kay!" He ran into the house with a loud whoop, slamming the screen door behind him.

Dani shook her head as she remembered what he'd said about Jack and how he believed dads ignored their children. What a sad lesson she'd inadvertently taught her son. A lesson that was undoubtedly more harmful in the long run than a car-theft movie.

"Thank you," she said quietly. "I should have realized tonight called for more than spaghetti and meatballs."

"Nothin' wrong with spaghetti and meatballs. In fact, were you to get it into your head to invite me to a spaghetti dinner tomorrow night, I sure wouldn't turn you down."

Dani had feared that making love with Jack would have complicated their relationship. Instead, it seemed to have made it even easier. Better, richer.

She thought about him in the morning, on her way to the library, during the day, while she chatted with patrons, date-stamped books, and put others away, and in the evening, when if he didn't show up, he'd call and she'd go into the bedroom, shut the door, and was grateful that they didn't have video phones when his sexy suggestions, drawled on that deep voice that vibrated all through her, made her blush like the teenager she'd once been.

"It's a date. A deal," she corrected quickly, earning a flashed, wicked grin at her slip as they followed Matt into the house.

"Deals are what you make when you buy a car, or plea-bargain a jail term. What I'm talkin' about, Danielle, darlin', is definitely a date."

The smile he bestowed on her definitely made up for her earlier less-than-stellar day. Which brought her mind skimming back to that horrid supermarket tabloid. "Did you happen to drop by the market today?" she asked with studied casualness.

"Yeah. But it wasn't real necessary, since the phone didn't stop ringing all day. I was amazed so many people in town actually read that rag."

"I think they mostly read the headlines." She studied him cautiously. "Aren't you angry?"

"Hell, if I let every negative thing people said about me get me riled up, I'd have gotten myself an ulcer a long time ago." He shrugged. "Besides, I make a livin' tellin' lies myself."

"You write fiction. Newspapers are supposed to deal in fact."

"No halfway-intelligent person considers that thing a real newspaper." Jack looped his arms around Dani's waist, drew her to him, and sniffed. "Don' worry about it. I'm sure as hell not. 'Specially when I have my girl in my arms." He nuzzled her neck. "Damn, but you smell extra good today."

"Thank you. But I think it's the cookies."

"Cookies?" He lifted his head and glanced over at the plate. "Hot damn. Are those chocolate chip?"

"Are there any other kind?"

"I knew I should have married you way back then."

*You know you're going to have to tell him,* that little voice piped up again.

"We were both too young for marriage," she repeated what her father had told her then, and again just the other day when she'd confronted him about sending Jack away.

"Probably," he agreed, sobering for a moment. "I sure as hell wasn't that good a husband material back then." He flashed that devilish pirate's grin. "But I gotta tell you, *chère*, if you'd promised homemade chocolate-chip cookies every once in a while, I sure would've considered giving it the old college try."

"Now who's easy?" she murmured.

"*Mais* yeah. And along those lines, I guess this is where I tell you my other great idea."

"I'm almost afraid to ask."

"How about we let the boys go sit down in front, where they'll probably want to anyway, so they can get an up-close look at the car wrecks, while you and I hang out in the balcony and neck?"

Having had to sneak around that summer, they'd never done anything so normal as neck in a movie-theater balcony. Actually, now that she thought about it, Dani realized she'd never done that with anyone.

She laughed, feeling unreasonably young and carefree for a woman who, just a few weeks ago, had nearly been homeless with a mountain of debts. She still didn't have her own home, and while she was continuing to chip away at Lowell's debts, her life was ever so much richer than it had been before she'd returned home to Blue Bayou.

Even her relationship with her father, while still suffering from the revelation about Jack's reason for leaving the bayou, was beginning to open up. Last night, when he'd come into the kitchen while she'd been sitting at the table, balancing her checkbook, he'd told her that he was proud of how well she'd grown up. She'd been so surprised by that revelation her fingers had stumbled on the calculator keys, clearing the entire column, forcing her to begin again. But it had been worth it, just to hear those long-awaited words.

"You're right," she decided with a smile of her own. "That may be the best idea you've had yet."

"And just think," he said as he gave her a quick hot kiss that ended far too soon but still left her head spinning, "the night's still young."

"I was thinking," Dani said to Matt two days later, as they drank frosty glasses of lemonade beneath a spreading oak that took up most of Orèlia's backyard after she'd gotten home from the library, "that as soon as we get settled into the apartment, perhaps we ought to take that trip to the animal shelter."

His blue eyes widened with blazing hope. "We're really gonna get a dog?"

"Unless you'd rather have a cat."

"Nah. Cats are okay, I guess. Mark Duggan has this really weird Siamese cat who'll fetch spitballs, which is kinda neat. But mostly cats just lie around. They don't play with you like a dog does."

"Then I guess we'd better make it a dog."

"Do you really, really mean it?"

"I really, really mean it."

"Wow, thanks, Mom!" He flung his arms around her, nearly making her spill her drink. "You're the greatest mom in the whole world. The universe, even."

"You're going to have to walk him," she warned.

"That'll be fun." He paused. "You mean a real dog, don't you?"

She didn't understand. "As opposed to a make-believe dog?"

"No. I mean we oughta get a mutt. Like Turnip. Jack says they're the best. If we get us some fluffy little dog that wears pink bows and gets its toenails polished like Danny's mother's dog, all the kids'll probably make fun of me when I'm walking her and I'll have to fight again."

"You will not fight again," she said sternly. "But you don't have to worry, because I honestly cannot imagine painting a dog's toenails." Dani glanced down at her sandaled feet that were in dire need of a pedicure and couldn't remember the last time she'd managed to find time to paint her own toenails.

"Can we get him his own bowl? With his name on it?"

"I don't see why not. Of course you'll have to come up with a name."

"Yeah." He turned thoughtful. "We ought to get a boy dog. That way he can make puppies with Turnip. Wouldn't that be way cool?"

"It's certainly something to consider," Dani said, torn between being pleased such a simple idea could make her son so happy and wondering how Jack would take to having a litter of puppies running around Beau Soleil. Let him be the one to shoot the idea down, she decided.

"Boy, I can't wait for Jack to get here, so I can tell him."

They were having dinner at his house again tonight, just the two of them. Anticipation sent ribbons of desire, like streams of shimmering light, flowing through her veins.

When the GTO pulled up in front of the house, Matt went racing toward the car while Dani stayed beneath the comforting shade of the ancient oak and enjoyed the sight of Jack unfolding himself from the driver's seat.

Just as he had, that summer, he filled Dani's mind. She couldn't stop thinking about him. Her first thought in the morning was how she wished she was waking up with him beside her; her last thought at night was while her bed didn't seem at all empty when Lowell had left, now, knowing that Jack was a good six miles away, sleeping alone at Beau Soleil, made the guest bed seem as vast and arid as the Saraha. In those long hours between waking and sleeping she thought of him as well—hot, erotic, wicked, wonderful thoughts.

For the first time in years, Dani was totally aware of her body. Every nerve, every pulse, every pore was vividly, almost painfully alive.

Still, if it was merely sex, she wouldn't have been so worried. What concerned her, as they began to find time to slip away together, was that she'd come to view it as lovemaking.

Watching the way he really listened as Matt danced around him, unable to control his boyish exuberance, she thought, not for the first time, what a good father Jack would make.

Dani knew she should tell him. She'd tell herself that a dozen times a day. Then, just as often, she'd tell herself that they needed time. Time to see if these feelings were real, or merely a product of romanticized memories of a forbidden, teenage love affair.

Dani had learned the hard way that fairy tales only happened between the pages of books and in the movies; she was living proof that women who made the mistake of believing in happily-ever-after endings were more than likely to end up disappointed.

But being back here in Blue Bayou with Jack again had her remembering just how seductive happiness could be. And it terrified her. Both for herself and her son, who was, just as she'd feared, becoming so very close to Jack. Too close, perhaps. But watching him open up from an intelligent, often too-studious child into this eight-year-old ball of boyish energy, Dani didn't have the heart to limit their time together.

Besides, it was obvious that they were good for each other; the brooding, self-absorbed man she'd found that night she'd first gone out to Beau Soleil was gone, replaced by a warm, caring, generous person who laughed easily and often.

She'd tell him. Soon, Dani promised herself. She just needed a little more time.

"You're awfully quiet tonight," Jack murmured as they drove through the bayou that evening. "Rough day?"

"No. Just busy. I was just thinking."

"Now, that can get you in trouble."

She smiled as he'd meant her to. "I owe you an apology," she said.

"You don't owe me anything."

"We both know that's not true. I shouldn't have ever accused you of using Matt to get to me. You're obviously very good for him, and I appreciate you spending so much time with him."

Jack shrugged. "I like hangin' out with him. He's a great kid." He tugged on the ends of her hair. "You did good, sugar."

"I should've done better."

"Life's full of *should-haves*. If you let them, they'll just eat you up."

"I suppose you're right."

"Believe me, I'm an expert on the subject."

It had crossed Jack's mind while watching Dani's son single-handedly making a double cheeseburger, chocolate shake, French fries, and a chocolate ice-cream sundae disappear the other night, that he hadn't had any nightmares or woken up in the middle of the night in a cold sweat since Danielle had first come out to Belle Soleil and he'd cooked her supper.

In fact this morning, when he'd been drinking some chicory-flavored coffee and watching the sun rise, he had the strangest feeling that something was wrong. No, not exactly wrong, but different.

It wasn't until he'd finished his second cup that he'd realized that something was missing: the survivor guilt that had seemed to have become a part of him was no longer grinding away at his gut.

Also, except for the occasional beer, he'd just about stopped drinking, and since he didn't want to expose Danielle's son to secondhand smoke, he hadn't had a cigarette in hours.

He almost laughed at the realization that, despite the effect she was having on his hormones, Danielle Dupree was actually good for his health.

"So, you'll be movin' into the apartment soon."

"Next week. Orèlia offered to sit with Matt once school's out while I'm at work."

"Couldn't imagine you'd find anyone better."

"I know." Dani sighed. "She also suggested Daddy stay at the house with her, rather than move with us."

"Makes sense, what with her bein' a retired nurse and all. Besides, the place might look like a warehouse for the Smithsonian, but even with all the stuff she's managed to cram into it, she's still got a lot more room than you will in that apartment."

They turned a corner and Beau Soleil came into view, gleaming like a fanciful dream in the gloaming. " 'Specially now that you've promised Matt a dog."

"I suppose you're right," she said on a soft sigh as he parked in front of the house. "It's just not what I'd originally planned."

Not what she'd written down on her lists, Jack supposed as he went around the hood of the red car and opened her passenger door. "You know what they say, *chère*."

When she was standing beside him, he turned her in his arms, fitting her against him, thinking, as he had so often these past weeks, what a perfect fit they were together. "Life's what happens when you're making plans."

He slipped a hand beneath her sunset-hued top and watched desire rise in her eyes as he caressed her. "And speaking of plans . . ."

"I'm giving Michael a woman in this book," Jack announced to Nate, Alcèe, and his brother Finn, who'd returned home for the fish fry out at the Callahan camp. A more typical south Louisiana bachelor party would more likely include a trip to the city, where everyone would get drunk and work their way through the French Quarter strip clubs. But having known Alcèe for most of his life, Jack had figured the former priest would undoubtedly start trying to "save" the girls five minutes after they'd ordered their overpriced, watered-down drinks and just put a pall on any passing of a good time.

So, it had been decided that they'd hold the party out at the camp. They'd do a little fishing, Jack would cook the catch—or some shrimp he'd bring along just in case—play some cards, and rag Alcèe about being the first of the longtime friends to take the fall into matrimony.

"Big surprise." Nate snorted. He leaned back, put his boots up on the railing, and took a swallow from one of the longneck bottles of Dixie beer Jack had sitting on ice in an aluminum tub. "The guy goes through women like Tiny Dupree goes through a mess of crawfish."

Since Tiny probably weighed about three-eighty soaking wet, and was the all-time Cajun Days crawfish-eating champion, that was saying something. It was also pretty much the truth. There might be a lot of violence in his books. But Jack hadn't scrimped on the sex, either. Which, his agent had told him, was partly responsible for his large female readership.

"Not that kind of woman. You know, *the* woman."

"Son of a bitch." Nate dropped his legs down to the deck and gave Jack an incredulous look. "You're not gonna marry the guy off?"

"Well, not right away."

Jack might admittedly have romance on the mind lately, but he wasn't a fool. Part of the fictional DEA's appeal to men was his success with the ladies, while female readers seemed to have decided that he was merely soothing his broken heart while waiting for that one special woman who could make him forget his bride had been blown up in a car bombing meant for him.

Besides, since his own road to romance had been goddamn rocky, Jack saw no reason why his character should have it any easier.

"Maybe eventually," he tacked on with extreme casualness.

Jack watched the comprehension dawn in his brother's intelligent blue eyes. Nate might be the only male Callahan who hadn't become a cop, but he was no slouch at detecting, either.

Alcèe eyed Jack over the rim of a glass of iced tea. "This wouldn't have anything to do with a certain gorgeous librarian, would it?"

Jack rocked back on his heels. "It just might. I gotta tell you, bro, I haven't felt this way about another woman since Yeoman Rand." He sighed fondly at the long ago adolescent memory.

Nate's lips curved. "You fantasized about Yeoman Rand? From *Star Trek?*"

"Sure. When I was twelve, I used to imagine that the *Enterprise* was on the way to a top-secret mission on Alpha Centauri when they received a distress call from an uncharted planet."

"Which was undoubtedly a trap," Alcèe suggested.

" 'Course it was," Jack agreed. "Set up by a race of aliens who'd become so inbred they needed to leave their planet and find new blood."

"Blond blood," Nate guessed.

"Naturally. So, in my adolescent fantasy, they'd captured Yeoman Rand and were going to take her back to their actual planet, which was in a parallel universe, to use her as a sex slave."

"What did you know about sex slaves when you were twelve years old?" Alcèe challenged.

"I was a prodigy." Jack grinned at his friend, who shook his head and grinned back. "Besides, I've always had an active imagination, me."

"So," Nate continued the story, "you leaped in like Captain Kirk and rescued the lady."

"I sure as hell did." Jack nodded. "I just happened to be passing by in my snazzy two-seater star cruiser. She was, needless to say, extremely grateful."

"I can imagine." Nate shook his head. "No wonder you became a writer. To think I used to settle for sneakin' looks at Finn's *Playboy* magazines."

"The Playmates were damn sexy," Jack allowed. "But they were no Yeoman Rand. I used to spend a lot of time fantasizing about the two of us gettin' naked, but I sure never gave any thought in those days to settling down and raising us a batch of little yeomen."

"You givin' any thought to it these days?" Alcèe asked.

"I might be." For some reason, ever since the night he, Dani, and Matt had gone to the movies, Jack hadn't been able to get the image of her carrying his child out of his mind. It was nearly as appealing a fantasy as the one where he carried her over the threshold of some Caribbean resort hotel room and undressed her slowly, bit by lacy bit, teasing them both to distraction while they made love beneath a big white tropical moon.

"Son of a bitch," Nate repeated. "Well, this is unexpected."

"Think how I feel."

"I couldn't imagine. Jesus. My big brother's in love."

"Keep it to yourself. I haven't told Dani yet."

"Got any plans to do that? Or are you just gonna let her read your book when it's published and figure it out for herself?"

"I've got plans. I just haven't figured out what they are yet. . . .

"You know," he mused, "when I first bought Beau Soleil, I figured it was a nice 'in your face' gesture to the judge. The bad kid he'd run out of town coming back a success, living in the house he'd been kicked out of, romancing the daughter he'd been told to stay away from."

"That's an understandable feeling," Alcèe said. "Not exactly the most admirable, but it'd be hard not to resent the judge for what he did to you."

Since Alcèe had once been in the business of forgiving sins, Jack figured he'd have managed to turn the other cheek. And he sure as hell wouldn't have nursed a grudge as long as Jack had.

"But then things started to change. And I realized I didn't want Danielle 'cause I'd been told I couldn't have her. I wanted her for herself. Which got me to thinking that maybe we were both supposed to come back here, at this point in our lives, to be together the way we couldn't be back then."

Alcèe nodded and pulled the tab on another cola can. "The Lord moves in mysterious ways."

"Whether it's God, or fate, or destiny, I'm just damn grateful."

Jack polished off the beer and reached for another. Since they were spending the night at the camp, he didn't have to worry about drinking and driving, something he hadn't done since that summer he'd stolen Jimbo Lott's patrol car.

"I know it's gonna sound stupid, but sometimes, late at night, after I've taken Dani back to Orèlia's, I'll sit out on Beau Soleil's *gallerie*, picture the two of us laughing in the house, loving in it, and sittin' out in our rocking chairs, watching our grandkids play with Turnip's grandpups, and you know what?"

"Goin' back to DEA starts sounding real appealing?" Nate suggested.

"No. I start thinking that it's kinda a nice picture."

"Jesus, Jack, that's so damn domestic it gives me the chills."

"I'd expect nothing less from a man who believes commitment is what happens when the men in white coats show up at your door with a straitjacket and tranquilizer gun. And speaking of domesticity, how's Suzanne? I've been meaning to ask you how the skirmish over flatware turned out."

"Last I heard, she'd switched gears and ended up going with Chantilly, which wasn't even in the early running, but I won't have to worry about paying for it, since she got fed up waiting around for me to propose and got herself engaged to some old boyfriend she met during their Ole Miss graduation reunion weekend."

"Sounds like you escaped yet again."

Nate had often said that he'd just as soon go skinny-dipping with a bunch of gators than settle down for the rest of his life with one woman. Remembering how he'd once felt much the same way, Jack was looking forward to the day his brother had to eat those words.

He glanced over toward Finn, who was standing off by himself at the far end of the deck, nursing the same glass of tonic water he'd poured nearly an hour ago. He hadn't entered into the conversation. In fact, now that he thought about it, Jack doubted Finn had strung ten words together since he'd picked him up at New Orleans's Louis Armstrong Airport.

He pushed himself out of the chair and went over to join his older brother.

"Well?" he asked.

"That's a deep subject," Finn murmured, his gaze directed out over the bayou, where black clouds scudded across the deep purple sky.

"Ha ha ha. And to think people say you don't have any sense of humor."

"I hadn't realized people said anything about me."

"Christ, you can be literal." Jack shook his head, wished for a cigarette and remembered he'd thrown his last pack away after figuring that he'd cut back so far to keep from smoking in front of Matt, he may as well just quit the rest of the way. "I was speaking rhetorically. Though, thinking about it, there was a bit of a buzz around here when you got yourself a second invitation to the White House after nabbing that serial killer last month." The first had come in the prior administration when Finn had foiled an assassination attempt.

"I nailed him too damn late."

"Finn, you rescued two women from that guy's house. And I don't even want to think about how many more he could have nabbed if you hadn't stopped him."

"Try telling that to Lori Hazelton's mother."

The nineteen-year-old woman had gone missing at the San Diego county fair. Her mutilated body had later been found in Griffith Park. "You had no way of knowing ahead of time that she'd been targeted as a victim by some sadistic pervert."

"Lori was the first." Finn pressed his glass against his temple. "And, goddammit, she wasn't the last."

"No. But as tragic as those murders were, things could have ended a helluva lot worse if you hadn't tracked the monster down."

His brother's only response to that was a shrug. Of the three of them, Finn had always been the hardest on himself. Jack had taken on the role of the troublemaker, the rebel without a cause, as Dani had described him, though in reality, he'd been a helluva lot closer to a rebel without a clue.

Nate had always been the easygoing one that everyone liked, the flirtatious Callahan with the quick smile and deceptively laid-back manner. Finn had been the perfectionist whom Jack had often thought was intent on living up to their larger-than-life father's image.

An anvil-shaped cloud moved across the thin sickle slice of moon, signaling that hurricane season was just around the corner. "There's always one who haunts you," Finn said after a long pause.

"Yeah." Jack knew that only too well. He'd certainly had his share, including a once stunning Colombian woman he could still picture draped artistically across her wide white bed, her beautiful face battered nearly beyond recognition, the front of her silk ivory nightgown drenched in blood.

"You know, maybe you ought to try doin' what I did to exorcise them."

"What's that?" Finn said with a decided lack of interest which suggested he didn't believe he'd ever get rid of his personal phantoms.

"Get yourself a woman. I realized the other day that I've just about quit having nightmares since Dani came home to Blue Bayou."

Finn turned his gaze to Jack, treating him to that same deep, hard stare he'd give him back when he was fifteen, the Christmas vacation Jack came home at two in the morning with his breath reeking of beer and the rest of him smelling of pot.

"Never thought I'd hear you use *home* and *Blue Bayou* in the same sentence. . . . So, looks like you're finally putting down roots," he murmured, proving that he had been listening to the conversation, after all.

"Though there's a part of me that's still scared to death of doing somethin' to fuck it up, I guess I just might be."

"Because of Dani."

"Yeah."

Finn thought about that for a long silent moment. "Works for me," he decided.

# 22

*The Holy Church of the Assumption* was filled to standing room only for the ceremony, proof of how many lives Alcèe, in his quiet way, had somehow touched. The bride was beautiful, as all brides are supposed to be, with stars shining in her eyes; the groom, who'd looked uncharacteristically nervous while waiting at the altar, couldn't stop beaming once he'd managed to survive the double-ring ceremony.

Since weddings always made Dani a little weepy, she ducked into the rest room of the parish hall where the reception was taking place to refresh her makeup—she knew she should have forgone the mascara—when Desiree Champagne came out of one of the stalls.

The merry widow's artfully tousled cloud of black hair, which definitely hadn't been styled at the Shear Pleasures, gave her the look of having just made love amidst hot silk sheets. Her doe eyes were emphasized by a deft hand with liner, her complexion was cream, her lips red. And her body was draped in a royal blue silk wrap dress that hugged her voluptuous curves.

"Hello, Dani." The brilliant smile didn't quite reach the brunette's eyes, which skimmed over Dani's reflection from her head to the toes of her red sandals. "You're certainly looking well. Small-town life seems to agree with you." She washed her hands, then pulled a gold monogrammed compact out of a Prada bag Dani figured probably cost at least two month's worth of groceries and began powdering her nose. "I can see why Jack hasn't had time to visit his old friends lately."

"He's been very busy with the house."

Desiree's answering laugh was rich and throaty. "I suppose that's as good an excuse as any."

She laughed again, richly, her eyes dancing with that same rebellious mischief Dani had seen so often in Jack's gaze. No wonder they were drawn to each other, she thought. They were two gloriously attractive rebels.

"You're looking beautiful as always." Dani had always believed in giving credit where credit was due.

"I've always cleaned up real well." A Liz Taylor-size diamond flashed as she fluffed her hair. More diamonds blazed at her earlobes.

She took a lipstick from the bag and touched up her crimson lips. "I don't believe in beating around the bush, Dani, so I'm going to say this right out; I wish to hell you hadn't come back to town."

"I'm sorry you feel that way."

"Oh, it's okay." The dress slid off Desiree's shoulders when she shrugged, just enough to tantalize male interest. Dani wondered if it were accidental, or if she'd practiced the gesture, and decided it really didn't matter since she'd never be able to pull it off in a million years. "We've never been all that serious. I'd just gotten spoiled having him all to myself."

"Should I say I'm sorry? About cutting into Jack's time with you?"

"Don't say it if you don't mean it."

"Then I won't."

Teeth so perfect they could only be caps flashed in a dazzling smile that even Dani couldn't entirely resist. "Good for you." Desiree took a pack of cigarettes out of the bag. "This isn't exactly the most private place in town. Why don't we find ourselves a little corner and catch up?"

"I'm sorry, but I really should be getting back. Jack's going to be wondering where I am."

"Let him." She held the pack toward Dani, who shook her head. "It's good for men to realize women won't come when they snap their fingers."

"Jack's not that way."

"No. He isn't." Her expression turned serious. "Look, Dani, watching the way Jack was looking at you all during Alcèe's wedding, it's obvious that the two of you have picked up right where you left off that summer."

"You knew about that?"

"Of course. Jack and I never had any secrets from each other."

"Were you . . ." Dani pressed her fingers against her mouth, cutting off the question.

"Fucking him back then?"

She refused to react to the word she suspected Desiree had used as a test. "It doesn't matter. It was a long time ago and none of my business if you were."

"Of course it was. Because you loved him. And he loved you."

Part of Dani wanted to avoid this woman who'd experienced Jack's clever mouth and wonderfully wicked hands; who'd taken him inside her, just as Dani herself had done only hours ago after last night's rehearsal dinner. The other part of her was honestly curious about what, if anything, Desiree knew about Jack's feelings back then.

"I suppose we could talk for a few minutes in the contemplation garden," she suggested. "Catch up on old times."

This time Desiree's laugh held no humor. "Sugar, with the exception of a couple of fund-raisers you never would have invited me to if Jimmy Ray hadn't had more money than God, you and I never had any old times."

"But you and Jack did?" Dani asked as they left the building by a back door. The garden, located between the church and the rectory, had been designed for quiet contemplation and prayer. Short, leafy green hedges created private hideaways, and Dani and Desiree chose one farthest away from the reception.

"Jack's a lot like this bayou," Desiree answered obliquely as she sat down on a wrought-iron bench and lit a long slender cigarette. "Still waters and all of that. He doesn't reveal all that much, but that doesn't mean there's not a lot of depth there. . . .

"He nearly killed my stepdaddy once," she said on a stream of blue smoke.

"Oh?" That single word was all Dani could manage.

"With a bat right against the back of his head. He was coming home from baseball practice, and I think he might have killed him if my mama hadn't come by about then and started clawing at him like a wildcat." She shook her head. "Christ, that was not one of my better days."

"Why did Jack hit him?"

"Because he caught him raping me in the woodshed outside our house."

Dani gasped even as she wondered how any woman could state such a dreadful thing in such a matter-of-fact way.

"Oh, it wasn't the first time. And I sure wasn't a virgin, because

Jack and I had been screwing around for months. Lord, we were horny kids," she said on a soft laugh.

Dani didn't want to think about that. "Still, your stepfather had no right to do such an evil thing. Was he arrested?"

"No, because I didn't want to press charges. My reputation wasn't exactly polished sterling even then, so I figured no one would believe me. Jack wanted to put the bastard in jail, but he reluctantly agreed to go along with me, since he didn't have a helluva lot of faith in Jimbo Lott to arrest his second cousin, which my stepdaddy happened to be.

"So Jack cleaned me up and told me everything was going to be okay, threw some of the old man's stuff in a duffel bag, dragged him half conscious to the car, drove him to the Mississippi state line, and tossed him out alongside the road with the warning that if he ever came back to Blue Bayou again, he was a dead man."

She drew in on the cigarette. "I don't know if you've ever witnessed it, but Jack's temper is a scary thing. The madder he gets, the icier he becomes. Then he blows sky high. He's the proverbial fire-and-ice guy. Well, that day he was pretty much both, and I, for one, certainly bought the idea that he was capable of cold-blooded murder. I guess my stepdaddy figured he'd best stay out of Dodge, too, because he never came back."

"You must have been relieved," Dani murmured, wondering why Desiree was telling her such a personal story. "And grateful."

"Hell yes, I was grateful. 'Course my mama was pissed off. She didn't tell anyone he was gone, so she could keep collecting his Social Security disability check. He'd gotten himself a bad back, working construction, but that never stopped him from beating the shit out of her. She managed to pull the wool over the bureaucrats' eyes for about six months before they caught on that it wasn't him endorsing the checks and put her in jail for fraud."

Dani wrapped her arms around herself to ward off the inner chill. She'd spent her own teen years feeling sorry for herself, unhappy that she couldn't connect with her distant father, that he couldn't seem to love her. But to discover that only a few miles away, this woman had been living in hell, definitely put things in perspective.

"I'm sorry. I can't imagine how awful all that must have been for you."

"Well, of course you can't. Since you were living like a princess up at Beau Soleil. Though," she said, on afterthought, "I'll have to give you credit for not bein' one of those rich bitches who loved to gossip about me and would snicker whenever I'd walk past them in the school hallway. And you always treated me like a lady at your parties. 'Course you wouldn't have ever invited me in the first place if it hadn't been for Jimmy Ray tossing so much money in your husband's coffers, but at least you didn't snub me."

She drew in a deep, seemingly resigned breath. Blew it out on another cloud of thick blue smoke. "Since my mama died a few years ago, no one knows this story about my stepdaddy but Jack and me. And I'm only telling you so you'll understand how things are between the two of us.

"There was a time, when we were kids, that for reasons of our own, we both felt like outsiders. Which built us a bond that's held all through the years. I'll always be grateful to Jack for what he did that day and I'll always be there for him. But I'd never do anything to cause him unhappiness, which is what I'd be doing if I even tried to get between the two of you.

"My life was a little rocky for a while, but that all changed after I married my Jimmy Ray, and I don't care what his hateful, vindictive children who never paid any mind to him when he was alive believe, I loved that man dearly and took good care of him while he was dying of lung cancer. Just like he took real good care of me." Her eyes grew moist as she twisted the diamond ring. "Jimmy Ray and Jack were the only two men who ever did care about me, and I'll love them both till the day I die.

"Jack might not have told you, since, like I said, he's not all that forthcoming, but he's been through some rough times himself these past years, and they've taken their toll on him. But he's still the most standup guy I've ever met. And the most honest, which is kind of ironic when you consider he spent years working undercover."

She stubbed out the cigarette in her empty champagne glass. "He's never been one to judge anyone, which is lucky since I sure as hell haven't been a saint, but I think all those years of living a lie is probably the reason that he flat out can't abide anyone lying to him."

She stood up with a lithe, catlike grace, making Dani think yet again how much Desiree and Jack had in common. Both of them radiated sex. "Of course you don't have to worry about that, sugar. It's not that you could be keeping anything from him. Since your life these past years has pretty much been an open book, played out in all the newspapers."

Dani didn't, couldn't, respond.

"Would you think me out of line if I offered one little word of advice?"

"I suppose not."

"I'm not going to share details, because it's Jack's story to tell, but he was burned pretty badly by a woman down in Colombia. If there's anything you're keeping from him, anything at all, perhaps about that summer, you'd best tell him yourself. And soon. Before someone else does."

The ice in Dani's blood spread outward to encase her heart. "Is that a threat?"

"Of course not." Desiree's eyes flashed with irritation. "It's merely a warning. I told you I'd never do anything to cause Jack pain. But unfortunately, not everyone loves the guy as much as I do, and secrets have a real funny way of not stayin' buried."

With that she began to walk away, hips swaying in a smooth seductive way Dani couldn't have managed if she practiced for a hundred years. She was halfway to the church hall when she turned. "Did I mention that I'd worked for a while in New Orleans?"

"I believe I've heard something about that."

Desiree waved her cautious response away with a flick of her wrist. "It's not what you're thinking. I worked retail for a time, selling cosmetics in a drugstore in the Quarter. It was just an itty bitty little place on Conti Street, hardly big enough to turn around in and certainly nothin' fancy." Her gaze zeroed in like a laser on Dani's. "But you'd be surprised by how, every so often, I'd see someone from home come in there to buy something. I didn't work there long. Just a couple months in the fall. Not long after Jack took off to California."

Her words tolled like one of the buoys out in the Gulf that warned ships against going aground. It was obvious she knew something about Dani's pregnancy. Dani might have put it down as a lucky guess if she hadn't mentioned that pharmacy where she'd bought the home pregnancy test. Of course, Desiree had no way of knowing which way the test had turned out. But still, if she knew Dani's secret, someone else might, too. It was just getting too risky. Especially now that she and Jack were actually beginning to be seen together, almost like a couple.

No, she corrected, exactly like a couple.

She'd tell him, Dani promised herself. Tonight. Then all she could do was pray he'd understand that at the time she hadn't believed she'd had any other choice but to give her child—their child—up for adoption.

Which had never happened. Because even though she'd changed her mind and had decided not to let her father force her into signing those final papers, her infant girl had tragically died before she'd lived a day. And Dani, who'd yet to turn eighteen years old, had left the Atlanta maternity home for unwed mothers, forced to spend the rest of her life grieving for the daughter who'd been her only source of comfort during those long and lonely months of her pregnancy.

"Orèlia told me a little about Alcèe," Dani said as they swayed together to a slow, seductive ballad. She couldn't translate all the French, but it sounded sad. Probably a love song, she thought, remembering what Jack had said about all love affairs being tragic. "About his drinking problem. And his leaving the priesthood."

She glanced over at the tall lean man who was dancing with his bride, his expression that of a man who'd stumbled across his own platinum mine. "It's so nice things worked out for him."

"Anyone deserves happiness, it's Alcèe," Jack said. "Though there was a moment, just before Jaycee began walking down the aisle, that I was afraid he might pass out on me."

"Nervous grooms are one of those stereotypes that seem to be true."

"Seem to be," he agreed.

The music was singing in her head and her heart seemed to be beating in unison with his. Their thighs brushed as she followed his steps. He was a good dancer. Perhaps not as flashy and schooled as Lowell had been, but steady, competent, yet not entirely predictable. A woman would feel secure in his arms. In his life. But he'd still surprise her from time to time, which would, she considered, keep things from getting boring.

Dani compared herself to Desiree, who was doing a pretty good job of singing along with the band and wondered if Jack ever compared the two of them and found her boring. Which she'd be bound to be next to the glamorous widow.

"Is getting married really that stressful for a man?" she asked, genuinely curious. "Is it so hard to give up your freedom?"

"Probably no harder for a man than a woman." He pressed his hand against her lower spine and drew her closer. "And I doubt if Alcèe felt like he was giving up his freedom. My guess is that he considered today the price a guy has to pay for a piece of his own personal heaven."

His answer was definitely not what she'd been expecting, proving yet again his unpredictability. Dani never would have guessed he'd view marriage so positively.

"Then why would he be so nervous?"

He slid his leg between hers, spreading heat. "Because he's afraid of failing. Of disappointing her. Of not living up to the man she believes herself to be marrying."

"Maybe that's part of the bargain," she mused. "Disappointing your partner but loving each other enough to work it out and move on." Something that certainly hadn't happened in her own marriage.

"You may be right." His hand slid up her back; his fingers tangled in her sleek blond hair. "And speaking of moving on, what would you say to cutting out of here early?"

"Before the bride and groom leave?"

"This place is packed, they won't miss us." He touched his lips to that surprisingly sensitive little hollow behind her ear he'd discovered the first time they'd made love. "Besides, they wouldn't notice us if we were to hang around and throw rice. Not tonight."

No. It was obvious Mr. and Mrs. Bonaparte only had eyes for each other. Still, Dani had been brought up to observe protocol. And to be perfectly honest, even having decided that she could no longer keep her secret from Jack, she wasn't in any hurry to break the news that she'd cost him the chance to be a father, if only for the few too brief hours their child had lived. There would have been a time she wouldn't have believed he'd even care. She now knew she would have been wrong.

"Why don't you weigh this into your decision-making process," Jack said when she didn't immediately respond. He lowered his head. The brief public kiss was not nearly as hot and primal as others they'd shared. But still made her head swim and her knees weak.

"How fast did you say that shiny red car of yours could go?" she asked when she could speak again.

He laughed and skimmed the back of his hand down her cheek, her neck, and across her collarbone bared by the dress's neckline. "Believe me, *chère*, I'm gonna be pushing it to the red line tonight."

Driving like the hotshot drag racer he'd once been, with one hand creating havoc high on her thigh beneath her hitched-up skirt, the other on the wheel, Jack ran all three red lights through the center of town, which fortunately, was deserted with nearly everyone at the wedding reception. Even with him driving at seemingly the speed of sound the short drive out to Beau Soleil seemed to take forever.

Finally, just when Dani was about to beg him to pull over, he screeched to a stop in front of the house. When her fumbling fingers couldn't unfasten the seatbelt, he reached over and yanked it apart, then pulled her to him, capturing her avid mouth, burying his hands in her hair.

Her scent swam in Jack's head, passion pounded away at him. He wanted to feel her hot and naked beneath him, he needed to feel her perfumed flesh against his skin, wanted her hands to stroke his body as he'd caress hers until all control disintegrated.

Starved for her taste, having spent both the wedding and the reception semi-hard, Jack nipped and sucked on her succulent lips, then stabbed his tongue between them, where it tangled with hers, making her moan even as her own greedy mouth ground against his.

Her hands raced up and down his back while his kneaded her breasts; she tore at the buttons of the starched white shirt he'd worn for the occasion, he yanked down the zipper at the back of the flowered dress that was sexier than anything she'd worn since coming back to town.

Needing to touch her, to taste her, he dragged the dress down her arms, unfastened the bra—which today opened in the front, thank you, God!—and ripped it off her.

She cried out and arched against him as he took a breast into his mouth, sucking ravenously while his hand delved beneath her short skirt. She was so hot he was surprised her panties hadn't gone up in flames. Finding the damp silk a poor substitute for the dewy flesh beneath, he dragged them down her legs. As eager as he, Dani helped him pull them off.

"It's not fair," she moaned as he skimmed a finger along her slick cleft.

The windows were steaming up and it had begun to rain, the sound of the drops splattering on the metal roof and streaming down the window.

"What's not fair?"

"All you have to do is look at me and I want you. Say my name and I melt. Touch me and any self-restraint I thought I possessed is scorched away." Her sharp intake of breath and the way she arched against his seductive touch, opening for him as he exerted a gentle pressure, seconded her ragged words.

"What makes you think it's any different for me?" He managed, without ceasing his stroking caress, to free himself, then dragged her hand down to his cock, which thrust upward from the open zipper.

Dani skimmed a fingernail down the length and had him biting back a groan. When she curled her fingers around him and caressed the ridged tip with her thumb, his entire body tensed with anticipation. Then she began to stroke him, and the last ragged thread of Jack's control snapped.

He dragged her onto his lap, pushed those legs that had been driving him crazy all day apart, and surged upward into her with a strength that made her cry out.

And then she was riding him, her thighs pressed against his, leaning back against the steering wheel to achieve the deepest penetration as she ground against him. They rocked together, fevered, devouring, filling the car with breathless words and cries and the raunchy scent of uninhibited sex.

In the instant before release, when his entire body felt like a spring too tightly wound, Jack looked at her—pearly breasts shimmering in the moonlight, her dress up around her waist, the muscles of her slender thighs taut, her eyes gleaming in a way that could have gotten her burned at the stake during the days of witch hunts—and knew he'd never see a more erotic sight than Danielle Dupree at this moment.

Grasping her waist, digging his fingers into her perfumed and powdered flesh, Jack surged upward, deeper still, all the way to the back of her womb, then came in a violent, shuddering climax of his own.

# 23

*It was the scream* that woke her.

Dani and Jack had finally managed to drag themselves out of the car and into the house, where, like the insatiable teenagers they'd once been, they made love in the hedonistic Jacuzzi tub Jack had installed, before stumbling, nearly boneless, into bed. By then it had been too late, and she'd been too drained to initiate the conversation that was so long overdue. Thanks to Matt being at a five-day baseball camp, this was the first time Dani had been able to spend the entire night at Beau Soleil, which allowed her to put it off just a little bit longer.

*I'll tell him in the morning*, she vowed. *When we're both fresh and can think straight.*

Having made the promise to herself, Dani drifted off to sleep and dreamed of Jack. Since night in the bayou was far from silent, at first she'd thought the terrifying sound, which resembled a cry a nutria would make when being ripped apart by a hungry alligator, had somehow incorporated itself into her hot, erotic dream.

But it wasn't a nutria. Nor was it a dream. It was all too real. And it was bloodcurdling. She jerked up, nearly falling out of bed, then, breathless, her splayed hand against her bare breasts, viewed Jack, who was drenched in sweat and sitting bolt upright as well.

"Jack?" Dani could tell that he was somewhere else. Somewhere far from her; somewhere deadly and terrifying.

"Jack, wake up." She combed her fingers through the damp strands of silk jet hair, pushing it away from his forehead. "You're dreaming."

She cupped his chin in her hand, turning his head toward her. His eyes were open, but he was staring right through her, as if she had no more substance than air.

"It's a only a dream," she repeated. "A nightmare." She wrapped her arms around him, appalled that he was trembling. "It's all right."

She watched as his gaze gradually focused and was more than a little relieved when she realized he was back from that dark and dangerous place he'd ventured without her.

"It's all right." With her heart still pounding like a rabbit's she managed a faint, reassuring smile.

"Shit." He turned away so he was sitting on the edge of the bed, palms braced on his knees. Turnip, who'd been sleeping in her usual position on the floor at the foot of the bed, whined her worry and licked the back of his hand. "I'm sorry, Danielle." His voice was roughened with self-disgust. "You must have been scared to death."

"Just for a second until I realized what was happening." Her own breathing was beginning to return to normal. "I was having the most wonderful dream." She skimmed a hand down his wet back. "Yours must not have been nearly as nice."

"No. It wasn't." He squeezed his eyes shut. Tight. When he opened them again, Dani shivered at what she saw in the dark tawny depths. "I used to have the nightmares all the time. Even when I was awake. But I haven't had them since I quit drinking heavily. Not since you came out here that first night."

"I believe that may just be the nicest compliment you've ever paid me." She shifted so she was sitting beside him and touched her hand to his cheek. "Do you want to talk about it?"

"*Non*. Not really." He dragged his hand through his hair, which was loose around his moon-shadowed face, giving him the look of a fallen angel. An angel whose weary eyes were giving her a glimpse of his own private hell. "But since it appears I haven't exactly put it completely behind me, and I'm hopin' like hell you'll risk sleeping with me again, I figure you deserve the truth about what I did. What kind of man I am. Even if you may take off runnin' after you hear."

"I won't." She couldn't imagine anything he could tell her that would change how she felt about him. "And I know what kind of man you are."

"You only think you do."

"Don't insult my intelligence, Jack. I do know you. Besides," she said, looking at the huge head the dog had thrust under his hand, "Turnip obviously adores you, and you know what they say about dogs being an excellent judge of people."

Jack's expression managed to be both fond and frighteningly grave at the same time. "One could also argue that this particular dog has lousy taste. After all, she does drink out of the toilet."

"She also growled at Jimbo Lott when we ran into him outside the market the other day."

"Well, there is that." He scratched the dog behind her ear, easing her concern and causing her to turn boneless and sink to the floor in obvious dog bliss. "You know I was a DEA agent."

"Yes.

"I worked undercover. Which doesn't always involve playing by the book. I had to constantly improvise, and every so often it became a case of doing to others before they could do what they were trying to do to me."

"You were doing your job. An important job."

He shook his head at her naïveté. "Maybe you're not getting the drift. I've killed people, *chère*."

After what Desiree had told her, Dani wasn't as surprised as she once might have been. "Were they trying to kill you?"

"Hell, yes, but—"

"Well, then, you didn't have any choice."

"That's what the investigators said when I came out of surgery."

"You had surgery?"

"Yeah, after getting shot up. But I got off easy. Because of a stupid, brief fling I had in Colombia, both my best—and only—friend in the world and the woman ended up dead."

Dani vaguely wondered what he meant by brief, then decided it didn't matter. "That must have been terrible for you," she soothed.

Having been wondering how to tell her, Jack considered that this was turning out to be too easy. And he damn well hadn't trusted anything easy since he'd been thirteen.

"I'd like to hear what happened," she said quietly.

"It's not pretty."

"Newsflash, Callahan. I'm not some pampered princess who's breezed through life without pain. Without making my share of mistakes. I mean, if you want to get technical, I suppose you could consider me partly responsible for Lowell's death."

"How the hell do you figure that?"

"If I hadn't married him, he wouldn't have been elected. If he hadn't been elected, we wouldn't have gone to Washington, and he wouldn't have become so power hungry he'd do anything to further his career. If I'd been a better wife, a better lover—"

"Sugar, if you were any better lover, I would have dropped dead of a heart attack tonight out in the car."

She smiled at that. Then just as quickly sobered. "My point was, that if my husband hadn't gotten bored with me, he wouldn't have left me for another women, so he wouldn't have been moving into the Watergate that day, and been standing there on the sidewalk when her piano fell on his head."

"You realize, don't you, that's a load of crap?"

"Most days. But sometimes I wonder how much of our lives is determined by our own actions, and how much is due to fate."

"We create our own fates." It's what Jack had always believed. Until Dani had come back home and had him wondering about things like fate and destiny. "That weasel the judge married you off to locked in his fate when he was too blind and too stupid to realize how special his wife was."

"That's a very nice thing for you to say."

"It's the truth." He sighed heavily. Then picked up his sordid story, determined to get through it once and for all, so they could put it behind them and move on with the rest of their life together. "I was in Bogota, with my partner, Dave," he began slowly. "We were checking out rumors of a submarine supposedly bein' built by the Colombian drug traffickers."

"Bogota's seven thousand, five hundred feet in the Andes and at least a hundred miles from any port."

That earned a reluctant smile. "Can't fool a reference librarian. And it's two hundred miles."

"Why on earth would they build a submarine there?"

He shrugged. "Best we figured, it was easier to conceal the construction. The blueprints we found tended to suggest they'd planned to transport it on tractor-trailers in three sections to the coast.

"Dave and I spent a lot of nights staking the place out, and one night, when we'd run out of sports to talk about, we got started on women. He told me all about Trish, his wife, and I told him about you."

"Me?"

"Yeah. Oh, not everything. Just the good times. After a while we took turns—one sleeping, the other standing guard—and that conversation had gotten me feelin' a little mellow, so I remember looking up at that sky filled with whirling stars and thought about them bein' the same ones you might be looking up at, and it made me feel not quite so alone.

"Anyway, we didn't much believe it was gonna turn into anything, because, hell, even by drug-dealing standards this wacky idea was off the charts. But it turned out they'd gotten some engineers from the Russian mafia, and some ex-patriot Americans to work on it, and damned if they weren't actually building a sub capable of carrying two-hundred tons of cocaine across an ocean. The plan was to carry it down in pieces, then assemble it in the port of Cartagena.

"The operation didn't start out that big a deal. We weren't getting any kingpins but we also didn't want to take the chance that they'd actually pull the plan off. Also, we figured if we nabbed some of the middle guys, with enough pressure, we could turn one or more of them, and if we were lucky, they'd give us the names of some dealers higher up the food chain.

"Dave and I were playing L.A. dealers down there lookin' to score. We'd been hanging around the resorts for a few days, being real visible, tossing money around, acting like your typical asshole California drug hotshots."

"I wouldn't think it would be a good idea to make yourself so noticeable when you were supposedly trying to buy illegal drugs."

"Hell, sometimes it seemed as if a third of the people went down there to score drugs, another third were there to sell them, and the rest just looked the other way and tried to stay out of the gunfire. Believe me, everyone knows what's goin' on. And Dave and I got a lot better service from the hotel staff and cab drivers when they thought we were dealers than we would have gotten if they'd known we were DEA."

"Didn't it get hard?" she asked quietly. "Always living a lie?"

"*Mais* yeah. It got damn hard. But I'd been doin' it so long, I'd forgotten it wasn't the way other people—real people—lived their lives."

Dani thought guiltily about her own lie and didn't respond.

"So, things were looking pretty good. Problem was, when we showed up at this warehouse at the docks in Cartagena, neither of us had any idea that we'd already been made. Because I fucked up." It still ripped him to shreds. Even after all this time.

"Anyone can make a mistake."

"Yeah, and mine was thinkin' with my dick. I'd gotten involved a few months earlier with a woman in Barranquilla. She was a reporter who covered the cartel and worked as a part-time DEA informant."

"I didn't think reporters worked that way."

"Not in the States. But this definitely wasn't the States. So, I figured it was the best of both worlds, I could get laid regular, and every so often she'd give me some useful information about drug-trafficking. What I was too stupid to realize was that she was playing both ends against the middle, collecting money from us for information, while working for the cartel. We later learned she was the mistress of one of the traffickers and was only sleeping with me to try to learn whatever she could about our operations down there."

"I don't believe that," Dani said.

"Why not? It's the truth."

"She may have been after government secrets the first time. But after that, if she was in your bed, she was there for mind-blowing sex."

He laughed, and although he still didn't buy the idea of any outside force shaping lives, he also couldn't help wondering what he'd done to deserve a second chance with this woman. She was good for him. And he liked to think he was good for her, too.

"Well, whatever her reasons, she set us up, though she didn't get away scot-free." He figured even if he ever escaped the ghosts, he'd never entirely forget the sight of the woman he'd foolishly trusted lying dead on the bed where he'd spent so many pleasurable hours. "Her lover killed her. I suppose because he was afraid she might be as disloyal to him as she'd been to me.

"When we walked into that warehouse, all hell broke loose, and for a while it was like the shoot-out at the O.K. Corral. Then our backup blew the door, and when it looked like they were actually gonna be on the losin' end, they scattered like roaches. Well, Dave and I had a lot of time and effort invested in this, so we chased a pair of them down the waterfront, onto the beach. One of them grabbed this poor terrified tourist who just happened to be in the wrong place at the wrong time and was holding a gun to her head, so we backed off.

"That's when Dave got shot from behind. It didn't take any shooting skill, he just got ripped open with an automatic rifle. He wasn't wearing a bulletproof vest, because, just like when my dad was shot, it was too damn hot. And besides, it's a little hard to hide one of those suckers beneath the skin-tight tropical silk shirt he'd worn to fit the California image.

"I was trying to drag him off the beach when I got hit. Next thing I knew it was twelve hours later and I was waking up in the hospital."

"How badly were you hurt?"

He shrugged. "Not that bad."

"Twelve hours is a long time to be unconscious."

"Well, there was some surgery involved to dig some lead out of my chest and fix a collapsed lung, but I was out of there in time to take Dave's body home to his widow."

"I'm glad you're not doing such dangerous work anymore."

He shrugged. "I lost my stomach for it after that." He gave her a long look, relieved when he didn't find any horror on her face. "So, now you know why I quit. Why I'm back here."

"As sorry as I am about what happened, I can't be sorry that you came back to Blue Bayou." She lifted a hand to his cheek, her light touch feeling so much like a brand, Jack was amazed he couldn't hear the sizzle of burning flesh. "So we could find each other again."

She leaned forward and touched her mouth to his. Her lips softened. Parted. The soft little sound she made in her throat, half sigh, half moan, had desire pooling hot and heavy in his groin. Minds emptied. Tongues tangled. Hearts entwined. His fingers tangled in the silk of her hair. Her lips were warm, heady and unbearably sweet. Jack could have kissed her endlessly.

He dipped his tongue into the slight hollow beneath her bottom lip. When she shuddered in expectation, he pressed her back down onto the mattress and into the mists.

She didn't tell him. Oh, she had lots of excuses, after that horrible story about his lover and partner having been killed, Dani hadn't had the heart to tell Jack that he'd also lost a child he'd never known about. Then there was the fact that after their long night of lovemaking, they'd gotten up late, then made love again in the shower, putting her way off schedule, causing her to open the library late.

Since there weren't any patrons waiting, she took advantage of the peace and quiet and was preparing her monthly budget report for the parish council when Jack walked in, looking much more upbeat than he had last night when he'd shared the story of his final DEA operation.

"Come on, *chère*," he said. "I'm taking you to lunch."

"It's not even eleven o'clock."

"Brunch, then."

"I really have to get these done before Tuesday night's council meeting."

"It's a long way to Tuesday." He reached over her shoulder, pressed Save, then closed the file. "And only two blocks to the courthouse."

"We're having lunch at the courthouse?"

"Brunch," he reminded her, as he took her purse and keys from her desk drawer. "And no, we're not eating at the courthouse. I figured we'd go out for a bite afterward."

"After what?" He had his arm around her waist and was walking her to the front door.

"That's a surprise." He closed the door behind them and locked it.

"The parish council isn't paying me to sleep in late, then have lunch with you twenty minutes after I finally get to work," she argued.

"Don't worry about that. Nate knows all about me stealing you for a bit. He thinks it's a great idea."

"Are all the Callahan brothers crazy? Or is it just you?"

"I don't know about Nate and Finn," he drawled as they turned the corner. "But I'll confess I'm crazy." He tangled his hand in her hair, which she'd worn loose today, and kissed her, right out on the sidewalk in front of Espresso Express, to the obvious delight of customers sitting at the little tables outside. "Crazy about you."

"I was wrong," she muttered, even as her lips clung a moment too long for a public kiss.

" 'Bout what?" He smoothed her hair and gave her a bold grin.

"You haven't reformed. You're still Bad Jack, the devil of Blue Bayou."

"Probably," he allowed cheerfully. "Which, since you're still *ma 'tite ange*, balances things out just fine."

"Arrogant," she muttered without heat.

He skimmed a finger down her nose. "And right."

Was there any woman in the world who could resist that slow, sexy smile? Dani wondered as they cut across the park to the courthouse. And why, she wondered as she enjoyed the faintly possessive weight of his broad hand on her hip, would any woman want to?

When, without giving it any thought, she touched Captain Callahan's horse's nose, Jack caught her hand and lifted her fingers to his lips. "We already have all the luck we need, us."

His voice was low, and thick with the Cajun patois she'd discovered it always took on when his libido was heating up. It wasn't the only thing getting warm; the light touch of his mouth was setting off sparks against her fingertips. It was so easy for him, she thought. One touch, one look, and she was melting.

"You're not the only one," he murmured, proving yet again his ability to read, if not her mind, at least her expression. "You do the same thing to me." Even as she knew it was asking for trouble, Dani glanced down and viewed the proof of his statement. "Which is probably why," he said, with that wicked humor she'd come to love gleaming in his tawny eyes, "we'd better get inside before I'm tempted to take you right here on this sweet-smellin' freshly mowed lawn."

"Jimbo Lott'd love that," she muttered, her desire temporarily dampened by the thought of Blue Bayou's sheriff. "He could arrest us for indecent exposure and any other number of charges."

"He'd probably like to. But Jimbo's not gonna be in a position to be arresting anyone for a long time."

She looked up at him, surprised and puzzled.

As he held the heavy door open, Jack's broad grin was both boyish and utterly self-satisfied, reminding her of how Matt had looked when he'd caught that fly ball during baseball tryouts.

Dani was surprised to see Jack's two brothers standing in the rotunda with the sheriff and another man she didn't recognize. Nate wasn't smiling, but his expression revealed the same satisfaction she could see on Jack's face; if looks could kill, Jimbo Lott would have put all of them six feet under, while Finn's expression gave absolutely nothing away.

Dani remembered Finn Callahan as having been big for his age. That hadn't changed. He'd grown up to be a big man. But unlike the way so many former high school athletes would go to fat, he was as strong, solid, and muscular as when he'd played football for the Blue Bayou Buccaneers. His black hair was cut almost military short, he was wearing a blue suit, white shirt, and red tie, all of which were amazingly unrumpled for a steamy Louisiana summer day. His eyes were a riveting Arctic blue she suspected could chill to ice, but they warmed as she approached with Jack.

"Hey, Dani," he greeted her. "It's been a long time."

"Too long." She hadn't known Finn as well as Jack or Nate, but remembered how things around the house had always calmed down whenever he'd come home from college. Even in his teens he'd possessed a quiet strength that invited confidence. He still did.

More puzzled than she'd been when Jack had dragged her from the library, she skimmed a dismissive glance over Lott, who was inexplicably carrying a raincoat, even though the day had dawned sunny and summer steamy, then offered a polite, half smile to the man standing on the other side of the sheriff, a man nearly as large as Finn, whose face looked like ten miles of bad road. This was a man Dani would never want to meet on a dark street.

"This is Lee Thomas," Finn introduced him. "Lee, this is my brother Jack, and the prettiest lady in Louisiana, Danielle Dupree."

"It's a pleasure to meet you, Miz Dupree," Thomas said, his soft musical cadence suggesting Georgia roots.

"It's nice to meet you as well," Dani said in her best tea-party manners, even as she continued to wonder what in the world they were all doing here. "Are you with the FBI, too?"

"No ma'am, I'm with the United States Marshals Service. We're sort of the jack-of-all-trades when it comes to federal crimes and prisoners. I worked with Finn a while back when I was assigned to the Missing and Exploited Children's Task Force."

"I see," she said, not really seeing anything at all. This was getting curiouser and curiouser.

"Good to meet you, too," he said, shaking hands with Jack. "Finn's told me all about you."

"It's all lies," Jack said easily. "The Marshal's Service handles the Witness Protection Program," he told Dani.

"Well, that's certainly interesting," she said, still not having the faintest idea why Jack had dragged her to the courthouse.

"We like to think so." Lee Thomas's teeth flashed in another smile which softened the harshly carved lines of his face and made him oddly attractive. "I've been workin' on a joint effort with the Justice Department, DEA, and the FBI on this one case that's particularly interesting. It involves a New Orleans mob family."

"Really?" She felt a prickling sensation at the back of her neck.

"Yep," Finn said, looking a bit smug, Dani thought. "The Maggione family, as a matter of fact."

"There's this guy who's worked for them as a cocaine mule off and on over the years that we're currently baby-sitting until he testifies at a bunch of trials," the marshal continued the explanation. "The family businesses have pretty much been on life support since Papa Joe died, and we think, thanks to what we've learned from this informant, we'll be able to finish them off. Then Finn called me and asked me to do some digging, and damned if your daddy's name didn't come up."

"My father's name?" Light-headed from fear, Dani grasped Jack's arm. "But he's already served his sentence. He's on parole."

"Oh, yes, ma'am. I sure know that. I also know that the governor's office is working on his pardon right now."

"Pardon?" Afraid she'd heard wrong, afraid to hope, she looked up at Jack, who nodded in confirmation. "I don't understand."

"Turns out the judge was set up and framed by Lott and a former member of the state legislature, who was, until he was picked up in Baton Rouge this morning, a gambling industry lobbyist," Jack revealed.

"But why would anyone want to frame my father?"

"Papa Joe's grandson was coming to trial for grand-theft auto and attempted murder. Since there was no question about him being guilty—he'd left DNA all over the guy's car—the verdict was pretty cut and dried. Unless they could get a friendly judge to assure a mistrial. Framing your father was the easiest way, short of killing him, to get him off the bench," Finn explained. "Lucky for him, the old man was never one to advocate violence when another method would work just as well."

"According to our informant, the sheriff wasn't that wild about the idea," the marshal revealed. "Seems he wanted to pull the judge over for speeding one night, jump him, drive him a few miles out of town, shoot him, and toss him in the bayou for the gators to take care of."

Dani's gaze flew to Lott. He glowered back, his reptilian eyes seething with venom. Then her gaze moved down to his wrists, which, she noticed for the first time, were handcuffed beneath the raincoat.

"I always knew you were despicable. I just never realized how truly evil you were," Dani told the sheriff.

"That's not all," Finn said. "The fire at the library wasn't exactly an accident after all. The fire marshal found evidence of an accelerant in the crawl space above the apartment's kitchen."

Dani's blood chilled at the idea of someone purposefully setting fire to the home she and her son had planned to move into. "But the fire wasn't ruled arson."

"Not officially," Nate agreed. "Because we didn't want to tip our hand. Interestingly enough, we found some explosives in Lott's garage and a store in Lafayette that sold him the alarm clock he used as a timer. We also have two witnesses who place him at the scene the night before the fire, and a third, who'll say that he heard the sheriff suggesting doing whatever it took to make sure the judge didn't have any reason to come back here where he might start digging around."

"There's a plane waiting in Baton Rouge to take the sheriff to D.C., where he'll be formally charged with an entire laundry list of offenses, including a little drug-trafficking business he had going on the side," Lee Thomas said. "I'd say he's going to be put away for a long, long time."

Dani's eyes swam. She opened her mouth to speak. Stopped. Shook her head and tried again. "I don't know how to thank you."

"Finn and I are just doin' our job, Miz Dupree, putting the bad guys behind bars where they belong."

"It's still such a glorious surprise. Does my father know?" she asked Finn.

"We told him this morning. Although it isn't standard operating procedure, since these are special circumstances, I thought the judge might like to come along when we picked Lott up. He said he was feeling a bit peaked this morning and thought he'd pass, but the satisfaction of knowing he'd been vindicated was enough."

Even concerned as she was about her father's health, Dani's heart soared. She hugged Finn and kissed him. Then did the same to Lee Thomas.

Jack was pissed off, just a little, when the federal marshall held her just a heartbeat too long.

Christ. Who was he trying to fool? He didn't want any other man's hands on his woman for any length of time. But, since the marshal had come through for them, and put the last piece into place that cleared the judge, Jack decided he'd let him live. This time.

"Well, guess we'd better go congratulate the judge," he said, snaking his arm around Dani's waist. Mine, both the gesture and his gaze said. "You'll probably want to be there when the governor calls him."

Finn grinned at his brother's uncharacteristic possessiveness while Lee Thomas wisely backed up a step.

"So," Jack asked Dani as they walked out of the courthouse, "how come you didn't give Lott a few choice parting words?"

"I considered it. But then I decided he wasn't worth letting myself all upset."

"Good call."

She looked up at him. "You did this, didn't you?"

"I'm out of the cops-and-robbers business, remember?"

She stopped beside the horse that had definitely proven lucky today. "Jack. I want to know."

"Hell, all I did was get the ball rolling by giving Finn the name of the mule and where they could probably find him and suggesting he may be willin' to cut a deal to get himself put into the government-protection program. Finn and I knew in our guts it was Lott, but getting the proof took a bit more time. My original plan was to just have Finn shoot the bastard and save the taxpayers a lot of money, but Nate, he thought that might be overkill and counseled restraint."

"I'm glad he did. Since I'd hate to have to start visiting you in prison." Her eyes shimmered. "I owe you, Jack. More than I can ever pay back."

"Oh, I wouldn't worry about that." He grinned down at her and dropped a light kiss on the tip of her nose. "We're two intelligent people, you and me. I bet if we put our heads together, we'll think of somethin'."

# 24

*So," Nate asked,* the next afternoon, "you pop the question yet?"

"No." Jack shook his head as he stood on the sixteen-foot-tall ladder and trimmed in the paint along the ceiling. "I was going to the night of Alcèe's wedding, but then we sorta got sidetracked."

Nate countersunk a nail on the doorframe of the cabinet he'd built to hide the oversize television. "From the way you two were dancing, I'm not at all surprised by that."

"It wasn't sex that kept me from telling her. I'd planned to earlier, then I decided to put it off until morning. Then I ended up having one of those old nightmares and woke up in a sweat, shouting my head off."

"I can see how that might sour the mood."

"Oh, she was real good about it." Jack dipped the brush in the paint bucket and wished for a cigarette. "Said all the right things, and all, but I decided that it must have freaked her out a little, so I decided to wait till today. Soon as I get this wall done, I'm goin' over to the apartment and help her hang pictures. Matt's off at some group baseball camp that's supposed to help the boys bond as a team, so I figure I'll have the rest of today and all night to convince her."

"Sounds good to me." Nate cocked his head at a sound filtering up the stairs. "Is that the front door?"

"Yeah. I got the chimes hooked up yesterday. It's probably the FedEx guy. My agent called and said he was sending over some contracts for me to sign."

"You don't have to come down," Nate said. "If you stop trimming before you get to the corner, you'll end up with brush marks. I'll get it."

Jack had worked in some of the more dangerous places on the planet. He'd dodged death more times than he'd cared to count. But those DEA operations had been a walk in the park compared to the idea of proposing marriage. Having used visualization techniques successfully in the past to ensure a successful outcome, he was running over the words he'd so painstakingly written down, making sure he'd memorized them so as not to fuck things up when the sound of Nate clearing his throat pulled him back to the present.

"I think you'd better come downstairs, Jack."

His brother's voice was strained. His expression more grim than Jack had ever seen it. Except at their daddy's funeral. Fear struck right at his heart.

"Is it something 'bout Danielle? Is she okay?"

"Yeah." Nate dragged a hand through his shaggy, sun-tipped hair. "It's about Dani. And she's okay, so far as I know. But there's someone here I think you need to meet."

The words were directed at Jack's back as he raced down the stairs two at a time. When he hit the foyer, he came to an abrupt stop, feeling as if he'd just been gutshot. As impossible as it was, a young Dani, looking exactly the way she had back in her early teens, was standing there holding a newspaper in her hand.

"Are you Mr. Callahan?" She may be a dead ringer for a younger Danielle, but her voice revealed no trace of Louisiana.

"Yeah." He knew he was staring but couldn't help himself.

Turnip was doing her happy welcome dance all around the girl, but the dog could have been as invisible as the ghosts supposedly haunting Beau Soleil for all either one of them paid attention to her.

"I read about you. And this house." She held up the tabloid story.

"I see." Jack could not drag his eyes away from those wide blue-green hazel eyes and the sleek slide of blond hair. "Actually, I don't," he admitted.

"I'm sorry." She blushed prettily, and despite knowing absolutely nothing about adolescent girls, Jack thought she possessed a bit more poise than most. "I should have explained." She drew in a deep breath. The hand she pulled through her long hair was trembling, evidence that she wasn't as calm as she was obviously trying to appear. "My name is Holly Reese. . . . And I think . . . well, I believe you might be my father."

* * *

The apartment was finally almost looking livable. Oh, there were still boxes stashed away in the bedroom closet, there might not be as much room as there had been in Fairfax, and it certainly wasn't Beau Soliel, yet it was still home. Dani couldn't wait until Matt returned from baseball camp and saw all the team pennants she'd tacked up on his bedroom walls.

She decided to reward herself for a job well done with a long luxurious bubble bath and was lying back in the tub, her freshly washed hair wrapped in a towel, eyes closed, cooling slices of cucumber on her lids, when someone began pounding on the door.

"Danielle," Jack shouted, "open this door!"

Fear struck like a laser straight into her heart, her first thought being that something had happened to Matt. She sat up, causing the cucumber to fall into the water.

"Goddammit, Danielle," he called again. "I know you're in there."

She leaped from the velvet cling of perfumed water, leaving wet footprints on the tile floor. She'd laid her clothes out on the bed, but far more concerned about her son than how she looked, she grabbed her worn, ancient terrycloth robe from the hook, threw it on, and went racing to the door.

She flung it open, took one look at the murderous scowl on Jack's face and knew that whatever he'd come here about, it couldn't be good.

"What is it?" Her heart beat even faster. She reached out an arm which he brusquely pushed aside as he strode into the apartment. "Is it Matt? Is he hurt?"

"So far as I know Matt's fine." His eyes were hard as agate, his mouth as grim as she'd ever seen it, his words growled through clenched teeth. But relief that he'd not come here about her son had Dani relaxing marginally. Which, she discovered, was a fatal mistake.

She'd thought him dangerous when she'd first tracked him down at Beau Soleil. But a different kind of danger was emanating from him. For the first time since returning home to Blue Bayou, she was looking at the man he'd told her about. The man who'd willingly worked in the shadowy, deadly drug underworld; the man who'd killed the bad guys before they could kill him.

She swallowed, her mouth dry from fear. "Jack . . ." She held out a trembling hand. He ignored it. "What's wrong?"

"Wrong?" He spat the word at her. "How about the fact that I'm not real wild about being played for a goddamn fool?" His large hands took hold of her shoulders, his fingers dug painfully into the flesh beneath the terrycloth. She was about to tell him that he was hurting her, when his next words choked the complaint off in her throat. "Why the hell didn't you tell me we had a daughter?"

The blood drained from her reeling head in a rush. Dani swayed as her knees went weak and would have fallen if he hadn't been holding her so tightly.

"H-h-how . . ." She couldn't talk. Couldn't think. Her mind whirled. "Who told you?"

"You're going to love this." His coldly vicious smile lacked the easygoing warmth she'd come to love. Fire and ice, Dani remembered Desiree saying. "Our daughter showed up at Beau Soleil today."

White dots like the flutter of moth wings danced in front of her eyes. "That's impossible," she whispered raggedly.

"Dammit, don't try to lie your way out of this, Danielle. The timing matches up with her age and she's the spitting image of you. Hell, Nate could see it the minute he opened the door."

"It can't be." She shook her head, unable to make sense of this while her stomach was in her throat and her mind felt as if it'd been hit with a sledgehammer. "Jack." When the moths turned into a blizzard, she grabbed hold of his arms to keep from falling to the floor. "Please let me sit down." His muscles tensed beneath her fingers. "I'm going to faint."

Apparently seeing that about this, at least, she was telling the truth, he dragged her over to the couch she'd bought at an antique shop he'd taken her to in Houma, pushed her onto the cushions it had taken her two nights of sewing to cover with pretty magnolia-printed fabric, and shoved her head between her bare knees.

"Take a deep breath."

The indrawn air burned her lungs. Despite outside temperatures in the nineties, she was cold. So cold.

The towel came unwound as he pressed harder; her damp hair fell over her shoulders and face. She was shivering like a woman stumbling through an Arctic blizzard.

"Keep your head down and don't move. I'll be right back."

She couldn't have moved if she'd wanted to. As she continued to take the deep breaths that became less painful and began to clear her head, Dani heard the heels of his cowboy boots striking like hammers on the wooden floor. There was the sound of water running from the kitchen, then he was back.

"Here." He took hold of her hair, dragged her head up, and shoved a glass into her hand. "Drink this."

A little water splashed over the rim and onto her bare leg as her unsteady hand lifted the glass to her mouth. The water was cool against her throat, and helped clear out the lingering clouds of vertigo.

"Thank you," she managed.

"Don't thank me; I just don' want you passin' out on me till I get the truth." He sat down in an overstuffed chair across from her that still needed recovering and pulled a cigarette pack from his shirt pocket.

"I thought you'd quit," she said before she could stop herself.

He speared her with another of those icy looks. "And I thought I could trust you. Seems we both were wrong."

He struck the match on the sole of his boot, lit the cigarette, and inhaled. "Okay," he instructed, "start talking."

He sounded as if she were one of his prisoners he was interrogating. Dani realized on some level that while he had every right to be upset, she should be angry that after how close she'd thought they'd become, he had so little trust in her, but at the moment she was too confused to try to stand up to a man who was undoubtedly an expert at intimidation.

"I don't know where to start."

"The usual way to start a story is from the beginning. Why don't you try that?"

"All right." She drew in a ragged breath and tried to compose her thoughts. "I didn't find out I was pregnant until after you left."

"But you chose not to tell me."

Unable to bear the coldness in those eyes that had only ever looked at her with warmth, Dani looked down at her hands. "I didn't know where you were."

"You could have asked my mother."

"I didn't think you'd want to know," she said softly. Miserably.

He slammed his hand down onto the table beside the chair. "Goddammit, look at me when I'm talking to you."

She lifted her chin and returned her gaze to his. "I didn't think you'd want to know," she repeated with a bit more strength. "After all, you were certainly there when the condom tore. But instead of sticking around to make sure everything would be okay, you took off right after I'd told you that I loved you."

"You know why I left."

"Now." The part of her who'd survived being deserted by the man she loved, then given birth to a child, only to have it die, the person who'd gone on to endure a passionless marriage and not crumble when publicly humiliated in front of the entire country, rose to help her deal with this latest personal disaster. "At the time I had no way of knowing that my father had blackmailed you into leaving."

"Did *Maman* know?"

"Yes." The pain that shot into his eyes echoed within her. Dani knew that what he was obviously viewing as his mother's betrayal must hurt nearly as much—if not more—than what she'd done. "Your mother supported my father's decision that I go away, have the baby, adopt it out, then go on to college."

"What a nice, tidy little plan you all worked out," he said dryly. "Interesting that no one thought to ask my opinion."

"How could I have known what you wanted?" she asked on a flare of heat. "You never said anything about loving me, or wanting anything more than just sex. You have to understand how things were. I was seventeen, Jack, a naive and in many ways a very immature seventeen. I didn't have any legal rights, and when my father and your mother began pressuring me to give up my child—"

"Our child."

She dipped her head in acknowledgment of his gritty correction. "They convinced me that my desire to keep *our* child was a schoolgirl's romantic fantasy. That giving it up for adoption would be the right thing to do. For everyone involved, especially the baby who deserved to be raised in a loving family with a mother and a father."

"She had a mother and a father." He drew in on the cigarette, exhaled smoke on a long, frustrated breath. "Or could have, if everyone hadn't decided to keep my daughter a secret."

"I'll admit that was horribly wrong. I didn't see it then, but I do now. There was just so much pressure coming from all directions. My father found a home for unwed mothers, and Marie drove me there. There were forty of us living in the house, and while I'm sure it wasn't nearly as harsh as that camp you were in, the rules were horribly strict—we weren't allowed to ever use our last names, have phone calls or visitors, except for our parents, and we were only allowed to go outside for three hours on Saturdays, and even then we had to always be with another girl.

"We had weekly counseling sessions, which were a joke, because they all centered around how trying to raise a child would ruin our lives, that we weren't emotionally prepared to be mothers, and how there were all these wonderful, loving parents just waiting for our babies.

"I've blocked some of that time out, but I do remember lying in bed, night after night, hoping that you'd come and rescue me—"

"Which would have been a bit difficult. Since I had no idea where you were. Or why."

"I know. As I said, I was naively romantic back then. I also had these terrible dark days when I'd think that they were right, that if I was foolish enough to get pregnant, I didn't deserve to have a child. Because I wouldn't be able to take care of it, and keep it safe."

Dani pressed a hand against her stomach as old feelings of shame she'd thought she'd overcome twisted inside her. "It wasn't until I was pregnant with Matt that I realized I'd undergone some sort of brainwashing. . . .

"Really," she insisted when he arched a mocking brow. "Not one minute of our prenatal training had ever offered a single piece of information on how to take care of our babies after they were born. Because adoption was a foregone conclusion. We were nothing more than a business to them, part of a profitable, child-procurement process."

"Maybe you ought to be the one writing stories," he suggested. "You could write this one as the heroine being a pregnant Oliver Twist character."

"That isn't a very nice thing to say."

"Perhaps you haven't noticed, *chère*, but I'm not exactly in any mood to be nice." The endearment was as frosty as his gaze.

"I was honestly going to tell you, but things kept happening. . . . No," she admitted on a soft, shuddering sigh, "that's not the truth. I kept putting it off because things were going so well and I was afraid when you learned the truth, you'd hate me."

"So you thought that would be an appropriate response?"

She could see the trap. "It might have been, if you didn't understand—"

"What I understand is that you lied to me, Danielle."

"It wasn't exactly a lie. More a sin of omission."

"You lied. Hell, why should I believe you ever would have told me if it hadn't come out? If she hadn't shown up at Beau Soleil?"

This was what Dani was finding more confusing about this entire horrible event. "That's impossible," she insisted. "She couldn't be at Beau Soleil."

"Why not?"

"Because she died, dammit!" Dani leaped to her feet. "Before she was a day old. Which broke my heart and is one of the reasons I put off telling you. Because there was nothing that could ever be done to set things right, and from how you were when I first saw you, along with the nightmares, I just kept telling myself that you'd already had enough death in your life!"

Nerves had her shouting at him when what she wanted was for him to hold her, and for her to told him back, while they figured out some way to get through this pain together.

He ground the cigarette out in a little crystal dish and pushed himself out of the chair. "There's no point in keeping this farce up, Danielle. Unless you've got an identical twin out there you didn't tell me about, who got knocked up the same summer you and I were goin' at it, there's no denying the girl is yours."

"It's impossible," she repeated through lips that felt like stone. She'd seen the death certificate. And had cried her eyes out for weeks afterward. "I'd changed my mind. An hour after she was born, the lawyers arrived at the hospital with the consent forms. But I realized, after having carried her for all those months, after having brought her into the world, there was no way I could ever give her up.

"I was exhausted from nearly twenty hours of labor, confused, and more scared than I'd ever been in my life, even more than when I first realized I was pregnant and I had no idea what, exactly I was going to do. But I did know I was going to take her away with me!" She slapped a hand against his chest, angry and aching and nearly as shaken as she'd been that long ago day.

"Sure you were." She felt the spike of his heartbeat beneath her fingertips. "The same way you were going to tell me."

"I was."

Their eyes clashed. A sizzle of electrical charge zapped through her, and as she watched the black of his pupils widen, like molten obsidian flowing over topaz, she knew that Jack felt it, too.

"Goddammit, what is it about you?" His face could have been chiseled from granite. His jaw was clenched, his mouth a hard grim line. "You've kept my child from me, lied through those pretty white teeth, continue to deny the truth, even when I've confronted you with irrefutable proof, and in spite of all that, I still want you."

Dani felt another moment of dizziness. If any other man had looked at her the way he was looking at her now, with such lust-edged anger she'd be terrified. But as a familiar warmth curled through her, she didn't fear Jack. She loved him. And wanted him. Desperately.

She knew he'd seen the answering hunger on her face when his hold on her tightened, like a black velvet bond and he drew her closer, so close she could feel the heat rising off his body. His very aroused body. The short robe had loosened and the feel of denim against her bare skin was unbearably erotic.

"I want you, too," she whispered.

His curse, in French, was vicious as his mouth swooped down, crushing hers, demanding retribution, capitulation, fueling the flames that had been smoldering beneath all that ice. He splayed his hand against the back of her head, refusing to allow her to escape the plundering kiss.

Her breath was nearly knocked out of her as they fell onto the couch, his body pressing her deep into the pretty flowered cushions.

His mouth ravaged hers, his lips sped over her face, his teeth scraped the cord in her neck as she twisted beneath him. His fingertips, roughened by work, scraped against her nipples, drawing a ragged moan; her teeth nipped his bottom lip, making him curse.

Jack wanted to hate her. Needed to love her. The dual hungers burned through him as they rolled off the couch and onto a needlepoint rug blooming with soft pastel flowers. Lifting himself above her, he looked down into her flushed face. Her eyes were emerald with passion, her shallow breath was coming in quick pants, her perfumed body slick.

"Jus' so we don't have any misunderstandings about what's happening here afterward, tell me again. That you want me."

"I course I do. I always have."

If the way she arched against his roving hand was any indication, about this, anyway, she was telling the truth.

"Say it." He skimmed a hand over her, from her breasts to the soft folds of flesh that were hot to the touch. She was warm and wet and ready for him. "Say 'I want you to fuck me, Jack.' "

"Jack, please, don't make me—"

"Say it."

He could see her heart in her moist green eyes, and if he hadn't been trying so hard to hate her, the hurt he'd inflicted would have broken Jack's own heart.

"I want you, Jack."

"The rest." He pressed his hand against her, drawing forth a long, throaty moan. "Say the rest."

"I want you to fuck me."

When the words were torn from her on a stifled sob, Jack discovered that an attack of conscience didn't necessarily diminish rampant lust. Having gotten his answer, he yanked down the zipper on his jeans and surged into her.

She cried out, then wrapped her long legs around his waist as he pounded into her like a man possessed. The ripe scent of passion filled the air as mouth to mouth, hot flesh slapping against hot flesh, they moved together, driving each other to the brink of sanity. Then beyond.

She came first, with a strangled cry, the climax shuddering through her. As the inner orgasmic tremors surrounded his cock, clutched at him, a red haze shimmered in front of Jack's eyes. He gave one last deep thrust, then, clenching his teeth to keep from calling out her name, he flooded into her.

Afterward, he lay sprawled on her limp body, feeling as if the air had been sucked from his lungs. The sex, as always with Dani, had been hot, but this time, instead of leaving him feeling as if he could outrun speeding bullets and leap skyscrapers in a single bound, Jack was overcome by regrets too numerous to calculate while his body was still throbbing inside her, his mind was covered in thick dark clouds and his heart still felt as if it had been shred to ribbons.

Because he wanted to stay here with her, to gather her into his arms and try to understand what she'd been thinking and feeling back then, as well as her reasons for having deceived him this summer, he levered himself off her.

"I'll let you meet her," he said as he refastened the jeans he hadn't bothered taking off. Hell, Jack figured he'd probably had more finesse in his teens than he had just now. "Since she deserves to know her mother. And you're going to have to pretend to care. For her sake."

"I do care." She'd wept while they'd made love. No, while they'd fucked, he corrected grimly since love had had nothing to do with the hot coupling that had edged as close to violence as he'd ever want to feel with any woman. That it had happened with her only made it worse.

Her face was wet and tearstained as she sat up and tugged the short robe closed. "I still can't understand how this can be true, how she could have been alive all these years. But maybe there was a mixup at the hospital. . . ."

"Give it a break, Danielle," Jack said wearily. "The bottom line is that you gave my child away—"

"Our child," she corrected quietly as he had earlier.

"You gave her away without so much as a backward glance. Without letting her know her father. Hell, she has two uncles she's never met because of you."

Dani was on her knees now. "My God, Jack, you know how much I missed growing up without a mother, how hard it was for me never being allowed to so much as mention her name, let alone talk about her with my father. How could you believe I'd abandon my own daughter?"

It was, he allowed, a good point. And one he'd have to consider later, after the lingering shock of today's revelation had worn off, his head had cleared, and he was able to think everything through.

"How did she find you?" Dani asked on a tear-clogged voice when he didn't respond. "How did she know? Where is she now?"

Jack didn't want to talk about this anymore. Couldn't, without risking crying himself. "She's with Nate at Beau Soleil. I'll let her answer the rest of your questions when you meet."

"When? Tonight?"

"I don't know." Since it was too painful looking at that beautiful tearstained face that was both wretched and hopeful at the same time, he turned and walked away. As he shut the apartment door behind him, Jack did not look back.

If he had, he would have seen Dani slump back down to the rug she'd been so excited about finding only last week, her slender shoulders shaking as she buried her face in her hands and sobbed.

# 25

*It didn't take Dani* any time at all to figure out that it wasn't likely Jack would be so furious, or so willing to condemn her, without a very good reason. Following on that conclusion was the understanding that whatever had happened that summer, her father was behind it.

Taking a shower to wash off the scents of sex and despair, she threw on a pair of shorts, T-shirt, and sandals, and wove her wet hair into a loose braid. Not taking the time to put on any makeup, she drove straight to Orèlia's, finding the judge alone, puttering around the garden as he'd begun doing the past couple weeks since he'd begun getting a bit stronger. And, she'd thought optimistically, less negative.

Dani did not bother with pleasantries. "Father, we need to talk."

He glanced up from weeding the flowers around the brick patio, taking in her red-rimmed eyes and puffy face. "You look terrible. Are you coming down with something?"

"No. You don't have to worry. I'm not contagious." Dr. Ancelet had warned that a virus or infection another person might be able to easily throw off could be fatal for her father.

"I wasn't thinking about that." He stood up, pulling off the gloves. "Believe it or not, I was concerned for you."

"I think it's a little late for that." Her heart was pounding in her throat, her ears, her head. "Jack had a visitor out at Beau Soleil today."

He arched a brow at her formal tone. "Oh? Something about that foolish ghost story?" He poured a glass of iced tea from a pitcher on a wrought-iron patio table. "Would you like some tea?"

"No. I don't want anything but the truth. I didn't meet her, but apparently she was a child. A thirteen-year-old girl who amazingly, according to Jack, looks a great deal like I did at her age."

"Ah." He nodded.

"Is that all you have to say?"

"Did this girl happen to say who she was?"

"I didn't get her name."

How could she have let Jack leave without finding that much out? Dani agonized. What if her daughter ran away before they had a chance to meet? To talk? What if she left before Dani tried to find a way to explain something she couldn't comprehend herself?

"But she alleges that she's my daughter. Which we both know is impossible. Since my baby died."

He didn't respond. He didn't have to.

"That *is* what happened, isn't it, Father? My baby died. You did, after all, show me the death certificate." It had read Baby Jane Doe. Dani had wept that her father had not even consulted her about the baby at least being given the Dupree family name.

"There's no point in using that tone with me, Danielle. Since it's obvious that you already know the truth."

"But that's just it!" she shouted, amazed to find herself on the verge of crying again when she wouldn't have thought she'd have any tears left after this horrid afternoon. "I don't know. Oh, I thought I did. But now I realize that everyone was lying to me."

"Not everyone. Only some of the staff at the hospital, who were well paid to keep silent."

"The adoption social worker didn't know?"

"I did what I thought best on a need-to-know basis. And she didn't need to know."

"Who signed the consent forms?"

"The nursery room nurse. She agreed with me that it was the best thing for all concerned."

"What about the people who took my daughter? Did they know?"

"No. I was concerned that if they knew the truth, their consciences might overtake their good sense and desire for a child and they'd back out of the adoption."

"I see." She pressed her hand against her stomach, which was roiling. "And Marie?"

"There was no way I was going to let her know the truth. She eventually would have notified Jack, or regretted having lost the chance to be a grandmother to her first grandchild. It was a risk I couldn't take."

"There you go again!" Dani was trembling like a leaf. "Putting yourself at the center of things. Pulling the strings as if people were only puppets for you to control."

"You were my daughter. I knew what was best for you. Besides, the night before you went into labor, you told one of the nurses that you were thinking of keeping the baby."

"That's right. I was."

"Which was why," he said patiently, "I had to arrange for you to believe the child had died. So you wouldn't ruin your life. Your entire future."

"Oh, God." She dragged a hand down her face. Drew in a deep, shuddering breath. "I've tried to live up to your expectations. I've tried to be the exemplary daughter, to always do what you wanted, to somehow make us into some kind of idealized *Father Knows Best* family—"

"Your father did know best."

"No." Dani shook her head. "You didn't know anything about me. About what I wanted, what was right for me, because you never loved me enough to get to know you."

"That's not true."

"Don't lie." She felt the ice begin to flow over her heart, allowing her mind to cool. Her thoughts to calm. "I'm not leaving Blue Bayou, because I'm not going to let you chase me away from the home I've made for my child.

"My children," she said, thinking with wonder that it appeared to be true. That she did, indeed have a daughter she'd never known about, a child who'd been cruelly kept from her. And somehow, she was going to have to convince both Jack and her newly found daughter that she'd never knowingly abandoned her.

"What you did was evil and manipulative and there is no way I'm going to let either of my children anywhere near you."

"Danielle—"

"Don't." She knocked away his outstretched hand. "I don't want you to touch me. I don't want you to speak to me." She turned to leave. "And I don't want to ever see you again for the rest of my life."

He called out again, and although his weakened tone tugged familial chords and played on her conscience, Dani kept walking toward the Volvo she'd parked at the curb.

It was the sound of glass shattering that had her turning around to see that he'd dropped the tea. Then, grabbing the edge of the table with one hand, his chest with the other, as she watched in horror, the judge collapsed to the patio, pulling the glass-topped table down on top of him.

What if she'd killed him? As badly as her father had hurt her, as angry as she'd been, Dani knew she'd never be able to forgive herself.

"I knew about his heart," she said to Orèlia, who'd arrived home from grocery shopping during all the excitement. "I knew how easily he could die."

As soon as she'd seen her father collapse, Dani had rushed to him, frantically trying to remember the CPR course she'd taken at a Fairfax fire station while dialing 911 on her cell phone. She'd managed to get an aspirin down his throat and was on her knees, pressing on his chest, struggling to count out the rhythm over the screaming inside her head when the paramedics arrived after what seemed like a lifetime but had only been, she'd learned later, four minutes after her call.

They'd taken over with brisk efficiency, the man setting up a portable monitor and ripping open her father's shirt to place the defibrillator paddles while the woman snapped an oxygen mask on his face and began installing a breathing tube in his throat.

Dani's heart dived and her blood pressure spiked when she viewed her father's heartbeat wiggling all over the monitor like fluorescent green worms.

She knew that if she lived to be a hundred, she'd never forget the sight of his body jerking upward when they zapped the electrical charge into it. The paramedics established an IV, lifted him onto the rolling gurney, and rushed him into the ambulance. Dani had gone with them, while Orèlia promised to follow in her car.

He'd gone into fibrillation again as they'd careened through the streets, siren wailing, tires thudding joltingly against the cobblestones she had, until then, considered charmingly picturesque.

The moment they'd reached the ER, she'd been abruptly shut out of the process; as the double doors slammed closed, cutting her off from her father, Dani was nearly overwhelmed with guilt.

Fortunately, Orèlia, foregoing any concern about speed limits, had arrived right behind the ambulance, taking care of the admission paperwork when Dani had been too numb to answer. After promising Dani she'd be right back, she had taken off to find out what exactly was happening to the judge behind those doors.

"He's not dead, *chère*," she said now as Dani paced the nearly deserted waiting room outside the ER.

"Not yet, maybe. But I saw his heartbeat on the monitor. It was all over the place. How can anyone survive that?"

"People have, and worse. You're not a doctor, you. So don' go jumpin' to conclusions. And sit down. You're making me nervous with all that walkin' back and forth. Besides, you look like you're gonna pass out any minute."

Dani managed a weak, humorless laugh at that diagnosis. "It appears to be the day for that," she murmured as she nevertheless sank down onto an obnoxiously orange couch. "Were you able to find out anything?"

"They've got the judge stabilized and are movin' him up to surgery."

"Surgery? I thought Dr. Ancelet said he was too weak to be a good surgical candidate."

"I'm sure they wouldn't be operating if they didn't think it was the best thing to do," the older woman assured her.

"Can't I see him, just for a minute? Talk to him?" Dani couldn't bear the thought of her father dying without her having a chance to apologize. He'd caused a great deal of emotional and personal pain, but didn't deserve to die for his actions.

"Darlin', you know I love you to pieces, but right now you'd just be in the way. Your daddy's in good hands. Seems there was a surgeon from Tulane in town to do some fishing tomorrow with the ER doctor. They called him at the Plantation Inn, where he's staying, and he came right over." She patted Dani's hand. "Isn't that lucky?"

"I'm sorry, but I'm having trouble finding anything about this day lucky."

As Dani struggled not to cry, she looked across the room and saw a little boy, running a toy truck back and forth across the green-and-white tile floor. His pregnant mother sat patiently nearby, reading a paperback romance novel. She'd told Dani she was waiting for her husband, who was in the ER getting a fish hook removed from his cheek. The pirate on the cover of the novel reminded Dani of Jack, which only increased her misery, while the sight of the boy and truck made her think of her own son.

"Do you think I should bring Matt home from baseball camp? Just in case?"

"I'd let him stay," Orèlia decided. "The camp's a big deal for the boy, and it'd take at least eight hours to get him down here. He's due home tomorrow. If the judge's gonna die, it'll probably be in the next few hours, so Matt would miss sayin' goodbye anyway even if we could get someone to drive him back to town. If he lives, there'll have been no point in disrupting his life."

"His life has been nothing but disruptions for the past two years."

"*Non*. It may have been shaken up, true enough. But you've provided a lot of stability for the child, Danielle. And it shows." She stroked Dani's hair in a soothing, reassuring way Dani had so often, during childhood, fantasized a mother doing. "Why don't I call Jack? He can come hold your hand."

"Jack wouldn't walk across the street to talk to me, let alone hold my hand."

Orange painted eyebrows flew up nearly to the birdnest hair. "*Comment sa se fait?* Did you two have yourselves a little lover's quarrel?"

"It was a lot more than a quarrel." Dani rubbed her temple with her fingertips. "It seems our daughter showed up at Beau Soleil today. Needless to say, he was surprised."

"He's not the only one." Orèlia's eyes widened and her raspberry red mouth made a little O of shock. "How could that be? Did you tell him he was mistaken?"

"At first. But I wasn't exactly standing on very firm ground having never told him I'd been pregnant in the first place."

"I can see that would be a problem," Orèlia said with a thoughtful nod. "But since the poor little *bébé* died—"

"She didn't." Dani sighed, thinking how strange it was that this should be the happiest day of her life, but was, instead, turning out to be one of her worst. "Father lied."

Orèlia exhaled a slow whistle. "Well. I wish I could say that I couldn't believe such a thing, but I suppose, knowin' the judge, it's not totally out of character. Have you met her? Your daughter? What's her name? Where is she now?"

"She's at Beau Soleil with her father and uncle, I was too shocked to ask her name, and if Jack has his way, I'll probably never meet her."

"*Non.*" Orèlia discarded that idea with a wave of her hand. "He's just angry, he. And hurt. Not to mention his male pride havin' been damaged. But Jack Callahan is a good man, Danielle. He won' try to keep your daughter from you. And it's obvious he loves you, so you'll see, all this will blow over quick enough."

Remembering Jack's face, as he'd walked out of her apartment and her life, Dani couldn't be nearly so optimistic.

She moved upstairs to another waiting room outside the CCU, which is where they told her her father would be taken after surgery and discovered the room was well named. It was as if her life had been put on hold; there was nothing to do but wait and see how this cruel trick that had been played on her was going to end. The magazines were old. Over the many months recipes and coupons had been clipped out of them, which hadn't left all that many articles intact. Not that she could have concentrated anyway.

She tried reading about the problems of the sandwich generation, stories of women tending for ill, aging parents while raising children of their own, but all that did was make her focus even more on how she could well end up discovering a daughter and losing her father all on the same day. Which she suspected, wasn't exactly the thrust of the article.

She jumped up when Eve Ancelet appeared in the door, a tall, distinguished-looking man at her side. They were both wearing green surgical scrubs.

"He's doing fine," Eve assured her.

"If he was fine, he wouldn't be here," Dani snapped. Then immediately apologized.

"Don't worry about it," the doctor brushed her apology off. "This is a stressful time, and heaven knows, hospitals aren't the most calming of places." She introduced the man as Dr. Young, who was, indeed, on the surgical staff at Tulane.

"Your father suffered an incident of arrhythmia," Eve explained. "Which is simply an irregular heartbeat. They're actually quite common and many are harmless, but given the fact that the judge is already suffering from dilated cardiomyopathy, Dr. Young and I both felt that he could benefit from an implantable defibrillator."

"I thought you said he wasn't strong enough for surgery."

"This surgery isn't all that intrusive, as surgeries go," Dr. Young said. "Earlier models were about the size of a pack of cigarettes, were implanted beneath the skin of the abdomen, and required open heart surgery to attach the electrodes to the heart. The latest model, which your father received, is much smaller, can be placed beneath the skin of the chest, and only requires a single electrode that can be routed into the heart through a vein."

"The defibrillator has a tiny computer which uses the electrode to constantly monitor the heartbeat," Eve picked up the explanation. "If it detects even a minor arrhythmia, it activates the built-in pacemaker to restabilize the heart's rhythm. If that fails, it delivers a jolt to the heart."

Dani didn't think she'd ever forget the sight of her father being violently jolted back to life by those EMTs. "Isn't that incredibly painful?"

"Not nearly as much as the muscle-contracting jolt delivered by the more traditional defibrillators you're probably thinking of," Dr. Young said.

"In fact unlike first-generation models, which could only deliver a maximum jolt several times a day, this one starts out small," Eve said. "Then, if necessary, builds, but, as Dr. Young told you, it's nothing like what you saw done to your father. In fact, patients report that the low-level charge, which often does the job, is barely noticable."

It was as if they were a medical tag team. Dani kept looking from one to the other, trying to see if there was anything they might not be telling her.

"Does this mean you expect more incidences?" she asked, thinking what a mild word that was for such a horrific event.

"There's a strong possibility," Eve allowed. "Though this has upped your father's chances for a longer life considerably, Dani. As I told you during our meeting in my office, while medication can reduce the mortality rate of ventricular tachycardia by fifteen to twenty-five percent, the implantable defibrillator cuts it down as low as two percent."

Dani asked more questions, received answers that had her feeling better than she had when she'd arrived, although she was still horribly concerned.

The doctors left. The shift changed. New nurses, their manner brisk and efficient, came on duty. Dinner trays were delivered and picked up again. More doctors arrived on the floor to put on starched white lab coats and make evening rounds. The waiting room began filling up with other patients' family members who'd come for visiting hours.

Orèlia brought Dani cups of tea and coffee and cola from the vending machine she kept forgetting to drink, food from the cafeteria she couldn't eat since it would have been impossible to swallow with a lump that felt as solid as Captain Callahan's statue stuck in her throat.

She heard a Code Blue announced and felt as if her own heart stopped as the team rushed by the waiting room door to the CCU.

"Who is it?" Dani asked the gray-haired woman manning the nurse's desk.

"Don't worry, *chère,*" the nurse assured her with a sympathetic smile. "It's not the judge."

A cooling relief rushed through Dani. A relief that was fleeting as the waiting continued.

Watching the clock, she knew that outside the hospital, night would be beginning to settle over the bayou. Inside the walls it remained constant day, the alien world lit by a complexion-draining fluorescent light. Having grown accustomed to the restful night music of bullfrogs, owls, and crickets, Dani was intensely aware of not just the loud noises, like those disembodied voices that seemed to never stop crackling over the intercom, but the softer sounds, as well. The swoosh of rubber-soled shoes, the tap of fingers on the computer keyboard, the sound of the elevator opening and closing, the click of beads and murmured prayers of a rosary being said in French from somewhere down the hallway, the occasional soft moan drifting on the antiseptic scented air, all conspired to spark at her nerves like fingernails being dragged down a chalkboard.

Gradually the visitors drifted away, leaving Dani alone in the waiting room with Orèlia. The shift changed again. And still she hadn't been allowed to see her father.

A nurse came and told Dani the judge was sleeping. "Why don't you go home and do the same thing yourself?" she suggested gently. "Get some rest so you'll be fresh for your father in the morning."

"I'll be fine," Dani said. "And I'm staying."

The nurse took one look at the determination in her eyes, exchanged a glance with Orèlia, who shrugged, then, with a resigned sigh, returned to charting meds.

Much, much later, feeling guilty that she was subjecting Orèlia, who refused to leave while Dani remained at the hospital, to the same interminable waiting, Dani arranged with the nurse for her to be able to use one of the empty rooms.

"I'll just take a short nap," the older woman promised. "So long as you promise to wake me if anything happens."

Dani promised. And her vigil continued.

She was standing at the window, staring out over the bayou, to where she could just barely make out the distant lights of the ships on the Gulf waterways, twinkling like fallen stars, when she realized she was no longer the only person in the waiting room. Steeling herself for bad news, she slowly turned toward the doorway, her knees nearly buckling when she saw Jack standing there.

# 26

*He looked every bit* as beat up as Dani felt. His hair was loose and looked as if he'd been thrusting his hands through it, his face, heavily shadowed by a midnight dark beard, was drawn and his eyes weary. But he was still the most wonderful sight she'd ever seen.

"I just heard," he said. "Actually Nate did. There was a news bulletin on the radio."

"Oh." When she hadn't been worrying about her father, Dani had been going over what she would eventually say to Jack. She'd rejected innumerable lines, but none had been as insufficient as that single word that had just come out of her mouth.

"Have you been alone all this time?"

She glanced around the waiting room as if surprised by the question. Brushed at the heavy wrinkles across the front of her shorts. "No." Determined to manage more than a stumbling monosyllable, she added, "Orèlia's been with me. I made her go take a nap."

He nodded, seeming as uncomfortable with this conversation as she was. "That's good. That she's been here. And that she's resting."

"Yes."

They were standing there across the room from each other. Exhausted and frightened and relieved that he'd come, all at the same time, Dani couldn't decide whether to weep or throw herself into his arms. So she did neither.

"I brought her," he said, breaking the silence that had stretched between them.

"You did?" Feeling as if she were having an incident of arrhythmia herself, Dani looked past him into the hallway.

"She's downstairs with Nate. I wanted a couple minutes to prepare you."

Dani opened her mouth to speak, but her throat was burning and the lump was back, blocking any words. She bit her lip, fought for composure and tried again. "Thank you."

He cursed. A rough, French word that needed no translation and seemed directed inward. Then, shaking his head, he opened his arms. *"Viens ici, mon coeur."*

Dani didn't need a second invitation. She flew into those strong outstretched arms like a sparrow winging toward safety in a hurricane. And when she felt them tighten around her, holding her close, she knew she'd come home.

"I'm so sorry," she said against the front of his shirt.

"I know." She felt his weary sigh ruffle her hair. "Me, too."

"You?" She lifted her eyes to his. "You don't have anything to apologize for."

"I didn't believe you. I was rough with you." He frowned as he took in the bruises on her upper arms.

"No." She touched her palm to his rough cheek. "You not believing me was my own fault for not having been truthful from the start. As for what happened, that was every bit as much my doing as yours." She managed a faint, wry smile. "It was also rather thrilling, while it was happening."

When she felt the deep rumbling chuckle in his chest, Dani knew that it was going to be all right. That they'd be all right.

"I know you have a lot of questions."

"They can wait." He raked a hand through his hair, then touched his palm to her cheek. "I should have been there."

And would have been, she knew now. If only she'd told him. "Of course you're right. I made a terrible decision."

"You were too young to be making any decisions under so much pressure. What I hate is the idea of you having gone through all that alone. I should have been with you when our child was born. I should have taken care of you. All the way back to Beau Soleil, I kept thinking of all the things I could have done to change things. If I'd stayed—"

"You had no choice."

"That's not true. Looking back on that day, I know that even if your father had made good his threat, my *maman* would have survived. She was a strong woman who'd overcome losing her husband. Losing her job wouldn't have been the end of the world.

"I should have stayed," he repeated with more strength. "Because I loved you. And you loved me. We may have been too young for marriage, but we would have made it work. Somehow."

Dani didn't know which surprising statement to take first. "You loved me?"

"*Mais*, yeah. Oh, I'd fought like hell against it. But that last night I realized that what we had going for us was a lot more than just sex."

"The night we made our daughter."

"Yeah." He took another deep breath, then frowned at his watch. "We need to talk. Make plans. But I figure we've got about two minutes before Nate and Holly get up here—"

"Her name's Holly?"

"Yeah." His smile lit his tawny eyes and warmed her heart. "You're gonna love her, *chère*." He brushed his lips against her temple. "And she's going to love you." Skimmed them down her cheek. "Just like I do."

They were the words she'd waited thirteen years to hear. And they were even more glorious than in her most romantic fantasies. Dani was about to tell him that she loved him, too, had always loved him, when his roving lips met hers and she was lost.

She sank into the kiss, twining her arms around his neck, going up onto her toes to kiss him back. He pulled her hard against him and held her as if he'd never let her go. As if she had any intention of going anywhere, Dani thought as her mouth clung and her heart soared.

"Hold that thought," he said, putting his hands on her shoulders as he broke off the kiss. And not a moment too soon, as Dani heard Nate clear his throat.

She braced herself as Jack ran his hands down her arms, soothing her inward tremors. Then he shifted to stand beside her and she was looking into a young face that was familiar and foreign at the same time. As she stared at this beautiful blond child poised on the brink of womanhood, a tangled blend of joy and panic clogged her throat. The years spun away and she was holding her little girl in her arms, pressing her lips against the downy fuzz atop the infant's head.

Then the doctor had snapped at the nurse who had, without thinking, broken the maternity home rules by allowing the unwed mother even that brief, fleeting moment to bond with the baby she'd carried beneath her heart for nine long months. Dani had wept after they'd snatched her daughter away and rushed her from the cold sterility of the delivery room.

She'd held firm when the grim-faced lawyers ganged up with the woman who ran the home, using every argument against her keeping her baby, even going so far as to call the judge to try to reason with her.

Then she'd screamed when, after sneaking down the hallway to the nursery before dawn the next morning, she'd been told that her baby hadn't survived the night. Refusing to believe it, she'd hysterically demanded to see her child. This child, she realized now with wonder.

They'd called a doctor, who, while two burly orderlies had held her down, injected her with something to calm her down. When she finally emerged from her drugged stupor two days later, her father had been waiting with her daughter's death certificate.

After leaving the hospital, her breasts aching from the pills they'd given her to dry up her milk, Dani would have the same dream every night. A dream that it had all been a horrible mistake, that Jack had returned home from wherever he'd gone, had been thrilled to discover he was a father, had proposed right on the spot and the three of them had all left the hospital together, their daughter dressed in a ruffled pink dress, little white socks on her pudgy feet and one of those stretchy baby headbands, to begin a new life together.

The dream had become more infrequent over the years, especially after Matt had been born, but it always returned on the anniversary of her first child's birth.

Now, wonder of wonders, it was turning out not to be a dream after all, and Dani couldn't say a word.

"Holly," Jack said, jumping into the breach to rescue her, "this is your mother. Danielle, meet Holly."

"Hi," Holly said. Beneath a poise beyond her years, Dani sensed nerves as tangled as her own.

"Oh, baby." Dani felt her eyes mist. "I want to hold you."

Holly's blue-green eyes, which were like looking into a mirror, were moist and shiny as well. "I think I'd like that," she admitted on a voice that was more child than woman.

Dani was across the room without having been aware of moving and gathered her daughter close, holding her to her breast as she'd dreamed of doing so many times.

When she'd finally accepted that what Jack had told her was true, Dani had been terrified that her child would, at worst, hate her. At best, resent her for having abandoned her. But as she felt the slender arms wrap around her waist, she allowed herself a glimmer of hope.

"Where have you been all these years? How did you know to come here to Blue Bayou? To Beau Soleil? Did you come with your"—she could not yet say the word *parents* in regard to anyone but she and Jack—"the people who adopted you?"

Holly opted to answer the last of Dani's breathless, rapid fire questions first. "My parents died when I was nearly ten. They were sailing off Depoe Bay—that's in Oregon—when their boat capsized."

Dani rubbed circles against Holly's slender back. "That must have been terrible."

"It was. I was sent to live with my uncle in Oceanside, he was in the Marines, but I'd never met him because I guess he and my dad, my adoptive dad," she corrected with a quick look Jack's way, "didn't get along real well."

"He was your dad in all the ways that counted," Jack said. "No one's going to try to take that away from you, *chère*."

Relief flittered across her face.

"Does your uncle know where you are?" Dani knew she'd be frantic if Matt just took off and left home.

"No. But he wouldn't really care."

"Of course he would," Dani said, feeling the need to stick up for this man she'd never met, if only to reassure her daughter that she was loved.

"I really don't think so, since I haven't seen him for the past couple years."

Dani exchanged a startled look with Jack, who nodded. "They got a divorce," he revealed, helping Holly out a bit with catching Dani up to date. "Apparently his wife had kids from a previous marriage and didn't feel any responsibility to her brother-in-law's child. And it was tough for him, since he's in the military and has to move around a lot."

Dani was certain there must be some sort of family hardship circumstances that would have gotten him out of the Marines, but didn't remark on this possibility since she didn't want to hurt her daughter any more than she'd already been hurt.

"So where have you been since then?" she asked, dreading the answer.

"In foster care," Holly said in a matter-of-fact way that broke Dani's heart. "Uncle Phil signed away custodial rights, so I could have been adopted out, but people don't want older kids, so that wasn't much of an option."

Dear Lord. How was she ever going to make this up to her? Dani wondered miserably.

"I told her that there're lots of people who'd love to adopt a *jolie fille* like herself," Jack revealed. "Not that she has to worry 'bout that, now that she's got us."

"Absolutely," Dani agreed, trying to read Holly's face to see what she thought about this. She desperately wanted to assure her that she had a family, a family who loved her, but still wasn't certain of how much resentment the girl might be harboring. How could she not, after all she'd been through? Dani's stomach fluttered.

"Why don't you pretty ladies sit down and have yourself a nice get-acquainted talk," Jack suggested. "While Nate and I go get you some pop from the vending machines."

Holly ordered a Diet Pepsi, as did Dani, who didn't really want anything but understood that Jack and Nate were leaving them alone to talk without an audience. She was grateful for their sensitivity until the heavy silence descended as soon as they'd left the room.

"This is harder than in my dreams," Dani murmured.

"Mine, too," Holly agreed.

Dani looked at her, surprised. "You dreamed about me? About us?"

"All the time. Sometimes I thought you were a famous opera star who traveled the world and couldn't take care of a baby. I used to watch PBS all the time, wondering if one of those ladies singing at the Lincoln Center might be my mom." She smiled a little shyly. "I know it's not cool for a kid my age, but I like opera."

"So does your grandfather Dupree. He always used to play it in his chambers. Sometimes loud enough that he could hear the music from the bench, but low enough that no one else in the courtroom other than his bailiff could."

"What's his favorite opera? Composer?"

Dani lifted her hands in a helpless gesture. "I'm afraid I don't know."

"Is he going to die tonight?"

"I hope not. The doctors seemed optimistic." She sighed at the thought of what her father had done. How many years he'd cost them all. "Let's sit down, shall we?" She took her daughter by the hand, led her over to the couch, which, rather than the obnoxious orange of the ER waiting room, was the color of a ripe lime.

They turned toward each other, knee to knee, face to face. "I'm assuming, from what you said about my father, that Jack explained some of the circumstances surrounding your birth."

Holly nodded. "Yeah, he pretty much told me all the facts. About you doing what the adults had convinced you was for the best, then you changing your mind about keeping me, and your father fixing it so you'd think I'd died."

"That's pretty much it." How strange it seemed to have the most traumatic time of her life condensed into a single concise statement.

"But what he couldn't tell me about how you were feeling, because he didn't know, you did."

"Me?"

"In your letter."

The letter! It had been the first one, and she'd spent days agonizing over what to say, finally writing the final draft the night before her daughter was born, sharing with her unborn baby the truth—that she'd been conceived in love and would always live in her mother's heart. She'd tried to explain, as best she could, why she was giving up custodial rights and how she hoped that her child would someday understand that her actions had also been born in love. Of course she'd changed her mind the next day. But it hadn't mattered, because she'd lost her child anyway.

"That's how I found you," Holly explained. "You wrote about growing up in Beau Soleil, and about how some day you'd love to introduce me to another part of my heritage, so you were going to register with that place that links up children with their adoptive parents, if they both want, when they're eighteen. You said you wouldn't try to find me, in case I didn't want my life disrupted, but that you'd always be there for me."

"That's true." Dani bit her lip to keep from bursting into tears. "I gave the letter to the social worker to give to your adoptive parents, but when I could start thinking straight again, I assumed it had been thrown away." As impossible as it seemed, Dani wondered if a part of her had continued to know, in some secret part of her heart, that her daughter was still alive. Perhaps that's why she'd felt moved to write those letters every year. Letters she couldn't wait to share with her newly found daughter.

"Well, I guess it wasn't thrown away, because I found it when I was about eight and was snooping around in a box in my parents' bedroom closet. I'd always known I was adopted, so it wasn't like it was any big surprise and I don't know why I stole it, but later I was glad I did, since it gave me something to hold on to the past two years in the foster homes. I couldn't wait to turn eighteen and could register to be matched up with you."

Dani silently blessed the social worker who, for reasons only she would ever know, had secretly gone against the judge's orders and passed on that fateful letter. "But you're not eighteen."

"I know. But once I saw the picture of Beau Soleil on the front of that newspaper, I knew where to find you, so I decided not to wait any longer."

"You ran away?"

"Yeah." Holly shrugged slender shoulders clad in a hot-pink top that looked as if it'd been created from shrink wrap. "A few days ago."

"Where were you living?"

"In San Diego County."

"That's so far away. How did you get all the way to Louisiana?"

"I hitched to Yuma, Arizona, because I was afraid to buy a bus ticket in case the police were looking for me. Then I took the bus from Yuma to here."

Even though she'd obviously survived the experience, Dani's blood turned to ice at the idea of her beautiful, young, vulnerable daughter hitchhiking. "That was horribly dangerous," she scolded in the tone she had seldom used with Matt. "I don't want you ever hitchhiking again."

Holly surprised her by laughing at that. She brushed her sleek slide of hair behind her shoulder. "Yes, Mother. . . . I still have the Pooh bear," she volunteered. "He's been restuffed twice. Mom said it was my favorite baby toy."

More memories flooded back. Dani had bought the bear at a toy store during one of her rare Saturday afternoons away from the home.

"That's so nice to hear," she managed to say on a voice clogged with emotion.

Surely it couldn't be this easy?

"I want you to know," Dani said, "that I'll understand if you resented me. Even if you still do."

"No. You did the right thing," Holly said, the bright laughter fading from her eyes as she turned serious. "Mom and Dad were wonderful and I loved them and they loved me. I'm not sure I ever would have contacted you if they hadn't died."

Dani ignored the little twinge of hurt and concentrated instead on the fact that her daughter had known at least ten years of happiness. "I understand," she said mildly.

"But I've been dreaming of this ever since they died, and I had to go live with Uncle Phil and Aunt Sara." Tears sparkled in her thick gold lashes. "But this is even better than I dreamed because I never, ever thought I'd find both my father and mother at the same time."

"It's been a strange set of circumstances," Dani murmured, thinking how all the turmoil in her life these past years had brought her back to Blue Bayou so she could find Jack again and the daughter they'd created that long-ago summer could find them.

"Yeah. Jack told me about the piano."

From the choked sound in Holly's voice, it was obvious she was trying not to laugh. But because the Steinway had been one of the stranger strings fate had pulled, Dani couldn't keep her own lips from quirking at the absurdity. "It sounds as if you and Jack had quite a conversation."

"We've been talking since I showed up. Well, except for when he came into town to tell you."

Studying her carefully, Dani was relieved not to see a hint of concern in the girl's expression. Obviously Jack had kept their personal troubles to himself.

Holly sighed. "He's so wonderful."

"You won't get any argument from me about that," Dani agreed.

"I asked him if he loved you. And he said he always had."

"That's handy, since I love him, too."

"Are you going to get married?"

Dani knew that it was more than just idle curiosity that had Holly asking the question. "He hasn't asked me yet."

"He will," Holly asserted with a childish conviction. "And if he doesn't ask you, you'll just have to propose to him."

"How old are you, anyway?" Dani asked with a faint smile, knowing the answer all too well. "Twelve going on thirty?"

"Everyone has always said I'm very mature for my age."

She would have had to have been, Dani thought sadly, to have experienced the loss of her parents, the breakup of another home, and the subsequent years in the revolving door of the foster-care system.

A nurse appeared in the doorway, accompanied by Nate and Jack, who'd returned with the cans of soda. "The judge is awake and asking for you, Ms. Dupree. Dr. Ancelet says you can visit for five minutes."

"I won't be long," she promised. She gave Holly another hug and experienced wonder that it felt so right. So natural.

"I'll be here."

Dani touched her fingertips to her daughter's smooth cheek. "I think those are the most beautiful words I've ever heard."

# 27

*Dani's heart,* which had been floating on air, took a crash dive when she walked into the CCU and saw her father looking swallowed up by the narrow hospital bed. His complexion was the color of library paste, his hands, lying limp on the sheets on either side of him, were spotted and blue-veined, and lank strands of white hair revealed a great deal of his scalp.

He'd always seemed so bold, so strong, so larger than life. Even after she learned of his heart disease, the force of his personality had kept her from realizing exactly how old he was. Oh, she knew that he'd married her mother late in his life, knew that he was now nearly seventy-eight, which didn't necessarily have to be all that ancient in these days of medical miracles such as the one humming away in his chest. Unfortunately, he looked every one of those years, and more.

She pulled a lime green vinyl chair that matched the waiting room couch up to the bed, sat down, and took one of those aged hands in both of hers.

He opened his eyes, which, amazingly, considering how the rest of him looked, were still filled with life.

"Hi, Daddy." She squeezed his fingers, which felt like chicken bones beneath her touch. "You gave us all quite a scare."

"They said you gave me CPR." His voice was raspy, but, like his eyes, not as frail as his body. "Probably saved my life."

"I think that's an exaggeration."

"Maybe it is, maybe it isn't." His eyes narrowed as he gave her one of those probing looks that had always brought witnesses and opposing counsels into line. For a long moment the only sound in the room was the beeps of the monitor and the faint hiss of the oxygen being fed into his system by a nasal tube.

"Why didn't you just let me die?"

"Don't be ridiculous. You're my father."

"Not exactly an exemplary one," he muttered.

She shrugged, refusing to hold a grudge on this day of miracles. "It's not easy being a parent. We all make mistakes."

"Have you met her?" he asked. "Your daughter?"

"Yes. And she's wonderful. Her name is Holly and she's sweet, beautiful, resourceful." Dani frowned a little when she thought about the hitchhiking. "I can't wait for you to meet her."

"Does she know what I did?"

She couldn't lie. "Yes. But she didn't seem as bitter as I might have expected. And I'm sure we can get past that, Daddy. If you want to. And we all try.

"We're going to be a family, Jack and Matt and Holly and me, and we'd like you to be part of it." Dani was not going to let the fact that Jack hadn't yet asked her to marry him get in the way of beginning the life that had been stolen from them. "I'm getting married at Beau Soleil." She figured if they all worked at it together, they could get the garden ready in no time. "And I want you to be there."

"Then you'd better not waste any time," he said. "Since I could keel over again any day."

"No, you won't, because while I've been going crazy worrying about you all day, you've been getting a brand-new shiny computer put in your chest. You're the judicial model of the six-million-dollar man and I'm not about to let you die for years and years."

"Anyone ever tell you that you can be damn bossy from time to time?" he asked without heat.

"I guess I take after my father. So you may as well get used to it." Her expression sobered. "I'm still not happy about what you did, but I love you and if there's anything the past two years has taught me, it's that life is too precious to waste."

She leaned forward, kissed his dry papery cheek, then stood up when the nurse appeared beside the bed, signaling that her time was up.

Dani squeezed her father's hand again, reassured when he squeezed back. She was almost to the door when she heard him rasp out her name.

She turned. "Yes, Daddy?"

"I'm damn proud of the woman you've become, Danielle. Your children are lucky to have you. Jack's lucky. And so am I."

Her answering smile was slow and warm and filled with all the joy she was feeling. "I know, Daddy."

Jack was alone when Dani returned to the waiting room.

"Where is everyone?" she asked.

"Nate took Holly down to the cafeteria for a midnight breakfast. I swear, for such a little thing, she's got an appetite that puts Turnip to shame."

"Lucky for Holly that her dad's a great cook."

"I'd say we're all pretty lucky. So, how's the judge doing?"

"He's certainly looked better, but I talked to the charge nurse after I left the room and she says his prognosis is very good."

"That's more good news."

She nodded. "Yes. It is. . . . He told me he was lucky to have me."

" 'Bout time." Jack stepped forward. Stopped. Never in all his years of undercover work had he been this nervous. "Remember me tellin' you how I thought about you while I was in Colombia?" he began, wondering why it was that words that could come so tripplingly off the tongues of his characters, seemed to be lodged in his throat. *Maybe you* do *need a ghostwriter, Callahan,* he thought with grim humor.

"Of course. It was when you were in the mountains with your partner."

"Yeah. Then, and a helluva lot of other nights as well. And I haven't stopped thinking about you—and us—since you've come back to Blue Bayou. And you know what I've decided?"

"What?" She seemed to be holding her breath. Hell, she wasn't the only one.

"Your marriage didn't really break up because your husband slept with his chief of staff and was, to the core, pretty much of a louse. I think you would have gotten divorced whoever you married."

"Well, that's certainly flattering." The soft smile took any complaint from her words.

"It's the truth. And it would've been the same way for me, if I'd ever gotten married. Neither one of us could have been happy with anyone else, because deep down inside, we would have been wanting each other."

"I can't argue with that, since the same thought has occurred to me."

"Good, because I'm willin' to wait till the judge is out of here to make an official announcement, but I want to marry you, Danielle. I want us to make ourselves a family with Matt and Holly, and maybe another baby or two, if you think that'd be a good idea, and have all our children grow up at Beau Soleil where their pretty *maman* did.

"I want to go to sleep every night with you beside me and wake up every day the same way. I make enough money to support us in pretty good style, but if you want to keep your job at the library, that'd be great, too."

"I would, absolutely, but—"

"Terrific," he said, cutting her off. Now that he'd begun, he wanted to state his case before she had a chance to think of any objections. "Fortunately, thanks to Hollywood, you'd have a rich husband who can afford all the nannies we'd ever need. Did I mention the movie folks have bought book number five?"

"I didn't think you'd finished with the fourth."

"I haven't." He raked his fingers through his hair, took another deep breath, and crossed the small space between them to stand in front of her. "But only because my hero is waitin' for the drug dealer's daughter to admit she loves him. How 'bout it, *chère?* Does she? Or doesn't she?"

"She does." Dani lifted her hand to his face. "With her entire heart."

Jack drew her into his arms with a deep sigh of relief. "Then you'll marry me? As soon as possible?"

A dazzling smile bloomed on Dani's face; her eyes were wet and brilliant, but Jack knew that this time her tears were born of happiness. "I was beginning to think you'd never ask."

# River Road

*To Jay—*
*who never complains about living in a house*
*populated by imaginary people, taught himself to cook*
*so I don't have to live on cereal while I'm deep in a book,*
*and is always there to point out the rainbow whenever*
*I begin fussing about storm clouds.*
*I love you.*

# 1

*Washington, D.C.*

*Finn Callahan hated bad guys,* criminal lawyers, bureaucrats and cockroaches. At least the bad guys had provided him with a livelihood as an FBI Special Agent for the past thirteen years. Why the good Lord had created the other three remained one of those universal mysteries, like how the ancient Egyptians built the pyramids or why it always rained right after you washed your truck.

"It's not like I killed the guy," he muttered. The way Finn saw it, a broken nose, some bruises and a few broken ribs didn't begin to equal the crimes that scumbag serial killer had committed.

"Only because two agents, a Maryland state trooper and a court-appointed shrink managed to pull you off him before you could," the woman behind the wide desk said. There was enough ice in her tone to coat Jupiter. Her black suit was unadorned; her champagne blond hair, cut nearly as short as his, barely reached the collar, and her jaw thrust toward him like a spear. Put her in dress blues and she could have appeared on a U.S. Marine recruiting poster.

"I've spent the past hour on the phone with Lawson's lead attorney. Unsurprisingly, he wants to file assault and battery charges. And that's just for starters. I'm attempting to convince him to allow us to handle the matter internally."

Unpolished fingernails, trimmed short as a nun's, tapped an irritated tattoo on the gleaming desktop.

Finn had no problem with women in the Bureau; he'd worked with several and would have trusted his life to them any day. Hell, even James Bond had gotten a woman boss when Judi Dench took over as M. Finn didn't even have any problem with ice queens like Special Agent in Charge Lillian Jansen.

He did, however, have a Herculean problem with any SAC who wasn't a stand-up guy. From the day she'd arrived from the New York field office, Jansen had proven herself to be far more interested in the politics of the job than in locking up criminals.

"It's a helluva thing when an SAC takes the side of a sicko killer over one of her own men," he muttered.

"Christ, Callahan," the other man in the office warned. James Burke's ruddy cheeks were the hue of ripe cherries, suggesting that Finn's recent behavior hadn't been good for his blood pressure problem. A faint white ring around his mouth was evidence he'd been chugging Maalox directly from the bottle again.

"You're out of line, Special Agent," Jansen snapped. "Again."

Leaning back in the leather swivel chair, she dropped the sword that had been hanging over his head for the past forty-eight hours—ever since the killer it had taken Finn nearly three years to track through eight states had made the mistake of trying to escape from the hospital, just as Finn dropped by to see how the court-appointed psychiatric evaluation was going.

"I will, of course, have no choice but to turn this incident over to OPR."

The Office of Professional Responsibility was the equivalent of a police force's internal affairs bureau. Since many of its investigators possessed a guilty-until-proven-innocent attitude, a lot of agents tended to distrust the OPR right back.

The idea of being thrown to the wolves made Finn's gut churn, but unwilling to allow Jansen to know she'd gotten beneath his skin, he forced his shoulders to relax, schooled his expression to a mask, and although it wasn't easy, kept his mouth shut.

"You're scheduled to be questioned tomorrow afternoon at three o'clock. You are, of course, entitled to be represented by legal counsel."

"Now there's an idea. Maybe I can get one of those worms making up Lawson's legal dream team to represent me. Of course, the only problem with that idea is since Lawson's a gazillionaire sicko with bucks out the kazoo, I doubt any of those scumbags would want to take on the case of a middle income cop who got pissed off at their client for raping and killing coeds."

Ronald Lawson had murdered eight college women scattered across the country from California to Maryland. Finn's recurring nightmare was that there were still more missing women he hadn't yet discovered who could be linked to the guy.

"We would have had eleven victims if Callahan hadn't gotten to Lawson's house when he did and found those girls locked up in his basement." A chain-smoker, Burke's voice was as rough as a bad gravel road.

"That's part of my problem." Frustration sharpened the SAC's brisk voice. "The Georgetown girl's parents are close personal friends of the Attorney General. In fact, the AG and his wife are her godparents. They heard about Lawson's attempted escape on the nightly news and are pressuring the AG to allow Callahan's outrageous cowboy tactics to slide."

Finn shot a sideways look at Burke, whose expression told him they were thinking the same thing. That perhaps he just should have put his gun barrel into the guy's mouth and pulled the trigger in those midnight hours when they'd descended on Lawson's Pontiac mansion. Every cop in the place would have sworn on a stack of bibles that deadly force had been absolutely justified.

He'd always been a by-the-book kind of guy, the type of FBI agent Efrem Zimbalist, Jr. had played on TV, but sometimes the laws protecting the bad guys really sucked.

"How about we come up with a compromise?" Burke suggested.

"What type of compromise do you have in mind?" Jansen asked.

"Callahan takes a leave of absence until this blows over. Say, two weeks."

"That's not enough time for damage control. Four weeks suspension," she countered. "Without pay."

Finn had been staring up at the ceiling, pretending disinterest in the negotiation. When he realized Burke wasn't countering Jansen's proposal, he shot the SAC a savage look.

"Fuck that." He rubbed knuckles which had been bruised when they'd connected so satisfyingly with Lawson's jaw. *You are not*, he instructed his itchy fist, *going to screw this up worse by punching a hole through that damn trophy wall.* A wall covered with photographs of SAC Lillian Jansen with seemingly every politician in town. "I'll take my chances with OPR."

"Dammit, Finn, it's not that bad an offer." Burke plowed a hand through thinning hair the color of a rusty Brillo pad. "You haven't taken a real vacation in years. Go home, do some fishing, unwind, and when you come back all this shit will have blown over."

They both knew it'd probably take another Hurricane Andrew to blow this particular shit pile away.

"If I were you, I'd take your squad supervisor's advice." Jansen folded her arms across the front of a jacket as black as her heart.

Finn suspected that not only was she enjoying this, she was just waiting for him to squirm. *Not in this lifetime,* his expression said.

*Want to bet?* hers said right back. "If this goes any further, my recommendation will be to terminate you."

And she'd do it if it'd help her career. Hell, she'd probably run over her own dog if it'd get her a promotion to ADIC. Of course she didn't actually have a dog; that would take some kind of personal commitment—and from what he'd seen, the woman was only committed to her swift climb up the Bureau's political ladder.

"Two weeks." *Forget Hurricane Andrew.* Finn needed a tornado to come sweeping out of Kansas, swoop down over K Street, and drop a damn house on Lillian Jansen.

"Four." Her lips actually quirked a bit at the corners, hinting at the closest thing to a smile he'd witnessed since her heralded arrival from New York. She held out her hand, palm up. "And I'll take your weapon and shield."

Feeling Burke's gaze on him, the silent plea to make nice radiating off his squad commander like a physical presence, Finn swallowed the frustration that rose like bile in his mouth, took his .40mm Glock from his shoulder holster and resisted, just barely, the urge to throw it onto her desk.

When he failed to manage the same restraint with his shield, all three pairs of eyes watched the leather case slide off the highly polished surface onto the carpet. Finn hoped Jansen would ask him to pick it up, so he could suggest where she could plant those thin, pale lips.

"Do you know the trouble with you, Callahan?"

"No. But I have a feeling you're going to tell me."

"You've begun to believe your own press. There are those in the Bureau, including your former SAC, who may be impressed by your appearances on *Nightline* and your dinners at the White House. But as far as I'm concerned, you have a very bad attitude toward authority. You also take your work personally."

"And your point is?"

She glared at him with nearly as much contempt as he felt for her, then pressed a button on her intercom. "Please send in security to escort Special Agent Callahan out of the building."

"I'll do that," Burke offered quickly. It was obvious he wanted to get Finn out of the office before things got worse.

"It's not your job," Jansen said.

"A superior stands by his men." His tone clearly implied the SAC did not. If Jansen's eyes were frost, Burke's were flame.

Finn was willing to take the heat himself, but didn't want to cause a longtime friend any more problems. Especially since he knew Burke had put a second mortgage on his Arlington house to pay for his three kids' college tuition and couldn't afford a disciplinary suspension.

"Jim, it's okay."

"The hell it is," the older man shot back. "This whole mess stinks to high heaven." He pinned the SAC with a hard look.

Clearly unwounded, she merely shrugged in return. "You have ten minutes," she told Finn.

Finn turned on his heel with military precision, and had just opened the office door when she called his name. Glancing back over his shoulder, he imagined a black widow spider sitting in the center of her web.

"If I were you Callahan, I'd spend the next month sending out resumes. Because if and when you return, you'll be transferred to another field office, where—if I have anything to say about it, and believe me, I do—you'll be reassigned to desk duty."

Oh, she was good. Coldly efficient, deadly accurate, hitting right on target. She knew he'd rather be gut shot than spend the rest of his career stuck in some dreary outpost, shuffling papers. Finn would bet his last grade increase that, instead of playing Barbie dolls and having pretend tea parties like other little girls, SAC Jansen had spent her childhood drowning kittens.

He heard Burke clear his throat, another less-than-subtle warning. But Finn refused to justify her threat with a response.

Since his work had always been his life, he didn't have any hobbies, nor had he bothered to accumulate any superfluous stuff that might clutter up either his desk or his life. He cleaned a few personal effects from his desk and was out of the building in just under eight minutes.

# 2

*Los Angeles, California*

*The bedroom was bathed* in a shimmering silver light. A sultry sax crooned from the stereo speakers hidden in the walls, a bottle of champagne nested in a sterling ice bucket beside the bed, and the warm glow of candles cast dancing shadows of a man and a woman against the walls.

"I dreamed about you," the woman said. She went up on her toes, her arms twining around his neck. "Hot, deliciously wicked dreams."

His hand fisted in her long auburn hair, pulling her head back to give his roving mouth access to her throat. "You're not alone there, darlin'," he drawled with the cadence of the Louisiana South. "I've been walking around with a hard-on since the moment you sashayed into that Vegas wedding chapel looking like a Hell's Angel's wet dream."

Her low, breathless laugh vibrated with sexual excitement. Amanda had known the black micro-skirt and studded, shaped jacket worn with nothing but perfumed and powdered flesh underneath had been an outrageous thing to wear to a wedding. Especially when you were the maid of honor. But it *had* been Las Vegas, and the minister marrying this man to her half sister was a decidedly untalented Elvis impersonator.

Two hours later, after a surfeit of champagne cocktails blended with a little Valium, the bride had passed out in the honeymoon suite while the maid of honor and groom were two floors below, screwing each other's brains out.

Three weeks later, back in the mansion on River Road, they were still at it. "What is it about black leather that makes men so horny?" Amanda asked.

"It wasn't the leather. It was you. Christ, I've never seen a woman who looked more ready to be laid. You were wet and hot and in heat. I've never *wanted* a woman the way I wanted you. Hell, after banging you every chance we get, I still want you even more than I did that day."

"Then take me," she purred. "Now."

"Now," he agreed. Buttons scattered across the floor as he ripped open the scarlet-as-sin dress that fit as if it'd been sprayed onto her gleaming flesh, and dragged her down onto the bed.

Wrapping her legs around his hips, Amanda encouraged him with ragged gasps, breathless cries and earthy sexual suggestions. He peeled the dress off her slick body, revealing an ivory teddy that was a surprisingly innocent contrast to the dress lying in a crimson puddle on the carpet.

He left the bed only long enough to strip off his trousers, then chuckled as Amanda's eyes widened at the huge bulge beneath his silk leopard printed bikini briefs. "See something you like, sweetheart?"

"There's definitely a great deal to like," she murmured.

He laughed appreciatively as he rolled her stockings down her legs, then used them to tie her wrists to the ebony bedposts.

Having recovered from her surprise, she gazed up at him, her green eyes limpid pools of desire. "There's nothing I won't do, Jared," she said, her voice throaty with sex and sin. "Nothing I'll say no to."

His hand stroked her, exploring, arousing. Kneeling over her, he followed the hot path with his lips. Engrossed in the moment, in each other, neither heard the French doors opening.

"Well, I'd hoped my husband and sister would get along." The icy British voice was like a splash of cold water on a blazing fire. "But don't you two think you're overdoing it a bit?"

"Vanessa!" The man leaped from the bed. "You weren't due back from Cornwall until next week."

"I found the country boring." The heat in the woman's eyes was a direct contrast to the chill in her voice. "Everyone tromping around in Wellies and shooting poor, defenseless birds out of the sky."

Amanda sighed. Obviously the fun was over for tonight. "Well, I suppose I should be leaving." Scenes with betrayed wives were so utterly boring. "Unless," she suggested wickedly, "you'd care to join us, Van."

A flush rose like a fever in the betrayed woman's peaches-and-cream complexion. "You're an amoral slut. Just like your mother. It's no wonder Father divorced her and deserted you."

"Sticks and stones," Amanda drawled. "And for the record, our dear papa married your mother for the same reason your husband here married you. For your money."

Both sisters ignored Jared's stuttered attempt at a protest. Amanda's accusation was true and all three people in the bedroom knew it.

"Since it appears you're not going to take me up on my invitation, if one of you could just untie me—"

Jared Lee moved quickly to do just that, as if he couldn't wait to get her out of his house, out of his life. But before he could untie the stubborn knot in the first stocking, his wife pulled a small but potentially deadly pistol from her Coach bag.

"Vanessa, what in God's name do you think you're doing?" he gasped.

"Isn't it obvious, darling?" She pointed the gun at the most vulnerable part of his anatomy. "I'm going to ensure you never betray me with this cheap piece of trash again."

He flinched and went ghost white. His hands instinctively dropped to his crotch. "You wouldn't."

"Jesus, Van," Amanda complained. "I can't believe you're being so middle-class uptight about a little infidelity."

Vanessa's chin lifted. "Perhaps if you were to actually marry that man whose ring you're wearing on your finger, sister dear, you'd understand my feelings better." She shot a scathing glance at her husband. "Quit trembling, Jared."

The injured wife was gone, replaced by the twenty-six-year-old CEO of Comfort Cottage Tea. "I believe, since I have use of them myself on occasion, I'll let you keep your testicles. For now. So long as you keep them at home. Where they belong."

"I promise, darling. This was just a small slip. I never planned to be unfaithful, but I was missing you so—"

"Don't embarrass yourself further by lying," she cut off his weak excuse.

He looked so desperate, Amanda was starting to feel sorrier for him than she did for herself. She, at least, was capable of standing on her own two feet. She couldn't remember the last time she'd been afraid of anyone or anything. Least of all this British bitch who'd bought herself an alcoholic Southern philanderer.

Finding the domestic drama increasingly tedious, she had just freed one wrist when the sound of a gunshot shattered the night and the smell of cordite overpowered the vanilla scent of the candle.

Pressing her hand against the lacy bodice of the bloodstained teddy, Amanda slumped back against the pillow.

Jared crumbled to the floor in a dead faint while his wife held the smoking pistol, a satisfied smile on her face as she looked down at her rival.

Silence descended. The candle sputtered out, plunging the room into darkness.

"Cut!" the director called out.

"Cut," the first assistant director called out.

"It's about time," Julia Summers complained. "There's a limit to how long a person can hold their breath, Randy."

"You're a professional, love." Randy Hogan's Australian strine bespoke outback roots. "I had every faith in you."

"I may be a professional, but I'm not Houdini." She tugged against the other stocking. "Could someone please untie me before my shoulder gives out?"

"Only if you'll agree to let me take you out to dinner," Shane Langley said.

A former baseball player who'd used his appearance as Mr. October on a Men of the Minor Leagues calendar to catapult him onto the cast of a daytime soap opera, he'd been asking Julia out since joining the cable network's prime time *River Road* cast three months ago. She'd been turning him down just as long.

"After what you did?"

"I have no idea what you're talking about."

"Springing that damn porn movie prosthesis you got from the props department on me without any warning."

"Surely you're not talking about Mr. Happy?"

She shook her head as one of the prop women loosened the stocking. "Mr. Happy?"

"He's aptly named." He retrieved his slacks and pulled them up his legs. "Come home with me tonight and I'll prove it."

"Shane, it's a good twelve inches long."

"A *very* good twelve inches." Boyish dimples flashed in cheeks tanned surfer bronze. "That's why women call him Mr. Happy."

"You're incorrigible." Along with a loyal audience, Shane had brought his penchant for obnoxious practical jokes with him to prime time. The *River Road* set hadn't been the same since his arrival.

Finally freed, Julia left the bed and slipped into the silk robe that Audrey, the wardrobe mistress, was holding out to her. "I hope you and Mr. Happy have a lovely evening, but I'm exhausted. Besides, I need to study my Bond script tonight."

As soon as this fifth season was wrapped up, she was going to Kathmandu to fulfill a childhood dream.

She'd been eight years old when her cousin had talked her into attending a 007 film festival in Santa Cruz. Watching Ursula Andress rise goddesslike from the sea in *Dr. No*, and having been taught by her parents that no dreams were impossible, Julia had decided, on the spot, to grow up to be a Bond Girl. After she'd gotten a little older and had actually read the novels the movies were based on and realized they were fiction, her goal shifted from *becoming* a Bond Girl to playing one in the movies.

Last month she'd beat out more than a hundred eager hopefuls, including Felissa Templeton, the actress who played Vanessa, for the role. Julia felt a little guilty about that, but Felissa had assured her that she was thrilled for Julia. When she'd added that she was far more interested in "serious work that will allow me to stretch as an actor," Julia hadn't bothered to take offense at the catty little dig.

"I've got an idea," Shane said. "How about I drop by your house with a pizza? We can run through your lines together over a bottle of wine. Then we'll take it from there and if you're suddenly moved to have your way with me, I sure as hell won't resist."

Before she could turn him down again, Randy clapped his hands. "Before you all rush off, I have a surprise for you, boys and girls." He paused for dramatic effect. "We're ending this season on a four-hour two-parter that'll be packaged as a TV miniseries and shown back-to-back on consecutive nights. And the budget's been expanded to include a location shoot."

"Where?" Shane asked.

"For how long?" Julia followed up.

"This time next week, we'll be shooting in Blue Bayou, Louisiana."

"Where is that? I've never heard of it," Felissa Templeton said in a petulant tone far different from her character's upper-class British accent.

"It's a charming little hamlet in southern Louisiana. You'll love it," Randy assured her. "It's very romantic, with mysterious dark water, fireflies flitting through the hanging Spanish moss—"

"Mosquitos, alligators, tropical heat," Felissa cut him off, exchanging a look with Julia, who was equally unenthusiastic about this news.

"Don't be so pessimistic. Wait until you see the house we'll be using. As for how long," he addressed Julia's question, "depending on whether or not the weather cooperates, we'll be there two weeks. Three tops."

"Two weeks? But Amanda's going to die. Why do you need me to come along?"

"She's not exactly going to die."

"Please don't tell me we're reprising the vampire plot from the first season." It had taken two hours in makeup every day to prepare for her role as the lawyer-turned-vampire, until a mad scientist lover had invented a super sunscreen that allowed her to join the living once again.

"Don't worry, love, you won't be growing fangs again. But Warren's come up with an exciting new twist in the story line. You're going to love it." He patted her cheek as if she were a five-year-old, then framed his hands in front of him. "I can see another Emmy gracing your mantel for this one."

"I don't have a mantel. Has Kendall seen it?"

"You know we don't do anything without running it by the big guy. He loves it. Which is why he's authorized the extra spending. After the last sweeps ratings, Warren can probably do whatever he wants."

Warren Hyatt was a twenty-eight-year-old wunderkind who'd been lured away from the Sci-Fi channel. Julia liked him, even though his story lines tended to push the envelope even for the most fantastical soap opera. Since demographics had shown the off-the-wall stories had a huge appeal to younger viewers, his star was definitely on the rise.

"So what is this new story line?" she asked Warren who was leaning against a wall, clad in unpressed chinos and a polo shirt that had seen better days. He was madly scribbling on a yellow legal pad.

"It's a surprise," Randy broke in. "But don't worry, love. We'll get things wrapped up in time for you to take off for the dark side of the moon."

"Kathmandu."

He tipped down his Armani sunglasses and looked over the top of the dark lenses. "Do they get *Variety* there?"

"I strongly doubt it."

"Any Starbucks?"

"Probably not."

"How about Foster's?"

"That'd probably be a no, as well."

He shook his head and pushed the glasses back up. "Any place without Aussie beer, *Variety* or frappuchinos may as well be the dark side of the moon."

This from a man who'd grown up in a place where people were outnumbered by kangaroos and poisonous snakes. Although technically her contract had three weeks left to run, Julia had hoped to wrap up her part in the next two days, since Vanessa had just put a bullet through Amanda's heart.

"I don't get it. If Amanda's not going to die—"

"We'll discuss it in more detail later over pasta," Randy promised. "Kendall's corporate jet is landing as I speak, and he wants to meet with all of you tonight, at La Roma."

Julia rubbed at the headache that had just shot into her temples. Last year, Dwyers' Diapers, the conglomerate that had owned *River Road*, had been acquired in a hostile takeover by Atlantic Pharmaceuticals.

From day one, Charles Kendall, a senior vice president of Atlantic, hadn't been able to resist sticking his unimaginative thumb into the series. After firing the show's producer, he'd declared himself the new executive producer.

He was also an ass pincher and an advocate for bringing back the casting couch. Neither of those qualities endeared him to the female cast members, though Audrey, in wardrobe, had told Damien, Julia's makeup man, that the script girl had seen one of the actors, Margot Madison, getting out of the back of Kendall's stretch limo the last time he'd visited the studio.

"Her blouse was fastened wrong," Damien had passed on with obvious relish. "And her hair looked as if she'd been in a wind tunnel."

"That's mildly intriguing. But none of our business." Having been on the hurting side of gossip too many times in the past, Julia was not going to help grow false rumors.

"Audrey said the knees of her stockings were ripped. I'll bet she'd been trying to blow her way into the bad girl slot that'll open up if you leave."

"*When* I leave," Julia corrected. After her futile admonishment not to pass on tales, the increasingly exaggerated story had added grist to the ever-grinding *River Road* gossip mill for days.

Three more weeks, Julia reminded herself. Then she'd be off this soap opera merry-go-round, on her way to Nepal.

# 3

*After leaving his office,* Finn stopped by his Crystal City apartment, which was as barren of personal effects as his desk, to pick up the suitcase he always kept packed and a stack of well-worn Ian Fleming paperbacks. Still fuming and wanting to get out of Dodge, he turned in his door and elevator keys to management, then left the building without a backward glance.

With Van Halen's "Sinner's Swing" screeching from the CD player, he headed his black Suburban southwest toward Louisiana, returning to the small bayou town he once couldn't wait to escape.

Because like it or not, the sorry truth was that Finn Callahan, the hotshot Special Agent who'd earned a medal for valor in the field from one president and had dined at the White House with another, had nowhere else to go.

Julia smelled them before she saw them. Dashing into her dressing room for a quick shower to wash off the fake blood, she was hit with a sweet, head-spinning scent. She stopped, stunned at the dozens of roses so darkly red as to be almost black, covering every flat surface, including the floor.

"Damn it, Shane, this is getting out of hand," she muttered. Just last week he'd filled her dressing room with heart-shaped helium balloons. The week before that, it had been a gorilla-gram that turned out to be a Chippendale dancer beneath the furry uniform. The other women on the set had throughly enjoyed the show. Julia, who resented any time taken away from work these days, did not.

"Shane?" a voice asked from behind a towering arrangement that would have been perfect for a Mafia don's funeral. "What makes you think it's him?"

"Graham!" Julia was nonplussed to see the man whose marriage proposal she'd turned down six months ago. "What are you doing here?"

"I felt we left things unsettled. We need to talk."

*Be firm. You won't do either of you any good by going back on a decision you know is right.* "I believe we're all talked out, Graham," she said gently.

At least she was. She hadn't ever intended to get involved with the British-born UCLA professor. Not seriously. And she still couldn't quite figure out how they'd gone from having a glass of wine to him proposing marriage.

It had begun innocently enough after she'd spoken to Graham Sheffield's class, when, surrounded by a subtle cloud of discreet aftershave, he'd walked her to her car—a snazzy BMW convertible Dwyers' Diapers had presented her with after *River Road* had led the ratings pack every week during its second successful season.

Accustomed to self-absorbed actor wannabes, Julia was flattered when Graham insisted on walking across an acre of melting parking lot asphalt to hear her opinion on why the bold strokes and rakish wit of the Bond films was only one of the reasons they'd led the marketplace during the 1960s and '70s.

"I enjoyed your presentation a great deal, Julia. I know my class certainly benefited from hearing an insider's view of the acting business." His voice had been part Sean Connery, part Pierce Brosnan and totally 007. Julia could have listened to it forever. "It seems a shame to say good-bye," he murmured.

When he casually plucked the door opener from her hand, she'd wondered if he was actually going to try to keep her from leaving. A moment later, she realized that he was merely intending to open the car door for her. He seemed to be a man of flawless manners.

Those manners didn't prevent him from moving closer, until she was close enough to smell coffee and wintergreen on his breath. "Are you doing anything this evening?"

Looking up into his eyes, which were the color of Hershey bars and possessed the adoring appeal of a cocker spaniel—two of her favorite things—Julia decided to forgo trying out the do-it-yourself bikini waxing kit she'd bought.

Over the next months he proved himself to be a man of taste, refinement and civility. Unfortunately, Julia had discovered that she was bored to tears by refinement and civility.

Their relationship hadn't been a total loss, though. She had learned to brew a decent cup of Earl Grey tea.

"I've belatedly come to the conclusion that your going to Kathmandu for a few weeks might be a good thing for us," he said now. "You know what they say about absence making the heart grow fonder."

Of course, there was another little saying about *out of sight, out of mind*, which she chose not to bring up.

"Oh, Graham." Julia sighed.

He was, beneath all that stuffy Oxford reserve, a nice man. And so sensitive. Too sensitive, she'd often thought, to succeed in the competitive world of Hollywood. He'd once admitted that he tended to take rejection too personally, which was why he'd opted to teach the craft of acting rather than attempt to establish a career of his own.

"Don't worry, darling, I'm not going to rehash all the old arguments about why we're perfect for one another." His smile was as infinitely reasonable and patient as the man himself. It was also, she thought with a flash of pique, just a tad condescending. "I just wanted to give you a little going-away gift before you left town."

"That's very sweet of you. But this is hardly a little gift." It looked as if a Rose Bowl float had blown up. Another thought occurred to her. "How did you get past security?"

"Bernie remembers we're a couple." *Even if you don't*, his tone implied.

"Not anymore," she tried again.

He appeared truly puzzled by her continued refusal to date a man many women would consider a great catch. Graham Sheffield was handsome, wealthy, worldly, and could, he'd informed her that first evening together, trace his family roots back to the English Tudors.

"Is there someone else? Shane Langley, perhaps? Is that why you assumed the roses were from him?"

"I only assumed that because he's got a thing for practical jokes." She told him about last week's balloon incident, then, after assuring him that the only man in her life right now was James Bond, managed to ease him out the door.

She was in and out of the shower in record time, threw on a pair of jeans and a T-shirt and ran to the parking lot, where her name, stenciled in white at her reserved slot, still gave her a secret thrill.

Bernie was in his usual spot in what was laughingly referred to as the guardhouse. At the sound of the BMW's engine, he glanced up from his paperback. He grinned at her, his missing teeth giving him the look of a cotton-haired jack-o'-lantern. Julia waved. He'd been sitting in this booth since the days when people thought television would be a passing fad, so there was no point in trying to explain that he shouldn't let anyone through the gates without the proper authority.

Besides, she knew how charmingly persuasive Graham could be, especially when he wanted something.

Her irritation about the upcoming location shoot and her discomfort at finding her former lover in her dressing room eased as Julia pulled into her driveway forty-five minutes later. Her robin's egg blue bungalow, located on Venice Beach, was cozy and bright and gave her a front row seat at the continually entertaining scenery right outside her door.

The purity and simplicity of the Craftsman style also appealed to her aesthetic sense and was immensely soothing, especially for someone who'd grown up with beaded curtains, velvet beanbag chairs, crystals hanging from all the windows, and furniture carved from grapevines which, while earning her father more money than a respectable hippie should possess during that stage of his artistic career, had also been incredibly uncomfortable. Hence the beanbags.

She'd bleached the pine floors herself and painted the walls a cheery yellow that brightened in the morning to the hue of freshly churned butter. Now, at the end of the day, it was deepening with the rich gold and bronze colors of the sunset streaming into the living room from the French doors leading out to the beach.

Toeing off her sneakers, she began leafing through the mail. There was a water bill, which seemed to get higher every month, which she found a bit ironic since an entire ocean lay just outside her front door, a postcard reminding her of an upcoming teeth cleaning, and an official looking envelope assuring her that either she or someone named Martin Stevenson from Salt Lake City may have won a million dollars.

She tossed another postcard, inviting her to a preview of the Fall Color Extravaganza at Elizabeth Arden's, onto the tile countertop.

"Maybe I can get a makeover for when the Prize Patrol shows up at the door," she murmured as she retrieved a bottle of white wine from the refrigerator. After pouring herself a glass, she took the rest of the mail out onto the postage-stamp size patio.

She discarded an offer for a preapproved new credit card, and put aside a book club announcement she'd need to respond to before leaving the country.

An impossibly gorgeous blonde wearing a bikini skimmed by on Rollerblades, deftly avoiding a collision with a Lycra-clad bicyclist, who nearly twisted his head off his neck watching her skate away in the opposite direction.

Lovers strolled along the beach, arms wrapped around each other, seemingly oblivious to the outside world; joggers ran along the hard-packed sand at the water's edge. The tarot card readers were doing a brisk business, and the tide continued to ebb and flow as it had for eons.

But after pulling a photograph from the final envelope, Julia felt her world tilt on its axis.

The photo, computer printed onto inexpensive white copy paper, showed her lying against the pillows, a crimson bloodstain spreading across the bodice of an ivory silk teddy that clung to the tips of her breasts. Her eyes were closed.

Beneath the picture someone had typed: *You make a stunningly beautiful corpse, Amanda, darling. Love and kisses from your #1 fan.*

Puzzled how a photograph taken only a few hours ago could have gotten through the mail system so fast, Julia turned the envelope over. The blood drained from her head when she saw that it hadn't been postmarked.

Which meant the photographer had been at her house. Even worse, since the scene where Vanessa shot Amanda had been the final one of the day, if Graham hadn't held her up at the studio, she might have arrived home just as the photographer had been putting it through her mail slot.

She leaped to her feet. She scanned the beach, searching for . . . whom?

Several months ago, shortly after the beginning of the year, she'd begun receiving a flurry of letters from someone who declared himself her number-one fan. While they hadn't overtly threatened her, they'd become more and more possessive sounding. Enough that she'd begun to lose sleep, waiting for what, she hadn't really known. Which was what made the entire experience so unsettling.

Then, for some unfathomable reason, they'd suddenly stopped. Now, it looked like the letter writer was back.

There was a loud knock at her front door. Julia jumped and dropped her wine glass, which shattered into crystalline shards as it hit the stone patio.

# 4

Twenty hours and innumerable gallons of coffee after leaving D.C., Finn passed the blue and white sign welcoming visitors to Blue Bayou, Louisiana. Though the town and its people had changed dramatically since antebellum days, some things remained the same: according to the sign, the Rotary still met at Cajun Cal's Country Café on Wednesday evenings and the Daughters of the Confederacy at the Blue Bayou museum and bookstore on Saturday mornings.

Gaslights still glowed along oak-lined, cobblestoned Gramercy Boulevard, the planters edging the brick sidewalk overflowed with early fall color, and at one end of the lushly green town square, the twin Gothic spires of the Church of the Holy Assumption lanced high into the sky. At the other end of the square a majestic Italianate courthouse boasted tall stone steps, gracefully arched windows, and lacy cast-iron pilasters. The courthouse had served as a hospital during the War Between the States, and if one knew where to look, it was possible to find minié balls still lodged in the woodwork. A red, white, and blue Acadian flag waved beneath the U.S. and state flags on a towering pole in front of the courthouse, and a bronze statue of one of Finn's ancestors, war hero Captain Jackson Callahan, graced the lawn.

What had once been reported to be the largest flag in the state snapped in the breeze in front of the weathered, gray American Legion building, where military men had been shooting pool, sucking suds, and avoiding talking about the battles they'd fought since the War of 1812. Back when he'd been alive, Finn's father, Big Jake Callahan, had marched as flag bearer with the veterans in the annual Fourth of July parade.

Marching behind the honor guard in his Boy Scout uniform, Finn had watched his father with a young boy's pride and wondered how he'd ever measure up. Years later, there were still times when he secretly worried about that.

He turned the corner onto Royal Street, which boasted one of the state's best rows of single-story antebellum offices, and pulled the Suburban up to the curb in front of the office with *Callahan Construction* written on the window in black script. Below that, in a smaller font, was *Nate Callahan, mayor*.

Finn wasn't surprised his youngest brother had grown up to be a politician. Nate had, after all, been blessed with his *maman's* good looks and his daddy's gregariousness. The combination had helped him win the award for selling the most Scoutarama tickets year after year.

Nor was it surprising he'd become a contractor. Back when they'd been kids, while his older big brothers were playing cops and robbers and having quick draw shootouts with cap pistols, Nate had been dragging home old boards he'd unearthed in the swamp, to build the jail.

Finn opened the door and walked inside.

"Well, look what the cat dragged in." A blonde wearing a pink-and-white striped spandex top looked up from painting her fingernails. "Hey, Finn. We didn't expect you back home so soon."

"I didn't expect to be back." He glanced into the adjoining office, which was empty. "Where's the tycoon?"

"Tycoon." She snorted. "That'll be the day. Your baby brother has always had this really warped idea that it's more important to be happy than rich."

Lorelei Fairchild and Nate had gone steady for a couple months back in high school; she'd strutted around in a sequined red, white and blue uniform and tasseled white boots, tossing her baton up in the air while his brother threw passes for the Blue Bayou Buccaneers football team.

She blew on her wet, glossy nails, then waggled them at him. "What do you think? It's Passionate Pink."

"It's sure bright enough." The color was like bubble gum blended into Pepto Bismol, but even Finn, who'd never claimed to understand the female mind, figured that wasn't the answer Lorelei was looking for.

She held her hand out at arm's length to observe it herself. "It is, isn't it?"

"Is Nate around?"

"Sorry, sugar, you just missed him. He's off gettin' some old bricks to use out at Beau Soleil before all those people descend on the house."

"I thought Jack and Dani were off on a belated honeymoon."

"Oh, they surely are. Jack finished his book and sent it off to New York City last week. So, as we speak, the newlyweds are in Hawaii, basking in the sun, lounging around on the beach, drinking mai tais and eating passion fruit." She sighed with dramatic envy and gazed out the window into the gathering darkness, as if imagining herself lying on some coral tropical beach.

"Why would people be coming to Beau Soleil if Jack and Dani aren't there?" His brother had spent the past several months restoring the magnificent Greek Revival mansion that had once belonged to Danielle Dupree's family.

"They're from Hollywood."

"So?"

"Didn't Jack tell you?"

"If he had, I wouldn't be asking, would I?"

Finn resisted the urge to grind his back molars. On the rare occasion he'd returned home over the years, he'd noticed with regretful nostalgia that the belles who'd wrapped themselves in clouds of floral femininity while flattering and flirting weren't nearly as common as they'd been when he'd been growing up. A clever belle could charm a man around her manicured little finger, but trying to carry on a conversation with this female named for a mythical siren was flat out exhausting.

Her peppermint pink lips, perfectly matched to her fingernails, which in turn matched the stripes in her top, curved upward, revealing sparkling white beauty queen teeth. "Remember when Jack's first book, *The Death Dealer*, was made into a movie?"

"Sure." He also remembered Jack and the production company had taken some hits for violence for that one.

"Well, seems he made friends with this Hollywood director who needs a plantation house for location shooting here in Louisiana, and since Beau Soleil's vacant, what with him and Dani in Kauai, and Holly and little Matt staying with Orèlia . . . he's such a darling little boy, isn't he? And Holly is just the sweetest thing."

"They're both great kids. Jack and Dani are lucky to have them." Finn figured Tolstoy could have written *War and Peace* in the time it was taking Lorelei to get around to letting him know where his other brother was. "So this Hollywood guy is filming a television show at Beau Soleil?"

"He surely is. And it's none other than *River Road*. Mama and I were just tickled pink when we heard that, because it's our very favorite show. Why, we've never missed an episode. In fact, we have ourselves a bet about whose baby Amanda's carrying. I think it's Saxon's, which makes the most sense since he's her fiancé, but Mama insists she got pregnant the night her Jag broke down and she had to walk to that roadhouse to call for a tow truck, and ended up makin' love on the pool table with the sexy bartender after the place closed. Winner has to buy the other lunch at the Neiman Marcus Café in New Orleans."

She paused for a breath and eyed him speculatively. "You're a detective. Which do you think? I've lost the last three bets and I'd dearly love for Mama to have to be the one to spring for the chicken salad this time."

"Sorry. I can't help you since I've never heard of the show."

Morning glory blue eyes widened. "Gracious, darlin', where on earth have you been? Why, I thought everyone and their dog watched *River Road*. It does, after all, have international distribution. *TV Guide* says it's a huge hit in France and Japan."

"I've been a little busy." *Tracking down a stone cold killer.*

"Well, it's only been the hottest thing on television for the past five years. Shane Langley is even prettier than Brad Pitt. He plays the ne'er-do-well Southern rogue, Jared Jefferson Lee, who married Vanessa this season. Comfort Cottage Tea's been in her family forever. Her daddy—who's also Amanda's daddy—died when he keeled over while playing tennis at his club. Some say he was murdered, which I suspect is going to be another story line next season. Or maybe they killed him off because Keith Peters, the actor who played him, didn't get his contract renewed.

"Jared married Vanessa for her money. He used to be a lawyer, but lost his license to practice after he got caught embezzling funds from one of his clients to pay his gambling debts. Of course, he doesn't really love Vanessa, and started sniffing after her half sister Amanda ever since they met at their wedding—Vanessa's and Jared's, not Jared's and Amanda's—so I think they're going to have an affair.

"Which is really a good plot twist since, like I said, Amanda's showing signs that she's pregnant. She's engaged to Saxon Elliott, the town doctor, and he's a sweetheart, but he just isn't hunk material like Jared. Why, every time that man walks into a room, my heart just goes pitterpat." She tapped her fingers against her perky breasts.

"Havin' them all here is going to be the most exciting thing Blue Bayou's ever experienced. Mercy, everyone has just worked themselves into an absolute tizzy over it."

The idea of the entire town of Blue Bayou worked into a tizzy was too much even for an FBI Special Agent to contemplate. Maybe he'd just lay in some groceries and hunker down out in the swamp until the Hollywood crew packed up and returned to Tinseltown.

"They're hiring local people to be extras," she continued breathlessly. "Mama and I are going to the tryouts. Mama's got herself a new hat that she's sure will help her get selected, but bless her heart, of course I'd never tell her to her face, but all those feathers make it look like a giant canary molted all over her head. I don't think that's exactly the look those TV people are going for.

"I'm hoping to get picked for one of the fancy dress ball scenes, but I can't decide whether I should wear my Miss Crawfish Days tiara, or the one I won for being crowned Sweetheart of the Shrimp Fleet last year. The crawfish one is taller and more ornate, but I am partial to the Shrimp sweetheart because it's more sparkly. Mama's lobbying for the Sweet Potato Princess crown. Which do you think I should choose?"

Finn was *so* in over his head here. "I haven't any idea." Inspiration struck. "What did Nate say?" If there was ever a man who knew the right thing to say to a woman, it was his baby brother.

"He suggested I go with the one that gave me the most confidence."

"Sounds good to me. And Nate is where?"

"Oh, didn't I tell you? Why, he's down in Houma."

"When do you expect him back?"

She shrugged. "Not for a couple days."

"Do you know where he's staying?"

Her pink lips turned down. "Sorry, hon."

"That's okay. Just give me his cell phone number."

"Sure." She glanced at a Post-it stuck on the monitor of her computer. As she read off the number, Finn wrote it down in the notebook he used for investigative notes. "But it's not going to do you any good to call."

"Why not?"

"Because he never turns it on. It frustrates folks no end, but he says if he turned it on, then people would call him."

Hell. That definitely sounded like his laid-back baby brother. "I don't suppose he happens to keep the keys to the camp here at the office?"

"You're in luck, sugar; there's an extra set in the top drawer of his desk."

She tilted her teased cloud of pastel blond hair toward the adjoining office. "I'd get them for you, but"— she wagged her pink-tipped fingers at him again—"my nails are wet."

Pressing a palm against her jackhammering heart, Julia went back inside the bungalow to answer the front door, locking the patio door behind her. Her breath escaped in a relieved whoosh as she viewed the familiar face on the other side of the peephole.

"Warren!" She flung open the door. "Come in! What a lovely surprise. Would you like some wine? I have a bottle of Chardonnay from that Sonoma Valley winery where we filmed the scene where Amanda pushed her grown stepdaughter into a vat of grapes."

"I'd better not. I noticed this morning that I was looking a bit jaundiced, so I'm staying clear of alcohol until I can get a blood test to check for liver damage."

*River Road*'s head writer was a card-carrying hypochondriac. Since his various life-threatening illnesses never impacted his work, everyone took his little neurosis in stride.

He'd been pitching film ideas to her for months, and been turned down each time, so he now seemed a bit puzzled by her enthusiasm. But apparently living by the *carpe diem* bumper sticker he'd stuck onto the lid of his laptop, he decided to seize the moment.

"I really believe I've come up with the perfect vehicle for you this time, Julia. I hoped you might get a chance to read it on the flight to Louisiana."

"Isn't that a good idea," she enthused, as if he'd just informed her he'd written both the Declaration of Independence and *The Great Gatsby* since she'd seen him last. Taking his arm, she pulled him into the bungalow, closed the door behind him, and double locked it. "I'm dying to hear all about it!"

She flashed him her most delicious smile and hoped that this script would be a departure from his usual ideas, which invariably had her playing an exaggerated version of her *River Road* vixen role.

"I think you'll like it. I've been thinking a lot about what you said, about my last story being too over the top."

"Oh, I didn't mean that in a bad way. Why, I'm sure an actress with a wider range could have handled it wonderfully." She patted his arm. "I just didn't believe I had the range to play a bisexual prostitute serial killer possessed by Satan."

"You would have been terrific," he insisted again. "But I decided your suggestion of playing against your soap image was a good idea. So I went back to the drawing board and came up with this cool woman-in-jeopardy script."

"A woman in jeopardy?" Sirens sounded in her head as he held the slender stack of bound papers toward her.

"Yeah." He grinned his pleasure at having come up with a new story he thought she'd accept. "In this one you're a movie star being stalked by a crazy guy who's confused your movie roles with real life and keeps sending you threatening letters."

"A stalker?" This was not amusing.

"He's an obsessive fan." Since she still hadn't taken the script from him, he turned to the first page. "It opens with the actress opening a letter and finding a photograph of herself in the shower."

It wasn't exactly the same as the "dead Amanda" shot, but close enough. Even as she told herself that she was overdramatizing a coincidence, Julia tightened her fingers around the dead bolt key, the way she'd learned in her self-defense class, and tried to convince herself that she'd have no compunction gouging Warren Hyatt's smiling blue eyes out to save her life.

# 5

*The sight of the weather-bleached cypress camp*—built planters' style, on stilts—stirred long-forgotten memories. His father teaching him to check the traps, an uncle teaching him to cook, hanging out here with his brothers back in their teens, drooling over a stack of *Playboy* magazines and arguing whether they'd rather be stranded on a desert island with the pretty, peaches-and-cream sorority girls of the SEC, or the PAC 10's sun-gilded beach bunnies.

There were also memories not as sweet. Like sneaking out here the night before his father's funeral and getting tanked on the bottle of Jack Daniel's he'd filched from the bottom drawer of the oak desk in the sheriff's office.

Big Jake Callahan had kept the unopened bottle in the drawer as a reminder of his wild past and a daily test of the vow he'd made to quit drinking the day he'd proposed to Finn's mother.

The Jack Black was the first and only thing Finn had ever stolen in his life, and guilt had roiled in his gut along with the whiskey, sorrow, and most of all fear of how he, now the eldest Callahan male in the family, could even think of filling his father's size thirteen boots.

Finn pulled up next to the screened porch. Because of the constant conflict between water and land in this part of the country, there were times when the only way to the camp was by boat. Now there was a narrow, twisting road that Nate had recently graveled. Of course, one good storm and the road would turn right back into a waterway.

He unearthed the Spic and Span and spent the first thirty minutes cleaning the refrigerator, tossing out all the green mystery items he figured had been left behind after the bachelor party Jack had thrown for a friend a couple months ago. He put away the groceries he'd bought at the Cajun Market, where everyone had been eager to tell him all about the Hollywood people coming to town. Apparently Lorelei hadn't been exaggerating when she'd said folks were in a tizzy.

Next he unpacked. Swept the floor. Changed the sheets on the moss-stuffed mattress, then poured some vinegar into a pan and used the classified section of *The Times-Picayune* to wash the windows.

Finally running out of domestic chores, he pulled the tab on a can of RC Cola, went out onto the porch, propped his feet up on the railing, and settled down to watch the lightning bugs. Cicadas were singing their high-pitched night song; bullfrogs croaked a bass accompaniment.

"So," Finn said as night descended over the bayou, "what the hell am I going to do for the next three weeks and six days?"

Warren appeared nearly as upset by the photograph as Julia.

"Ohmigod." His eyes darted around the room like nervous birds trying to escape. "Your stalker's back. But now he's threatening to kill you!"

Hearing it out loud made it sound incredibly far-fetched. Like a new plot twist on *River Road*. She watched him press the fingertips of his right hand against his left wrist and suspected he was checking his pulse rate.

*If you're not careful, you're going to become as neurotic as Warren.*

Six months ago, while working on a story line about Amanda's fifth husband dying of a heart attack—which may or may not have been poison induced—he'd been rushed to the UCLA Medical Center with palpitations he'd been convinced was angina.

Then there was last year's subplot which conveniently did away with her fourth husband, Helmut Heinz, the Swiss ski instructor she'd rashly married on a whim after sharing three bottles of après-ski champagne. Helmut had been blackmailing her, threatening to tell oil baron J.C. Honeycutt, husband number five, that she'd still been legally married when she'd walked down the aisle for the fifth time.

When Warren began writing the scenes giving the ski instructor blinding headaches and attacks of vertigo, leading up to a fatal embolism, he began to suffer his own symptoms.

"I just know it's a brain tumor," he'd fretted to Julia, who'd driven him to the hospital and kept him company during the CAT scan which revealed nothing wrong.

He was lucky she was leaving the show; if Amanda wasn't scheduled to die from the gunshot wound Vanessa had inflicted on her, there was an outside chance Amanda would go through with her pregnancy—despite one abortion and two miscarriages, not to mention that fake pregnancy she'd used to nab husband number three. And Warren would undoubtedly suffer sympathetic morning sickness.

She didn't even want to think how he'd survive a subsequent fictional labor and delivery.

"Someone must have been on the set today, Julia."

"A lot of people were on the set today, Warren."

Whenever the script called for Amanda to strip down to her underwear, every male on the crew seemed to find a reason to show up for the taping. One of them must have brought a camera.

After the show had first launched five years ago, making Amanda a household name, a supposedly nude photograph of her ended up on the Internet, ratings soared into the stratosphere and she'd won the dubious honor of actually passing Pamela Anderson and Tommy Lee as the most downloaded photograph by males eighteen to thirty-four. Which, her agent had assured her when she'd complained about the invasion of her privacy, was a good thing.

"Surely you don't think one of the *River Road* family is your stalker?"

"No, I can't believe that." She took a deep breath and made herself sound calm. "I'll admit the thought flashed through my mind when I first opened the envelope. But I get all sorts of weird viewer mail." Just this week she'd received a half dozen proposals, three times as many propositions, and one warning, scrawled in the margin of a yellowed page torn from a bible, that God punished adulteresses.

"You only get your mail after it's been screened by all those people the network hired to answer it. When was the last time you got a viewer letter here at home?"

Good point. "It's probably just another stupid practical joke."

"If it is, it's not very funny."

"Practical jokes at the expense of others are never funny. I'm sure I haven't been threatened, Warren." The more she said it out loud, the more she began to believe it. "You have to promise me you won't say anything about this at dinner."

"But Julia—"

"Promise," she insisted. "It'll only stir things up unnecessarily and some waiter might overhear and call the *Enquirer* and it'll just give the tabloids more fodder." She hadn't been able to go into the grocery store for two weeks when the shower picture had shown up at supermarket checkout stands all over the country.

He nodded, but the worry in his eyes didn't give Julia a great deal of confidence.

Two hours later, in a private dining room in a trendy Melrose restaurant, Julia's concerns were justified.

"Someone sent Julia a death threat today," Warren announced.

The buzz of conversation up and down the table instantly went silent. Every eye turned toward her.

"I'm sure it was just a practical joke." Damn. They hadn't even gotten through the antipasto course. She explained about the photograph in as few words as possible, putting the most positive spin on it she could.

"If it is just a joke, it's sure not very funny," Shane responded to her theory.

"I hate to break this to you, Shane, but neither was Mr. Happy. And how about when you glued the silverware to the table at Margot's birthday party?"

The former Diva of Daytime frowned at the memory. "That was decidedly in poor taste."

Somewhere between forty and forty-five, Margot Madison was fast approaching the age when actresses tended to disappear from television and movie screens. And on those occasions they did get roles, their characters certainly didn't have the hot sex scenes Margot had built her early career on.

"Maybe it wasn't meant as a threat," Shane suggested. "You could have a secret admirer on the crew."

"That's probably it." Julia was grateful to have a new theory. And it made sense. Just last season, the head cameraman had taken to leaving little chocolate hearts and tapes of country songs he'd written about her in her dressing room. He'd quit the show and moved to Nashville when John Michael Montgomery actually bought one of his twangy ballads about a cowboy who'd lost his wife and house to another man, his truck to the bank, but thank God he still had his drinking buddies, his horse, and his good ole one-eyed hound dog, Duke. He'd been very sweet and Julia still missed him. She'd never been filmed as flatteringly as she had during the six months of that country boy's crush.

"No doubt Warren's just bein' a big neurotic sook again," Randy said. "But there's no use taking unnecessary chances."

"You're too important to the show," Charles Kendall weighed in from his power seat at the end of the long table. "We certainly can't afford to lose you."

*Fortune* magazine had reported the corporate vice president to be thirty-five years old, but his receding hairline made him appear older. His body, beneath the dark charcoal gray suit that stood out on Melrose Avenue like a blizzard in January, was pudgy and out of shape. His eyes tended to be a bit shifty and his manicured hands didn't look as if they'd ever done anything more physical than punch the buttons on his television remote.

When she'd first met him, Julia had been surprised such an unimpressive man had achieved so much power at such a relatively young age. Until Damien—who seemed to be tapped into every gossip line in Los Angeles—informed her Kendall was the son of the corporate founder's second wife by a previous marriage.

"I'm flattered. But I'm still leaving at the end of the season," Julia reminded him.

When she'd first announced her decision to quit the show, he'd assumed she was merely angling for more money, and had flown into town in his corporate jet, taken her out to dinner, and offered a fifty-percent increase per episode.

When she'd explained that her decision to leave wasn't based on income, but on a once-in-a-lifetime career opportunity, he'd doubled the first offer.

She'd politely but firmly turned that down, as well.

He'd tried reasoning. Cajoled. Then finally resorted to shouting, which certainly hadn't been any way to change her mind. Julia had remained resolute.

With visible reluctance, he'd finally accepted her decision and assured her that she was welcome to return to the show if things didn't work out on the big screen. Then, as they'd left the restaurant, he'd pinched her butt.

"You're still under contract until the end of the season," he now reminded her. "We're launching a breakthrough new drug during the Louisiana story segment. We need your high visibility to ensure strong initial sales."

"What *is* the story?"

"You'll all be given the scripts on a day-to-day basis, the night before each day's taping," Randy informed them. "We'll be taping all four episodes over the next two weeks."

"That's two a week," Shane complained.

"Not only is he *People Magazine*'s sexiest man of the year, he can count, too," Margot murmured.

Shane gave her an uncharacteristically annoyed look. "My point was that it's not a great deal of time for me to get a handle on my character's motivation."

"This isn't *King Lear,* darling," Margot drawled as the busboy cleared away the now-forgotten plates. "You're playing a sleazy Southern alcoholic opportunist who's led around by his wandering cock. Surely that's not such a stretch."

The smile she flashed him over the rim of her martini glass was laced with acid. She and Shane had been an item three years ago, when they both worked on the soap *All My Tomorrows*. She'd been a fixture on daytime. An icon. He'd been the brash newcomer who'd figured out that if he had an affair with the actress who got the most screen time, she'd undoubtedly push the writers for meatier parts for her lover. Which was exactly what happened.

A flush rose from the collar of his body-hugging black silk T-shirt. "If anyone's an alcoholic—"

"Now, now, mate," Randy jumped in to smooth feathers before they became irreparably ruffled. "I'm sure Margot didn't mean anything personal. Did you, love?"

"I damn well did." The waiter had returned with the entrees. The older woman tapped the rim of her empty glass with a long fingernail, ordering her third drink of the evening.

"Can we stop the lovers' quarrel and get back to Julia's problem?" Warren asked peevishly. "I'm beginning to get a migraine." He paled. "Or perhaps this time I really do have a brain tumor."

"I'm sure that's not the case," Julia assured him. "It hasn't been that long since your CAT scan. And I really can't believe this is a serious threat."

"Nevertheless, there's no point in taking unnecessary chances," Charles Kendall said. "Perhaps we should notify the authorities."

That was the last thing Julia wanted. "Surely that's not necessary." Since police reports were public documents, there'd be no way she could keep the disturbing photograph out of the news, which could inspire copycat threats.

"You don't want to call the cops." Randy immediately supported her case, and Julia could have kissed him. "Call them and the story will hit like a shower of shit, and the next thing you know, we'll be overrun by those supermarket jurnos. Why don't we just close the set and hire additional security?"

"Security costs money," Kendall muttered. As if realizing he'd made it sound as if money was more important than Julia's life, he added, "But a little extra expense shouldn't enter into the equation." He reached beneath the pink tablecloth and patted her thigh. "The important thing is to keep our star safe."

Julia was tempted to jab her fork into the soft hand that lingered on her leg. She didn't buy his concerned act for a moment; Charles Kendall would make Scrooge look downright generous.

He was constantly complaining about expenses, seeming unable or unwilling to understand that *River Road*'s glamorous style was a great part of the show's success. People might claim to be interested in simpler things these days, but if ratings were any indication, they continued to be fascinated by wealth. Particularly when those rich characters were behaving as badly as *River Road*'s inhabitants did. And Amanda was definitely the worst of the lot.

Outargued and outvoted, she ended up spending the next two days with a former cop turned private detective and bodyguard. Julia suspected he probably didn't spend all that much time detecting; it would be a little difficult for a man with the girth of a sperm whale who'd adopted the 1980s *Miami Vice* pastel look to pull off surveillance without being noticed.

"There's no way he's coming to Louisiana with us," she informed Randy the night before the flight. "I doubt there's a seat on the plane wide enough for him, and that aftershave he bathes in is killing my sinuses." Apparently no one had informed him that not every woman was wild about an Aqua Velva man.

Realizing she wasn't going to budge on this point, Randy called Charles at his suite at the Beverly Hills Hotel. During a hastily called summit meeting, the powers-that-be of *River Road* unanimously agreed to leave the Hulk behind in Los Angeles.

That was the good news.

The bad news was that Julia was still going to be stuck with a bodyguard.

# 6

*Finn felt like a guy who'd been shipwrecked* on a desert island. When the bass boat that had been roaring up the channel cut its engine and began drifting toward the camp, he had to restrain himself from jumping into the water and pulling it the rest of the way into the dock. Bond Girl Pussy Galore, stripped down to suntan oil and a smile, could not have been more welcome than Nate.

"It's about time you got around to paying your big brother a visit." He put down the well-worn copy of *From Russia With Love* he'd first read in the eighth grade. 007 and the beautiful, Garbo-look-alike Russian corporal who'd been employed to seduce him had just boarded the Orient Express.

"It's only been three days." Nate tied up the boat.

"You and I must be living in different time zones, because it feels like I've been stuck out here for a month."

"Time flies when you're having fun," Nate said agreeably. The sun was setting into the water in a blaze of red. "How's the fishing goin'?"

"Lousy." Finn hated fishing.

"You could always try shooting them out of the water."

"That's against the law."

Nate shook his head. "Christ, you can be literal. Well, no matter, because I brought dinner." He lifted some bags from the bottom of the boat. "I've got us some red beans, rice, a nice fat chicken, and some of the Cajun Market's spiciest boudin."

"Since when did you learn to cook?"

"Actually, anything 'sides burgers, grilled sausage or take-out pizza is a stretch," Nate admitted with a quick flash of his trademark grin. "But I figured you might like making one of Dad's old recipes while I spin you a tale. And make you an offer you won't be able to refuse."

Finn didn't trust his brother's offhanded tone. Years of dealing with criminals had him listening more to what Nate *wasn't* saying than his actual words. He was holding something back, which was totally out of character for his normally forthright brother.

Finn wondered all through supper what Nate was up to, but figuring that his brother would spill the beans when he was ready, he enjoyed the stories of small town life which sounded like an alien planet when compared to the world he'd been living in.

Three hours later, as the moon rose in the dark purple sky, Finn finally got his answer.

"You want to deputize me?" he asked incredulously.

"Just for a few days."

"I already have a job."

"Which you're currently on leave from."

"I'm going back." Finn was damned if he was going to let SAC Jansen banish him to the FBI's version of Siberia.

"Of course you are. But you've still got three and a half weeks in exile. I'm only asking for two of those weeks. Besides, you've already told me you're getting antsy out here."

Actually, he was on the verge of going stark raving mad. Still, Nate's offer wasn't any more appealing than drowning worms.

"I got stuck with one of those celebrity baby-sitting jobs years ago when I worked for the Manhattan office, and hated it. I swore I'd never do another one."

The Supermodel had been the daughter of the dictator of some obscure Carribean island. The guy had received death threats from a band of rebels, and rumors in the intelligence community said they might try to kidnap the daughter as a bargaining tool. So the local cops brought in the FBI as a CYA maneuver.

She'd run him ragged. It was bad enough that she'd insisted on going to seemingly every store and nightclub in the city; she'd also pulled every feminine trick in the book to seduce him. She'd only been in the city for five nights, but it had seemed like a year.

"Yeah, I remember. And I still doubt many guys would think spending twenty-four hours a day with a woman built for sin was much of a hardship," Nate said. "But this'll be different."

"Sure it will. And the Sox'll win the Series next year."

"Christ, you're a cynic." Nate shook his sun-streaked head. "Look,

Jack's friend, this Hogan guy who's directed the movies made from his books, plans to shoot every day and into the evening. Since Blue Bayou doesn't have any nightlife to speak of, there'll be no reason for Julia Summers to leave the inn during her off hours. Besides, it pays damn well. Jack's not kidding when he says those Hollywood people throw money around like confetti."

"I've got all the money I need." Most of it tied up in stocks and bonds that continued to yield a nice little profit, making Finn glad he hadn't jumped on the tech and Internet bandwagon.

"Okay, let me put it this way." Nate ran a finger down the condensation on the neck of his Voodoo beer bottle. "I'm in a bind here. This isn't exactly the big city. Until I can find someone to replace Jimbo Lott as sheriff, the town's entire police force is down to two deputies, one who's pushing seventy and belongs on school crossing duty, the other who's fresh out of the police academy." He paused. "I don't suppose you'd consider taking the job."

Finn narrowed his eyes in what he'd been told was an intimidating glare. "Don't even think about it."

His brother shrugged. "That's what I figured you'd say. So, the thing is, the budget doesn't allow for me to hire extra private guys from out of town, but if I don't supply a bodyguard for Julia Summers, they'll have to take their dog and pony show somewhere else. And believe me, Finn, even if you don't need some of those bucks they'll be spending, Blue Bayou could sure as hell use them. If we don't get some additional funding, we may have to close down the after-school program at the Boys and Girls Club.

"Then there was last month's tropical storm, which turned the baseball diamonds at Heron Park back to bayou, so we've had to apply to the federal government for a loan to relocate them. Plus the prenatal nurse visitation program sure isn't cheap to run, and—"

"I get the picture." Having grown up in the remote bayou town, Finn knew how it had never entirely recovered after the oil bust. Jobs had been lost, people whose roots went back to the first Acadians had been forced to take jobs in the cities, and those who'd stayed had seen their income drop considerably. If Lorelei was right about them hiring local folks as extras, that could provide another much needed economic boost.

"So, who is this Julia Summers?"

"Obviously you've been spending too much time looking at

Wanted posters. She's the hottest thing on the tube these days. Back when Suzanne Bouchand and I were passing a good time together, before Suzanne got all carried away and started thinkin' about marriage, she used to make me watch it every Friday night with her."

Nate held out a glossy publicity photo of a modern-day Amazon lying in the surf wearing little more than two postage stamps and a Band-Aid. Her hair was a tawny red mane around shoulders that gleamed with glistening drops of sea spray and oil. Her glossy, kiss-me-big-boy lips were parted; her eyes, which were so green they had to be contacts, were darkly lined to emphasize their catlike tilt.

She had an old Hollywood sex appeal, like Rita Hayworth's Gilda who'd so sorely tempted poor old Glenn Ford. She also had *bimbo* written all over her.

"She looks like trouble." Only for family or country would Finn even consider spending the next two weeks with someone whose bra size was undoubtedly higher than her I.Q.

"Lorelei says she saw on *Entertainment Tonight* that Julia Summers is going to be the new Bond Girl."

"Well, shit, that impresses the hell out of me." She'd be perfect, he secretly allowed.

Ursula Andress had been the quintessential Bond Girl, the first of those beautiful women with the big breasts and double entendre names that were as integral to the stories as all the guns and gadgets. The actresses who'd followed had come close, though the more recent girls tended to be intelligent and athletic, as likely to exchange clever banter and engage in one-upmanship as they were to swoon in Bond's arms. While these women were definitely appealing, Finn took it as proof that political correctness had managed to get its tentacles even into the last true bastion of testosterone-driven fantasy.

"It's only fourteen days, *cher,*" Nate coaxed. "If you won't do it for me, how 'bout doin' it for the little kids of Blue Bayou?"

"Jesus, you're shameless."

Nate grinned. "I'm a politician."

"So, how serious is everyone taking this so-called threat?"

"The producer seemed concerned enough, but I got the impression he was more worried about some crazy fan disrupting shooting before they finished the season finale."

"I suppose I could call the L.A. cops and get their take on things."

Nate shook his head. "Won't help, since she refused to bring the cops into it."

"Why?"

"Beats me. Maybe she's worried about the press getting hold of the story and blowing it out of proportion."

"If that's the case, why the hell is she agreeing to police protection while she's here?"

"I got the impression she's still not that eager about the idea, but since she refused to let the private guy they hired in L.A. come with her to Louisiana, we were a last-minute compromise."

"Terrific." An uncooperative Hollywood type was all he needed right now. Still, it wasn't as if he had a helluva lot to do until he returned to D.C.

Fourteen days. A guy could probably survive anything for fourteen days. Except fishing.

"When are they due to show up?"

"They're arriving in New Orleans the day after tomorrow, then coming down here by limo. They booked all the rooms at The Plantation Inn and I'll be throwing them a little welcome cocktail party. They'll begin shooting a couple days later out at Beau Soleil."

"If they bring out the drugs, I'm going to have to bust them," Finn warned.

Nate sighed. "I'd expect nothing less. Which is why I've already warned them that Blue Bayou has a zero-tolerance policy." He paused, eyeing his brother with a suspicious caution.

"What now?" Finn asked.

"I promised the director you'd meet their plane."

"That was ballsy. What would you have done if I'd turned you down?"

His brother shrugged. "Never happen. If there's one constant in life, it's the fact that I can always count on my big brother to come through for me." His expression sobered. "I really do owe you one, Finn."

"Believe me, Nate, I intend to collect."

Finn shook his head as he checked out the photo again. If the actress fell into the bayou, at least he wouldn't have to worry about rescuing her from drowning. Not with the set of water wings she'd managed to stuff into that teensy-weensy gold bikini.

# 7

*As the airliner made its approach* into New Orleans, Julia couldn't decide whether she was looking at bits of land surrounded by water, or water dotted with hundreds of tiny little islands.

She turned to Charles, who was seated across the aisle.

"Please tell me that you didn't hire the Incredible Hulk's Louisiana cousin."

"Large is good. It's intimidating. Keeps the crazies from trying anything in the first place."

"If a stalker *had* tried to get to me, I would have been on my own. I've seen glaciers on the Nature Channel move faster than that guy."

"I'm sure the Blue Bayou deputy will be more to your liking," he said, his tone letting her know he was still less than pleased with her demand to leave the L.A. bodyguard behind.

Julia wasn't so sure about that. Using voice mail to monitor her calls, she'd received three messages from the cop before leaving for the airport.

"We're probably just trading the human blimp for Barney Fife," she muttered.

Granted, he hadn't sounded much like Mayberry's inept deputy. His voice had been deep and gruff, his instruction that she call him back terse. He'd also sounded increasingly frustrated with the situation. Well, that made two of them.

"Callahan assured me he's just what we're looking for. Besides, it's a sensible solution. A local cop is bound to spot any strangers showing up on the set who don't belong there."

Julia allowed it made a bit of sense, and reminded herself that it was only two weeks. She could probably survive anyone for two weeks.

She changed her mind the moment she entered the terminal. It wasn't his height that gave him away. Nor his body, which while even more substantial than the *Miami Vice* wannabe, appeared to have not an ounce of excess flesh on it. His black hair was cut military short, another giveaway, and certainly too short for her personal taste.

But it was his alert ice blue eyes, which somehow managed to scan the terminal while not appearing to move, that screamed out Cop. With a capital C. This was no Barney Fife. And if he was a small town deputy, she'd eat her Emmy.

Damn. Though Julia understood, on an intellectual level, that the majority of police put their lives on the line on a daily basis to protect citizens, and she certainly appreciated their efforts on her behalf, she'd spent too many of her formative years watching cops drag her counterculture parents, Freedom and Peace, off to jail in paddy wagons to be comfortable around them. She'd even been arrested herself once, though the charges were dropped after she'd spent a night in jail.

"You didn't tell me Kendall brought in the FBI," she murmured to Randy.

"He didn't."

"Then you want to tell me who else would be wearing a suit and tie in this heat?"

The New Orleans humidity had hit like a steamy fist the instant she'd entered the jetway. Amazingly, the man's white shirt didn't appear to have a solitary wrinkle. The full Windsor knot of his dark blue tie was precisely centered beneath his starched collar.

Randy followed her gaze. "He certainly does stand out. But what makes you think he's your bodyguard? Perhaps he's picking up a prisoner. Or his wife."

"He doesn't have a wife."

"How would you know that?"

"Just call it a hunch." Surely a man with a loving woman in his life wouldn't look so hard. A man with a family—wife, kids, and a mutt who'd dig holes in the lawn and fetch sticks—wouldn't appear so unrelentingly rigid.

Definitely FBI, Julia decided as he squared his broad shoulders and began walking toward them.

"Welcome to Blue Bayou, Mr. Hogan," he greeted Randy. "I admire your work." He held out a huge bear paw of a hand. His nails were neatly trimmed, not manicured, but squared to precision that suggested a controlling nature. "I'm Finn Callahan. Nate apologizes for not coming to the airport to welcome you himself, but something came up."

"Nothing vital, I hope." Charles's brow furrowed at the idea that something might disrupt their shooting schedule.

"Just a little dispute over some traps," Finn assured him, then turned to Julia. "Ms. Summers. If you'll come with me, we'll get your bags."

She gave him a sweet, utterly false smile. "How lovely of you to offer. But that won't be necessary, Special Agent Callahan."

Those killer blue eyes hardened and his dark head dipped in a slight nod. "Good guess."

"Oh, it wasn't that difficult," she said with a careless shrug. There was no way she'd let him know that her stomach had taken off on a roller coaster the moment she'd spotted him. "You're obviously not a local cop, and since I'm neither visiting royalty nor a member of the presidential family, that rules out Secret Service. Which leaves FBI."

And there was no way she could spend the next two weeks in close proximity with this man. "I'm terribly sorry about wasting your time by bringing you out here today, but I won't be needing your services."

"Dammit, Julia," Randy complained. "You can't refuse a bodyguard."

"I don't know why not." She flicked her tawny hair over her shoulder. "We are, after all, talking about *my* body."

Finn, who'd so far managed to keep his damn eyes out of trouble, couldn't quite resist this challenge to check out the body in question. Having rented a tape of last season's show last night—just to check out the cast of players he was going to be stuck with for the next two weeks—he'd admittedly been surprised by the woman now simply dressed in a waist-skimming white T-shirt and low-slung jeans.

That bikini picture, along with the over-the-top bad girl character she played and the news she was going to be the next Bond Girl, had given the impression that she was some larger than life sex goddess.

Even though he, more than most, knew appearances were deceiving—Lawson was Redford handsome, with a deceptively easygoing outward manner that had allowed him to lure the girls in the first place—Finn was having trouble picturing this slender woman as the voluptuous seductress he'd watched giving her pool guy the ride of his life in the shallow end.

The corporate honcho, Kendall, weighed in.

"It may be your body, but it's not your choice. Your contract with Atlantic Pharmaceuticals forbids any behavior that might jeopardize your ability to perform."

"That clause refers to off-the-set behavior," she argued. "It was only put in there by the insurance company lawyers to keep me from breaking my neck skiing or skydiving."

"Since the parameters aren't spelled out, the wording encompasses all dangerous behavior," he countered. "I've no doubt that the legal department would consider refusing protection after receiving threatening notes an unsatisfactory risk."

Finn had gotten her unlisted number from the director last night. Frustrated when all he'd gotten was her answering machine, he'd left his number so she could fill in the huge gaps Kendall had left out. When she hadn't bothered to return his calls, he'd spent the past eighteen hours getting more and more pissed. This conversation did nothing to improve his mood.

"If you don't want him, Julia, can I have him?"

When the Barbie doll blonde he recognized from the show's credits as Felissa Templeton put a French manicured talon on his arm and offered him a come-hither-big-boy smile, Finn decided Nate was going to owe him big time for this one.

They were beginning to draw attention. He turned to the others, who were watching the little battle of wills with undisguised interest.

"The limo's waiting to take you all on to Blue Bayou. Why don't you go ahead, and Ms. Summers and I will catch up with you at the inn."

It was not a suggestion, but an order. One which not a single person questioned.

"That's very good," Julia murmured as they headed off like a herd of sheep. "You didn't even have to pull out your gun."

"I tend to save my gun for the bad guys. Along with the bright lights and rubber hoses."

She folded her arms, drawing his attention back to those breasts, which while not as full as they appeared on TV, were still pretty fine. "That isn't terribly reassuring, since I suspect you consider the entire population to be bad guys."

"Potential bad guys," he corrected as he took hold of her elbow and without utilizing force, began moving her forward. "And for the record, I was playing sandlot ball with my brothers when the Feds busted your parents. Which means there's no way I could have been involved."

While he may be on the SAC's shit list and in OPR's sights, Finn still had friends at the Bureau, who'd stayed late and pulled her hippie parents' thick FBI jackets.

"You've obviously been reading old files. But that doesn't mean you have the slightest idea what really happened back then."

"Our situations may have been different, Ms. Summers, but I do happen to know firsthand how it feels to be a kid and have your entire world pulled out from under you."

What in hell had him telling her that? He'd been sixteen years old when Jake Callahan, Blue Bayou's sheriff, had heroically taken a bullet to save another man's life. His dad's death still hurt; Finn figured it always would.

A very strong part of him just wanted to let the woman have her own way. A stronger part, the sense of personal responsibility he'd learned from his father, knew that there was no way he was going to let her walk away with her life potentially in danger.

"Look." He reined in his frustration that she wasn't going along with the program. "It's obvious that we've got a problem here."

She tossed up her chin. A chin which, now that he was seeing it up close, was a bit too stubborn for classical beauty. "My only problem is that too many people seem to believe that just because I'm good at taking direction, I'll also take orders." A woven silver ring gleamed as she skimmed a slender hand through a wild riot of hair that looked as if she'd just gotten out of bed after a night of hot sex.

Finn told himself not to go there. 007 would know how to settle this: he'd toss off some sexy, witty line that would immediately charm the lace panties right off her. Or, even better, he'd just shut her up by hauling her against him and kissing her silly.

Finn momentarily wondered if those lush lips tasted as good as they looked, then ruthlessly shoved the forbidden idea back into a dark corner of his brain.

"I'm not real wild about our situation, either. But my brother's mayor of Blue Bayou and it just might hurt tourism if some nutcase decides to kill you while you're in town, which wouldn't bode real well for his reelection chances. So why don't we just lay our cards on the table and move on. I'll agree not to consider you an anarchist if you stop thinking of me as a storm trooper."

"I'm certainly no anarchist. And neither are my parents."

She did not acknowledge any willingness not to think of him as a storm trooper. The woman was really beginning to piss him off. Here he'd been willing to compromise, and she was still arguing. And, dammit, now she was marching away again.

"We obviously have different definitions." He fell into step beside her. "In my book, anyone who threatens to blow up a nuclear power plant isn't exactly into law and order."

"Did it ever occur to you that your so-called 'book' may be as fictional as my TV show? Besides, they were acquitted."

"Guilty people have been known to get acquitted."

Too damn often, to Finn's way of thinking. Unable to deny the strength of evidence against their client, which included two naked women locked in a dungeon in his basement, Lawson's damn dream team was now trying to ensure he'd end up in some cozy mental ward instead of the prison cell where he belonged.

"And sometimes innocent people are falsely arrested by overeager cops and prosecuted by ambitious politicians."

Finn rubbed at the boulder-size knot of tension at the nape of his neck. "Sort of like you were, when you were picked up for starting that riot in Sacramento last year?"

"It was hardly a riot. I'd merely joined a picket line of nurses demonstrating against losing more and more of their responsibilities to unlicensed hospital employees. It certainly wasn't our fault when some thugs hired by the other side started physically harassing us."

"You're the one who began the riot by wacking one of those so-called thugs with your protest sign."

"He knocked down a pregnant woman." She scowled at the memory. "After that, I'll admit things got a bit out of hand, but the case would have blown over if some overly ambitious district attorney hadn't been running for Congress on a law and order platform."

The newspaper articles he'd found on an Internet search stated the prosecutor had lost his election chances the moment the pictures of Julia Summers being loaded into a paddy wagon, along with a clutch of scrub-clad nurses—one who looked about to give birth to a ten pound basketball at any moment—showed up on the nightly news of every TV station in the state.

"We're not going to get anywhere arguing the United States judicial system," he tried to reason with her yet again.

Which was a joke. How the hell did you begin to reason with an actress who'd grown up on a hippie California dope farm, with parents who'd been too busy protesting the system and throwing red paint on army recruiters to ever get around to tying the knot like respectable people? And she appeared to be following in their protesting footsteps.

"The point I was trying to make was that I joined the FBI because I wanted to uphold the law. Not abuse it. But whether you believe that or not, given that clause in your contract, it appears you're stuck with a bodyguard until this production wraps up.

"As it happens, Blue Bayou's sheriff's department is currently shorthanded, so you can either take your chances with some Rent-a-Cop, or put up with me. Now, since I'm a straight-talking kind of guy, I'm going to admit that I'm not real wild about the deal either, since my lifetime goal was never to baby-sit some spoiled, argumentative Hollywood prima donna who never met a wacked-out cause she couldn't embrace."

Her chin shot up again. "Protecting nurses' jobs and patients' safety is not a wacked-out cause."

"Okay, I'll grant you that one." Finn's own maternal grandmother had been an LPN at the country's only remaining leprosarium in Carville. "But my point is that, just in case some nutcase out there has actually targeted you, your best bet to stay alive is with me. Because I'm the best there is."

"You're also more than a little arrogant."

"Thanks. I work at it."

"Oh, I think you're being overly modest, Special Agent. I doubt it takes any work at all."

She turned and began walking away again. Cursing beneath his breath, Finn reminded himself that he had two choices: Julia Summers or fishing. Which was no damn choice at all.

# 8

*Julia had been raised* in an atmosphere that celebrated the differences in people. Her parents had taught her at an early age not to stereotype and even without that early instruction, she'd witnessed the danger of such behavior firsthand when the government had painted her parents with that broad anarchist brush during her childhood.

Admittedly, they'd been social activists, embracing causes from saving the whales to stopping the war in Vietnam to the Equal Rights Amendment to reparations for American Japanese who'd been sent off to internment camps during the second world war. They'd also brought her up to fight for the rights of those who couldn't fight for themselves. But she'd always known that there was absolutely no way Peace or Freedom would have ever turned to violence.

"They don't even eat meat," she muttered to herself as they left the terminal in a black Suburban which, like his dark suit, screamed FBI.

When he slanted her a look, she realized she'd inadvertently spoken out loud. "My parents are vegetarians."

He nodded. "I know."

The simple acknowledgment only irritated her all the more. "Doesn't it bother you at all?"

"What?"

"That you make your living invading the privacy of your fellow Americans?"

"No. Because I don't consider investigating the bad guys as invading privacy. And while it may be hard for you to fathom, from what I've been able to tell, most Americans don't feel that way, either."

"Maybe they're just afraid they'll be thrown in jail if they admit their real feelings."

His only response to the careless accusation, which Julia regretted the moment it came out of her mouth, was a slight tightening of his fingers on the steering wheel.

"I recently closed a case," he said in a mild, dry, just-the-facts-ma'am tone. "There was this rich computer software mogul who hop-skipped around the country, picking up coeds and slicing them up. That would've been bad enough, but since killing apparently didn't give him a big enough rush, he'd keep them prisoner first, sometimes for weeks. Rape was probably the easiest of the stuff he put them through."

"Ronald Lawson."

"I guess you've heard about the case."

"It would have been hard not to, since it was all over the headlines when he was arrested. But I didn't follow it very closely." The murderous sexual crime spree had been too horrendous to think about.

"Then you probably missed the part about him keeping trophies of the killings." His voice remained matter-of-fact, making her wish she could see his eyes behind the dark glasses he'd put on against the glare of the setting sun. "The night we raided his house, we found this walnut box in the safe behind a painting. The painting was from Picasso's Blue Period.

"One of the things in the box was a wedding veil and a yellow bikini. Seems his fourth victim had planned to get married the next day, then she and her groom were heading off to Bora Bora for their honeymoon. Needless to say, she missed both the wedding and the trip. We figure it took Lawson about a week to get bored with her."

As an actress, Julia was accustomed to putting herself in other people's skins. She shivered as she imagined the pain and terror the woman must have experienced. "Agent Callahan—"

"You might as well make it Finn. Since it looks like we're going to be spending a lot of time together."

"I'm sorry. I may have exaggerated." She'd never felt smaller.

He looked over at her, his eyes still hidden by those damn glasses. "*May* have?"

"All right." She threw up her hands. "I definitely overspoke. My only excuse is that I'm very uncomfortable with all this. And my early personal experience with your agency wasn't exactly positive."

He seemed to consider that idea. Then merely nodded and returned his attention back to driving.

When they drove past a cemetery, Julia's mind flashed back to a long-ago day. Rainbow's End Farm had been a warm and loving place where adults had gone out of their way to make the children feel loved. And safe.

Then, when she was five, she'd been throwing sticks for Taffy, her cocker spaniel, when one of the sticks had gone sailing across the dirt road leading to the milking barn. As she'd watched in horror, the dog, in enthusiastic pursuit, had gone racing after it and was hit by a truck delivering propane to the farm.

That was the day she'd learned firsthand about death. She'd been uncomfortable with the subject ever since, which made her wonder what kind of man could talk about such evils in such a matter-of-fact tone.

She turned toward him, taking in a profile that looked as if it'd been hacked from granite. He was not conventionally handsome, but many women would consider his rugged looks very appealing.

His heavily hooded eyes gave him a somewhat sleepy look that was deceptive, and his nose had a slight cant, suggesting it'd been broken. If his broad jaw was any indication, when they'd been handing out testosterone, Special Agent Callahan had gone back for seconds. Oh yes, Julia could see the appeal—not that he was at all her type.

She'd always preferred artistic, sensitive men, fellow actors or musicians, and once, for a not-all-that memorable two months, she'd had an affair with a promising painter who'd called her his muse. Until he'd finished the last in a series of nude paintings.

Declaring himself creatively blocked, he'd moved on to greener, more stimulating pastures. But not before borrowing a hundred dollars she'd known at the time she'd never see again. She'd recently received an invitation to his one-man show at a gallery in Taos. But still no check.

Graham may have been boring. But at least he hadn't stiffed her.

As they crossed the Mississippi River, leaving New Orleans behind them, an unpalatable thought occurred to Julia.

"Are you carrying?"

He glanced over at her. "Carrying?"

"Isn't that what you call it? When you're armed?"

"Yeah." The corner of his mouth quirked. "That's what we call it. And I am. Carrying."

"I don't like guns." Even after having been mugged at the ATM last year, she hadn't considered buying a weapon, and had done a

PSA with Tom Selleck about firearms safety. Ironically, it had drawn a firestorm of criticism from both the NRA and gun control advocates.

"Now, there's a news flash," he murmured. "You might find yourself changing your mind if your secret admirer decides to re-create that photo. But don't worry. I usually try to read people their rights before I shoot them."

"Did anyone ever tell you that you have a bad attitude, Special Agent Callahan?"

"Finn," he reminded her. "And yeah, it's been called to my attention—recently, as a matter of fact. But unlike my arrogance, the attitude comes naturally."

It was the first thing he'd said she found herself unable to argue with.

Since her parents believed that travel was broadening, Julia had been all over the world. She'd heard Big Ben strike the hour in London, marveled at the Renaissance beauty of Florence, listened to the hum of prayer wheels in Tibet, and had awakened to the sun rising over Mt. Kilimanjaro in Kenya. But the Louisiana bayou was a world apart, as foreign as anywhere she'd ever visited.

They drove past seemingly endless waterways, root-laced swamps, and rivulets ribboning the marshland. Sun glimmered over the bayou, backlighting the hanging Spanish moss in ghostly gold.

"Like a magician extended his golden wand over the landscape," she murmured.

"Twinkling vapors arose. Sky and water and forest seemed all on fire at the touch, and melted and mingled together," Finn surprised her by quoting the following line.

"I hadn't realized they taught Longfellow at the FBI Academy."

"Sure they do. It's an elective, squeezed in between the course on how to beat up on suspects without leaving any bruises and the one on falsifying reports."

"The frightening thing is, I almost believe you."

"Even more frightening is that I almost believe you believe me. And now who's the one doing the stereotyping?"

Taking it as a rhetorical question, Julia didn't answer, though she secretly acknowledged his point.

"As for me knowing that poem, you can't grow up here in the

swamp without knowing the story of those two star-crossed lovers," he said. "There's an oak tree in St. Martinville that's supposedly where Evangeline waited for her Gabriel."

"So you grew up here?"

At first, when her question was met by silence, she didn't think he was going to answer.

"My parents moved here from Chicago when I was seven," he said finally. "But my mother's people were part of the original group of Acadians expelled from Nova Scotia in *le Grand Derangement*."

"That must have been quite a change for you."

He didn't respond.

"Well?"

"I'm sorry." The steel curtain had drawn closed again. "Was that a question?"

"Never mind." Julia refused to admit she was the least bit interested.

He sighed. "Sure, it was a change. But when you're a kid, your family's more important than where your house is located."

Remembering what he'd said about playing sandlot ball with his brothers, Julia was about to ask him about his family when he leaned forward and punched on the CD player. The down and dirty sound of Kiss's "Love Gun" came screaming out of the speakers, essentially cutting off any further conversation.

As unhappy as he was with this baby-sitting assignment, Finn was even more disgusted with himself for nearly sharing personal stuff he never discussed with anyone else. Despite being an actress, which wasn't exactly the most down-to-earth career in the world, and that episode with the nurses, she hadn't followed all that closely in her parents' hippie footsteps.

And although he'd throw himself off the Huey Long Bridge before admitting it, the fact that she was slated to be the next Bond Girl was pretty cool.

Out of the corner of his eye, he watched her drinking in scenery as different from L.A. or that bucolic commune she'd grown up on as Oz, and remembered how uprooted he'd felt when his father had brought his family to Louisiana, wanting to raise his children in a safe place, away from the mean and dangerous city streets.

Finn was a little surprised she'd so immediately honed in on what he'd been feeling when he'd first arrived in Blue Bayou. But an actress was undoubtedly accustomed to trying on different roles. Even that of a seven-year-old boy.

He wondered if such behavior had become second nature; wondered how a person would ever know whether or not they were seeing the "real" Julia Summers; wondered if she even knew herself who the real Julia Summers was—then reminded himself it didn't matter.

His job was to keep her safe. Which he had every intention of doing. Then, after sending her off to Kathmandu, he could return to the life he'd been forced to put on hold.

After all the miles of swamp and waving green fields of what Julia supposed was sugar cane, they drove across an iron bridge and came to a blue and white sign welcoming them to Blue Bayou.

"It's very different from the other towns we've passed," she volunteered over the earsplitting music. The other communities had all stretched out on a narrow strip along the road, while Blue Bayou appeared to be laid out in squares, tree-lined cobblestone streets setting off pretty parks with bubbling fountains and lush gardens.

"That's because most of the other communities grew up along the road, to save valuable land for crops. Blue Bayou's patterned after Savannah."

They were driving through neighborhoods of brightly colored cottages and small, cozy white houses with wide front porches where people were sitting in wicker chairs beneath lazily circling ceiling fans. Several of them waved to Finn, who lifted a hand in response.

"A mix of Creole, Acadian and Native Americans had lived here for a long time, but they'd been scattered along the bayou like everywhere else. Then a rich Creole planter visited Savannah for a wedding and liked it so much, after he came home, he hooked up with an African-American architect and this is what they ended up with. They named it *Bayou Bleu*, after all the herons that nest on the banks, but over the years it became Anglicized."

"It's charming."

"I suppose it is." He seemed a bit surprised by that idea. "When I was a teenager, I thought it was about as dull as dirt."

Julia found herself unwillingly identifying with him. "It's hard at that age to live in a place where everyone knows your parents. Do yours still live here?"

"They died."

"I'm sorry."

"So was I," he said, putting a damper on any further attempt at conversation.

She'd already discovered that whenever a topic veered into the personal, he clammed up. Which was fine with her. Since she'd never see him again once shooting ended, she didn't need to know his life story. Though it was sad about his parents. Julia couldn't imagine a world without Freedom and Peace in it. She also wondered if the Callahans had died together, and whether their deaths might be what he'd been talking about when he'd said he knew what it was to be a kid and have the world pulled out from under you.

Not that she was all that interested. Just naturally curious.

They passed the VFW hall which, if all the trucks in the parking lot were any indication, was doing a bang-up business. The bumper stickers—*Thank a Vet For Your Freedom, I Don't Care How You Did It Up North, Coon Ass and Proud,* and *Real Men Don't Shoot Blanks*—were yet more proof that she was no longer in California.

He pulled up in front of The Plantation Inn, which reminded Julia of a scaled-down Twelve Oaks. "It's beautiful," she murmured appreciatively. "Like something from a movie set."

"The original inn, which housed troops during the Union occupation, blew away during a hurricane in the 1980s. It was a lot plainer, and the owners decided rebuilding in this style might appeal more to tourists."

As she entered the inn, Julia decided the owners were right. The lobby boasted huge bouquets of hothouse flowers, lots of rich wood, exquisite antique furniture, and leafy plants. Though she barely got a glimpse of it all on her rush to the elevator.

"Shouldn't we check in?" she asked as Finn put the coded card in the elevator slot and punched the button for the third floor.

"It's all taken care of."

The elevator door opened directly onto a corner suite which provided a view of the bayou in one direction and the flickering gaslights of what appeared to be the town's main street in the other.

"You know, I want very much to be annoyed at you." She walked over to the gold silk-framed windows and drank in the sight of the water, which was gleaming a brilliant copper in the final rays of the setting sun. "But if you had anything to do with me being booked into this suite, I'm willing to overlook your manhandling me through the lobby."

"There you go, exaggerating again."

"What would you call humiliating me by dragging me across the floor in front of the entire cast of *River Road*?"

"I'd call it doing my job. And I wouldn't think any woman who'd strip naked in front of the entire world could be that easily humiliated."

"The entire world doesn't show up on the set. I also always wear a bodysuit or flesh-colored bikini. Besides, I was brought up to believe the human body is nothing to be embarrassed about."

He gave her another of those slow looks that suggested he was recording her vital statistics for a Wanted poster. "I suppose that depends on the body in question."

The statement, coming from left field, left Julia at a loss for words. Finn Callahan was unlike anyone she'd ever met, and she couldn't quite figure out how to handle him.

But Amanda could. There wasn't a male alive who was a match for her feminine wiles. Julia had always left her character on the set, but as his slow, judicious scrutiny tangled her nerves, she decided to make an exception.

"Gracious, Special Agent," she purred. "Is that a compliment?"

"Merely an observation. You undoubtedly realize you're a stunningly beautiful woman. Otherwise you wouldn't have auditioned for that Bond Girl role."

"It's a great part. Even if it's a little intimidating following in the footsteps of Kim Basinger and Terri Hatcher."

Damn, why had she told him that? He was undoubtedly an expert at latching onto any little weakness and using it against a suspect. Not that she was a suspect. So why did she feel like one?

"I don't think you have anything to worry about," he said, his tone dry and matter-of-fact. "So what's your name going to be?"

"You'll laugh."

"No, I won't."

Julia supposed he was telling the truth. After all, the FBI wasn't known for its sense of humor. "Promise?"

"Look, if you don't want to tell me, fine. I was just making idle conversation."

"I doubt you've had an idle conversation in your life," she countered. "It's Carma Sutra."

He didn't laugh, but his chiseled lips quirked again in that way that softened the rugged planes of his face a bit. Julia was waiting for him to say something, anything, when the phone on a Queen Anne desk across the room rang.

He beat her to it, snatched up the receiver, barked out a brusque, "Callahan," listened a moment, then held it out to her. "It's for you."

"Why, what a coincidence. Considering this is, after all, my suite."

The call was from the director, reminding her of tonight's welcoming party in the inn's library. "Of course I remember," she assured Randy. "Yes. Seven-thirty." She stifled a sigh. "I'll be there."

Julia couldn't decide which she found more annoying: The idea of having to squeeze herself into a sexy, Amanda-style cocktail dress and toe-pinching shoes so she could chat up the natives, or Finn answering her phone.

"You're not going," he said after she'd hung up.

She lifted a brow. "I beg your pardon?"

"Nice take. It's the same duchess-to-peasant tone Amanda used with her yoga instructor, right before she got naked and taught him a new twist on the cobra pose."

That episode was from the beginning of last season, when *River Road* had been switched from its usual slot of Monday night to the supposedly dead zone of Friday. To hopefully keep their target audience at home on date night, Amanda had blazed through men like a brush fire in the Hollywood Hills.

"My, my, you *have* been doing your homework."

"I figured I should get a take on all the players." He rocked back on his heels. "So, which were you wearing in that scene? The nude bodysuit or the flesh-colored bikini?"

"Why don't I just leave that to your imagination? If you even have one."

He rubbed his jutting jaw. "Now that you mention it, I can't recall receiving one with my gun and shield when I graduated from the Academy."

Oh, he was a cool one. If they ever made a movie about that serial killer he'd tracked down, Tommy Lee Jones would be a shoo-in to play him. Jones might have a good fifteen years on Finn Callahan, but she couldn't think of any other actor who could portray so much rigidly controlled energy.

"Perhaps we can work on that imagination problem." Amanda rose from inside her and skimmed a fingernail down the front of his shirt.

Long dark fingers circled her wrist as he plucked her hand from his chest. "Just so we won't have any misunderstanding, as appealing as you admittedly are, for the next two weeks you're a case, like any other. Though you do smell better than most."

"Damned with faint praise." Even though she'd been attempting to jerk his chain, Julia was a bit miffed by his rejection. "Are you saying you're not interested?"

"I'm saying that I may be more selective than the men you're used to in L.A."

"Well, that's certainly to the point. And less than flattering."

Having always believed herself more like her calm, collected mother rather than her intense, passion-driven father, Julia was surprised to discover he'd tapped into a hidden temper.

"It wasn't meant to be flattering. Or an insult. I was merely explaining why, if you're expecting to ease small town boredom by having hot sex with your bodyguard every night, you're going to be disappointed."

"Believe me, Callahan, a woman would need a great deal more imagination than I possess to expect hot anything from you."

"Good shot." Even though he acknowledged the hit, it irked her that he didn't appear gravely wounded. Nor did he suggest proving her accusation wrong.

"Thank you." She tossed her head. "And while we're laying our cards on the table, you should know right off the bat that not only have I taken self-defense training, I also don't intend to allow anyone or anything to keep me from living my life. Which is why I'm going to that party tonight."

"Good idea." His tone said otherwise. He took hold of her chin, lifted her face to the lamp light, and skimmed a calloused finger beneath her eyes. "You look like someone's slugged you."

" Is that an example of your detecting skills?" She'd seen the shadows herself this morning, glaring evidence that unwilling concerns about her stalker's possible return had disturbed her sleep. Obviously the concealer she'd paid a small fortune for at Saks had worn off.

"I don't have to be a detective to see you haven't been sleeping. I'd think, since you have a busy day tomorrow, you'd want to go to bed early."

"I seem to recall suggesting something along those lines. But you turned me down." Because his touch was distracting her more than hers had appeared to affect him, she moved away. "And I don't really want to go, but it's part of the job description. The parish commissioners want to meet Amanda. How do you think it'd affect your brother's election chances if she doesn't show up?"

Good point, Finn thought reluctantly, torn between loyalty to his brother and his assignment. He also found it more than a little interesting that she referred to her character in the third person, as if she were making a mental distinction between them.

She tilted her head, studying him. "What are we going to tell people?"

"About what?"

"About what you're doing here with me."

"Why do you have to tell anyone anything?"

"Because for some reason, since I appear in their living rooms every week, people are unreasonably curious about my life and it's always best to have a story ready."

A *story*. It did not escape his attention that she didn't suggest telling the truth.

"Why don't you just say we're friends?"

"I don't know." She looked up at him. "That may be a bit beyond my acting ability, but I suppose I could try." She glanced down at a diamond-studded watch, yet another reminder to Finn that he and Julia Summers lived in entirely different worlds. "Now, if you're through throwing your weight around, Special Agent, I believe I'll unpack and get ready to dazzle."

As she left the room, even though he'd professed a lack of imagination, Finn had no difficulty hearing the bell signaling the end of round three.

# 9

*She had to be out of her mind.* She didn't even like Finn Callahan. So why had she thrown Amanda in front of him?

"Because you're not certain you can handle him," Julia decided as she wiggled out of her jeans. Even in Los Angeles, where you could throw a stick on Rodeo Drive and hit a dozen women more beautiful than she was, Julia was more accustomed to fighting men off than having to work to get their attention. "Amanda's tougher."

It wasn't as if he hadn't noticed her, she mused as she pulled the T-shirt over her head. A seamless flesh-hued bra followed. Stripped down to a pair of panties, she opened the suitcase some unseen bellman had delivered to her room, shook the wrinkles out of the dress she'd packed specifically for this party, then dashed into the adjoining bathroom to touch up her makeup.

A thought occurred to her as she was brushing on mascara. "What if he doesn't like women?"

She dismissed that idea the moment it entered her mind. He might be frustratingly remote, he might have ice water in his veins. But he was the least gay man she'd ever met.

Amanda could have him begging. On his knees. With that mental image providing some much needed amusement, Julia returned to the living room.

Finn had figured that since she seemed to view the party as yet another acting gig, she'd be dressed to kill. He'd definitely hit that one right on the money.

As she strolled out of the bedroom with a sultry, hip-swinging walk wearing—or not wearing was probably a more accurate description—a black outfit designed to make any male still alive below the waist swallow his tongue, Finn decided men were going to be walking into walls all over Blue Bayou.

The strapless top had been cut off just below her breasts and was connected to a hip-hugger skirt with two narrow black lace panels.

"Well?" she asked. Finn wondered how she managed to twirl on those ankle-breaking ice-pick high heels to show a mouthwatering expanse of bare back. "Do you think I'll help your brother's reelection chances?"

She wasn't going to get to him. She was a case, a favor for Nate. That was all. It was all he'd allow it to be.

As she completed the circle, Finn had to remind himself he'd outgrown thinking with his glands a very long time ago.

"If he claims credit for bringing you to town, he's definitely going to get all the male votes in the parish."

"Well, that's a start. Perhaps he can work on the women's votes himself."

"I don't think he'll have any problem with those. I do have one question."

"Oh?"

"How does that top stay up?"

"That's for me to know." She combed a hand through her hair, the gesture doing interesting things to her breasts, which Finn figured must be as bare as her back beneath that skimpy strip of material. When she smiled he felt a punch of something hot, lethal, and decidedly unwanted in his gut. "And you to find out."

"I guess some mysteries are destined to remain unsolved." Unreasonably tempted to touch, Finn slipped his hands into his slacks. "We need to talk before we go downstairs. I want you to give me a rundown on all the players."

She shook her head and sighed. "You really do have a one-track mind, Callahan." Silk swished against smooth, bare thighs as she sauntered over to the fruit basket on the desk. "It's been a long day and I skipped lunch. I'd better eat something so the alcohol won't go to my head."

She plucked out a Red Delicious apple and held it out to him. "Would you care for a bite?"

Because both the gesture and the throaty purr were so blatantly Amanda-suggestive, Finn laughed. "I think I'll pass."

"Suit yourself." She shrugged and exchanged the apple for a ripe yellow banana, peeling the fruit with exaggerated slowness. "Where shall we begin?"

"With the photograph. Do you still have it?"

"No. I threw it away. And before you jump on my case about preserving evidence, I'd managed to convince myself it was only a practical joke."

"Yet it upset you enough not to want to keep it."

She shrugged her bare shoulders. "I don't keep junk mail, either."

When those perfect white teeth bit into the flesh of the banana, obscene thoughts ricocheted through his mind. Did she realize what she was doing to him? Hell, of course she did. The woman was a pro.

"What about the blonde?"

"Felissa?"

"Yeah. How do you two get along?"

"We don't run in the same circles—she's into the nightclub party scene—but we have a good working relationship."

"No professional jealousy?"

"Not on my part."

"How about hers?"

Julia considered that. "She's competitive, as everyone who lasts in this business has to be, but I don't think she stays awake nights counting lines to see which of us has more. And she's a very good actress."

"But she's not going to be the Bond Girl."

"True. And while I suspect she must have been disappointed about that, she says she never expected to win the role anyway."

"She was up for the part?"

"Yes."

"So you beat her?"

"It wasn't anything personal. They simply wanted another look."

"Hot, dangerous, black widow sex."

The director had used the same description. "There's always a measure of danger in a Bond film. I play a biophysicist who's an undercover *SPECTRE* agent assigned to assassinate 007, but falls in love with him instead. I think it also may have helped that I've had some martial arts training."

"Really." He sounded unconvinced.

"After I was mugged last year, I took a self-defense class at the gym. There was a woman there who introduced me to ninjitsu. I'm certainly not any expert, but I know some moves."

"Do your parents know their daughter's learning to be a ninja warrior?"

"Ninjitsu is far more about defense and spirituality," she countered. "Real ninjas, like in the movies, don't exist anymore. It may have helped me win the part, since they wrote it into the story. A stunt woman's going to be doing all the long shots, of course, since I'm not that proficient. But I believe what clinched my getting the role was the fact that I've not only seen all the movies, but read the books, as well. So, I know Bond's back story."

"You've read Ian Fleming?" He didn't bother to mask his surprise.

"There you go again, stereotyping."

"Profiling."

"Whatever. I'll bet you were guessing Jackie Collins."

"It fits. You're both part of the Hollywood scene."

"Please. I am as far from whatever people mean when they say the Hollywood scene as anyone in the business can possibly be, but actually I enjoy Collins. I also read Kafka. And Longfellow." She smiled sweetly. "I've very eclectic tastes."

"So it seems."

"I also realize some people consider James Bond merely a cartoon character, but that's only because there've been some bad movies made. The books are just filled with wonderful details about 007's spiritual and physical fluctuations. And *From Russia With Love* just happened to have been one of President Kennedy's top ten favorite books."

"How do you know that? You weren't even born when Kennedy was alive."

"You're not the only one who can do your homework. I know everything about the character and the stories."

"Okay, I'll bite," Finn said, amazed that he and this woman might have anything in common. "Who's the only man 007 answers to?"

"That's too easy. It's M, of course. Head of MI6. And it hasn't always been a man. Bernard Lee played M from *Dr. No* to *Moonraker*, then was replaced by Robert Brown. Their relationship was always a bit of a roller coaster, but things turned really ugly when Bond pushed him too far in *License to Kill*.

"The third M to play the part is Judith Dench, who's marvelous. She doesn't care for Bond's attitude, but thinks very highly of him. Is any of this pertinent?"

He shrugged broad shoulders more suited to an NFL linebacker than a federal agent. "You never know what's pertinent. Which is why it's best to cover all the bases."

"Felissa's no threat."

"I've heard that before. Had you gotten threats before winning the Bond role?"

"Of course I have. It comes with the territory, when you play a woman who'd seduce her stepsister's husband so she can claim he's the father of her child. Just last week, a woman in Blockbuster slapped me because Amanda had held her third husband's nitroglycerin pills out of reach when he was having his fatal heart attack."

"Does that happen a lot? People confusing you with your character?"

He wouldn't appreciate the charge that he seemed to fit in that category, as well. Though that wasn't surprising, since she kept throwing Amanda at him.

"Viewers occasionally blur the lines between fiction and reality."

"Terrific. So we're looking at several million potential suspects who'd like you dead."

"You have such a way with words, Callahan. If what I've seen so far is any indication, I've no doubt you have people lined up around the block to confess to crimes they haven't committed."

The accusation merely bounced off those wide shoulders. "Tell me about the pretty boy who plays Jared."

"Shane? He's definitely ambitious and wouldn't hesitate to sleep his way up the Hollywood ladder, but he's basically harmless and would never commit violence to get ahead. It also wouldn't make any sense for him to kill me, since his character's recent adultery with Amanda has really boosted his on-screen time."

"But you're leaving the show. He's probably not real keen on the idea."

"I wouldn't know. Why don't you ask him?"

"I will. What's your relationship with him?"

"I find him somewhat amusing, though I'm no fan of his practical jokes. But he shows up each day with his lines memorized, he doesn't eat garlic before a lovemaking scene, and our chemistry is good on-screen, which is important in a soap. And before you ask, I'm not sleeping with him, if that's what you're getting at."

"Have you ever?"

"No." She dared him to challenge that statement, but he merely shrugged again and seemed to take her at face value.

"How about the director? Ever sleep with him?"

"What are you? The morality police?"

"I wouldn't care if you and Hogan dress up like Tarzan and Jane and swing from the chandeliers. I'm just trying to get a handle on where the guy fits on a suspect list."

"He doesn't belong on it in the first place. Randy has a wife and six children."

"Some women might not be bothered by that."

"I'm not one of them." Julia felt the anger bubbling up and managed to control it. "Besides, he's not the type of man to commit adultery." Her eyes narrowed. "Or are you so suspicious of everyone, you're incapable of imagining someone staying true to wedding vows?"

"Sure, I believe in fidelity. But not everyone does."

"My relationship with Randy is strictly professional, Callahan."

"News flash. There's not a man on the planet who could keep his thoughts strictly professional around you."

"Really?" She tilted her head, intrigued by the idea she may have just found a chink in his armor after all. "Does that include you?"

"I said I wasn't interested. I didn't say I was dead. So, let's talk about the actress who plays the former hooker."

"Margot." Realizing that he intended to work his way through the entire list of cast and crew, Julia let out a frustrated breath, leaned back in the chair, crossed her legs, and wished she'd just picked up the damn phone and gotten this interrogation over with last night.

# 10

*Julia recognized Nate Callahan immediately.* His eyes were a warm and inviting lake blue rather than Finn's lighter, chillier hue; his appealingly shaggy hair sun-tipped chestnut instead of black; his body, toned in a way that suggested physical work, lankier and more loose limbed than his brother. But there was no mistaking the resemblance in the masculine self-confidence surrounding him like an aura.

"You have a lovely town," she said after he'd welcomed her to Blue Bayou.

"We like it." His grin was quick and charming. "And the scenery's sure gotten a lot prettier in the past few hours."

"Aren't you sweet?" She smiled up at him. "And ever so much more agreeable than your brother."

"Handsomer, too."

She appeared to give that appropriate consideration, then fluttered her lashes in a blatantly flirtatious Scarlett O'Hara look that would have gotten her kicked off the most amateur middle school production of *Gone with the Wind*. "I do believe I ended up with the wrong brother."

"If you want to pass a good time, you probably did. But if you want to keep some nutcase from harassing you, you couldn't be in better hands, Ms. Summers."

"So Agent Callahan has already told me. And it's Julia." She glanced over at the clutch of people standing across the room, watching them with interest. She slipped her arm in his. "Since this is supposed to be a getting-acquainted party, why don't you introduce me to your parish council?" she suggested.

She was more than a little frustrated when Nate gave his brother a questioning look.

Even more irritated when Finn said, "Go ahead. Just don't leave the room."

Julia blew out a breath. "Why don't you go spread some of that Southern charm around, Callahan, while I mingle with the natives?

"Your brother," she fumed to Nate as they crossed the floor, "is, without a doubt, the bossiest man I've ever had the misfortune to meet."

"He can be a little heavy-handed, from time to time," Nate allowed. "But there's nobody better in a crunch. Once, when I was in the third grade, this gang of big kids kept stealing my lunch money. I didn't tell my parents because it was so damn humiliating. But you can't get anything past Finn. He found out what was happening, went over to the park where they were playing a little after-school one-on-one, and cleaned their clocks. They never bothered me again."

"Why am I not surprised he resorted to violence?"

Obviously the man had possessed industrial-strength testosterone even as a schoolboy. She had never been the least bit attracted to men who opted for brawn over brains.

"That's the only thing those thugs would have understood. Hell, half of them later ended up in prison and I suspect it's just a matter of time before the others join them. I was damn lucky to have my big brother looking after me. You are, too."

Julia didn't want to be rude and argue with her host, but the only answer she could come up with was a muttered *humph*.

Finn was watching her ooze charm to the parish council, all of whom appeared appropriately starstruck, when a sloe-eyed brunette wearing a clingy red dress came up to him. Margot Madison, Finn mentally clicked through the *River Road* credits. The former madam of River Road's only brothel, turned romance writer.

"As hunky an addition as you are to our little family, Agent Callahan, you do realize, of course, that your presence is totally unnecessary," she said, dispensing with any polite opening conversation.

"Is it?"

"Of course. It's obvious Julia doesn't need a bodyguard. Because it's just as obvious that she sent that photograph to herself."

"Why would she want to do that?"

"To garner attention. We actors are outrageously egocentric. We can't bear not to be in the middle of the spotlight. God knows, Julia's certainly done whatever it takes to boost her career. Now that the buzz about her winning that Bond Girl role is beginning to die down, I've been expecting her to pull some stunt to get herself back in the news."

"It's a little difficult to take a picture of yourself from across the room without anyone noticing."

"She undoubtedly had an accomplice. Perhaps her agent. Or publicist. Or maybe even that stuffy acting professor she was dating for a time." She shrugged. "Julia's an actress. She wouldn't have had any trouble talking some man into helping her out."

Finn couldn't argue with that. "Is that what you'd do?"

"Absolutely." She smiled up at him. "Are you shocked?"

"I don't shock all that easily."

"I wouldn't guess you would. I saw the clip on the news after you apprehended that horrid serial killer." Her eyes glittered with avid interest. "I imagine you've seen a great many unsavory things in your career."

Her voice went up a little on the end, turning the comment into a question. Finn wasn't surprised; civilians seemed ghoulishly drawn to murder. And serial killers were the most fascinating of all.

"None suitable for cocktail party conversation. So, you were telling me about why Ms. Summers would send that photograph to herself?"

"Tell me, Special Agent, do you have to practice that just-the-facts-ma'am tone, or does it come naturally? Never mind." She waved her question away. "You'll have to forgive me. I have an unfortunate habit of being facetious when I'm excruciatingly bored. . . .

"Why would Julia fake a threat to herself? The answer is obvious, darling. Because it makes such juicy headlines. We all like to pretend that we hate the tabloids, but the truth is that we have a parasitic relationship with them. We need them to keep us in the public eye as much as they need us to fill their tacky little pages every day."

"I suppose a death threat might be the kind of story the *Enquirer* or *Star* could get their teeth into."

"Oh, they could masticate on it for months." Her crimson lips curved in a smile that was more predatory than friendly. "What our

Julia lacks in acting ability, she definitely makes up for in imagination."

"I don't know anything about acting, but she seems pretty good."

The dress slid off a shoulder as she shrugged with calculated insouciance. "It's not that difficult if you're playing yourself. Believe me, Amanda and Julia could be twins separated at birth." She tossed back her champagne and snagged another glass from the tray of a passing waiter.

She swayed a little as she leaned toward him, worrying Finn that he might have to keep her from falling flat on her face. "Let me tell you a little shecret about television." She was beginning to slur her words, suggesting she'd had some warm-up drinks before coming downstairs to the party. "The schedule for an hour-long weekly series is so grinding, there's not a lot of room for an actor to stretch. If you're not playing yourself, you're going to make it a helluva lot harder than it need be."

Her words had Finn recalling a scene he'd watched where her character, who was being blackmailed by Amanda for some reason the tape hadn't made clear, had hired a buffed up, not-all-that-bright romance novel cover model to kill Amanda. The plan fell apart when the would-be assassin fell in love with his victim and refused to go through with the crime.

"I've been married five times," she revealed. "Six if you count Everett Channing, whom I made the dreadful mistake of marrying twice. Every one of those marriages has made it into the story line of the daytime soap I starred in before I moved to *River Road*. So have several of my affairs. As I told that officious little IRS man who audited me last year, that dalliance in Rome with the Italian shoe king was merely creative research, which I had every right to deduct."

Finn would have loved to have been present for that audit. "Thanks for your take on the situation, Ms. Madison. It's been very helpful talking with you."

"Any time, Agent Callahan." Her slow, blatantly sexual appraisal suggested she might be considering him a new research project. "You'll find I'm a very accommodating woman." With that gilt-edged invitation hanging in the air, she wove her way unsteadily through the crowd over to the open bar.

It was obvious that Margot Madison was jealous of Julia Summers.

However, Finn reminded himself as he watched Julia laugh appreciatively at something Nate had said, jealousy didn't necessary preclude the actress from being right.

"Welcome to Blue Bayou." The blonde holding the flute of champagne toward Warren had a beauty queen's smile and a cover girl's body shrink wrapped into a pink floral silk dress. A rhinestone-studded tiara rested atop a cloud of pale blond hair. "I'm Lorelei Fairchild. And I'll bet you're Warren Hyatt."

"That's right." Because it would have seemed rude to refuse, he accepted the champagne, deciding to dump it into one of those potted palms at the first opportunity. "How did you know?" People usually didn't pay attention to the writer. Especially in a room of actors.

"Because you're the most intelligent-looking man here." Dimples deep enough to drown in flashed charmingly. She leaned toward him, as if about to share a deep secret. "I do so admire your work."

"You do?" He found himself holding his breath, waiting for those magnificent breasts to pop out of their scant covering.

"Of course. I'm all the time tellin' Mama, 'Mama, that Warren Hyatt is a literary genius.' "

"Really?"

"I surely do. Mama, of course, agrees. She's a huge fan, too. She absolutely adored the story line where you killed that Swiss ski instructor, but I think my favorite, until this latest triangle with Vanessa, Jared and Amanda, of course, was the one where that alien from outer space landed in River Road and snatched Amanda right out of her snazzy red convertible and beamed her up to his ship to take her back to his womanless planet to save their species."

That had been one of his personal favorites. "You didn't think the premise was too over the top?"

"Why, of course not!" She looked askance at the idea. Forgetting all about any potential damage to his liver, Warren took a sip of champagne. "I thought it was absolutely inspired. And sexy as all get out. I especially loved how you had her escape by pretending she was actually going to go through with having hot alien sex with him." She flashed another of those smiles that caused him to go a little light-headed. "If you promise not to tell a single solitary soul, I'll share a little secret."

"I promise." The scent emanating from acres of creamy skin was making his head spin. At that moment, Warren would have agreed to anything.

"That's always been a personal sexual fantasy of mine."

"To be beamed aboard a spaceship?"

"No, silly." She skimmed a glossy pink fingernail down his sleeve. "To be taken against my will and ravished."

"Really?" he croaked.

"Well, not in actuality. I mean, I certainly wouldn't want some stranger to drag me into an alley, strip my clothes off and rape me in real life, but I do fantasize about a handsome masked man breaking into my bedroom at night and having his way with me. Why, just thinking about it gives me goose bumps all over, if you know what I mean."

Her light laugh flowed over him like warm honey as he imagined that lush body. All over.

"Well, of course you do. Since you're the one who wrote the story line in the first place. I haven't been able to sleep since I heard you were coming to town. I just kept lying all alone in bed, hoping that I'd get a chance to meet the one man who truly and deeply understands women's secret desires." She sighed and pressed her hand against a magnificent breast. "You must be a purely wonderful lover."

That did it. He was definitely going to faint.

"Oh, dear. Are you all right?" Feminine speculation instantly turned to concern. "Gracious, sugar, you've gone as white as Stonewall Jackson's ghost."

"I'm fine." He took a deep breath. "The flight from L.A. was a bit bumpy. I think it's probably just a touch of lingering airsickness."

"Oh, don't you just hate that?" Glossy pink lips that matched her nails turned down in a sexy little moue. "I have a stomach like iron. Mama says it's as hard as my head, but she used to get butterflies something awful whenever we flew. They'd start flapping their wings even before she got on the plane. It got so she just couldn't travel anywhere, except on Amtrak, which really upset her because Mama does so love to visit new places, bless her heart.

"I swear, we tried everything: pills, hypnosis, those little wristbands with the magnets on them, why, we even got Nate to take us out in his boat, deep into the swamp where we paid this wonderful old juju woman to do a voodoo spell for her, but nothing worked.

"I can't tell you the despair we were in. Then, thank heavens, I found this miracle cure on the Internet and since we figured we didn't have anything to lose, we gave it a try." She smiled brilliantly. "It worked like a charm. Mama's never had a lick of trouble since."

"You found a miracle cure on the Internet?"

"Oh, it's just filled with the most interesting information, sugar. Why, you can't imagine. Anyway, the cure's as easy as pecan pie. You just splash some Southern Comfort into a glass of flat ginger ale and swallow it all down at once. The ginger ale settles your stomach while the whiskey calms you down."

She looked up at him through her lashes. "Maybe your wife or girlfriend can mix one for you before you fly next time."

A sledgehammer would have been more subtle. Warren began to worry that this was another of Shane's practical jokes. He quickly scanned the room, but the actor was busy charming a clutch of blue-haired old ladies, and didn't seem to be paying any attention to them.

"I guess I'll be mixing it myself, since I'm not married. And I don't have a girlfriend."

"Really?" Salome could not have looked more seductive when asking for John the Baptist's head than Lorelei Fairchild did as she nibbled speculatively on her glossy pink thumbnail. "You're still looking a tad pale," she diagnosed. "Perhaps we should get you back upstairs to your room so you can lie down."

Warren's first thought was that if he wasn't dead and in heaven, he must be hallucinating.

And even on the outside chance he was still breathing and this wasn't a joke, and this blond belle bombshell was actually suggesting what he thought she was suggesting, he reminded himself that energetic sex could kill you. He'd learned that firsthand when, a week before his twelfth birthday, his father keeled over from a heart attack at a mere forty years old while making love to his mistress in a suite at the Plaza on an alleged business trip to New York.

After the funeral, he'd heard his uncle Paul say that they'd been forced to go with a closed casket because the undertaker hadn't been able to wipe the smile from Warren Senior's face.

Deciding not to look a gift breast—horse, he corrected, dragging his wandering eyes from those lush white globes which, if they weren't real, were the best silicone job he'd ever seen—in the mouth, Warren reminded himself that life was filled with risks. Forgetting about his possible liver disease, he tossed back the champagne.

"You are," he said as the alcohol went straight to his head, replacing the blood rushing hot and thick to lower regions, "the most stunningly Southern woman I've ever met."

She flashed another of those beauty queen smiles that he decided would be the inspiration for the new character who'd replace Amanda as *River Road*'s vixen. "There you go, making my toes go as tingly as they did while I was watchin' Amanda being licked all over by that horny alien."

She was every sexual fantasy he'd ever had, all wrapped up into one luscious, sweet-smelling female body. Since he couldn't think of a single solitary line to fit this amazing occasion, Warren stole one he'd written for that womanizing Southern scoundrel, Jared Lee.

"Let's go upstairs, darlin'," he drawled, "and I'll make the rest of you tingle."

*Carpe diem.*

# 11

*Finn was keeping an eye on Julia* while scoping out all the players in this little drama he'd landed in, when Felissa Templeton sidled up to him. "Well? Have you figured out which of us is trying to kill Julia?"

"What makes you think it's someone from inside the show?"

"Oh, it's always someone the victim knows," she said airily. "I've made enough women-in-jeopardy movies to know that."

"Who do you think it is?"

"Margot, of course."

"That's interesting. Since she believes Ms. Summers is threatening herself to attract more publicity."

Felissa laughed. "Of course the old bitch would say that. She hates Julia's guts."

"Because Ms. Summers took over her bad girl role?"

"That's very perceptive of you."

"Thanks."

"So, you've watched the show?"

"I've seen a few episode."

"Which ones?"

"One where your character and Amanda have a cat fight and fall into the fountain at Amanda's fourth wedding."

"Oh, that was fun." Remembered pleasure shone in her eyes. "Julia's just lucky Warren wrote that scene for me. Margot undoubtedly would have held her under."

"She hates her that much?"

"Mostly she just wants Julia off the show."

"How about you? Do you want her gone?"

"Well, of course I do, since playing the good girl is excruciatingly boring, and the bad girl gets the majority of lines each week and most of the press, besides. But there's no earthly point in trying to run her off since she's already going, isn't she?"

"I hear you tried out for the Bond Girl role."

"Every actress in Hollywood probably tried out for that role."

"But Julia got it. Does that bother you?"

"In the beginning, I suppose it did, just a little. But I've gotten over it. Especially since Warren's promised to give Vanessa an evil twin. Or better yet, multiple personalities. While those are admittedly getting a little overdone, I just know he'll be able to create a new twist that could earn me an Emmy when one of the personalities starts killing people and poor, suffering Vanessa goes on trial for murder."

As ludicrous a plotline as that might be, Finn decided it wasn't that different from Lawson's lawyers' attempt to pull an insanity defense out of their legal hats.

"There they go."

He followed her gaze across the room to where Margot Madison and Charles Kendall were slipping out the French doors.

"They've been having a fling now for the past month," Felissa revealed. "It's my guess that she's doing a bit of horizontal lobbying to get him to reprise *her* old bad girl role. With the emphasis on *old*. Personally, I think she's wasting her time. Charles may write the checks and sit in the executive office, but Warren pretty much has carte blanche when it comes to *River Road*'s story line. So long as ratings stay as high as they are, he'll be allowed to write just about any plot he wants. Which is why, if Margot had any sense, she'd seduce him instead."

Her gaze shifted to the bespectacled writer who was standing on the edges of the crowd, appearing absolutely enthralled by Lorelei, who'd squeezed her voluptuous curves into a flowered dress that fit like a sausage casing. If she took an even halfway deep breath, she was definitely going to provide the entertainment for the evening.

"Damn," Felissa muttered.

"What?"

"It looks as if I'm about to lose a bet with Randy. I said it'd take at least an hour for Miss Gator Gulch over there to entice Warren to write her into the script. Randy bet she'd pull it off in under thirty minutes, which means I owe him a weekend at Las Costa."

As Finn watched Lorelei and Warren leave the room together in a cloud of pheromones, he decided it was getting more and more difficult to tell real life from *River Road.*

"So, what do you think?" Nate asked an hour later.

"I think after this bash, you'll be elected mayor for life," Finn said.

"The parish council certainly seems happy enough. Of course, Mrs. Robicheaux's probably gonna have to go out and buy poor old Henri a Seeing Eye dog first thing in the morning, since his eyes seemed to have become detached from his head and glued to Julia Summers's very appealing body."

"I noticed. Unfortunately for him, so did Marie Robicheaux."

"Henri will be sleeping in the doghouse for sure, tonight . . . She really is something, isn't she? Julia, not Marie."

"Yeah. She's something all right. She's a pain in the ass."

Nate looked at him curiously. "I thought she seemed real nice. Not at all full of herself, like I figured some Hollywood star could be."

"She's an actress," Finn reminded his brother. "She can probably be anyone you want her to be. She's also on her good behavior with you."

"More's the pity. You sayin' she's being bad with you? And you're complaining? *Mon Dieu, cher,* I'm worried about you."

"Look, I watched the show. The woman can turn the charm off and on without missing a beat."

"You talking about the woman? Or the character she plays?"

"Both, since she seems to have been pretty well typecast. The lady's probably as phony as that two-headed coin you had back when you were seventeen and thought you might become a magician."

"I wasn't all that interested in magic. I was interested in Christy Marchand, who had herself a big old crush on David Copperfield. I convinced her I could make her float on air."

"And did you?"

"Hell, no. I never much got past palming quarters in the teach-yourself-magic book. But Christy didn't know that. And we sure passed a good time that summer. Lord, she looked good in that pretty harem magician assistant's outfit."

"You talked Christy Marchand, the class valedictorian who grew up to be a NASA scientist, into wearing a harem costume?"

"I billed myself as The Swamp Swami, so the costume fit the theme. And I didn't have to do all that much talking, since I was the closest thing to Copperfield in Blue Bayou. I'll admit, I didn't care whether she levitated or not. I just wanted to get past second base."

"So did the ploy work?"

"Far be it from me to besmirch the honor of Southern womanhood, but since you're my brother and I know it won't go any further, I like to think back on that as the summer of my Grand Slam."

They shared a laugh.

"So," Nate said, "do you believe the lady's really in danger?"

"I've heard various theories tonight. But personally, if forced to take a guess, I'd say no."

"But you're not taking any chances."

Finn thought of those other women he hadn't been able to protect. "No," he said. "I'm not."

"Home sweet home." Julia stepped out of her heels the moment they entered the suite and padded over to the minibar. "Your brother's a nice man."

"Everyone's always said so."

"I'm going to have some juice. Would you . . ." Her voice trailed off as she glanced at him over her shoulder and saw he'd picked up the shoes. "Oh, great." She cast a frustrated glance up at the ceiling. "It's bad enough I'm stuck with Dudley Do-Right. Do you also have to be Felix Unger?"

"Do you have something against neatness?"

"No. But obsessive neatness is another entirely different matter. It's a definite sign of repression."

"I suppose you learned that on the commune?"

"No. Psych 101." Her pretty Manolo Blahniks looked oddly fragile in his big hands. She snatched them away.

"Ah." He nodded. "Well, that certainly makes you an expert."

"You're not that hard to read. Don't take this wrong, Callahan, but you're a bit of a walking cliché."

"That's one of the nicer things I've been accused of over the years. If you're trying to insult me, you're going to have to do better than that."

"How about you only view the world in black and white?"

"What's wrong with that?"

"In case you haven't noticed, the rest of the planet has moved on to Technicolor."

He shrugged. "Call me old-fashioned."

"That, too," she muttered. "I'll bet you even dream in black and white."

He wondered what she'd say if he told her that tonight he'd be dreaming of green eyes that could turn from a soft Southern moss to blazing emerald in a heartbeat. Of hair so bright it looked as if it'd burn his fingers if he gave into the urge to dip them into those lush fiery waves. Of creamy porcelain flesh he suspected felt a great deal warmer than it looked.

"Got me," he said easily. Because he was tempted, too tempted, he turned away, opened the closet by the suite's living room door, and took out a spare sheet and pillow.

"You're sleeping on the couch?" she asked as he tossed them onto the antique reproduction sofa. "Why? The suite has two bedrooms."

"They're too far apart."

Those remarkable eyes widened, just a little. "Surely you don't actually believe I'm in danger?"

"I don't know." There was no point in getting her overly concerned, but neither was he going to encourage her to shrug off a potential threat.

"Well, that's certainly honest."

"I may not always tell you what you want to hear, but if I say something, you can count on it being the truth. There's no way of knowing whether that picture was some guy's socially inept way of expressing admiration, or a threat against your life. But while you're stuck with me, as you so charmingly put it, I'm not taking any chances."

Their eyes met. And held, just a moment too long.

"Well. I don't exactly know what to say to that."

"How about good night?"

She looked prepared to argue. Finn figured she wasn't accustomed to taking orders. Tough.

"Good night, Callahan."

She put the shoes down in order to open the minibar, took out a bottle of orange juice, and disappeared into the larger of the two bedrooms.

As the door shut behind her, Finn let out a long, weary breath. "Good night," he murmured. He was about to pick up the ridiculously spindly shoes when her words came back to him. What the hell, he decided. And left them where she'd dropped them.

* * *

Julia had just come out of the shower when her cell phone trilled. She threw on a robe, went into the adjoining bedroom, and located it in the bottom of her purse. Afraid it might be Graham, trying yet another shot at a reconciliation, she was relieved when the caller ID displayed her mother's cell phone number.

The door from the living room opened. During a long, mostly sleepless night, Julia had decided she'd exaggerated Finn's size. Now, looking at him taking up nearly the entire doorway, she realized he was actually even larger than the image that had tormented her sleep.

"So where are you, and how's the harmony and light tour going?" Although the thick terry cloth robe concealed far more than that dress she'd taunted him with last night, Julia felt vaguely uncomfortable. She turned her back on him.

"Oh, just wonderfully," the familiar rich, warm voice responded. "We're in Coldwater Cove. It's a charming little Victorian town on the Washington peninsula. People in the Northwest have always been more in tune with nature than some other parts of the country your father and I have visited over the years."

Julia's parents, Freedom and Peace, had been part of a group of flower children who'd drifted down the California coast when Haight-Ashbury had become too commercially artificial for their tastes. They pooled their funds to purchase a small dairy and, proving surprisingly entrepreneurial for hippies, they'd used the proceeds from milk and ice cream sales, along with ticket revenues to an annual summer solstice music festival, to fund their artistic projects.

For people who'd professed an aversion to private wealth, many had done quite well for themselves: among their ranks were a world-famous balladeer, two Pulitzer Prize winners—one a novelist, the other a poet—and a silver craftsman whose work was featured at Neiman Marcus and Saks.

Her parents had achieved their own measure of fame. One of her father's grapevine chairs had appeared in a retrospective of chairs as art at the Smithsonian, two of his paintings hung in New York's Museum of Modern Art, and a recent pictorial in *Vanity Fair* had shown one of her mother's woven blankets hanging on the wall of the President and First Lady's Texas ranch house.

Her mother gave a thumbnail sketch of their travels, then asked, "How are things in Louisiana?"

"So far, so good." Better now that Finn, apparently deciding her mother offered no threat, had returned to the living room.

"I'm glad to hear that." Julia could hear her mother's slight exhaled sigh. "You know I try not to interfere in your life, dear. But the reason I'm calling is that I'm worried about you."

"Me? Why?"

"I had a dream about you last night. Your aura was decidedly muddy."

"My aura's fine. All those mountains in the Northwest must be screwing up your signal."

"Laugh all you want," her mother said mildly. "But the vibrations coming from your way are decidedly unstable."

"I hadn't realized you'd begun predicting earthquakes." The smile in Julia's voice took the sting from her teasing words.

"Don't I wish. If I could, we would have been prepared for yesterday's tremor."

"Tremor?" Julia hadn't heard anything about a tremor in Washington state. "Are you all right?"

"We're fine. Though it was a bit exciting, since we were crossing the Evergreen Bridge at the time. . . . I was just about to get to that, dear," she said to someone Julia heard talking in the background. "Your father's unhappy because that troll candle you bought us the summer we sold my jewelry on the Grateful Dead tour fell off the dashboard. His head broke off. The troll's, not your father's."

Julia remembered the summer well. She'd been twelve and although she'd grown up surrounded by free love, it was the first time she'd ever been kissed. Woodstock McIntyre, whose mother sold tie-dyed T-shirts and Electric Kool-Aid from the back of a battered old Ford Econoline, had put his tongue in her mouth and touched her breast. Well, he'd touched her nipple, since she hadn't had anything resembling a breast at the time.

He'd then blabbed that fact to all his stupid friends, making her, for a brief time, consider joining a convent.

"Oh, you wouldn't want to become a nun," her mother had said when she'd found Julia crying her eyes out in the back of the VW minibus. "We're pagans. Although," she'd tacked on thoughtfully, "I believe Rainbow Seagull became a Buddhist nun for a time when she was living in Tibet. If you'd like, I could ask her—"

"What I want," Julia had wailed as only a girl whose life had been ruined could, "is breasts."

Charm bracelets had jingled as her mother had run a beringed hand down Julia's red hair. "And you'll have them. In their own time."

"Easy for you to say," she'd muttered into a pillow stuffed with organically grown cotton and lavender. Adding insult to injury, Woodstock had pointed out that Julia's mother—who'd be the last person to flaunt her sexuality—was really, really built.

"The candle's wax," she said, dragging her mind back from that day of adolescent humiliation that she could almost laugh about now. "Can't he just heat it up and shape it back together?"

"I suggested that. But he insists it wouldn't be the same, since he'd always know it was flawed."

Julia reminded herself that those idyllic families resurrected from television archives and given a new life on Nick at Nite had never existed. The Cleavers and the Brady Bunch were as fictitious as *River Road*. But even knowing that, there were times when she wondered what it would have been like to grow up in the suburbs with Donna Reed for a mother. What many now called New Age had been her parents' normal lifestyle for more than three decades, and despite their success, they mostly continued to live as they always had.

But these days, rather than driving the Volkswagen Julia remembered so fondly, they traveled in a luxurious bus that had been tricked out at the factory with all the comforts of home. Replacing the 70s perky-faced daisies, peace signs and anti-war slogans which had covered the original VW, her father had painted a mural of bearded wizards casting spells, fairies with shimmering wings who danced on sunbeams and slept amid petals of lush flowers, while fire-breathing dragons guarded the mouths of secret caves.

This wonderland was overseen by stunningly beautiful goddesses who floated above the scene in filmy, translucent pastel gowns and never suffered bad-hair days. Characteristically, when he'd bought this whimsical house on wheels, he'd written checks equal to the sticker price to local charities.

Her parents had been together thirty-five years, yet had never married. "Starhearts and soulmates don't need cold administrative documents to sanctify their love," Freedom had always proclaimed in his big, booming voice.

"And a piece of paper can't keep love alive," Peace always serenely pointed out.

The more Julia witnessed so many of her friends' marriages crash and burn, or even sadder yet, slowly, quietly fade into disinterest, the more she appreciated her parents' relationship. She'd never met two people more suited to one another, alike in every way, so bonded it was impossible to think of one without the other.

"You are keeping that malachite necklace I sent you close by, aren't you?"

"Yes, Mother," Julia said dutifully. The variegated green stone was supposed to break into two pieces to warn her of danger, which would admittedly be difficult to notice since she'd forgone wearing it around her neck and now carried it in her purse in a small black velvet bag.

"And the bloodstone?"

"Absolutely. Along with the obsidian, the turquoise, and the falcon's eye." There were nearly enough rocks in her purse to make up her own quarry. Remembering her mother's claim that the Danish blue falcon's eye would help her maintain control of her life, Julia idly wondered if she should dig it out.

After passing on her love to her father and promising to be extra careful, at least until the new moon, she hung up and returned to the bathroom to blow her hair dry and brace herself for whatever outrageous scenarios Warren had thought up for Amanda this time.

The morning cast meeting did not start out on a high note.

"What the hell is this?" Margot, looking a bit ragged around the edges, waved her copy of the revised script.

"It's the new story line I told you about, love," Randy said blithely. "Warren's come up with a ripper of an idea. Amanda's going to time travel back to the Civil War after Vanessa shoots her. We'll be a shoo-in to win our time slot in the sweeps."

"The hell with the sweeps." She stabbed the page with a long crimson fingernail. "Who is Fancy?"

"Fancy's who Amanda is in a past life."

"I'm going to be Amanda's *mother?* Do I have to remind you that it's stipulated in my contract that I won't play anyone's mother?"

"The mother's a bonzer part. She's wonderfully neurotic and needy. Gives you a chance to really chew the scenery."

"I'd like to chew Warren's neurotic ass." She glared around the long table. "Where the hell is the little prick, anyway?"

"He called and said he's running a bit late. But he's on his way down."

"Sounds as if Warren's the one who may need protecting," Felissa drawled. "I do hope he didn't use up all his strength doing the nasty with that airhead blond bimbo last night."

"She's not an airhead." Warren entered the conference room, looking, Finn thought, more than a little smug. "Or a bimbo. And there's no need to be crude."

"Pots and kettles, darling," Felissa tossed back. "It was obvious that the overteased bleached blonde was just a small town slut looking for a fame fuck."

"She's not a slut." Finn wanted to remain as far out of the dynamics of the *River Road* cast as possible, but there was no way he was going to allow this woman to insult a friend. "She's just . . ." Shit. How the hell did you explain Lorelei to anyone who'd grown up north of the Mason-Dixon line?

"Southern," Warren supplied.

"Absolutely," Finn agreed.

"If we're through discussing Warren's sex life, I'd like to return to the subject of this new script." Margot pushed the pages away as if they were contaminated. "There's no way the audience—and all my fans—are going to accept me as any grown woman's mother."

"People married younger in those days," Warren argued. "Your character was a child bride, forced by her father into a marriage of convenience with a much older cotton planter."

She muttered a short, rude curse and returned to skimming the pages. "Wait a goddamn minute! Amanda seduces my husband? Her own father? That's just sick, Warren."

"He's your second husband, which makes him her stepfather. And her name's Fancy," he reminded her.

"Whatever her name is, she's getting to sleep with *my* fiancé the night before he goes off to war," Felissa complained, leafing through the pages. "Why can't I seduce Margot's husband?"

"Because the audience would never believe it, since you're playing the Melanie Wilkes role."

"And Julia gets to be Scarlett?"

Felissa's tone was as much of a storm warning as the rumble of thunder out over the Gulf. Finn could tell the writer knew he'd made a tactical error with that comparison.

"Fancy's not at all like Scarlett," he backpedaled. "She's really a Confederate spy who has to determine if her mother's new riverboat gambler husband is secretly selling the plantation's cotton to the Northern army."

"So now I'm going to be married to a traitor?" Margot looked on the verge of going ballistic.

"I don't know if he's a traitor or not. I still haven't decided."

"Well, whichever, I absolutely refuse to compromise my character." She turned toward Kendall, who was seated on a sofa a few feet away from the table. "Tell him he has to change the script, Charles."

"I'll tell him no such thing." His eyes were hard as stone. "The story line stands as written."

"But my contract—"

"Has so many holes in it, it may as well have been written on Swiss cheese. Atlantic Pharmaceuticals' lawyers teethed on the *Art of War* and they love going into battle, so if I were you, I'd think twice about challenging this story line. And if you get it into your head to sulk in your dressing room, the way you did last month when you balked about that scene in the country club where Amanda threw champagne in your face, I'll fine you a thousand dollars for every minute you tie up shooting."

Fury drew her face into harsh, ugly lines. "You're an ungrateful bastard."

Kendall's face was just as hard. "You swore on your dear old granny's memory that you didn't have any ulterior motive in going to bed with me. I took you at your word. If you were lying, sweetheart, it's your problem, not mine."

Margot flung the bound pages across the room, shot Julia a white-hot look of hatred, then stormed out as dramatically as one might expect from a former daytime diva.

"Just another day in paradise," Julia murmured. "If you had any sense at all, Callahan, you'd escape now. While you still can."

# 12

*That was a nice thing to do,"* Julia said thirty minutes later after the story meeting ended.

Finn stepped back, allowing her to enter the elevator first. "What?"

"Standing up for that woman Warren left the party with last night."

"She's a friend," he said simply. He stuck the keycard in the slot that made the elevator bypass the lower floors. The doors closed.

"And that's important to you."

It didn't sound like a question, but Finn answered it anyway. "Yeah."

"That's nice."

"Is that a compliment?"

"Merely a statement."

They rode up in silence, side by side, both watching the numbers above the door light up.

"I lied," Julia said as they entered the suite.

"About what?" He wondered if she was going to confess she'd staged the threat.

"It *was* a compliment."

"Okay."

"Okay? That's it?" She folded her arms. "Perhaps spending all your time with police types and criminals may have left you a bit socially challenged, but it's customary, when one receives a compliment, to respond in kind."

"You want a compliment?"

"I didn't say that." Her answer was a bit too quick. It had sure sounded that way to Finn. "I merely pointed out that your answer was a bit curt."

"Just give me a minute to think of one."

Finn wondered if there were any words of praise this woman hadn't heard, and for some insane reason wanted to try to come up with something original. Which was one of the lamest ideas he'd ever had. Pretty words had always come trippingly off Nate's tongue and he figured Jack must do pretty well in that department, since the middle Callahan brother earned his living as a writer these days, but Finn had never been one to wax poetic.

"Forget it." She shook her head in disgust, stomped into the adjoining bedroom, and shut the door between them. It wasn't quite a slam, but it was damn close.

Finn shook his own head. Sighed heavily as he took his notebook from a suit jacket pocket.

No matter what else was going on in his life, he'd never had any trouble concentrating on a case. He'd developed the ability to shut out everything and everyone around him back when he'd been cramming for tests in a college dorm that made *Animal House* look tame by comparison.

But as he reviewed the details of the conversations he'd had downstairs last night, the words on the lined pages seemed to blur, replaced with an unbidden mental image of him and Julia Summers rolling around on the moss-stuffed mattress at the camp.

The moment Julia saw Beau Soleil, she was enthralled. "It's stunning."

"It looks just like Tara," Felissa said.

"I'll bet it's being eaten by termites," Margot said. Faced with being fired, she'd shown up for work this morning but it was obvious to everyone that she wasn't at all happy with her situation.

"It used to be," Nate, who'd come along to open the house for them, said. "But my brother thinks he's managed to run them off. He's been restoring the house for months, and though it's probably a lifetime project, if you'd seen the place when Jack started, you'd be amazed it looks this good."

Julia put the names together. "Your brother's Jack Callahan? *The* Jack Callahan? Who wrote *The Death Dealer*?"

"Yeah. That's him."

"I absolutely love his books. I cried when his DEA hero's wife was blown up in a car bombing meant for him, and I keep hoping he'll find a nice woman to fall in love with. Is it true the stories are autobiographical?"

"I honestly don't know. Jack doesn't talk all that much about his days in the DEA. You'd have to ask him."

"Is he going to be living in the house while we're here?"

"He's on a belated honeymoon. His wife's family owned Beau Soleil for generations before Jack bought it. Our *maman* was the housekeeper here when we were kids."

"Sounds as if there's a story there." A fairy tale, she suspected.

"One with a happy ending." Nate's smile was quick and warm. Julia was a little unnerved that it didn't affect her nearly as much as a mere quirk of his older brother's harshly cut lips.

She wasn't sure what she was going to do about Finn Callahan, but since things between them had been silent and uncomfortable since she'd walked out on him yesterday morning, she didn't think she could stand to spend the next two weeks in a state of undeclared war.

She looked up at Finn. "You didn't tell me your brother was Jack Callahan."

"You didn't ask. And it's not germane to our situation."

Deciding that it was impossible to have a normal social conversation with this man, Julia gave up on any idea of a truce and turned back to Nate. "I love the double front stairs."

"Aren't they cool? The practical reason for the design is that because the women's hoop skirts were so wide, there wasn't room for two people to walk up them side by side. They also served to keep social order, since if a man saw a woman's ankles back in those days, he was duty bound to marry her. Having men go up one side and women the other prevented an escort from seeing a lady's legs when she lifted her hoop skirts to climb the steps."

"Hoop skirts." Felissa sighed happily, obviously pleased with the idea of wearing antebellum-era costumes.

Margot, on the other hand, seemed determined not to find anything positive about the experience. "Corsets," she muttered.

Julia sighed with resignation. The last time Margot had been in a snit, she'd disrupted not only the mood among the cast and crew, but the shooting schedule for over a week, as well. If this season-ending project ran late, she'd never make it to Kathmandu in time.

Things fell into a pattern over the next three days. Finn and Julia drove in silence to Beau Soleil each morning to meet the rest of the cast, who arrived by van from town. By the end of the first day, Finn had come to realize that acting involved a lot more than smiling pretty for the camera and shedding your clothes.

He sat nearby as Damien, the magenta-haired makeup man, chattered like a magpie while transforming Julia into *River Road*'s siren. Next her hair was brushed, teased, and sprayed into a sexy tangle of curls. Finally, while Finn waited outside her trailer, Audrey, the motherly wardrobe mistress, would dress her in period costumes that looked as if they weighed a ton and were probably even more uncomfortable than Damien's crotch binding leather pants, which had to feel like a sauna in this heat.

Then she'd spend hours waiting while people blocked scenes, arranged lighting, and myriad other things just to shoot a scene that maybe would last five or ten minutes. If things went well.

He began to recognize the transformation into Amanda. It wasn't that she turned from some ordinary person into Wonder Woman. Julia Summers was a naturally stunning creature, albeit with surprisingly uneven features—there was that feline slant to her eyes, her nose was a bit too pug, her lips too large, the chin too stubborn. But somehow they all fit together perfectly.

It was, he decided, watching Fancy flirt with her mother's husband, as if an already bright light inside her flared even hotter when the camera turned on her. Even on those occasions when she'd have to repeat the same lines again and again, she somehow managed to make them sound fresh each time.

At the end of each scene, Damien would leap to action with his brushes, powders and potions; the hairdresser would struggle to tame her curls, which were made even more wild by the unrelenting humidity; and the waiting would begin again.

And all the time, while Margot bitched about anything and everything, and Felissa fussed about the heat, Julia didn't utter a word of complaint.

That she was universally liked by the crew was obvious. It wasn't that surprising, since she appeared to take a genuine interest in them. Finn watched her ask a cameraman about his new son and ooh and aah over the snapshots the man proudly whipped out of his shirt pocket, commiserate with the script girl about her husband's infidelity, and encourage an electrician to adopt a puppy for his daughter's birthday from a Golden Retriever rescue group she'd made a fund-raising appearance for.

She was even gracious to the townspeople who'd been hired as extras, obligingly posing for pictures and signing autographs for the locals, who were openly enthralled. Finn recognized several of them and couldn't help noticing that not only did Lorelei show up in more than a few scenes, she also disappeared with the writer during the lunch break.

After they returned to the inn at the end of the day, Julia would order a light supper from room service and disappear into the bedroom, where he could hear her rehearsing her next day's lines aloud. Then, mere hours later, the process would begin again.

The third day of shooting dragged on, the final scene shot late at night in the plantation cemetery. Finn stood in the shadow of a broken-winged angel, watching her. Silvery moondust streamed over the bayou graveyard, illuminating tombs that stood like mute white ghosts in the ethereal glow. Julia/Fancy was wearing a clinging moss green dress which, though not entirely true to the period, could have been created from the mist that curled in clinging tendrils around her bare arms. She'd left her fiery hair loose, allowing it to curl over pearlescent shoulders.

"So you've come," a deep male voice echoed out of the thickening fog.

"I hadn't realized I had a choice." She tossed her head, and there was an adversarial edge to her honeyed Southern drawl. "Since you've put Belle Terre under Yankee occupation."

"Of course you have a choice." Captain James Farragut emerged from behind one of the tombs, wearing a uniform of Yankee blue. With his well-trimmed blond hair and beard, shiny brass buttons, and boots polished to a brilliant sheen, he could have stepped off a Union recruiting poster. Fancy O'Halloran had hated him on sight.

Thunder rumbled like Northern cannon fire in the distance. "During my stay here, you can meet me wherever I say, whenever I say, and I won't order my men to burn your beloved plantation house to the ground when we leave," he said matter-of-factly. "Or you can refuse, and I'll turn you and your sister over to my men, many of whom are rough farm boys who don't have any idea of how to treat a lady."

"And you do?" Her tone suggested that she found it unlikely any man from New York City would have the faintest idea how to treat a genteel Southern woman.

His boots crunched on the crushed oyster shell gravel as he approached. "Absolutely."

They were standing face-to-face now, her skirt pressing against his thighs as he backed her up against a crypt, pinning her between the damp stone and his body.

Lightning flashed, brightening the scene to a daylight brilliance for a fleeting heartbeat of a second. Watching her closely as he was, Finn saw her faint shudder when the captain's fingers skimmed over her bare shoulders. With anticipation or fear, he couldn't tell.

"Of course," Farragut mused as his touch trailed lower, tracing the rounded curve of her upper breast, "one could argue that any woman who'd meet a man all alone in a deserted cemetery at midnight isn't really much of a lady."

The sky opened up. Rain fell in a torrent, as if being poured out of a bucket. Fancy cried out as he roughly tore the last of her pretty, pre-war dresses down to her waist, but when he dragged her to the ground and began unfastening his wool trousers, she reached beneath her filmy skirt—exposing a mouthwatering length of stocking—and retrieved the derringer she'd stuck in a lacy garter.

"If you lay a hand on me again," she said, pointing the weapon directly at his groin, "or so much as touch a hair on the head of my sister or any other woman on this plantation, I swear, you'll be carrying your manhood back to New York in a basket."

If he hadn't known that this soap opera vixen had grown up on one of the last surviving flower child communes in northern California, Finn might have believed that Julia Summers was a true Steel Magnolia of the South.

They glared at each other for a long, tension-filled moment. The Union captain's eyes glittered with dangerous male intent. The rain had turned her dress nearly invisible; the thin wet material clung to her curves.

An instinctive male response to the provocative sight uncoiled in his loins; Finn ruthlessly reined it in.

"Rebel slut," Shane Langley, playing Captain Farragut, spat the words, then lunged at her again.

As the thunder boomed around them and the rain fell, Fancy pulled the trigger.

"Cut!" Randy's voice broke the night.

"Cut," echoed the assistant director.

The artificially generated storm abruptly ceased.

"Stone the bloody dingoes." The hard-driving Australian director bestowed the first compliment Finn had heard him hand out in three days of filming. "You pulled that scene off in one take."

"It was either that or let you rain on me for the rest of the night." Julia took hold of Shane's hand as he pulled her back onto her feet.

"I'll see you all back on the set at nine A.M. sharp. Julia, luv, you're due in makeup at seven."

"Dammit, Randy. That's only six hours from now. How do you expect me to get my beauty sleep?"

"I'd suggest you sleep quickly," the director responded.

"Don't worry, darlin'," her co-star said, his own natural Mississippi drawl more suited to a Confederate uniform than Union blue. "You're already drop-dead gorgeous."

"Flatterer," she muttered, slipping her arms into the robe Audrey held out to her.

"It's the God's own truth." He lifted his right hand.

"Isn't that sweet." She patted his cheek, her smile luminous. "But I'm still not sleeping with you."

He shrugged good-naturedly. "Can't blame a guy for trying."

No, Finn agreed silently. With the image of those long, firm legs replaying in his mind, he doubted there were many men who wouldn't attempt to parlay that scene into the real thing.

Julia didn't so much as spare him a glance as he followed her to her trailer; didn't say a word when he walked in right behind her as if he had every right to be there. Though he was grateful for her apparent change in attitude, Finn didn't trust her seeming acquiescence.

"God, I feel as if I've gone ten rounds with Mike Tyson," she complained. "In a mud pit. And I'm going to have bruises all over my butt tomorrow from that damn gravel."

Since he'd discovered that she had a habit of talking to herself, most often when she was preparing for a scene, Finn didn't respond.

She turned her back on him and shrugged off the robe, letting it slide down her body onto the floor. The wet, muddy dress that revealed more than it concealed followed, leaving her in a muddied corset and lacy silk pantaloons that might have come from a nineteenth-century Victoria's Secret store. "If you're going to insist on hovering over me like some oversize bullmastiff guard dog, you may as well make yourself useful and get me out of this damn straitjacket so I can breathe again."

The corset was white floral satin, heavily boned and laced up the back. It looked uncomfortable as hell, but winnowed her waist down to an unbelievably narrow size he figured he could span with his fingers. Fingers that were practically itching to touch her.

"Why don't I call Audrey?" he suggested.

"Because she's had a long day since Randy got it into his head to change costumes every two hours, and she still has tomorrow's wardrobe to get ready."

She flashed him a deliberately provocative look over her bare shoulder. "Which leaves you to undress me."

The pink ribbons tied at the back of her wasp-slender waist were wet and muddy. Deliberately testing his self-control, Finn drew them through the loops slowly, allowing his fingers to brush against perfumed flesh that felt like cool satin to the touch.

Neither spoke. But the higher he got, the more he sensed the tension that had been stretched nearly to the breaking point between them these past days begin to ease. When his knuckles brushed against her spine, not by accident, but design, he heard a slow languid sigh escape from between her lips.

"What did you think?" she murmured.

"About what? Lift up your hair so I can unlace these top ones."

She did as instructed, revealing a slender neck he found unreasonably erotic. "About the scene."

"I think it was getting pretty hot." He slipped the ribbon through the final loop. "Until you shot the guy's balls off."

"Did that make you wince? Want to grab your own?"

"Yeah."

"Good." There was a rasp of smooth silk against harsh denim as she leaned her nearly naked body back against him in a way that sent the last of the blood rushing straight from his head to his boxer shorts.

Finn knew the move was calculated when she looked up at him, her sexy come-and-kiss-me lips tilted up in the same smile he'd watched her use two days ago when her character had seduced her sister's Confederate Army fiancé before sending him off to fight for a losing cause.

"My gracious," she said in Fancy's slow magnolia drawl. "Is that your gun, Special Agent Callahan? Or are you just glad to see me?"

"What the hell do you think?" Because he suspected it was what she wanted, Finn refused to be embarrassed by his body's response and move away.

Buns of steel earned from daily yoga workouts wiggled against him in a way meant to test his resolve. Oh, she was good, Finn decided as he ground his teeth and forced his sex-crazed mind to run through the entire 1978 Yankees lineup. He was trying to remember who'd replaced the injured Willie Randolph at second base late in the season, when Julia gave him another smile, more wickedly seductive than the first.

"It's nice to know you're actually human, darling. I was beginning to wonder." With that less than flattering remark, she let her damp red hair fall back over her shoulders, held the corset against her breasts, and disappeared into the bathroom.

When he heard the shower turn on, Finn imagined her naked, imagined himself joining her in that compact shower, smoothing the fragrant soap that clung to her skin over her lush curves.

As his mind wandered into forbidden territory, flashing pictures that would make the old *Playboy* magazines his brothers used to snitch from him back in high school seem tame by comparison, Finn leaned his head against the wall and reminded himself that if he allowed his rampant hard-on to drag him into that shower with her, he'd undoubtedly be breaking every rule in the book. Along with some that hadn't even been written yet.

But that crack about not being human was pissing him off. What the hell did she think he was? Some sort of sexless android? Just because he didn't believe in giving in to temptation and mixing work and pleasure? Of course, he'd never been so tempted, either.

Finn had been threatened, shot at, and had even foiled an assassination plot that had earned him an ugly knife gash in the thigh and an invitation to the White House to have dinner with the President and First Lady. Unfortunately, he was beginning to fear that guarding the woman soap opera fans loved to hate might end up being the most dangerous assignment of his career.

He could protect Julia from her obsessed star-stalker.

But who the effing hell was going to protect *him* from *her*?

On the other side of the closed door, as the shower cubicle filled up with fragrant steam, Julia's reckless mind imagined Finn Callahan's broad, capable hands moving all over her wet slick body, touching her, doing all the erotic things he'd done in her dreams.

Leaning her head back against the shower wall, she lifted her face to the water and sighed. It was going to be a very long two weeks.

# 13

*Julia woke feeling cranky* and out of sorts after having spent the night tossing and turning, suffering unwanted erotic dreams about Finn, one of which had included a hoopskirt and a vat of warm honey.

The silent drive to Beau Soleil did nothing to ease her headache. When they arrived Margot looked hungover and was her typical acid self, deriding the room service waiter who'd taken all of ten minutes to bring her coffee to her suite, the van driver for "purposefully trying to hit every goddamn pothole in the goddamn road," and Warren for writing such "godawful drek."

Warren appeared unwounded by both her barbs and her stiletto sharp glares. He was deep in some creative zone, madly scribbling on a legal pad, undoubtedly changing the script yet again, Julia thought with a sigh.

Shane, who, if one could believe a barb Margot had thrown at him, had disappeared from the inn's bar last night with a cocktail waitress, caught up on missed sleep while Randy went over the script, blocking out scenes he intended to shoot today.

And all the time Finn remained beside Julia, as large and silent as the Sphinx.

Clouds were gathering out over the Gulf, dark portents of a possible storm, making Julia very glad Randy had decided to shoot the indoor ballroom scene, which flashed back to a time before the war, today. The light was an odd yellow, making Beau Soleil gleam more gold than alabaster. It truly was a stunning house, though Julia couldn't imagine ever thinking of it as home. To her it would be like living in a museum.

Dreading the prospect of another day laced up like a Christmas goose, she entered the trailer that served as a temporary dressing room. Someone had left a manila envelope with her name on the table. She sighed and opened what she took to be yet more revisions to the script. Blood rushed from her head in a dizzying rush when she saw the photograph. Sound roared in her head. Then everything went black.

The next thing she knew, she was lying on the couch.

"Wait here," she heard Finn say from what sounded like the bottom of the sea.

As if she were capable of getting anywhere without crawling. Julia looked up at him, but the way he was going in and out of focus only made her more dizzy, so she shut her eyes.

A moment later, a cold washcloth was laid on her forehead.

"Take a deep breath."

She managed a shallow, shuddering intake of air that cleared away a few of the mental cobwebs.

"Again." When she felt his fingertips against her throat, Julia realized he was checking her pulse.

She took another, more efficient breath.

"Good. Another." The deep, self-assured voice, the reassuring stroke of his fingers as he brushed her hair off her cheek, the coolness of the damp cloth against her skin, all began to calm her. "The color's coming back to your cheeks."

She knew. She could feel it. Her heart, which had been pounding against her ribs like an angry fist, began to slow to something resembling a normal beat.

"I feel so foolish," she murmured. "I never faint." She'd once gotten a little light-headed when she'd stood up too fast after giving blood, but had felt fine again after eating the cookie the nurse had given her.

"There's a first time for everything. You're going to have to start having something besides coffee and half an orange for breakfast."

"Easy for you to say. You don't have to squeeze into a spandex catsuit in a couple weeks."

After winning the role, she'd belatedly realized the downside of becoming a Bond Girl. Her body was going to be up on that huge screen, inviting audiences all around the world to criticize every blemish and lump. Which was why she'd hired a personal trainer, a sadistic Russian immigrant she suspected must have run a gulag back in his homeland.

"Besides, I've skipped breakfast my entire life and never fainted before."

If her eyes hadn't been closed, forcing her to rely more on her other senses, if his hand hadn't still been on her face, she might have missed the way he stiffened ever so slightly.

"Never?" His voice was gritty, even for him.

"Never."

"Could you be pregnant?"

That made her open her eyes. "No."

"You sure?"

"Since I haven't been paid a visitation by some angel bringing glad tidings lately, I'd have to be six months pregnant, so yeah, I'm pretty sure I would have noticed by now. Besides, I'm on the pill."

"You haven't had sex for six months?"

"Gee, Callahan. Is that germane to our situation?"

"Touché." A flash of humor momentarily brightened his eyes, then just as quickly faded, replaced by concern. His lips had appeared to quirk, just a little, and thinking back on those disturbingly erotic dreams, Julia wondered what they would taste like.

Which was also not germane to the situation, she reminded herself.

"Maybe I'd better call a doctor." Her stomach fluttered when he brushed a wayward curl off her cheek.

"That's not necessary." She pointed toward the photograph lying face down on the carpet. "You might want to take a look at that."

Anger moved in waves across his face as he viewed the photograph, computer printed exactly as the first one had been. Having surreptitiously watched him nearly as carefully as he'd been watching her, Julia had looked beneath the stoicism he wore like a coat of armor, and begun to sense Finn Callahan could be dangerous. Now, taking in the muscle jerking in his dark cheek and the whiteness of his knuckles as he clenched and unclenched his right hand, she belatedly realized that if you were one of the bad guys, he could be deadly.

"How do you think he took it?" she asked, swallowing her fear. She would not allow some stalker to make her feel helpless or vulnerable. She sat up and pushed her hair back from her face with both hands.

He held the photograph by the edges. The better, she guessed, to protect any fingerprints that might be on the paper. "My best guess would be, since we were alone in here, he was outside the window."

That idea caused goose bumps to rise on her flesh. Despite an outside temperature in the low nineties, with a humidity nearly as high, Julia began to shiver. She wrapped her arms around herself, partly for warmth, partly in an unconscious gesture of protection.

"You probably think I'm acting like a ninny."

"Why would I think that?"

"Well, I do spend a great deal of my life performing for a camera, and, as you've already pointed out, I shed my clothes on a regular basis, so I suppose a single still shot shouldn't be so upsetting . . ."

"But this is different," Finn guessed. "Because those scenes were carefully scripted and professionally acted." He brushed his fingers along the top outline of her lips, which she was pressing together to keep from quivering. "Having some stranger filming your ordinary everyday private moments without any warning or permission would be enough to make anyone a little jumpy."

"I think what took me by surprise was that if someone on the cast isn't playing a very sick joke, my stalker's back."

"From last week, right?"

"No." She rubbed her eyes with the heels of her hands. "Before that."

"Before . . . When? And why the hell don't the police have a record of any stalker?"

"There wasn't any official report made, because he didn't quite fit the criteria for a stalker. He didn't make any threats, never tried to get too close to me. If he had, I'd know who he was.

"Since the photos were flattering, with equally flattering comments written beneath them, I decided it was merely a fan with a crush and not worth dragging the police into."

"That's what they're for, dammit. I can understand how you might be reluctant, given your background, to go into a police station, but believe it or not, cops do have other duties besides beating up civilians at traffic stops and setting up speeding traps to catch you when you're driving too fast to the airport."

"I went to traffic school," she muttered, irritated but unsurprised he knew about that. "Paid the fine and did my time."

"I know. The instructor said it was the only time in his memory that someone stuck all Saturday in the basement of a church brought home baked brownies to class."

"It was my birthday. My parents were at some jazzfest in Sedona—that's in Arizona—"

"Yeah. I've been there. Pretty little place."

"It's more than pretty. It's spectacular with all that red rock and impossibly blue sky. Did you know it's the red of the rocks that makes the sky look so blue over the canyons?"

"I've never heard the theory, but it makes sense . . . And you're changing the subject."

"I'm merely responding to your crack about the brownies. I didn't want to celebrate alone, so I baked some from my mother's famous recipe and took them along for the class lunch break."

He lifted a dark brow. "I'll bet that made the second half of the day a lot more mellow for everyone."

"They weren't laced with anything. Geez, Callahan, even if I did drugs, which I never have, you must have a really bad opinion of me to think I'm that stupid."

"I don't think you're stupid. I also didn't think you'd actually done it. I was just—"

"Making a joke?"

Hell, Finn thought. What kind of opinion of him did she have if she found that idea so impossible? "Yeah. But not because I'm not taking this seriously."

"Of course you take it seriously. From what I've been able to tell, you're a textbook firstborn. You take everything seriously. And the only reason I didn't get the joke was that I wasn't expecting it."

Humor lit her remarkable eyes. "Perhaps we could work out some sort of system for you to warn me when one's coming up," she suggested. "Hold up a sign, perhaps. Or maybe a code word that'll serve as a clue."

When she smiled, Finn realized that despite what he'd said to Nate about her being a pain in the ass, he was actually starting to like—and admire—Julia Summers. "Clues never hurt," he murmured with a practiced casualness.

And speaking of clues . . .

He studied the picture more closely, seeking some small clue to the photographer. It had been taken by a digital camera, printed on the type of inexpensive white computer paper that could be bought at any office supply store.

"Is it like the others you've gotten? Either the first time or last week?" He didn't see any point in suggesting that having thrown the earlier one away hadn't been the most prudent thing to do.

"I'm no expert, but it looks like the same paper and the same printer. The flesh tones are off in the same way."

"You have a good eye." The skin above and between the corset laces was more pink than the pale ivory of a true redhead. More rosy than he knew hers to be.

Beneath the photograph her stalker had typed, *I'm very disappointed in you, Amanda. You should choose your lovers more carefully.*

"He thinks we're lovers," Finn said, more to himself than to her. A suspicion that had undoubtedly been fueled by this seemingly intimate moment which her stalker had frozen in time.

"It appears so."

"He—or she—is also jealous."

"Surely you don't think it's a woman?"

His gut told him it wasn't. But . . .

"I'm not ruling anyone out."

She tried to hold the shiver in, but accustomed to watching for the smallest of details, he caught it. Wanting to reassure, he took hold of her shoulders.

"It's going to be okay."

Hell. He'd known it was a mistake to touch her. From the way her eyes widened, Finn knew she felt the same flash of heat, the sizzle of nerve endings.

"I'll keep you safe."

"I know." For a woman who had grown up surrounded by free love, an actress who could slip with silky ease into the skin of a siren, her green eyes were surprisingly innocent. "You may not be the easiest man in the world, Callahan. And I'm not even sure I like you. But I do trust you."

It would be against every tenet he believed in if he gave into the temptation to take that wide, generous mouth. The safest thing to do would be to take his hands off her. Unfortunately, if he'd been a fan of safe, he would have made his mother happy and become a corporate lawyer instead of a cop.

His fingers stroked, soothing the knots at the base of her neck. His eyes delved deeply into hers, hoping he'd find the refusal that would stop him before he stepped over the line.

"Callahan . . ." He knew he was lost when she lifted a hand to his cheek. Knew the same smoke that was clouding his mind was billowing in hers.

The hard-won control Finn had forced himself to take on so many years ago deserted him. Knowing what he was about to do was wrong, knowing it would create even more problems, he lowered his mouth to hers, stopping just a breath before contact.

Her eyes were deep green pools. A man could drown in them, if he wasn't careful.

She recklessly wrapped her arm around his neck and closed the distance.

# 14

*The first touch of lips* was like being punched in the gut with a velvet fist. The way she drew her head back just enough to stare up at him assured him that she'd felt it, too.

The little voice of caution, of conscience, he was usually able to count on deserted him. All Finn could think about was how much he wanted to strip that T-shirt and tight, low-slung jeans off her body and touch her. All over. Taste her. Everywhere.

As dangerous as that idea was, even worse was the realization that she wanted him to do exactly that.

Since he'd already broken his rule about getting involved on the job, Finn decided to deal with the consequences later—when his body wasn't throbbing, his blood had cooled to something below the boiling point, and his brain wasn't clogged with her scent.

She shivered, not from cold, not from fear, but anticipation. And that was his undoing.

This time he dove headlong into the kiss, dragging her right along with him. Tongues tangled, teeth scraped, arousal flared. His hands streaked over her, desperate to touch. Melting against him like heated wax, she encouraged him with soft sighs, low moans and dazed whimpers.

He tangled a hand in her hair and pulled her head back, allowing his mouth access to her smooth white throat. When he touched his tongue to the hollow where her pulse was pounding hot and hard and fast, Finn imagined he heard a hiss of steam.

Dark desires drummed in his head. Erotic images of all the things he wanted to do to her, with her, flashed through his mind like strobe lights, blinding him to anything and everything but her.

He wanted her. He wanted to press her back against the cushions, wanted to feel those long, slender legs around him; he wanted to bury himself deep within her, taking, possessing, claiming. That was just for starters.

Battered by hunger, by need, Finn forced himself to back away now, while he still could.

A little cry of protest escaped her lips as he broke the heated contact. Ruthlessly reining in his runaway desire, he nearly groaned as he took in the sight of her—eyes still a little soft-focused from lust, wine-sweet lips parted, her face flushed the soft hue of the late summer roses his mother had loved to tend in Beau Soleil's gardens.

"Wow." She pressed her fingers against her lips as she stared up at him. Her voice was ragged, her breathing hard.

She wasn't the only one. His chest was heaving like a man who'd been on the verge of drowning and pulled to safety just in time. Which was pretty much the case.

Finn pushed himself off the couch and put a safety zone of about five feet between them.

"I owe you an apology."

"You tell me you're sorry you kissed me, Callahan, and I'll forget I'm a pacifist and slug you." Her chin tilted up in that way he was beginning to enjoy. Her voice and her breathing steadied. "You liked it while it was happening. A lot."

Despite having just caused himself one helluva problem, her spark of spirit made him want to grin. Which was odd. He couldn't recall the last time he'd grinned.

Nate, of course, was well known for his lady-killing boyish grin, and Finn had heard more than one woman describe Jack's bold, cocky one to be a pirate's, dark and wickedly appealing. But to Finn's knowledge, no one ever mentioned his smile when describing him.

In fact, one frustrated former lover had, just before their brief affair ended, accused him of hiding all his feelings—if he even had any—behind a damn impenetrable stone face. He hadn't challenged her accusation since she was pretty much right. Any FBI Special Agent who revealed emotion wouldn't last long on the street, or in the Bureau. If there was a way to compartmentalize his feelings, Finn hadn't found it. Not that he'd ever looked all that hard; his life, both professionally and personally, had always suited him just fine.

So how was it that both seemed to be spinning out of control at the same time?

The thing to do now was to prioritize. First he'd regain control of this immediate situation with Julia. Then he could tackle the problem of how the hell he was going to get through the next week and a half.

"Sure, I enjoyed it." He might not volunteer information, but neither did he lie. "You're a dynamite kisser." Because it was too tempting to kiss her again, Finn sought something, anything, to say to cool things down. "Of course, I suppose I shouldn't be surprised. Since you've had a lot of practice."

Finn could have taken out his Glock and shot himself the minute he heard the words coming out of his mouth. If either Nate or Jack had heard him screw up like that, they'd probably be on the floor howling with laughter.

Instead of crumbling into a little puddle of hurt feelings, she fired right back at him. "Correction: *Amanda's* had a lot of practice. If you can't tell the difference by now, you're even more clueless about the opposite sex than you let on."

"Okay." *You can defuse this situation*, Finn assured himself. *Hell, you aced hostage negotiation and terrorist training. Handling one woman, even one who was as pissed off as this one seemed to be, should be a piece of cake.* "You're right. I misspoke."

"Now there's a governmental bureaucratic word for you," she muttered.

"I may be clueless when it comes to women—"

"*May* be?"

Finn forged on. "I may be one of the most socially inept guys you've ever met—"

"Oh, believe me, Callahan," she interrupted him again, "you win the crown."

He ground his teeth. "The thing is, you're understandably upset right now. And probably, although you've been doing a bang-up job of hiding it, a little scared. I had no right to take advantage of you that way."

"You weren't taking advantage of me. I wanted you to kiss me. Are you going to try to tell me that you haven't wondered what it would be like? That you haven't been at all curious?"

Truth warred with the desire to get out of these treacherous waters, he was already in way over his head. "Sure. But I shouldn't have allowed it to happen."

"Allowed?" That had her on her feet in a flash. "You *allowed*? Listen, you insufferable, arrogant—"

"Dammit, you've got a short fuse."

"Only when I'm forced to be locked up in close quarters with a bossy, humorless control freak." Her finger jabbed against the front of his shirt; Finn grasped her hand and held it against his chest.

He sighed heavily, then tried again. "Look, I'm probably all you've accused me of and a lot more. I also think you're gorgeous, sexy as hell, not to mention being a very nice woman."

"Nice," she muttered. Finn was encouraged when she didn't yank her hand away. "A glass of wine with a shrimp salad at the beach is nice. TV weather forecasters are nice. The guy who greets you at Wal-Mart is paid to be nice. Excuse me if I don't find *nice* that huge a compliment. As for being gorgeous, I honestly don't see it, though others seem to. But I can't take credit for great genes. My mother's stunningly beautiful."

"I know." Once again, Finn could have bit his tongue off. For someone who *never* spoke without thinking first, he was definitely bypassing his brain today.

"That's right." She shot him a frustrated look. "You've been busy digging up dirt on me and my family, so you've undoubtedly seen all our mug shots."

"As a matter of fact, I have. Are you going to slug me if I say yours looked pretty damn good?"

"For a woman with a number across her chest." A reluctant smile teased at the corner of her lips. "Damn it, Callahan, you really do know how to sweet-talk a girl, don't you?" It was her turn to sigh. "I can't believe we're even having this conversation. I can't believe I kissed an FBI agent. I especially can't believe that even as irritated as I am at you right now, I want to do it again."

That made two of them.

Kissing her had been a huge mistake. Instead of easing his hunger, now that he knew she tasted every bit as good as she looked, he was starving for more. Forbidden fruit was always the most appealing.

"Probably not as much as I do." In a gesture more suited to Nate, one he would have groaned at only a few days ago, Finn lifted their joined hands and skimmed a light kiss over her knuckles. "The thing is, it can't go anywhere."

"What makes you think I want it to? We're just talking a kiss here, Callahan. Basic physical attraction. Did you hear me say anything about needing orange blossoms or ever-afters?"

"No. But don't most women want them?" Frustrated, he rubbed the bridge of his nose. If he screwed up his work as badly as he had this, he wouldn't be able to get a job as a meter maid.

"A woman doesn't necessarily need marriage these days to be fulfilled."

"I know that." He had women friends in the Bureau who'd drilled that into him. "What's your favorite Fleming novel?"

"What?" She blinked at the apparent sudden change in subject.

"Your favorite Bond book. Which is it?"

"That's easy. *On Her Majesty's Service*. Why? And what's yours?"

"It changes. I suppose right now I'd have to say *Thunderball*." Finn could definitely identify with the disgraced spy who was sent off to a health farm for two weeks to get his act together. "And it's interesting that yours just happens to be the one book in which the guy gets married."

"His wife also gets killed in the end. Which blows any theory you might try to be formulating about my reading tastes and my own personal feelings about matrimony."

"Okay, maybe you'll follow in your parents' footsteps and skip taking the vows, but I'm pretty good at profiling and I'd peg you as the type of woman who believes in the happily-ever-after kind of storybook love."

"Don't you?"

"I believe in it for some people."

His parents came instantly to mind. Jake Callahan had doted on his dark-eyed Marie and she'd openly adored him. In fact, there'd been times when their penchant for public displays of affection had embarrassed the hell out of their three sons.

"Now you have me curious." She tilted her head. "Are you saying you've never thought about spending the rest of your life with one special woman?"

"Not really."

He wasn't like Nate, who was open about his desire to go to his grave playing the field, but Finn's work precluded any sustained relationship.

His last had been in the early days of his hunt for Lawson. He'd been dating a bright, ambitious senatorial aide who, while her work might keep her up on the Hill until all hours of the night, was not at all pleased when he stood her up for one of the inaugural balls.

He'd been notified that another girl's body had been found in the desert outside Las Vegas, the MO too close to the first murder in San Diego to be ignored. In his rush to catch the first plane out of National, he'd forgotten to call the aide, which had resulted in a blistering message on his voice mail, complete with sexual suggestions that were as physically impossible as they were graphic.

Since then his relationships had been kept to brief, no-strings affairs with women he knew well enough not to risk playing sexual Russian roulette. Sometimes they'd go out to dinner, have a few drinks, then return to her place for some hot steamy sex, after which, more often than not, he'd return to his own apartment before morning.

Other times they'd skip the preliminaries and go straight to the sex. Since the women were every bit as career driven and no more interested in a long-term relationship than he was, everyone stayed happy.

After his brother Jack's wedding a couple months ago, there were times when Finn had tried to imagine himself settling down with a wife and kids. He could see himself possibly getting married. Someday. Years from now, when he was retired, settled down, and wanted companionship for his old age.

"So, how about you?" he asked, partly because he wanted to move the focus away from him and partly because he was curious. "Is there some special guy in your life these days?"

She seemed to be living alone in her Venice house, but that didn't necessarily mean she wasn't involved with someone. He hadn't had time to do an in-depth investigation.

"Do you honestly believe that if I was in an intimate relationship, I would have kissed you like that?" She shot him a seething look. "You're the hotshot profiler. Do you think I'm the kind of woman who'd cheat on anyone I cared about?"

"I take it that's a *no*."

Julia folded her arms. "One thing I love about you, Callahan, is how good you are at reading subtleties."

The bitch of it was, he'd always been good at picking up nuances. But it was difficult to think clearly when his body craved her and his mind was so full of her all there was room for was hunger. He'd spent the past nights twisted into a pretzel on that hard, too-short couch, unable to get his mind off the woman sleeping just on the other side of the bedroom door.

Did she sleep in the nude? Or in some slinky bit of Hollywood siren's satin? Right before dawn this morning, he'd imagined her in a brief bit of lace and silk designed to make a man's mouth water.

He'd envisioned skimming his hands over her slender curves, thought about how he'd nudge the thin straps down with his teeth. A mental picture of her sitting in the middle of that king-size bed, amid tousled sheets, the bit of froth clinging provocatively to the rosy tips of her breasts, had filled his mind.

Two hundred push-ups later, he'd still been edgy, itchy, and, although it wasn't her fault he couldn't keep his mind reined in, a little angry at her for his inability to do so.

He shook his head. "It would be a mistake."

She didn't need to ask what he meant. "Perhaps. But I've always believed that we regret most the things we don't do. Things we're left wondering about after the opportunity has passed."

Finn didn't have to wonder what being with her would be like. Even before he'd made the mistake of kissing her, he'd known that sex with this woman would be hot and explosive. And dangerous. A need this strong could make a man weak. Vulnerable.

"Point taken. But we're talking about more than just sex. Even if I didn't have a rule about mixing my personal life with my professional one—"

"This isn't exactly professional. Despite what you keep saying, I'm not an official FBI case you've been assigned to. You told me that you agreed to baby-sit me as a favor to your brother. That, to me, seems to move it into the personal arena."

He blew out a breath. "Do you have to argue every little point?"

"When something's important to me. I was brought up to question the status quo and never take things at face value. And in case you haven't dug up a copy of my yearbook, I also happened to be captain of my high school debating team."

"Now why doesn't that surprise me?" Finn's brain was finally beginning to clear. "Yeah, I want you. Any man in his right mind would. I haven't felt this way about a woman since I fell for Jaclyn Smith when she was one of the Angels."

Her eyes narrowed. "I have difficulty picturing you watching *Charlie's Angels*."

What did she think? That he'd spent his adolescence glued to PBS? "Hey, I wanted to be a cop. So I watched a lot of crime shows." When she arched a challenging eyebrow, he grinned again. "Actually that one was a lot better with the sound off."

Her light laughter touched her eyes and made them sparkle appealingly. "There may be hope for you yet, Special Agent."

"That's debatable."

"You're a hard man, Callahan."

"I'm a realist."

"A pessimist," she shot back without heat.

She'd splayed her hands on her hips, drawing his attention to bare flesh as smooth and tasty-looking as cream. All-too-familiar smoke clouds began billowing again in his mind.

"Dammit, don't you own anything big and baggy and ugly?"

The humor in her gaze brightened to delight.

Finn saw the exact moment she remembered. The light in her eyes went out, like a candle snuffed out by an icy winter's wind.

"Well, at least I can't say you're not a distraction," she said on a soft, exhaled breath. "For a minute I'd almost forgotten what you're doing here."

She pressed her fingers against her eyes. "Okay, I admit it. Whoever he is, he's got me scared."

He hesitated, reason warring with the need to comfort. This time when he took her in his arms, it was to soothe rather than arouse.

# 15

*Two hours later,* while he watched Julia flutter around the ballroom dance floor in a scandalous scarlet gown, flirting outrageously with the men and scandalizing the women, Finn decided that while she may look as delicate as a magnolia blossom, the lady definitely had a steel core. Not a single person would ever guess that she'd received another threat this morning.

Except, of course, the person who'd slipped it into her trailer.

They'd pulled out all the stops today. The room, which Jack had restored to its original glory earlier in the year, was crowded with the cast and extras from as far away as Lafayette.

The women's hoopskirts swayed like colorful tulips as they danced in the arms of formally dressed men to the sounds of a string ensemble hired from New Orleans.

Finn was standing on the sidelines, watching her take advantage of a break in shooting to get her picture taken with one of the extras, an elderly woman dressed in mourning, when Nate came up to him.

"She looks good."

"She always looks good." Finn frowned at the scores of Blue Bayou parish residents who had come out to Beau Soleil to watch the goings-on, as they'd been doing every day. Even knowing that having a movie company come to town was on a par with waking up one morning and finding Disney World had moved its magic kingdom to your front yard, he wasn't comfortable with the crowds.

Unfortunately, his arguments to Kendall and Hogan to close the set had been rejected. Making matters worse, a crew from *Entertainment Tonight* was scheduled to arrive this week. Apparently showing stars mingling with local folks made for good TV.

"You thinking of calling in reinforcements, now that she's gotten that second photograph?"

"I don't know."

"With so many people on the cast knowing about that first photograph, it's going to be hard to keep it under wraps." Nate said what Finn had already been telling himself.

"It's just Kendall, Hogan and the primary cast. At least it's supposed to be. To everyone else, we're sticking to the friends story."

"Looks like you're getting to be pretty close friends." Nate's quick grin belied the seriousness of the topic. "I watched the two of you earlier, between takes. You probably had a dozen people between you, but you could have been the only two people in the room."

"I'm just doing my job."

"Come on, Finn. You're talking to your brother here. A man who's pretty damn good at picking up women's signals. And she's broadcasting at 100,000 watts." His gaze skimmed over Finn's face, taking in the bags beneath his eyes, his unshaved jaw. "She's not the only one."

"Sleeping with her would mean putting aside my personal code of ethics."

"I've always admired you, big brother. But I hadn't realized you'd become a monk since leaving home."

"I'm supposed to protect her. Not take advantage of her vulnerability."

"I can understand that." Nate nodded. "And it's a good excuse. But why do I get the feeling that it's not just Julia you're trying to protect?"

The woman had not only disturbed his life, she'd unsettled his entire universe. For as long as Finn could remember, he'd been the rock. The big brother Jack and Nate could turn to when they'd had problems, or fucked up, which Jack had done a lot more often than Nate. Though Finn had always suspected that his youngest brother had had his own way of dealing with their father's death.

He'd become the responsible one; Jack had turned rebel. Nate, who was the most gregarious of the three, seemed to decide that it was his duty to ease those horrendous days with unrelenting smiles, easy humor and charm.

Nate had been the only one of the Callahan boys who could make their mother smile through her tears. And less than a decade later, when she'd been dying of breast cancer, it had been Nate who, despite her protests, immediately dropped out of college and moved back home to be with her. Marie Callahan had died with her eldest and youngest sons at her side, smiling at some foolish joke Nate had made.

Finn figured he'd always owe Nate for that one. He also knew that, like all of them, Nate had inherited Big Jake's Irish tenacity and could, in his own cheerful way, be as unrelenting as water carving away at a stone.

"My life's messed up enough right now," he said. "I've got the Wicked Witch of the West back in D.C. to contend with, and even if Jansen wasn't in the picture, my career takes up all my time and energy. Besides, there's no future in getting involved."

"Who's saying anything about a future? Ever think about just loosening up and enjoying the moment, *cher?*"

Nate was smiling but Finn thought he heard a hint of friendly censure in the mild tone.

"No." As if sensing his gaze on her, Julia looked up from a discussion of the script with the writer and director. When her lips curved in a luscious Bond Girl smile, Finn nearly forgot he knew how to breathe.

*Oh, God.* He was so getting to her, Julia thought. Having become attuned to Finn in the few days that they'd been forced together, it had seemed perfectly natural to feel his gaze from across the room. He stirred her senses, warming her blood as if he was touching her with those big wide hands, instead of his eyes.

Did he know what he did to her? How he made her feel? Most men had a strong sense of their seductive powers. The majority, at least in Los Angeles, seemed to possess an inflated opinion of their ability to charm a woman into their beds.

But Finn was a different breed entirely. Julia was beginning to come to the conclusion that he didn't have any idea how he could turn her to mush with one of those hot, hungry looks. Beneath the uptight suit and tightly controlled, Joe Friday attitude, she sensed untapped passions. He was not an easy man to know. He'd be a difficult man to love.

*Love?* She shook her head. What a ninny she was. She'd obviously been working on a soap opera too long; if she didn't watch out, she'd become as susceptible to suggestion as Warren.

Dragging her gaze from Finn's, Julia was trying to focus on what the writer was saying—something about adding lines to one of the non-speaking extra's parts—when she heard a sudden buzz move through the group of Civil War-costumed extras, sounding like a swarm of hungry bees.

Eyes turned toward her. A few at a time, then more, until she felt as if she were in the crosshair of some hunter's rifle.

When she saw the tabloid paper being passed around, a cold chill skidded up her spine.

"I think it's a lovely idea," she assured Warren. "And yes, it'd be great PR. Small town beauty queen 'discovered' in the steamy Louisiana bayou." The locals were now studying her with the fascination an entomologist might observe a new and rare type of beetle. "Would you do me a favor?"

"Sure," he said, looking a bit puzzled by her sudden shift in topic.

"Would you go get that paper that seems to be causing such a stir among the extras?"

"Sure," he repeated. She watched him exchange a few words with a middle-aged woman who was currently reading the tabloid. When his eyebrows sketched up like blond wings and he shot her a surprised—no, make that shocked—look, Julia prepared herself for whatever pack of lies the paper had printed this time. Even braced as she was, she was stunned by the tabloid Warren reluctantly handed to her.

There, on the front page, was the photograph of Finn unfastening her corset.

*River Road's Vixen in Ghostly Bayou Tryst With Rebel Lover From a Past Life!* the headline screamed.

"Oh, God." She turned the page, skimming down the text. "This is preposterous."

There was another photograph of her taken in the plantation's cemetery, with the mist swirling around her legs, Shane's hand—just his hand, no other identifying features—on her breast. The implication, of course, being that the same man who was unlacing her corset on page one was caressing her in a graveyard in the photo on page two.

"Finn's supposed to be the ghost of a Confederate soldier who's been waiting for me to return to Beau Soleil for more than two hundred years?"

"It's quite creative," Warren allowed. "I wish I'd thought of it."

"Oh, God," Julia repeated. Surely people wouldn't take such an outrageous story seriously?

Well, she'd wanted to tap Finn's deep-seated passions. As she cautiously lifted her gaze and found him continuing to watch her in that steady, unblinking way of his, Julia feared he'd probably hit the roof. Anyone would resent such lies, especially someone who'd neither asked nor wanted to be thrust into the public spotlight.

As he'd been doing from the beginning, he surprised her.

"Well," he drawled as he scanned the pages she'd reluctantly shown him, "at least they're not saying I'm Big Foot."

Her relief at having dodged that bullet was short-lived. Five minutes later, during another break in shooting while Finn tried to track down the tabloid's source, Julia was sitting on a stool in the plantation house's kitchen, having her makeup touched up, when Randy came into the room and held out his cell phone.

"It's your mother."

"My mother? What's she doing calling on your phone?"

"She tracked me down. Apparently there's an emergency."

Julia's blood chilled. "Hello, Mom?"

"Julia, darling, I'm so relieved to have found you."

"What's wrong? Is it Dad?"

"Oh, no, dear. I'm sorry, I didn't mean to frighten you. No, it's just that your father and I were passing the market on the way to this wonderful little crystal store that has the most spectacular selection of rose quartz I've seen in a very long time, when I felt this strong urge to go inside."

"You've seen the paper," Julia guessed.

"Yes. They're actually quite flattering photographs, for a tabloid. Of course you've always had a lovely back. . . . Is it true? About the ghost?"

"Of course not!" She'd no sooner scoffed than Julia remembered her mother believed in ghosts. Along with fairies and Druids and all sorts of spirits that went bump in the night.

"Oh." Peace sounded vaguely disappointed. "What about the man?"

"Believe me, Mom, I'm not having a location affair."

"That's not what I asked. I was merely inquiring about him."

"The photo's from a scene we shot in the plantation cemetery. It's Shane's hand. He's playing a Yankee captain."

"A Yankee as in a Civil War Yankee?"

"That's it. Warren added a time travel thread to the story line."

"What a wonderful idea!" Pleasure shimmered in Peace's warm voice. "How does this OBE occur?"

Julia had never believed in out-of-body experiences. Until this morning, when Finn had kissed her and she'd felt herself capable of floating right up into the sky. "Amanda gets shot and goes into a coma."

"Comas are a common way for people to use astral projection to work out karmic structures in their physical lifetime," her mother said matter-of-factly. "I'm pleased Warren did his homework. Who's the other man?"

"What other man?"

"The one unlacing your corset."

Julia's breath caught. Her mind whirled as she struggled to decide how much, exactly, she could admit to this woman who'd always been able to know when she was lying.

"He's just a man."

"That's not what I sensed. There's something very intimate about the photograph, darling."

"Of course it's intimate. I was in my underwear. Finn was just helping me with my costume."

"Finn. He's Irish?"

"Half Irish. The other half is Cajun."

"My goodness." Peace exhaled a breath. "That's quite a passionate combination."

"If you met him, you certainly wouldn't think so," Julia hedged, desperately hoping her mother couldn't read her mind as the memory of that kiss flooded into it.

"I don't want to argue, dear, but I believe you're wrong. Why, the paper nearly singed my fingertips . . . Just a minute. Your father's speaking to me."

Julia strained to hear the conversation, but all she could catch was Peace's usual smooth tone being overridden by her father's louder, stronger one.

"Julia, this is your father," a deep bass boomed out.

"Hi, Daddy. How's the harmony tour going?"

"It's probably our most successful yet. The mood's been contagious; I even caught one of the sheriff's deputies who'd been assigned to the festival singing along to 'White Rabbit.'"

"I wouldn't have expected a cop would be a Jefferson Airplane fan."

"That's exactly what I thought at the time. But don't change the subject. I want to know about this man who's laying hands on my daughter in front of the entire world."

"It wasn't the entire world. We were all alone in my trailer and—"

"That's even worse. Your mother says it's serious."

"No offense, but I think Mom's crystal ball must have gotten cloudy. Finn's just a friend, Daddy."

"Finn? He's Irish?"

"Half," Julia repeated what she'd told her mother.

"Your great-grandfather was Irish."

"I know, Daddy."

She vaguely remembered her parents taking her to Galway to meet her father's maternal grandfather when she was five. He'd had lush white hair, a smile that could charm the fairies, and a sweet tenor voice that sounded like music on the Irish breeze. During their month-long visit he was never without peppermints in his scratchy wool shirt pocket, just for her.

"Emotional people, the Irish." This from a man who lived on the edge of his own bold emotions. A man whose paternal grandfather was a Russian cossack.

"He's a friend," she said again. "I think you'd like him." And pigs would sprout gossamer wings and start soaring over the bayou.

"That remains to be seen."

"What?" Every atom in Julia's body went on red alert.

"We're coming to Louisiana."

"Why on earth would you want to do that?"

"To meet your friend, of course. And make sure he's good enough for my little girl. I've got to run, sweetheart, this damn cell phone signal's breaking up." It sounded perfectly clear to her. "See you in a few days."

He ended the call, leaving Julia listening to dead air.

"What on earth was that all about?" Wondering what they put in the water up in Coldwater Cove, Washington, Julia had the strongest feeling that her father was actually coming here to grill Finn.

It couldn't be. Could it?

Just last week, she'd been wishing that her parents had been a bit more like the Cleavers or Jim Anderson, that unrelentingly calm, utterly sane sitcom father who always knew best.

Of course in those old sitcoms, even the adults didn't appear to have sex lives. As for their children . . . She could just imagine how Jim Anderson would have responded to his Princess rolling around with some boy in the back seat of a '55 Chevy. Or on a couch in a trailer.

*Be careful what you wish for.*

Right on the heels of that idea came another more unsettling one. How Freedom, the former political radical who'd been arrested innumerable times for protesting the system Finn Callahan had sworn to uphold, would respond to his daughter's relationship with an FBI Special Agent.

"What happened?" Her makeup man, Damien, brushed color into her right cheek with deft strokes of his sable brush. "This morning you were absolutely glowing. Now you look as if you're coming down with some nasty tropical bayou fever."

Julia scowled into the lighted mirror. "Well, that's certainly flattering."

"If you want flattery, call the president of your fan club. My job is to make you beautiful. Which usually isn't such a chore."

"It's been a long day."

"True." He performed the same magic on her left cheek. "But you've had long days before. You worked twenty hours last year when that idiot editor's assistant managed to erase half the week's work. But even then you didn't look so washed out." He squeezed a little concealer from a tube and began dabbing it beneath her eyes. "My guess is that it's got something to do with Mr. Tall, Dark and Grim."

"He's not grim." It was the third time in the past two hours she'd felt the need to defend Finn. "Just serious."

"Seriously grim. Close your eyes."

Julia did as instructed. He set the concealer cream with powder, then skimmed a little mascara onto the ends of her lashes. "Don't furrow your brow that way, darling. It'll give you premature wrinkles. You've been licking your lips again," he scolded as he touched up the color.

"My mouth keeps getting dry." Every time she looked at Finn, who was currently waiting outside.

"So does mine. Big macho brutes do that to me." He stood back and studied her. "Apparently they affect you the same way. At least this one does."

"He's just a friend."

"Really, Julia." He huffed out a breath. "How long have we been together?"

"Nearly five years."

"Which is probably longer than most Hollywood marriages. And haven't I agreed to go traipsing off to Kathmandu with you?"

"It's not exactly a sacrifice. You're being very well paid."

"Money isn't anything. There's no way I'd spend three months of my life in a country where such a large percentage of the eligible males are Buddist monks, if I didn't adore you to pieces. Is your boyfriend coming with us?"

"He's not my . . ." She sighed as his knowing gaze met hers in the mirror. "I don't know what Finn is, exactly." That was definitely the truth.

"He's gorgeous, is what he is. In a supersize, rough-hewn cop sort of way. He reminds me of what you might get if you took Tommy Lee Jones's DNA and stirred in some Hulk Hogan. Don't worry, you'll be able to decipher your feelings a lot better after you sleep with him."

"What makes you think I haven't?"

"Because the pheromones in the air are nearly lethal. You're exuding so much sex on the set, it's a wonder the fire marshal hasn't shut us down for endangering a historical site." He fanned himself with the sable powder brush. "And your incredible hulk is a walking testosterone bomb waiting to explode."

"He's not my hulk. Besides, it would be a mistake," she repeated Finn's analysis of their situation.

"That failed playwright you were seeing when you first came to *River Road* was a mistake. Along with the last three artists and that pudgy, out-of-shape Welsh folk singer who sang naked."

"Ian sang about stripping away the trappings of our lives. About getting back to our natural selves."

"If *my* natural self looked like Humpty Dumpty, I sure as hell wouldn't go stripping off my clothes in public. I'd also like to see him try to pull that act off back home on those Welsh moors. Believe me, once Mr. Stiffy got frostbite, the guy would change his act faster than I can say Ricky Martin."

"Mr. Stiffy?" She lifted a brow at him in the mirror. "You've been talking to Shane, haven't you?"

"We haven't exchanged two words since I told him he ought to lighten up on the Botox because he's starting to look like a Ken doll. Personally, I think he's homophobic, but it could be he's just narcissistic."

She suspected Damien might just be right. She also wondered if all men named their penis. Then she thought of Finn. *Not in this lifetime.*

"And to get back to my point about your having lousy taste in men," Damien said, pursing his own lips as he dipped into a pot and brushed some gloss onto her mouth, "let's not forget the deadbeat married poet—"

"Let's also not forget that I did not know he had a wife," she interjected firmly.

"I seem to recall three wives, actually. There was the art dealer in Paris, the editor in Stockholm, along with the heir to that silver fortune in Guadalajara. And it was obvious he had you pegged for number four, so you could help continue to support him in the style to which he'd become accustomed. And I don't even want to think about the time you wasted with that English professor."

"He reminded me of Cary Grant playing Henry Higgins." She'd always been a sucker for *My Fair Lady*. "Or Connery's James Bond."

"The man was definitely no 007. What he was, dear heart, was a mistake. Just like the others. On the other hand, the guy who fills out that size forty-eight long suit so deliciously is more along the lines of riding a boat over the edge of Niagara Falls."

"That sounds like a huge mistake." A dangerous mistake, she reminded herself.

"It could well be." He brushed a bit of iridescent powder over the crest of her breasts, which were plumped up to spill over the deeply cut neckline of her ball gown by a heavily padded bra that made her feel as if she was wearing the Golden Gate Bridge on her chest. "But think of the rush on the way down."

"Think of crashing on the rocks and breaking to smithereens."

Now that she'd had more time to think about it, Julia had decided Finn was right about not taking things further. After all, using Damien's boat analogy, they were two ships passing in the night. The *Titanic* and the *Lusitania*. "My life's too complicated right now. I don't need a man making it worse."

"Everyone needs a man, sweetcheeks. They're the cherry on top of the hot fudge sundae, the whipped cream atop the crème brûlée—"

"Crème brûlée doesn't have whipped cream."

"You make it your way, I'll make it mine." He began to put away his pots and jars. "Besides, if you're telling the truth about not wanting to get involved with the big guy, it looks as if you may be off the hook."

Julia followed his gaze out the window, to where Felissa was looking up at Finn as if she was a sleek Siamese cat and he was a giant bowl of cream.

It took her a minute to recognize the emotion that shot through her. And when she did, it was staggering. She, who could not recall ever feeling jealousy toward anyone for anything, suddenly felt like scratching the actress's hyacinth blue contacts out.

And that was just for starters.

# 16

*What took so damn long?"* Finn demanded when Julia came out of the trailer.

"Should I be flattered I was missed?" He recognized her smile. It was the same one Amanda pulled out whenever she was about to screw someone. Literally or figuratively.

He folded his arms. "I'm being paid to guard your body. Which is a little difficult to do when you won't light anywhere."

"I wasn't in there that long."

"It seemed like a lifetime." He glanced across the room and groaned as Felissa met his eyes and licked her lips.

Julia laughed. "What's the matter, Callahan? Can't you handle a little flirtation?"

"That's more than flirting. The woman's like that rabbit in the commercials. She just keeps on coming."

"Perhaps you can take out your gun and shoot her. I'll bet that'd do the job."

"Bullets would just bounce right off. She's got a steel exterior."

"I can't believe she's that much of a problem." She shrugged. "After all, as a cop, you're undoubtedly used to throwing your weight around from time to time. And you're a lot bigger than she is."

"So she pointed out."

He still couldn't believe she'd shared that sordid little story about having made a porno flick back when she'd been a struggling actress. The director, apparently, had assured her she was a natural at giving blow jobs. If that hadn't been bad enough, she'd actually come right out and assured him that if Julia couldn't handle his "obvious endowment," she'd love to help him out.

Julia tilted her head at the muttered comment he'd meant to keep to himself. Then gave him a slow, speculative gaze that followed the same path that earlier female appraisal had taken. The difference was that the blond barracuda's hadn't stirred any feelings. That was definitely not the case this time.

"So?"

"So what?"

"Are you? Larger than the average bear, so to speak?"

"That's for me to know." He tossed her own words back at her. "And you to find out."

"Don't look now, Special Agent, but you just made another joke." Her eyes laughed up at him. "If you're not careful, people may just figure out there's a human being beneath that suit. And speaking of suits . . ."

She laced his fingers with hers in a casual, uncalculated gesture. "I have this teensy little problem I need you to help me out with."

Her hands were slender and soft as she led him up the metal steps into the trailer. He'd watched them pouring tea for the Yankee captain and been struck by their natural grace. He'd also wanted them on his body.

A mistake, he warned himself yet again. As he breathed in her seductive scent hanging in the air, he forced himself to remember that.

"Let me get this straight," he said, five minutes later. "You want to take me shopping."

"That's right." She smiled encouragingly.

"For new clothes." He didn't bother blocking off the scowl.

"Not an entire new wardrobe. Just something a bit less imposing."

"I would have thought imposing would be a good look for a bodyguard."

"It's a great look for a bodyguard," she agreed quickly. Too quickly. Her smile was bright and decidedly forced. "I know I'd certainly think twice—more than twice—before trying to get by you."

"So what's the problem?"

"While it's a great look for a bodyguard, it's not exactly the right look for my lover."

"I'm not your lover."

"Well, I know that, and you know that. But, well . . ." She began twisting her fingers together.

"Well?"

"My parents don't know that. They think we're—"

She paused, seeking the right word—"involved."

Ah. "The tabloid," Finn guessed.

"Yes." She let out a long breath. "They called me earlier. From Washington. The state, not the capital."

"I see." Actually, Finn didn't see anything at all, but wanted to get to the bottom of whatever had rattled her.

"They wanted to know who it was undressing me on the front page of the *Enquirer.*"

"I wouldn't think that would matter to them."

"Not matter?" Color that had nothing to do with the makeup guy's work flooded into her cheeks. "They're my parents. Wouldn't you be interested in some man who was unfastening your daughter's corset?"

"It's a moot point since I don't have a daughter."

Her frustrated sigh ruffled a lock of hair that had fallen over her eyes and she shoved it back with an impatient hand. "Don't play word games with me, Callahan. You might be bigger than I am. And armed, but I just happen to have been seventh-grade regional Scrabble champion."

"I'm impressed."

"You should be. Though Woodstock, the former champion, wasn't," she admitted.

"His name was Woodstock?"

"It seemed normal at the time. His mother, Enlightenment, was friends with my parents. We grew up together."

"It figures. So how come you don't have a goofy name?"

She lifted a brow. "Excuse me?"

"I wouldn't think two people named Peace and Freedom, who had a friend named Enlightenment, would have settled for an ordinary name for their daughter who is anything but ordinary."

Julia smiled a little, deciding to take that a good way. "Thank you."

"You're welcome."

"And while I hate to burst your little stereotyping-profiling bubble, I happen to have been named for my grandmother," she informed him loftily. "Who also wasn't the least bit ordinary. She was a jazz singer. My father practically grew up on the band's tour bus."

"Why does that not surprise me? What was her name?"

"Julia Rose Summers.

"You're kidding." He looked suitably impressed. "I've got all her songs on CD and a handful of vinyls I can't play because I don't have a turntable, but I still like taking them out of the jackets and looking at them. Holding them. They're a lot more substantial feeling and the jackets are large enough to show off the art."

"That's what Daddy always says," she murmured, a bit surprised that this man would have anything in common with Freedom.

"God, your grandmother was The Monterey Rose. Wow." He skimmed his palm over his hair. "Her cover of 'They Can't Take That Away from Me' is even better than Lady Day's, which was pretty damn great itself."

"I'll tell her you said so. She toured with Billie Holiday for a while in Europe."

"I know. I paid a small fortune for some bootleg studio cuts from when the two of them were just fooling around, doing riffs together. So, she's still alive?"

"She owns a club in Carmel."

"I'll have to try to get there one of these days. Does she still sing?"

"On special occasions."

"Hey, any time The Rose sings is a special occasion."

It was the most enthusiasm she'd witnessed from him thus far. It also made him seem far more human. In fact, he reminded her of her paternal grandfather, Rose's second husband, a steady, solid, easygoing man who didn't say much and had spent much of their marriage driving the tour bus back and forth across the country. The Rose's first husband had been a sax player who'd abandoned her as soon as she told him that they'd made more than just music together. Seven months later, Julia's father had been born.

"So tell me about Woodstock," Finn said, returning the conversation to its original track.

"Why? He's not my stalker."

"Maybe not, but I'm curious."

"Why?"

He shrugged. "Why don't you just humor me?"

"And here I thought I'd been doing that all along," she said dryly. "He was just a boy I had a huge crush on. The only reason I entered the competition was because he was in it. He'd been sixth grade champion the year before and I figured if we practiced together he'd finally notice me."

She sighed. "It was not one of the highlights of my life. It was also where I learned boys don't like girls to beat them."

"Maybe boys feel that way, but I'm perfectly willing to admit you can probably beat me at Scrabble. But I'd leave you in the dust at Clue."

"I should hope so, since you're a detective. I doubt if it would have made a difference even if I had let him win by pretending I didn't see that triple word score. Because the only thing he was interested in at the time were breasts. And I didn't have any."

Enjoying her tale, Finn tried to remember the last time he'd been amused by anything. Three years ago, he decided. Before Ronald Lawson had decided to take up a new hobby.

"He's probably eating his heart out now."

She laughed softly at that. "Actually, he moved to L.A. and became a plastic surgeon. He's very popular; a lot of the breasts you see in the movies are his."

"But not yours."

"No." She looked down at the front of her nineteenth-century gown. "If they'd only had Wonderbras when I was growing up, my entire life could have been different. Woodstock might have fallen madly in love with me, we might have gotten married, had children—"

"And set up housekeeping on Sunnybrook Farm."

"You don't have to make fun of me. Just because you don't want marriage and a family."

How the hell did they get from shopping to Scrabble to talking about marriage again? "So what was this favor you wanted from me?"

"It's just a small one. Teensy, actually. My parents, like any loving, caring parents, are understandably interested in knowing more about the man they think I'm in love with."

"Love?" Finn blinked.

"Yes." Her chin popped up in that way he recognized all too well. "And you don't have to behave as if I'd just exposed you to plague. I didn't say I *was* in love with you. I merely said they *believe* I'm in love with you."

"Because of some tabloid piece of crap?"

"No. That would be ridiculous."

To Finn's mind, the fact he was even having this discussion was ridiculous.

"I suppose the picture didn't help," she allowed. "But it's mostly my mother's vibes."

"Vibes."

"Yes. My mother's an intuitive." Her look dared him to challenge that remark.

"Okay."

"You're laughing."

"Do I look like I'm laughing?"

"No. But since nobody can possibly be as serious as you appear to be, I've decided that you must keep your laughter on the inside."

"How did you guess?" His tone was dry as dust. "It's dancing a happy jig right now with my inner child."

She crossed her arms beneath those breasts he thought were just about perfect. More than a handful was overkill, anyway. "I find it difficult to believe you even have an inner child. I have the feeling you were born thirty. And grim."

Well, that was certainly flattering. Finn was on the verge of being pissed, when he remembered that they'd be a lot better off if she didn't like him. That would prevent a repeat of that kiss he never should have allowed to happen.

"Nailed that one," he said mildly. "And for the record, I wasn't laughing about your mother. In fact, I've used psychics before in my investigations."

"You? Mr. Just-the-facts-ma'am Callahan?"

"I'll try whatever it takes to bring the bad guys to justice." So it sounded corny. It was the truth. "Some of the psychics have been obvious frauds, with others it's a toss-up whether they were right or just lucky. Then there's that third group who can't quite be defined, but seem to have something going for them. I'm willing to accept that your mother might fit into that third category. So, what did you tell them about me?"

"I told them the truth. That we're not in a romantic relationship."

"Then what's the problem? And what does all this have to do with your wanting to go shopping?"

"They didn't believe me."

Finn could see this one coming, like a bullet headed straight toward him in slow motion.

"So they're coming here," she said when he didn't respond.

"Here?" Everything inside him stilled. "To Blue Bayou?"

"Here," she confirmed. "To Blue Bayou. To meet you."

*Jesus H. Christ.* Finn knew his feelings about this little bombshell must have shown on his face when her tawny brows drew together.

"I realize that socializing with hippies is not exactly something you'd normally do—"

"Try never." He'd never bought into the concept of reincarnation, but if those mantra chanters really were on to something about making redemption for past sins, he must have been a real prick in his previous life.

She exhaled a long, frustrated breath that once again drew his eyes to her breasts. "Believe me, Callahan, when my father finds out you're an FBI agent, he's going to hit the roof. Which is why we're going to have to give you a makeover."

"A makeover?" Her words jerked him out of a fantasy of spreading whipped cream over that flesh revealed by the low neckline and taking a very long time to lick it off. Finn folded his arms. "Guys don't get makeovers."

"Of course they do. I've seen it on *Oprah*."

He rolled his eyes. "The woman could do an entire week around transvestites, but I still wouldn't put on panty hose and a dress."

"You really do have a rotten attitude." When she tossed her head, the sun streaming through the blinds of the trailer turned her hair to flame. "Look, why don't we just call this entire bodyguard thing off? It's not like those photographs were specific. I'll admit they had me a little unnerved, but when I think about it more clearly, I realize I'm undoubtedly just overreacting.

"So, why don't you just get back in that Suburban and go back to Washington? When my parents arrive, I'll tell them we broke up. Which they'd undoubtedly believe since I'm sure the idea of my getting involved with a cop, let alone an FBI agent, has never entered their realm of possibility."

*Here's your out.* Finn felt like a guy teetering on the edge of a pit of quicksand. One false move and he'd be stuck.

"My going back to D.C.'s not an option." He wasn't about to reveal why he couldn't return to work. Yet. *Damn.* "Look, I have clothes out at the camp I own with my brother. Why can't I just wear those?"

"Are they casual?"

"Even I don't fish in a suit."

"I have trouble picturing you fishing."

That made two of them. "I've got T-shirts. And jeans."

"Let me guess. The T-shirts have FBI lettering on them and the jeans are creased to a knife edge."

He couldn't believe he'd been forced into a situation where he had to defend his wardrobe. "I happen to work for the FBI—"

"A fact I'm attempting not to wave in my parents' faces. Besides, has it ever occurred to you that working for the FBI is what you do? Not who you are?"

"No. It hasn't." He'd always defined himself by his work; Finn wasn't certain he could separate the man from the agent, which was a moot point since he didn't want to try. "As for the jeans, that's the way they come back from the cleaners."

She sighed dramatically. "Come on, Callahan. Be a sport. Don't tell me a big, strapping man like yourself is afraid of a little shopping trip. Or would you rather I just go into the city alone and pick up some things?"

Short of tying her up, he doubted he could keep her from doing exactly that. Not wanting to let her out of his sight, and afraid of what kind of clothes she might choose just for spite, with eyes wide open, he took that fatal step. "Let's just get it the hell over with."

As if never expecting any other outcome, she smiled. Not an Amanda hit-you-in-the-groin smile, but a quick, pleased Julia one that aimed directly at the heart. As it hit the bull's-eye, Finn imagined the huge sucking sound he heard was the quicksand closing in around him.

# 17

*Since there was no way* he was going to let her drag him around like a trained pup in his own hometown, after the shooting wrapped up for the day, and she'd changed into a short denim skirt and a striped knit top that left one shoulder bare in a way that made him want to bite it, Finn drove them to the city.

"I adore New Orleans," she said as the lights of the skyline grew closer. "The food, the music, the atmosphere—"

"We're not here to play tourist," he warned as they crossed the Mississippi.

"Spoilsport."

"I believe we've already determined that. And for the record, it's one of the things I do best. So, here's the plan. We're going to go into the store, snag what we need, and get the hell out and back to Blue Bayou."

"Whatever you say." Lord, he could be bossy. Along with a whole new sartorial look, they were going to have to work on his attitude. Because right now the coiled, controlled male energy radiating from him just screamed FBI. "Of course, your ordeal will be over far more quickly if you promise not to argue about every little thing I pick out."

Seconds passed. He was looking straight ahead and for a moment she thought he hadn't heard her over the Van Halen screeching from the speakers.

"You're not going to try to put me in a Grateful Dead T-shirt are you?"

"Of course not. Unless you're prepared to discuss the significance of their concert posters on the seventies pop art scene."

His sideways stare set her straight on that.

"I didn't think so," she said. She'd never met a more unlikely Deadhead. Though the pounding seventies metal rock hinted at possibilities. She would have pegged him more as a Sinatra guy.

"There is no way I'm going to let you dress me up like some throwback from Haight-Ashbury. I'm willing to make some concessions to the situation, but the clothes have to be conservative."

"Absolutely."

"And regular guy sneaks. None of those sissy Birkenstocks."

"I wouldn't think of it."

"Okay." He nodded, apparently satisfied.

"And I'd suggest you not mention to my father you think Birkenstocks are for sissies. You may consider him a throwback to the sixties, but even those critics who don't like his art have always raved about the primal male power of his work."

"Believe me, if there's one thing I have no intention of discussing with your father, it's primal male instincts."

"Good." It was her turn to nod.

With his attention turned back to his driving, Finn missed seeing Julia's lips curve in a faint smile of anticipation.

His internal radar went off the scale as they entered the trendy boutique in the lobby of the five star hotel she'd had him drive to on Canal Street. When she plucked a shirt from a rack, Finn decided the time had come to stand his ground.

"No way."

"You said you wanted something conservative."

"The frigging shirt is pink!" he hissed. How conservative was that?

"Actually, it's Tropical Rose," the saleswoman, a sleek blond fortysomething said. "A preppy favorite."

"It's lovely," Julia said. The smile she bestowed upon the woman suggested *What can you expect from an uncivilized barbarian?* "But not quite what we're looking for."

She held a polo shirt up against Finn's chest. "Oh, I like this one."

"Good choice." The woman nodded. "Bastille Purple. It's one of our more popular colors this season." Finn had the feeling it was the same thing she'd say whatever a prospective customer selected.

"I can see why," Julia said. "It's very attractive. A bit like crushed merlot grapes. And the name is so evocative, don't you think?" she asked Finn.

"Oh yeah, Bastille has a real nice ring to it. If you like thinking about filthy mobs and public beheadings."

"Don't be sarcastic. Come over to a mirror and see how well the deep color contrasts with your eyes. Perhaps if you were to just try it on . . ."

The speculative look in Julia's gaze was almost as terrifying as the idea of showing up in Blue Bayou in a preppy pink or purple polo shirt. Finn grabbed her elbow and dragged her behind a nearby display of mannequins that looked as if they were posing for a GQ cover. "There is no way in hell I'm wearing anything on that rack."

"I thought we had an agreement."

"Our agreement was for you to pick out something conservative."

"I doubt if there's a more conservative store in all of New Orleans. Why, I have it on good authority that Republicans love these shirts."

"I find it hard to believe you even know a Republican."

"I know you."

"Apparently you didn't inherit your mother's intuitive talents. I'm an Independent." He folded his arms across the white dress shirt that had always suited him just fine.

"What a surprise." Her sweet smile couldn't quite conceal her own sarcasm. She exhaled a resigned breath. "All right. They may not exactly be you."

He'd learned not to trust her easy acquiescence.

She began rifling through a rack right next to them and pulled out a pair of tweed pants with suede inserts on the inside of the thighs. "How about these?"

"I categorically refuse to wear the same pants Elizabeth Taylor wore in *National Velvet*." Those were even worse than the prissy pink shirt.

"It's the Equestrian look. I saw a report about it on *Fashion Emergency*. It's predicted to be a very popular trend this fall."

He folded his arms. "Do I look like a trendy sort of guy to you?"

"No," she admitted. "You look like a cop."

"I am a cop. And I'm willing to play along, within limits, but from here on in, I'm picking out my own clothes."

"Nothing that requires a tie. And those wing tips have to go."

Did every damn thing have to be up for negotiation? "I can live with that. But I don't do tassels." He'd seen her eyeing the tasseled cordovan loafers when they'd first come in the store.

"No tassels," she agreed.

That settled, Finn went hunting at a midprice department store down the street. "Don't you want to try them on?" Julia asked as he grabbed a pair of jeans from the first rack they came upon.

"No need." He scooped up a pair of black T-shirts, then headed over to the shoe department. Although Julia hadn't put a stopwatch on him, she guessed he'd managed to gather up a new wardrobe, including crew sox, in under five minutes.

"They'll fit."

"Why don't you humor me?"

"What the hell do you think I've been doing since you got this cockamamie idea?"

"Please? You're not exactly average size. What if we get back to Blue Bayou and discover they need alterations?"

He cursed without heat. "I don't want to leave you alone."

"I could come in the dressing room with you."

"Yeah, you and me together in an enclosed place with me taking off my clothes. That's about the worst idea you've had yet."

"Haven't you ever heard of restraint, Callahan?"

"Yeah. But it's not a word I'd use in regard to you. Let's go."

She was beginning to learn to recognize when she'd hit the stone wall of Finn Callahan's resistance.

"I'll pay for them," she said when he pulled out his credit card and put it on the sales counter.

"The hell you will."

"You're only buying them because I wanted you to wear something other than that suit." She picked up the AmEx card and put her own down in its place. "So, it's only fair I should pay."

"I've been buying my own clothes for some time." He snatched the green card from her hand, slapped it onto the counter again, and held her platinum one out to her. His expression could have been hacked from granite.

"Oh, do whatever you want." She snatched her card back with a huff. "Though it's ridiculous, since you won't even be wearing them that long."

The salesman's head jerked up like a puppet's, making Julia realize how he'd misinterpreted her statement.

She couldn't resist.

"It's not as if you haven't earned them, sugar," she drawled in the same voice Fancy had used to lure her sister's longtime fiancé into that one-night stand before he headed off to war in his newly woven Confederate gray uniform with the snazzy epaulets. "Why, you've already exceeded the money-back satisfaction guarantee Madame Beauregard promised me when I booked your services. It's just amazing what a girl can find in the Yellow Pages these days."

Her finger trailed up the back of his hand, slipping beneath that starched cuff that was still, after an excruciatingly long day, amazingly white and stiff. Nearly as stiff as he'd just gone. "And just think, the night's still young."

From the way Finn signed the charge slip, in a bold, rough scrawl as black as his expression, Julia suspected that she wasn't exactly going to receive a standing ovation for this performance.

"That was real cute," he ground out from between gritted teeth as they left the store.

"I'm sorry." Julia was already regretting her actions, but if only he hadn't been so damn autocratic! "It was just a spur-of-the-moment thing."

Silence.

"You have to admit that clerk's expression was priceless. Who would have guessed that anyone in a town where strippers dance in club windows, women flash their breasts to get Mardi Gras beads tossed to them from a float, and one of the most popular tourist spots is a voodoo museum, could be shocked by anything?"

Thunderheads of frustration darkened his face. "You let the guy think I was a damn . . . gigolo."

"I know. And that was terrible of me." Her smile encouraged him to see the bright side. "But at least he thinks you're a very good gigolo."

# 18

*Undeterred by the anger* radiating from him in waves, Julia put her arm through his as they walked toward the parked SUV. A green trolley headed toward the Garden District rumbled past, bell clanging. "It's getting late," she said with studied casualness. "What would you say to having dinner before we go back to Blue Bayou?"

Finn assured himself that the only reason he was willing to go along with this obvious stalling tactic was that he was hungry. Also, as good as the inn's fare was, he was getting sick and tired of room service every night. "I suppose you've already made reservations?"

"Of course not. And I'm disappointed you'd even think me capable of such subterfuge, when we both know you're the one in charge."

"Yeah, right." As he watched her curvy butt climb into the Suburban, Finn knew he was getting closer and closer to a line he'd sworn not to cross. A line which, once he was on the other side, he would never be able to go back across.

The damn thing about it, he thought as he twisted the key in the ignition, was that he was having a harder and harder time remembering why that would be such a bad thing.

"I do have a suggestion where we might eat," she said.

"Now there's a surprise," he said dryly.

As her perfume bloomed around them on the warm, sultry air, Finn ignored the little voice in his mind asking if he really thought he was in charge of anything in his life these days. He didn't want to know the answer.

He'd expected her to choose some fancy place with snowy tablecloths, formally dressed condescending waiters, tasseled menus written in French, and ridiculously inflated prices. Instead, they ended up at a crowded, noisy place above a strip joint. The lack of any outdoor sign suggested it catered to locals, and while he didn't do a head count, one glance told him that the place was undoubtedly violating fire department occupancy limits.

The tables crowded together were covered in white butcher paper, the spices in the best gumbo he'd tasted since his mother's were hot, the jazz cool. If he wasn't still so pissed off about the gigolo thing Finn would have been enjoying himself.

"Are you intending to speak to me anytime soon?" Julia asked as the waiter—an African-American who appeared to be at least in his nineties, who'd greeted her with open affection which suggested this was not her first time here—took away their bowls and delivered their entrees: shrimp rémoulade for her, a huge platter of étouffée for him.

"I'm not sure you want me to."

"Don't you ever give in to impulse?"

He put his fork down, leaned back in his chair, and looked straight at her mouth. "More often than I'd like lately."

Before she could question that, a female tourist dressed in shorts, a T-shirt in Mardi Gras colors of purple, green and gold that read LET THE GOOD TIMES ROLL and sporting a bright yellow perm that made it look as if she'd put a wet finger in a light socket, pushed her way through the crowd to their table.

"I knew it was you!" she crowed. "Why, the minute you came in, I told my husband, that's Amanda from *River Road*. Didn't I, Leon? Didn't I say it was Amanda?"

"Sure as heck did," the beanpole thin man agreed in a West Texas twang. "Howdy, Miz Amanda." If he'd been wearing a cowboy hat, he would have tipped it. "We don't want to be interrupting your supper—"

"Don't be silly, Leon," his wife waved away his apology with a plump hand laden down with turquoise and silver rings. "Why, everyone knows Amanda doesn't eat. I think she's suffering from anorexia," she confided to Finn. "She's been getting skinnier and skinnier ever since she started taking those energy booster pills Dr. Wilder got her hooked on.

"Dr. Wilder used to be married to Amanda's best friend Hope, whose career as a fashion designer was destroyed when Amanda seduced that professor at River Road College into inventing a formula that made that stuck-up Hope's fashions disintegrate during her big important runway show in Paris, which left her so embarrassed and depressed she drowned herself in the Seine, which opened the way for the doctor to marry Amanda. But then he got murdered, leaving Amanda the chief suspect, since they'd been playing doctor themselves for months."

She beamed at Julia. "That suit you wore for your testimony at the trial was just the prettiest thing, and you were so clever to wear pink because it made you look a lot more soft and vulnerable than you are.

"Why, by the time you finished telling your story, you had even the district attorney in tears. And I was bawling my head off. Wasn't I, Leon?"

"She was crying so hard she couldn't cook supper that night," the man confirmed. "We had to eat out at The Chat and Chew."

The woman shoved a cardboard disposable camera toward Finn. "Would you take our picture with Amanda? The girls back home at the bunco babes' club in Rattler's Roost will never believe I actually met her, otherwise."

Finn exchanged a quick glance with Julia, who seemed to repress a sigh, then smiled. Unlike the other ones he'd witnessed, this did not quite reach her remarkable eyes. She stood up beside the woman.

"Not here. Between us . . . Leon, move aside so Amanda can squeeze in." She bumped an ample hip against her husband, nearly pushing him into a waiter carrying a tray of Hurricanes. The waiter's deft steps, as he dodged just in time, saved them all from a rum and passion fruit shower.

"Okay, honey." She flung an arm around Julia's shoulder, as if they'd been best friends since childhood. A woman seated alone at a nearby table obligingly leaned out of the picture frame. "On the count of three, everyone say *fromage*."

Finn shot the picture, then another, "just in case," the woman instructed. She'd taken back the camera and was on her way toward the door—probably to take it to the nearest Fotomat, Finn figured, when she turned back toward the table.

"Are you anyone?" she demanded on afterthought.

"*Non*," Finn said, borrowing from his mother's bayou French. "I'm jus' Miz Amanda's Cajun gigolo, doin' my best to make sure she passes herself a good time in our Big Easy."

The woman's eyes widened. "Did you hear that, Leon?" she asked as they waded back through the crowd to the door. "Didn't I tell you that girl was nothing but poor white trash? What sort of woman would hire herself a gigolo? And what kind of man would service women for money?"

If Leon had been given an opportunity to respond, his answer was droned out by the band.

Alone again, those damn pouty lips that had been tormenting him since before he'd been stupid enough to kiss her, curved in a brilliant smile. "Why Agent Callahan, I do believe you shocked her."

"I didn't plan to. It just came out."

"Did you see her face?" Julia laughed. "Maybe you should give into impulse more often."

He considered that. "I don't think so."

"How do you know if you don't try?" The legs of her chair scraped on the wooden floor covered in sawdust as she stood up and held out a hand. "Do you have any idea how long it's been since I've gone dancing?"

Those long legs were close enough he could bite her thigh. Since he was sorely tempted to do exactly that, Finn settled for the lesser of the two evils. Besides, the piano man was pounding away on a raucous Jerry Lee Lewis song that wasn't the least bit conducive to romance. Not that the impulses bombarding his body had anything to do with romance.

It was only sex. A man could live indefinitely without sex. Look at the Dalai Lama. And the pope, though he might not really count since how much temptation could there be when a guy spent all his time in a city pretty much devoid of women?

There had to be other males who managed it, though.

Somewhere in the world.

The dance floor made the rest of the place seem downright roomy. Naturally, instead of staying on the perimeter of the crowd, like any sensible person, she headed straight toward the very center, where bodies were packed together like a tangle of the night crawlers he and his dad used to hunt for bait with a flashlight.

She'd no sooner stopped and turned back toward him when "Great Balls of Fire" segued into a slow, plaintive soul sound.

Terrific. If he hadn't been sitting knee to knee with her since they'd arrived, Finn might have suspected she'd bribed the band just to torture him a little more.

Determined to prove that it didn't take a religious calling to control his dick, Finn yanked her against his chest.

She twined her bare arms around his neck and melted against him like she had during that mind-blowing kiss.

"Mmmm. Nice."

Impossibly, more couples crowded onto the dance floor. Hell, if they got any closer together, she'd be inside his suit. Her nipples felt like little berries against his chest and her stomach pressed against his erection. When desire twisted in his gut and caused a painful tightening in his groin, Finn gritted his teeth and fell back on the mental trick to control rampant teenage lust that Father Dupree had taught his varsity baseball team.

Her fingers absently stroked his neck as she hummed along to the bluesy ballad about love gone wrong. Trying to concentrate on the batting order of the 1975 World Champion Cincinnati Reds wasn't working a damn bit better than it had when he'd was sixteen.

"Favorite Bond line," he said, seeking something, anything to keep his mind off how perfect she felt against him.

"That's hard. There are so many . . . Perhaps when Dimitri Mishkin asks 007 how he wants to be executed, and he complains about there being no chitchat or small talk and says that's the trouble with the world. 'No one takes the time to do a really sinister interrogation anymore. It's a lost art.' I love his dry wit under pressure." She twined her arms more closely around his neck. "How about yours?"

Finn decided this had been a bad idea, as he envisioned the command center getting audiovisual with Bond and Holly Goodhead in the nose cone of the spaceshuttle in *Moonraker*. The final scene, where Q, when asked what Bond was doing, responded, "I think he's attempting reentry, sir."

"You're right, there's too many to choose."

She continued to sway, humming along with the music and driving him crazy.

"Finn?"

It was the first time she'd called him by his name, and the way it sounded, all soft and breathy, affected him more powerfully than raunchy sexual words cried out in the heat of passion ever had.

"What?"

"I really am sorry I embarrassed you back at that store."

"Forget it." He slid his hands down her back, allowing them to settle against the warm, bare skin at her waist. "It's no big deal. Besides, I got even."

"It's not the same thing. I'm used to people confusing me with Amanda and thinking the worst. But you were upset. You probably won't believe me, but I'm usually much more circumspect. Especially in public, among strangers.

"When I'm with friends, that's different. But even then I can't remember another time when I purposefully set out to make anyone uncomfortable. I mean, one of the things that drives me crazy about Shane's penchant for practical jokes is that they're at the deliberate expense of others, which is one of the few good things about my possible stalker, since it's made him give them up for the time being, but—"

"Would you do something for me?" Finn broke in.

She looked up at him. "What?"

"Shut up."

Assuring himself that he couldn't get into that much trouble on a public dance floor, even in the Big Easy where hedonistic pleasures had been turned into a profitable tourist industry, Finn lowered his mouth to hers.

Unlike his first kiss, which had swept through her like a tropical storm, this was like sliding into a warm lagoon. He took his time, the tip of his tongue skimming along the seam of her lips, encouraging hers to part. Which they did. Willingly. Eagerly.

His clever mouth was devastatingly controlled. And tormentingly slow.

*Hurry*, she wanted to beg him as he tilted his head, changing the angle of the kiss. *Before I remember all the reasons why this would be a mistake*.

There'd been so many times over the past days Julia had gotten the feeling Finn could read her mind. But now, if he sensed her need, intuited her impatience, he didn't reveal it. Instead, with slow, sure hands he stroked her back, sending her floating on rising tides of sweet desire.

The smoky room seemed to dissolve, like sea foam beneath a warm sun. She was lost to him. Absolutely, utterly lost. Time stopped; they could have been the only people on the dance floor, on the planet as they swayed together, breaths mingling in a slow, undemanding meeting.

When he began to hum along with the sultry, sad sound of the tenor sax, vibrations thrummed from his mouth deep into her moist, needy core. The heat of his body warmed her from breast to thigh; his mouth continued to seduce her until they seemed of one shared breath as he took her deeper, then deeper still. Then, just when she was on the verge of drowning, he retreated.

She pressed her fingertips against her tingling lips. "Does this mean you forgive me?" she asked when the power of speech returned.

"I've never been one to hold a grudge." He took hold of her hand and kissed her fingertips. "Life's too short. And you taste too damn good."

She shouldn't have had that glass of wine after such a long day. The way he was looking at her made her head reel, her throat go dry, and her knees turn all wobbly.

They'd stopped any pretense at dancing.

He wanted her. Julia didn't need Amanda's extensive experience to know when a man's mind was on sex. And Finn Callahan wasn't just any man.

When the band broke into a drum-banging rockabilly, he put his hand on her back and began walking off the dance floor. "You've got an early call and you've already had a long day. We'd better get back to town." Julia was a bit surprised when his tone suggested he was no more eager to call it a night than she was.

They were back out on the sidewalk again and Finn had just unlocked the passenger door when a biker, clad in skintight black leather pants, a Harley-Davidson T-shirt, and enough chains to stretch from here to the Moonwalk, called out to her.

"Hey, Amanda, I gotta know, are you gonna get an abortion?"

Julia flashed one of her professional smiles. "Now, I'd just love to tell you, darlin'," she answered in Amanda's smoke and honey drawl. "But if I breathed so much as a single solitary word about the plotline, those mean old producers would have to kill me."

He laughed at that and blew her a kiss.

Their attention on the biker, neither Finn nor Julia noticed the woman who'd kept herself out of the photograph exiting the restaurant. She was in the shadows, watching them intently as Finn opened the Suburban's door. She failed to smile at Julia's little joke; indeed her expression was murderous.

"It must get old," Finn said as they drove away from the restaurant. "Losing your privacy."

"I've gotten used to living in a fishbowl. Besides, it's a trade-off."

"It'll probably get worse after the Bond movie comes out." Finn figured even a minor royalty from her Bond Girl poster profits could be enough to set a person up for life.

"Perhaps. But I'm hoping people's attitudes might change a bit since a 'movie star'"—she made little quote marks in the air with her fingers—"is viewed a lot differently than a TV actor. Viewers invite us into their homes every week. They invest a lot of time—sometimes years—and emotional energy into the characters. So, I think they get to feel like part of the family."

"A dysfunctional family."

"True. But that's what keeps people tuning in every week."

"That, and you wearing those bodysuits and taking all those steamy showers."

"That, too." She laughed, clearly not apologetic of what some strident feminists had blasted as a role that exploited female sexuality and demeaned the strides women had made in the workplace.

Once they left the bright lights of the city behind, night closed in on them. Clouds had drifted in from the Gulf, concealing the moon. The fields of sugar cane and forests of cypress stretched outward from both sides of the road like ghostly shadows.

"It really is like another world," she murmured as an owl swooped silently down from a snag, flashing across the fog-softened yellow beam of the headlights. It snatched up a field mouse that hadn't quite managed to make it across the pavement to the safety of the cane field, before being swallowed up again by the dark. "Like from a movie. The world time forgot." She turned toward him. "Do you miss it?"

"It's impossible to miss something you're never really away from. The land may not look all that substantial, but roots grow deep here. Once the bayou's in your blood, it never lets go."

"But you don't live here. Is it because there's not enough challenge?"

"There're a lot of challenges that come with living in the swamp. But I guess I just felt too confined."

"Plus it's difficult to get people to view you as an adult in the town where you grew up," she suggested. "Even when I go home to the farm, I'm still Peace and Freedom's little girl."

He shrugged, deciding that they might actually have this in common. "It's not that I mind being regarded by everyone as my father's son—"

"But you wanted more. More autonomy. More excitement. And sometimes you feel a little guilty about that," she guessed, "even though it's as perfectly natural as the tide flowing out to sea, or a flower reaching for the sun."

"Are you actually comparing me to some daisy?"

"Are you always so damn literal?" She exhaled a long sigh. "Okay, like a tree reaching for the sun. A giant sequoia. Is that better?"

Despite her teasing, he sensed she was genuinely interested. "It's not the excitement." He'd never been particularly introspective, but took a moment to consider her suggestion.

"If I wanted excitement, I would've been a street cop. Or joined a SWAT team. I always knew I'd be in law enforcement, but I also knew I wasn't an adrenaline junkie. I suppose I chose the FBI because I enjoy solving puzzles."

"And because you're a red, white and blue patriot—"

"Anything wrong with that?"

"Of course not. There you go, jumping to conclusions, trying to pigeonhole me into some neat and tidy counterculture box."

"Nothing neat or tidy about you, sweetheart."

"Since I've had such a lovely evening, I'm going to pretend that's a compliment. And for the record, my parents brought me up to love my country."

"Sure they did. That's why they spent so much of the seventies bucking the system and promoting anarchy."

"Anarchists do not create working, cooperative societies. Rainbow's End Farm was not only financially successful, it's as close as you can get to a pure democracy. It's because they love this country that they felt the need to speak out when they believed things were going in the wrong direction. But this isn't about them."

"Could have fooled me. I thought our little shopping trip was about pulling the wool over their eyes."

"Maybe I just wanted to go dancing. And it's not that I'm trying to hide that you work for the FBI, I just don't see any point in rubbing it in their faces."

"I don't see why that'd be any big deal. Since if they do think there's anything going on between us, instead of setting the record straight, you're going to lie and say we broke up."

"I don't want them to worry about me, which they'd do if they knew why we're really together. Besides, it'd only be a little white lie."

"Black, white"—he shrugged—"it's still not the truth, the whole truth, and nothing but the truth."

"That may work fine in court, but this is a personal matter."

"Maybe you're not giving them enough credit. Let's say, for argument's sake, that we were involved—"

"Involved like sleeping together?"

"Involved like involved. We're talking hypothetical here. My point is that, even if they were to believe we're in an intimate relationship, they shouldn't get all uptight about what I do for a living. Aren't flower children supposed to be open-minded when they're not smoking dope or having free sex?"

"It's been a very long time since my parents dabbled in illegal drugs, and while you probably won't believe this, they've always been monogamous."

"How would you know?"

She folded her arms. "Because they told me. And we've always been absolutely honest with each other."

"Until now."

She shot him a look. "Touché."

"For some reason I can't figure out—except for the possibility I've gone nuts and don't realize it—I'm willing to go along with this little charade of yours," he said. "To a point. But I'm still convinced it's a waste of time." Looking out into the well of darkness, Finn broke another rule and shared a thought with her. "I can understand and even admire your desire to protect your parents from worrying about you because you love them—"

"Unequivocally."

He believed that. This was not a woman who did—or felt—anything by half measures. "But there's still one thing we have to get clear. If it comes down to a choice between your safety or protecting their feelings, there's not going to be a choice. Is that understood?"

"You're one of the few men I've ever met who says precisely what he means."

"Perhaps you need to meet a different type of man."

"I have." The smile she bestowed on him was designed to dazzle. And did. "And with that we come full circle, back to why you became an agent in the first place. Deep down inside that gruff exterior is a man who cares, Finn. Sometimes too much."

She turned toward him, her eyes skimming over his face. "This last case was hard on you."

"Yeah."

"Because you feel you should have caught the killer sooner?"

"Most cops would feel the same way."

"But it ate at you. You lived the case day and night for three years. You lived in Lawson's head. Every woman you saw on the street, in a bar or a restaurant, riding on a bus or across the aisle in a plane, all became potential victims. You looked at them the way he would. Thought of why he might pick out any one of them, imagined what he'd do. And then you found them when he was finished with them, and you were the one who became their voice. You were the one who spoke for those dead women, but even that didn't quite ease your conscience."

"They wouldn't have been dead if I'd caught the guy sooner."

"True. But did you ever consider how many you saved? Not after you captured him, but during that time? I looked the case up on the Internet last night. You were right on his trail nearly the entire time."

"Not close enough."

"You can't know that. The two of you obviously became close, in a fashion. If you were in his head, he was undoubtedly in yours. And if that's the case, there could have been times you don't even know about when you were close enough that he sensed you following him, and didn't dare make his move. Nights the women who might have ended up his victims got home safely. Because of you."

Even the shrink Burke had sent him to after his little blowup hadn't suggested that.

"I never thought of it that way."

"Perhaps you should."

Finn didn't respond as they drove through the night in silence. But he did wonder.

# 19

*Several of the cast* and crew were still in the bar and called out to Julia to join them when they returned to the inn, but she begged off, claiming she still had lines to memorize before morning.

Warren was sitting at a table in the far corner, deeply engrossed in conversation.

"Well, they certainly seem to be getting along well," Julia murmured in the elevator, more to herself than to Finn. She liked Warren a great deal and worried about his being hurt by someone who might only view him as her ticket out of the bayou.

"Who?"

"Warren and that local blond cheerleader-type belle he's been spending his evenings with. The one with the mother who wears that horrid hat that looks as if a bird died on it."

"The belle is Lorelei. Her mama with the hat is Miss Melanie."

"You're kidding."

"Nope. And not only that, Miss Melanie's sister is Miss Scarlett."

"Well, fiddle-dee-dee. And I thought folks on the commune saddled their kids with tough names."

"Lorelei and Miss Melanie are loyal fans."

"So they tell me. Mercy, I didn't think I was going to be able to get a word in edgewise between the two of them." She nailed Lorelei's breathless accent as she fanned herself with her hand. "Lorelei's certainly doing all right for herself. After Warren was so obviously smitten with her the night of the welcome party, he started writing her lines, which just goes to show that the casting couch hasn't entirely been tossed out with the old studio system. Though in this case, I suspect it's the actress who's manipulating things."

"Lorelei isn't like that. She may play the belle, but that's because she actually is one. What you see is pretty much what you get, and if she sleeps with a guy it's because she likes him."

"She seems to like you well enough."

"We go back to high school. She knows Nate better."

"So I gathered. If the hat lady can be believed, their wedding's in the planning stages."

He laughed at that idea. "Miss Melanie's been writing out the guest list and choosing the songs and flowers since Lorelei was five and Nate was six. For a lady with a cotton candy exterior, she's your quintessential steel magnolia. I can't see her giving up until her daughter's safely married off."

"Safely. What an odd way to put it."

"You weren't around when Lorelei got herself engaged to some Baton Rouge banker with a gambling problem, who got himself in debt to the mob. Her Shih Tzu got kidnapped. The thugs left a letter in his little wicker bed suggesting she was next if her rat of a fiancé didn't cough up the bucks."

"What happened?"

"Nate calmed her down, found where they were keeping the dog, and brought him back home."

"What happened to the fiancé?"

"That's not so clear. Some folks say he's in the Witness Protection program, working as a caddy at a country club in Tucson. Others say he ran off with one of the mobster's daughters and is hiding out in Little Rock working as a hospital orderly. There's also another theory that he's had plastic surgery and is selling bibles door to door in Kansas."

"Who says small towns are boring?" she said with a smile as they entered the suite, which seemed to have shrunk in the past few days. It was nearly claustrophobic tonight, the tension rising as thick as morning fog over the bayou.

"Would you like a nightcap?" she asked.

"Thanks, but I don't drink."

"I noticed that at dinner, but thought perhaps it was because you were on duty."

"No. I don't drink, period."

She tilted her head and studied him. "Is there a story there?"

"Not really."

"Then I'd guess it's because you don't want to risk giving up control."

"Don't you think you've done enough psychoanalyzing for one night?" There was no humor in his half smile.

"Sorry. Professional hazard." She took two bottles of mineral water from the minibar and held one out to him. "I enjoy tinkering with characters, taking them apart, getting beneath the surface to see how they work."

"I'm not a character."

"Of course you are." She took a long drink and told herself that her dry throat was only due to the heat. "As much as I detest putting people into neat little boxes, everyone does pretty much fit an archetype. You're a classic romantic and literary staple: tall, dark and silent."

"And yours would be?"

She didn't stop to ponder the question. "Artistic. A bit unconventional. Occasionally given to flights of fantasy. But grounded, in my own way."

"This from someone with a purse full of rocks."

Was there anything he didn't notice? "They're crystals. From my mother. And it's not that I actually believe in them."

"No?"

"No. It's more like I don't disbelieve." She shrugged as she tossed the bag in question onto the sofa. "Besides, what harm can they do?"

"How about give you a very sore shoulder from lugging them around?"

"Good point." She rubbed the shoulder in question. "I don't suppose you know anyone who'd be able to work the kinks out?"

"Why don't you try sleeping it off? If it's still sore in the morning, have Hogan call a masseuse."

"I could do that. But mornings are so hectic, what with hair and makeup, script changes, dry-blocking, and beginning to tape the scenes. Perhaps it'd be easier if you could give it a try for me tonight. I know I'd sleep ever so much better if my body were more relaxed."

"I'm not a masseuse."

"How hard can it be? All you have to do is put your hands on me. And begin rubbing."

He looked at her long enough to make her blood pulse with expectation. Julia could tell he was definitely tempted. "I'll get you an aspirin."

Foiled again. "Dudley Do-Right lives," she murmured. "Have you ever considered moving across the border and joining the Mounties?"

"Nah. The uniform sucks."

"Some women like a man in uniform." He'd look fabulous.

"Maybe. And the Mounties are good enough cops—"

"They always get their man."

"It's a catchy motto. But their uniform reminds me of an operetta."

"*Indian Love Call*. Nelson Eddy and Jeanette MacDonald." She grinned when he looked surprised. "My parents used to act out those old musicals with friends in the farm's theater."

"Why do I have difficulty picturing your parents as Mickey Rooney and Judy Garland putting on a show in the barn?"

Because they'd been getting along so well, the sarcasm grated more than it would have before. "If you'd seen Mama Cass and Jerry Garcia in *Take Me to St. Louis*, you might change your mind. Maybe you can't imagine it because you're a snob.

"Yes, you are," she said when he arched a challenging brow. "A cop snob. You think that just because you carry a badge and arrest bad guys, you're better than the rest of us flawed civilians."

"That's bullshit."

"I don't think so. And you know what, Callahan? You're also the male version of a cock tease."

He went very still. "What the hell are you talking about?" His shoulders were stone, his eyes fierce and narrowed.

"You kissed me the other day. And again, tonight in the restaurant. Kissed me like you wanted me."

"What man wouldn't want you? Besides, you're the one who keeps telling me I ought to give in to impulse once in a while."

"That's all it was? An impulse?"

"Sure. You're a sexy woman, and I've spent the better part of a week watching you shed your clothes and get down and dirty with enough guys to make up a basketball team."

"Surely a hotshot detective like you ought to be able to tell the difference between real life and fantasy."

"Sure. But playacting or not, it's still hot. It gets a guy to thinking about things."

"A guy? Or you?"

"Me. Ever since you got off that damn plane, I've been thinking about all the things I wanted to do with you. To you."

She watched his mouth draw into a grim line and remembered the way it tasted. Tantalized. Tormented.

"But I've been working overtime to keep things professional. Then you flutter those Scarlett O'Hara eyelashes and wheedle me into taking you into the city—"

She couldn't deny it. "Is it so wrong to want to escape another evening locked in protective custody?"

That wasn't the whole story. The truth was that she'd wanted to be alone with him away from Blue Bayou and *River Road.* She'd wanted him to hold her again. Kiss her again. And that was just for starters.

"This suite isn't exactly Angola Prison. Then you drag me to that club—"

"I was hungry."

"Sure you were. But you'd hardly taken a bite when the next thing I know, I'm out on the dance floor and you've wrapped yourself around me like some damn Bourbon Street hooker—"

His mouth slammed shut. But it was too late. Julia felt the color drain from her face. The sharp pain in her heart.

"Well." She drew in a shaky breath and fought against the tears. She hadn't wept over a male since Woodstock. Then again, she couldn't remember being both so hurt and furious as she was now. "You've certainly made yourself very clear."

"I didn't mean it." He caught her arm as she tried to escape into the bedroom with some pride intact. "Dammit, Julia, you've just got me frustrated and angry at myself and—"

"You're frustrated?" Her voice rose a full octave, like Jeanette MacDonald's had when singing those duets with Nelson Eddy. *"You're* frustrated?" she repeated. "What about me? Do you think it's easy for me to have a man keep acting like he wants me—"

"That wasn't acting. I did. I do."

"Shut up and stop interrupting me. You keep coming on to me, Callahan, then you back away, hiding behind your shiny gold badge. Some people might consider you a hero, but I think you're a coward. You're afraid of your own feelings. You're afraid to take a chance."

She glared at him when he didn't respond. "Well? Don't you have anything to say to that?"

"You told me to shut up."

The sound that came from deep in her throat was somewhere between a growl and a scream. "I've had it with you, Callahan. First thing tomorrow, I'm going to insist that you be fired. Then I'm going to refuse to show up on the set if you're anywhere in the vicinity."

"That's stupid."

"Not as stupid as some of the things I've been doing lately." Like letting a stiff, stuffed shirt Neanderthal creep past her defenses into her mind. And, dammit, heart.

"I'm going to go to bed now. Alone. And don't worry, you're off the hook where my parents are concerned, too." She dragged a hand through her hair, appalled that it was trembling. "You know the ridiculous thing about all this?"

"What?"

"Ever since they called, I've been worried about how you'd view them. Concerned that they wouldn't measure up enough to overcome your obvious prejudice against them. But the truth is, I had it all backward.

"No matter what you may think, my mother and father are good people. Caring people who might not show up at the Episcopal Church on Sunday mornings, or vote a straight Republican ticket, or have dinner at the country club, but they're real and honest and neither one of them has a prejudiced bone in their body. Which is why they're too good to even waste their time with a rigid, controlling, inconsiderate jerk like you."

Didn't anything get to him? He was standing there, as rigid as the statue of the soldier she'd seen in front of the courthouse down the street. Could he really be so unfeeling? "I'm going to bed."

"That's a good idea."

"And tomorrow you're going to be gone."

When he didn't respond, Julia swept from the room, threw herself onto the bed, and squeezed her eyes tightly shut to close off the hot tears brimming at the back of her lids.

There was a loud thud from the other side of the wall. Then nothing but the sound of cicadas singing their lonely songs out in the bayou.

She wasn't going to talk to him. During the night, while Julia had been tossing and turning, she'd vowed that if Finn was still there in the morning, she'd simply walk off the show. Let Kendall the ass-pinching executive producer deal with that, she'd decided.

Until she came out of the bedroom and saw Finn sitting at the table, wearing his stark FBI suit, looking even worse than she felt. His eyes were heavily lidded, his uncharacteristically unshaven jaw shadowed, and his shirt, wonder of wonders, was actually rumpled, as if he'd spent the night in it.

Sympathy stirred. Just a little.

He didn't look up from the laptop computer he was tapping on. An incredible aroma wafted from a waxed bag on the table beside the computer. "What do you know about Atlantic Pharmaceuticals?"

As she sat down across from him, Julia reminded herself that she'd always considered the silent treatment more than a little juvenile. "Not much. Only that it bought out Dwyers' Diapers last year, which made it owner of *River Road*. And that Charles Kendall could be the poster boy for nepotism. Why?"

He poured her a cup of coffee from the carafe, added the perfect amount of cream and two sugars, and handed it to her. His knuckles were bruised, explaining that hole in the wall that hadn't been there yesterday. "Did you know they're about to launch a new drug?"

"Now that you mention it, that's what this on-location shoot is all about. The episodes are airing during sweeps, at the same time Atlantic's launching the drug."

"Providing a huge built-in audience for its advertising blitz," Finn guessed.

"That'd be my guess." She took a sip of the chicory coffee she was becoming accustomed to. "For someone who didn't earn his own wealth, Charles is terribly tightfisted. The only reason I can imagine him springing for this end-of-the-season increase in budget is because Atlantic's got a real winner on their hands this time."

"Or a real loser."

She thought about that for a minute, then shook her head. "If it were possible to sell a loser product with an advertising blitz, we'd all be drinking New Coke and driving Edsels."

"Maybe he doesn't have a choice."

Now he'd piqued her curiosity. "Why do you say that?"

"There's a rumor on the street that Kendall's ass is on the line, because it looks as if Atlantic Pharmaceuticals' new wonder drug is going to tank, big time."

"Street as in Wall Street?"

"Yeah. Atlantic's hoping a huge promotional campaign during your two-night season special will prevent a stock free fall."

"That's quite a lot to expect from a soap opera."

"True. But it turns out Kendall also promised his stepfather, who happens to be CEO, that he can get you back for another season to help keep the hype up for the product's first year. It appears you're a commodity, sweetheart."

"Like potatoes and pork futures," she muttered. "I've already informed him that there's no way I'm returning to the show."

"If the rumors are true, you could probably name your own price."

"I'm not leaving for money," she told him the same thing she'd already told Charles Kendall innumerable times. "I'm leaving for a role I've dreamed of since I was eight years old. I'm also moving on because I'd enjoy the chance for a role where I actually got to keep my clothes on for an entire scene. . . . So what's this drug that's going to tank?"

"An antidepressant."

"Atlantic already produces an antidepressant. You can't turn on the television without seeing the commercials."

"Yeah, but this is different, because it's for animals."

"Animals?"

"Yeah. Specifically cats."

Abandoning the last of her irritation, Julia laughed. "How on earth do you diagnose a depressed cat when they mostly lie in sunbeams, feel superior to their owners, eat and sleep?"

Finn's grin was slow and, perhaps because he shared it so seldom, unreasonably appealing. "That's pretty much what the focus groups said."

"I'm impressed you were able to find that out," she allowed. Something occurred to her. She looked at the computer. "You didn't do anything illegal, did you?"

The smile turned to a scowl. "Hell, no."

"Good."

A strained silence settled over them, broken only by the tapping of the keys and the cheerful chirps of a bird outside the window. Having been brought up in an environment that believed in clearing the air, Julia was uncomfortable with this lingering, silent conflict.

"I've been thinking about what you said," Julia carefully waded into the dangerous conversational waters. "About us sleeping together."

"And?"

"And I've decided that you're right . . . Are those donuts?"

"Yeah. Nate brought them by while you were in the shower."

"I think I've just fallen in love with your brother."

"You and at least half the women in the Western world."

"He's sweet and sexy and considerate. Women find those traits appealing."

"As opposed to rigid, controlling and inconsiderate?"

"I may have exaggerated just a bit, because you made me so angry. But the fact remains that we're too different, that our worlds are too far apart, and we'd never be able to make a relationship work outside of bed. Maybe not even there."

"Want to bet?"

"All right. Maybe we'd be compatible in bed. Maybe you'd be the best lover I've ever had and maybe I'd make you forget any other woman you'd ever slept with. Maybe we'd set the sheets on fire and burn this place down. But what if things got complicated?"

"There's no 'what if' about it. Sex complicates things."

"That's exactly my point. We only have a few more days here, then we'll be going our separate ways, so why risk any messy entanglements?"

"Why indeed?" he murmured, reaching into the bag for a glazed bear claw.

"Then we're agreed?" As he took a huge bite, Julia reminded herself that Carma Sutra's wardrobe did not allow for an extra ounce. "That if I allow you to stay, there'll be no more kissing?"

"If you allow it?"

Interesting how he could intimidate with a mere lift of a brow; he was probably a crackerjack interrogator. She took another sip of coffee. "Well, you are working for me. Technically."

"Technically, I'm not working for anyone."

"You're being paid to be my bodyguard."

"As it happens, I had the check from the production company made out to the Blue Bayou after-school recreation program. If I don't stick it out, the kids are going to be the ones who pay the price."

"Stick it out. Well, that's certainly a flattering way to state it. So, you're putting up with me to help some kids?"

"No. I'm putting up with you because my brother asked for my help, and I don't believe in letting family down. I'm putting up with you because despite the fact that you can be a pain in the ass, I don't take threats lightly and I want to keep you alive long enough to watch you wear that catsuit in the new Bond flick.

"But the number one reason I'm putting up with you is because I'm discovering that you're not anything like the prima donna television star I was expecting."

"Gracious, Special Agent, that comes awfully close to flattery."

"Take it any way you like it. It's a fact."

"I believe I'll take it as a compliment, then, since you're so stingy with them. I'll also admit that for a rigid, controlling, blue-suited government storm trooper, you can be rather nice. At times. Which is the only reason I'm putting up with you. Well, that and the fact that you're a dynamite kisser."

"You're not so bad yourself."

"So, are we friends?" Like Finn, she'd never been able to hold a grudge. It took too much emotional energy and was a waste of time.

"Sure." He shrugged. "Why not?"

"Now there's a ringing endorsement." She rested her elbows on the table, cupped her chin in her palms, and looked at him over the bag of donuts. "Want to seal it with a kiss?"

"Nope." He brushed the crumbs into his palm and dumped them back into the bag.

"Surely you're not afraid of a friendly little kiss between friends?"

"No. But you might want to be. Because if I touch you right now, I'm going to have you."

It was neither threat nor promise. Merely, Julia realized, like so many other things Finn said, a statement of fact.

"What if I touch you?"

"Same thing goes. My libido's hanging by a ragged thread, which is not a good thing, since I need to stay coolheaded until the film wraps and you're safely off to Kathmandu."

"Still, it seems we should celebrate this new stage in our relationship somehow."

"Have a Krispy Kreme." He pushed the bag toward her.

Drawn by the aroma of forbidden warm fat and sugar, she gave up trying to fight temptation, chose a chocolate-filled donut, bit into it, and nearly wept with pleasure. "Oh, God. . . . Okay, you're safe. Because I think I may just ask your brother to marry me."

"If anyone could make him tumble, it'd probably be you. But he's vowed to play the field until they bury him in the Callahan family tomb. Nate views commitment as something that happens when the guys show up with a straitjacket and a one-way ticket to a rubber room."

"He'll change his mind," she predicted blithely. "When the right woman comes along."

"She'd better bring a length of rope to hog-tie him. Because he won't go down easily." He leaned toward her. "You've got chocolate on your mouth." A long finger set her skin to sizzling as he touched the corner of her lips.

When he sucked the chocolate he'd gathered off his fingertip, she felt herself melting. Bone by bone. Atom by atom. "You're doing it again." Her voice was uncharacteristically fractured.

"Yeah." He skimmed a thumb along her jaw. "It'd help if you told me to keep my damn hands to myself."

"It'd help if I *wanted* you to keep your hands to yourself." She drew in a deep, painful breath. "But I don't. I want them on me. Everywhere. All the time."

"Damn." He slowly shook his head. "Don't you have any natural defenses?"

"Of course. At least I did. Until you came storming into my life."

This time his curse was rough, and as ragged as her nerves. A tension as heavy as the rain falling outside the silk-draped windows rose to hover between them.

He leaned closer.

So did she.

His lips were a mere whisper away from hers, which parted on a slow sigh that was half surrender, half anticipation.

His eyes darkened, like molten obsidian flowing over cobalt.

They both jumped apart as the shrill demand of the phone shattered the expectant silence.

"Saved by the bell," he muttered as he scooped up the receiver.

"That's not funny."

"I wasn't trying to be funny. . . . Yeah, she's here with me. Yeah, we'll be right down." He hung up without any polite good-byes. "The shooting schedule's been changed again."

"There's a surprise."

"Instead of the Confederate attack scene, they're going to shoot some more footage inside Beau Soleil." He paused. "It's the scene

Hyatt added yesterday. The one where the Yankee captain rapes Fancy."

Upping the sexual content of the movie one more notch, Kendall and Warren had decided to inject the scene into the early part of the time-travel story at the editing stage, so it'd occur before the confrontation in the cemetery when Fancy pulled the gun on him.

It was just another scene. Just acting. But Finn knew he was in trouble when he hated the idea of any other man putting his hands on this woman.

# 20

*Damn.* Her lipstick was smeared. Oh well, a little smeared Max Factor was definitely worth the kiss that had smeared it. Lorelei smiled to herself as she repaired the damage in the mirror of the rest room assigned to the extras.

"Isn't this just the most fun?" she asked the elderly woman standing next to her. "I cannot believe I'm actually going to be in a movie."

The woman, seeming intent on tucking wayward strands of gray hair beneath a bonnet, ignored her.

"Are you from around here? I don't recognize you."

"New Orleans." The woman's voice was deep and sounded as if she'd spent decades smoking. Her hands, on the other hand, didn't appear nearly as old as her face, which Lorelei took to be the work of the makeup people. She thanked her good fortune—and *River Road*'s writer—that she hadn't been assigned the role of this elderly widow.

"Oh, then you probably don't find this nearly so exciting, since New Orleans is pretty lively itself. Out here in the sticks, watching paint dry can be considered entertainment. Of course, there was that little flap a few months ago when the sheriff got arrested, but everyone knew he was a crook, so it was more a case of him finally getting his comeuppance rather than a surprise. Then, of course, Jack Callahan moved back to town and bought Beau Soleil. You've probably heard of him. The famous writer?"

That earned a muffled grunt.

Undeterred by her listener's seeming lack of interest, buoyed by a night of lovemaking and the prospect of actually getting to speak real lines today, Lorelei chattered on.

"His stories are horribly dark, and not at all what I'd usually read.

I tend to like books with happy endings. But Jack's are very well written and exciting, though I'd certainly recommend reading them with the lights on. Why, after I read *The Death Dealer*, every time I heard a little noise outside the house at night, I was sure it was a Colombian drug kingpin coming to murder me in my bed."

She trilled a laugh at the absurdity of that idea. "As if any drug kingpin would bother coming to Blue Bayou. As I said, the only real criminal to set foot in town for ages was the sheriff, who's doing time in Angola right now. I hear they have him in solitary, which isn't surprising since even though he was a bad cop, he was still technically a member of law enforcement, which I'm sure didn't exactly endear him to the rest of the inmates."

As she paused to take a breath, the woman, apparently satisfied with her hair, turned and walked out of the rest room, closing the door behind her.

"Well." Lorelei's breath ruffled the blond fringe of curls tumbling over her forehead. "Some people just have no manners." She couldn't imagine anyone, even someone from the city, being so rude. "Obviously a transplanted Yankee," she decided. Thanking her lucky stars that her mama hadn't given birth to her north of the Mason-Dixon line, Lorelei patted her own hair, flashed her best beauty queen's smile at her reflection, then satisfied, followed the woman out of the rest room.

Julia did not take the sight of Warren waiting at the steps of her trailer when they arrived at Beau Soleil as a good sign. She was right.

"We're adding a scene," he announced.

"I know. The rape one."

"No, another."

Her stomach sank. "Dammit, Warren, if we keep this up, we're going to run over schedule."

"Maybe just a bit," he allowed.

"More than a bit. At this rate I'll be lucky to get to Kathmandu before the wrap party. In fact, I'm probably in danger of being the only support hose–wearing septuagenarian Bond Girl in history."

"Now you're exaggerating."

"Gee, with perception like that I'm surprised you're not a writer."

"Snapping at me isn't going to speed things up," he said, clearly wounded. "It's not my fault Kendall keeps tinkering with the script."

"I suppose there's a good reason?"

"Sure. He decided he wanted more outdoor footage for visuals, so I came up with a scene where Fancy drives out into the swamp to meet with her mother's husband, the blockade runner."

"I can't keep track. Is the husband working for the Blue or the Gray now?"

"Both. He's a double spy, mostly working for himself. Both sides are paying him for information. Fancy's going to seduce him into giving her some of his ill-gotten gains to save Beau Soleil."

Julia rubbed her temple, where a headache warned. "Please tell me she's at least not going to be wearing curtains."

"And have people accuse us of stealing from *Gone With the Wind?*"

"Why on earth would anything think that?" Julia glanced over at the buggy that looked suspiciously like the one Scarlett had been driving when she'd gone out to the sawmill and nearly gotten herself raped, which had, in turn, resulted in her husband's getting shot when the men had been duty bound to defend her honor. "What makes you think I even know how to drive a carriage?"

"I thought you told me you'd grown up on some kind of farm."

"I did. And I had a pony cart, but I'm not at all sure it's the same thing."

"Don't worry," Randy, who'd arrived to join in the conversation, assured her. "We'll use one of the stunt doubles for the actual driving. That way we can shoot your shapely arse climbing into the carriage and your knockers as you climb back out."

"You have such a way with words." Julia could feel the irritation simmering just beneath Finn's impassive exterior and realized once again how alien all this must be to him. She'd never met a man less suited to the Hollywood life.

"I'm no writer, but I do know how to frame the bloody shots that helped get you that Bond Girl gig," Randy countered without heat. "The carriage scene'll be great. The big guy was all for it when Warren thought it up."

Julia shot Warren a look. "Thanks a lot."

"It actually makes more sense this way," he argued. "When she comes back from the drive, all mussed and smelling of sex, the Yankee will decide to take some for himself."

"Why don't we just let Amanda return to the twenty-first century?" Which would allow *her* to leave for Nepal.

"We're not sure she's going to go back to the present."

"What?" Julia stared at him.

"Kendall's considering keeping her in the coma for the rest of next season."

"How are you going to explain that a different actress is lying in the hospital bed?"

"We might not have to. After all, *Bewitched* didn't make a big deal of switching Darrens. Or we'll write something in about her being horribly disfigured—perhaps Vanessa shot her twice, once in the heart, then her face—and when the bandages come off, voila, all the reconstructive surgery has left her looking different."

"That's not very realistic."

"If viewers wanted real life they could tune into CNN or C-Span, rather than visiting River Road," Randy pointed out.

Kendall came out of Margot's trailer just in time to hear that statement. There was a telltale lipstick stain on his collar.

"I agree that it'd be better if we didn't have to resort to such tactics, Julia. But I talked with Atlantic's board of directors this morning. There's already a huge buzz about the film out there. They've authorized me to make you an offer that would more than make it worth your while to return for a sixth season."

"I promised Dwyers' Diapers, when I signed my first contract, that I'd stay until there were enough episodes in the can for syndication," Julia reminded him. "We're finishing up our fifth year. So, I'm leaving." Her tone was mild, but firm. "It's not that I haven't enjoyed playing Amanda, but—"

"I know, I know." He threw up hands she didn't like to think about having been all over Margot's surgery-enhanced body only moments earlier. "You need to stretch creatively."

Julia refused to take offense at his voice, heavily laced with sarcasm. "Yes." She refused to back down from his challenging gaze. "I do."

"A Bond movie is not exactly *Sophie's Choice*."

Julia smiled sweetly. "Neither is *River Road*. At least in the Bond film, the only man I'm going to bed with is 007."

"She's got you there, mate," Randy said on a bark of a laugh while Kendall glowered.

Warren lingered after the others left to begin getting ready for the day's shooting. "I know you've got to start hair and makeup, but may I have a couple minutes of your time? It's kind of important."

"Sure. What's up?"

"I was hoping we could talk. Privately." He glanced up at Finn, with a wariness he might have approaching a snarling rottweiler. Clearly uncomfortable, he cleared his throat. "It's personal."

Julia wondered what fatal disease he was coming down with now. If she were a betting woman, she'd put her money on malaria or yellow fever. "All right. We can talk in the trailer."

She turned to Finn. "Why don't you go get some coffee? I'll be fine."

"Of course you will," he agreed mildly. "And I'm staying here."

Now, there was a surprise. She sighed as he checked out the inside of the trailer, as he had every day before letting her enter. It might have bothered her, had it not been for the all too vivid memory of opening that envelope and knowing her stalker had been there. She hadn't noticed anything missing, but remembering what Finn had told her about Lawson keeping souvenirs, she wondered if she should take a more careful look around. Had he roamed the two rooms, touching her things? The idea made her skin crawl.

"What's the problem?" she asked the writer, after he'd turned down her offer of iced tea or soda.

"What do you know about spontaneous combustion?"

"Not all that much." She didn't mention she'd experienced it the first time Finn had kissed her. "Why?" Suspicion stirred. "Please tell me you're not going to write it into the script?"

"No. Like I said, this is personal." He took a deep breath. Dragged his fingers through his hair. "Sometimes I think it's going to happen to me."

"Spontaneous combustion?"

"Yeah. I realize that it's not all that common for people to burst into flame—"

"I don't believe it's ever happened." It took a herculean effort not to laugh. "Though Ripley might correct me on that."

"I wouldn't want to get in the record books that way."

"Warren." She patted his hand. "I was joking."

"Oh." The problem was, he didn't seem to be. "It's whenever I'm with Lorelei. My skin gets all hot and though I haven't taken my temperature, I'm sure it must be around five hundred degrees. And when she touches me . . ." He blushed fire-engine red. "I swear, Julia, I nearly burst into flame right on the spot."

"Oh, Warren." Julia lifted her hand to his hot cheek. "You don't have to worry. It's not possible to actually burn up from being in love. Though sometimes it can feel like it," she allowed.

"That's what Lorelei says. But I was worried. More about her than myself. I really care for her. If she caught on fire because I'd burst into flame, I'd never forgive myself."

"I honestly don't think you have a problem. Actually, you sound pretty lucky."

"I am." The broad smile cleared the concern from his freckled face. "I can't believe a woman like that would be interested in a guy like me."

"Don't be silly. She's the lucky one," Julia said, meaning it.

While Julia was busy reassuring Warren, Finn was standing at the base of the steps, monitoring the stopwatch feature on his watch when Lorelei came up to him, looking like a strawberry ice cream cone in her pink hoopskirted dress.

"Hi, sugar. Someone told me Warren came over this way."

"Yeah. He's inside, talking to Julia."

"Oh. I guess I'll just have to wait, then. He's promised me more lines, and I have to admit I'm anxious to see if he got them approved. He thinks I have a good chance at a real future in television."

"That's nice."

"Mama and I are thinkin' of moving out to Hollywood so I can focus on my career."

"Good for you." He cast a glance at his watch. Two minutes, Hyatt had said. They were now approaching six. And counting.

"Of course, if that fails, I can always become an astronaut and go into outer space and walk naked on the moon."

"Works for me." Okay, that was it. Sixty more seconds and . . . "What did you say?"

Lorelei pouted prettily. "If you'd been paying attention, you wouldn't have to ask that."

"Sorry. My mind's on other things."

"*One* other thing, anyway. And it's okay that you didn't hear me. I understand." She smiled up at him. "I think it's wonderful about you and Julia."

Finn narrowed his eyes. "What about Julia and me?"

"That you're an item, of course. Why, it's as obvious to everyone as the nose on your face." She fanned herself with the lace-trimmed fan looped around her wrist. "Gracious, there's so much energy bouncing around when you two are in a room together, it's like being inside a pinball machine. . . .

"This is turning out to be such a wonderful thing for everyone, isn't it?" she said when Finn didn't immediately respond to the pinball machine comment. "Not only in the romance department, but mercy, it's amazing how everyone's gotten a job. Even people who'd probably never, in a million years, get work in Hollywood. Like that woman over there." She pointed her fan toward an elderly woman dressed in mourning. She frowned thoughtfully. "I wonder who she is. It's obvious that she's not from around here."

That got Finn's attention. "You sure?"

"Of course. She hasn't spoken a word to anyone since the first day. And she's always off by herself during breaks. I tried to have a conversation with her earlier and she just cut me off cold. I don't know why she's even here in the first place, unless it's because she's obviously such a Julia Summers fan."

"Why would you say that?"

"Because I noticed her yesterday. She's always watching her."

Finn studied the woman closer. The fixated way she was staring at the trailer reminded him of the way Jack's dog, Turnip, stared at a steak bone. The intensity in her gaze made the hair on the back of his neck stand up in a way he hadn't felt since he'd approached Lawson's suburban torture chamber.

"You don't recognize her?"

"That's what I've been telling you," Lorelei said in a huff. "For pity's sake, Finn Callahan. If you'd just pay a little attention. . . ."

He could tell she was just winding up when the metal door opened and Julia came out, followed by Warren.

"You've got the extra lines," he told Lorelei.

Her eyes filled and she beamed like a beauty contestant who'd just been crowned Miss America. "Oh, you are so sweet, sugar, I don't know how I'll ever make it up to you."

He blushed beneath his freckles. "Maybe if we put our heads together we can think of something."

"I'll just bet we can," she chirped.

It was all Finn could do not to roll his eyes as they walked off together, seemingly joined at the hip.

"They seem happy," Julia murmured.

"Seems Hyatt's promised to make her a star."

"It's an old story. There are certainly still men who misuse their power in Hollywood, but he's not one of them. Of course, she'll need more than looks to succeed, but she's very beautiful, in an ultra spun-sugar sort of way. I can almost hear little hearts over her *i*'s when she talks."

"She's been that way as long as I've known her. Which, thinking about it, was back about the same time she won her first Blue Bayou title when in the second grade."

"That young." Julia didn't envy the other woman at all. She couldn't imagine trading a moment of her childhood for a tiara and satin sash. When she was seven, she'd been running barefoot through meadows, wading in crystal creeks, and riding her sweet old mare, Buttermilk, bareback.

"Her mother got her started on the pageant trail when she was just a baby in Georgia, then they kept it up when they moved here. She's got a photograph on the office desk of Nate crowning her. I can't remember how, exactly, he got roped into it, but if the sappy, puppy dog I'm-in-love look on his face was any indication, he didn't consider it a hardship. In fact, it was sort of like the one he's got now."

Her gaze shifted to where Finn's brother was deep in what appeared to be an intimate conversation with the continuity girl.

"He's not in love," Julia determined. "It's more like friendly lust." She looked up at Finn. They both felt the jolt as the atmosphere became charged. "Not that there's anything wrong with lust, of course."

"Not at all." Pheromones. He was being battered by them, just like being inside that pinball machine Lorelei had mentioned. "Anyone ever tell you that you've got one helluva sexy mouth?"

"All the time." Those lips that had been tormenting his sleep curved in a slow, sexy Amanda/Fancy smile designed to hit a man between the eyes. And lower. "But I can't really take credit since I inherited it from my mother."

"Sounds like your dad's a lucky man." He was surprised he could still speak, being bombarded from within as he was.

"He is. My mother's a very special person. Would you stop looking at me like that?"

"How am I looking at you?"

"Like you want to ravish me."

"I do. How about you? Would you like to be ravished?"

"Absolutely." She tipped her face up in feminine invitation. "And that's just for starters."

He dragged his hands down his face to keep from putting them on her. Then reminded his scorched brain why he was here at Beau Soleil, with her, in the first place.

"Keep that thought. Meanwhile, see that woman over there? The one dressed all in black?"

She scanned the group of extras. "Yes."

"Do you know her?"

"I can't tell. She's turned away. Should I go over—"

"No." He suspected he was being overly cautious. But better that, than putting Julia in harm's way and finding out the hard way that the woman was carrying a weapon. "It's just something Lorelei said." He shook his head, deciding that his detecting skills were getting rusty if he was finding clues in Lorelei's breathless monologues. "Apparently she's been watching you."

The woman began moving away toward the cemetery. "Although technically we're an ensemble cast, Amanda's pretty much the star of the show." Julia shrugged. "A lot of people watch her."

The first assistant director, who was in charge of keeping all the planned scenes shot on time, called for the extras to gather on the *gallerie*. The old woman moved slowly, almost painfully, her back hunched, her head down, as if carefully watching her step as she crossed the shell gravel. She sure didn't look like much of a threat. But then Finn thought of those blazing eyes.

"Do me a favor."

"All right," she said without pause.

"Don't you want to hear what it is?"

"Not particularly, since I can't think of anything you might suggest I wouldn't say yes to."

"Damn, you're not making this easy."

"It hasn't been easy from the beginning."

"No," he agreed in a deep sigh. "It hasn't. Keep away from her, okay?"

"You're kidding." She glanced over at the group of extras, then back up at Finn. "You're not, are you?"

He shrugged. "It's probably nothing. But there's no point in taking chances."

Obviously she thought he was being overly cautious. He could read the doubt in her gaze. But then her attention drifted back to the extras and, as if sensing her appraisal, the woman raised her head. When their gazes met, Finn could practically hear the sizzle of heat.

"Ouch." Julia breathed, after the woman looked away, breaking contact.

"Yeah," Finn said.

"I don't think she likes me."

"You don't have to be a detective to see that."

"She's probably just another one who confuses me with Amanda, like the woman who hit me in the video store. Then there was a heavyset black-haired woman who looked as if she was about to murder her husband and throw him in the bayou the night of the welcome party."

"Marie Robicheaux. She's always been jealous and obviously didn't like the way her Henri was looking at you. Nate and I were thinking that we sure wouldn't want to be in that car on the drive home."

"That's too bad." She sighed. "Amanda's such a dual-edged sword. People always want to meet her. She is, after all, far more interesting than me."

"Not from where I'm standing."

She smiled at that. "Ah, but as you've already pointed out, you're a man of discriminating tastes."

"You've got that right."

The morning air was lush with perfume and promise. That same promise was echoed in Julia's eyes as she looked up into Finn's. The world paused as the planet seemed to cease spinning.

"What were we talking about?"

"I don't remember." If she didn't stop looking at his mouth that way, he wasn't going to be responsible for his actions.

Hell, there was no point in lying to himself. Whatever happened, he damn well would be responsible. There were lines to draw, barricades to keep up, and since he wasn't getting any help from her, he'd have to keep things from getting out of control himself.

"Amanda," he remembered, feeling a flash of relief as his brain kicked back in. "We were talking about her. And that old woman."

"That's right." She looked downright disappointed that he'd forced the change in mood. And while he didn't like being the one to put those shadows in Julia's eyes, she'd be a whole lot better off disappointed than dead.

He called out to Nate, who was leaning a hand against one of Beau Soleil's white pillars while his other toyed with the ends of the woman's dark hair.

After saying something that earned a smile from her, Nate strolled across the yard to join them. He was whistling.

"Would you stay here with Julia?" Finn asked his brother. "There's something I want to check out."

"Sure. Anything I can do?"

"Just don't let her out of your sight."

He flashed a grin down at Julia. "That's sure no hardship."

Julia smiled back up at him, wishing just a little that if she had to fall for one of the Callahan brothers, it would've been this friendly, uncomplex one.

# 21

*I've never met a man quite like your brother,"* Julia said to Nate as she watched Finn walk away. "Has he always considered himself responsible for the entire world?"

"Pretty much," Nate said. "Even before our dad was killed."

"He was killed?" She remembered Finn telling her his parents had died, but when he'd refused to offer specifics, she'd opted not to push. "In an accident?"

"No." For the first time since she'd met him, his expression turned sober. When his eyes shadowed and his mouth grew into an uncharacteristically tight line, Julia sensed that there was more to Nate Callahan than the easygoing, smooth talking Southern male she'd first taken him for.

"He was murdered. I was twelve, Jack was thirteen, and Finn was sixteen when it happened. Dad was Blue Bayou's sheriff."

"Finn said you'd moved here from Chicago."

"Yeah. The ironic thing was, Dad had brought us here because he thought it'd be safer than Chicago. Even before that day, Finn was the big brother Jack and I could always depend on.

"I couldn't count the number of kites he retrieved from trees or fishing lines he untangled. He was also the one with the stash of *Playboy* magazines that pretty much defined our adolescence."

She smiled at that, as he'd meant her to, then watched Finn disappear around the corner of the house.

"He'll be okay," Nate promised, picking up on her tension. "If there's one guy who can take care of himself, it's Finn. Like I said, he was probably born responsible, but after Dad was gone, he stepped into the role of man of the house as if it were the most natural thing in the world."

"It must have been difficult for him."

"Probably was. But he's never uttered a word of complaint. Not then, or anytime since. At the time, I'm not sure any of us realized how hard it must have been on him, trying to become a father when he was still really a boy himself, he."

His Cajun accent had deepened and the subtle, seemingly unconscious change in syntax told Julia it was an emotional topic for him. Which was probably why Finn, who was the least open individual she'd ever met, had refused to discuss it.

Julia's heart ached for the boy Finn had been as she pictured him doing his best to fill what must have been an enormous void in the Callahan family.

"What happened? How was your father killed?"

"Oh, *mon Dieu,* that was a bad day." He dragged a nicked and calloused hand through his sun-tipped hair. His gaze momentarily grew distant, giving her the impression he was reliving it. Then he sighed and shook his head, as if to rid it of painful old memories. "He was at the courthouse testifying in a domestic abuse case, when this crazed, drunk swamp dweller with a beef about his family situation came storming into the courthouse to murder the judge.

"Dad threw himself in front of the bullet. The judge lived. Dad died. And our lives changed forever."

She couldn't imagine how she'd feel if it had been her own father. She'd certainly watched Freedom put himself in danger enough times, including that occasion he and a group of Greenpeace activists had piloted their small boats back and forth in front of a Japanese fishing fleet working the waters outside San Diego. Two boats had been swamped. The Coast Guard, called in to rescue the protestors, had not been at all pleased.

"That must have been horrendously hard on all of you."

"*Mais*, yeah. At least I had two big brothers I could talk to and count on, but Finn, who'd always been steady as a rock, just seemed to get tougher. And quieter.

"I'm not tellin' tales, since everyone 'round here knows it, but Jack started rebelling pretty bad then; these days they'd probably call it acting out. In some ways he had it the roughest since he'd been there when it happened, and while it doesn't make a lick of sense, I've always had the feeling he blamed himself for not having done something to stop it."

"That's sad. That a boy would think such a thing."

"Even sadder that he'd continue to think it as a man. He's moved on these days, though. Looking back on it, I guess I was pretty much in denial. *Maman*, who'd never worked a day in her life for wages, went to work as the judge's housekeeper right after Dad's death.

"It's his daughter Jack married. They had a fling one summer when they were kids, her father and my mother broke them up, then they got back together this year after her marriage fell apart and her husband died. Anyone can see they belong together."

"That's sweet. I suppose, in a small town like this, people's lives are probably pretty connected." Not so unlike Rainbow's End Farm, she thought.

"They tend to be."

"I imagine Finn has a lot of old friends who still live here."

"Sure." He shrugged, then got her drift. "Finn never dated anyone seriously, Jules. At least none that I know about. And I sure as hell never saw him get as close to any other woman the way he is with you."

"Perhaps no one else in Blue Bayou has needed a bodyguard."

"I don't have to tell you that it's more than that."

"Perhaps." It was going too fast, she thought. Too fast and to where? That was the question she couldn't answer. "It's complicated."

"Now you sound just like Finn. It doesn't have to be complicated, *chère*. Not unless you let it." He linked their fingers together in a casual, friendly sort of way. "You like him, he likes you, neither one of you is married, or engaged, or even going steady." He paused. "You're not, are you?"

"No."

"Then there's no reason for you not to just quit fighting it and pass a good time."

He made it sound so easy, Julia thought, and a rush of relief flooded through her as she watched Finn walking back toward them.

"She's gone."

"Gone?"

"Yeah." Frustration was etched onto the rugged planes of his face. "Like into thin air. There's something else."

Julia was almost afraid to ask. "What?"

"Kendall's going to check more carefully, but she doesn't appear to be on payroll."

* * *

"I don't like this," Finn muttered as he and Nate watched Julia climb into the black, single-horse carriage.

Today's dress was rich green and trimmed in dark gold. It might not be made of drapes from the plantation house, it might be satin rather than velvet, but it would be hard for anyone watching not to think of *Gone With the Wind.* Despite Warren Hyatt's denials, even Finn could tell they were trying to tap into that viewership.

Like the scarlet ballgown, the low, round neckline displayed the crest of her creamy breasts; the upsweep the hairdresser had spent nearly an hour creating, only to cover it with a forest green bonnet, showed off a long, slender neck adorned with an emerald ribbon.

As clouds, pregnant with rain began to darken the sky, Finn dragged his hand down his cheek and realized he'd forgotten to shave. What the hell was the woman doing to his mind?

"They're going to get a stunt woman to do the actual driving," Nate reminded him. "And you're going to be right here. What could happen?"

"If there's one thing I've learned over the past thirteen years, it's that anything can happen." Thunder rumbled; lightning forked on the horizon. "And usually does."

He'd no sooner spoken when another thunderclap shook the air with the roar of a cannon. The dappled gray gelding suddenly reared up, front hooves pawing at the air. Before the wrangler could grab the bridle, the horse took off like a bullet, dragging the carriage behind him.

"I knew it!" The reins were dragging ineffectually on the ground. Wishing he'd gone with his gut, which had been screaming that the new scene was not a good idea, Finn took off running, Nate right behind him.

Hoping to cut the horse off before he got to the bayou, Finn caught up with the carriage about fifty yards from the water. Lunging forward, powered by a mighty burst of adrenaline he managed—just barely—to grab the streaming mane. Using every bit of strength he possessed, he pulled himself up onto the horse's back just as the sky overhead opened up.

"Whoa, dammit!" Mindless of his own safety, he leaned down and gathered up the dragging reins, then yanked on them. Hard.

The damn horse, tearing toward the still water as if trying to outrun the devil himself, didn't stop.

More adrenaline flooded Finn's mind, causing time to seem to crawl to the speed of a televised NFL replay. Hooves hammered into the ground, throwing up clods of soggy turf.

"Goddammit, I said whoa!" No longer caring whether he broke the damn animal's neck, Finn yanked on the reins even harder.

They were less than a yard from the edge of the bayou. An alligator began moving with surprising speed out of the way, sliding into the water like a log that had rolled down the slope.

Two feet.

One.

The muscles in Finn's arms and shoulders were burning. They were down to mere inches when the horse attempted to jump a fallen snag. He cleared it with room to spare, but the axle broke as the carriage bumped jerkily over it. When one of the front yellow wheels fell off, both horse and carriage came to a sudden, bone-rattling stop.

"Thank God." Finn threw the reins to Nate—who'd amazingly stayed right behind them, revealing the lightning speed that had once made him one helluva base stealer. He slid off the broad back and pulled himself into the carriage.

"It's okay," he assured Julia, who had somehow stayed on the seat. Her fingers were gripping the sides of the carriage with such strength Finn had trouble uncurling her fingers. "You're okay."

She was trembling as Finn drew her into his arms.

Nate whistled. "Well, that was certainly close."

"Too damn close." Finn ran his hands, which were none too steady, over her shoulders, down her arms.

"Would you do me a favor?" Julia asked in a ragged voice.

"Anything." With his blood pounding furiously in his ears and his lungs feeling as if they were on fire, Finn would have moved heaven and earth to get her anything her heart desired.

"When I get my voice back enough to grovel, would you please not rub in the fact that I ever complained about you being here in the first place?"

"I won't say a word about it. But I am going to tell Hogan that you're through for the day."

"Oh, you can't do that!" Color returned to her too-pale cheeks, like red roses blooming in a field of snow. "We're already so behind schedule. If we break off shooting, it'll add at least another day before we can wrap."

"In case you didn't notice, you were nearly killed." The bonnet had fallen off during her wild ride. Finn pushed her tumbled hair back from her face, which he framed between his hands. "I'd say that calls for an afternoon off."

"He's right," Randy, who'd caught up to them, said. "You've got a real emotional rape scene coming up, Jules. I need you in top form."

"I'm a professional." She lifted her chin in that way Finn was deciding was more effective than the loudest shout. "I'm not going to fall apart just because of a little accident. Just give me some time to get my hair redone and—"

"Dammit, Julia. We all know you're a bloody trooper," the director complained. "So I'm ordering you to take the rest of the day off."

"My flight leaves for Kathmandu in less than a week, and I intend to be on it. I also intend to complete all my scenes. Which means there's no time for any days off."

They both looked at Kendall for confirmation.

"We'll resume shooting first thing tomorrow morning," he decreed.

"You realize, of course," Finn muttered as he helped Julia into the Suburban, "that you're all flat out nuts."

"And your point is?"

He shook his head, then touched his fingers to her cheek, skimming them along her jaw, down her throat, and over her shoulders. "You're all scratched up."

"I suppose it's from the tree branches the horse ran beneath."

"Probably." She flinched as he lightly pressed a deepening bruise at the soft flesh where her shoulder connected with her neck. "We should have the ER doc check you out."

"I don't want to go to the hospital."

"Dammit, I don't want to argue with you about this."

"I don't want to argue, either. Because quite honestly, I don't think I have the strength for it. It'll take twenty minutes to get to town, but news travels a lot faster and I'm really not up to running the gauntlet of reporters who'd show up at the ER. Besides, I'm sure all I've got is a few scratches."

He turned the key in the ignition. "I didn't realize you had a medical license."

"I'm not a doctor," Julia allowed. "But I did play one on TV. A guest spot on *ER* last season," she elaborated at his sideways glance.

Concerned for her well-being, he refused to smile. "Cute. Real cute."

"Please? Surely you learned basic first aid training in the FBI?"

"That was Boy Scouts."

"Let me guess. You were an Eagle Scout."

"Yeah, I was. Want to come up to my place and see my merit badges?"

Her light laughter at one of his rare attempts at humor was warm and rich. He owed Nate big time for bringing her into his life, if only for this brief, fleeting time.

"Unless we try sneaking in through the kitchen, we're not going to get past any reporters staking out the inn," she pointed out as they drove away from Beau Soleil.

Hell. And she really didn't seem all that badly injured.

"You've got a point. I'll take you out to the camp."

"The camp?"

"Where I was staying before Nate brought me back to town to be with you. It's been in my family for generations. It won't be easy for anyone unfamiliar with the area to find, so I doubt we'll be bothered by the press. But if you've got any wound that can't be cleaned with soap and water, the deal's off."

"That sounds wonderful."

Better than wonderful, Julia thought. The chance to be alone with Finn all night long was sublime.

Understanding why Sweet Nell fell in love with Mountie Dudley Do-Right, she leaned her head against the back of the seat, closed her eyes, listened to the rain pinging on the roof, the swish, swish, swish of the windshield wipers, and smiled with anticipation.

# 22

*Because her velvet carriage shoes* were too impractical for walking across the boggy land, Finn carried her to the cabin, the full satin skirt flowing over his arms. Although it was only a few yards from the oyster gravel driveway to the door, they got drenched again on the dash from the Suburban.

He carried her into the bathroom. "Give me a call when you're out of those wet clothes and we'll take care of any cuts."

After he'd left her alone, she'd managed to strip out of the heavy green dress before being stymied.

"Finn?"

"Ready?" He opened the door.

"Almost. But I could use some help again with the wet laces."

Julia was accustomed to wearing far less than the corset and lacy white pantaloons on a set surrounded by men. But this was so, so different. The way Finn was looking at her caused her breath to back up in her lungs.

She had the feeling the same desire was written all over her face. He'd changed into a gray T-shirt and jeans and looked so good. Better than good. He looked big and tough and sexy as hell. If he'd chosen to be an actor instead of an FBI Special Agent, he would have had producers willing to run over their grandmothers to cast him in their films.

"So you do own something else besides that suit."

"It's a little hard to drown worms while wearing a suit."

"Why do I have trouble picturing you fishing?" she murmured with a half smile, proving yet again that she could hit pretty close with those characterizations of hers. "Why did you let me drag you shopping?"

He shrugged. "You'd been working damn hard. So far, Hyatt's written you into every scene. I figured you deserved a break. An evening on the town."

"Our first date."

"I guess you might call it that."

At least it wasn't a total denial. He didn't smile enough, she mused. She'd have to work on that.

"You've taken over my mind." His voice was rough and husky with need, a shared need she felt all the way to the marrow of her bones. He began plucking the pins from her hair, allowing the curls that hadn't escaped during her wild ride to tumble over her shoulders. "I can't stop thinking about all the things I want to do with you."

"I'm having trouble coming up with a reason why that isn't a good thing." She drew in a quick, unsteady breath that revealed he wasn't the only one unsettled by all this.

"That makes two of us." Finn's stomach was tying itself into tight knots. "I want to give you fair warning before this goes any further."

"This?" Seeming amused, she arched a brow.

"You. And me." He put his arms on her shoulders and turned her around, giving him access to the corset ribbons. "And sex."

"Ah. Well, that's certainly laying your cards on the table."

"I'm a straight-talking guy. If you want hearts and flowers and pretty speeches, you'd be better off with Nate." Though if his silver-tongued playboy brother laid one of his clever hands on this woman, he'd have to shoot him.

"I like Nate. He's probably the most naturally charming man I've ever met, but nice, too—which is a bit of a surprise, since most men who are women-magnets are insufferably egotistical." She glanced back over her shoulder, her eyes as green as a tropical lagoon and just as inviting. "But I don't want Nate. I want his big brother."

"It can't go anywhere."

"You think not?"

"I know not."

"Because we're too different?"

"Yeah. For starters."

"Sounds as if I've got a lot of strikes against me," she murmured.

"Not you." How could she think that? "Us. Together."

"You may be right." She sighed. "I've always thought the reason my parents get along so well is that they're so much alike. They share so many things in common."

"Which we don't."

"No, we don't." She brushed some wayward curls away from her face with an uncharacteristically nervous hand. Her breath hitched. "But it doesn't seem to matter all that much right now, does it?"

"No." There was no point in lying. Finn reminded himself that they were both adults. They knew how the game was played. "It doesn't." He drew in a deep breath. "There's something you should probably know about me."

"I know everything I need to know."

"Not everything. You don't know why I'm here. In Blue Bayou."

She glanced back over her bare shoulder. "You didn't come home to go fishing?"

"I hate fishing. I came home because I didn't have a choice. I'm working off four weeks suspension, for beating the shit out of Ronald Lawson."

He could tell she was surprised by that. "When you arrested him?"

"No. When he tried to escape from the hospital where he's being mentally evaluated. It admittedly wasn't the right thing to do, but it was damn satisfying. Then things got political and"—he shrugged—"here I am."

"That's not right." He assumed she was referring to his lapse in control. But it was her turn to surprise him. "That you were suspended for keeping a killer off the streets. Personally, if I were the Director of the FBI, I would have given you a commendation."

"I suppose that's only one of the reasons why you'll never be FBI Director."

"It's just as well," she said on a slight sigh. "Since I can't imagining explaining such a career change to my parents . . . So, is that all? No confessions about beating little old ladies with rubber hoses for operating unlicensed bingo games in nursing homes? Or hauling in people for not paying library fines?"

"The FBI doesn't arrest citizens for overdue library books. And I don't believe I've bludgeoned any old ladies in, oh, at least six, maybe eight months."

"I'm ever so glad to hear that." As the last lace was undone, she turned around. "And now that we've cleared the air, I certainly wouldn't object to your kissing me."

He gathered up a handful of fiery hair as soft as thistledown and felt himself growing hard when he imagined it skimming over his thighs.

He'd been walking around in a constant state of arousal since she'd landed in Louisiana. Need was eating away at his insides. The sensible thing to do would be to shut up and satisfy both their lust and curiosity, so they could move on.

"No strings," he said, wondering which of them he was warning.

"No strings," she agreed, her voice as breathless as his was roughened. "We'll keep things physical. Enjoy this time together and each other; then when it's over, we'll both move on."

"The Bureau makes us get yearly physicals," he volunteered. "I had mine a couple months ago. Everything was okay. So you don't have to worry about any sexually transmitted diseases."

"I had to get one for the studio insurance. Same here."

"Okay. So, now that we've taken care of the health disclosure issue, let me make absolutely sure we're both on the same page, here."

"For heaven's sake, Finn." Her frustrated sigh ruffled a curl that had fallen over her eye. "If you make every woman jump through hoops like this, I'm amazed you get any sex at all."

"Not every woman is looking for a long-term relationship."

"I'm off to Kathmandu in a few days. How long-term can this be?"

Good point. "Okay, so what you're saying is that you're willing to have hot, steamy sex with me for as long as you're here in Blue Bayou, then when the film wraps, we'll just shake hands and you'll trot off to Nepal. No harm, no foul."

"Did anyone ever explain that not every conversation has to be an interrogation? Yes, that's exactly what I'm saying. Except for one point."

"I knew it." Here came the *but*, the loophole in her argument.

"If we're going to be having all that hot, steamy sex, I think a good-bye kiss would be more appropriate than a handshake. We're both adults, Finn. We're unattached, I want you, and you want me. I may be an actress, and I might have grown up on a commune, but inside this Bond Girl body is a very levelheaded woman."

"The Bond Girl body is dynamite." He touched his lips to hers and drew forth a sigh. "But it's the woman inside it that's been driving me crazy." After all, it was the damn wondering that was causing the tension between them. Since sex could never quite equal the fantasy, it was only logical to get it behind them. "I'm going to have you, Julia. And when we're done, your head is going to be anything but level."

She grinned at that. "Promises, promises." Touched her hand to his face. "Does this mean we're finished negotiating the terms of our brief, hot, sexual affair now?"

"Yeah. I guess so." She was making him feel a little foolish for trying to do the right thing.

"Good. And since we don't have any Krispy Kremes handy, how about sealing this deal with a kiss?"

Since he was only human, and male, Finn finally surrendered, deciding to take Nate's advice and just take what he'd been craving for too long.

He covered her mouth with his as he carried her into the bedroom, then stood her beside the same bed in which his grandmother had been born. The bed his mother had been conceived in. The bed a horny teenage Finn had brought girls to, where they'd enthusiastically rolled over the mattress, eagerly learning the basics of sex, but none of the subtleties.

He'd gotten better over the years, more skilled, less selfish, more caring of his partner's needs and desires. But never had anything felt so perfect, so right, as being in this place at this time with this woman.

Instead of the usual fumbling of zippers and buttons, and shirts that got caught up on eager arms, their undressing was like something from the movies, all soft fades and slow dissolves.

"It smells like a garden," she murmured as he laid her down on the mattress.

"That's because it's stuffed with moss and herbs."

She smiled up at him. Sweetly. Endearingly. Looking, he thought, almost like the young girl he imagined must have driven all those farm boys to distraction. "I like it."

"I'm glad."

Since he'd been standing on the edge of this towering cliff for too long, Finn had imagined whenever he'd pictured this moment—which he had, too many times to count—that he'd just dive in headfirst.

But now that the moment he'd tried like hell to avoid was finally upon him, Finn found that he didn't want to hurry. He wanted to draw things out, to pleasure them both.

He drew her to him, stroking her hair with one hand, while the other cupped her exquisitely lovely face. His lips brushed feathery kisses against her lids, which fluttered shut at his touch, then against her cheeks, and that soft, fragrant place behind her ear.

He touched his mouth to hers, moving back and forth, tasting, teasing. All his edgy hunger faded as he allowed himself to bask in this gentle, undemanding meeting of lips, mingling of breaths.

Time slowed. Then seemed to stop. The past spun away, back into the mists; the future seemed a lifetime away. There was only now. Only her. Only him.

Julia lifted her fingertips to his mouth, tenderly touching his lips. Exploring the harsh lines of his face, skimming over his hair.

Outside the wind moaned, the rain hammered on the tin roof, and thunder grumbled. Inside there were soft sighs, low moans and murmured words.

He nuzzled at her ear and wondered that any skin could be so silky. Nibbled his way across her smooth bare shoulders, then licked a wet path down to her breasts and brought the blood simmering to the surface.

"I want to know what you want." His words vibrated against soft skin. She was so soft. So sexy. So impossibly tempting. "What you need."

"You." She slid her hands down his chest, her fingers skimming though the scattering of dark hair that arrowed down to his cock, which felt as if it might erupt at any moment. "Oh, God, Finn, I want, I need, you."

"We'll have each other soon enough, *chère*." Determined to maintain control, he caught her hand and continued on his leisurly, erotic journey. His mouth grew hot, his hands possessive. "But meanwhile . . ."

Having been ready for fast, flaming sex, Julia found herself falling under the spell of his slow, sensual exploration. He was scattering kisses over her stomach, the inside of her thigh, the back of her knee, which, amazingly, seemed to be directly connected to other, more vital body parts.

She should have known a man like Finn, who focused on the smallest detail, would be thorough. His hands and mouth were everywhere, caressing, feasting, an agonizingly slow journey from her lips to her toes, discovering hidden, secret flashpoints of pleasure. And everywhere his lips touched, he left tormenting trails of fire and ice.

She couldn't bear it much longer. Julia's body craved; her heart hungered. When he pressed his mouth against the heat between her legs, the keen edge of his teeth scraping against the ultra-sensitive flesh, his tongue diving deep, she felt a flood of hot moisture and moaned.

Hungry for him, desperate to taste him as he was her, with a greedy sense of wonder, Julia pulled away, just long enough to shift position on the soft fragrant mattress so they mirrored each other, hands shaping the swell of hips, hungry mouths closing over straining shaft and bud.

His thumb parted the sensitive pink folds, and pressed down at the same time he thrust his fingers deep inside her.

Her eyes flew open and she cried out his name as she shattered.

She was limp. Boneless. A hurricane could have swept through Blue Bayou and she couldn't have moved a muscle to save herself.

"I need to . . ." She couldn't think. Couldn't talk. Her fingers stroked his sex which was, like the rest of him, decidedly oversized. If her mind wasn't scattered into little pieces all over the floor, she might have been concerned about how on earth she was ever going to handle that. "*You* need to . . ."

When she lifted her head off his thigh and pressed her dry lips against the nobbed tip of his penis, gathering in the wet gleaming evidence of his readiness with her tongue, Finn fisted his hand in her hair.

"Don't worry about me. For now, just relax. And take."

How did he expect her to relax when he was creating such havoc in every atom of her body?

He shifted their positions yet again so she was lying on her back, looking up at him, wondering if she'd ever seen a more perfect male specimen. He was a large man, but had not allowed himself to soften. She couldn't detect an ounce of superfluous flesh on his body; he reminded her of Michelangelo's *David* that she'd seen in the Accadamia in Florence.

But this man was not marble. He was strong, hard muscle, dark skin that smelled of musk, rain, vaguely of horse, and male power. And for this stolen time together in Blue Bayou, he was hers.

He braced himself on his elbows and, looking into Julia's eyes, slowly lowered himself onto her, the weight of that magnificent body pressing her into the mattress. Julia loved the strength of his long legs, the beguiling power emanating from his every pore, the taste of herself on his lips as he kissed her—hard and long and deep.

He slid his fingers into her again, widening her, preparing her. Then he rubbed his penis against her still tingling clitoris, first back and forth, then in tiny circles, refusing to stop even when she whimpered and begged for release. She twisted beneath him, hands gathering up fistfuls of sheet, inarticulate pleas falling from lips he was bruising with his kisses.

But there was no need for words. A Trappist monk, cloistered for a century, would have had no trouble hearing the need in her ragged voice.

Her climax lasted longer this time, like waves rolling onto the shore, crashing against granite cliffs.

"Beautiful," he said in a rough sound that was half groan, half sigh. "I could watch you like that forever." He bent his head, brushed his lips against hers as he took his cock in his hand and guided it into her welcoming warmth. The first touch of flesh against flesh was like an electrical shock.

"Please don't stop," she murmured when he paused. Her hair looked like tongues of flame as she tossed her head on the pillow. "I want you to take me, Finn." As lovely as those earlier climaxes were, and they had taken a bit of the edge off her hunger, she still wanted all of him. And now.

She closed her eyes and bit her lip as the broad flare of his penis pushed past the opening.

"Hell. I'm hurting you."

"Never." She exhaled a breath and pressed a palm against his lower back to prevent him from pulling out. "I love it." She arched her back, lifting her hips even higher and exhaled another deep, soothing breath. "May I please have some more, sir?"

He laughed, the sound rumbling from his chest like friendly thunder. "Since you ask so politely, how can I refuse?"

He pressed on, inch by solid inch, filling her, stretching her.

"Ah," he breathed as her body responded, wrapping around him like a greedy fist to draw him in even deeper. "You feel so good, baby. All hot and wet . . . Hold on."

His mouth covered hers in a hard, mind-blinding kiss as he thrust the rest of the way into her, all the way to the hilt. He was thick and full and vital, filling her body as he'd already filled her heart.

Finn stilled for a moment, giving her body time to adjust to the erotic invasion. "You okay?"

"Better than okay," she said in a pleased little sigh. "I've never felt so good in my life."

He smiled at that, against her mouth, and said, "How about going for a personal best?"

He began to move, rocking against her, slowly at first, then faster, harder, deeper, punctuating each thrust with her name.

This time they came together. Julia cried out against his neck; her legs tightened around his hips. She could feel his thighs go rigid, the contractions that convulsed inside her, his release, the spasms racking his body in a vigorous series of pulses.

She didn't know how long they lay there, chest to chest, legs and arms entwined, hearts beating in unison, her body sparking with sharp spasms of aftershocks, listening to the rain on the roof and Finn's labored breathing against her neck.

If the world came to an end this very minute, she couldn't complain. Because she'd already been to Paradise.

"I didn't know you spoke French."

"I don't." He touched his lips to hers with a gentleness that belied the power he'd just brought to their lovemaking.

"My parents believed in widening horizons," she said against his mouth as he amazingly, started things stirring inside her all over again. "I could speak three languages before my tenth birthday."

"Good for you."

"My point is . . . oh, God, I can't believe what you do to me," she sighed when his hand trailed up her inner thigh. "Anyway, I know French. And you were speaking it."

"It's Cajun French." He gave her a surprisingly playful nip on the chin. "I was nearly eight when I started learning it, so it doesn't come as naturally to me as it does to Jack and Nate."

Then there were all the years at the Bureau when he'd worked to rid his voice of any trace of his bayou roots, wanting, needing to fit the FBI's All-American prototype. Finn closed his mind to his work; determined that this stolen night be only about them. "It only comes out when I disengage my brain."

"You ought to disengage your brain more often, because I like it. It's sexy. And all those other things you said you were planning to do to me were pretty good, too." She ran a finger down the side of his face, dipping into the cleft in his chin. "Tell me some more."

"Why don't I just show you?" he suggested.

"Oh, good idea." Her arms wrapped around his neck, surrendering to the fantasy, to Finn.

# 23

*Although the idea had originally bothered him,* Finn had wanted her from the beginning. And now he'd had her—again and again, and it had been better than he could have imagined. The problem was, as he lay with her in his arms this morning, listening to the bayou come awake outside, Finn idly wondered what it would be like to keep her.

Dangerous thinking, that. Impossible thoughts. The deal they'd made was for no strings. No commitments. And he was a man of his word.

"Well," she murmured as the bedroom began to light up with a rosy glow, "that certainly should have done it."

"Yeah." He touched his lips to the top of her head.

"These next days should be much easier, don't you think? Without all that sexual tension between us?"

"Yeah." She had a little birthmark, shaped almost like a heart, at the back of her neck. Finn bent his head and kissed it.

"Where did you get that scar?" she asked.

"Scar?" He nuzzled his face against her breasts.

"The long, dangerous-looking one on the inside of your thigh."

"Oh, that." Since it wasn't his favorite subject, he skimmed the tip of his tongue across her nipple in an attempt to distract. "It's nothing."

"Finn." She arched her back, offering that creamy flesh to him even as she refused to drop the question. "I want to know."

"It wasn't anything." He switched to the other breast and felt her shiver beneath his mouth. "I just got in the way of a knife." He didn't mention that knife had been intended for the president, and he'd managed to get the would-be assassin before the guy could get to the protective ring of Secret Service guys.

She leaned back to look at him, breaking the warm contact. "You said you joined the FBI because you didn't need the adrenaline rush of being a cop, so I haven't thought about your work as dangerous."

"It's usually not." Neither was he about to bring up the Bureau's Hall of Honor for agents lost in the line of duty. "Sometimes things just happen."

"Things like being stabbed."

"Yeah." The mood had definitely changed, and not for the better. Sighing, Finn picked up his watch, which was lying on the bedside table. "It's getting late. I'd better shower."

"Would you like some company? After all, I was brought up to be an environmentalist, and saving the world's resources—like water—is very high on our agenda."

Finn was amazed at how little it took to make him want her all over again. "Well, if we're saving the world . . ." He scooped her from the bed and carried her into the bathroom. As the room filled with steam and his head filled with her, Finn decided there was a lot to be said for environmentalism.

The rape scene Finn had not been looking forward to watching was filmed just before they were to break for lunch.

Langley, in his role of the Yankee captain, caught Fancy's arm as she entered the front hall, which boasted a mural depicting the story of the Acadians being driven from Nova Scotia and ending up in the Louisiana swamp. It was one of the hallmarks of the house, which Jack and Nate had gone to a lot of trouble and expense to restore.

"Where the hell have you been?" the actor demanded.

She pulled free, removed her bonnet, and tossed it onto a table. "Out."

When Langley's eyes, filled with scorn and lust, crawled over her, Finn, who wasn't wild about the fact the guy kept getting to put his hands all over Julia, begrudgingly admired his acting talent. It was hard to believe that the edgy, dangerous army officer was actually a flirtatious ex-baseball player from Tupelo.

"You were with a man," the Yankee accused.

"Don't be silly." She brushed by him and headed toward the stairs. "Perhaps Yankee women are different, but we Southern ladies are quite content with our own company. We don't always need to have a man around, telling us what to do."

"You don't quite understand, do you, Fancy?" He snagged her arm again and jerked her back toward him. "So long as I'm here, you damn *will* have a man telling you what to do. Because you're under house arrest."

"Why fiddle-dee-dee," she tossed the words Finn had watched her fight against saying at him. "That little old detail must have just slipped my silly female mind."

"Don't waste your time playing the fluttery Southern belle. Your mind's a damn steel trap," he countered. He pulled her against him, hard. "As for your body . . ." He trailed his fingers down her throat, over the crest of her breasts. "It gives a man ideas."

Even knowing it was coming, Finn flinched when she slapped the actor. "Take your ideas and your filthy Yankee hands somewhere else, Captain."

She lifted her skirts and was nearly to the first landing when he caught up with her. When he hit her and Julia/Fancy fell crumbled at the Yankee's feet, Finn's jaw tightened, even knowing that the actor had pulled the punch.

"*Mon Dieu*, that looked real," Nate murmured.

"Yeah."

His brother slanted him a look. "You okay?"

"Sure," he lied through his teeth. "Why wouldn't I be?"

"I sure as hell would have a hard time watching someone mistreat any woman. 'Specially one I had feelings for."

"They're just acting." Finn unclenched his hands, which had fisted.

When the damn Yankee ripped the front of the dress—which had been designed to tear away—down to her waist, he heard a low snarl and realized it had come from him.

"Down boy," Nate warned. "They're just acting."

"Yeah." Finn exhaled a breath and forced himself to stay where he was.

But damn, it was difficult as he watched one of the Yankee's hands grasp her breast. When the other reached beneath her skirt, he knew he'd never be able to look at Beau Soleil's staircase the same way again.

She was fighting him, kicking her firm, smooth legs, pounding her fists against his back, twisting her head to avoid the harsh demands of his mouth. He backhanded her again, once, twice, a third time, knocking the fight out of her long enough to clamp both her wrists in one hand and yank them high above her head. She tugged helplessly, but could not free herself.

"That's it, keep fighting, love," Finn heard Hogan saying. "You may be a slut, but you've always chosen who you give it away to. You've too much Southern pride to allow yourself to be taken without your consent."

Knowing the director could give instructions without worrying about the boom microphone picking up the sound because this part of the scene would be scored, Finn wondered what the hell kind of music went with rape. Lawson had favored chants and Japanese drummers. The search of his mansion had uncovered the CDs in the stereo in his media room, and speakers in the walls and ceiling of his dungeon.

Finn felt the rage rising up again. Rage and despair, which were a goddamn pisspoor, not to mention dangerous, combination.

"You shoot this guy and you'll kill my reelection chances." Nate's words might suggest a joke, but the low, serious voice was nothing like his usual easy tone.

"Shit," Finn muttered as the camera went in for a close-up of her lovely, tortured face. He shoved his left hand, which had instinctively gone to the grip of the Glock at the back of his jeans, deep into his pocket, rattling change. "I fucking hate this."

"You're not responsible for those girls' deaths, *cher.*"

Not at all happy that anyone, even his brother, could read his thoughts and his heart so well, Finn shot Nate a hard, sideways look. "I wasn't talking about them."

It was the sympathy in those unusually sober eyes that got to Finn. "Weren't you?"

"No." He jammed his right hand deep into the other pocket and was grateful when Nate didn't challenge his lie.

"Are you sure you're all right?" Julia asked for the third time.

"Of course." Or he would be, if people quit harping on it. "And shouldn't I be asking that of you?" Finn took hold of her hand and felt another low surge of anger rumbling through him. "Your wrist is bruised."

She shrugged. "I'm a redhead. I bruise easily."

"I was on the verge of shooting Langley," he surprised himself by admitting.

"You're not serious." Her wide eyes scanned his face.

Finn shrugged, wondering grimly why the hell his brain disengaged whenever he was around this woman. "No." He wasn't totally convinced himself that he wasn't serious, and that worried him. Just a little. "Besides, as Nate so succinctly pointed out, I'd ruin my brother's chances for a second term if I murdered some hotshot Hollywood actor."

"Well, that's certainly a good reason not to commit homicide." She managed a smile at that, even though her eyes continued to hold little seeds of worry.

"Look, I have something to say to you," Finn said awkwardly. "But I don't want you to get the wrong idea. Because it doesn't have anything to do with that scene you just finished." The scene that had taken sixteen goddamn takes and ground his nerves to dust. "Well, not in any prurient way."

"There's something to be said for prurient. Under the right circumstances. With the right person."

"Remember what I said about wanting to ravish you?"

"I do and you did. A woman would be unlikely to forget the most memorable night of her life, Finn."

"It *was* good, wasn't it?" He allowed himself to get momentarily sidetracked by his own memories.

"The best. And you know what? I'm discovering I'm insatiable. Because I want to do it again."

"That's sort of along the lines I was thinking." He paused. "I want to be alone with you. Now."

"Thank God." A half laugh tumbled out in a shuddering breath of shared need. "But we don't have time."

"Not to do it right." He closed his hand overs hers. "But I at least want to kiss you. Hard and deep and long. And while you might be used to public performances, I'd prefer not to have an audience."

When he lifted her hand and kissed her palm, a dark and dangerous thrill skimmed through Julia. "I left my script in the trailer," she said breathlessly. "I need it to rehearse my lines for the next scene, whatever it turns out to be." The way Warren and Charles kept switching everything around, it could be any one of the handful still left to film, and endless ones yet unwritten.

As they crossed the yard to where the trailers were parked, Julia was aware they were being observed by most of the crew and a great many of the extras.

She also realized they were undoubtedly fueling the tabloid coverage of their relationship. But right now, with need battering away at her, she decided that since they were already so blatantly ripping off Margaret Mitchell's classic novel, she might as well take yet another page from Scarlett O'Hara's book, and worry about the consequences tomorrow.

They'd no sooner entered the trailer when Finn grasped her waist, lifted her off her feet, pressed her back against the door, and captured her mouth.

Staggered by his heat and speed, Julia put her hands on his shoulders, wrapped her legs around his hips and hung on for dear life. His mouth was hot and thrillingly greedy, his fingers dug deeply, possessively into the flesh beneath her dress. Flesh that was burning so furnace hot as she slid down his hard, aroused body, willing her legs to hold her, she was amazed the material hadn't burst into flame.

Her head spun, her heart hammered as her mouth opened to his; when he thrust a hand beneath the yards of billowy emerald material, her blood began flowing molten in her veins.

"God, I love how hot you get," he ground out as he cupped her with one of his large hands. "And wet."

Needing to touch Finn as he was touching her, Julia reached between them, but the hand that wasn't creating havoc between her trembling thighs caught hold of her wrist.

"It's not that I'm trying to re-create that scene on the stairs, but if I let you touch me, *chère*, you're never going to make it back to the set," he warned. His deep voice, harsh with hunger, vibrated through her like a tuning fork.

He captured the other wrist and lifted them both above her head, effectively holding her prisoner. "You know that, don't you? That I'd never force you. And that watching you act that scene with Langley wasn't what made me hot."

"Of course I know that," she managed to say as his free hand coursed up her inner thighs, only the thin layer of her ruffled pantaloons between them.

She drew in an sharp, expectant breath as his hand dipped beneath the waistband. "Because I know you," she managed in a weak, thready voice that sounded nothing at all like her usual strong, confident one.

She'd been so, so wrong when she'd accused him of being clueless about women. The way he'd driven her to more orgasms than she'd ever had in one night, along with the way he was skimming gathered moisture over her outer lips, making her burn, making her ache, proved that this was a man who knew how to please.

A jolt of lighting shot through her when he skimmed a fingertip over her clitoris. When he began moving it up and down, the slight abrasion feeling like the finest grade sandpaper, she arched her body toward him, needing more.

"Finn . . . Please . . ."

"Just relax, *chère.*" His mouth took hers again. When he rubbed the heel of his hand against her, her body began to throb, drenching the cotton beneath his stroking touch. "Let it come."

As if she had any choice, Julia thought as he pressed harder, faster, causing her breath to clog in her lungs. When he slid first one, then a second finger deep within her, she choked out a whimpering little sound of need.

Her body clenched at him, ripping a groan from deep in his chest, assuring her that despite his seemingly enormous control, Finn was every bit as needy as her.

She closed her eyes, surrendering to the erotic sensations ricocheting through her. Those treacherous fingers were deep inside her, moving in and out. In and out. In. Out.

All it took was a final, wicked skim of a fingertip to send her into the void. Arching against him, clinging to him like a drowning woman. Julia sobbed out Finn's name as the climax shuddered through her.

Drained, she sagged against him; if he hadn't released her hands to catch her, she would have fallen to the floor.

"Oh, my God. That was definitely one of the best ideas you've had yet. You know the only thing that bothers me about this?"

"What?"

"We wasted so much time trying to pretend we weren't attracted to each other. Do you realize how many more times we could have done this?"

"We'll just have to make up for quantity with quality."

She laughed as she framed his face with her hands and lifted her lips to his lightly, more promise than proper kiss. "Absolutely."

# 24

*After making some quick repairs* to her hair and makeup, and ensuring that her legs would indeed hold her, Julia went back to work, only to learn that Charles had called yet another meeting in Beau Soleil's magnificent library.

"Julia's right about us running late," the producer announced from behind a wide cherry desk Julia suspected was a genuine period antique. "We're too far behind. We're going to have to return to the original script."

As Julia tried to recall which one that was, Warren bristled. "You're the one who keeps demanding major changes and new scenes."

"You'll just have to make the scenes we've got left more layered, so they reveal more changes in the plot and character arcs. There's no reason why we need all these characters. Like that blond housemaid you've written in, who's going to be serving Fancy breakfast in bed tomorrow. Why the hell do we need that scene? Other than the fact that you're screwing the actress?"

"My personal relationship with Lorelei Fairchild has nothing to do with this," Warren argued, a hot flush rising from his collar. His eyes, behind the thick lenses of his glasses, were uncharacteristically hard and resolute. "Lorelei just happens to be a natural-born actress and I think she could add a lot to the story line. But the main reason I wrote that scene was to give us a chance to actually show Fancy in bed with her stepfather. So far we've only alluded to it."

"The audience isn't dense, mate. They've got the picture," Randy said.

"True," Kendall said. "Still . . ." He rubbed his double chin and turned toward Warren. "I suppose it would be stronger if we actually show her willing to do whatever it takes to save Belle Terre. Including sleeping with a man she detests."

"A man who's feeding information and supplies to the Yankees," Warren reminded him. "A man she's plotting to kill."

"I don't buy it," Julia complained. "Okay, maybe the audience can understand her need to save not only the home that's been in her family for generations, but her way of life, as well. But you're making her horribly unsympathetic having her sleep with a man she despises and intends to murder."

"Ah, but that's her dilemma," Kendall said. "She doesn't despise him anymore. She loves him. Which makes her more conflicted about her intention to do murder."

"She loves him? Since when?" Julia snatched a script from the desk and began leafing through it, trying to find some part she might have missed. That's what she got for being so distracted. She'd never had a problem concentrating until now. Until Finn.

"Since I just decided it," Kendall said, looking more than a little pleased with himself. "The war's winding to an inglorious end, her stepfather's been promised land and property, but he's wily enough to realize that he's already suspected of dealing with the other side. Which is why he's going to have to start winning people over. Beginning with Fancy."

"Why Fancy?" Margot said a little petulantly. "His wife was important in society before he married her. Why doesn't he just stay faithful? That will still allow him to end up with her property when the war's over."

"Because it's becoming more and more obvious that the North's going to win the war. Which means she'll no longer own any property," the producer said patiently. "It'll become the spoils of war."

Julia wondered if she should be worried when she could actually, almost, follow his line of reasoning. "But he can still end up with it because the victorious U.S. government is going to give Belle Terre to him for services rendered?" she asked.

"That's it." Warren beamed at her as if she'd just correctly answered the million dollar question.

"But his wife's blood runs Confederate gray," Felissa argued. "Once *she* discovers he's been dealing with the enemy, why won't she rally their neighbors against him? I may not have a college degree, but even I know lynchings were not uncommon after the war."

"She won't be able to rally anyone, because he and Fancy are going to make sure she isn't going to be alive."

"You're going to kill the wife?" Margot looked less than pleased by this latest twist.

"Oh, it's a crackerjack of a death scene," Randy assured her. "You're going to love it."

"Are you saying Fancy's turned traitor now, too?" Julia scowled at that new twist.

"It's a soap," the producer reminded her. "Which means no one is who they seem and the plot can turn on a dime."

"Wait just a damn minute!" Margot said as an unpalatable thought occurred to her. "If the wife is going to be murdered, does that mean my modern day character will be killed off, too?"

"Of course not," the producer said, not quite convincingly. "You're vital to the show. Especially if Julia insists on leaving."

"I *am* leaving," Julia said under her breath. What did she have to do? Have the words tattooed on her forehead?

"What about *my* character?" Felissa demanded. "What's she supposed to be doing while all this is going on?"

"She's going to almost die in childbirth. But fortunately for her, Fancy saves her life by delivering the baby."

"How am I going to have a baby? I haven't been pregnant."

"No problem." The producer waved her complaint away with a pudgy hand. "We'll simply tweak the time line, to allow more months to have passed."

"She hasn't seen her fiancé since the beginning of the war," Julia said, backing Felissa up. "And there's been no indication she's slept with any other man. Soap or not, it would be nice to have some semblance of continuity. If the war's almost over, this has to be the world's longest pregnancy. Whose child is it? And what's she carrying? A baby elephant?"

"Sarcasm doesn't suit you, love," Randy chided. "As to who the father is, we'll just keep the audience guessing."

"Which means you don't know," Felissa accused.

"It's Warren's job to figure it out." A pinky ring flashed gold in the sunlight streaming through the French doors as Charles waved away her complaint. "My job is to come up with plot devices that resonate with an audience. And childbirth is right up there with weddings and death scenes."

"I'll grant you that," Julia said. "But I thought you wanted to cut back on scenes. What you're suggesting will only add more." She was never going to get to Kathmandu at this rate.

"Not that many. We'll just work a little later each day. You said you wanted Fancy to be more sympathetic," he reminded her. "What's more sympathetic than delivering a baby while a battle's raging outside the plantation house?"

"Reviewers are going to think we've gone flat out nuts," Julia complained.

"It's the audience that counts. And they've proven over the years they'll buy anything where your character's concerned. Besides, what do you care? You keep saying you're not going to be here."

"I'm not."

"Then it's none of your concern. All you have to worry about is showing up on time and knowing your part. Because the better you've memorized your lines, the faster the shoot will go and the sooner you'll be on the way to your new life."

Ten minutes later Julia was still fuming, walking off her frustration, muttering about the ridiculousness.

"Thank you," she said to Finn as she stopped at the water's edge several hundred yards from Beau Soleil.

"For what?"

"For not offering advice."

"Are you kidding? All I know about your business is that you have to be nuts to want to do it. No offense intended," he tacked on quickly.

"None taken. Because it's true." She folded her arms and sighed as she watched a trio of blue herons walking along on their stilted legs. One ducked his feathered head into the water and speared a small striped water snake, which disappeared into his long beak.

"It's just so frustrating." She sighed and willed the anger to drain out of her. He was standing behind her; when she leaned back against him, he looped his arms lightly around her waist and leaned his cheek against the top of her head.

"I might not be an expert on show business, but I do think I'm getting a handle on how to take your mind off it."

Her lips quirked. He'd loosened up so much since they'd met. Or perhaps she'd quit expecting the worst from him.

"Think so, huh?"

He turned her toward him, drew her against his chest. "I know so." His lips nibbled at hers, tasting, teasing. She'd just gone up on her toes, twining her arms around his neck, when the distant roar of a diesel engine captured her reluctant attention.

"Oh, no."

"What now?" She felt him tense, as if prepared to protect her against invading vandals.

"They're here. Freedom and Peace." How could her parents' impending visit have slipped her mind? Because, she thought, as the huge fancifully painted bus drove into view, her mind was filled with Finn. "My parents."

After exchanging greetings and kisses and being enveloped in her father's arms like a cub embraced by papa bear, Julia said a silent little prayer and introduced her parents to Finn, and him to them. Her father was dressed in his usual black shirt and jeans. Like country singer Johnny Cash, who'd owned one of his paintings, Freedom had sworn to wear the color until no American lived in poverty. He'd added a touch of color since Julia saw him last: a small red, white and blue Stars-and-Stripes patch over his chest pocket.

His hair, which he'd tied back with a leather thong, was long and beginning to be streaked with gray, which was also a surprise since she'd never actually thought of her father as a grown-up. He was a long way from being old yet, but it was odd to think of him no longer being young.

Peace, on the other hand, could have been Julia's slightly older sister. Her hair was still a burnished auburn, her body, beneath the flowing sunset color tunic and skirt, as shapely as ever. The faint lines extending out from her soft, moss-hued eyes were evidence that she smiled easily and often.

"Mr. Callahan." She extended a slender hand. "We've so been looking forward to meeting you."

"It's good to meet you, too, Mrs. Summers."

"Oh, please, call me Peace," she said, her melodious voice singing like a silver bell. "All our friends do." She tilted her head. "You're an earth sign."

"So I've been told."

"And Julia's air."

"Is that so?"

"Yes. Everything's individualistic, of course, and I'd have to do your chart, but they can often balance each other beautifully."

"Earth signs can also tether airs to the ground," Freedom growled. He extended his hand, which was scarred and nicked from years of chiseling his famous chairs before turning to paint and canvas. "Callahan." His tone was frankly skeptical, his eagle-sharp dark eyes openly appraising this man he wasn't yet prepared to welcome into his daughter's life. "So, you've known our Julia long, have you?"

"Daddy," Julia murmured.

"Not as long as I'd like," Finn said, surprising Julia by lacing their fingers together at his side in a show of solidarity.

"Isn't that lovely, dear." Peace's soft eyes pleaded with her husband to make nice. "I remember you saying much the same thing to my father."

"I don't recall anything like that." He didn't take his gaze from Finn.

"Oh, you did." Julia thought it was the first time in her entire life she'd heard her mother fudge the truth. "The day I brought you home to meet my parents."

Family lore had Julia's maternal grandfather, a San Francisco investment banker, less than thrilled when his daughter, Katherine, broke off her marriage to a corporate lawyer for Jonathon Summers, a love-bead-wearing, pot-smoking, long-haired hippie Deadhead Berkeley war protestor who had the nerve to claim he was going to support the two of them by carving furniture from discarded grapevines.

The older man had hit the roof, thrown them out of his Pacific Heights mansion, cut off Katherine's trust funds, and refused all contact with the couple until Julia's birth melted the ice he'd encased himself in since that day he'd stubbornly let his daughter walk out of his home and his life.

"No." Freedom had never been one to shade the truth. Not even for social niceties. "What I told him was that he was an uptight, pampered Republican establishment capitalist crook living in the lap of luxury off the backs of honest, hard-working laborers."

"Well, there was that," Peace allowed, sharing a faint smile with Julia. "But you did inform him that we were going to spend the rest of our lives together, whether he liked it or not."

"And I meant every word. Including the crook part, but especially the part about the rest of our lives." Julia watched the male antagonism he'd been radiating toward Finn soften as he looked down at his partner of more than thirty years.

Then he returned his attention to Finn, who appeared respectful, but not a bit intimidated. "I think the bus may have a leak in its air hose. I don't suppose you'd know anything about engines."

"A bit." It wasn't exactly a lie. Finn had helped his brother change the spark plugs on Jack's old GTO back when they'd been kids.

"Then let's go take a look at it." Freedom turned and walked toward the fancifully painted home on wheels, clearly expecting Finn to follow.

"It'll be all right," Finn assured Julia, easily reading her concern. He touched his hand to her cheek, bent his head, and brushed a quick kiss against her lips, which had the power to curl her toes.

"Your Finn seems nice," Peace murmured. "His aura is very intense, but that can be a good thing. So long as all that force is directed toward good."

"Oh, it is," Julia assured her.

"Of course it is. That would be obvious to someone without any intuition." She combed her hand through the slide of hair that fell to her waist in the same style she'd worn as a young girl handing her heart to a man who'd bring his own brand of force into her life. "I'm also relieved to see that you've given up dating weak, undependable men."

"They were artists. Creative men. Like Daddy."

"Whether they were creative is for others to judge. But believe me, darling, they were nothing like your father. It's possible for a man to be artistic and strong. Your father is. They were not."

Good point. "So how come you never mentioned that before?"

"Because we all have to make our own choices and mistakes. I'm also finding it amusing that you'd follow in my footsteps when you decided to fall in love."

"I'm hardly following in your footsteps, since I'm certainly not in love with Finn." Julia might have grown up in an open environment, but she wasn't prepared to discuss her lustful feelings for Finn with her mother.

"Whatever you say, dear," Peace said mildly. She ran her graceful hand down Julia's riot of curls. "My father was less than pleased I'd fallen in love with a bohemian spirit. I doubt yours is thrilled with the idea of his only daughter giving her heart to an FBI agent."

"I haven't given anyone my heart," she insisted. "And how could you tell he's FBI? The tabloid didn't mention him being a Special Agent. And besides, he isn't wearing a suit."

Peace laughed at that. "Darling, the man doesn't have to wear a suit to reveal who he is. It's as plain as those riveting ice blue eyes."

"Damn. Finn said it wouldn't work," Julia muttered.

"Is everything all right?" Her mother's smile faded as she looked at Julia with maternal concern. "Is your stalker back? Is that how you and Finn happen to be together?"

"I don't know." She was not surprised that her mother had put two and two together. "I've received a couple of strange notes, so Finn's watching out for me as a favor to his brother, who's the mayor. But I can't believe it's anything really serious." She glanced warily over toward the back of the bus, where both men appeared intrigued by the engine. "What do you think Daddy will do?"

"I have no idea. Which is one of the more interesting things about living with him. However, there are two things I do know."

"What are those?" Julia asked apprehensively. A crew from *Entertainment Tonight* was arriving in Blue Bayou this afternoon, so a fistfight between her father and her lover was not what she needed right now.

"Your father has never been anything but fair. And," Peace's speculative gaze skimmed over the men, "your Finn can certainly handle anything Freedom plans to dish out."

"Oh, God," Julia moaned.

Freedom had never minced words. He did not now. "You realize you're not fooling anyone."

"I'm not trying to," Finn said mildly.

"I'm assuming my daughter knows you're a Special Agent."

"Yessir. She does."

"So, she's in on the subterfuge, too?"

"It's not exactly subterfuge," Finn hedged. "She wanted to protect you and your wife."

"Us? How?"

"She's received some letters that may or may not be threatening."

"Her stalker's back?"

"I don't know," Finn said honestly. "But I promise you, sir, if that's the case, I won't let anything happen to your daughter."

Freedom gave him a long hard look. "I suppose I'll have to trust your word on that. At least you look up to the job of keeping Julia safe." He rubbed his jaw, his gaze still on the engine. "Are you sleeping with her?"

"I don't want to be rude, sir, but I believe that would be between Julia and me."

"She's just a baby."

"Your baby, perhaps," Finn allowed. "But she's a grown woman. Capable of making her own choices."

"Like sleeping with an FBI agent." Freedom dragged his hands down his face. "Christ. If I was a religious man, I'd believe this was divine retribution."

"For past crimes?" Finn hoped they weren't going to get into that. He really wasn't up to a lecture on the excesses of the government against free-thinkers.

"In a way." Freedom finally glanced over at Finn. "Peace's father was Winston Stanford. As in Stanford, Worthington, Madison, Young and Moore."

Finn exhaled a slight whistle. The man was one of the most prestigious names in investment banking and well known for his philanthropy. "As well as Stanford University."

"None other, though he's a distant relative several times removed from Leland Stanford. Julia's mother was a student at the university when she met me at a peace rally."

"I'll bet the guy was tickled pink when she brought you home to dinner."

"We didn't make it through the cocktail hour." Because it had been decades since he'd spent a miserable week drying her tears and assuring her that everything would be all right, Freedom smiled a bit at the memory. "He mellowed once Julia was born." That brought up another thought. "Are you planning to get my daughter pregnant?"

"Not intentionally."

"Not intentionally," Freedom murmured. "Do you have any intentions at all where my daughter's concerned?"

"I intend to keep her safe until she leaves for Kathmandu. If you're talking about any future between us, I care about your daughter a great deal, but I doubt that's in the cards."

They were too different, their lives worlds apart. Even if he was prepared to settle down, which he wasn't, Julia Summers would be the last person he could imagine leading a life of comfortable domesticity. Especially just when her already strong career was about to take off.

"Well." Freedom thought on that for a long, silent moment as they both went back to studying the diesel engine with all its belts and wires and hoses. "At least I'll have to give you points for honesty."

"I don't lie, sir. And I'd never lie to Julia."

"Dammit, don't call me sir." Freedom shot him his most irritated look yet. "The name's Freedom." He shook his head and made a disgusted sound. "FBI," he muttered.

Another silence settled over them.

"So," Finn said finally, "did you really bring me over here to talk about the engine?"

"Hell, no."

"Good. Because I don't know a damn thing about it."

"Neither do I." Freedom slammed down the fire-breathing-dragon-painted hood. "It's been ages since I had a good Cajun meal. You know any place around here that's decent?"

"Cajun Cal's is as close as you're going to find to my *maman's* cooking."

"That may not be saying much. How good a cook was your mother?"

"The best, sir. Freedom," Finn corrected at the pointed look, managing to get the name out without choking.

"Then let's go."

They were headed back to the women when Freedom stopped and shot Finn a look that would have made any FBI interrogating agent proud. "Let's get one thing straight, Special Agent Callahan. You hurt my baby girl and I'll track you down, wherever the hell you are, and rip your miserable cop heart out with my bare hands."

"Sounds reasonable to me," Finn agreed.

# 25

*For Julia, who'd been so anxious* for her time in Louisiana to hurry up and end, it was as if the final days of shooting had grown unwanted wings. They were working longer hours, starting at dawn and working long after sundown, after which she'd return to the suite, take a bubble bath Finn would run for her, then lie moaning on the bed while he massaged the day's tension out of her, which usually turned into an entirely different kind of tension reliever.

The nights were also far too short. Although they shared a bed, nestled like spoons, Julia feeling warm and happy and secure in his arms, she came to resent the time she had to waste sleeping.

Peace and Freedom had remained in Louisiana, but didn't spend much time at Beau Soleil. Her father, declaring that the bayou had stimulated his muse, took his easel out into the swamp each day, capturing the rich wealth of nature of the mysterious moss-draped land and in his own bold strokes way, revealing the deep currents that ran beneath seemingly still dark waters.

While Julia's father painted, her mother talked herbs and potions with local traiteurs, whose magical healing ways went back centuries.

Besides the dinner at Cajun Cal's, which was every bit as good as promised, they'd had lunch together once, and dinner twice. Julia was relieved that Freedom and Finn had forged some sort of truce. The energy surrounding them reminded her a bit of how her childhood marmalade cat, Pussy Galore, had responded when she'd brought home a mangy stray that seemed to be part Pekinese, part Dachshund, and, her detractors had said, part drowned rat. After a bit of hissing and snarling, Pussy had reluctantly allowed the dog into the fold but usually kept one eye on her. Just in case.

They were coming down to the final wire. Unless Charles changed his mind yet again, there was only one more scene to shoot. Then came the wrap party, which everyone really needed after such a grinding schedule, then at last she'd be going back to L.A. And finally, Kathmandu.

"I'm going to miss this," she murmured as she and Finn sat facing one another in the tub.

"They don't have bathtubs in Nepal?" Her legs were stretched out between his. He lifted her foot and began doing some clever magic with his thumbs against her arch.

"I'm sure they do." She leaned her head back and closed her eyes, her mind drifting, her body melting as he switched to her other foot. "But I doubt they come so well accessorized. If you ever decide to leave the FBI, you could definitely have a career turning women to mush."

"Nah," he decided as he abandoned her feet to trace the contours of her breasts with his fingertips. "As appealing as I may have found that idea in my twenties, I guess I've just become a one-woman gigolo."

"I meant you could give massages for a living." Her senses were pleasantly fogging.

"I'm not sure it'd be as much fun, getting paid. Besides," desire sparked as his thumbs skimmed over her nipples, "you're the only woman I want to put my hands on."

He'd changed so much, she mused as her mind floated and her body warmed beneath those large, wickedly clever hands that had learned all her sensual secrets and discovered more she hadn't even known were possible.

At first, the only time he'd seemed to lower his barricades had been in bed. It was the one place he'd allowed his emotions free rein, making Julia occasionally wonder what her chances were of keeping him in bed forever.

Still, although the walls would go back up again each morning, they didn't seem as high or as thick as they'd initially been. He'd never be as gregarious as his brother Nate. Or as devilish as his brother Jack was said to be. But he'd begun to loosen up, laughing easily and often; touching her hair, her face, holding hands with her in front of the crew, even in front of the *Entertainment Tonight* crew, which resulted in a breathless Mary Hart advising the world that even as she was set to play super spy James Bond's latest lover,

Carma Sutra, it appeared Julia Summers had found a real-life hero of her own.

"And you're the only man whose hands I want on me," she said now, sucking in her stomach as he trailed a fingertip between her breasts, over her stomach to lightly tug the curls between her thighs.

"Good." He scooped up some bubbles with the hand that wasn't creating such havoc beneath the water, and began spreading them over her breasts. "God, you're gorgeous."

"You're pretty gorgeous yourself," she murmured as she sank lower into the water. Into seduction.

"How can you tell? Your eyes are closed."

"Believe me, I've memorized every glorious inch." No wonder Warren had been concerned about self-combustion. If she wasn't a levelheaded woman, she might worry about it herself.

"Open your eyes."

It took an effort, but she managed to do as he asked.

"Look at this." Her breasts were draped in iridescent lather, but he'd left her ruby-hard nipples bare. The sight of his wide, dark hand against those snowy bubbles, against her fair skin, was the most erotic thing she'd ever seen. "Did I ever tell you that I was a soda jerk for a while?"

"I don't believe it came up," she said raggedly, as those fingers inside her began seductively moving in and out.

"Breaux's Drugstore had a fountain. Before I was old enough to get my driver's license, I used to build hot fudge sundaes for pretty girls." He skimmed a thumb over first one taut peak, then the other. "That's what you remind me of, two scoops of French vanilla with whipped cream and red cherries topping them off. Sweet and indulgent and very, very tasty."

His lips closed over her nipple, battering her senses with the tug of his mouth, which connected directly to the dark sensation between her legs. Not wanting to come alone, needing to share everything, she rolled over on top of him, taking him deep inside her, embracing him as they both slid under the water.

---

They were on their way to Beau Soleil for the final day's shoot when Finn's cell phone rang. He flipped it open and tensed when he saw the caller had blocked his identity. "Callahan."

"Finn?"

"Jim? What's up?" Figuring Jansen had been busy trying to get rid of him while he'd been away, Finn braced himself for the worst.

"I've got some good news and some bad news," his superior told him.

"Give me the good news first."

"Jansen's gone."

"What do you mean, gone? Wait a minute, let me guess. Someone threw water on her and she melted?"

"She's been transferred. Well, more like demoted to desk duty out in the hinterlands. So far out, I figure it'll take her about fifty years to crawl her way back up to Boise."

She'd come from Idaho on her rocket ride up the Bureau's ranks. It appeared her rocket had crashed and burned.

"Why? What did she do?"

"It was more a case of what she didn't do. She didn't pay enough attention when Lawson fired his counsel and hired himself a female lawyer."

"He's entitled." Finn had thought it had been a stupid move when he'd heard about it the other night on the news, but if dumping the dream team weakened Lawson's defense enough to ensure his conviction, he was all for it.

"Sure, but then she stalled when brass told her to move the guy out of the hospital to a more secure facility."

"Because she wanted to keep him in her jurisdiction." And garner all the press that would entail, Finn supposed.

"It'd be my guess she didn't want to lose the headlines," Jim Burke said. One of the reasons they'd always worked so well together was that they often thought alike. "But she miscalculated badly."

Finn felt everything in him still. "You're not telling me he tried to escape again?"

"No." The drawn breath was easily heard across the miles. "I'm telling you he *did* escape."

"Fuck," Finn ground out, causing Julia, who'd been studying her script, to look over at him. "Anyone know where he's gone?"

"He seems to have gone to ground. Remember that house he had in North Carolina?"

"In the mountains around where he grew up." They'd found his fourth victim in the well in the back yard.

"We tracked him to a truck stop at the North Carolina-Virginia border. We're guessing he's headed home."

"Hell, the ground there is riddled with limestone caves." If Lawson stayed put, it could take years to find him.

"We've got agents headed there now. And the state cops have brought out dog teams. I'm trying to get your suspension overturned so you can get in on the hunt, but you know the red tape involved. Jansen built up a pretty strong political base, which seems to be lobbying to shift the blame to the guys who were assigned to guard Lawson, so it may take a day or so."

"They might have screwed up, letting him get away. But it was her command." Which meant the SAC should have been prepared to accept responsibility.

"Standing by her men wasn't in her playbook," Burke said, telling Finn nothing he hadn't thought for himself innumerable times. "Since you know Lawson best, the director's bound to want you on the case."

"Yeah. I want me on the case, too." After his supervisor promised to keep him up to date, Finn flipped the phone closed again.

"Was that about Lawson?" Julia asked.

"Yeah. He escaped."

"So I gathered. And you're going after him."

"Yeah. After you're safe on the plane for Kathmandu."

He could sense she was prepared to argue, and appreciated when she didn't challenge his choices.

"You'll get him," she said calmly.

"Yeah." Finn couldn't allow himself to consider the alternative. He worried momentarily that Lawson might actually come after him, then decided that he wouldn't go to the trouble of escaping only to risk showing up here in the media spotlight.

Hell. The guy was turning out to be just like the killer in all those Halloween movies: just when you thought for sure he was a goner, he'd leap up, knife in hand, for another sequel.

He'd find him, Finn vowed. And this time, if he was lucky, Lawson would give him the excuse to end things once and for all.

"All right, everyone," Randy said as everyone gathered to shoot the kidnapping scene. "Since time is money, and I know everyone's eager to take off on holiday, we're going to attempt the impossible and pull this off in one take. Julia, you'll be in the cemetery, digging up the silver you'd hidden there at the beginning of the war.

"The Yankees are holding your stepfather prisoner. You plan to buy his freedom with some of the sterling, then use the rest to finance a new start in Texas, where you've heard people don't ask questions regarding others' backgrounds.

"With the cannons booming, you don't hear the men creeping up behind you in the fog. When you do become aware of them, it's too late. You're captured by a group of rebel deserters who've concocted a plan to kidnap you and finance their own trip west by selling you to a brothel in New Orleans."

"A brothel?"

"A brothel," he agreed. "Worn out by the trials and tribulations you've undergone, on the brink of starvation because the Yankees have burned your fields and taken all your livestock for their army, you can't bear the idea of further degradation. So instead of fighting for your freedom, you pull the derringer from your garter and shoot yourself through the heart."

"I don't believe that."

The director shot Julia a frustrated look. "You don't believe what?"

"That Fancy wouldn't fight. This is a woman who's done whatever it took for survival. She's within days—perhaps even hours—of this nightmare being over. And now she's giving up?"

"You've never heard of metaphors?" Charles challenged in that bull-like way Julia hated. "She's been defeated. Like the South. She's a woman in ruins. Like Belle Terre. Fancy symbolizes the excesses of the antebellum era finally brought to its knees."

"I agree with Julia," Warren spoke up, as he had been doing more and more. Julia wondered if he was merely starting to understand his power, or if perhaps his relationship with Lorelei Fairchild had boosted his self-confidence. "Which is why I wrote Fancy fighting like a wildcat."

"That's the way I see it," Randy seconded. "Not only do we get another Fancy fight scene, which audiences will love, but since we need to get the story line back to modern times, it'll be more dramatic if the renegade soldiers take her hostage. Then, when she escapes, she can make that leap back to the twenty-first century."

"I don't like it." Kendall folded his arms in a show of the Golden Rule: he who owns the gold, rules. "Since Julia insists on leaving *River Road*, there's no point in having her return. We'll still get back to the twenty-first century by killing her off in the Belle Terre cemetery, which will result in her dying while lingering in that coma."

It was the first time the producer had actually acknowledged she was leaving the show. Julia was relieved he'd finally seen the light. But Amanda had been good for her and she intended to remain true to character, flawed though it might be, until the end.

Warren insisted, "Neither Fancy nor Amanda would kill themselves. They're survivors. Fancy has survived a war; certainly she isn't going to view being kidnapped by a bunch of thugs as the end of the world. Particularly since she has a way of getting men to do what she wants. She'd probably seduce each and every one of them, or at least promise them sex, then hold them at gunpoint with their own weapons and escape."

"Viewers want retribution," Kendall said stubbornly. "Fancy has betrayed everyone in her life. She deserves comeuppance."

"Why don't we try it this way first, mates?" Randy suggested. "Then if it doesn't work, suicide's still on the table. The extra riders we've pulled in for the kidnapping are already here, so we might as well shoot the scene for insurance. Because if it turns out you're wrong, Kendall, and the suicide scene doesn't work, it'd cost us a bloody fortune on wasted days while we rounded everyone up again."

"All right." Charles was obviously less than pleased with this suggestion. Julia suspected the only reason he was willing to concede to even try the scene her way was that time was money and they were wasting too much of it standing around here arguing. "When you put it that way, it seems only cost effective to give it a try."

Not even attempting to conceal his satisfaction with having won that argument, Randy turned toward Julia. "All right, love, here's the setup. You're in the cemetery, placing flowers on the grave of your sister's fiancé, having realized too late that it's him, not your stepfather, you love. Will ever love. You throw yourself on his grave—"

"Isn't that a bit overly dramatic?"

"You're bleeping right it is. Which is why it works. So, because you're weeping, you don't hear the thunder of the horses' hooves at first. When you do, you look up—wiping your tears from your face—expecting it to be those hated Yankees soldiers returning to Belle Terre after the battle.

"Instead, you're thrilled to see the group of men in tattered gray uniforms who you believe have broken through the battle lines. The cannon fire is growing closer; you realize that the war is finally coming to an end and you're looking forward to a new start.

"But that's not to be. They've already planned to kidnap you. Both sides think you've been spying on the other, but these are blokes without principles or scruples, so they're just going to hold you hostage until the war ends, then hand you over to the victors. For a price, of course."

"Of course," Julia murmured.

Randy and Warren then began arguing that it might be a good idea to have Fancy seduce her captors. Fortunately, they finally opted for the cliff-hanger ending of just having her kidnapped. As patient as Finn had been, Julia knew he would have been less than thrilled watching the seduction scenario played out.

# 26

*Watching Julia being kidnapped* by Confederate thugs might not be as bad as watching the rape scene on Beau Soleil's stairs, and definitely not as heart wrenching as when the horse and carriage had been tearing toward the water, but Finn sure couldn't call it entertainment.

"All this is starting to make whatever she's going to go through on that Bond movie look like kiddie's play," Nate observed as one of the rebels dressed in tattered and bloodied gray yanked her off the mound of dirt that had been brought in to look like a freshly covered grave, and pulled her astride his horse.

"We've always ended each episode with a bit of a cliff-hanger," Warren, who was standing nearby, said. "And a big one at the end of the season. Viewers have come to expect it."

"Well, they're definitely not going to be disappointed with this one then," Nate said.

Finn didn't say anything. His eyes remained riveted on the riders and horses as they raced away into the fog, which was even thicker than usual this morning. He could barely see his hand in front of his face. That hadn't deterred Hogan, who'd declared it only heightened the suspense and besides, if it did prove a problem, computers could take care of it in editing.

"Cut," Hogan called out.

"Cut," the assistant director echoed.

"And that's finally a wrap," the director said, making Finn all too aware of the fact that Julia would be leaving tomorrow.

In the beginning, he'd been looking forward to that day. When things had been different. When he hadn't known how much more satisfying his days were when he began them with her smile, how much more pleasurable his nights were when he spent them making love to her. And how much enjoyment she brought to all those hours in between.

She did more than just rile up his glands; she filled his senses, balanced him in a way he hadn't felt in a very long time. Since a young woman had been found murdered in San Diego's Griffith Park and had set off the thirty-month nearly round-the-clock chase for Lawson that had consumed not just his every waking hour and most of those he should have been sleeping, but his mind. She'd been right about them becoming linked in some eerie way. Somehow Lawson's thoughts had become his, writhing in his brain and before his mind's eye like poisonous snakes.

Finn had dreamed of the women, all young and pretty and filled with life when the killer had picked them up at the local watering spots around the universities, and taken them to whatever home he'd been living in at the time. Julia had once accused him of only viewing the world in black and white. What he hadn't told her, hadn't told anyone, was that whenever he'd look down at one of Lawson's victim's bodies, discarded like old rags onto a trash heap, he'd pictured her last days of life in vivid, blinding Technicolor, down to the last horrendous detail.

He'd forced himself to watch every minute of their autopsies, acknowledging that they were more than mere files that were piling higher and higher on his metal desk. Although it was by far the most difficult thing he'd ever done, and hoped it was the most painful thing he'd ever have to do, he'd attended their funerals and assured their weeping mothers and shell-shocked fathers, whose suffering made his own inconsequential by comparison, that the monster who'd brought so much misery to so many, would be brought to justice.

"Justice," he scoffed now. The only real justice would be to put Lawson in a cage with all those grieving parents and sisters and brothers, and walk away.

Nate glanced over at him. "Did you say something?"

"No," Finn responded brusquely, as he always did when this subject came up. But somehow, when he hadn't been paying close attention, his internal walls had begun to crumble. "I was just wondering at what point vengeance becomes justice. And vice versa."

"I suppose it depends on your point of view."

"Yeah. I suppose so."

"You got him once," Nate said. Finn had told him, and only him, about Burke's call. "You'll get him again."

"I fully intend to." The riders had returned. At least four of them had. But hadn't there originally been six? "How long has she been gone?"

Nate blinked at the sudden shift in topic, then followed Finn's gaze to the wrangler, who was unsaddling the horses. "I don't know. Five minutes, maybe. Six?"

The short hairs at the back of Finn's neck prickled. Never a good sign. "However long it's been," he said, "it's been too damn long."

Julia blinked her eyes, attempting to focus through the shadows. She had no idea where she was or any memory of how she'd gotten here. The last thing she remembered, she'd been flung over the back of a horse that was thundering through fog as thick as a gray velvet theater curtain.

"It's about time you woke up," an unfamiliar voice said. "I was getting afraid you'd overdosed."

Was she awake? Or dreaming? Had she fallen off the horse? That might explain the maniac who was pounding away with a sledgehammer inside her head.

He mentioned an overdose. Which was impossible, since she'd never done drugs. But maybe she'd been given drugs? Was she in a hospital? She tried to focus through the dark shadows, but everything was blurry, as if viewed through dirty glass.

It didn't feel like a hospital. Or smell, sound, or look like one. There were no bright lights, no busy activity out in the hallway, no disembodied voices paging doctors over the intercom, no low, steady beeping of monitors or distant sound of televisions from adjoining rooms.

There was no rattle of metal trays outside her door, which made her realize she was hungry. And instead of the smell of antiseptic, the air, drenched with moisture, was thick with the rank odor of mildew.

Her arms and shoulders felt as if they'd been yanked out of their sockets. Had she fallen off the horse during that kidnap scene? She tried to ease the ache, only to discover that she couldn't move. Someone had tied her wrists to the rusted iron headboard of a narrow bed, in much the same way Amanda had been tied to the bedposts in that scene they'd shot before leaving Los Angeles.

Julia struggled to steady her breath. Tried to concentrate. She seemed to be in a cabin that was nothing like Finn's cozy camp. The mold and musty smell suggested it had been deserted for a very long time. If there were windows, they must have been painted black, because the only light coming into the room was a stuttering thin sliver that managed to shine through a gap in the rotting boards.

How long ago had she been unconscious? Minutes? Hours? Days?

"I know this is a cliché. But where am I?" Her throat was sore and raspy. "And who are you?"

"You don't need to know either of those things," said a gruffer male voice coming from the shadows. "You just need to know that if you follow the program and don't try anything funny, everything will be okay."

Julia found nothing funny about her situation.

"Are you my stalker?"

"I've never had to stalk a woman in my life." He sounded honestly affronted. Terrific. An overly sensitive kidnapper, who was undoubtedly armed. That's all she needed.

"If you're after ransom, you're never going to get away with this," Julia warned. "In case no one has informed you, kidnapping is a federal offense. You're going to have the FBI after you. And believe me, those guys take their jobs very seriously." Oh, God. Finn. He must be going crazy.

"The FBI? Is she right, Jimmy?" the first voice asked. "I don't want the Feds after me. I thought we were just gonna pick up some extra dough."

"I told you not to use names," the first man snapped back. "And hell no, she's not right." Julia heard the strike of a match. The acrid scent of burning sulfur stung her nostrils.

"She's just trying to do a number on you."

"It's not like we're *really* kidnapping her."

Julia wondered who he was trying to convince: her, or himself. She could read the lack of conviction in his voice. At least one of her abductors was concerned about what he might have gotten himself into. Surely she could talk her way out of this. And if not her, Amanda.

The deep purple shadows kept her from being able to see them. "What would you call this?" she asked. "If not a kidnapping?"

"Think of yourself as our guest," the second man suggested.

"Gee, I was certain I'd sent in my RSVP declining this fun party."

*Stall*. Even without windows, it was dark enough in the cabin that she suspected it might be approaching twilight. Surely Finn would be showing up to rescue her at any moment.

"If it's just money you want, perhaps we can work out some sort of deal."

"Are you saying the TV network will pay to get you back?" the man who was not Jimmy asked.

"I don't know about them." This was no time to get herself into deeper trouble by telling a lie they could prove false. *Stall*. "But my parents would be willing to pay whatever you're asking."

"Your parents are fucking hippies," Jimmy scoffed. He exhaled a thick stream of smoke into the humidity-laden air as he laughed. His cigarette was not the kind you could buy in any store.

"We saw them when you all came into Cajun Cal's," the first man volunteered.

Another clue. They'd been at the Cajun restaurant. They didn't sound as if they were locals. Then again, neither did Finn. Except when they were making love and he allowed his control to slip.

"They may be hippies, but they're rich hippies," she said. "One of my father's chairs was in the Smithsonian and Harrison Ford owns one of my mother's weavings."

"Big deal," Jimmy scoffed, but she could tell he was interested. Now she just needed to get him to nibble a bit on the bait.

"I think so. Not everyone gets in the Smithsonian."

Hard heels that sounded a bit like cowboy boots hammered on the floor as he came out of the shadows to stand over her. Along with the pot, she breathed in male sweat and an acrid scent that could have been nerves. "If you don't shut up, I'm gonna put a gag in your mouth."

He was obviously edgy, and Amanda had been in jeopardy enough times for Julia to know that even the best laid plans often blew up in your face. He was obviously not comfortable with this situation, which made her suspect he was not your everyday garden variety criminal, out for a fast buck before moving on.

And that made him all the more dangerous.

*Think*, she told herself. *There's a way out of this. All you have to do is think of it*. She closed her eyes again and narrowed her whirling thoughts down to one succinct question: *What would a Bond Girl do?*

* * *

Where the hell was she? A trio of Jim Lafite's hounds were baying in the woods. A helicopter donated by the Louisiana Fish and Game Department swept back and forth over the bayou, rotors churning. Half the town of Blue Bayou was out searching for her; the other half was hovering around Beau Soleil, watching. And waiting.

"This is even more interestin' than watchin' them shoot that movie," Jean Boudreaux said as he sat on a log and watched the beehive of activity.

"A whole bunch more," Frenchie Hebert, his best friend for more than seventy years, agreed. "That was pretty much stop and go, stop and go, all day long. I've decided I don' want to ever be no movie star, me."

Jean shot him a look. "Like you'd have a chance in hell to be a movie star."

Frenchie spat a stream of tobacco juice, hitting an RC can one of the searchers had dropped onto the ground. "Maybe I could. Maybe I couldn't. But 'at's beside the point, since I'd never do it. Hell, makin' a movie's more damn boring than sitting on a rock waiting for your trap to fill up."

"*Mais*, yeah," Jean agreed. His attention drifted from the sixties model cherry-red GTO that had just pulled up in front of Beau Soleil with a squeal of brakes, to that blond actress who was built like a brick shithouse. "But all the women you get would probably make it worthwhile."

Frenchie considered that for a minute as he zeroed in on Felissa Templeton's ass when she bent over to take a Dr. Pepper can out of an ice-filled trash can and hand it to a sheriff's deputy from Point Coupée parish. "Guess it would, at that," he said as he pulled a pouch from his shirt pocket and stuck another plug of Apple Jack chew between cheek and gum.

Jack Callahan was in a hurry, but took the time to open the GTO's door for his wife before heading across the yard on long, purposeful strides.

"I heard on the radio driving here from the airport," the middle Callahan brother told Finn. "What can I do?"

Finn shook his head in frustration. Hours had passed without a sign of her. The horses had returned of their own accord, giving no clue as to where they'd been.

"Just what everyone else is doin', I guess. Sign up for a quadrant and start covering ground." He glared out over the miles of low land

and water. It was going to be dark soon; he didn't want to think of her somewhere out there with gators and snakes and God knows what kind of two-legged animal.

"How was the honeymoon?" he thought to ask.

"Pretty damn great. 'Specially since I never thought I'd ever be havin' one, and if anyone had asked my opinion even a few months ago, I'd have said the whole concept was a chick thing." Despite the seriousness of their situation, Jack flashed one of his trademark killer smiles. "Turns out they're not bad for guys, either. When this is over and we get Julia Summers back safe and sound, you might want to give it a try."

Finn shot a look at Nate. "What have you been telling him?"

"Not a thing." Nate held up his hands. "I swear. Do you really think I'd interrupt a guy on his honeymoon just to tell him you'd fallen hard for the newest Bond Girl?"

"It wasn't Nate," Dani Dupree Callahan offered as she joined the brothers. "It was Ed Pitre down at the gas station. And I think it's wonderful. Jack and I are so happy, I want everyone to feel the same way, and it's high time you found someone to love."

"Find being the definite concept," Finn muttered, deciding this wasn't the time or place to argue about his feelings. Especially when he hadn't sorted them out for himself.

"I'm so sorry." Dani hugged him. "But it'll be okay."

Finn had always liked Dani, from the time she'd been a skinny little thing with braces and blond hair down to her waist who'd follow after Jack like an adoring little puppy dog. Both of them had been through some tough times, which was why Finn was real glad things had worked out for them.

"It's my goddamn fault," Finn repeated as he had for hours. "Sorry about the language, Dani."

"Don't worry about it. It's a stressful situation." Finn appreciated her not bringing up the fact that Julia's disappearance was eerily similar to the case he'd devoted three years of his life to.

"You had no way of knowing this was going to happen," Nate said yet again. Unfortunately, his family role of comforter wasn't working today.

"It was my job to know." Finn's lips were pressed in a grim line, his thoughts even darker than his expression. "I was supposed to be protecting her, dammit."

Julia's mother joined them, having just completed a live interview with WGNO News out of New Orleans. "She's all right," Peace said. "A little frightened, as anyone would be under the circumstances, but she's keeping her head."

"See that in your crystal ball, did you?" Finn immediately regretted his rash words. She'd been incredibly calm and supportive, proving that when she'd decided to take on a new name, she'd chosen well. "Hell, I'm sorry." He raked a hand over his hair. "That was out of line."

"It's an upsetting situation. You're right to be a little unnerved. Heaven knows, I hate to think what Julia's father would be doing if he couldn't be out walking off his anger." Freedom was out with Jim Lafite and his bloodhounds.

Something occurred to Finn. "If you can read her mind—"

"Actually, I can't. It's more a case of sensing her feelings."

"Close enough. Can you get a sense of where she is?"

"I'm sorry, it doesn't work that way," Peace said regretfully. "Besides, I'm so unfamiliar with Blue Bayou, anything I'm picking up probably wouldn't mean anything to you."

"Why don't you give it a shot?"

She sighed, then ran her hand through her hair in a gesture Finn had seen Julia make a thousand times. "It's dark." She closed her eyes and went into what seemed to be a slight trance. "There are trees. And dark water all around." She opened her eyes again and looked up at him. "That's not much help, is it?"

No. Not when the sun was slowing sinking into the bayou and everything around them for miles was all trees and water.

"That's okay." It was his turn to try to reassure her. "I figured it was worth a shot."

"There is something else," Peace ventured.

"What's that?"

"She's not alone."

Since he had no idea what he was dealing with, Finn had no way of knowing whether that was a positive thing, or negative. It could be incredibly dangerous for anyone, especially someone who had no swamp experience, to be alone at night on the bayou. On the other hand, depending on what her kidnappers had planned, Julia might be better off taking her chances with the gators.

# 27

*Unsurprisingly, for this part of the country,* there was no electricity in the cabin. A kerosene lantern on a rough wooden table added a petroleum stench to the muggy air and cast spooky shadows on the wall. The light also drew moths that beat their wings against the glass panes and mosquitoes that seemed to think she was an all-you-can-eat buffet.

The two men were playing cards. After that brief conversation when she'd regained consciousness, they hadn't said a word to her. But the younger man, the one who wasn't Jimmy, kept casting nervous glances her way. Nervous, and, Julia thought, familiar. It was the way men looked at Amanda.

The unmistakable chords of the *William Tell* Overture suddenly overcame the frogs and cicadas from outside. Jimmy snatched a cell phone off his belt. Julia found it a bit ironic that a kidnapper would choose the Lone Ranger's theme song for his customized ring.

"It's about time you called," he barked out. "Yeah, we've got her."

"What?" She watched him frown. "A week? How the hell do you expect us to keep her under wraps for a week with everybody but the nationalfuckingguard out looking for her?"

A *week?* Julia bit down her panic; it wouldn't help. *Think, dammit!* While she didn't have a single doubt that Finn would find her, the idea of being out here in the middle of nowhere with these two men for a week was impossible. Her captors had said they wouldn't hurt her, but since they'd already proven themselves capable of criminal behavior by obviously drugging her, bringing her here, tying her up and holding her hostage, she didn't put a great deal of faith in either one of them to tell the truth. The man named Jimmy let out a long, harsh string of curses.

"Dammit, I can't hear you," he complained. "The reception's shit here. We must be too far from a cell tower. Let me go outside."

Without giving her so much as a glance, he left the cabin.

With Jimmy gone, Julia's odds for escape had just gotten fifty percent better. *You can do this*. Between Amanda and Carma Sutra, escape was not only possible, it was almost guaranteed. She hoped.

"Excuse me?" Julia hated the way her voice sounded so frail. So vulnerable. Never let your opponent sense your fear, her ninjitsu instructor had drilled into his students. Easy for him to say. She doubted he'd ever been tied up in some remote bayou cabin with the *Deliverance* twins.

When the other man didn't appear to hear her, reminding her that there was a delicate balance between making herself heard and speaking loud enough to bring Jimmy back into the cabin, she cleared her throat and tried again. "Excuse me?"

"What?" He cast a quick, nervous look at the door. Obviously she wasn't the only one concerned about the other man returning to find them talking.

"I'm thirsty." Although her eyes were burning from the smoke, she looked up at him the way Amanda did whenever she was luring a hapless male victim into her sticky, dangerous web. "I don't suppose you have any water?"

"I'm not supposed to talk to you."

"It must get old." She shook her head regretfully on the bare mattress that was undoubtedly crawling with all sorts of creepy disgusting things she didn't want to think about. "Having Jimmy tell you what to do."

"He isn't the boss of me."

"Isn't he?" she asked sweetly. "He certainly seems to be running the show. You're not the one taking the important phone call right now, are you?"

"That's because someone has to be in charge."

"Of course." She suspected he was parroting Jimmy and hoped that somewhere, perhaps deep inside him, he'd harbor a bit of resentment. "But why can't it be you?"

"Because it's always Jimmy."

"Why?"

"Why what?" He looked confused.

"Why has Jimmy always been the one in charge?"

"Because I'm dumb. Jimmy's the smart one. He even goes to college."

"Really." She couldn't quite keep the skepticism from her voice.

"He does," he insisted. "UCLA."

Even as she realized he'd just given her a clue, Julia's mind whirled. Could these men have actually followed her here from Los Angeles? Was one of them her stalker? That didn't make sense, since Jimmy was obviously working for someone. Maybe her stalker? Since when did stalkers hire accomplices?

Perhaps she was being held for ransom. It wasn't an impossible idea. Considering all the press her movie contract had gotten, perhaps someone had decided the studio would be willing to pay big bucks to get her back. Which just went to show what they knew about Hollywood. If she wasn't in Kathmandu on time, the producer would replace her quicker than you could say "Bond. James Bond."

She thought back on what Finn had told her about Charles assuring his father that he'd have her on board for a sixth season. Surely he wouldn't risk prison just to keep her from getting on that plane so she'd lose the Carma Sutra role and, in his mind, have to return to *River Road*. Would he?

Deciding to sort all this out later, once she was free, she turned her thoughts back to escaping. "Well, he might go to college, but you're definitely the handsome one," she purred, drawing forth a blush that shone like hot coals in the dim sooty light. "Besides, I think you're selling yourself short in the brains department."

"You do?"

"Oh, I certainly do, sugar. Personally, it seems to me that you're every bit as smart as Jimmy. Even smarter."

"He's always been the smart one," he said doggedly. "And I've always been dumb. In school he could figure out the letters in the books, but they always looked screwed up to me."

"That doesn't make you dumb." Obviously this man was not her letter writer. "Only dyslexic."

He frowned. "What's that?"

"It's a disorder that makes it difficult to read. Didn't anyone ever test you?"

"Got tests," he muttered. "Failed 'em all, which is why I dropped out in the eighth grade. It just got to be a bummer, you know?"

"I can imagine," she said, her voice oozing with sympathy. "But it really is a very real condition that interferes with the ability to recognize written words. We did an episode on the subject just last season."

"Hey, I saw that." She could practically see the cartoon lightbulb flash on over his head. "You had a one-night fling with that guy you met when your Jag crunched his minivan. The one who taught special ed classes."

Julia didn't point out that it had been her character who'd had the steamy one-night stand. If he was blurring the lines, so much the better.

"You know," she said conversationally, "this situation reminds me of an episode we did two seasons ago. Maybe you saw it—the one where I was kidnapped aboard an alien's mothership?"

"Yeah. Wow. You were really sexy when you were showing that outer space guy where to touch a woman."

"Thank you." She shifted a bit on the mattress, arching her back as best she could, drawing attention to her breasts which, thanks to the corset Audrey had lashed her into this morning, appeared nearly as lush as a Playmate's.

"My arms are getting so horribly sore," she complained. "Can't you untie me just for a minute so I can get my circulation back?"

"Jimmy said you had to stay tied up until we get the order to let you go."

Her spirits took a nosedive at the thought of staying tied up for days. Julia resolutely pulled them back up. "So Jimmy isn't the one giving the orders? Does this other man have a name?"

"Well, sure he does. Everyone has a name."

"Would you happen to know what it is?"

"Jimmy didn't tell me. And I didn't ask, since it's none of my business. Knowing stuff gets you in trouble, like when my pals Sam and Matt decided to hit that 7-Eleven and shot the clerk. I wasn't even there when they did it, but because I'm the one who bought Sam the damn gun, the DA sent me to prison as a co-conspirator. So now I'm out and all I want is enough money to buy me a car. The bus service in L.A. really sucks. I've got my eye on a lime green Charger I figure I can fix up and run at the drags."

Terrific. She was being held hostage for a nineteen seventies muscle car. "Why would anyone hire you and Jimmy to kidnap me and keep me here?"

"I don't know. I just do what Jimmy tells me to do. Then I can't get arrested, 'cause I don't know nothing."

"Surely you must have overheard something. Perhaps I can help out your memory," Amanda suggested silkily.

"Nah. I don't think so."

"Oh, I think I could, sugar," she drawled, tossing in a little Lorelei Fairchild. That belle routine had worked gangbusters with Warren, who was so far beyond this man in intelligence they could have been born on different planets.

"How do you figure to help my memory when I don't got one in the first place?" He was clearly tempted. He also knew something he wasn't saying. Every time he lied to her, his eyes went darting all over the room like nervous birds trying to escape.

"Sometimes we have things in our minds, but we just have to know the way to get them out. Why don't we play a little game?" Her lush tone and come-and-get-me-big-boy gaze returned his attention to her.

His broad brow furrowed. "What kinda game?"

"It's like Truth or Dare, but with a twist. We ask each other questions, and if you guess the answer, I have to give you a kiss. If I answer yours, you get to kiss me."

He folded his arms across his chest. "That's all we're talkin' about?" His eyes narrowed to slits. "Just a kiss?"

Deciding he might not be quite as dumb as she'd first suspected, Amanda smiled her most dazzling smile. "Just for starters. It's like *Jeopardy*."

"Don't watch *Jeopardy*. I like that millionaire show, 'cause you got more time to answer the questions."

"We'll play like that one, then," she assured him. "The more questions you answer, the more you win."

She was looking up at him through the fringe of lashes Damien had darkened with several layers of mascara. Had that been only this morning?

"Guess that sounds like an okay deal."

More than okay; she could see the anticipation glowing in his lust-filled eyes.

"Doesn't it?" Amanda could be slick, aggressive, shrewd and decidedly mercenary. Even, on occasion, under the right circumstances and the proper motivation, kittenish. But she was definitely at her best when she turned meltingly, implicitly sexual. "So, if you'll just be a sweetheart and untie me—"

"Maybe I don't want to. I've never fucked a woman when she was tied up before. It'd be just like bein' one of them porn stars. Sometimes I think I could be real good at that. Mr. Timex is just as big as them on the videos."

Julia categorically refused to ask.

"Don't you wanna know why I call my johnson Mr. Timex?" he asked slyly.

If there was any bit of information she could go her entire life without learning, it was why this swamp creature had named his penis. Damn. "Only if you want to tell me, sugar," Amanda cooed.

" 'Cause it takes a lickin' and keeps on tickin'." He winked and put his hand on the crotch of the filthy jeans he must have changed into after discarding that scratchy wool uniform. "Which you're about to find out."

"Now, doesn't that sound like fun?" It was all she could do not to throw up at the idea. "But this bed is awful narrow and I'll bet the springs just squeak to beat the band, which doesn't bother me all that much, since all my attention's going to be on giving you a good time. But you might not want Jimmy to hear what's goin' on in here."

She watched the wheels grind exceedingly slowly as he followed that thought to its logical conclusion. If she couldn't get this idiot to untie her soon, Jimmy would finish his conversation with whoever had hatched this plot and she'd lose her chance to escape.

"If I untie you, you gotta promise me you won't try to escape," he finally decided.

"Oh, I surely do," she said. "In fact, I'd cross my heart, if my hand was free." She forced an Amanda smile she had never felt less like in her life.

She nearly wept with relief when it turned out that whoever had tied her had used a basic slip knot, which allowed the rope to loosen swiftly. She took a breath that was meant to calm, tried to remember what her ninjitsu master had taught her about staying centered, then stood up on legs that were decidedly wobbly.

She skimmed her fingers over his prickly jaw, around his chin, managing to dodge the mouth that had been aimed for hers. The idea of this man kissing her nearly made her gag, but Julia reminded herself that it was only acting, something she did every day.

Her hands continued down his chest. She toyed teasingly with his belt buckle, then knelt in front of him. He was watching her with a fixed, unblinking look that reminded her of an alligator watching a nutria.

She could do this. It was only acting.

She unfastened the buckle, and slid the stiff, stained denim down his thin legs. Mr. Timex stirred beneath the yellowed white cotton briefs. Drawing in a calming breath, Julia drew the briefs down his legs.

She cast a cautious glance up at him. He'd closed his eyes, waiting. Anticipating. His pants were down around his ankles, like shackles.

It was now or never. She took another deep breath, then found her center, aligning herself as she'd been taught—mind, heart, will, and intention. Then she jerked on his ankles, pulling him off his feet in a move that might not be textbook ninjitsu, but effective.

He landed flat on his back with a thud, causing Julia to cringe when the back of his head connected with the cypress planks, and she hoped she hadn't killed him. She was relieved when she pressed her fingers against his throat and found a pulse, then used his belt to hog-tie him. It was nearly the same ploy Amanda had used to escape that horny alien. When she got out of here, Julia was going to kiss Warren for having written it.

She opened the door gingerly, relieved when it didn't squeak. She couldn't see Jimmy, but could hear his voice coming from the shadows around the corner of the cabin. He was arguing loudly, and from his tone, she suspected he was not coming out on the winning side.

"If you're not going to get out here and take the bitch off our hands, I'll just take care of the problem myself," he shouted.

Julia suspected that his method of taking care of "the problem" would not be a good thing.

She'd practiced the ancient act of silent walking in her classes, though she'd never expected to use it, and she was extremely grateful for her training as she slipped through the shadows away from the cabin. Whenever she stepped on a branch or accidently splashed through water, she reminded herself that her instructor had taught her that some noise was all right. After all, nature was not entirely still.

While she had no way of knowing where she was or where she was going, she did know that she didn't want to be out here all alone when the sun, which was a great deal lower in the sky now, went down.

Her actions might be considered foolhardy, but taking her chances with the bayou seemed far preferable to trusting Jimmy to release her.

Once she was about a hundred yards from the cabin, she began to move slowly, cautiously, down the narrow road, cringing at the crunching sound of her nineteenth-century slippers on the clamshell gravel. But to leave the road would be risking sinking into the swamp.

"It'll be okay," she assured herself, stifling a scream as a gator floated past her in the dark, silent water. They definitely looked less threatening out at Beau Soleil, when she was surrounded by people. And, of course, when she was with Finn, who had his gun and could shoot one dead if it decided to eat her.

Finn—he was going to be frantic. And, she feared, furious at himself. Then there were her parents. She'd wanted to save them from worrying; now they had something far worse to be concerned about.

She'd have to make it up to them when she got back to Blue Bayou safe and sound. And she would be all right, Julia insisted. Because the alternative was unthinkable.

# 28

*"There's something funny going on,"* Finn said to his brothers when they'd gathered to devise a new plan. There were miles of swamp; locating Julia once it turned dark would be like finding the proverbial needle in the haystack.

"What's that?" Nate glugged from a plastic bottle of water, then wiped his mouth with the back of his hand. Despite the ominous dark clouds gathering overhead, searching was hot, sweaty work.

"Nearly every guy, and a lot of the women, too, have been dragging their asses all over this place today." Even that magenta-haired make-up guy had stripped off today's skintight purple leather pants, changed into some uniform trousers Audrey had given him, and had hardly stopped long enough to take a piss.

"It's not surprising that we'd have so many volunteers. It's obvious everyone likes Jules," Nate said. "With good reason."

"Kendall hasn't joined the search." Finn said what had been nagging at his mind for the past couple hours. Nate and Jack glanced over at the producer, who was away from the others, talking into a cell phone. Which wasn't unusual; his ear had been practically glued to the thing since he'd arrived in Blue Bayou. Nor was his obvious irritation with whoever was on the other end of the line unusual; he'd already demonstrated himself to be impatient and unpleasant.

"He's not in real good shape," Jack said. "I'm not sure he'd last five minutes."

"And he hasn't seemed like the type to put himself out for anyone else," Nate said.

"True enough. But you'd still think he'd at least pretend to show some concern."

"Are you suggesting he has something to do with this?" Nate asked. "That doesn't make any sense. She's too important to the show."

"The show just wrapped for the season," Finn pointed out. "And she's not coming back."

Nate frowned. "All the more reason why he's not a real strong suspect. He doesn't have a dog in this fight anymore."

"How about insurance?" Jack asked. "Does the show carry a policy on her?"

"Yeah." Finn had already looked it up the night he'd found out about the cat pills. "A million dollars, which is chicken feed for a place like Atlantic Pharmaceuticals. It runs out the same time her contract does. Tomorrow."

Jack blew out a breath. "I've seen people killed for a lot less back when I was workin' DEA."

They both had.

*We'll find her,* Finn vowed. As they resumed searching, he found himself desperately praying to a God he'd thought he'd stopped believing in sometime between Lawson's fifth and sixth victims.

The sun was blood red and going down as Julia came around a corner and saw the building. It was weathered, the paint was peeling, the metal roof rusted, and the plank door had been faded by time and sun to a dingy rust color. It was the most beautiful thing she'd ever seen.

She muttered a heartfelt "damn" when her skirt caught on a bush, causing her to fall to her knees. Again. Fighting back tears—she couldn't waste energy on anything that wasn't going to get her back to Blue Bayou, to Finn—she pushed herself to her feet and resumed stumbling toward it.

The interior of the building was dark and cheerless, smelling of sawdust and despair. A tall, lean African-American man who didn't look at all suited to such a depressing place stood behind the bar. Behind him on the wall were dark bottles, dim lamps and dusty bottles of wine. And a baseball bat, which she assumed he must use to keep order.

Not that it appeared any of the bar's clientele was capable of causing any trouble. Hunched over their drinks, they looked as if life had defeated them and they were just waiting for the final bell. There were a few muttered complaints as the sun entered with her, then most went back to contemplating the universe in their glasses, as if answers could be found in the brown depths of whiskey.

Strangely, now that she was reasonably safe, fright came crashing down on her. The whippet-slender man came out from behind the bar in seconds, catching her shoulders with firm, capable hands as she swayed.

"Please," she managed. She'd put her teeth through her bottom lip during one of her many falls, and suspected it must be terribly swollen by the way she had trouble getting the single word out. She swallowed and tried again. "May I use your phone?"

Finn found her safe, thank God, in the tiny room the bartender of the No Name called an office. She was sitting on a cracked vinyl couch that looked as ancient and abused as the men who were sitting on stools out in the bar, cradling a cup of tea in her hands. Her hair was a wild, matted tangle around her shoulders, her dress was torn and muddy, and more mud and bruises darkened her face and arms. She'd never looked more beautiful to him.

"Carma Sutra, I presume?" he asked with a calm that belied his pounding heart.

"It's about time you showed up, Special Agent," she said with the same feigned casualness. There'd been no disguising the joy and relief that had flooded into her eyes, the same joy and relief that had swept over him.

"Are you all right?" He sat down beside her and cupped his hands over her shoulders. Her face was scratched and a large bruise in the shape of a handprint darkened her cheek, infuriating him.

"I am now." She lifted a hand to the cheek of this man she loved. "Because you're here."

She managed to give him an edited version of events. There was no point in bringing up the details about her undressing her captor; it wasn't germane to their situation.

He called the state police on his cell phone, gave them the new location to search, then tipped her face back, a finger under her chin. "I should have been there for you." His touch was tender, but a fury hot enough to melt glass blazed in his eyes. "In the swamp."

"You're here now." She curled her fingers around his wrist, and lay her throbbing cheek against his palm. "That's all that matters." She sighed. "I don't suppose they're at the cabin anymore."

"Probably not. But it doesn't matter: they're not going to be able to get away with every cop in the state looking for them. And when we find them, I'll get them to tell me who hired them."

Looking at his face, Julia didn't want to think about how he'd conduct that interrogation. "I know you're angry—"

"That's putting it mildly."

"—but you have to promise me you won't bring out the rubber hoses." She was kidding. Mostly. "If not for me, for your own career. You're just coming off suspension, Callahan. I'd hate to be responsible for your losing your shield for good."

"I'll try to restrain myself. For you."

He kissed her on the brow. Julia could feel the anger in him slowly fading away, just as the fear that had left her feeling so shaky began to dissolve. It was so good to be with him. Amazingly, and as impossible as she would have thought it a mere two weeks ago, they were good together.

The sight of her being carried out of the office and across the floor garnered the attention of every grizzled barfly in the place.

"You don't have to do this," she insisted. "I can walk."

"Of course you can. But maybe I like the idea of sweeping you off your feet."

"Why, gracious, Special Agent, are you suggesting that there's a romantic lurking inside that big, manly body?"

"I guess there is now."

He paused just long enough to introduce her to the man behind the bar, Alcèe Bonaparte, who was a childhood friend of all the Callahan brothers. Then took her outside to the Suburban and buckled her up with the tenderness and care one might expect for a precious child.

"By the way," he said mildly, "I had Nate move your stuff from the inn to Beau Soleil. I want to keep you under wraps until it's time to put you on the plane."

There'd been a time when Julia might have considered his behavior highhanded. No longer. "Are you sure it'll be okay with your brother and his wife?"

"Actually, it was Jack's idea, and Dani was all for it. They just got back this afternoon." He twisted the key in the ignition. Then turned toward her. "Damn."

"What's wrong?"

"I forgot something."

He was looking at her that way again. That hot, bone-melting way she knew would still possess the power to thrill her in her nineties, when the only Bond Girl role she'd be able to win would be 007's grandmother.

"What?" she asked in a whisper as her mouth went dry.

"This." He bent his head and kissed her with the slow, deep reassurance they both needed.

Peace wept openly when Finn returned her daughter to her, safe and sound. Freedom's eyes gleamed with moisture.

"I owe you, man." He held out his hand and in the handshake that followed, both men knew their previously cautious relationship had just been cemented.

Finn introduced her to the rest of his family. She could see both Nate and Finn in Jack, but this middle brother was edgier, his eyes darker, cheekbones sharper, his personality seemingly roughly honed. His flowing black hair had been pulled back into a ponytail which, along with his gleaming gold earring and rakish grin, had her thinking of the pirates that had once hidden out in this bayou after raiding Spanish ships on the Gulf.

His embrace was so easy, so natural, that Julia suspected he was a toucher. There was nothing sexual in the gesture, and as he introduced her to his wife, it was obvious that Danielle Dupree Callahan was the only woman in the world for him. Love, devotion, and pride radiated from every male pore.

Dani was slender, with warm hazel eyes and a slide of blond hair that stopped at her shoulders. "I'm so pleased you'll be staying with us," she said with a welcoming smile. "Jack and I thought you'd like our room." When Julia started to protest, she held up her hand. "I insist. As you no doubt noticed while you were filming in the house, the upstairs is still in what will undoubtedly be a lifetime renovation, and the guest room is filled with paint cans. Besides, my clever husband installed a bathtub I suspect would be considered decadent even in Hollywood."

Julia was filthy, sore, and felt like something that had been dragged out of the swamp. The tub clinched it. "That sounds wonderful."

While Julia, Peace, and Dani chatted about house renovations, Finn checked out the group who'd gathered for her return. They all seemed openly and honestly relieved, including Kendall. Which left Finn without a suspect.

Even as he assured himself that Julia would be safe once she was on the way to Kathmandu, Finn knew he wouldn't feel comfortable until whoever had orchestrated the kidnapping was behind bars. But meanwhile, Lawson was out there . . .

Once again he was forced to wonder if Lawson had come after him, and decided to use Julia as a pawn. That idea was gaining more credence when a slight movement behind one of the tombs got his attention.

"Shit! I knew it," he shouted. "Take Julia into the house and stay with her," he instructed Nate as he sprinted toward the cemetery, Jack right on his heels.

"What on earth?" Julia stared after them.

"I guess he just cracked the case," Nate said with what Julia found to be amazing aplomb under the circumstances.

When he put his hand beneath her elbow to usher her into Beau Soleil, she shook off the light touch. "Whatever's happening, I want to watch."

"The back upstairs windows look out onto the cemetery," Dani said. "You can watch from there, so Finn won't be distracted worrying about you."

Remembering that wicked looking scar on his thigh, Julia allowed herself to be convinced. She'd no sooner entered the house when the threatening sky opened up.

"What if whoever it is has a gun?" Julia fretted.

"If he tries to use it, he's in trouble. Finn's a crack shot," Nate assured her. "He and Jack used to have quick draw shootouts with cap pistols when they were kids. Jack was fast, but Finn was like lightning."

Real guns were a long way from cap pistols. Dear God, surely they weren't going to have a shootout in Blue Bayou's cemetery? Even Warren wouldn't have come up with such a thing.

Julia dragged her hands down her wet face, then leaned forward, trying to see him through the thick gray curtain of falling rain.

# 29

*Where the hell was she?* Finn ran through the cemetery, rain blinding his vision, knowing that if he failed, the hunter who'd been stalking Julia and arranged to have her kidnapped would return another day, more determined than ever. Even more focused on his prey.

When he caught a glimpse of a bit of black dodging around a marble obelisk, he lifted the Glock, prepared to shoot, when a chip of marble blew off the wing of the angel atop the tomb behind him. Finn dodged behind it.

"Nothing like an old-fashioned gunfight to get the blood racing," Jack said conversationally as he joined his brother behind the tomb. "Do we know who we're chasing?"

"No. But if she's really an old lady, I'll eat my shield." He took a deep breath. "On the count of three."

"Got it," Jack agreed.

"One . . . two . . . three." Finn darted out, bending low as he charged the obelisk, Jack right beside him, just like back when they'd been kids.

The extra who was once again dressed in widow's mourning lifted her heavy skirts and began running across the sodden turf, past the tomb of Andre Dupree, who'd won Beau Soleil in a bourré game before the War Between the States. The two Callahan brothers chased after him, beginning to close the gap.

"FBI," Finn shouted. "Stop or I'll shoot." It might sound like a television show cliché, but once in a blue moon it worked. He also wanted to be sure he identified himself as a law officer if he ended up shooting the guy. Which seemed like a damn good idea right about now.

He was close enough he could hear the shooter's labored breathing. It was down to inches. Finn reached out the hand that wasn't holding the pistol, his fingers brushing black taffeta. The guy tried to dodge a low black iron fence around a pair of gravestones and slipped on the wet ground. As he struggled for his footing, Finn launched himself airborne, the same way he had gone over the opposing team's defensive line for a touchdown back at LSU.

They went down together. When the shooter's gun skittered across the gravel, Finn kicked it out of reach. Then he put the barrel of his own Glock, the backup piece to the one he'd had to hand over to Jansen, against the attacker's temple.

"Maybe you didn't hear me," he said. "I said to stop."

"Fuck you," the male voice shot back.

"I think I'll pass," Finn ripped off the jet bonnet and the gray wig, grabbed hold of the short hair, and slammed the shooter's face against the ground. "But I bet there'll be lots of guys up at Angola who'll be more than happy to take you up on the invitation."

He pulled a pair of the handcuffs he was never without from his pocket, yanked the man's hands behind his back, and captured his wrists.

"Nothing like the satisfying click of metal on metal," Jack said approvingly.

"You can say that again. Now, here's what we're going to do," Finn told the man lying beneath him. "I'm going to read you your rights. Then we're going to get up. And if I were you, I wouldn't try anything funny, because I'm really pissed off at bad guys in general these days, super pissed at cretins who get their rocks off hurting women, and you can't even imagine, in your worst and darkest nightmares, how pissed I am at you in particular, and how I'd love an excuse to blow your head off."

"You wouldn't dare," the man said. "Not with all these witnesses."

"Want to bet?" Finn countered. "Maybe you aren't tapped into the Blue Bayou gossip line, 'cause if you were, you would have heard that I'm on disciplinary suspension for beating up a perp. I probably would have killed him, but two FBI agents, a Maryland State trooper, and a court-appointed shrink managed to pull me off him before I could."

Finn's emotions, usually so steady, were on a hair trigger. "Get up." He jerked his prisoner to his feet, aimed the pistol directly at the center of his back, and pushed him forward.

As frightened as Julia had been to find herself tied up in that cabin, it was nothing compared to hearing the sound of gunshots from Blue Bayou's cemetery. Despite Nate's assurance that his brother would be all right, Julia was flooded with relief when she saw the trio headed toward the house. She flew down the stairs and out the door, heedless of the rain.

"Are you all right?" She raced to Finn, intending to throw her arms around his neck, but was stopped by the sight of the treacherous pistol in his hand.

"I'm fine. But I'll be a lot better when this creep's behind bars."

She took a closer look at the woman clad in black mourning. "Graham? Is that really you?" With the wig and bonnet off, it certainly looked like him. "What on earth are you doing here?"

"What do you think I was doing?" Graham Sheffield asked peevishly. "I was protecting my property."

"Property?" Julia stared at his face and wondered why she hadn't seen through the makeup and women's clothing to the man who'd proposed on their first date. Perhaps because her mind had been so filled with Finn.

"You're mine, Julia. You've always been mine. And you knew it, too, or you wouldn't have slept with me."

Hell. If she'd known he was going to bring that up, Julia might have wished for Finn to shoot him back in the cemetery.

"I knew we were meant to be together the first time I tuned into *River Road* and saw you making love to that ski instructor in the hot tub at the resort. I knew he wasn't good enough for you. Which he proved by blackmailing you a few months later."

"Graham, that was Amanda."

"Well, of course it was," he huffed. "I can tell the difference. I am, after all, your number one fan."

Her heart hitched as the reality hit home. "It was you who sent me those letters?" Something else clicked in. "That's why they stopped coming after I came and talked to your class."

"Of course. I didn't have to write anymore, because you were in my life. Where you belonged." His eyes narrowed. "Where you still belong. I love you, and although you may have problems with commitment, you know you love me. I want us to spend the rest of our lives together."

"Great way you had of showing it," Finn said as a pair of cop cars arrived, lights flashing, sirens screaming. "Having a woman kidnapped and held hostage in some filthy cabin is not the way to get her to fall in love with you."

"I needed time alone with Julia, away from distractions. So I could convince her that we're soulmates." Despite the fact he was covered in mud, despite his hands being handcuffed behind his back, his voice slid back into that patronizing royal tone that she suspected his British ancestors had used with their serfs. "And, of course, I couldn't let her leave for Kathmandu."

"Because you'd stand out like a sore thumb if you tried to stalk her there," Jack said.

"Watch over her," Graham corrected stiffly. "I am not a common stalker."

"Who were those men?" Julia asked.

"James was one of my students. The other one was his brother."

"A brother who'd served prison time for conspiracy in an armed robbery and shooting." Julia's temper flared.

"James didn't mention that," he said defensively.

"Did it ever occur to you that you were putting me at a terrible risk?"

"Of course I realized there was an outside chance of your being injured, but then I could have taken you back to L.A. and cared for you."

"And if I'd died?" How had she not noticed how mentally disturbed Graham was? "Did you think of that?"

"Naturally. But that was a risk I was prepared to take."

Julia shoved wet curls out of her eyes. "*You* were prepared to take? What makes you think you had any right to play with my life?"

"You belong to me," he insisted yet again. "If you were too stupid or stubborn to realize it, then you deserved whatever happened."

"If you couldn't have her, no one could," Finn said. Unfortunately, he'd seen that mind-set before.

The professor nodded, as if the idea was perfectly rational. "Indeed."

"By the time you get out of prison, you're going to forget what a woman is," Finn said. "I'm going to make sure the DAs here and back in California throw the book at you. We're talking stalking, kidnapping, assault with a deadly weapon—"

"It's an air gun," Graham sniffed. "I would think any law enforcement officer worth his salt should be able to tell the difference."

"Sure I can. It's a Webley Nemesis. I suppose you thought you were being cute, choosing a model named for the Greek goddess of retribution."

"It seemed appropriate," Graham agreed. "Under the circumstances."

Finn shook his head and cursed softly. "You're also looking at attempted murder of a police officer, along with a shitload of other possible charges, including littering since there are pellets all over the cemetery."

"You know, you could save two states a lot of money by just feeding the bastard to the gators," Jack suggested.

"That's not such a bad idea." Finn rubbed his jaw.

"You wouldn't dare." Graham's tone lacked conviction and for the first time, his situation seemed to hit home.

"Want to bet?"

"You're an FBI Special Agent. You can't just assassinate someone."

"Relax, Sheffield. I'm not going to kill you. But only because you're not worth the trouble it'd cause me." He reached into the pocket of his wet jeans, dug out his car keys, and tossed them to Jack. "Why don't you put this guy in the Suburban and we can take him to the state cops in Baton Rouge?"

"Works for me," Jack said. Finn knew his brother had made the right decision to get out of the DEA after the near-fatal shooting that had taken the life of his partner, along with a lot of other innocent people. But it was obvious that Jack was enjoying playing cops and robbers again.

Finn took Julia aside. Excitement over for now, the others went back into the house, giving them some privacy. "I noticed you didn't exactly jump in and beg me not to shoot him," he said as they watched Jack walk Sheffield toward the SUV.

"That's because I wasn't worried. You promised me you wouldn't resort to unnecessary violence. And you're a good man who takes your oath to uphold justice seriously."

Despite the seriousness of what had happened, Finn felt himself smiling. "This from the woman who thinks cops are lower than pond scum."

"I may have been a little misguided about that."

"May have been?"

"All right. I was wrong. It's obvious that you and your brother are two of the good guys." Graham was now in the back seat of the Suburban. "Why are you taking him all the way to Baton Rouge? Doesn't Blue Bayou have a jail?"

"Sure. But since the department currently consists of one grandmotherly dispatcher, who sits behind the desk and crochets afghans, a deputy on the long side of seventy, and another fresh out of college who's as green as new grass, the jail's mostly being used as a place for drunks to sleep it off. Oh, and last month Jack and Dani's daughter Holly had a sleepover in the cells."

"Well, that does it. You have no right to make any more cracks against life on the commune, since a slumber party in a jail is more off-the-wall than anything my parents ever came up with."

"It was all Jack's idea. He's pretty much reformed since he and Dani got back together, but there's still a streak of bad boy in him."

"Lucky Dani."

"Jack's the lucky one. Fortunately, he knows it."

"That's nice." She'd always been a sucker for a love story. Which was probably partly how she'd ended up on a soap.

As the rain began to pick up again, they stood there, Julia looking up at Finn, him looking down at her. They were drenched to the skin but neither noticed. She felt the heat rise and wouldn't have been surprised if they'd been engulfed in clouds of steam.

"I don't suppose, after all you've been through, that you'd feel like going into New Orleans tonight?" he asked.

In all honesty, she'd rather take a long hot bubble bath to wash the swamp from her hair and skin, and then spend the night in bed with him. But then it occurred to her that Finn was a very traditional man. Perhaps he was taking her out for a night on the town to tell her, on her last night in Blue Bayou, how much he loved her. To tell her he couldn't live without her. Maybe even, she thought with a secret thrill, to propose.

"I'd love that," she agreed as heady anticipation sang like a siren's song in her blood.

The bathtub might not be true to the antebellum period, but it was wonderfully hedonistic. Julia soaked for a long time in the perfumed water, breathing in the fresh, fragrant sea mist scent of candles and luxuriating as the Jacuzzi jets bubbled away her aches and pains.

Not wanting to keep Finn waiting when he and Jack got back from

Baton Rouge, she finally forced herself to abandon the bliss of the tub and was sitting at a skirted dressing table, putting on her makeup, while her mother perched on the edge of the antique bed.

Having packed only that one outrageously bare Amanda cocktail dress she'd worn to the parish council welcome party and casual clothes, Julia had been trying to figure out what she was going to wear for what might turn out to be the most important night of her life, when Dani had offered to lend her a dress she'd brought home from Hawaii. Made of gleaming white silk ablaze with scarlet poppies, it was a dress made for celebration. For seduction. It was hanging on the back of the closet door, a colorful promise of the night to come.

"I love him, Mama," Julia said.

"I know darling," Peace said gently. Julia had been grateful when Dani had insisted her parents spend the night at Beau Soleil so they could all have some time together before Julia left the country. "I was fairly sure when we talked on the phone while your father and I were still in Coldwater Cove. It was obvious the moment I saw you."

"Well, it sure wasn't obvious to me."

"Perhaps you were in denial, since Finn's so different from all those men you'd tried to love."

"Perhaps," Julia allowed. Deciding to forgo blush since her cheeks were already flushed with the heat of the bath and anticipation, she smoothed some taupe shadow on her eyelids. "But it certainly hit home when I realized I might never see him again."

The idea had struck, while she'd been stumbling through the swamp, with such a clarion ring of certainty, she'd been amazed that she hadn't seen it coming. "I've been trying to tell myself that the only reason I responded to Finn so strongly was because he was an FBI Special Agent."

"Because Finn was an agent, you automatically saw him as an enemy?"

"I felt that way at the time." Now she realized that she'd needed to dislike him because the alternative of such a strong initial reaction would have been to fall in love with him. Which she'd gone ahead and done.

"I'd hoped we taught you more tolerance," Peace chided softly.

"It wasn't just me," Julia muttered. She took a sip of the herbal tea her mother had brewed. "Finn wasn't exactly flattering toward any of us."

"Nor your father toward him," Peace admitted. "Believe me, you would not have wanted to be in the bus with Freedom on the drive down here. Fortunately, they seem to have found a common ground in their love for you."

"Do you really think Finn loves me?"

"Absolutely." Julia would have felt more positive about her mother's declaration if it hadn't been accompanied by such a serious expression. "But I'm not that sure he's ready to accept the idea yet. And he's an incredibly stubborn man. Which is another thing he has in common with your father.

"It wasn't easy convincing Freedom that he was not going to ruin my life by taking me away from my wealthy, pampered, lonely existence. Of course he was also trying to protect his own heart, afraid I'd run back to Daddy at the first little problem." She took a blue stone from a small box. "This is the same love-enhancer stone I used to help your father see the light. It's been waiting all these years for you and Finn."

Although she didn't quite believe in magic spells and potions, Julia could have sworn her palm warmed when she held the lapis lazuli in her hand.

She'd just finished dressing when Dani came into the bedroom. "Wow," she said. "My poor brother-in-law is a goner."

"It's the dress. It's wonderful." Julia twirled on strappy red sandals with ice pick heels, causing the short skirt to flare around her thighs. The halter top dipped below the waist in back; and crystal earrings brushed her bare shoulders.

"The dress is gorgeous, and it fits as if it was designed with you in mind. If you're planning to entice Finn into proposing, you're definitely wearing the right ammunition."

"Is it that obvious?"

"Only to a woman who's been there recently." Dani exchanged a smile with Peace, who was beaming with maternal benevolence. "I'm so pleased for you and Finn. He's a good man. Strong, solid, steady. What you see is what you get."

"Not always," Julia murmured.

Dani nodded, seeming pleased with that assessment. "So he's let you in."

"A little. He's not an easy nut to crack."

"No, I imagine he wouldn't be. I also imagine the effort will be well worth it, in the long run. I hope you don't mind me telling you that there were times I wished I could fall in love with him."

"But you couldn't."

"No. Oh, I dearly love Finn, but it's the same way I do Nate. As brothers. My heart's always belonged to Jack."

"You're a lucky woman."

"Boy, do I know that. Though Jack sure didn't make it easy. But I suppose anything—or anyone—worth having is worth a little effort."

The front door slammed. "Hey, Mom," a young voice called out. "Guess what me and Holly did while you were gone."

"I'll be downstairs in a second, darling." Dani's smile touched her eyes, revealing gold flecks in the soft hazel. "Looks as if the honeymoon's over; it's time to return to real life. I'm so glad to have met you, Julia. We'll have to make sure we have lots more time to visit when you return to Blue Bayou."

"I'd like that. Oh, and I hate to argue, when you've so generously given up your room and lent me this drop-dead gorgeous dress, but I think you're wrong about something."

Dani lifted a blond brow. "Oh?"

"I'd say your honeymoon's not likely to ever be over."

"What a lovely thing to say. I'm going to have to thank Finn for the gift of such a wonderful sister." Dani hugged her, exchanged another smile with Peace, then left the room.

"Holly and *I*," Julia heard her correcting her son as she went down the curving staircase to the first floor. "Come into the kitchen and we can make some fudge while you catch me up on everything."

"Holly's got a boyfriend . . ."

"I do not," a teenage girl's voice countered. "We're just friends."

The conversation faded as the kitchen door closed behind the family trio. Julia had been too focused on her career these past years to really think about children. But now that she was in love, she definitely wanted to have children with Finn. Someday.

There was no point in rushing things, she reminded herself. After all, Finn hadn't even broached the L word, except for that evening she'd talked him into going shopping, and he'd seemed appalled at the idea. She hoped that would all change tonight.

Thirty minutes later, Julia was growing impatient. How long did it take to drive into Baton Rouge and back?

Leaving her packing, she wandered out into the garden outside the ballroom. The long Southern day was finally drawing to a close; the perfume of roses and jasmine hung seductively on the still air.

She'd bent to sniff an unfurled scarlet rose when she realized she was no longer alone. She turned, the welcome smile fading on her face when it wasn't Finn, but one of the local movie crew. The snug T-shirt hugging a muscled chest read *Louisiana Lighting Lights Up Your Life*.

"Hello," she said, a little surprised. She'd thought everyone had packed up and left.

"Hey, Miz Summers." His voice was friendly, molasses thick with the sound of the South. "I didn't mean to bother you."

"You're not. I was just enjoying the sunset."

"Sure is a nice one," he said agreeably. "And this is a real pretty place to spend it." He gestured toward the rose she'd been smelling. "That'd look awfully nice in your hair. Go real well with your dress. Want me to cut it for you?"

"Oh, that's not necessary." She'd already taken Dani and Jack's bedroom; she wouldn't feel right about raiding their garden.

"No problem." He whipped a knife out of his pocket and moved toward her.

# 30

*"Damn, that sure as hell felt good,"* Jack said as he and Finn returned from Baton Rouge.

"Yeah. Not as good as putting my fist through the guy's face, but it's nice to know he's going to be spending a lot of years as a guest of the state."

"Maybe he can start a little theater group in Angola," Jack suggested. "That actor and his brother were something, weren't they?"

They'd been caught by a state trooper as they'd been racing for the Texas border. *"Dumb and Dumber,"* Finn agreed. "But the older one looked like he could be dangerous."

"Julia was smart to escape. Beauty and brains are a great combination." Jack grinned. "And I should know, having an exceptional woman of my own."

"Dani would have to be exceptional to put up with you. And yeah, Julia's pretty damn special, too."

"I sorta figured that out, since it'd take more than a drop-dead gorgeous face to bring my big brother down. So, are you gonna pop the question tonight?"

"No."

Jack shot him a surprised look. "Why not? It's obvious you're crazy about her. It's just as obvious she thinks you hung the moon. You're both single, unattached, available. And let's not forget she's leaving for Kathmandu in the morning."

"Which is only one of the reasons why I'm not going to ask her to marry me."

"Excuse me if I've got things a little confused. I'm still running on Hawaii time and probably a bit jet-lagged, not to mention worn out from days of hot, steamy sex with my bride on every private beach we could find.

"But while Nepal is admittedly not right around the corner, it's still on this planet and planes do fly there. Besides, it's not like she's going to be moving to the place permanently."

"It wouldn't work out."

"Christ, and Mom always thought you were the smart one. How do you figure that?"

"My life is with the Bureau. In D.C. Hers is in Los Angeles."

"Big deal. So get yourself transferred. I've no idea why you'd want to stay in the Bureau after the past few years, especially after what that Jansen woman did to you, but the FBI does have a field office in L.A. Or maybe you could just set up housekeeping somewhere in the middle."

"Like here?"

Jack shrugged. "It's a nice little town. A good place to raise a family."

"In the first place, I can't transfer to L.A. because I've got to track down Lawson. In the second place, I doubt the newest Bond Girl is real eager to start having kids."

"No reason to hurry," Jack said easily. "Have you even talked to her about it?"

"Hell, no."

"Then you have no way of knowing, do you?"

"We're too different."

"*Mais* yeah, you are. You're a man; she's a woman. It's what keeps life interesting, *cher*."

"She's rich."

"So am I. Probably a lot richer than her. And you're still willing to put up with me as a brother."

"I don't have any choice. You're family. I'm stuck with you. Besides, it's different when the woman has the money."

"Bullshit. I loved Dani when she was rich, I loved her when she was poor, thanks to that lying son of a bitch she let her daddy talk her into marrying, and I love her like crazy now. Money doesn't have a damn thing to do with it. Never knew you to be a quitter, you. Aren't you the one who was always tellin' Nate and me that obstacles were just opportunities in disguise?"

"That's what Dad used to say."

"And he was right," Jack said as they pulled up in front of Beau

Soleil. "The woman loves you, Finn, which is amazing, when you stop to think that she's one of the most gorgeous, soon-to-be famous females on the planet, and not only do you lack my smoldering dark good looks or Nate's boyish sex appeal, you can be a real pain in the ass sometimes."

"Thanks."

"If a brother won't be honest with you, who will? Don't let her walk away. Not without giving it your best shot. Because believe me, you could end up spending years regretting it."

Finn knew that Jack was speaking from personal experience. It had taken more than a dozen years for him and Dani to find their way back to Blue Bayou and each other. "I'm taking her out to dinner."

"That's a start. You goin' dancing, too?"

"Yeah. I figured we might."

"Good." He nodded approvingly. "Women like that. Not only is it the closest a guy can get to a female without gettin' horizontal, if you pop the question on the dance floor, she's less likely to turn you down, bein' how it's more public and all."

"I told you, I'm not popping any question. I'm in no position to get married, what with Lawson on the loose again."

"Nobody says you have to go to the altar tomorrow," Jack pointed out. "The idea is to make things official before she goes off to Kathmandu, meets some guy who isn't afraid of commitment, and gives up on you."

"I'm not afraid of commitment." It was Nate who'd rather go skinny-dipping in a bayou filled with hungry gators than allow himself to be tied down. "But I don't have any right to ask any woman to put her life on hold for however long it takes me to track Lawson down."

"I'm bettin' she'd be willing to wait."

"Maybe. But I don't want to force the issue and put her on the spot. Especially since we agreed going in to keep things casual."

"If you fight crime with the same speed, I'm amazed you ever get anyone behind bars."

"Good point. I sure as hell took too long with Lawson."

Jack grimaced. "Hell, that's not what I meant."

"I know." Finn sighed. "It's just proving real hard to put behind me. Especially now that the sick son of a bitch is on the loose again."

"You can't say the guy isn't providing you with job security."

"Yeah." The thought of resuming the hunt that had gobbled up his entire life for so long was goddamn depressing.

In a rotten mood for a guy in love, Finn went up to Jack and Dani's room, irritated to find Julia gone.

"She's in the garden off the ballroom," Dani told him. "At least she was, last I saw her."

Determined to make the most of their time together, Finn vowed to put Lawson out of his mind. At least for tonight.

Until he entered the country garden and saw the object of all his vexation chatting easily with Julia, who seemed unaware of the fact that the Brad Pitt look-alike holding that rose out to her was one of the most infamous murderers since Jack the Ripper.

Julia could not understand what was happening. One moment she was chatting pleasantly with the friendly lighting tech who'd cut a rose for her, the next she was being pulled against his chest, the glittering blade of a knife held against her throat.

"Hello, Special Agent Callahan," the man holding her drawled. "Fancy meeting you here."

"Funny. That's what I was about to say to you." Finn determinedly kept his voice calm even as banshees screeched in his head.

"It's such a small world, isn't it?" Ronald Lawson said pleasantly, as if they'd merely met in Beau Soleil's fragrant garden for an evening chat.

"And getting smaller by the moment. How about you let the lady go?"

"Surely you jest. And don't go making any heroic moves, Callahan. Or I'll slice her fragrant white throat."

Finn's remarkably calm eyes met Julia's. "How are you doing?"

Following his example, she struggled against rising hysteria. "I've had better days."

"Haven't we all," he murmured. "It's going to be all right."

Because it was Finn, Julia believed him. "I know."

"So it's true what they said on *Entertainment Tonight* about this being your woman?" Lawson asked.

"Yeah. And you harm one hair on her head and you're a dead man."

"Is that any way to talk to someone who's gone to so much trouble to come visit you?" Lawson's arm tightened around her; Julia fought the dizzying vertigo that was accompanied by a metallic taste of fear and forced herself to stay still. If she allowed herself to so much as tremble, she could die. "Besides, you're not exactly in a position to be making demands now, are you, Special Agent?"

"Let her go, Lawson. She doesn't have anything to do with this. It's between you and me."

"Just like old times. But there's one important difference now."

"And what's that?"

"Before, you didn't have any real weakness. Indeed, there were times when I wondered if you were even human, the way you kept doggedly tracking me, day and night, week after week, month after month. Bringing me down was all you appeared to cared about."

"It was."

"But now there's something else. Someone else. Which is what's going to make my revenge all the sweeter. When I first decided to escape, I was interested in only two things. Being free. And killing you. But now I've decided to let you live."

"That's real big of you."

"Thank you. I rather think so, as well. Unfortunately, you may not be so appreciative after you've watched what I have in mind for your girlfriend."

"Let her go," Finn repeated.

"Why would I want to do that? It's not as if I've anything to lose. I'm already under indictment for all those other killings."

"The reason you don't want to do it, is that whatever sick tortures you could possibly conceive will pale in comparison to what I'll do to you."

"You'll have to catch me first." The sly smirk in Lawson's voice turned Julia's stomach. "Besides, you'd never do anything outside the law. You're Mr. Black and White, go-by-the-book, law-and-order Special Agent."

"I'm not a Special Agent anymore."

"Of course you're not. And I'm not one of the country's Ten Most Wanted."

"It's true." Finn held up a broad hand. "I'm just going for my wallet here. So, don't go getting upset or jumpy or anything."

"I'm not at all upset. Actually, I'm almost giddy with anticipation."

Finn pulled his wallet from his jeans and flipped it open. "See. No shield."

Lawson's eyes narrowed. "Mary Hart didn't say anything about your quitting the FBI."

"Obviously she doesn't have the latest scoop, which isn't all that surprising, since *Entertainment Tonight* isn't exactly investigative hard news. So, is that how you knew where to find me?"

"It was quite serendipitous, actually. When I was taken to the infirmary for a heart irregularity, one of the nurses had the television on. Imagine my surprise when your ugly face showed up on the screen."

"There's not much that surprises me these days, but I'll admit I wouldn't have expected you to get away with that old infirmary escape ploy," Finn said dryly.

"You've always underestimated me, Callahan. The same way my attorneys did. They actually believed I was insane."

"I never thought that."

"No, you always understood that my proclivities were merely a lifestyle choice. My new attorney didn't believe me mad, either. She understood how I'd been framed by a desperate FBI that was under pressure to make an arrest."

"You weren't framed. You tortured those women for no other reason than your own amusement. Then when they were no longer entertaining, you killed them You know it, I know it, and if she'd had half a brain, your attorney would have known it, too."

"Well, the bitch doesn't know anything now."

"You killed her." Finn's tone was flat. Unsurprised.

Lawson shrugged. "She'd served her purpose by getting me moved to the infirmary. Once I was out of the hospital prison ward, she was superfluous baggage. It was a shame, really."

"That she had to die?"

"No. Her death was predetermined from the start. The pity was that I didn't have time to do it right, to play with her, watch her beg. One snap of the neck and she was gone. It was like stepping on a roach."

Julia had meant to keep her mouth shut, but that cold disregard for a life, for a woman who'd foolishly made a fatal mistake, drew a soft moan from between her lips.

"I'd conceived a much nicer time for us," he assured Julia. He touched his lips to the corner of her tightly set mouth without taking his eyes from Finn. Her skin crawled. "Unfortunately, it looks as if I'm going to have to alter my plans. Again."

"You're not a stupid guy, Lawson. You've got to realize you'll never get away with this," Finn warned. "So why don't you just put that knife down and we'll end this right now. Before it gets deadly."

"Haven't you ever heard of suicide by police? The way I see it, my options are beginning to narrow. I can take your slut with me as a hostage, but she'd only slow me down. Though I would so enjoy knowing that you'd have to live the rest of your life with the knowledge that you put her in harm's way in the first place."

"Just let her go," Finn said doggedly.

"I could get this over with quickly," Lawson mused aloud. "If I slashed her throat, you'd have to shoot me. Which would make it a win-win situation for both of us. You'd get your man—again—and I'd avoid years lingering on death row followed by an immoral, state-supported murder, where the small-minded people who could never conceive a brilliant widespread crime spree like the one I pulled off, would take my life as easily as they might put down a rabid dog—"

"Good comparison."

"Well, well." Julia's blood, already ice, chilled several degrees colder when Ronald Lawson actually chuckled like the monster he was. "It appears I misjudged you in one respect, Special Agent."

"What's that?" Finn asked with the rigid self-control that had frustrated her from day one, but which she'd learned to respect. The same control that she knew would allow her to escape this nightmare.

"I never would have taken you for a man with a sense of humor, even a dark one. Particularly at a time like this. Here's a little test for you, Callahan. Let's see if you still have the speed you did when you were a running back. Why don't you try to stop me before she dies?"

Julia felt the warning prick right below her earlobe, followed by a warm trickle of blood.

Fighting panic, she looked at Finn, whose icy blue eyes counseled her to remain still. Ceding control wasn't easy, but Julia trusted him with her life. Then she felt another prick of the glittering steel blade beneath her jaw.

"You should have paid more attention to your history classes, Lawson." Finn's words were directed at the killer, but his eyes were on Julia's. "You would have learned about the fate of a certain Captain Farragut of the Union army, who made the mistake of overstepping his bounds. Of taking more than was offered to him."

With the synergy of mind they'd seemed to share, Julia recognized what Finn was referring to: they were going to act out the scene she'd played with Shane. But this time the bullets in the gun were going to be real.

"Farragut was a sick son of a bitch who got off on abusing his power," Finn continued conversationally. "Sometimes he traveled with Sherman, other times he went on ahead as a scout, or came in behind as a one-man looting machine. He saw the spoils of war as his just reward for preserving the union. He also had a personal plan that could have come right out your playbook, Lawson. Rather than slaughter all the women prisoners, he'd turn them over to his troops for a bit of entertainment. For some reason, those men felt empowered by rape and plunder."

"I can certainly identify with that."

"I'm sure you can. But Farragut made his mistake by going after the wrong woman. Just like you've done today."

*Now* she read in his eyes. Trusting him implicitly, Julia allowed her rubbery knees to sag, going limp as she'd been taught in self-defense class.

Lawson cursed as the sudden dead weight pulled him off balance.

There was a swoosh of air as the silvery slash of the knife just missed her face.

In a blur of speed, Finn pulled his pistol from the back of his jeans. The shot rang out, sharp and loud enough to silence the cicadas. In a half crouch, the gun in both hands, he looked just like James Bond to Julia's shell-shocked senses.

Dark crimson blood bloomed across the front of Lawson's shirt. His eyes were wide with surprise and fury. But he wasn't dead.

"Drop the knife," Finn ordered.

Instead, the killer's fingers tightened on the handle.

Blood began trailing from beneath Lawson's shirt sleeve, trickled over his hand, and dripped from the blade of the knife.

The knife clattered to the crushed-shell path that wound through the roses.

"You wouldn't shoot an unarmed man," Lawson said.

"You sure about that, are you?" Finn's lips twisted in a half smile that was both grim and challenging.

"You play by the rules, Special Agent. That's your fatal flaw. Because some of us make our own rules." Julia's breath backed up in her lungs as he pulled an ugly pistol from behind *his* back.

Another shot shattered the soft, darkening evening.

Lawson stiffened, then fell face first to the ground, like an oak tree surrendering to the ax.

When Finn held out his arms to Julia, she flew into them.

"It's okay, baby." He pulled her tight against his chest, as if he'd never let her go. As she clung back, Julia hoped he never would.

# 31

*After what seemed like forever,* the FBI Special Agents who'd been dispatched from the Baton Rouge field office finally left Beau Soleil. The medical examiner had taken away Lawson's body, and Dani was already planning how she was going to change the garden she'd so recently planted, to rid it of the killer's presence.

"God," Julia said in a long, weary sigh when they were finally alone. "I feel as if I've landed in a road company production of the *Perils of Pauline*."

"It's all over now," Finn assured her.

"Thanks to you."

"No. That fiasco in the garden was my fault. Lawson never would have come here if it hadn't been for me."

"You know, you're really not responsible for everything that happens in the universe," she said mildly. "Besides, it's all over. And, though I would never wish for anyone to die, I think it worked out for the best, because that horrid evil man will never be able to hurt anyone again."

After a brief silence, Finn said, "I know I promised to take you into the city, and I will, if you still want, but—"

"I'd rather be alone with you. Back at the camp."

"Great minds," he said. "How long will it take you to pack?"

She glanced over at the open suitcase on the bed. The one she'd begun to pack while waiting for him to return from Baton Rouge. "I'm almost done."

"Good. I figured if we take your stuff with us, in the morning we can just leave for the airport from there."

"What if I don't want to leave?"

"Seems to me you don't have much choice. You made a deal, sugar. That studio's expecting Carma Sutra to show up in Nepal ready to go to work. And I'm going back to D.C."

She hated that he sounded so reasonable, when she was feeling anything but. Hated the way the warm, open-hearted sexy male she'd come to love was fading away right in front of her eyes. In his place was that unnaturally calm, rigidly controlled FBI Special Agent she now knew he played as a part, much the same way she'd played the unrelentingly amoral Amanda.

"We have, as Nate would say, passed a good time, you and me," he said. "But the time's come to move on. Neither one of us made any promises."

"Of course we did." Impending heartbreak warred with good old-fashioned anger in her breast. To keep from weeping, Julia concentrated on the latter. "We may not have said the words out loud, but we made promises. With our bodies. And our hearts."

"Just because you sleep with someone doesn't mean you're pledging to spend the rest of your life with them."

"That's all it was to you?" She couldn't—wouldn't—believe it. "You just were sleeping with me?"

"We said no strings," Finn reminded her.

"Maybe we both lied," she dared to suggest. "Without meaning to."

He cursed, softly, without heat. Sighed like a man carrying a heavy burden. "It wouldn't work."

"Why not?"

"We live in different worlds. I'm beer and boiled shrimp. You're champagne and caviar."

"You don't drink," she reminded him. "I've never liked caviar, and champagne makes me sneeze. And on top of all that, your snobbery's showing through again if you're going to hold my career against me."

"Are you saying the new Bond Girl would be happy being the wife of an FBI agent?"

"Are you proposing? Or is that a hypothetical question?"

He looked up at the ceiling as if seeking strength—or divine intervention—and made a sound somewhere between a curse and a groan. His expression, when he returned his gaze to hers, was not encouraging.

"Look, you're talking to a guy who spent three years tracking down a serial killer. You were right about Lawson being in my mind. I ate, slept, and lived the bastard. He was all I thought about. All I cared about."

"He's dead."

"You think he's the only one out there? My work's too demanding, too all-consuming to allow for emotional involvement."

"Whether you want to admit it or not, Callahan, you're already emotionally involved. Besides, we've been through this before. Being an FBI agent is what you do. Not who you are."

"There's no difference."

"If that were true, it'd be the most purely pitiful thing I ever heard. We may come from different backgrounds, and you might have chosen to be a cop, while I became an actor, but deep down inside, where it really matters, we're more alike than either of us ever could have imagined."

She looked up at him earnestly. "I love you, Finn Callahan. I didn't plan for it to happen, and if anyone had ever told me I'd fall in love with a bossy, oversized—"

"I sure didn't hear you complaining about my size the other night when you were screaming my name into the pillow to keep from waking up the entire inn."

"Arrogant," she muttered. "But it does suggest there's some hope for you, that you can make a joke at a time like this. As bad as that one was."

"It's either laugh or shoot myself."

Julia was trying not to think about Finn shooting anyone. The scene with Lawson was still too fresh in her mind. "I know you're not a coward," she tried again. "I can't understand why you won't admit you love me."

"Hell, yes, I do!"

"You don't have to shout."

"I'm not shouting." But he did lower his voice several decibels. "Of course I love you, dammit," he shot back. "Okay? Are you satisfied? Happy now?"

"Let's just say I'm a bit less unhappy than I was a minute ago. But less happy than I would be if you seemed at all pleased with the idea."

"Look." He scraped his palm over his short-cropped hair. "I love you. You know it, I know it, I'll bet every damn person in south Louisiana knows it. Hell, even Lawson spotted it right off. But sometimes love just isn't enough."

"And sometimes it's all you need. Do you think it was easy for me, realizing I'd fallen in love with a man whose work could get him killed? Every time you walk out the door, I'll probably think back on that scene with Lawson and wonder if this is the day you don't come home to me. But dammit, if I can live with that, if I'm willing to love an FBI Special Agent, you can certainly put up with an actress for a wife and two ex-hippies for in-laws." There, she'd said it. She'd actually gone past love straight into marriage. And she wasn't the least bit sorry.

"Christ, you can be a stubborn, argumentative female."

"And you can be a rigid, obtuse male who can't recognize the best thing that ever happened to him when it's staring him right in the face."

"You *are* the best thing that's ever happened to me, which is why I'm probably going to spend the rest of my life kicking myself. But I'm trying to do the right thing here."

"The stupid thing." She blew out a breath as she realized she wasn't going to get anywhere tonight. His mind was made up, his size thirteen feet set in stone. Oh, Julia had no doubt that she could, with time, change his mind. Eventually. But since he seemed unwilling or unable to budge at the moment, she was wasting precious time.

"You think you're doing the right thing, but what you're really doing is making a huge mistake."

"It wouldn't be my first."

"No. And lucky for you, I'm not going to let it be your last. But meanwhile, time's flying, Callahan. Surely you can think of a better way to pass what little we have left."

Julia was relieved when Finn at least let her win that argument.

Each lost in private thoughts, wrestling with "what ifs," neither spoke much on the drive out to the camp.

"Just tell me one thing," she asked as they entered the cozy cabin.

"What?" he asked cautiously.

"When you knew you loved me."

"I don't know, for sure. I kept telling myself that I didn't want you. That you weren't my type. That a man would be a fool to get tangled up with a woman like you."

She arched a brow. "A woman like me?"

"It's a compliment," he said, wondering what it was about this woman that could so easily turn his brains to grit and tangle his damn tongue.

"You thought I was Amanda."

"Yeah, and you didn't do anything to change my mind about that in the beginning. Then Margot said you were one and the same—"

"Margot? You were discussing us with Margot Madison?"

"You," he said. "I was discussing *you* with her." Hell, why didn't someone just give him a goddamn shovel so he could dig this hole he was burying himself in a little deeper? "There wasn't an *us* yet. It was the night of the welcome party."

"The night you informed me that your tastes were too selective for a woman like me. And that if I was expecting to ease small-town boredom by having hot sex with my bodyguard every night, I was going to be disappointed."

"Damn, you've got a memory," he complained.

"It comes naturally. Sort of like your rotten attitude." She folded her arms. "So, what did Margot tell you about me?"

"That you and Amanda were pretty much the same character."

"I see. And you believed that."

"Yes. No." He rubbed the back of his neck where a boulder-size knot of tension had settled. "Hell, I don't know. Maybe in the beginning. But not later. That's when I started making promises to myself. That I wouldn't allow myself to touch you, even when every fiber in my body wanted you so badly, I was spending twenty-four hours a day aching from it."

"Good." She nodded her satisfaction, clearly not willing to let him off the hook anytime soon. "What other promises did you make?"

"That I wouldn't make love to you. That I wouldn't let it get serious, that I could keep it casual. That I wouldn't want you more than I wanted to take my next breath. Wouldn't need you more than I needed to breathe."

"Well." She blew out a short, surprised breath. Then her eyes narrowed suspiciously. And, he thought, a little dangerously. "Did you have your brother write that for you?"

"Hell, no. I haven't had Jack write me lines since I was sixteen and wanted to ask Mary Jo McCarthy to the Spring Fling."

"You had a twelve-year-old write your pickup lines?"

"Hey, he happens to have been a prodigy. But even Jack couldn't put down on paper a tenth of how I feel about you."

"Well," she repeated, mollified. "Why don't you tell me, then? In your own words?"

Julia watched him draw in another deep breath, and her heart went out to him. But she held her ground.

"I love you. More than I ever thought I would love any woman. More than I wanted to." He smoothed his hands over her bare shoulders, down her arms, then back up again. "I doubt if there's a minute in the day that I don't want you. Or a fleeting second during the night that I don't want to reach for you."

The emotions he kept so tightly locked inside him poured out, swamping her. How could he not see? she wondered as she tilted her head, parting her lips, inviting him to deepen the kiss, which he did, degree by weakening degree, until she felt herself going limp.

"I want you now." Her head fell back as he trailed his lips down her neck. "Then I'll want you again." His teeth nipped at her earlobe while his hands moved cleverly, tenderly over her breasts. "All night long."

"Yes." She lifted her hands to his shoulders and allowed herself to sink even more deeply into the tantalizing warmth. "Yes." Not wanting to ruin their last night together by arguing, she surrendered without hesitation. Without regret. "And yes."

True to his word, Finn made love to her all night long, hot flashes of devastating heat that had her bucking on the fragrant mattress, nails digging into his bare back, her own hot skin slick with passion.

Although she never would have imagined it that afternoon she entered the terminal and saw him standing there, looking so huge, so formidable, they fit together perfectly, their bodies attuned to each other even after the smoke clouded their minds and flames scorched their senses. As if determined to claim her, to brand her as his own before he sent her away, Finn abandoned control and allowed the primitive, possessive male to break free.

His greed was dark, thrilling, almost violent as he took her ruthlessly to peak after devastating peak. She'd never before dreamed that need could be so driving, so turbulent. Never dared dream that she'd so willingly lose herself in anyone, or that helplessness with a person you trusted implicitly with your body, your heart, your life, could give birth to its own special strength.

A crimson harvest moon sailed across a midnight sky as they plundered, all speed and heat and force, until finally, just before dawn, hands gentled, lips turned tender. The pace slowed. Sweetened. When he slipped into her, smoothly, silkily, Julia opened for him, taking him as fully as he'd taken her.

Later she lay nestled in his arms, her cheek against his chest, cozy as a kitten and feeling just as boneless. "You've ruined me, Special Agent."

He idly brushed some damp spiral curls away from her face. "Should I apologize?"

"Of course not." She pressed her lips against his cooling flesh. "It's just that it could never be the same with any other man. Ever again." He felt her smile. "So, I guess you're stuck with me."

Finally surrendering to the events of the past eighteen hours, she drifted off. Gathering her close, not wanting to lose a moment, Finn watched her sleep as the pale shimmers of silver light signaled the dawning of a new day. The day he'd once been so looking forward to. The day he'd send her away.

# 32

*You realize, of course, that you're an idiot."*

Finn blinked against the burst of sun that came flooding into the room as the window shade snapped up. "Jesus." He rubbed the heels of his hands against his burning eyes, vaguely surprised that there was a part of his body that could still feel pain, when he'd been working so hard around the clock to numb it. "What the hell do you think you're doing?"

"Sorry," Nate said, his easy tone dripping with insincerity. "We figured you might like knowing that it's nearly noon."

"So?" Finn reached down and picked the Jack Daniel's off the floor to pour himself another drink. Then frowned when he realized the bottle was empty. No problem; like any good former Eagle Scout, he'd prepared for this contingency.

"So, drinking by yourself is a good way to get into trouble." About this, Jack was definitely the voice of experience of the three Callahan brothers. "Drinking before noon shows you're already there. And sinking fast."

"This from the man who singlehandedly nearly turned Blue Bayou dry by drinking up all the booze in the parish when he came back home." Finn stood up, swayed as the bourbon swam in his gut and head, and sat heavily back down again.

"True. Fortunately, the love of a good woman turned me around. You might want to give it a try sometime."

"It's too late." God, what he'd give for a drink. Wondering what his chances were of talking either of his brothers into getting the backup bottle from the kitchen cupboard, Finn ran his tongue around fuzzy teeth that had been numb for the past eight days. At least he thought it had been eight days. It had been hard to tell with the hurricane shutters closed and the shades down. Which had been just the way Finn liked it. "I screwed things up. Big time."

He felt something wet push its way beneath his hand and didn't have to open his eyes to know it was Jack's oversized mutt's nose. The dog had gotten the name Turnip, because one day this past spring, she'd just turned up in Blue Bayou. The same way Julia had. But the dog had stayed and she'd gone.

"So unscrew them," Nate advised. "It's only been ten days."

"Ten?" Obviously he'd lost two somewhere in one of those bottles.

"Yeah. Ten. Which is not exactly a lifetime."

"It just seems that way in idiot years," Jack said. "This is something else I'm an expert on. Time doesn't stop just 'cause you shut down, *cher*. The old world jus' keeps on a turning. It took me thirteen years to get Danielle back. That what you plannin' to do? Wait thirteen years?"

"I figured I should give Julia some time." He said what he'd been reminding himself of ever since he'd watched her plane turn into a little silver speck in the sky, then disappear out over the water.

"Time to find herself another guy?"

"Time to make sure she knows what she wants."

"Yeah, the woman seemed real indecisive," Nate drawled.

"Besides, this movie is a big deal for her." Liking this excuse, Finn nodded slowly, gravely, wishing he hadn't when the rock pile that he'd been building stone by stone, drink by drink, shifted, causing a few boulders to come crashing down behind eyes that felt like burning coals. "I don't want to distract her."

"Remind me to stop by Holy Assumption and tell Father Benoit to call the pope and ring the bells," Nate said. "Because Blue Bayou's just got itself a brand-new martyr buckin' for sainthood."

"Saint Finn," Jack piled on. "Has a nice ring to it."

"So, I take it the reason you two came all the way out here was to tell jokes?"

Jack held up the empty bottle. "This isn't any joke, Finn."

"I know." Finn cursed. "Hell, I don't see how you did it. Bein' a drunk isn't a whole lot of laughs."

"Spend enough time unconscious and you don't notice."

"Obviously I've been underachieving." He rubbed his jaw and tried to remember when he'd last shaved. About three days ago, he decided. When he'd put the razor away after damn near cutting his throat. "I'm going to have to crawl, aren't I?"

"Remember that old eight ball I had when I was a kid?" Nate asked.

"Sure. You believed those messages like they were God speaking to you from a burning bush."

"It hit things pretty much on the money most of the time," Nate said. "It told me I was going to lose my virginity to Misty Montgomery. And I did, two days later."

"I always figured that said a lot more about Misty's reputation than any magic in some dime store toy," Finn said. "Weren't many guys Misty didn't play hide and seek with beneath those bleachers."

"We're getting off track. The thing is, if I still had that sucker and asked, is my big brother gonna have to grovel to Julia, it'd probably answer that signs definitely point to yes."

"Groveling's definitely in the cards," Jack seconded his brother's appraisal. "Lucky thing you've been probably gettin' a lot of practice down on your knees worshiping at the porcelain altar since you decided to take up drinking."

The throwing up had been worse than the jackhammers in his head. Finn might have been wrong about a lot of things in his life, but sticking to RC Cola hadn't been one of them.

"Jesus, you're a million laughs. Maybe you ought to start writing comedy instead of thrillers."

"Might as well. Seein' I've got me a clown for a brother."

Finn glared at him. Jack crossed arms which were pretty damn big for a guy who spent most of his days at a computer keyboard, and stared right back.

"If you two are going to start pounding on each other, I'm leaving," Nate threatened. "Because if I hang around, I'll get dragged into the damn thing and there's no way I'm gonna risk getting my pretty face broken." He flashed a quick grin. "Hey, maybe I'll go to Nepal and see if I can talk a certain sexy red-haired Bond Girl into changing her mind and goin' for the handsome brother."

Finn snarled. Then lunged.

Nate might have been able to dodge the attack if it hadn't been for Turnip, who, always wanting to be right in the middle of things, got in his way. He landed sprawled on the floor, facedown.

When blood began gushing from his nose, Nate roared in outrage.

Then grabbed his brother around the ankles and yanked him down.

Finn hit the wood. "Goddammit," he growled, "you never would have been able to pull that off if I wasn't plowed."

Jack stayed on the sidelines, watching the flailing fists and swinging elbows as they rolled around the camp floor uncharacteristically littered with old newspapers, fast food bags and underwear. Turnip was jumping happily around them, tail wagging to beat the band.

Obviously it must be true what they said about marriage and fatherhood settling a guy down, Jack mused, as Nate connected with a surprisingly strong left hook. There'd been a time, not all that long ago, when he would have swung the first fist, been the first on the pile. Now he was just content to play spectator. Until a crunch of bone on bone made him flinch.

"Okay, that's the bell." He grabbed his brothers by the shirt collars and shoved them in opposite directions. "Get to your respective corners before someone gets hurt."

"That's the plan," Finn muttered.

"Christ, you're pathetic," Nate shot back. "Getting all liquored up because you're afraid of a woman."

Finn looked on the verge of beginning World War III, and Jack decided the time had come to get things moving toward their logical conclusion. "Okay, here's what we're going to do." He yanked Finn to his feet. "We're going to sober you up, then drive you into New Orleans and put you on a plane to Kathmandu, where you will grovel like a dog with its belly in a rut so the woman will agree to save you from a life of booze and despair, living beneath some bridge in a cardboard refrigerator box and gettin' mugged by bag ladies."

He shot a look at Nate, who'd pushed himself to his feet and was pressing the back of his hand against his nose in an attempt to stem the flowing blood.

Shit, Jack thought. He'd better get Finn out of here and on a plane quick, before the prettiest Callahan brother realized that his big brother had broken his nose.

"Give me a hand," he told Nate. "Since the water pressure's shit out here, which rules out a decent shower to sober our big brother up, it's time for a swim."

Finn was cursing a blue streak when they tossed him into the bayou with a mighty splash. Turnip, thinking this was some new game of fetch her master had invented, dove right in after him.

* * *

Although it took some doing, Finn found Julia's parents in San Antonio, at an arts festival at the Riverwalk. Peace greeted him warmly. Freedom did not.

"You broke my little girl's heart." The artist's booming voice drew a startled glance from a pretty blonde selling handcrafted candles in the next booth.

"I'm sorry." He'd never spoken truer words. "I didn't intend for that to happen."

"Road to hell's paved with so-called good intentions." Freedom glanced down at his wife. "I'm sorry."

She sighed. Resigned. "I know. A man's gotta do—"

"What a man's gotta do."

Thinking it was odd that this hippie artist was quoting John Wayne, Finn didn't see the fist coming straight at him until it was too late. Knowing it was deserved, he didn't try to get out of the way; just stood there and took it right on the chin.

"I'm sorry about that, man," Freedom said, rubbing his knuckles. "But you deserved it after making my baby girl cry."

"I can't argue with that," Finn said. "If Julia and I are lucky enough to have a daughter, I'd have to do the same thing if some guy hurt her."

"Are you saying she's pregnant?"

"Darling," Peace interjected, "that's not your concern."

"Of course it's my concern. I'm her father. I'm only looking out for her welfare."

"I do believe those are the same words my father used when he threatened to disown me if I left the house with a long-haired, pot-smoking, hippie draft dodger."

"Times change," Freedom said. "Fathers don't. So?" he asked Finn again. "Did you get our Julia pregnant?"

"No." Not yet. But the idea was unreasonably appealing. One of these days. After she'd gotten her movie career on firm footing.

"But you're going to marry her?"

"If she'll have me, sir. Freedom," Finn corrected when Freedom's eyes narrowed dangerously. He did not point out that the older man had never seen fit to marry Julia's mother. Still, he'd never seen two people more suited to one another. Except the woman he was determined to win back and him. "That's why I came here. I thought you should be the first to know."

"Isn't that sweet?" Peace said. "And don't worry, Finn dear, of course Julia will have you. You may have to grovel a bit, but you'll win her over." She took a small blue box out of an oversized woven bag.

Inside the box was a stone, much like the ones Julia lugged around.

"To enhance your powers of persuasion," Peace explained.

"Thanks." He didn't really buy into the magic rock theory, but as he left the Riverwalk, headed for the airport, Finn figured he needed all the help he could get.

# 33

*Kathmandu was set in an emerald valley* shaped like an oval bowl. The city, encircled by green terraced hills dotted by small clusters of red tiled-roof houses, temples and shrines, was the most exotic and fascinating showcase of cultures, art, and tradition Julia had ever witnessed. There hadn't been a day for the past two weeks that she hadn't wished Finn was there to share it with her.

She was sitting on a rock away from the others, drinking up the atmosphere during the lunch break, when she saw him walking up the dirt road toward her. At first she thought she was imagining things. That he was merely the product of wishful thinking, a mirage born from her nightly dreams of him.

Hope fluttered delicate wings in her heart. Because she wanted to run to him, to throw her arms around him, to kiss him and never let go, she forced herself to stay where she was.

"Perhaps you need to get a new atlas," she said. "Because you're a little off target. This isn't Washington, D.C."

"Tell me about it. It's not the easiest place to get to." Finn had given up trying to count how many means of transportation he'd taken, beginning with the jet out of New Orleans and ending with a taxi driver who'd bartered the mileage fare like a camel dealer, then refused to use the meter. And just maybe, fifty years from now, he might be able to laugh about the hour he'd spent packed onto a bus where the animals had outnumbered the humans.

"But well worth the effort," she suggested.

Because he wanted to go to her, to pull her into his arms and kiss her silly, Finn dipped his hands into the pockets of his jeans. "It really is gorgeous."

"Isn't it? There's a legend that says this entire valley was once covered by a lake until the Bodhisattva Manjushri raised his sword of wisdom and sliced a passage through the mountain walls, which drained the water and allowed for the first settlements."

He rocked back on his heels and looked out over the valley that seemed to exude its own energy force. "That's very interesting."

"I thought so . . . what are you doing here, Finn?"

"I came to see you. You look great, by the way. You're going to be the best Bond Girl on record."

"Thank you."

"Great outfit, too," he said, obviously stalling. "You remind me of Emma Peel. Or Catwoman. But better."

"What is it about men and catsuits?" she murmured.

"You could wear a burlap bag and you'd still be gorgeous."

This wasn't getting them anywhere. "Shouldn't you be back to work? Surely the FBI didn't extend your suspension time?"

"No. I took a leave of absence."

"I see. For how long?"

"Forever. I quit."

"I see." It was taking a huge effort to keep that polite, distant smile on her face. "What are you doing now? Besides traveling?"

"I went into business for myself. Actually, with my former boss. Turns out he was ready for a change, too. This way there'll be someone to share the work, which will give us both more free time. Jim and his wife have an empty nest, what with their kids in college, so they decided to take up golf together."

"That's nice." Personally, she'd never understood why anyone would want to spend a perfectly nice day chasing a little white ball around, but it was always nice to hear about a marriage that was still obviously so strong after many years. "So you'll be working as a professional bodyguard?" Even as she loathed the idea of him guarding any other woman's body, Julia had to admit he'd be perfect.

"No. Yours is the only body I ever wanted to guard." Her smile turned a bit more genuine as she realized they were, once again, thinking the same thing. "This is more along the lines of corporate security. There's a lot of need for it these days."

"I imagine there would be. So, I suppose you set up office in D.C."

"No. That was never my home. Just a place I kept my clothes."

"Blue Bayou?" That seemed a bit far-fetched.

"No. I've got an office in L.A."

"Oh." *Oh, God.* She pressed a hand against her chest, over her heart, which was pounding against her sternum. She was just getting so it didn't hurt all the time; Julia wasn't sure she could take him reopening the wound. "Any special reason that out of all the cities in the world, you chose that one?"

"Dammit, of course there is," he said in an unusual flare of temper. Then he cursed softly beneath his breath. Scrubbed a hand down his face. "Nate said you were going to make me grovel."

"It's no wonder Nate's so popular with the ladies," she said mildly. "Since he obviously knows a great deal about female behavior."

"He also has one helluva left hook."

"So I see." Because she couldn't just sit there like moss on a rock, while the man she loved was so close, so real, Julia stood up and touched her fingertips to his bruised cheek. His right eyelid was almost swollen closed. His chin. "Did Nate do all this damage?"

"Most of it. The chin's your father's right uppercut."

"My father *hit* you?"

"Yeah. But it's okay because I deserved it."

"Well, I'm not going to argue with that. But my parents are in San Antonio." She'd just talked to them last night. "What were you doing there?"

"Asking Freedom for his daughter's hand."

"What?" How could a man who seemed so rigid, so set in his ways, prove to be one surprise after another?

"I figured, after you told me the story about how he went to your mom's father, well, it sounded like a family tradition or something, and hell, I just wanted to try to do things right."

Of course he would. Julia was trying to think of something, anything, to say when he pulled a small box from his pocket, went down on one knee, and handed it to her.

Julia slowly opened it. "A tiger's eye?"

"Damn. Wrong box. That one's from your mother. To me. She said it'd help my powers of persuasion." He dug a little deeper and came up with a second one. This time when she opened the lid, Julia drew in a quick, sharp breath.

The stone was small, certainly nothing that would draw cameras on the red carpet on Emmy or Oscar night. But it sparkled like moonlight on ice and was set in an antique white gold setting.

"It was my mother's," Finn explained. "Since I was the oldest son, it came to me after she died. I wasn't sure I'd ever have use for it. Until you."

She took the ring from its bed of midnight blue satin and slipped it on her finger. "It fits."

"Obviously a sign."

"Or you had it sized."

"Well, I suppose that's one possibility."

Julia suspected he had. "You were so sure I'd say yes?"

"I was hoping." He stood up again, towering over her, hands jammed deep into his pockets. "I haven't eaten a decent meal since you left. I haven't slept, haven't been able to think straight, until I sobered up and managed to focus long enough to figure out what I wanted to do for a job, once I realized there was no way I wanted to go back to jumping political hoops and having my life eaten up with lowlife scum who aren't worth the bullets it takes to get rid of them."

"Sobered up?" One more revelation in a day of surprises. "But you don't drink."

"I did. For ten days. I thought it was eight, but Jack and Nate say ten. Since I was unconscious a lot of the time, I took their word for it."

"You got drunk because of me?"

"No. Because of me. Because I was stupid enough to stand by and let the best thing in my life get on a plane and go halfway around the world, without me telling her that I wanted to be the one she came home to. That I want to be the one she'll make babies with, if she wants them—"

"Oh, she definitely does."

"Good. Because I want to get them a big stupid dog who'll shed all over the furniture and chew up your scripts. I want to build a swing set in the backyard and stay up all Christmas Eve night putting together Hot Wheels tracks and Barbie dream houses.

"I want to teach them the joy of growing with parents who love each other more with each passing day; a home like we were both lucky enough to have when we were kids. And I want to hold hands while we walk on the beach when we're both old and gray, watching our grandbabies run in the surf and collect seashells, and showing them the whale migration."

"That's quite a scenario," she murmured when he paused for a breath.

"There's a lot more, but it'll take at least the next fifty years to tell it. Hell, I haven't even gotten to the hot sex part yet." His voice was roughened with a depth of emotion she'd once mistakenly thought him incapable of. "I never thought I was a greedy man. But I want it all, Julia. I want everything. But I only want that, will only ever be able to have it, with you."

She felt the tears welling up in her eyes. "Jack didn't write that for you."

"Hell, no." He looked affronted she'd even think such a thing.

Julia drank in the bruised and battered face of the man she loved, the man who'd made love to her with such exquisite patience, the man who'd so heatedly ravished her their last night together in the cabin. The man who'd stubbornly sent her away, then made her wait for so many days for him to see the light. To realize they belonged together.

The man who'd gone down on one knee and opened himself up to her in a way she knew hadn't been easy for him.

"Well," he demanded. "Could you please just put me out of my misery and say yes, dammit?"

It might be petty of her, but Julia loved the frustration that was etched all over his rugged face. Then again, she loved everything about Finn Callahan.

Julia laughed as she flung her arms around his neck. "Yes, dammit."

# Magnolia Moon

*To Patty Gardner-Evans,*
*for all the years. (Sorry about*
*the gator; maybe next time.)*

*And, as always, to Jay,*
*with love.*

# 1

*New Orleans, Louisiana*

*I've always adored a Libra man,"* the blond purred.

"Have you now?" Nate Callahan grinned and drew her closer. There were few things in life more enjoyable than making love to a beautiful woman.

"Oh, absolutely." Cuddling up against him, she fluttered her lashes in a way only a true southern belle could pull off. "Why, a Libra man can charm the birds out of the trees and flatter a girl right out of her lace panties."

"It wasn't flattery, *chère*." He refilled her crystal champagne flute. "It was the absolute truth."

Nate had always enjoyed females—he liked the way they moved, the way they smelled, their soft skin and slender ladies' hands. From the first time he'd filched one of his older brother Finn's *Playboy* magazines, he'd flat-out liked everything about women. Fortunately, they'd always liked him right back.

He toyed with a blond curl trailing down her neck. It was a little stiff and hadn't deflated much during their session of hot, steamy sex, but Nate was used to that, since most of the women he dated favored big hair. Big hair, big breasts, and, he thought with a pleasant twinge of lust, big appetites for sex.

"Your moon is in the seventh house." She trailed a glossy coral nail down his chest.

"Is that good?" He skimmed his palm down her back; she arched against the caress like a sleek, pampered cat.

Outside her bedroom, a full moon rose in a star-studded sky; inside, flames crackled cozily in the fireplace and gardenia-scented candles glowed.

"It certainly is. You're ruled by Venus, goddess of beauty."

"Seems that'd fit you better than me, sugar." He nuzzled the smooth curve of her shoulder. His accent, always more pronounced when romancing a woman, turned thick as Cajun gumbo. "Bein' how you've gotten more beautiful every year since you won that Miss Louisiana crown."

"I was only first runner-up." She pouted prettily.

"Officially," he allowed. "But everyone in the state knew the judges were obviously blind as swamp bats."

"You are so sweet." Her laugh was rich and pleased.

Nate's mind began to drift as she chattered on about the stars, which, if he were to be perfectly honest, didn't interest him. He'd never thought much about lunar signs until the afternoon he'd shown up to give the blond astrologer a bid on remodeling her bedroom.

Although he'd arrived ten minutes late at her Garden District house, he'd gotten her out of the shower; she'd shown up at the door, breathlessly apologetic for not being ready, prettily flushed, and smelling of jasmine. It was only later, when he'd remembered that her hair hadn't been wet, that Nate realized he'd been set up. Having always appreciated female wiles, he didn't mind.

She'd hung on to his every word as he'd suggested ways to open up the room—including putting a skylight over the bed—declared him brilliant, and hired him on the spot.

"You are," she'd sworn on a drawl as sweet as the sugarcane his granddaddy used to grow, "the first contractor I've interviewed who understands that a bedroom is more than just a place to sleep." She'd coyly looked up at him from beneath her lashes. "It is, after all, the most important room in the house."

When she'd touched a scarlet fingernail to the back of Nate's hand, warm and pleasant desire had ribboned through him.

"You've been so sweet. Would you do me just one teensy little favor?"

"Sure, *chère*. If I can."

Avid green eyes had swept over him in a slow, feminine perusal. "Oh, I think you're just the man for the job."

She'd untied the silk robe, revealing perfumed and powdered flesh. "I do so need to exorcise my horrid ex-husband's memory from this room." The robe dropped to the plush carpeting.

That had been six months ago. Not only had Nate done his best to exorcise her former husband's memory, he'd done a damn fine job on the remodeling, if he did say so himself. Lying on his back amid sex-tangled sheets, Nate looked up at the ghost galleon moon, decided he'd definitely been right about the skylight, and wondered why he'd never thought to put one over his own bed.

"Of course, Venus is also the goddess of love." The *L* word, slipping smoothly from her coral-tinted lips, yanked his wandering mind back to their conversation.

"She is?" he asked with a bit more caution.

"Absolutely. Make love, not war, is a phrase that could have been coined with Libras in mind. You became interested in women at a young age, you make sex a rewarding experience, and will not stop until your lover is satisfied, even if it takes all night."

"I try," he said modestly. She'd certainly seemed well satisfied when she'd been bucking beneath him earlier.

She smiled and touched her lips to his. "Oh, you not only succeed, darling, you set the standard. Libras also rule the house of partnerships."

"Now there's where your stars might be a little off, sugar." He stroked her smooth silk back, cupped her butt, and pulled her closer. " 'Cause I've always enjoyed working alone."

It wasn't that he was antisocial, far from it. But he liked being his own boss, working when he liked, and playing when he wanted.

"You weren't alone a few minutes ago, and you seemed to be enjoying yourself well enough."

"I always enjoy passin' a good time with you, angel."

"If you didn't play well with others, you wouldn't have run for mayor." She rolled over and straddled him. "Libras are not lone wolves, darling. A Libra male needs a permanent partner."

Nate's breath clogged in his lungs. "Permanent?"

Having grown up in South Louisiana, where water and land were constantly battling, with water winning most of the time, he knew that very few things were permanent. Especially relationships between men and women.

"We've been together six months," she pointed out, which exceeded any previous relationship Nate had ever had. Then again, it helped that she'd spent most of that time away, selling her astrology books at New Age festivals and talking them up on television talk shows around the country.

Doing some rapid calculation, Nate figured they'd probably been together a total of three weeks, and had spent most of that time in bed.

"I've been thinking," she murmured when he didn't respond. Her clever fingers slipped between them, encircling him. "About us."

"Us?"

"It occurred to me yesterday, when my flight was cruising at thirty thousand feet over New Mexico, that we should get married."

*Married?* Having not seen this coming—she'd certainly never shown one iota of domesticity—Nate didn't immediately answer.

"You don't want to." Danger sparked in her voice, like heat lightning flashing out over the Gulf. She pulled away.

Sighing, Nate hitched himself up beside her and saw any future plans for the night disappearing.

"It's nothing to do with you, *chère*." His cajoling smile encouraged one in return. "But we agreed goin' in that neither of us was the marrying kind."

"That was then." She left the bed and retrieved his shirt from where it had landed earlier. "Things change." The perfumed air swirled with temper. "The moon is also a mother sign."

"It is?" Nate caught the denim shirt she threw at him. Christ, he needed air.

"Yes." Her chin angled up. Her eyes narrowed to green slits. "Which is why Libras often repeat the same childlike behavior over and over again in their relationships."

It was a long way from charming to childish. Boyish, Nate might be willing to accept—in the right context. But he hadn't been a child since that life-altering day when he was twelve and a liquored-up, swamp-dwelling, gun-carrying idiot had blown away his father.

"If I didn't know better, I might take offense at that, darlin'." He bent to pick up his jeans from the loblolly pine floor; one of his boots came sailing toward him. "*Mon Dieu,* Charlene." He ducked the first one and snagged the second out of the air an instant before it connected with his head.

"Do you have any idea how many proposals I get every month?" She marched back across the bedroom and jabbed her finger against his bare chest.

"I'll bet a bunch." Nate reminded himself that he'd never run into a situation he couldn't smooth over.

"You damn well bet a lot!" His chest now bore little crescent gouges from her fingernail. "I've turned down two in the past six weeks—from men who make a hell of a lot more money than you—because I was fool enough to think we had a future."

"You're a wonderful woman, *chèrie*," he tried again, hopping on first one foot, then the other, as he pulled his pants up. "Smart, beautiful—"

"And getting goddamn older by the moment," she shouted.

"You don't look a day over twenty-five." Thanks to a Houston surgeon whose clever touch with a scalpel had carved a good ten years off her face and body.

When she began coming toward him again, Nate backed away and yanked on his shirt. Not pausing to button it, he scooped his keys and wallet from the bedside table and shoved them into his pocket. "Twenty-six, tops." He debated sitting down again to pull on his boots, then decided not to risk it.

"It's not going to work this time, Callahan."

A champagne glass hit the wall, then shattered. She tossed her stiff cloud of honey blond hair. "If I'd taken the time to do your full chart before hiring you, I never would have let you seduce me."

Deciding that discretion was the better part of valor, Nate wisely didn't point out that she'd been the one who'd dropped the damn robe.

"I would have realized that you're suffering from a gigantic Peter Pan complex."

Peter Pan? Nate gritted his teeth. "I'll call you, *chère*," he promised as he dodged the second flute. PMS, he decided. "Later in the month. When you're feeling a little more like yourself."

A banshee could not have screamed louder. Nate escaped the suffocating room, taking the back stairs two at a time. Something thudded against the bedroom wall; he hoped to hell she hadn't damaged the new plaster job.

Feeling blindsided, Nate drove toward his home on the peaceful bank of Blue Bayou, trying to figure out where, exactly, an evening that had begun so promising had gone offtrack.

"Peter Pan," he muttered.

Where the hell had she come up with that one?

The full moon was brighter than he'd ever seen it, surrealistically silhouetting the knobby bayou cypresses in eerie white light. Having just survived Hurricane Charlene, Nate hoped it wasn't some weird portent of yet another storm to come.

# 2

*Los Angeles*

*Oh, God,* doesn't that hunk just jump-start your hormones?"

L.A. homicide detective Regan Hart glanced up at the billboard towering over Sunset Boulevard. "Not really." He was too blond, too good-looking, and even with that ragged hair and scruffy beard, somehow too perfect. Regan preferred men who looked as if they had some mileage on them.

"Any woman who doesn't respond to Brad Pitt needs her head examined," Vanessa Kante, Regan's partner, said on a deep sigh. "Not to mention more vital body parts."

"My head and all my other body parts are working just fine, thank you." At least Regan assumed they were; it had been a while since they'd been subjected to a field test. "And in case you've forgotten, you're married. Aren't you supposed to be directing those leaping hormones toward your husband?"

"I'm married, not dead. Part of the reason our marriage is so strong is that Rhasheed doesn't mind who I lust after, so long as he's the one whose tall, lanky bones I'm jumping when I get home." She shot Regan a knowing look. "Since you've been in a crappy mood all shift, I take it the Santa Monica plastic surgeon wasn't exactly Mr. Right."

Regan heaved out a breath. "He wasn't even Mr. Maybe if a meteor hit Santa Monica and we were the only man and woman left on earth I might just maybe consider having sex with you only to perpetuate the species. Enough said."

"Sorry."

She shrugged. "I don't know why I even let you fix me up with him in the first place."

"Perhaps because it's been too long since you've had sex that didn't involve batteries?"

"It's not that easy. First of all, we're living in the land of gorgeous women, where every waitress is a Cameron Diaz wannabe and any female over a size two is a candidate for liposuction."

"I'm not a size two. And Rhasheed likes me just the way I am."

"What man wouldn't? I've seen stone-cold killers swallow their tongues when you sashay into the squad room." A dead ringer for Tyra Banks, Vanessa even dressed like a supermodel. "And besides, Rhasheed grew up in Nigeria. You keep telling me the brothers like their women with curves."

"That's what he tells me, and if actions back up his sweet-talking jive, it's true. I think it's one of those Neanderthal things about looking for a woman who'll make a good breeder, even during famine. But Rhasheed says it's mainly so he'll have something to hold onto so he won't fall out of bed."

"Then I'm out of luck with Neanderthals, too. All my adolescent growth hormones went into my height, so I didn't have any left for curves. As Dr. Bill felt obliged to point out when he suggested I consider implant surgery."

"Ouch. I never realized he was such a silver-tongued devil."

"It wouldn't have worked out anyway. If guys aren't intimidated by a woman who wears a pistol to work, they just want to hear gory war stories about dead bodies."

"Which kind was Dr. Bill?"

"The first. We were out on the dance floor for about two minutes when he admitted he couldn't handle getting that close to a woman who was wearing a Beretta beneath her jacket."

Van shot her a disbelieving look. "Tell me you didn't actually wear your sidearm on a date?"

"I got a call while I was in court to testify on the Sanchez case, saying one of the Front Street Crips had some info on that Diamond Street gangbanger who was killed while collecting drug taxes for the Mexican Mafia. Would you go into that neighborhood unarmed?"

"I'll have to give you that one."

"Besides, I looked pretty damn good. I was wearing that suit you talked me into buying last week."

Van had unearthed the designer knockoff at Second Hand Rose, a trendy consignment boutique on Melrose. The label read "Armini," the simple change in vowels keeping the counterfeit police from declaring the suit illegal. It was also several hundred dollars less expensive than the original.

"Couldn't you have left the gun in the trunk of your car?" her partner asked.

"And have it stolen like Malloy's? Boy, wouldn't that be a career booster."

Just last month Devon Malloy, a rookie B&E detective, had left his pistol in the trunk of his car to keep it away from his kids. Unfortunately, his car had been stolen, and the gun ended up being used in an armed robbery that had left a liquor store clerk wounded. By the time IAD eventually got through dragging Malloy over the coals, he might still be a cop, but any chances of advancement were nil; if he stayed on the force, he could look forward to spending all his days on pawnshop detail.

"Actually, it was kind of funny," Regan said. "We were slow-dancing, and every time he'd pull me close and try to cop a feel, his fingers would hit cold steel. After the third time, he suggested we call it a night. Not only was I crushing his libido—apparently it's a little disconcerting to go out with a woman who can shoot your balls off—but the metal in my Beretta was screwing up his *qi*. Whatever that is."

"It's feng shui. In Taoist thought, everything is made up of *qi*—or energy. It's the essence of existence."

"And here I thought that was DNA."

The rain was picking up. Regan turned on the wipers, which dragged across the glass with a rubbery squeal like fingernails on a chalkboard. LAPD never retired their crap cars; they just assigned them to her. The heater hadn't worked for six weeks. By the time it got repaired, the weather would have warmed up, and she wouldn't need it. Which, she thought darkly, was probably exactly the department's reasoning.

"Hey, there are a lot of things in this world we can't understand," Van said. "If it wasn't for feng shui, I wouldn't have gotten pregnant."

Regan shot her a look. "You got pregnant because when you and Rhasheed were off cavorting in the tropics, you had one too many mai tais and forgot to use birth control."

"True. But before we went to Kauai, between the stress of his job and mine, we were having some sex problems—which is why we made the reservations at the Crouching Dragon Inn in the first place."

"Ah yes, the sex palace."

"You make it sound like someplace with mystery stains on the sheets and porno movies playing on a TV bolted to the dresser. The Crouching Dragon Inn was designed on the feng shui principle that we should live *with* nature rather than against it, so it was constructed for all the bed and beach *qi* to flow properly. As soon as we got there, all our problems just flew out the window. Except for going to that luau, we made love all week."

"So you said." From the play-by-play her partner had shared, she was amazed Van had still been able to walk when they got back from Hawaii.

"All that positive loving energy sent out a special frequency that allowed Rhasheed's essential elements to come together with mine and create Denzel's life force."

"It's called a sperm swimming up to fertilize an egg."

With the exception of certain truisms such as full moons make the crazies come out, and you always get a floater the day you're wearing new shoes, Regan didn't believe in feng shui, voodoo, fate, or anything else that she couldn't see with her own eyes or touch with her own hands.

After she'd been set up to be killed by a gang who was tired of her hauling in their dealers, the psychologist the department had forced her to see had blamed her skepticism on all those childhood years waiting for her father to return home from Vietnam. In her child's mind he would walk in, declare her the most beautiful, lovable little girl in the world, get down on one knee just like the prince did in Cinderella, beg her mother to remarry him, and they'd all live happily ever after.

None of which had ever happened. Unfortunately, Lieutenant John Hart, U.S. Marines, had never returned from Vietnam. Her mother, who'd filed for divorce before Regan was born, had returned to her law practice when Regan was a week old, leaving her in the hands of a continuously changing series of nannies and housekeepers who never quite lived up to Karen Hart's standards. When her father never showed up in a suit of shining armor to sweep his daughter onto the back of a prancing white steed and take her away to his palace, Regan had decided fairy tales belonged in the gilt-edged pages of books, not in real life.

In a way, she'd always thought that youthful disappointment had served her well. The very same realism and skepticism the department shrink had advised her to overcome was what made her a good cop.

"Birth's a miracle." Van repeated what she'd been saying since the day the little pink cross had shown up on the test strip. "Rhasheed said he knew I was pregnant that morning when I began glowing from the inside."

"You sure you didn't get confused about what you were putting in your mouth, and swallow your mag light?"

"Very funny. The glow was the red lightwave from baby Denzel's heart." She patted her rounded stomach, which had been showing her pregnancy for the past two months.

Regan shook her head. "Only in L.A. would cops be into New Age."

As happy as she was for Van, Regan wasn't looking forward to losing her as a partner. But Van and her husband had decided a homicide detective's twenty-four/seven lifestyle wasn't exactly family friendly and she'd decided to leave the force in another six weeks.

"Feng shui isn't new. The concept goes back eight thousand years." Van turned in the passenger seat toward Regan. "Maybe you should have a master check out your apartment. You've been under a lot of stress lately."

"I'm a murder cop. Stress comes with the territory."

"Which is why you need to find something that helps."

"What would help would be for the good citizens of Los Angeles to take a forty-eight-hour ceasefire."

"Russell Crowe's going to show up in the squad room in full breastplate and sandals before that happens," Vanessa said dryly. "You know, I took a class last month with the guy who advised Donald Trump to change a set of French doors at Mar-a-Lago to the other wall. If you weren't so hard-minded, you might actually like him."

"I don't need an architectural adviser. I just need to close the Lancaster case. And the fact that Donald Trump wants to pay some so-called building wizard big bucks to tell him to tear out some doors is just proof that some people have more money than sense."

"I hope you didn't tell Dr. Bill all this. He lives by feng shui."

"I know. We had to wait an hour for a dinner table that faced the right direction." An hour she'd spent nursing a glass of wine and eating bar mix. "Give me some credit. I merely told him that the mental vision of scalpels cutting into my breasts had the same negative effect on me that guns seemed to have on him. So, since cold steel seems to be destined to come between us, we might as well give both our *qi*s a break and make it an early night."

"I was really hoping you two would work out. What about the Century City investment banker? Mike something? He was good looking."

"His name was Mark Mitchell." Regan had met him after a real estate developer got shot execution style in a parking garage. Since Mark had discovered the body, Regan had interviewed him, then given him her card in case he thought of anything that might prove useful to the investigation. He'd called that night to ask her out. She'd declined, not wanting to cross the professional/personal line she'd always firmly maintained.

It hadn't taken long to apprehend the shooter, a bumbling first-time hit-for-hire guy. The day the jury found him guilty, she'd received another call from Mark Mitchell. This time she'd made the mistake of taking him up on his offer of a late dinner.

"He kept an iguana named Gordon Gekko in his bedroom." And revealed he'd always viewed the "Greed is good" character Michael Douglas played in *Wall Street* as a role model.

"That is a little weird," Van allowed. "You could always go out with someone on the force."

"I'd rather shoot myself than date a cop." She'd no sooner spoken when she wished she could take the words back. Rhasheed was an L.A. county sheriff's department deputy. "Hell, I'm sorry. Rhasheed's an exception."

"He's special, all right." Van's smile showed she hadn't taken offense. "We were supposed to go out tonight to celebrate the fifth anniversary of when we met."

Then they'd gotten called out on what could well prove a wild-goose chase. It was tough enough to have a normal life when you were a street cop. Homicide detectives might as well forget about relationships, romance, or any type of social life, especially on weekends, when the majority of murders occurred.

On the rare occasion she stopped to think about it, Regan found it ironic that she could have grown up to be so different from her mother, but still end up in a career that discouraged marriage and a family.

She checked out the block-long white limousine gliding past. When she'd worked in Vice, she'd busted a prostitution ring doing a bang-up business using limos as rolling motel rooms. Since this one had a Just Married sign in the back window, she let it pass.

It was turning out to be a peaceful night in the City of Angels, almost as if the city had done an aerial spraying of Valium, but neither Regan nor Van commented on it, since another Murphy's Law of police work declared that unspeakable evils would befall anyone who said, "Sure is a quiet night."

The rain streaking down the windshield of the black-and-white patrol car had driven most of the drunks, batterers, and robbers indoors, leaving only the neighborhood's homeless sleeping beneath soaked newspapers and plastic garbage bags. The souvenir shops selling Marilyn Monroe posters, movie clapboards, and maps to stars' homes were closed, their heavy metal shutters drawn down.

There'd been a time, before Regan was born, when the area that made up her precinct had been the glittering home of the motion picture industry. Glamorous movie stars had dined at the Brown Derby, drank champagne from crystal flutes, and attended premieres at Grauman's Chinese Theater in limousines. But T-shirt shops, check-cashing joints, and pornographic bookstores had invaded the once elite neighborhood, and addicts, prostitutes, and homeless men and women were as common a sight as Japanese tourists.

Hollywood was beginning to make a comeback, but Regan knew that even if the area did succeed in becoming Los Angeles' version of New York's Time Square, the dispossessed would simply pack up and drift somewhere else.

"This tip had better pan out," she muttered as they cruised by the Rock & Roll Denny's. "Even the working girls have enough sense to come in out of this lousy weather."

Inside the bright, twenty-four-hour restaurant, forlorn prostitutes seeking relief from the rain hunkered in the booths, drinking pots of coffee, smoking packs of cigarettes, and rubbing feet sore from pounding the pavement in ankle-breaking five-inch platform heels, all the time keeping an eye on the street outside the restaurant window in the unlikely event a silver Lotus might happen to cruise by.

Unfortunately, the average john who frequented these blocks was no Richard Gere, and the *Pretty Woman* Cinderella story about the tycoon falling in love with the heart-of-gold hooker was so far removed from these mean streets it could have been filmed on Mars.

"Word is, Double D's back from Fresno to hit some guy from the Eighth Street Regulars who's been poaching on his territory." Van repeated the phone tip that had gotten Regan to leave the warmth of the station. The seventeen-year-old with the yellow sheet as long as a Russian novel was as elusive as smoke. "He's got a new girlfriend and is laying low at her grandmother's place. The old lady got busted two years ago for running a crack house with her son and grandkids."

"And they say the American family's in decline. How come Granny isn't in prison?"

"Because she looks like she should be baking cookies rather than cooking dope. The DA couldn't get the grand jury to indict."

Regan shook her head in disgust. She'd become a cop because she'd wanted to make a difference, to help make people's lives better. But lately she'd begun to feel like a sand castle at high tide. It seemed that more and more of the idealist she'd been when she'd first put on that blue LAPD uniform was getting washed away each day.

"You're doing it again," Van said.

"What?"

"Humming that damn song."

"Sorry. Sometimes it gets stuck in my head." Some people's minds grasped onto jingles; whenever her mind drifted, it tended to break into "You Are My Sunshine." She'd stopped noticing it years ago; others, who found it understandably annoying, weren't so fortunate.

A gleaming black Lexus with muddy license plates caught Regan's attention as it passed in the opposite direction.

The passenger was looking straight ahead. The driver turned his face, but not before she caught a glimpse of him. Adrenaline sparked like a hot electrical wire hitting wet pavement. "I'll bet my next pay grade that's our boy."

"Sure looked like him."

Regan made a U-turn, then cursed as a grizzled, bearded man clad in camouflage with an American flag sticking out of his backpack began marching across the street with the determination of the soldier he'd once been.

"Come on, come on." Her fingers tapped an impatient drumbeat on the top of the steering wheel. Having suffered from post-traumatic stress herself, she resisted hitting the siren.

Mad Max was a fixture on the street. Since he claimed to have served in Vietnam, Regan had once, in a rash moment, asked him if he'd ever served with her father. He'd taken a look at the photograph she always carried with her, shook his head, and rattled off a string of gibberish from a mind burned by drugs, alcohol, and God only knew what kind of flashbacks.

It had, admittedly, been a long shot. But Regan could never stop herself from asking.

She took off the second Mad Max cleared the lane. That the vet didn't even glance back when the siren began screeching said a lot about both the neighborhood and his life.

Regan caught up with the Lexus at a red light just past Hollywood High. Van tapped the car's description, license number, and tag into her computer. The light turned green.

The vehicle started out slowly, testing the waters. Testing Regan.

Every instinct she possessed told Regan this was the murder suspect who'd managed to elude her for the past forty-five days. If she didn't nab the kid in another two weeks, she'd be forced to write up a sixty-day report, the closest thing in the murder business to conceding defeat.

The Lexus picked up speed.

"Come on, dammit." The computer, ancient and as cranky as she herself was feeling, seemed to take forever.

"It's him." Van's voice was edged with excitement. "He and another gangbanger carjacked the vehicle after committing an armed robbery at the Hollywood Stars Motel."

"Guess the son of a bitch ran through the five bucks he stole from that old lady," she muttered.

Last month's beating death of the eighty-five-year-old woman had been the most heinous thing she'd witnessed during her twelve years working Los Angeles' meanest streets: five in a patrol car, a year lost to hospitals and office duty, a year in robbery, another in vice, and the past four in homicide. Regan was thirty-three years old, but there were times lately she felt a hundred. And counting.

She flipped on the lights, unsurprised when the driver rabbited. Regan took off after it, Code 3, blue lights flashing, siren whooping.

# 3

*Blue Bayou, Louisiana*

"So," *Jack Callahan asked his brother,* "how's the search for a new sheriff going?"

"Lousy." Nate frowned as he tackled another stack of evidence bags from the police property room. Since they'd been collecting dust for decades, he figured they should be properly dealt with before he could begin remodeling the office. Opening the bags was like unearthing an ancient city; the deeper he dug, the older the evidence.

"I wasted Monday morning interviewing yet another Dirty Harry wannabe from Shreveport, who opted for early retirement to save himself from being suspended for excess brutality on a prisoner. There's a lawsuit pending on that case, no surprise."

The envelope held a slug that, according to the accompanying papers, had been dug out of a wall.

"Do you remember when Henri Dubois and Julian Breaux fought that duel at Lafitte's Landing?"

"Sure." Jack dug into his brown paper bag and pulled out one of the thick muffulettas he'd brought along for lunch with his brother. "It was Mardi Gras," he said around a mouthful of deli meats and cheese. "They got the fool idea firearms were the best way to settle who'd get the first dance with Christy Marchand." He frowned thoughtfully. "I recall them both being too drunk to hit their targets, but I don't remember what happened next."

Nate skimmed the papers. "Dad arrested them, they pleaded guilty to disorderly conduct, and they were sentenced to give ten percent of their crawfish catch to the parish food bank for the next six months."

"That sounds like something the judge would come up with," Jack agreed.

"Not that there was any excuse for shooting guns off in a crowded dance hall, but I can kind of understand how they might have been moved to passion. I was in love with Christy myself in those days."

The Blue Bayou Mardi Gras queen had gone on to be Miss Louisiana, landed a job as weather girl on KATC in Lafayette, then began working her way up the network ladder through larger and larger markets. She was currently a foreign correspondent for NBC's nightly news, and although her long, dark hair was now a short, perky blond bob, Nate still enjoyed looking at her.

"That's not surprising, since you tended to fall in love with just about every girl in the parish on a regular basis." Jack took a swig from a can of Dr Pepper. "Though I have to admit, Christy was pretty cute. So, got any other hot sheriff prospects?"

"Don't I wish." Since the case had been settled a dozen years ago, Nate tossed the papers and the slug into the circular file.

"How about the guy who was just leaving when I got here? The goofy-looking long-haired guy with the gold stud in his ear."

"Strange criticism from a man who returned to town sportin' an earring himself."

"I'm not applying to be a cop. Besides, Dani likes it. She says it reminds her of a pirate."Jack flashed a rakish grin Nate had to agree was damn piratelike.

Jack had always been the most dashing of the three Callahan brothers. And the wildest, having earned his teenage nickname, Bad Jack, the old-fashioned way: by working overtime to be the baddest-assed juvenile delinquent in the parish.

"The guy was some sprout eater from Oregon who wanted me to know right off the bat that he refused to carry a gun because he was a pacifist. Then asked me if there were any good vegan restaurants in town."

"Not much call for tofu burgers here in hot sauce country."

"That's pretty much what I told him."

"Question is, why he'd want the job in the first place?"

"He's a former soc major." The scent wafting from the bag was mouthwatering. One bite confirmed that the sandwich tasted as good as it smelled. "Seems he's got new liberal ideas 'bout law enforcement that none of the other cities he's interviewed with seem eager to embrace."

"Let me guess. The theory is based on the idea that all those murderers and rapists up there in Angola Prison are merely victims of a harsh, vengeance-driven society."

"From the little I let him tell me, that's pretty much it."

"Hell, that's an old retread idea."

"Well, like I said, it probably isn't real popular in the cop community. Which was why he was willing to come all this way to interview."

"So he thought we were so desperate we'd be willing to end up with him by default?"

"That'd be my guess. I explained that even though the last crime spree was Anton Beloit's kid taking that can of John Deere green paint and spraying his love for Lurleen Woods on the side of every bridge in the parish, I'd prefer the chief law enforcement officer in Blue Bayou to carry a weapon. And know how to use it. He told me he'd have to think about it. I told him not to bother."

"Lucky for you Blue Bayou's a peaceful place."

"Since the town's entire police force consists of Ruby Bernhard, who mostly sits behind her desk and crochets afghans for her hoard of grandchildren while waitin' for someone to call in a crime so she can play dispatcher; Henri Pitre, who refuses to tell me his age, but has gotta be on the long side of seventy; and Dwayne Johnson, who's eager enough but green as Billy Bob Beloit's damn paint, I sure as hell hope things stay peaceful."

Nate studied the former-DEA-agent-turned-thriller-novelist over the top of the crusty round loaf of French bread. "I don't suppose you're startin' to get bored, being out of law enforcement these past few years?"

"Nope." Jack shook his head. "I figure it's damn near impossible to get bored with a perfect life with the world's sexiest pregnant wife, two terrific good-lookin' kids, a great dog, and getting to tell lies for a living."

The yellow dog in question lifted her huge head, looking for a handout. She swallowed the piece of cheese Jack tossed her in one gulp.

"Nice to hear you put Dani in first place."

"We might have taken a thirteen-year detour, but she's always been first. Always will be." Jack took another hit of the Dr Pepper. "You know, marriage could be the best invention going, right up there with the combustible engine. You might want to give it a try someday."

"No offense, bro, but I'd rather—"

"I know." Jack shook his head. "Go skinny-dippin' with gators. Anyone ever tell you that line's getting a bit old?"

Nate frowned. Three weeks later, and the debacle with Charlene still irked. "Do you think I have a Peter Pan complex?"

"Probably."

This was not the answer Nate had been expecting. Or hoping for.

"That's why it's gonna be so much fun watching when you take the fall, you," Jack said with a pirate's flash of white teeth.

"I wouldn't hold your breath, you. 'Cause it's not going to happen."

"That's pretty much what I said, before Dani came back to town. And I'll bet Finn sure as hell never imagined getting hitched to some Hollywood actress." Jack shrugged. "When it's right, it's right."

"Marriage might be right for you guys, but it's not in the cards for me. Long-term relationships are just too much heavy lifting."

"Never known you to be afraid of hard work."

"It's different in construction. Eventually things come to an end."

"I doubt Beau Soleil will ever be done."

"That's beside the point."

"And that point was?"

"When I'm building something or restoring an old house, eventually I have something to show for the effort, something I can be proud of. The more time you put into a place like Beau Soleil, the better it gets. The more time you put into a relationship with a woman, the more likely it is that you'll mess it up. Then everyone just ends up angry, with hurt feelings. The trick is to know when to bail, before you get to that pissed-off point."

Granted, he hadn't pulled that off with Charlene, but usually he was able to remain friends with a woman after the sheets had cooled.

"Never met a woman yet who didn't feel the need to change a man," he grumbled.

"Dani's never tried to change me. Guess that's 'cause I'm already perfect."

"Talk about telling lies." Nate looked out the window at the January rain streaming down the glass. "Do you ever just want to take off?"

"I did that thirteen years ago," Jack reminded his brother. "But like the old sayin' goes, there's no place like home."

"Easy for you to say, since you've been just about every place in the world."

"That's true." Jack studied him more closely. "Is there a point to this?"

"I've never been anywhere."

"You went away to college."

"Tulane's in New Orleans, which is not exactly much of a journey. And I came home my freshman year."

"When *Maman* was dying." Jack frowned. "I don't know if I ever thanked you for that—"

"That's what brothers are for. Finn was tied up with that manhunt, and you were off somewhere in the Yucatán Peninsula chasing dope dealers."

Since he'd loved his *maman* dearly, Nate had never regretted his actions. He was happy in Blue Bayou; it was where his friends were, where his life was. Life was good. And if truth be told, there wasn't anywhere else in the world he'd rather live.

But there were still times, on summer Saturday afternoons, when he'd be watching a ball game on TV and wonder whether if he'd stayed in school and not given up the athletic scholarship that had paid his tuition, he might have made it to the pros. After all, the scouts had called him a phenom, possibly the most natural third baseman since Brooks Robinson.

He stifled a sigh. Yesterday's ball scores, as Jake Callahan used to say. He tore open the last evidence envelope.

"Hey, look at this." He fanned the yellowed papers out like a hand of bouree cards.

His brother leaned forward. "Stock certificates?"

"Yeah. For Melancon Petroleum."

Jack whistled. "They've got to be pretty old, since Melancon must've quit givin' out paper certificates at least two decades ago. If they're real, I'll bet they're worth some dough. 'Specially now that the company's rumored to be bought up by Citgo."

"There's also a death certificate for a Linda Dale."

"The name doesn't ring a bell."

"It was thirty-one years ago. Back when Dad first got elected sheriff." Nate frowned. "She died of carbon monoxide poisoning."

"Heating accident?"

"No." His frown deepened. "Suicide." He flipped through a small ringed notebook. "But Dad didn't buy that."

"He thought she was murdered?"

"Yeah," Nate said.

"Blue Bayou's only ever had two murders that I know of. That one back when we were in high school, when Remy Renault got wasted and shot that tin roof salesman he found sleeping with his wife."

"I remember that."

He also remembered the long, hot, frustrating summer when Mrs. Renault hired him to mow her lawn and clean her pool. She'd liked to sunbathe topless. When he got a bit older and realized that she'd been purposefully tormenting him, Nate had been real grateful he hadn't been the one Remy found rolling in the sheets with the woman who'd made the models in Finn's *Playboy* magazines look downright anorexic.

He skimmed some more of the notes, written in a wide, scrawling script not that different from his own. "Seems Dad even went up to Baton Rouge, to try and get the state cops to come in on the case, but while he was gone, Dale's sister showed up and had the body cremated."

"Which would have destroyed any physical evidence he needed to make a case."

"Yeah. But the ashes aren't all the sister took away with her. There was a toddler in the house. Dad figured she'd been left alone about forty-eight hours. She'd obviously been scrounging for food; he found some empty cookie packages on the kitchen floor and an empty bread wrapper in her room."

"Shit. What about Mr. Dale? Where was he while all this was going on?"

"Appears there wasn't any Mr. Dale."

"Single woman havin' a baby out of wedlock sure wasn't unheard of three decades ago," Jack said. "But it could've created a bit of a stir in a small Catholic town like this one."

"That's what Dad thought." It wasn't that people were more uptight here than other places around the country; people in Blue Bayou certainly knew how to pass a good time. But whatever sexual revolution had taken place during the sixties and seventies had been kept behind closed doors.

"Linda Dale was a lounge singer at Lafitte's Landing. Seems like it would have been hard to save up enough money from whatever salary and tips she was making to buy all this stock."

"How much does it come to?"

Nate checked out the certificates again and did some rapid calculation. "The face value back then was twenty-five thousand dollars."

Jack whistled. "Which means that there's a thirty-three-year-old woman out there somewhere who's due a tidy inheritance. Though if Dale was murdered, it's strange the killer would leave the stock behind."

"The sister was from L.A. When Dad tried to find her, he ran into a dead end."

"That's not surprising. L.A.'s a big place."

"True." Nate picked up a small bound book. "But Linda Dale kept herself a journal, too. If we'd never known *Maman*, but she'd left behind somethin' that would tell us a little about her and then someone stumbled across it, wouldn't you want them to try to find you?"

"*Mais* sure. But finding her's gonna be a long shot. If Dad couldn't find this Linda Dale's sister back then, what makes you think you can after all these years?"

"He didn't have the Internet. Besides, we've got ourselves an ace in the hole. Our special agent big brother."

"Finn quit the Feebs."

"Just 'cause he left the FBI doesn't mean he lost his talent for trackin' people down. And since he's living in L.A., that's gotta make things easier."

Nate picked up the phone and began dialing.

# 4

*Regan called in to Dispatch,* requesting all available units in the vicinity to respond. While Van called off the intersections as they sped past them, she floored the gas pedal. The Crown Vic skidded around the corner and flashed through the rain-slick streets, the high-pitched wail of the siren shattering the night.

The police-issue sedan was no match for the Lexus, but the fact that she was a lot better driver was on Regan's side. Working against her was the twinge of fear in the back of her mind at each cross street. It had been seven years since the car chase that had nearly cost her her life, and she still had the scars.

Dammit, homicide detectives didn't do chases. They showed up after the killing and methodically began working a case that would take them from a dead body to a live suspect.

"Shit!"

There was a flash from the Lexus. A slug hit the windshield, shattering it into a spiderweb of cracks.

Regan's already hammering heart was flooded with a burst of adrenaline as the slug buried itself in the backseat. One of the reasons she'd worked so hard to make this division was because any adrenaline rushes were supposed to come from the thrill of putting together all the pieces of a crime so well that when she showed the finished picture of the puzzle to a jury chosen at random, those twelve men and women would find one human being guilty of murdering another. Murder cops weren't supposed to be risking the lives of innocent civilians, not to mention their own, by acting out the raging pursuit myth created by movie and television scriptwriters.

"Shots fired," Van reported.

"Shots fired," Dispatch echoed. "Ten-four."

"That was close," Van said.

"Yeah," Regan agreed grimly, trying not to think about the fact that her Kevlar vest had been supplied by the lowest bidder.

The chase had been picked up by at least five patrol cars. The screaming, flashing light parade, which was now hitting speeds in the sixties, left Sunset to barrel through a quiet residential neighborhood. Regan's murder books—a stack of three-ring binders that contained all the homicide cases she was currently juggling—went sailing onto the floor when she hit a speed bump full-on.

The Lexus took a corner too tight, tilting onto its right two wheels and looking in danger of rolling over; Regan backed off a bit to avoid crashing into it. No sooner had it settled back onto four wheels than it careened over the center line, sideswiping two vehicles parked on the other side of the street, taking out two mailboxes and a section of Cyclone fence. Brakes squealing, it came to a shuddering halt in the front yard of a tidy 1930s bungalow.

Two males exploded from the car and took off into the shadows.

"Suspects are on foot." Regan gave Dispatch their description, as best as she'd been able to tell from the spreading yellow glow of the porch light.

"Copy. All units, suspects are fleeing on foot. Ten-twenty. Officer needs assistance," the disembodied voice announced as Regan sprinted between two houses.

She was within inches of the passenger when he swerved and ran straight into a darkened swimming pool. Water splashed into the air and over the deck, drenching her already rain-wet sweatshirt and jeans.

"One suspect just landed in a pool," she reported into the radio, pinned to her sweatshirt. "You scoop out Flipper," Regan called to Van, who was on her heels. "I'll stick with Double D."

Having begun running years ago, to get back in shape after surgery and as rehabilitation, Regan was now nearly the fastest runner in the precinct. The only guy who could beat her was a former USC running back who had a good six inches on her and legs as long as a giraffe's.

Heart pounding painfully against her ribs, Regan dashed through a hedge. As branches scratched her hands and face, all her attention was focused on her perp. The *whop-whop-whop* sound of the police helicopter reverberating overhead told her the cavalry had arrived.

They beamed a light down on the scene, turning it as bright as day. "Freeze! Police!" she shouted, just like they'd taught her at the academy. Twelve years on the job, and she'd never seen it work. It didn't tonight. "Dammit, I said freeze!"

She managed to grab the back of his T-shirt, but since he was as wet as she was, half her age, and outweighed her by at least fifty pounds, he jerked free, scrambled to his feet on the wet grass, and took off again, clearing the fence like an Olympic hurdler.

Regan followed, ripping both her sweatshirt and her arm on the barbed wire along the top of the fence. The shirt bothered her more than her arm; she'd just bought it yesterday. "There's thirty dollars down the damn drain!" she cursed.

They pounded down an alley, splashing through the puddles formed by countless potholes, past huge dogs barking behind fences. Just when Regan was sure her lungs were going to burst, she launched herself into the air and nailed him with a flying tackle that sent them both skidding across what seemed like a football field's length of gravel. They finally came to a stop when they crashed headfirst into a group of galvanized metal trash cans.

"When a police officer says freeze, you're supposed to stop running!"

"How the hell I supposed to know you're a goddamn police officer?" he shouted back. "You ain't wearin' no uniform."

"I suppose you figured all those flashing lights and sirens were just a parade?" Hugely ticked off, she slammed her knee into his back, holding him facedown while a pair of uniforms arriving from the other end of the alley grabbed his arms and legs.

"The guy needs peppering," said one cop, who had to be a rookie. It was obvious he was having a grand time with all this. Regan was not.

"We don't need it." One absolute truism in police work was that you were always downwind from pepper spray. He'd find that out for himself, but Regan would just as soon not be in the vicinity when it happened. The perp's elbow slammed into her rib cage, nearly knocking the air out of her.

Once they'd finally gotten the suspect subdued, she said, "Congratulations. You win tonight's grand prize by racking up at least a hundred moving violations. That doesn't begin to cover the carjacking and motel robbery. And let's not forget the original murder and rape counts."

Regan snagged one of his wrists. Ignoring the string of epithets, all colorfully graphic, several anatomically impossible, she caught the other wrist, then yanked on the plastic restraints. While she missed the decisive sound of the old metal handcuffs clicking closed, the ratchet sound of the plastic teeth was still damn satisfying.

"What about my rights?" he shouted between curses. "I got rights, bitch."

She scooped wet hair out of her eyes. She was breathing heavily, but felt damn good. "You bet you do. Beginning with the constitutional right to be a boil on the butt of society. But in case you haven't figured it out yet, even most of your homeboys draw the line at killing a little old lady who never did anything but give you a job cleaning up her yard and made you a glass of lemonade."

With the help of the others, she yanked him to his feet and recited the Miranda warning she suspected he'd first heard in grammar school. Then, ignoring the pain in her solar plexus and the burning of the slice on her arm, she walked him down the middle of the street to one of the cruisers angled at the curb.

Tonight's bust, as satisfying as it was, would create a mountain of paperwork. She'd be lucky if she managed a couple hours sleep before having to show up at the courthouse tomorrow.

Six hours later Regan had showered, changed, and was hunched over her laptop keyboard, attacking the stack of report forms, trying to push yet more paperwork through the byzantine legal system.

You never saw television cops doing paperwork. Homicide cops on TV only handled one or two cases at a time, and except for the occasional season-ending cliffhanger, always managed to wrap up the crime in an hour, minus time for commercials. In real life, a detective was forced to juggle dozens of old cases while struggling to stay ahead of the deluge of new ones.

The motto of the LAPD homicide division was "Our day begins when yours ends." What it didn't mention was that it was not uncommon for a homicide detective to work around the clock.

"So," Barnie Williams, who was two months away from retirement and a house on the beach in Mexico, said from the neighboring desk, "this guy calls nine-one-one and says his wife saw a light on out in the garage. He looked out the bedroom window, and sure enough, there are some guys moving around in there, looking like they're loading up stuff.

"Dispatch explains that it's Saturday night, cops are all tied up with more vital shit, there's no one in the vicinity, but stay put and they'll send someone out as soon as possible.

"Guy says okay, and hangs up. A minute later, he calls nine-one-one again and says there's no hurry sending the cops out, because he just shot and killed all the guys in his garage."

He'd succeeded in capturing Regan's reluctant attention. "So, what happened?"

"Well, the shit hits the fan, and it takes less than three minutes for half a dozen cars to pull up on the scene, including Rockford and me, Armed Response Unit, and a producer and cameraman from that TV show *Cops*, who just happened to pick tonight to ride around with a couple patrol officers."

"Jones from Rampart," elaborated Williams's partner, Case Rockford. He was leaning back in his chair, hand-tooled lizard cowboy boots up on the desk. "And that rookie with the Jennifer Lopez ass that even manages to look fine in blues."

"Her headlights aren't bad, either," a detective from across the room volunteered.

"She spends her own bucks to have her uniform privately tailored," offered Dora Jenkins, a female detective. "If she didn't, her ass would look as big as Montana. As for the headlights, they're silicone."

"No way," Williams said.

"Way. She got them back when she was a Hooters waitress. The restaurant loaned her the bucks for the surgery."

"Are you saying those Hooters girls aren't naturally endowed?" another detective asked with mock surprise.

"So what happened with the guy who shot the robbery suspects?" Regan asked Williams in an attempt to return the typically wandering cop conversation to its original track.

"Oh, turns out they're all alive, and the department's own J.Lo and her partner get to make a bust for the cameras," Rockford replied. "They're happy as white on rice, but Barnie and I were majorly pissed, 'cause we were at the drive-through at Burger King and had just gotten our Whoppers when the call came in."

"I hate cold burgers," Williams muttered.

Rockford picked up the story again. "So Barnie gets in this guy's face and yells, 'I thought you said you killed them!' The man just stands there, puffing away on a cigarette, cool as can be, and says, 'I thought *you* guys said there weren't any cops available.' "

The story drew a mixture of laughs and groans. Wishing caffeine came with an IV option, Regan shook her head and returned to her typing.

"Hey, Hart," called a deep voice roughened by years of cigarettes.

Since another Murphy's Law of police work states that computers only delete reports when they are nearly done, Regan saved her work for the umpteenth time and looked up at the uniformed cop standing in the doorway.

"What's up, Jim?"

"There's a guy here to see you. Says it's personal."

"Obviously he doesn't know anything about cop shops." She glanced around at the bank of desks crowded together, files that no longer fit on desktops piled onto the floor beside them, telephones jangling, computer keys tapping, the cross conversations that kept anything from being personal.

"Should I bring him on back?"

"No need," a drawled voice offered.

The cop spun around, one hand going instinctively to his sidearm; Regan stood up, pulled her .38 from the desk drawer, and quickly skimmed a measuring look over him.

Six-two, one-ninety, blue eyes, brown hair. No scars, tattoos, or identifying marks that she could see. He was wearing jeans that looked faded from use, rather than any trendy stone or acid wash. His unabashedly becoming bomber jacket was unzipped, revealing a blue shirt that whether by accident or design matched his eyes; his leather boots were scuffed and, like his jeans, looked well worn. He was carrying a manila envelope.

He didn't look dangerous. Then again, neither had Ronald Lawson, that Robert Redford lookalike serial killer who'd finally been arrested by the FBI last summer.

"How did you get back here?" It was her street voice, controlled, but sharp enough to cut granite.

"Detective Kante was just coming in and was kind enough to show me the way."

A dimplelike crease flashed at Van, who'd just arrived with coffee from the espresso shop across the street.

"Hey, he came with a letter of recommendation." Van smiled up at the guy with the warmth of an old friend as she handed Regan the brown cardboard cup.

"A recommendation?" Regan lifted her brow, the only one of the three not smiling.

"From the FBI." He took a folded piece of paper from his shirt pocket and held it out. "Well, to be completely accurate, Finn's a former special agent. He said he worked with you on the Valdez murder."

Valdez was one of Lawson's victims, which could only mean the letter was from Finn Callahan. Regan snatched it from his hand and skimmed the few lines, which were as terse and to the point as the special agent had always been, merely suggesting that she might want to hear Nate Callahan out. It was signed "Just-the-Fucking-Facts-Ma'am-Finn."

Since Finn Callahan wasn't one for chitchat, Regan suspected he hadn't told anyone about the late-night argument they'd had after eighteen hours of canvassing the UCLA area in record-breaking heat, searching for witnesses in the Lawson case. Finn's cut-and-dried method of keeping conversation to the subject certainly allowed for more people to be interviewed, but she'd insisted that by allowing them to chat a bit, you often learned important facts the witnesses might not have realized they'd known. Regan rarely lost her temper, but too little sleep and too much caffeine made her blow up that night. She'd shouted at him, shoved impotently against his chest (the man was huge), and accused him of being Just the Fucking Facts Ma'am Finn Callahan.

He'd surprised her by laughing, and instead of causing things to escalate, her accusation cleared the air. From then on, they'd worked out their own version of good cop/gruff cop.

It had taken Finn another year to bring Lawson down, but the investigation had been a thorough one, with enough evidence gathered that had the killer been tried for the death of the UCLA coed, the DA would have won a conviction.

"I didn't know Finn Callahan had a brother."

"Actually, he's got two," Nate said. "There's another you might have heard of. Jack. He writes books."

That was putting it mildly. Jack Callahan was a former DEA agent turned blockbuster best-selling author. Touted as a new generation's Joseph Wambaugh, he'd soared to the top of the lists with his first novel. Regan had bought all his books for his women characters, who were more richly drawn than those written by most men. Especially former cops turned writers, who, even if they managed to make it past the Madonna/whore stereotype, too often seemed to portray females as victims.

"With both an FBI agent and a DEA agent in your family, you should be aware that wandering around in a police station can get you shot." Why was it the good-looking men were always the stupid ones?

"I realize that, officer."

"Detective." For some reason, Regan felt a need to establish rank in this case.

"Detective," he agreed. His blue eyes warmed; gorgeous white teeth flashed. "Which is why I enlisted Detective Kante's help."

"Want me to throw him out?" the desk cop asked.

Now that she knew the man standing in front of her was Finn's brother, Regan could see the family resemblance. "No, that's okay." His eyes were a deeper blue than Finn's chillier hue, his sun-tipped hair chestnut rather than Finn's black, and his body lankier and more loose-limbed. He was also more casually boyish, but the masculine self-confidence was all too familiar. It had surrounded Finn like an aura, it emanated from the gritty black-and-white author photograph on Jack Callahan's novels, and Nate Callahan, for all his outward, easygoing charm, possessed it in spades.

She reached for the phone.

"If you're calling Finn to find out why I'm here, he won't be able to tell you. Because he doesn't know."

Regan folded her arms across the front of her black silk blouse, angled her head, and narrowed her eyes. "Why not?"

"Because I didn't want to bother him with details."

Details. She already had so many damn details to deal with, she felt as if she was being nibbled to death by killer ducks. "Look, if your car got towed and you need help getting it out of impound, you're out of luck, because we don't do that here. Nor do I fix speeding tickets. If you want me to arrest someone, unless you're talking about a murder, I don't have the time to get involved, but you're free to file a complaint with the desk sergeant."

She picked up a heavy blue binder. The murder book contained everything she'd gathered during the course of her investigation, and she'd spent the few hours between last night's bust and this morning memorizing pertinent facts for today's court testimony.

He tucked his thumbs into the front pockets of his jeans, rocked back on his heels, and appeared to contemplate the matter. Regan had participated in countless interrogations over the years, and had learned from some of the best cops in the business, but she'd never met anyone who could draw a pause out so long.

"My car's back home," he said finally. "I don' know anyone who's been murdered, at least not lately, and except for the street crew that spent last night jackhammering through the pavement outside my hotel room window, I don't really have any complaints."

His slow, easy smile was a contrast to the thoughtful look he skimmed over her face. Even knowing that after all the surgeries she'd undergone, her facial scars were more imagined than real, she was still discomforted by such silent scrutiny. Especially from a man whose own face could have washed off a cathedral ceiling.

"As for why I came, well, it's a long story."

"Then you're really out of luck. Because I have to be in court in thirty"—she glanced down at her watch—"make that twenty-five minutes. And counting."

"That's okay. I'll ride along with you, and we can talk on the way."

"The LAPD police force is not a taxi service. And even if I were willing to allow a civilian to tag along, which I'm not, there wouldn't be any conversation, because I'll be going over the details of my testimony on the way."

"Finn's a stickler for details, too." The nicks and scars on the hand he skimmed over his hair seemed at odds with his pretty face. "We can talk over lunch."

"I wasn't planning to eat lunch." She'd be lucky to score a candy bar from the courthouse vending machine. "So, why don't we just cut to the chase, and you can tell me what you're doing here."

"Like I said, it's a long story. And personal."

"I don't want to offend you, Mr. Callahan, but unless you've committed homicide, I'm not terribly interested in your personal life."

"Not mine, *chère*. Yours."

Regan would have sworn there was no longer anything that could surprise her. She would have been wrong.

"It won't take very long," he coaxed when she didn't immediately respond. "If I wanted to dump it on you without any explanation, I would have used the mail and not bothered flying all this way. So, since my flight back home doesn't leave until this evening, how about I jus' come to the courthouse and we can talk after you wrap up your testimony."

His voice might be as smooth as whiskey sauce over a rich bread pudding, but she refused to be charmed. "They don't have phones in Louisiana?"

"Sure they do. Even in Blue Bayou. That's a nice little town in the south of the state, down by the Gulf," he volunteered. "I'm mayor."

"Good for you." He was certainly the antithesis of the stereotypical sweaty, overweight, south-of-the-Mason-Dixon-line politician wearing a rumpled white suit, seated on a veranda in a rocking chair, sipping from a silver flask of Southern Comfort. "And the reason you didn't just pick up a telephone and call was . . . ?"

"I thought you'd rather talk face-to-face."

She really did have to get going. Judge Otterbein, a stickler for time, ran his courtroom with the precision of a Swiss watch.

Once again he seemed to sense her thoughts. "I promise I won't say a word on the way to the courthouse."

The room had gone unnaturally quiet. Aware they were drawing the attention of every detective in the bull pen, she reached for the gray wool jacket draped over the back of her chair. Moving with surprising speed for someone so seemingly laid-back, he beat her to it.

"I can do that," she muttered, taken off guard as he held it out for her.

"Sure you can," he said agreeably. "But my daddy taught me to help a lady into her coat."

"I'm a detective, not a lady," she reminded him as she slid her arms into the sleeves. "And your father might want to think about joining the twenty-first century."

"Now, that might be a little hard for him to do. Seein' how he's passed on."

"I'm sorry. I didn't know."

He shrugged. "Don't worry about it. I'm not surprised Finn didn't mention it, since my big brother's not real talkative on a good day. Anyway, it was a long time ago."

A less observant woman might have missed the shadow that moved across his lake blue eyes. Regan didn't need her detective skills to spot the No Trespassing sign. Nate Callahan wasn't that old, she mused as they walked out of the station toward the police garage. Maybe thirty, thirty-one tops. So, how long was a long time ago?

Not that she cared.

Since the remote hadn't worked for weeks, she unlocked both car doors with the key. "Since I like and respect your brother, I'm willing to hear you out," she said. "But until court's adjourned, I have more important things to focus on. Say one word, and I'll have to shoot you."

"Works for me," he said agreeably as he climbed in beside her.

"Fasten your seatbelt." She jerked her own shut.

Neither spoke as they cruised into the steady stream of traffic, engine valves rattling. Since the teenage Front Street Crip defendant was the son of a city councilwoman, this was one of her more high-profile murder cases. TV news vans, their satellite uplinks pointed skyward, lined the street outside the courthouse. Wanting to avoid an appearance on the six-o'clock news, Regan pulled into the underground parking garage.

"I know I promised to keep my mouth shut, but you wouldn't shoot me if I say jus' one little thing, would you?"

"What?"

He turned toward her, putting his hand on the back of her seat. A standard seduction ploy that hadn't worked since she was fourteen and Tom Hardinger had copped a feel while they'd been sitting in the back row of the Village Theater in Westwood, watching *Indiana Jones and the Temple of Doom*.

Apparently undeterred by the gun in its holster on the waistband of her skirt, he leaned toward her, close enough so Regan could smell the coffee and Juicy Fruit on his breath. Close enough to make her muscles tense. Too close for comfort.

"You sure do smell good, *chère*."

"Detective." She cut the engine and climbed out of the driver's seat. "And I'm not wearing perfume."

His warm blue gaze fastened on hers over the roof of the car. Regan's stomach fluttered. Telling herself that's what she got for skipping breakfast, she ignored it.

"I know." His grin was slow and sexy and had undoubtedly seduced legions of southern belles. "Detective, *chère*."

Steeling herself against that bone-melting smile, she turned and began walking across the garage with long, determined strides, heels tapping on the concrete floor.

For Finn's sake, she'd listen to whatever Nate Callahan had to say, which she suspected wasn't nearly as personal or intriguing as he'd tried to make it sound. Then, before the sun sank into the Pacific, she'd send the man home and get back to chasing the bad guys.

# 5

*She was really something.* Oh, not his type, of course, Nate had been telling himself from the moment he'd walked into the squad room and spotted her sitting behind her desk, her forehead furrowed in concentration as she typed away at blinding speed. In fact, he wasn't even sure he liked her, which was unusual, since he tended to like most everyone he met. Especially females.

She was tall and willowy, but not at all skinny. Her arms, revealed by the short-sleeved blouse she'd covered up with her jacket, were firm in a way that suggested she worked out regularly. Her hands were slender, her long fingers with their unpolished nails looking far more suited to playing the harp in some southern drawing room than pulling a trigger.

Her lips, which were neither too thin nor kewpie-doll full, but just right, were unpainted. Her hair was styled in a short, thick cut in order, he imagined, to appear more cop than woman. But it wasn't working, because he figured most men—himself included—would be tempted to run their hands through those glossy strands.

The discreet pearl earrings were all wrong. Nate mentally exchanged them for gleaming hoops that would bring out the gold in her whiskey-hued eyes. She'd unbuttoned only the top button on her blouse, and in his mind, Nate unbuttoned another. Then one more.

What was she wearing beneath that unadorned blouse? Something cotton and practical? Or a bit of feminine fluff and lace? The mixing of the tailored charcoal wool suit and silk blouse suggested she was a woman of contrasts.

Her skirt was slim, ending at her knees when she was standing, but revealing an enticing flash of firm, stocking-clad thigh when she crossed her legs.

Like the earrings, the neat and tidy suit was all wrong for her. She was a woman born to wear rich jewel tones. Nate had no trouble imagining the smooth flesh of her breasts framed by emerald silk.

He listened as the defense attorney battered away at her for an hour, the woman's voice rising to stridency as she paced the floor in front of the witness stand, challenging everything about the investigation, attacking the chain of evidence, the veracity of the witness reports, Detective Regan Hart's possible personal prejudice.

"I do have a personal prejudice," Regan agreed.

At the table, the teenage defendant, wearing a suit so new Nate was surprised it didn't still have the price tag hanging from the sleeve, smirked.

"I'm prejudiced against the idea that a human life in some L.A. zip codes is worth less than one in a more affluent neighborhood; and that if several hundred American soldiers were killed in an overseas mission, politicians all over this country would be clamoring for a change in policy, yet when hundreds of citizens die every year in areas of this city that a politician never ventures into without police guard, and then only at election time—"

"Objection, Your Honor." The defense attorney popped up like a jack-in-the-box.

Regan didn't spare her a glance, just kept her gaze directed on the jury as she finished her declaration. "There appears to be a business-as-usual attitude toward murder. And I hope I'll always be prejudiced against the cold-blooded murder of a child."

"Objection," the attorney repeated with more strength.

"Sustained," the judge agreed. "Witness will keep her answers to the questions and refrain from making any speeches."

"I'm sorry, Your Honor." She turned back to the attorney. "Could you repeat the question?"

There was a ripple of laughter among the spectators. The judge frowned, and the bailiff warned everyone to be quiet.

The attorney, who looked angry enough to chew nails and spit out staples, tried again. "Do you have any personal prejudice against my client's race or socioeconomic status?"

Her expression didn't change, but watching her closely as he was, Nate saw the flash of irritation. "No."

The two women's eyes held, and Nate doubted there was a person in the room who couldn't hear the clash of swords.

"So," the attorney began again, "let's walk through what you did when you arrived on the scene. Step by step."

"If we're going to do that, we're breaking for lunch," the judge decreed. "Court's adjourned until one-thirty."

He slammed down his wooden gavel, signaling the midday recess. While Regan locked herself away with the DA, planning strategy, Nate went next door to a bar and grill, ate an order of wings, and watched a lissome blond on the bar television breathlessly report the latest in the case that seemed to have captured the city's attention. Although the DA had apparently fought it, television cameras had been brought into the courtroom, the better, he thought, for the defense attorney, who appeared prone to dramatics.

"Good-looking broad," the bartender said, watching a replay of Regan's testimony while spritzing seltzer into glasses for the lunch crowd. "For a cop."

Nate agreed.

"She comes in here every once in a while. Doesn't talk much, just orders a Coke, or maybe a glass of white wine at the end of the day. I figure she might be a former waitress, 'cause she tips real good."

Nate took a drink from his pilsner glass of draft. "What's the prevailing opinion on this case?"

"The evidence against the gangbanger is rock solid, but his mother has gotten her kid his own private dream team, so who knows how the jury's going to vote." He shrugged. "Folks seem to respond to star power."

Watching the jury as the questioning resumed after lunch, Nate worried about that. Unlike the defense, Detective Regan Hart's tone remained cool, matter-of-fact, and, like the rest of her, almost too much in control. While he wasn't any expert, he wondered if she might not be better off appealing as much to the jury members' emotions as to their heads. She was beginning to remind Nate more and more of Finn. What would it take, he wondered, to make the woman relax?

As she stepped down from the witness stand, Nate found himself wondering how cool and collected the detective would be when she learned his reason for coming here to L.A.

It was over. Despite some initial discomfort caused by Nate Callahan watching her so intently, Regan had managed to stay calm, cool, and professional. She hadn't let them see her sweat, and by the time she'd finished her testimony, everyone knew that the baby-faced defendant was guilty as sin. Regan knew it, the defense team knew it, the judge knew it, and you didn't have to be a psychic to sense that the majority of the jury members, who'd remained engaged but could no longer look the kid in the eye, had known it, too.

Which was why, of course, the defense attorney had suddenly asked for a recess minutes before the case closed. The deal was swiftly cut by those Great Compromisers, the lawyers on both sides.

Nate Callahan was waiting for her outside the courtroom. "Good job. You sure as hell impressed me."

"Thank you, Mr. Callahan, but impressing you is not high on my list of priorities."

"It's Nate," he said easily, falling into step beside her, adjusting his long-legged stride to hers. "You don't seem real pleased with the outcome."

She stopped in her tracks and looked up at him. "Why should I be pleased?"

"He's goin' to prison."

"For second-degree murder." She shook her head, still fuming. "What the hell does that mean? How can eight-year-old Ramon Consuelo be second-degree dead?" She raked a hand through her hair. "He's one hundred percent dead, dammit." She would have much preferred a slam-dunk win over a lousy, convenient plea bargain.

"You did your best," he said mildly. "Which Mrs. Consuelo seemed to appreciate."

"He was her last living child." Regan wondered how any woman survived the pain. "Her seven-year-old daughter was killed six years ago by a hit-and-run drunk driver who swerved into a group of kids waiting for the school bus. She lost a two-year-old daughter to AIDs back in the nineties. She hadn't even realized her drug abuser husband had passed the virus on to her until the baby was born HIV-positive. She's still alive; the baby isn't. Ramon was her last child and her only son." She blew out a long, slow breath. "And now she doesn't have him, either."

"It must be hard," he said. "Doin' what you do, caring like you do."

"Some days are harder than others." As were the nights when her sleep was haunted by those whose deaths she hadn't managed to avenge. "What time is your flight?"

"It's a while yet. We can talk over supper."

"Do you have a pen?"

"Sure." He reached into an inside jacket pocket and pulled out a ballpoint.

Regan ignored it. "Then write this down. I'm not having dinner with you."

Her hard stare seemed to deflect right off him. "You have to eat to keep your strength up for playing cops and robbers."

"I don't consider my job playing."

"It wasn't meant to be taken literally, detective. Anyone watching you in court today could tell you take your work real seriously."

"It's become almost a cliché," she murmured. "But there's a reason the idea of homicide detectives being the ones who speak for the dead is always showing up in books and movies. Because it's the truth." She slanted him a look. "But I suppose, being Finn's brother, you already know that."

"*Mais* yeah. Finn can be a serious one, he. But he's loosened up some since he got married."

"I heard about that." Regan had been amazed that the most serious man she'd ever met had married one of Hollywood's highest profile actresses. And not just any actress, but the new Bond Girl, for heaven's sake. You couldn't turn on a television these days without seeing some promo for the movie.

"He and Julia didn't hit it off right away, but they're sure happy now."

"That's nice." She meant it. Having had a front-row seat for the horrific things people who'd once been in love could do to one another, Regan had become a conscientious objector in the war between the sexes.

"It'll take a while to tell you my story," he said. "So, how about getting a couple burgers and going out to the beach? I've never been to the Pacific Ocean, but I hear it's real pretty."

That smooth-talking southern steamroller might work back home in Louisiana, but it wasn't working on Regan. "Look, Mr. Callahan—"

"Nate," he reminded her with a quick smile.

She waved his correction away with an impatient hand. "Why don't you tell me—as succinctly as possible—why you've come here, so I can get back to work, and you can go back to Big Bayou."

"It's Blue Bayou, like the old Orbison song. It was originally named Bayou Bleu, after all the herons that nest there, but over the years it's become Anglicized."

"How interesting." She didn't care about how the damn backwater town had gotten its name. She also wasn't sure this man knew the meaning of succinct. "Now, if we could just get down to business?"

"You know, sometimes it's not a bad idea to take a little break and clear your head." He skimmed a hand over her shoulder, which stiffened at his touch. "You seem a little tense, detective."

"What I am, is losing patience." The roughened tip of his fingers brushed against her neck, causing a spurt of her pulse. "And I don't know how things are done down in the bayou, but touching an armed woman without asking permission could get you shot here in the city."

"You thinking of shooting me?"

"The idea is becoming more appealing by the moment."

Because that lightly stroking touch stimulated hormones she'd thought she'd locked away in cold storage, Regan pulled away just as a detective she'd once worked with walked by. Her week with the man had been spent dodging clumsy passes, and the smile he gave her was close to a smirk, suggesting he believed more was going on here than a frustrating conversation.

"Look." Nate dipped his hands into his front pockets. "We're wasting a lot of that time you said you don't have, standing around this parking garage arguing. So, how about we just stop somewhere, pick up some supper, and drive to the beach, where I'll tell you a little story, then you can drop me off at LAX and I'll be out of your hair."

Regan sighed in frustration. Since he was turning out to be as stubborn as his eldest brother, they'd undoubtedly get things over with a lot faster if she just agreed to dinner.

Nate didn't appear the least bit surprised by her caving in, which only heightened Regan's irritation as she drove the two blocks to the Code Ten, a local cop bar and grill named for the police off-duty lunch code. After another brief argument, which she won, they each paid for their own burgers, then headed toward the coast.

# 6

*"This is real nice,"* Nate said a few minutes later as they sat on a bench on the Santa Monica pier. The air was cool and crisp, and scented with salt and faraway places. "And worth the trip."

"Which was about?" She took a waxed wrapped burger from the bag and nearly moaned at the scent of grilled meat and melted cheese. She'd become so used to skipping meals, she'd learned not to notice hunger pangs. Now Regan realized she was starving.

"Like I said, it's a little hard to explain. See, my daddy was sheriff of Blue Bayou when he was killed in the line of duty."

She'd just taken a bite, and had a hard time swallowing. Having attended more funerals than she would have liked, Regan knew how hard the loss of a cop killed in the line of duty could be on a community. She also knew how hard not having a father could be on a child.

"That's rough."

She'd been the only kid she knew whose dad had died. Oh, there'd been lots of divorced dads who only saw their sons and daughters on weekends, some that had taken off to parts unknown, and a couple of kids whose mothers had never married their fathers. But to have a parent, even one your mother had divorced, die? That definitely made you stand out. Different.

"Yeah, it was hard. But like I said, it was a long time ago."

"How long?"

"Nineteen years this May." The way he didn't have to pause and think suggested the memory was still fresh in his mind.

"And you were?"

"Twelve." His expression was uncharacteristically sober. "Anyway,

I was emptyin' out a storage room in the sheriff's office before doing some remodeling—I'm a contractor—"

"I thought you were a politician."

"Bein' mayor's a volunteer position. Contracting pays the bills—at least most months. Anyway, I was goin' through some old evidence envelopes when I came across something that belongs to you."

"That's impossible."

She'd been to Louisiana twice in her life. Once was five years ago, when she'd given a workshop about protecting crime scenes at a cop convention in New Orleans; the other was last month, when she'd flown to Shreveport to bring back a robbery/murder suspect.

"Your mother was Karen Hart, right?"

"I suppose you learned that from Finn."

"I did," he said on a smooth, genial tone that probably made him a dandy politician back home. "He was going on the information I gave him from an old police file. It's one of those funny coincidences, seein' as how you two worked together and all."

He'd just piqued her curiosity again. "What police file?"

"The one I got your *maman*'s name from."

"Look, Finn Callahan's a crackerjack detective. In fact, he's the best I've ever met. But even he can screw up occasionally. My mother was a partner in a law firm. She was not the type of person to end up in a police file."

"How old are you, detective?"

"I fail to see how my age is relevant to this conversation."

"According to this file, your mother had a sister. One who died and left behind a toddler who'd be thirty-three years old."

Regan took a sip of coffee she had no business drinking this late in the day. The caffeine would mean another sleepless night. "News flash, Callahan, I'm not the only thirty-three-year-old woman in the world. Besides, my mother was an only child."

He pulled a sheaf of papers from the manila envelope he'd been carrying when he came into the station. "Karen Hart's listed as Linda Dale's only living relative. Except for a girl baby named on her birth certificate as Regan Dale."

Regan hated her hesitation in taking the envelope from his hand. Shaking off an uneasy sense of foreboding, she forced her shoulders to relax as she skimmed over what appeared to be a valid police report from Blue Bayou Parish, Louisiana. Then she looked at the copy of the birth certificate. Linda Dale, whoever she was, had been twenty-five years old when she'd given birth to a seven-pound, three-ounce daughter. The father was listed as unknown.

"I've never heard the name Linda Dale. Or Regan Dale. My name is Hart. It's always been Hart."

"There's a photograph, too." He reached into the envelope again. "Linda Dale was a real pretty lady. You might find her a little familiar."

The photograph had obviously been taken in New Orleans; Regan easily recognized the ornate cast-iron grillwork on the front of the red brick building. The woman was wearing a red, white, and blue Wonder Woman costume, suggesting the picture had been taken either at Halloween or during Mardi Gras. The color had faded over the years, but there was no mistaking the face smiling back at her.

Impossibly, although the hair was a bright, coppery red, not brunette, it was her mother's face. It was also much the same face Regan had seen every morning in her bathroom mirror, until plastic surgeons had dug out the bits of metal that had torn apart her skin and sculpted her features into as close an approximation as possible to what she'd been before that fateful night she'd driven her patrol car into a trap meant to be a literal dead end.

There was another, more important difference between her face and the one in the photograph. Regan didn't think she'd ever experienced the depth of emotion glowing in Linda Dale's light brown eyes. It was obvious that the woman was madly, passionately, in love with whoever was holding the camera.

Regan felt Nate looking at her, waiting for some response that she refused to give him. "Interesting." Not wanting him to think she was afraid to look him in the eye, she lifted her gaze. "But it doesn't prove anything."

"She looks quite a bit like you."

"Somewhat like me," she corrected. "Her nose tilts up more than mine does, and her jawline's softer." Hers was more angular, her manufactured cheekbones sharper. "And her hair's a different color."

"Women have been known to dye their hair. It's still a pretty close resemblance."

"Even if we looked like twins separated at birth, it wouldn't prove anything. They say everyone has a double; in fact, there's a night bartender at the Code Ten who's a dead ringer for Julia Roberts." She did not reveal that this unknown woman could be a dead ringer for

Karen Hart, since that would only reinforce his ridiculous argument.

"The evidence folder says she's Linda Dale. Karen Hart's twin sister," he stressed.

"That still doesn't necessarily prove your point. If there weren't all sorts of ways to interpret evidence, court dockets wouldn't be so crowded."

"Good point." He tilted his head and studied her. Quietly. Thoughtfully. "Trust doesn't come real easy to Finn, either."

If he was telling the truth, the woman in the photograph was dead. But Regan felt a familiar, palpable emotional pull. While she was not a fanciful person, Regan knew that it was, indeed, possible for people to speak beyond the grave. She'd experienced it before, when the unseeing eyes of a murder victim seemed to be imploring her to find the killer who'd ended her life.

"Let me put it this way, Mr. Callahan: just weeks ago I sat next to a Christmas tree in the living room of a house that looked like a place the Beav might have grown up in, and listened to a woman insist that the last she'd seen of her four-year-old daughter was when she'd lost her at the mall on a visit to see Santa Claus.

"Two days later, I arrested her drug-dealing boyfriend for being a coconspirator in the mother's plot to kill the little girl for a thousand-dollar insurance policy. A third friend, whom we also indicted, had taken her from the mall and out into the desert, where he'd shot her in the head. She never did get to sit on Santa's lap. And it might have taken us years to get justice for her, if some teenagers hadn't been riding their new ATVs out on those dunes and came across her body.

"I've had to step over the body of a woman whose husband shot her while holding a knife at the throat of their toddler son. When we showed up in response to a neighbor's nine-one-one call, he hadn't even bothered to change his bloody clothes, but still swore he was innocent and insisted on lawyering up.

"I've seen children shot while playing hoops on a public playground, for no other reason than some other kid needed to kill a stranger to make it through some gang initiation. And I worked with your brother for twenty-four-hour days during one of the city's worst heat waves, trying to nail a sicko pervert who got his kicks torturing young women. No, Mr. Callahan, I do not trust easily."

He tipped his head again. The California sun, buttery bright even on this winter day, glinted on his short, spiky hair and turned the tips to a gleaming gold that not even the most acclaimed Beverly Hills colorist could have pulled off. Regan found it strange that she, who'd worked years to perfect her intimidating cop look, could be made to feel so uneasy by his silent scrutiny.

"You've definitely got a cop's brain inside your pretty head, Detective *Chère*."

She bit into a salty French fry. "And you've obviously got a chauvinist's brain inside *your* head, Mayor Callahan."

"For noticin' that you're a good-looking woman? It's a man's right to look at pretty things." He slid an appreciative glance over her. The light sparkling in his eyes could have been the lowering sun glancing off the water, but Regan didn't think so. "Doesn't necessarily mean he intends to do anything more without permission."

While she might not be Nicole Kidman, Regan had had men look at her before. Even after her cruiser had been turned into a shooting gallery. But somehow she'd gotten to be thirty-three years old without ever feeling in danger of melting. When his gaze lingered momentarily on her legs, she wished she'd worn her usual pantsuit rather than a skirt to court today. Which in turn made her furious at herself for responding like a giddy high school girl talking with the quarterback.

"A word of advice: don't hold your breath." Emotional need always made her defensive, which led directly to the safer emotion of anger. She crushed the burger bag. "Now if that's all the evidence you have to show me—"

"*Dieu*, are you always in such a hurry? Didn't anyone ever tell you that rushing around is bad on a person's system?" He shook his head as he took some more papers from the envelope. "These stock certificates would make Regan Dale a rich woman."

"They could also make you a rich man, since they appear to be bearer certificates."

"They don't belong to me." He looked affronted that she'd even suggest cashing them in. "I'm pretty sure they're yours."

As he held them toward her, Regan reminded herself that the devil didn't come slithering up to you with horns and a tail and reeking of brimstone; he came courting with engaging manners and a smooth, seductive smile.

"So you say. I still say you're wrong."

"Why don't you take them anyway? Do a little detecting. You might find something that'll make you feel different."

Regan knew otherwise, but there was no way she was going to let him accuse her of having a closed mind. "We'd better get you to the airport before you miss your flight."

His smile was slow, delicious, and in its own charming way, dangerous. "There's still time."

"It's obvious you don't know LAX. It was bad enough before the heightened security measures. Now it's a nightmare." She tossed the bag into a trash barrel.

"You know, the Pacific's even nicer than I've heard," he said as they walked back to the parking lot. "I appreciate you bringin' me here."

"Like you said, I had to eat."

Regan had no idea what those papers he'd shown her meant, but she was certain they didn't have anything to do with her. But still, the cop in her couldn't quite stop mulling over the what-ifs.

Nate Callahan seemed to have an instinct for knowing how far to press his case. He didn't bring the subject up again as she drove to the airport, but instead waxed enthusiastic about his south Louisiana home.

"Well, I can certainly see why you were elected mayor," she allowed as she pulled up to the curb designated for departing passengers. "You're quite an ambassador for the place."

"It's a nice little town." He unfastened his seat belt, reached into the backseat, and retrieved his overnight bag. "Pretty as a picture on a travel poster and real peaceful." He paused before opening the passenger door and gave her another of those slow perusals. Unlike the earlier ones, this didn't seem to have any sexual intent. "We jus' happen to be looking for a new sheriff. If you ever get tired of life in the fast lane, you might want to give us a try."

"Thanks for the offer, but I'm quite happy right where I am." That might not be the whole truth and nothing but the truth, but she saw no reason to share her private feelings with a total stranger she'd never see again.

Once again he surprised her with his speed, reaching out and slipping her shades off her face before she could react. "I'm not one to argue with a *belle femme*." Before she could back away, the roughened pad of his thumb brushed against the skin below her eyes. "But you look like you could use a little bit of R&R, Detective *Chère*."

"Dammit, Callahan—"

"Jus' making a little observation." He ducked away before she could push him out of the car. He was standing on the sidewalk, seemingly oblivious to the driver who was leaning on his horn behind them, urging Regan to move on so he could claim the spot. He reached back into the car, handing her the sunglasses and a white leather book he'd taken from his jacket pocket.

"What's this?"

"Linda Dale's journal. I thought you might like to read it. The details are a little sketchy—she wasn't a real regular writer—but it does mention her baby. And her sister, Karen Hart. I put my phone number on a piece of paper inside the front cover, just in case you want to call and compare notes once you're finished reading." He turned and walked away into the terminal.

The horn behind her sounded again, a long, strident demand. A uniformed cop standing on the curb blew his whistle and began heading toward her.

"All right, dammit." Resisting the urge to ticket the other driver for disturbing the peace—unfortunately, Nate Callahan had already succeeded in doing that—Regan shifted the car into gear and pulled out into traffic.

# 7

*So," Jack asked,* "how did it go?"

After arriving in Blue Bayou, Nate had driven out to Beau Soleil, the antebellum home Jack was in the process of restoring. Nate was the contractor, and so far the work had been going on close to two years; he figured it could easily take a lifetime to restore it to its former glory, but fortunately neither Jack nor Dani—whose family had owned the plantation house for generations before Jack had bought it—seemed to mind living in a construction zone. Somehow his brother's wife had created a warm and cozy atmosphere out of what could have easily been chaos.

The kids were upstairs doing homework, and Dani was sitting over in the corner of the former library, knitting. Or, as she'd explained to Nate, attempting to learn to knit, which wasn't nearly as easy as it had appeared in that big yellow *Knitting for Dummies* book she'd brought home from Blue Bayou's library.

"Not as bad as it could have." He bent over the custom-made green-felt-topped pool table, broke the balls, sunk two in a corner pocket, and called for stripes. "Not as good as it might have."

Jack leaned against the wall, paneled in a gleaming burled bird's-eye maple, and chalked his cue. "What's she like?"

"Smart." The ten ball disappeared into a side pocket. "And real pretty, though outwardly tough as nails, which I suppose a cop's gotta be." He banked a red-striped ball against the side and sent it spinning into the far corner. "She reminded me a lot of Finn. Before he fell for Julia."

"That grim, huh?"

"Not grim, exactly." He thought about that as he moved around the table. "She's like our big brother in that she obviously believes in truth, justice, and the American way. And she's definitely not like any of our bayou belles."

Jack laughed at that. "What's the matter, baby brother? Did the old Nate Callahan charm finally fail you?"

"I got her to hear me out." Memories of the unwilling flash of emotion he'd seen in her gaze when he'd touched that shadowed skin beneath her eyes had him, not for the first time, imagining touching her all over. Momentarily distracted, he missed the shot. "She also took the envelope we found in the evidence room."

"What did she have to say about the autopsy report?"

"Nothing, 'cause at the last minute I decided not to give it to her. She'd had a rough day in court, and I was already dumping enough on her, so I figured that could wait until she called."

"She might not be real happy with you, holding back that way."

"Then I'll just have to smooth things over."

"If she's as much like Finn as you say, I'm goin' to enjoy watching that."

Having spent a lot more years of his youth in bars and pool halls than Nate had, Jack went to work, sending three balls in quick succession thumping into holes.

Across the room, Danielle Dupree Callahan cussed as she dropped another stitch. She'd told Nate that the buttery yellow yarn was going to end up a baby sweater. But he sure hadn't been able to picture it from what she'd managed to knit so far.

"Think she'll actually call?" Jack asked. The solid three ball clicked off Nate's fourteen and sent the seven into the far corner pocket

"Yeah." Balls were disappearing from the table like crawfish at an all-you-can-eat buffet. "She's a detective, she. She'll be curious enough to call." He watched as Jack used the ball he'd missed to sink the eight ball. "You know, it gets old, having my hustler brother all the time beating the pants off me."

Jack's smile flashed. "Jus' one of the benefits of a misspent youth." He held out his hand. "You owe me twenty bucks, *cher*."

As he dug into his pocket for the money, Nate glanced up at the wall clock, calculated that it'd be about eight o'clock in Los Angeles, and wondered if Regan had gotten through the journal yet.

She had. As Nate Callahan had said, the journal entries were sporadic, occurring weeks, months, sometimes even years apart. After leaving home at seventeen to become the girl singer in a country band, Linda Dale had bounced from town to town, singing gig to singing gig, man to man, for seven years. She hadn't seemed to mind the nomadic life. Most of the men she'd gotten involved with were musicians, and while she appeared to set limits—bailing on relationships the moment they turned abusive—Regan began to detect a pattern. It appeared the woman was part free spirit, intent on enjoying life to the fullest, and part nurturer, needing to rescue lost souls (even those who might not want to be rescued) and take care of everyone around her.

The entries, Regan noticed as she ate her way through a pint of Ben and Jerry's Chocolate Chip Cookie Dough ice cream, seemed to come at the beginnings and ends of her romances, which gave the impression that when she was actually in a relationship, she was too busy living life to comment on it.

None of the men had been the prince in shining armor Dale professed to dream of; quite a few had been toads. But she'd remained upbeat, positive that somewhere out there in the world her true soul mate was waiting for her.

After a gap of nearly two years, an infant girl she named Regan came into the picture. And then things became really personal. Regan put her head back against her headboard, closed her eyes, and took a long deep breath.

The woman in her sympathized with the single mother trying to balance a singing career and a young daughter. The detective needed more. She turned to the next page and began to read again.

*January 1. J surprised me by slipping away from the gala. The champagne he brought with him to toast a new year in my dressing room was ridiculously expensive. It tasted like sunshine, all bright and sparkly, but didn't go to my head nearly as much as his promise: that this year we'd finally be able to live together openly. Our lovemaking, while necessarily quick and silent, was still every bit as thrilling as it had been that first time in New Orleans after he'd walked into the Camellia Club and changed my life.*

*January 15. I think Regan has picked up on my excitement. Sometimes I wonder if I made the wrong decision, choosing to raise her alone, to risk her growing up without the stabilizing influence of both a father and mother.*

*Of course Karen, for whom Regan has always been a sore subject, scoffed at me when I suggested that on the phone the other day and said something I couldn't quite understand about women needing men like fish needed a bicycle, which I took to mean that I was foolish to enjoy having a man in my life. In Regan's life. Then again, Karen has always been the most independent person I've ever known. My legal eagle sister makes the Rock of Gibraltar look like a tower of sand by comparison.*

*It was such a delight watching Regan spin around the room like a small dervish. She's such a sunny child. I like to think she's inherited my talent, but she already has so much more confidence than I did at her age. Sometimes more than I do now, I think. And while I know all mothers think their children beautiful and talented, I truly believe she could be a star someday. When I told her that soon she'll be dancing at our wedding with her new daddy, she giggled, flung her arms around me, and gave me a huge smack of a kiss. I can't remember being happier.*

*February 14. Valentine's Day. J and I managed to slip away to be together at lunch. We went out to our secret place and made love, and afterward he surprised me with a stunning heart-shaped ruby pendant. He said I'd had his heart from the day we met. As he's had mine. And always will. He fretted when I wept, but I assured him that they were tears of joy, not sorrow.*

*February 25. It's the waiting that's so hard. I understand, as I always have, that J's position is not an easy one, and I must remain patient. He came into the lounge with friends tonight, and just seeing him without being able to touch him—and be touched—is so impossibly hard. Soon, he tells me. Soon.*

*March 4. Regan's second birthday. J showed up this evening with a stuffed elephant. It's a silly, fanciful thing, covered with green, purple, and gold polka dots and wearing a Mardi Gras crown and beads. Regan loves it.*

"No." Regan snapped out a quick, harsh denial. She pressed the heels of her hands against her eyes, hard enough to see swirling stars. Emotions she couldn't begin to sort out crashed down on her as the disbelief she'd been trying to hang on to shattered.

Her heart was pounding hard and fast as she forced herself to continue reading, her eyes racing over the page.

*He seemed a bit distracted, which isn't surprising, since tomorrow's the day he'll finally tell his wife that he's leaving Blue Bayou. Regan and I will be leaving with him. Anticipation has me as giddy as if I've been drinking champagne from a glass slipper. I won't sleep a wink tonight.*

That was the final entry. Regan closed both the journal and her eyes as waves of emotion crested over her. She lifted a hand that felt as heavy as stone and dragged it through her hair.

She'd felt this way twice before: during those weeks she'd spent in the hospital, drugged to the gills, and again three years ago, when her mother had died suddenly and unexpectedly from a brain embolism. Karen Hart, L.A.'s own Wonder Woman, had finally run across something she couldn't control.

The thing to focus on, Regan told herself, was that she'd survived both. She'd surprised all the medical experts with the speed of her recovery, and she'd gone back to work despite the constant need for more surgery, just as she'd overcome the shock and pain of loss to take care of the funeral arrangements for her mother.

She dragged herself out of bed on legs that felt as shaky as they had during her early months of physical therapy, and opened the cedar trunk.

Fighting for breath, she took the elephant, which for some reason she'd named Gabriel, from the trunk. He was tattered and worn, as any child's favorite old toy would be. And while technically in a court of law he might be considered circumstantial evidence, since he couldn't be the only such toy in the world, Regan knew, without a shadow of doubt, that she was holding proof of Nate Callahan's claim.

The gilt crown had long since disappeared, and she remembered breaking the beads during a playground tug-of-war with six-year-old Johnny Jacobs. She'd ended up with the elephant, and he had gone home with a black eye that had caused her to be deprived of television for an entire week after the crybaby had gone home bawling to his mother.

Regan hadn't minded being banished to her bedroom; justice was more important than watching *Starsky and Hutch.* Her father would have understood, she'd insisted at the time.

Her father. The thought struck like a sledgehammer to the head. If

Karen Hart wasn't her mother, then John Hart was probably not her father, either. Unless, of course, he was the *J* in the journal?

Could he have been having an affair with his *sister-in-law?* The distance between Louisiana and California would have made it difficult, but then, there was no indication that Linda Dale had been living in Louisiana when she'd gotten pregnant.

And would a woman actually take the child her husband had fathered with another woman into her home, raising her as her own? Especially if that other woman was her own twin sister?

Regan didn't think many women would, but Karen Hart could well have been the exception. She might not have taken the child out of any sense of family or love, but she'd had a steely sense of responsibility. It also might have explained why Regan could not recall a single warm maternal moment spent with the woman she'd always believed to be her mother.

"Damn." A predawn light cast the room in a soft lavender glow. Regan pressed the stuffed toy against her breast, bowing her head against a sudden onslaught of pain. Had her entire life been built on a foundation of lies? And if not, what parts had been true, what parts false?

She picked up the piece of hotel stationery with Nate Callahan's telephone number and stared at it for a long time, trying to decide what to do next. Part of her wanted to call him, to ask the myriad questions bombarding her brain.

She removed the receiver from the cradle, dialed the 985 area code, then slammed it down again. She needed time. Time to absorb the shock. Time to decide her next move.

She had to get out of here. Had to clear her mind, start thinking like a cop, and not a woman who'd just had her world pulled out from under her.

Still numb, she changed into her running clothes, though a cold winter drizzle was falling and fog was blowing in from the beaches. As she began running through the still dark streets, Regan remained oblivious to the weather. The very strong possibility that the woman who'd fed and clothed her, put a roof over her head, and raised her, if not affectionately, at least dutifully, had also created a sham of a life, left Regan with a bitter, metallic taste in her mouth.

And so, beneath the thick gray clouds blowing in from the steely, white-capped Pacific, Regan ran. And ran. And ran.

# 8

A *breakout of gang wars* kept Regan working nearly around the clock, which, while exhausting, at least occasionally took her mind off her own problem.

She kept her secret to herself for nearly a month, viewing it on some distant level like a cold case she'd get to as soon as the hot ones were solved. Finally, after several marches by residents of the communities that were being torn apart garnered the attention of the press, politicians loosened the purse strings long enough to pay for more cops on the beat, which resulted in a string of high-profile arrests.

Once things seemed to have calmed down, Regan tracked down Finn, whose advice echoed what she'd been telling herself ever since Nate Callahan's visit. There was no way she was even going to begin to get a handle on her past if she didn't visit Blue Bayou—and the scene of Linda Dale's death—herself.

Regan made the travel arrangements. Then, after another long, early morning run on the beach, she called her partner. "Did I wake you?"

"Of course not." Van's groggy tone said otherwise. A male voice said something in the background. Regan could hear her telling Rhasheed who was calling. "So, what's up?"

"I'm going to be taking some leave time."

"Good idea. You've been working killer hours for too long. A break will do you good."

"I hadn't realized there was anything wrong with me." *Terrific. Could you sound any more defensive?*

"You haven't taken any real time for over eighteen months."

Nineteen. But who was counting?

"Where are you going?"

"Louisiana."

"Oh, lucky girl! New Orleans's got great food, great jazz, and lots going on, especially now with Mardi Gras coming up."

"I'm not going to New Orleans. I'm going to Blue Bayou. It's a little town closer to the Gulf," she said, anticipating Van's next question.

"I've never heard of it."

"I doubt if many people have. It's pretty small."

"How did you find out about the place?"

"I did an Internet search." The half lie caused a little pang of guilt. She *had* looked up the town's website, which had revealed what Finn had already confirmed: that Nate Callahan was, indeed, the mayor.

"How long will you be gone?"

"I don't know."

There was a longer pause. Regan could practically hear the gears turning in her partner's head. "This sudden trip wouldn't have anything to do with a man, would it?"

"In a way."

They'd known each other too long for Van not to realize something wasn't quite right. "Would you care to share what you're holding back on your partner and best friend?"

There was no point in trying to pretend everything was all right. "I can't. Not yet."

The curiosity in Van's voice changed to concern. "Anything I can do to help?"

Regan wasn't quite prepared to share details she didn't even know herself. "Thanks anyway, but I'll be fine. It's just some little misunderstanding I have to clear up. In case anything urgent comes up, I'm staying at the Plantation Inn."

"Sounds nice."

"I guess so." It was the only hotel in town. She recited the number she'd called to book her reservation, then, after reassuring Van that she really was fine, Regan began packing.

Fourteen-year-old Josh Duggan had never expected Louisiana to be so frigging cold. It had been snowing when he'd left Tampa, and he'd figured it'd stay warmer if he stuck to the southern states, but he'd been wrong. If someone didn't come along soon, he'd turn into a Popsicle.

He knew it was dangerous to be hitchhiking, but it wasn't like he had a whole lot of choices. After seeing the cop talking to the cook in the restaurant next to the bus station in Jackson, he'd been afraid to get back on the bus and had decided to take his chances with his thumb on the back roads, which was proving not to be the most brilliant idea he'd ever had.

So far only one car had passed on this narrow, lonely stretch of road. When he'd recognized the black-and-white as a trooper's cruiser, he'd dived into a ditch until it had passed. Now his clothes were wet and sticking to his skin, and he could feel the blood from the rock he'd hit his face on oozing down his cheek.

His stomach growled. He'd been promising it something to eat for the last twelve hours. Since he was down to about thirty-five cents, he was going to have to boost dinner. It wouldn't be the first time.

But first he was going to have to get to an effing town.

His spirits perked up just a little when something came looming out of the swirling gray mist. The roar of the diesel engine was unmistakable. But at the speed it was going, would it even see him in time? Josh was desperate enough to consider leaping in front of the cab when the eighteen-wheeler's air brakes squealed.

The semi came to a grinding stop about fifteen feet beyond him. He must have hurt his leg when he'd jumped into the ditch, because it hurt like hell to run on it, but afraid the driver would take off, he ignored the pain and sprinted on a limp past the two trailers to the cab. The big door opened. A man Josh would not want to meet in a dark alley was looking down at him. His eyes were black as midnight; a red scar started high on his cheekbone and slashed through a scrabbly thatch of dark beard. "What the hell are you doin' out here, kid?"

"Car broke down," Josh lied without a qualm. Everyone lied. "I was walking into town to try and find a mechanic."

Dark eyes narrowed. "Didn't see no car on the highway."

"I left it on a side road."

"Sure you did. You don't look old enough to drive."

Josh thrust out his jaw and met the openly skeptical gaze head-on. "I'm small for my age."

"That so?" The driver studied him for another long moment that seemed like a lifetime. "It's against regulations to take on passengers."

He jabbed a thumb at the sign in the window. "But hell, my old lady would kick my ass six ways to Sunday if she found out I left some skinny kid out in a frog-strangler like this." He shrugged. "Get on in."

Not waiting for a second invitation, Josh scrambled into the passenger seat. The rush of heat from the dashboard, mingling with the mouthwatering aroma that could only be doughnuts, made his head spin. "Thanks. I'd pay you for the ride, but—"

"Hell, I'm not interested in your money, kid. What I'd like is for you to tell me the truth, so I know whether or not I can expect the law to be comin' after you." He glanced up into the rearview mirror as if expecting to see flashing lights behind them.

Blue and red artwork snaked around huge arms the girth of tree trunks. Josh wondered if he'd gotten any of those tattoos in prison, then decided he didn't really want to know.

"I'm not some juvenile delinquent runaway, if that's what you're worried about," he lied.

If the driver picked up that cell phone fastened to the dash and called the cops, he'd be busted. Not that it'd do any good. They could drag his ass back to Florida, but he'd just run again. And again.

The driver didn't answer right away. Every nerve ending in Josh's body jangled as he plucked an empty Coke can from the cup holder on the dash and spat a huge stream of brown tobacco juice into it. "Don't much like the law," he said finally. He reached behind him and pulled a waxed Krispy Kreme bag from the sleeper. "You like doughnuts?"

"Who doesn't?"

The taste of the sugar-glazed fried dough nearly made Josh burst out bawling. Exhausted, he leaned his head against the window and watched the wipers sweeping the rain from the windshield. As the lonely sound of a train whistle wailed somewhere out in the heavy fog, he almost allowed himself to relax.

Nate was up on a ladder, ripping away some water-stained drywall, when she entered the sheriff's office. His built-in female radar detector had never failed him, and it didn't this evening. He glanced back over his shoulder at Regan Hart standing in the doorway of the former storage room.

Raindrops sparkled like diamonds in her sleek hair. She was wearing black jeans, sneakers, and a black Lakers jacket.

"I didn't expect to see you here," she said. No hello, nice to see you again, what a lovely little town you have.

"I was doin' a little work on the place."

"I came to see the sheriff. There wasn't anyone in the outer office." Her tone suggested she didn't approve.

"We're still looking for a sheriff. Mrs. Bernhard, she's the dispatcher, doesn't work after five. Her husband likes his supper on the table right on the dot, so he can eat it along with WATC's six-o'clock news." As he looked down into thickly fringed whiskey-colored eyes, Nate felt a familiar, enjoyable pull. "I never have figured that out, since it seems watching all that war, politics, and crime'd ruin anyone's appetite, but that's the way Emil likes it. And after fifty years of marriage, Ruby says it's too hard to teach her old man new tricks."

"The town doesn't have a night dispatcher?"

"Nope." She clearly did not approve. Nate shoved the claw hammer back into the loop on his tool belt, wondering how she could remind him so much of his big brother and still have him wanting to nip at that stubborn chin.

"What happens when a crime happens at night?"

"It rings into Henri Petrie's house. He's the senior ranking deputy. Mostly the only after-hours trouble happens at the No Name—that's a bar outside of town—or the Mud Dog, another local watering hole about a mile away from the No Name. Since Henri spends most every evenin' but Sunday at the Mud Dog playing bouree—that's a card game sorta between poker and bridge—he's usually already on the scene if trouble does break out."

He climbed down the ladder and noted her slight step back. Not only was she into control, she liked to be the one setting boundaries. Which wickedly made him want to press hers a little more.

"Though he's been complaining that being on call all the time is cuttin' down on his socializing, being as how he can't get drunk anymore, just in case something does come up."

"He wouldn't be the first cop to drink on duty."

"Probably true. But so long as I'm mayor, I'd just as soon he not." He saw the flash of skepticism in her eyes. "You're surprised."

"I suppose, if I'd given it any thought, I would've expected you to be a bit more laid-back when it came to law-and-order issues."

"Stick around a while, Detective *Chère*, and you'll discover I'm just full of surprises."

He could smell the rain on her hair. Accustomed to women who seemed to bathe in heady perfumes custom-blended in New Orleans, he'd never realized he could find the fragrance of rain and Ivory soap so appealing. Underlying the clean aroma was her own scent, which reminded him of those citrus candles his *maman* used to like, blended with freshly cut spring grass.

"It's real nice if you can have a job you enjoy, but that doesn't mean that everyone should go mixin' work and play. Especially when their job involves guns," he said with a slow smile that more than one woman had told him was irresistible.

Apparently they'd been wrong. Or, more likely, she was just a harder case than the average woman.

"But you do," she guessed with what appeared to be yet more disapproval. "Mix work and play."

Christ, the woman could be a hardass. Though, he thought, remembering how she'd looked marching away from him in that L.A. parking garage, as asses went, it was still a pretty fine one.

"Like I said, it's nice to have a job you enjoy. As for the drinking-on-duty rule, it's hard enough for the parish to make its liability insurance payments now. The last thing we need is a lawsuit from some city slicker who came down here to let off a little steam and got himself thrown into jail on a drunk and disorderly by a cop with whiskey on his breath."

"And you people prefer to handle things yourselves and leave outsiders . . . well, outside."

"That's pretty much the way it's always been down here," he said agreeably. If he didn't suspect that the weeks since he'd dropped his bombshell had been pretty damn tough on her, he might have let her know flat-out that he wasn't real thrilled with the way she seemed to be looking down not just on him, but on Blue Bayou as well. "How much do you know about the Cajuns?"

"I know who Paul Prudhomme is. And that I like Cajun food, and they have a reputation for partying."

"*Laissez le bon temps rouler*. That's the name of a song: 'Let the Good Times Roll.' " If her attitude so far had been any indication, he suspected it'd been one helluva long time since she'd *roulered* any *bon temps*. "It's pretty much a motto down here."

Nate wondered what it would take to get that cool, faintly sarcastic mouth to soften. He'd never kissed a cop before. The closest he'd come had been Jenna Jermain, a reporter who worked the police beat up in Ascension Parish. They'd passed a few good times before she'd landed herself a job on the *Houston Chronicle*.

"I read the journal," she said.

"I was hoping you would." He took another two steps forward; she held her ground. "So, you've come to Blue Bayou to track down some loose ends." Forward.

She didn't budge. The challenge was swirling in the air between them. "That's very perceptive."

"It's what Finn'd do." Forward. He felt a little tinge of victory when she finally retreated half a step.

"It's undoubtedly also what your father would have done, if he'd had the opportunity."

"Yeah." Her long legs, which seemed to go all the way up to her neck, were now pressed against the desk. *Don't like bein' boxed in, do you, sugar?* "He was a good man, my father. And a damn good cop."

"I suppose, never having met him, I'll have to take your word for that."

The little dig managed to get under Nate's skin and remind him that she hadn't come here to give a pleasant boost to his libido. Now that he'd gotten her attention, things could only get complicated, and he'd never liked complications. Which was why he still couldn't quite explain why the hell he'd put himself into the middle of this long-ago story and tracked down Linda Dale's daughter.

"Dad didn't believe the autopsy report," he revealed.

Although her expression didn't change, Nate thought she went a little pale.

"You have the autopsy report?" She sounded more pissed than shaken.

"Yeah." The look she shot him was way too familiar. Finn, who'd taken on the role of man of the house after their father had been blown away, hadn't let either of his brothers get away with much, and Nate had been on the receiving end of it too many times to count.

"And you didn't think that was important enough to share with me?"

"I wasn't even one hundred percent positive that you were the right woman." This time he was the one who took a step back.

"Yet you were sure enough to give me some of the papers."

He swore inwardly. "Not the ones that'd be real rough to read."

"And you felt it your job to protect my so-called delicate female sensibilities why?"

"It wasn' that way." Not exactly. "The autopsy report was an official crime document. The journal was a different matter. Jack and I figured that if our *maman* had died without us ever knowin' about her, and she'd left something like that behind, we'd want to read it."

"Did you?"

"Did I what?"

"Read it?"

"Hell, no. It wasn't any of my business."

Her eyes narrowed, studying him like he was some murder suspect in a lineup. "But you read the autopsy report."

"It was an official document. I'm a city official, so I figured I was entitled. The journal's personal."

"Yet your father obviously kept it for a reason."

"He didn't know where Linda Dale's sister took off to. And knowin' him, he probably wanted to keep it as evidence."

"In the event he reopened the case."

"Yeah. His notes, by the way, say he tried."

"As a rule, small-town police forces aren't equipped to handle a homicide."

"I 'magine that's the case. But Pop wasn't just some small-town, gut-over-his-shirt hack sheriff. He'd been a homicide cop up in Chicago and had a drawer full of awards."

"Most cops hang them on the wall."

"Dad never believed in skatin' on past accomplishments. He probably wouldn't have even kept the commendations and stuff if they hadn't meant a lot to *maman*. She'd always show them off to any of her relatives who'd bad-mouth her Yankee husband. After a while, they just shut up."

"Why, if he'd been working for a big force like Chicago, would he want to give it all up and come live in this . . ."

"Backwater hick town?" he supplied.

"It seems it would be a step down. Careerwise."

"Jake Callahan loved bein' a cop. Used to say he was born to the job. But his family was the most important thing in his life. *Maman* was homesick, and he figured Blue Bayou would be a nice safe place to raise his children. But I don' think it could have been easy on him in the beginning. From the stories he used to tell, he'd liked being a big-city cop, and I think the jury stayed out for a long time among the people here as to whether he was really going to try to fit in."

"Did he?"

"*Mais* yeah. He taught us boys that man was put on earth to help out his fellow man and to be part of a community, and that bein' a cop meant taking care of a community, and how organizing a youth baseball league, or taking an elderly widow a hot meal, or changing a tire on a pregnant young mother's car could all be, in their own way, just as helpful as rounding up stone-cold killers."

"Your father sounds like a good man."

"My father was a great man."

Her gaze shifted from his face, out the window to where the cobblestone streets wore a satiny sheen from an earlier rain and the sunset looked like red-and-purple smoke against the western sky. "What was the cause of death cited on the autopsy report?"

"Same as the death certificate," he hedged, even though he knew she was about to find out the answer herself. "Carbon monoxide poisoning."

She returned her gaze to him. "Was it listed as a natural death?"

Nate could tell that she had a lot more invested emotionally into the answer than she was letting on. He supposed cops, especially homicide detectives, grew used to death, but he also knew firsthand that the death of a parent was an entirely different thing. It was more personal. Even, he suspected, if you were talking about a mother or father you'd never known. Maybe Jack had been right; maybe he just should have left well enough alone and tossed the damn file into the trash.

"*Non*. It wasn't natural."

"That leaves either suicide or murder."

Jesus, did the woman have ice water in her veins? The only outward sign that he'd managed to score a direct hit was a quick blink of the eye. A train whistle sounded at the crossing just outside town. "The coroner opted for suicide."

Wishing that either of his brothers were around to handle this, Nate reached into the top desk drawer where he'd stashed the file, suspecting that if nothing else, her cop curiosity would eventually make her want to read it.

"Your father's not alone. Because I don't believe it, either. I'm going to want to see the house where she died."

"Now, there's going to be a little problem with that."

"Oh?"

"It got blown to pieces in a hurricane back in the nineties, and the land where it used to sit is now water."

"It figures." She shook her head and frowned as she read the top page with absolute concentration.

Nate was idly wondering if she'd give the same attention to sex when a sound like a bomb going off shook the building.

# 9

"*What the hell?*" He jerked his gaze from those tempting, unpainted lips to the window. "That sounded too close to be a rig explosion."

The oil rigs out in the Gulf had always been a hazard; his maternal grandfather had died on one before any of the three Callahan boys had been born. A cloud of smoke billowed over the top of the courthouse.

"Christ. It's coming from the tracks."

He turned back toward Regan. "You remember any first aid from your patrol days?"

"I passed a disaster response test six weeks ago."

"Good. Because we're gonna be needin' all the help we can get." He opened a desk drawer and threw her a badge.

"I don't need that," she said, even as she snagged the shiny sheriff's badge out of the air.

"Stuff like this tends to brings out the lookie-loos and Good Samaritans. There are going to be a lot of people getting in the way out there. This'll give you the authority to get rid of folks who don't belong or can't be of any real help."

Again proving that he could move damn fast when the occasion called for it, he was out the door like a shot, Regan right on his heels. Without waiting to be invited, she jumped into the passenger seat of the black SUV parked outside and pinned on the badge. It took them less than three minutes to drive to the redbrick fire station where Blue Bayou's fire and rescue department garaged its only pumper truck.

"There's not gonna be room for you in the truck." He was yanking on a pair of tobacco brown fireproof pants that had been folded down with tall rubber boots already inside them, so all he had to do was step into the boots and pull the pants up. "The keys are in the SUV." He grabbed a heavy coat and helmet. "I'll meet you out at the crossing."

Unlike the other narrow towns she'd driven past, which she'd supposed had sprung up in long narrow strips to save valuable waterfront land for crops, Blue Bayou had been laid out in grids. Sweeps of sunshine-bright yellow daffodils brightened squares fenced in fancifully curved wrought-iron fences, and trees lined the clean brick sidewalks. It appeared, as Nate Callahan had described it, a peaceful town.

There was nothing peaceful about the scene at the rail crossing. At least a dozen freight cars left a zigzagging trail along the muddy banks of the bayou. Broken railroad ties were scattered along the track, the metal rails shredded. On the far side of the track, a trailer from an eighteen-wheeler was on its side; farther down the other trailer was crushed and mangled, mute evidence that the semi had been hit trying to cross the track. The cab was upside down, the roof resting inches from the edge of the water; the glass lying on the ground had once been a windshield. It could have been worse. A lot worse.

"Thank God it was a freight," Nate said.

Regan nodded in agreement, not even wanting to think about the number of deaths and injuries there could have been if the railroad cars had been carrying passengers.

"I thought my furnace had blowed up," she heard one onlooker, who appeared to be at least in his eighties, say to another man. "I heard a bunch of grinding and then *boom*," he said. "Ol' Duke jumped clean off the *gallerie* and started barking." He pointed toward an old hound dog who was sniffing the air.

One of the train cars had knocked a utility pole down; its lines were tangled in a tall, moss-draped oak and sagged about ten feet above the top of the truck's cab. Sparks were flying, and as tree limbs burned, the lines drooped lower toward the cab.

"The driver's still in the truck," someone shouted. "There's an arm hangin' out the window."

"Can you tell if he's alive?" a fireman, whose helmet designated him as the fire chief, asked.

"He's not movin'."

"Christ," another fireman said. "There's no way to get the poor sucker out."

"We can't just stand by and let him die," Nate said.

"Can't run onto an accident scene with downed power lines, either," the chief said. "That's one of the first things they teach you in fire school."

A pair of state troopers arrived, sirens blaring, adding to the din. Walkie-talkies squawked. A crowd began to gather, as if to watch a Hollywood crew film a disaster-of-the-week movie.

"He's gotta have family," Nate argued doggedly, once again reminding Regan of his brother. Finn hadn't been one to back down from an argument, either; not when there was a matter of principal involved. "Mother, maybe. Wife. Kids." He pulled on his gloves. "I'm going in."

"You realize, of course, that truck could catch on fire any time," Regan said. Okay, so it was a pretty impressive gesture; it was also foolhardy as hell.

"One more reason to get the guy out. But I've probably got some time, since diesel fuel isn't as flammable as gasoline."

She knew that, but the knowledge didn't stop her from holding her breath as he cautiously ducked beneath the sagging wires. An odd hush came over the rescue workers as he dropped down on his belly and crawled the last eight feet.

"Hey," a voice called out from inside the cab. "We're trapped in here!"

Regan sucked in a sharp breath at the child's voice. Watching carefully, she actually saw Nate's shoulders tense beneath the heavy jacket.

"It's gonna be all right, *cher,*" he said matter-of-factly, as if train-truck collisions were an everyday occurrence in Blue Bayou. Metal screeched as the dented truck cab shifted, tilting precariously closer to the water.

"Shit, we're gonna drown!" the boy shouted.

"Don' you worry," Nate said again, his voice as calm as it'd been when she'd first met him in the station. "We'll be gettin' you out soon enough, you."

He yanked on the door. Nothing. "Shit, it's stuck."

"Can't use the Hurst," the captain pointed out. The Hurst, more commonly known as the Jaws of Life, could chew up metal like taffy. "You try takin' that roof off, you'll hit those wires for sure."

"How about goin' up from the floor?" another asked.

Nate shook his head. "We're sittin' on marsh, here. Even if we set it on blocks, they'd just sink into water. Then there's the little matter of starting up the gas unit while diesel's leaking from the tank."

He yanked again. Cursed again.

Nearby, another tree limb burst into flame as the power surged. The wires drooped even lower, nearing the upturned wheels.

"Anyone got a tow strap?" Nate called.

"I got a cable I use for towing breakdowns in the trunk of the cruiser," a trooper responded.

"That'll do. Go get it and bring it as close as you can." Once again Regan heard him talking in a low, soothing voice to the child inside the truck. "And Henri, why don't you back the ladder truck as near as you can get without hittin' those wires?" Which were currently lighting up the gathering twilight like Fourth of July sparklers. "And can someone toss me—very carefully—a blanket?"

Without giving it a moment's thought, Regan grabbed an army green blanket from a newly arrived ambulance and moved slowly, step by step, toward the cab.

"That's far enough, *chère*," he warned.

"If I throw it to you, it could hit the wires."

"If you get any closer, those wires could turn you into a crispy critter."

"Don't you watch TV? We cops get off on taking risks."

Though her voice was as calm as if she were writing out a speeding ticket, her nerves were jangling with adrenaline.

"That a fact?" Amazingly, his tone was as conversational as hers.

"Absolutely." The overhead wires crackled and sagged. Ignoring his warning, Regan bent lower until she was nearly doubled, and continued inching toward the truck. "Why, a day without danger is like a day without chocolate." Despite the chill, sweat was beating up on her forehead and between her breasts.

"I never heard it put quite that way before."

"Believe me, it's true." She shoved the blanket toward him. "It's in our blood."

"Thanks." He carefully pushed the blanket through the rectangular hole where the windshield used to be. "Hey, kid."

"Yeah?" The boy's tone sounded remarkably defiant, but Regan knew some people responded to fear with aggression.

"Put this over the driver as well as you can, okay? Then hunker down beneath it, because we're gonna have some flying glass in a minute."

Nate waited a moment for the boy to do as instructed. Then he shoved his gloved fingers through a hole in the driver's side window and tore the glass away. By now the trooper had arrived with the cable; the two men wrapped one end of it around the windshield post and the other around the bumper of the fire truck, which began slowly moving forward.

There was an ominous sound of groaning metal, and the cab tilted a bit, as if it might pull right side up. Just when Regan thought for sure they'd land in the water, the door broke off its hinges.

"Hey," Nate said, again to someone in the truck. "Good to have you back with us. Is anything broken?" There was a pause, then a mumbled response in a voice far deeper than the boy's.

"*Bien*. Now, here's what we're gonna do. You take my arm and climb out of here, real careful like, so you don't rock the cab. And I'll grab the kid."

A huge bearded man with the look of a renegade biker appeared in the open door and half jumped, half fell from the cab. Regan flinched inwardly when she heard the crack of a kneecap breaking, but the driver didn't have any time to indulge his pain.

The wires let loose, draping over the cab like Spanish moss just as Nate reached inside, grabbed the boy's denim jacket, and jerked him from the truck. They'd no sooner rolled aside when the cab burst into flames.

A collective cheer went up.

"Thanks, man," the grizzled driver groaned as a paramedic slipped a C-collar around his neck and strapped him onto a rolling half-backboard to protect his spine. "Weren't for you, my old lady'd be puttin' plastic flowers on my grave."

"Jus' doin' my job, *cher*," Nate said agreeably. "Wouldn't want you to get a bad impression of our little town." He put the boy onto his feet. "We'll be taking you into the hospital, too. Just to make sure."

Freckles were standing out like copper coins all over the kid's pale, thin face, but his brown eyes, as he folded his arms, were resolute. "Fuck that. I'm fine."

"Sure you are," Nate said in that mild, deceptively laid-back tone. "Problem is, I've heard of folks saying the same thing at accidents, then passing out without any warning. Wouldn't want to take a chance on you falling into the water and becoming gator bait."

"I'm not scared of any damn gators."

Regan wasn't sure if he was exaggerating or not. But having watched a special on alligators on the Nature Channel, she was uneasy about putting it to the test. Gangbangers she could handle, drug dealers she knew. But there weren't a lot of man-eating reptiles in the normally dry Los Angeles River.

"This your kid?" a paramedic asked the truck driver.

"I just picked him up." He looked decidedly defensive. Regan hoped it was only because he was worried about having violated the No Riders sign. "No law against giving people a ride. 'Specially when it's cold enough to freeze a well digger's ass and getting dark, besides."

"You have to wonder why a grown man was traveling with a child who isn't his own," Regan murmured.

"I was already there." Nate's serious expression revealed he shared her concern. He might not be a cop, and Blue Bayou might look like Louisiana's version of Mayberry, but obviously he'd picked up some sense of the dark side of the world from his brothers' work.

"If I were you, I'd have one of my deputies question him."

"Great minds think alike. Fortunately, I've got an officer capable of doing a bang-up job." He put his hand on her back in a possessive, masculine way that annoyed her. "Since the fog's really startin' to roll in and you don't know the way to the hospital, I'll drive you there."

She shook off the light touch. "Me?"

"You're the most qualified member of the force."

"Force? What force? This isn't my jurisdiction."

"Sure it is. I deputized you."

"Dammit, Callahan, this isn't the Wild West. You can't just put badges on people and make them part of your posse."

"I can, and I did." His expression sobered. "This needs to be done right. There's no way I'm going to put Dwayne on it. As for Henri, he's always tried real hard and done a good enough job, but Blue Bayou doesn't present a lot of opportunities to use real police skills, so even if he ever possessed any, they'd be real rusty about now."

"I didn't come to Louisiana to apply for a job. I already have one back in L.A."

"Where I'll bet you take protectin' kids real seriously." His gaze moved to the young teenager being loaded into the back of the ambulance.

Regan counted to ten. Reminded herself that she'd sworn to protect and to serve. Her professional duty might stop once she went outside her precinct boundaries, but her moral responsibility was an entirely different thing.

"Dammit." She folded her arms even as she felt herself caving. "That's not fair."

"Life's not always fair, detective."

"Tell me something I don't know." She had proof of that every day, even before she hit the streets looking for the bad guys. All she had to do was get out of the shower and stand naked in front of a full-length mirror.

"How about I make you a deal?"

"What kind of deal?"

"You help me out with this one little thing, and I'll do all I can to help you find out the facts about Linda Dale's death."

"A thirty-one-year-old case is about as cold as they get. What makes you think you can find anything out when your father couldn't?"

"He'd probably have had better luck if your aunt hadn't disappeared."

*Your aunt.* Even after she had read the journal over and over again, those words still rang so false. The ambulance pulled away from the scene, lights flashing, siren wailing.

"Besides, I've lived here all my life, me," he said, his Cajun syntax backing up his words. "I know everyone in the parish, which'll come in handy, since folks around here aren't real eager to answer questions from strangers."

"Small-town paranoia," she muttered.

"There you go, jumpin' to conclusions again. We tend to think of it as mindin' our own business. Now, I can understand why you won't do it for me, or even because, being an independent woman, you don't want any help digging up the truth 'bout your *maman*'s death. But I'm having a real hard time believing that cop who just risked her life for a kid won't want to do whatever she can to find out why that kid isn't sitting at home playing video games like he should be."

It was emotional blackmail, pure and simple. It also worked. "You really are shameless."

"You're not the first person to tell me that, sugar. But that's not the point here. That boy's puttin' on a good enough show, but beneath the surface, he reminds me of a whupped pup. I'd put hard money on the fact that he had a pretty good reason for running away."

"Hell. All right." She blew out a breath. "I'll do it."

"*Merci bien.*"

They drove together through the night, the headlights bouncing back against a dense wall of fog that surrounded the SUV, cutting them off from the outside world. Regan was grateful he was driving; she wasn't sure she could have told road from water.

"I suppose, having grown up here, you know your way around." She certainly hoped he did. She was in no mood for a moonlight swim.

"*Mais* yeah, though it's always changing." He leaned forward and punched on the radio, which was tuned to a station playing what seemed to be a sad song in French. "What was water yesterday could be land today. And vice versa."

"Then how do you know for certain where you're going?"

"Never gave it any thought." He seemed to now. "Guess it's just instinct. Like a homing pigeon returning to his loft. Once the bayou gets in your blood, I don't think you could ever get it out. Even if you wanted to."

"Which you don't."

"*Non.* Roots sink deep here. Sometimes I think 'bout taking off and exploring the world, but the truth is, mostly I'm pretty satisfied doing what I'm doin', where I'm doin' it."

Regan wondered how it would feel to be so at ease with yourself. So comfortable with your world and your place in it. As long as she could remember, she'd always pushed herself harder and harder, trying to please a mother who'd always been incapable of being pleased.

The police shrink she'd gone to, a bearded guy who seemed to be doing his best to look like Freud's twin—which made her wonder about his own identity problems—had suggested that it wasn't the ambush or the resultant injuries and lengthy recovery that had left her feeling constantly edgy and unable to sleep.

She was, he'd diagnosed, suffering from the impossible need to prove her worth not only to her remote, perfectionist mother, but also to the larger-than-life father she'd never known. The man who'd died a hero's death in a jungle halfway around the world.

"Which is, of course," the Freud wannabe had added, "impossible."

Perhaps. On one level, Regan understood that. She had, after all, minored in psychology in college. But on a deeper, more intrinsically personal level, she couldn't stop trying.

"That was a remarkable thing you did," she murmured. "Going in under those high-voltage wires."

"I wasn't alone. You were right there with me."

"Like I said, it's my job. Cops get paid to do stuff like that. I wouldn't think risking your life came under the job description of mayor."

He shrugged. "I wouldn't be able to live with myself if I hadn't tried to get him out of there. I lost my dad when I was twelve. The trucker's kids are going to have theirs. That's all that counts."

"It was still a brave thing to do."

The grin he flashed her was quick and devastating. And dangerous. His eyes, surrounded by soot and dirt, gleamed in the glow from the dashboard like the blue lights atop a police cruiser. "Don' tell me you just found something about me you can approve of?"

"Don't let it go to your head."

"I wouldn't think of it." They'd driven in silence for about five more minutes when he said, "You're probably used to all that."

"Guys with big heads?"

"No. Well, maybe you run into them from time to time, bein' how you live in L.A. But I was talking about wrecks, flashing lights, sirens. Injuries. Death."

"Detectives don't, as a rule, handle car wrecks unless there's evidence of a homicide." She'd thought about death, though. A lot. Her first week on the job, she'd spent hours on the phone after a shift trying to find a shelter and counseling for a woman who'd called 911 for a domestic abuse, then refused, despite two black eyes and a missing tooth, to press charges against her husband. A veteran cop had warned her against becoming too emotionally involved.

"Gotta hold back, Hart," he'd growled around a Reuben sandwich dripping sauerkraut. "The taxpayers of L.A. aren't paying you to hold people's hands and play counselor. If you want to be a social worker, then turn in your sidearm and go for it, because you're not going to be able to keep a cool head and maintain the judgment needed to do this job if you're too damn sensitive."

Easy for him to say. One of the reasons she'd gone into homicide was because she'd figured that if she switched to dealing with bodies, she'd be able to distance herself emotionally from her work. She'd been wrong. The dead often spoke a lot louder than the living. And they didn't stop just because she'd gone to sleep.

"I don't think anyone ever gets used to death." She wouldn't want to.

"Yeah." He pulled up in front of a redbrick building. "I read that in Jack's last book."

"That happens to be a yellow line you're parking by."

"I know." He cut the engine, pocketed the keys, took a placard reading "On Duty" from the center console, and tossed it onto the dash. She'd done it herself numerous times. Still . . .

"And the sign says it's reserved for police vehicles." At least he hadn't parked in the red ambulance zone.

"Then we're in luck, bein' how we're the police," he said reasonably. "At least one half of us is. The other half's fire, so I'd guess we have a right to park just 'bout anywhere we like."

"So how many tickets did you get before you were elected and able to award yourself the privilege of political office?" she asked as she climbed out of the SUV.

"I still get 'em. Blue Bayou runs on too tight a budget to let parking infractions slide." He opened the center console to reveal stacks of yellow slips of paper. "I save 'em up and pay 'em every month or so."

"Wouldn't it be simpler—and cheaper—to just park legally?"

"I suppose it would be. But just think of all the revenue the town'd be missing."

He'd placed his hand on her back again, in that casual way that suggested he was a toucher. Yet another way he was different from his brother; Finn had kept a privacy zone the size of Jupiter around himself. Regan suspected his new bride must really be something to have gotten past that man's emotional barricades.

"Besides, writing out tickets gives Dwayne something constructive to do during the slow times. He's one of our two deputies. Graduated from LSU last summer with a degree in criminal justice, and I think we're coming as a big disappointment. Sometimes I feel like I oughta pay some kids to go out and bash in mailboxes just so he'll have a crime to investigate."

If it were anyone else, Regan might have taken his words as a joke. Since she hadn't yet been able to get a handle on Nate Callahan, she wasn't at all certain he was kidding.

# 10

*The door whooshed open automatically.* The smell of disinfectant, blood, and stress sweat was like a fist in the stomach.

Regan hated hospitals. After her accident, when she'd been extricated from the crumbled mass of metal that had once been her police cruiser, she'd spent two weeks in ICU, another month on the surgical recovery floor, and weeks and weeks over the next two years undergoing reconstructive surgery and rehabilitation.

"You okay, *chère?*"

She hadn't realized she'd stopped walking until he'd turned around. "Of course." She had to remain calm. To think like a cop, instead of a victim. "Why wouldn't I be?"

"Now see, that's what I don' know." He laced their fingers together and skimmed his thumb against her palm. "Your hand's like ice."

"Because I'm freezing." She tugged her hand free. "I thought Louisiana was supposed to be warm."

"We have ourselves some cold spells in winter. It's the moisture that makes it seem colder than it really is; it seeps down deep into your bones." He brushed the back of his fingers up her cheek. "That's good."

"What?" She hated to keep backing away from him, but holding her ground would mean staying in too close proximity.

"Your color's comin' back. You were pale as Lafitte's ghost a minute ago."

"I was not," she lied. She'd felt the blood going out of her face as she'd gone light-headed. "I'd really like it if you'd keep your hands to yourself, Callahan."

"That's not gonna be easy, but I'll try my best."

"You do that." She resumed walking. "Who's Lafitte?"

"One of our more colorful citizens. A pirate. I'll tell you about him later, over supper."

"I ate at the airport." She hadn't wanted to waste precious time; the fast-food burger she'd eaten in the terminal sat like a rock in her stomach.

"It's a good story. You'll enjoy it."

The little exchange had given her time to adjust to being back in an ER. Her legs were much steadier as she walked toward a counter where a woman sporting an enormous orange beehive was chewing on the end of a pencil.

"Hey, handsome," the receptionist greeted Nate as they approached, "what's an eleven-letter word for 'having magnetism'?"

"Callahan," he answered without missing a beat.

She counted on fingers tipped in metallic purple. "Not that I'm arguing your point, *cher*. But that's only eight letters."

"Charismatic," Regan said.

The woman filled in the crossword puzzle squares. "That's sure enough it. *Bien merci*."

"I see the ambulance arrived," Nate said.

"It did. Truck driver's down the hall in X-ray. I figured somebody'd be wanting to talk with him, so I told the tech to take her time, so he wouldn't be able to take off for a while. Not that I imagine he'd make it far, with his truck wrecked and his leg broken the way it is. The bone's sticking clear through the skin. Must hurt like the devil."

It did, Regan thought, but did not say. A hideous memory of hearing the snap of bone flashed through her mind. "How about the boy?"

"He's in treatment room A. Lucky thing Tiny Dupree was mopping the floors when the ambulance showed up. He practically had to sit on the kid to keep him from leaving."

"Tiny's the Cajun Days crawfish-eating champion," Nate told Regan. "Probably weighs three-eighty soaking wet. So, the kid's okay?"

"He got himself some bruising across his ribs from the seat belt yanking tight, and a cut on his head, but that's all that showed up when he first came in. That's new, anyway."

"He has old wounds?" Regan asked sharply.

"*Mais oui*. He's got some old white scars that look real suspicious, if you ask me. Dr. Ancelet should be finishing up a more thorough examination any time now."

Regan wasn't surprised by any suspicious scars. Happy, well-cared-for children did not run away from home.

"We'd like to talk with Eve when she's done checking him over," Nate said.

"Sure 'nough." Her interested gaze settled on the badge Regan was still wearing. "So, *cher,*" she said, addressing her words to Nate, "I see you've finally hired us a new sheriff."

"I'm not the new sheriff." Try as she might, it was difficult not to stare at the woman's blinking red crawfish earrings.

"You're wearing a badge."

"That's just temporary, so I could help out at the train wreck."

"Terrible thing, that. If God hadn't had them in his hands . . ." The beehive bobbled a bit as she shook her head. "One thing medicine's taught me is that sometimes you're blessed with a miracle."

"Orèlia's husband was Blue Bayou's doctor just about forever," Nate explained, then introduced them fully.

The woman looked at her more closely through the rose-tinted lenses of the cat-eyed rhinestone-framed glasses. "I seem to recall my husband treating a little girl named Regan. It was a long time ago."

"Was he the only doctor in town?" She wondered if he'd signed Linda Dale's death certificate.

"*Non.* There was a new doctor, came here to work off his medical school bills through some sort of government program. He was a Yankee, from New York City, I think. Mebee Boston. Or Philadelphia. One of those northern cities. He just stayed a couple years." She nodded to herself. "He worked here at the hospital and picked up some extra money working as the parish medical examiner."

Which meant, Regan thought, that he would have been the one who wrote that death certificate.

"My Leon passed on two years ago," the woman continued, "leaving me to rattle around in our big old house where he used to have his office. For a while it wasn't too bad, what with Dani and her son Matt living with me."

"Dani's married to Jack," Nate filled in.

"And about time they finally got together, too," she said. "Well, like I was saying, Dani and Matt lived with me a while when they first came back to town, then when she moved out to live above the library for a time before marryin' Jack, her papa moved in so I could sort of keep an eye on him, bein' as how he has himself a heart condition. But he's back to work three days a week, which left me with too much time on my hands. I was going crazy, me, until Nate saved my life by fixing me up with this volunteer job."

"Orèlia exaggerates," Nate said.

"And the boy's too humble."

Regan couldn't help snorting at that.

"So, what do you do when you're not rescuing children from train wrecks?"

"I'm a detective, in L.A."

"Are you, now? Isn't that interesting?" Her appraising gaze shifted from Regan to a woman wearing dark glasses, who'd just come out of the swinging doors from the treatment rooms. "If this *fille* really isn't going to be the new sheriff, you need to send Dwayne down to the No Name and pick up Mike Chauvet," Orèlia told Nate.

"Does it have something to do with Shannon bein' here?"

"She says she ran into a door." It was Orèlia's turn to snort. "But this is the second time in the past ten days she's shown up in the ER. The first time she had a cracked rib. Claimed she fell off her horse, and bein' as how she was sticking to the story and the injury matched the excuse, Eve Ancelet couldn't do much for her, 'cepting give her a referral card to the free counseling clinic."

"Do you know if she went?"

"She did. Which didn't go over real well with Mike when he found out she was talking about their so-called private family stuff."

"Shit. Mike always was a goddamn hothead." A temper Regan wouldn't have thought him possible of possessing licked at the edges of Nate's voice.

"And as useless as tits on a bull," Orèlia said. "Lord knows what Shannon was thinkin' when she married him. She can sure do a lot better than that, she."

"Would you mind jus' waiting here a minute?" Nate asked Regan. "While I take care of something?"

"Sure."

Regan watched as he went over to the woman and said something she couldn't hear. He pulled off her sunglasses, the same way he'd done to Regan at the airport, and shook his head at the ugly dark bruise surrounding an eye red-rimmed from crying.

Regan had seen it all too often as a beat cop: a battered wife seeks medical care, maybe goes so far as to kick her abuser out of the house.

Occasionally she'd get brave enough to call the cops. But more times than she cared to count, the woman would inevitably end up taking the guy back. And the cycle of pain would begin all over again, inevitably spiraling downward, until in the worst cases, Regan would end up at the house investigating a homicide.

Obviously something Nate said struck a chord. The woman slapped him. Hard. Then, wrapping her arms around herself, she turned away.

"Anybody can talk her into escapin' a dangerous marriage, it's that boy," Orèlia, who was also watching the little drama, said. "Not many people can resist Nate Callahan once he gets an idea into his head."

"I've noticed. They seem close."

"They went together for a while in college. Back when Nate was playin' ball for Tulane. They were Blue Bayou's golden couple: the local boy headed toward a pro baseball career and the pretty, sweet prom queen who'd always wanted to be a first-grade teacher."

"Nate Callahan played professional baseball?" Not that she cared, but it did explain the easy, fluid way he moved. She was not the least bit surprised to learn he'd dated a prom queen. She suspected there were a great many cheerleaders and beauty contestants in the man's past.

"Played all the sports, he, but the big thing was his baseball scholarship. College recruiters were buzzin' around this place like bees to a honeycomb his senior year of high school. Like to drive his *maman* crazy. A lot of people who know a lot more than me about sports said he was a phenom—that's like a natural, but better, so they tell me—but then he ended up havin' to come home his freshman year."

Huh—he'd undoubtedly flunked out after too many frat parties.

Nate took the former prom queen in his arms; she threw her arms around his neck and clung. He held her tight for a long, silent minute, then curved his hands over her shoulders and put her a little away from him. His expression was warm and caring, but determined.

Shannon Chauvet blinked against the tears that had begun streaming down her face. Bit her lip. Then nodded.

Regan saw not a hint of seduction in his smile as he skimmed a knuckle up one of her badly bruised cheekbones, then dropped a quick kiss on her lips.

"Call Jack," he said to Orèlia when he returned to the counter. "Ask him to come get Shannon so she and Ben can stay at Beau

Soleil for a while. Then call the state police and ask for Trooper Benoit. Tell him you're calling for me, explain the situation, and tell him that I'm claiming that favor he owes me."

"Good idea." She reached for the phone.

"Harboring abused wives can be dangerous," Regan said. Violent husbands were often at their most volatile when the women finally got up the nerve to leave. "Shouldn't you have asked your brother if he wanted to take her in?"

"Jack won't mind. He and Shannon had a little bit of a thing back when they were kids, before Jack fell heart over heels for Dani. They stayed friends."

Both brothers had dated her? "Definitely a friendly town you have here," she said dryly.

"I told you it was," he reminded her, ignoring the dash of sarcasm.

"Jack may not mind, but what about his wife? Surely she won't feel comfortable with one of his ex-girlfriends sleeping in her house."

"Dani's got a heart as big as all outdoors," Orèlia offered.

"The important thing is to get her somewhere safe before she gets seriously hurt, or Ben, her fifteen-year-old son, gets hurt trying to protect her. Besides, Jack's thing for Shannon ended long before he and Dani hooked up," Nate said. "Since he gave his heart to Dani, he's become a born-again monogamist. She doesn't have anything to worry about."

"It looks as if you and Shannon stayed real good friends after your *thing*, too."

His eyes filled with humor. "Aren't you supposed to read me my rights about anything I say being used against me before you ask a leading question like that, detective?"

"Skip it." Disgusted with herself for asking, Regan gave him a withering look. "It's not germane to the situation."

"Germane." He chuckled and rocked back on his heels. "Damned if you aren't reminding me more and more of Finn, which tends to get a little distracting, since you sure smell a whole lot better."

He skimmed a finger down her nose.

"I believe we were talking about your brother Jack." That treacherous finger was now trailing around the line of her jaw. She batted at his hand. "And would you *please* stop touching me."

"Sorry. You had a little smudge of dirt on your face." He dipped his hands into the back pockets of his jeans. "And touchin' is jus' one of those natural things I do without thinking. Most women don't seem to mind."

"Maybe they just don't tell you they don't like it."

"Maybe." He considered that possibility. "But I don't think so. Women down here might have a reputation north of the Mason-Dixon line for being too accommodating, and I suppose, on occasion, some might be. But I've never met one yet who won't let a man know when she's not happy. We southern men are very well trained."

"What a sterling testimony to southern womanhood. Scarlett O'Hara would be so pleased."

"You've got a sassy mouth on you, Detective Delectable. Good thing I always preferred Scarlett over Melanie. As for Jack, the trick is going to be keeping him from cleaning Mike's clock for laying hands on Shannon. Which is why I'm having a state cop come make the arrest."

"That sounds like a sensible decision."

"Why, thank you, darlin'. I do have my moments."

The doors to the ER swung open again, and a slender woman wearing a white lab coat came out. She greeted Nate warmly, then drew back and looked at Regan. "I'm Dr. Eve Ancelet. I hear we have you and Nate to thank for saving that little boy's life."

"It's good to meet you. I'm Regan Hart, and I'm just glad I was able to help out."

"As am I." Friendly, intelligent eyes drifted to the badge. "Looks as if Nate's found the perfect person to be our new sheriff."

"I'm not the new sheriff."

"Detective Hart keeps tellin' me that she's going back to L.A. after she gets some personal business taken care of," Nate said. "I'm hoping to change her mind."

"Blue Bayou would be quite a change from Los Angeles." The doctor's gaze turned professional, and Regan knew her expert eye was taking in the faint tracing of scars.

"I suppose it would be," Regan replied equably.

"How's the kid doin'?" Nate asked.

"Fairly well, considering what he's been through. He's a little underweight, but I have no way of knowing whether or not that's a longtime problem, or something that's occurred recently during his time on the road."

"Did he tell you how long that's been?" Nate asked.

"He's claiming he doesn't remember anything prior to the accident, which could be valid, since retrograde amnesia certainly isn't unheard of after a blow to the head or even some traumatic incidents. But it's my guess he's attempting to avoid getting sent back home."

"Did the exam show any sign of abuse?" Regan asked.

"Several, actually."

Every muscle in Regan's body tensed. "What kind?"

"Small white circular scars over his back and chest."

Unfortunately, Regan had seen those before. "Cigarette burns."

The doctor nodded.

"Christ," Nate breathed, "that's out and out torture. What kind of person would do anything like that to a kid?"

"A monster," Regan said grimly. "What else?" she asked the doctor.

"Some longer, narrower scars across his buttocks. I'd say they'd been made with a belt or some sort of strap."

Nate looked as sick as Regan felt. All these years on the job but she'd never get used to the idea of anyone purposefully harming a child.

"What about sexual abuse?"

"There were no physical signs."

"Well, that's good news," Nate said.

"Not all abuse leaves evidence," Regan pointed out. Personally, she didn't have a very optimistic view in this case.

"True," Doctor Ancelet agreed. "And he's so closemouthed, it's hard to tell what he's running from. But he claimed all the truck driver did was give him a ride. I spoke with the driver, who didn't appear to fit any profile."

"Do you have experience with abuse profiling?"

"Actually, I do. Before I went into family practice, I was in a residency program specializing in the treatment of both abused children and their abusers, who, with the exception of sexual abuse, are often merely people who never learned parenting skills."

"Even if the driver's not a pedophile, he's still guilty of breaking regulations against taking on passengers," Regan insisted. "He could also possibly be charged with criminal recklessness at the crossing."

"The troopers are handling that, since the accident was on a state highway," Nate said. "The state cops will probably also question him about the kid. But meanwhile, we don't even know the accident was his fault. It was awfully foggy."

"I heard the whistle from your office. He should have heard it from the tracks."

"Maybe he made a major mistake. But you've got to give the guy credit for being a Good Samaritan by picking up the kid. What was he supposed to do, leave the boy alone out there and freezing?"

"He had to know he was a runaway," Regan argued doggedly. "He should have called the cops." She turned back to Eve. "I don't suppose the kid told you where he's from, either."

"No." The doctor shook her head. "I'm afraid his so-called amnesia struck again. I have a call in to the Department of Social Services. Hopefully once they get him temporarily settled somewhere, he might begin to open up."

When they entered the treatment room, the teen was sitting atop the metal examining table, clad in threadbare jeans and an OutKast rapper T-shirt. A huge man wearing navy blue coveralls and a custodian's name tag stood at the doorway, arms like tree trunks folded across his mighty chest. His speckled face, which appeared perpetually sunburned, was set in a forbidding scowl. Regan doubted many people would want to test him.

"How are you doing?" Regan asked the teenager after Nate had introduced her to the misnamed Tiny Dupree.

"Fine. Or I will be when I get the hell out of here."

"Hospitals aren't the most fun places," she agreed. "Just tell us where you're from, and we'll call and have someone come get you. You can be back home by morning."

His face and eyes hardened. "I already told the doc I don't remember."

"Well, I'm sure we'll be able to help you with that," she reassured him in her best Good Cop voice. "Have you ever heard of NOMEC?"

Those hard young eyes narrowed suspiciously. "No."

"It stands for the National Center for Missing and Exploited Children. It lists every child reported missing in America. I'm sure it won't take any time at all to find out who you are."

He met her mild look with a level one of his own. She'd seen that expression on the faces of kids who'd grown up in dangerous, violent homes. He wasn't the least bit afraid of the badge she'd pinned to her shirt. In fact, he seemed to be daring her to do her best.

"Cool. 'Cause it's a real bitch not knowing who I am."

"Well now," Nate entered the conversation. "I've got myself an idea. How 'bout you and me go get a bite of supper? I haven't eaten since noon, and after all that happened out at the crash site, I've got a powerful hunger."

"May I speak with you out in the hall, mayor?" Regan asked on a frosty tone.

"Sure." He squeezed the kid's too-thin shoulder. "We'll be right back."

"Like I care."

Regan turned on Nate the moment they left the room. "You dragged me into this, Callahan. So would you care to explain why you felt the need to interrupt my questioning?"

"I thought he might find it easier to talk to me."

"Because you're a man? I'm not surprised you'd take a chauvinistic view of the problem."

"I wasn't thinking about the man/woman thing." When his finger skimmed over the badge she'd yet to take off, Regan could have sworn the metal heated. "Given his situation, he might not feel all that comfortable with a police officer."

They were wasting time. As relieved as she was that they'd been able to get the driver and kid out of the truck, she hadn't come here to take part in any rescue operation. She certainly hadn't wanted to get involved with an uncooperative runaway. What she wanted, dammit, was to find out some facts about the woman who could very well be her birth mother.

Unfortunately, until this situation was taken care of, she wasn't going to have Nate Callahan's help. Only a few hours ago she wouldn't have thought she'd needed it, but having watched him in action, she realized that he could be an asset. Not only did he seem to know everyone in town, he also possessed some sort of aura, as if he was sending out brain-altering vibes that made everyone do exactly what he wanted.

No wonder he'd been elected mayor. Regan was just grateful he'd chosen to use that personality trait for politics, because if he'd decided to be a con man, he probably would have been a crackerjack one.

"Well?" Nate asked.

"You've got a point," she allowed. "But if he starts saying anything that could implicate anyone in a crime—"

"I promise I'll shut my mouth and save any further questioning for you so I don't mess up a court case."

It wasn't a bad solution. And right now it was the best they had. "Okay. Then let's get this show on the road."

She still didn't quite trust Nate Callahan, but didn't see that she had much choice. The thought of Dwayne the parking-ticket-writer tackling such sensitive questioning wasn't at all appealing.

# 11

*The cafeteria was small* and designed to cater more to staff than to family members of patients. Since it was past visiting hours, most of the Formica tables were empty. Someone was making French fries. The smell made Josh's mouth water.

The guy who'd dragged him out of the truck handed him a tray, then picked one up for himself. "You ever have crawfish étouffée?"

"Hell, no. Crawfish look like bugs. Who'd want to eat a bug?"

"They may not be real pretty. And you're right about them looking kinda buglike, which I guess is how they got the name mud bugs. But they sure taste good."

"I'd rather have a burger." His stomach growled at the thought of a huge hunk of ground beef dripping with mayo.

"One burger, coming up," the woman wearing a hair net and white apron standing behind the open pans of food said. "What you want on that, *cher?*"

"Everything."

"You know," Nate said, "I think I'll have a burger, too. But hold the onions." He shot Josh a grin. "Never know when you might have the chance to kiss a pretty girl."

"Like that cop?"

"Detective Hart?"

"Yeah. You got something going with the bitch? Like are you shacked up together or something?"

"Contrary to what you may hear on the radio these days, life's not a rap song," Nate said mildly. "Why don't you try calling her a lady?"

"What kinda lady packs heat?"

"An interesting one. And we're not shacked up together or anything. What gave you the idea that we were?"

"Don't know." He shrugged, wishing he hadn't brought it up. "She's kind of okay looking. For a cop."

"She's real pretty, cop or not. And she smells good, too."

She did. But not like she'd bathed in some too-sweet stink oil, like Josh's mother's old hooker pals. He looked around. This place wasn't exactly Mickey D's, but it was sure a lot better than some of the places he'd been eating in lately. Hell, back home if you turned your back on a bologna sandwich long enough to get a can of Dr Pepper out of the refrigerator, the roaches would carry it away.

"That sure was some wreck," Nate said conversationally. "Lucky thing nobody got hurt too bad."

"Yeah." Although he couldn't admit it, he was grateful to the guy for having saved him. Not that he was sure he deserved saving.

When he'd been younger and a lot smaller, his mother had gotten arrested for drug dealing and he'd been sent to live with his grandmother, who had never let alcoholism get in the way of her old-time fire-and-brimstone religion. She used to beat him with a leather strap, trying to knock the devil out of him, and although Josh didn't really believe in God or the devil or heaven and hell, deep down inside, he wondered if maybe the reason no one had ever wanted him was because he'd been born bad.

He tried to think of one person he knew who'd risk his life for strangers and was coming up with a big fat zero when the woman slapped a white plate onto the tray. The burger had been piled high with lettuce, tomato slices, and onion.

"Fixin's are on the table," she said. "You want fries with that, *cher?*"

"Sure he does," Nate answered for him. "And dessert."

"We got rice custard or molasses pecan pie."

"Got any vanilla ice cream for the pie?" Nate asked.

Her gaze flicked over Josh in a measuring way he'd come to recognize. "I suppose I can round some up. You gonna want whipped cream on the custard?"

"Darlin', you read my mind. We'll take both for the *jeune homme*, here, and I'll take the custard and some coffee."

"I don't want any of that rice crap," Josh said.

"Is that any way for a risk taker to talk?" Nate asked. "Joe, the cook, isn't quite up to my *maman*'s standard—she made a *riz au lait* that could make the angels sing—but his comes pretty damn close. Antoine's, up in N'Awlins, tried to hire him away last year, but his wife is a nurse up in ICU and neither of them was all that eager to leave Blue Bayou, after havin' lived their whole lives here, so we were lucky to keep him."

"They've always lived in one place?"

"Sure. Mos' folks around here were born on the bayou."

Josh figured that counting the foster homes and two residential treatment homes, he'd probably moved twenty times in his fourteen years. Everytime those envelopes with the flourescent red Overdue stickers would start coming in, his mother would pack up their stuff and they'd take off in the middle of the night. The last time his backpack had gotten left behind, along with class records from three previous schools, which always made it tough to enroll in a new one.

Not that his mother had cared if he showed up in class, but he did. Not only was school an escape, so long as he could survive the inevitable challenges from the bullies; the classroom was the only place he'd ever felt safe. And in charge of his own life.

"Okay," he said when he realized they were both looking at him, waiting for an answer. "What the fuck. I'll try it."

"Good choice," the woman said with a nod. "Maybe I should get you some soap, too. So you can wash out that potty mouth."

"She's got a point," Nate said as she retrieved their desserts.

"Excuse me, your Heinass."

"Cute." They carried their trays to a round table in the far corner of the room. The better, Josh figured, to conduct the interrogation.

Nate picked up a small bottle of red sauce and doused his fries and burger. "Want some peppers?"

"On French fries?" Josh reached for the catsup.

"Pepper juice goes on jus' about anything. You haven't tasted fried eggs till you've had them with Tabasco. We grow the peppers right outside Blue Bayou. Most kids grow up eating it as soon as they graduate off their *maman*'s milk. Guess you're not used to that."

"No."

"So that'd mean you're not from around here."

The burger was halfway to his mouth. Although it was one of the hardest things he'd ever done, nearly as hard as spending the past month on the run, Josh lowered it to the plate. "Did you bring me down here to feed me? Or pump me for that effing cop?"

"A little of both. But since you're on to me, how about we skip the questions till after supper?"

They ate in silence, the boy wolfing the food down as if he'd been starving for days. Which, Nate figured, could well be the case.

"You know," he suggested after a while, "Detective Hart is only trying to help."

"She's a cop."

"So?"

"So all she cares about is making busts and taking bribes."

"That's quite a negative viewpoint you've got goin' there. Did you pick it up on the streets? Or from someone you know? Like, maybe, your dad?"

"I never had a dad."

His face grew hard, once again reminding Nate of his brother. Jack had prided himself on being the hellion of Blue Bayou. The truth was, he'd just been hurting so bad, he hadn't known any other way to deal with his anger. Nate had been mad, too, but at twelve he'd been a lot more afraid of Finn than Jack was.

Besides, although no one would have ever said it out loud, as the baby of the family, Nate had been their *maman*'s favorite. Which was why it'd fallen to him to try to ease her hurt after that terrible day that was scorched into his memory.

"That must be tough. I lost my dad when I was twelve. About your age."

"He take off?"

The kid didn't agree about the age thing, nor did he correct him. So much for that ploy. "No. He passed on. But at least I got to know him for a little while."

"Yeah, some guys get all the luck." Ignoring the big red-and-white No Smoking sign just a few feet away, the teen reached into a pocket and took out a book of matches. "You got a cigarette?"

"No. Besides, this is a nonsmoking building, and you're too young to smoke."

"Am not. I'm just small for my age."

"Won't get a whole lot bigger if you smoke," Nate said. "And die of lung cancer by the time you're in your forties."

"Everyone's going to die of something."

"True enough. But me, I'd rather drop dead after makin' love to a *jolie fille* rather than go bald from chemo and hacking my lungs out."

"Is that how your dad died?"

"No. He was shot and killed by some crazy, mad-as-a-hornet swamp dweller tryin' to murder a judge." Nate sighed at the memory. "He was as big and strong as ever at breakfast, when he lit into me for getting caught up in a ball game and forgettin' to mow the lawn the day before. By lunch he was lying on the courthouse floor, bleeding to death."

"That sucks."

"Yeah."

A silence settled over them.

"Did it make you mad?"

"*Mais* yeah. I used to lie in bed at night and imagine going down to the jail with his service revolver—he was sheriff of Blue Bayou—and blowing the guy away. But my *maman* was real torn up about losing him, so I didn't want to make things worse for her by getting myself sent away to prison. 'Sides, like we say in bouree, you gotta play the cards you're dealt."

"What if you're playing against a stacked deck?"

Nate suspected the kid had been born with the cards stacked against him. "I don't know," he said honestly.

"You damn bet you don't. Like I said, some guys get all the luck." This time the silence lengthened. Grew deeper. "I don't even know who my dad was."

"That's gotta be tough."

"Nah." He drew in on a paper straw, making a loud sucking sound in the bottom of the milkshake cup. "I figured if she didn't know, I didn't want to. I never would have wanted any of those scumbags she brought home to be my dad, anyway."

"Brought? As in the past?"

"She died." She'd died of a drug overdose, but that wasn't any of this guy's business.

"I'm sorry, *cher*."

"Well, that makes one of us." The chair legs scraped on the vinyl tile as he pushed away from the table. As they returned upstairs, Nate figured it was a good thing he hadn't followed Big Jake Callahan into law enforcement, because he couldn't even get a confession out of a half-starved kid.

After leaving the teenager in the more than capable hands of Tiny

Dupree, Regan and Nate went to Eve Ancelet's office, where Judi Welch of the parish Department of Social Services was waiting.

"Hey, Judi," Nate greeted her with a hug. "Aren't you lookin' as pretty as a speckled pup?"

"Flatterer." She punched him lightly on the shoulder. "But actually, you're close. I've been sick as a dog all week with morning sickness. Which, in my case, is inaccurately named, since it pretty much lasts all day."

"Sorry to hear that, *chère*. But Matt must be real happy about the news."

"He is. Especially since he got a promotion last week," she said proudly. "He's now assistant bank manager. It pays enough to add another bedroom onto the house."

"Good for him." Given the choice between being thrown into a pool of piranhas in a feeding frenzy or spending his days wearing a suit and tie and sitting behind a desk counting other people's money, he'd go with the man-eating fish any old day. "How're the girls?"

She had three. When the third one, Angelique, had been born and he'd shown up at the hospital with flowers, Matt had jokingly said that he'd always wanted his own basketball team, but had gotten a harem instead. Since Judi had always been Blue Bayou's most outspoken, card-carrying feminist, Nate had been stunned when, instead of lighting into her husband, she'd laughed as if Matt had been doin' standup on *Letterman*.

Love, he'd figured, obviously scrambles your brain. Which was why he'd decided a long time ago to stay clear of it.

Regan watched their easy banter, noticing how the social worker didn't even back away when he brushed a curl off her temple. She'd bet *her* last pay raise they'd slept together. Reminding herself that it was none of her business if Nate Callahan had affairs with all his constituents, Regan yanked her mind back to business.

"Mrs. Welch is here to interview the boy," she told Nate.

"I figured as much. Not going to be easy," he said. "The kid's wearing pretty tough armor. I did manage to find out that his mom's dead. And he doesn't know who his father is."

"If he's telling the truth," Regan said.

"Well, since we've no idea who he is, DSS is going to have to take charge of him and find temporary placement," Judi said.

"He can come home with me," Nate said.

"You?" Judi appeared as surprised by the offer as Regan was.

"What's wrong with me?"

"You're not married," Judi pointed out.

"So? You never heard of single fathers?"

"Sure. I just never thought of you as being one." She tapped the tip of her ballpoint pen on her clipboard. "Are you actually volunteering to become a foster parent? Or to adopt the boy if it turns out he's available?"

"You said you needed a *temporary* home. I've got an extra room. And I think we understand each other well enough that we could get through the next few days without him burning down my house."

"Don't be so sure of that," Regan said. "He's at a ripe age for pyromania."

Nate thought of those matches the kid had taken out of his pocket. "We'll be okay." He hoped.

Judi frowned. "You haven't been prequalified."

"Got anyone else in town who is?"

"No. Well, there are the Duprees over on Heron, but they've already got three kids staying at their house along with their own two. And since the Camerons are currently between kids, they decided to take that vacation in California they've always dreamed of. The McDaniels just took a newborn last week, so she's pretty swamped."

"See," he said as if the matter had already been settled, "I'm the logical solution."

"That's very sweet of you to offer, Nate, but you're not in the system. I don't have the authority to just let you take him home like he's some stray puppy you picked up off the street."

"We've kinda bonded." Okay, so it was a stretch.

"He belongs in an official juvenile care facility."

"You mean a kid jail." Regan was surprised by the way his jaw tightened and his eyes turned hard. "Dammit, Judi, you know what happened to Jack when he landed in one of those."

"From what I've heard, it was difficult. But he survived and became a better person for it."

"He survived because he was a lot tougher than this kid, and because he'd come from a family who cared about him with a mother who never failed to show up on visiting day the entire year he was there."

"That was a boot camp for repeat offenders. I'm talking about a residential care center."

"Center, boot camp, they're still no place for a messed-up kid." He folded his arms, which, while not nearly the size of the gargantuan custodian's, were admittedly impressive. Regan suspected those rock-hard biceps and well-defined muscles came from swinging a hammer, not reps on some spa weight machine. "I may not be the perfect solution, but I'm a helluva lot better than one of those places."

"You'd have to get judicial approval."

"No sweat. Since Judge Dupree got himself reappointed to the bench, he can vouch for me."

Judi rubbed her forehead with her fingers. Sighed. Then gave him a warning look. "You know, this isn't going to be a walk in the park."

"I realize we're not talking about the Beav here. The kid might try to come off like Eminem, but deep down he's just a kid." He winked at Regan. "And if he gives me any real trouble, I'll have the detective shoot him."

Judi shook her head. "Lucky thing I know you well enough to know that you're joking. Some DSS workers might just find that statement worrisome."

"See? Who better to vouch for me than the lady in charge of placement, who knows me so well?" he said with one of those devastating smiles.

She studied him again. "Peter Pan and the lost boy," she murmured.

Peter Pan again? Obviously she'd been talking to Charlene. Nate had forgotten the two women had been on the high school prom court together. Terrific.

"All right. We'll give it a try," she said finally. "But I can't cut corners just because it's you, Nate. Since jurisdiction crosses parish and perhaps even state lines, depending on where the kid ran from, I'm going to have to make sure all the *i*'s are dotted and the *t*'s crossed."

"The judge is staying with Orèlia during the week to save himself the drive into town from Beau Soleil, so we can stop on the way to checkin' Detective Hart into the inn."

Regan held up a hand. "I don't need—"

"Of course you don't need me to drive you, *chère*," he cut her off. "But I figured you'd want to get down to working on that project of yours, which I promised to help with," he reminded her. "You can come along with me, and I'll have Dwayne drive your car over to the inn first thing in the morning."

"I'm not here for a vacation. I want to get an early start."

"The car'll be there before you get up," he promised. "Besides, you'll get a lot better break on the rate if I'm with you when you check in."

"Oh?" She arched a brow. "I suppose the night clerk is an old *friend?*"

The sarcasm slid right off him. "Well now, you know, she is. But that's not the reason I can get you a discount rate. The reason is that I'm part owner."

"You own a hotel?"

"Only about a third." He glanced at his watch. "But it's gettin' late, and I hate botherin' the judge at home, since it wasn't that long ago he had heart surgery. How about we just save the explanation for after we check you in?"

# 12

*Nate called the judge* to let him know they were coming. Ten minutes later, they were stopping in front of a white two-story house on the corner of a tree-flanked cobblestone street.

"I'll wait in the car," the kid said.

"Sorry, *cher,*" Nate said. "But you're coming in with us."

"I didn't hear anyone reading me my rights," he grumbled.

"And I didn't hear anyone putting you under arrest," Regan said mildly. "So why don't you make it easier on all of us and come along? Unless you'd rather the mayor call for a trooper to take you to the nearest residential facility."

Apparently deciding he was outnumbered and better off with them than in some juvenile detention center, he gave in.

"You didn't lock the door," Regan reminded Nate as they began walking up the front sidewalk.

"No need. This is—"

"A peaceful town."

"Got it on the first try."

"This house would cost a small fortune in L.A.," Regan said as they climbed the steps to the front door. "The porch is nearly as wide as my apartment living room."

"It was designed for sleeping outside during the summer," Nate said. "Back before air conditioning." He rang a doorbell that played the opening bars of "Dixie." "It's also good for sitting out, watching your neighbors, and chatting with folks that walk by."

"People still actually do that?"

"Not as much as they used to," he allowed. "But probably more than in the city."

"Sounds boring," the kid said.

Sounds nice, Regan thought. Unfortunately, if the citizens of her precinct were to try it, they could be hit by a stray bullet.

The judge might be old enough to be her grandfather and a bit frail looking, but his voice had the deep, sonorous tones made for projecting throughout a courtroom.

"Heard you're a detective," he said after Nate had introduced them.

"Yes, sir. I work homicide in L.A."

"So what brings you to town?"

"I was overdue for some R&R, and I've always enjoyed Louisiana." It wasn't exactly the truth, the whole truth, and nothing but the truth, but this wasn't a courtroom, and she hadn't sworn an oath.

"Most people go to New Orleans."

"I'm not most people, Your Honor."

He gave her a razor-sharp look she suspected he used to keep order in his courtroom. Then he turned to Nate. "So you need a temporary custody order."

"Yessir."

"You have any idea what you're getting into?"

"No, sir. Not exactly. But it just seems like the thing to do."

The judge shrugged. "You always were the soft one in the family. Just like your *maman*." His stern expression softened for the first time since he'd opened the front door. "She was a good woman."

"The best," Nate agreed. "*Maman* was the judge's housekeeper," he told Regan. "After my father was killed."

"I would have liked her to be more than a housekeeper. But Jake turned out to be too tough an act to follow."

Regan noticed Nate looked surprised by that revelation. "My parents had something special."

"That's what she said when she rejected me."

"I hadn't known you proposed."

"No need for you boys to know, since she turned my proposal down. Of course, she was real nice about it. No one in the parish sweeter than your mother." Appearing embarrassed by the glimpse into his personal life, the judge squared his shoulders, cleared his throat, signed the temporary custody papers with a flourish, then handed them back to Nate.

"This is just temporary," he warned the teenager. "You give Mr.

Callahan any trouble, and I'll rescind the order so fast your head will spin." He snapped his fingers to underscore the warning.

"Well, that scares the shit out of me," the boy muttered beneath his breath.

"What did you say?" The judge's voice cracked like a whip.

"I said, okay."

Eyes locked, and challenge swirled between the youngest and oldest males in the book-lined room. Regan let out a breath when the judge decided not to wield his authority to just ship the kid off right now.

"You've definitely got your hands full," he warned Nate.

"We'll get along fine."

"If he doesn't steal you blind," the judge muttered, as if the teenager wasn't standing right there in the room. "Always were too good-natured for your own good. Just like your mother."

"I'm proud to be compared to *maman*."

"Blue Bayou might be a small town," Regan said as they drove away from the house, "but the judge could hold his own on any bench in L.A." The teen was in the backseat, nodding along with whatever was blasting out of his Walkman earphones.

"You should have seen him in the old days. He's softened a lot the past few months."

"Seems he had at least one soft spot for a long time. You didn't know about his feelings for your mother, did you?"

"No fooling a cop," he said with a casualness she suspected he wasn't quite feeling. "That was a surprise. Though I suppose it does explain a lot of things. Like why he was always bailing Jack out of trouble and trying to straighten him out, like he was his own son. Looking back on it, I guess you could say he was giving him tough love. At least he didn't ignore him, the way he did Danielle."

"Jack's wife?"

"Yeah. I guess I didn't mention that part. She's the judge's daughter."

"Is everyone in this town connected?"

"Pretty much so, I guess. It's a small place, and people tend not to move away, or move in. So while there are some distinct circles, they all pretty much overlap."

"Which means that most of the people, of a certain age, anyway, would have known Linda Dale."

"Yeah. I'd suspect so." He glanced up at the rearview mirror, then over at her. "Which should make your cold case not as cold as it might be in the big city."

"True. It also suggests that if she didn't commit suicide, whoever murdered her may still be living in Blue Bayou, which makes it personal." For both of them, if Dale did turn out to be her mother.

"Yeah."

Having come to the conclusion that things really were different in the South, Regan didn't bother to argue when Nate insisted on seeing her up to her room. Which meant, of course, that they had to take the teenager with them so they wouldn't risk him rabbiting the minute he was alone.

"Shit, you two are paranoid," he muttered as he slumped across a lobby boasting huge bouquets of hothouse flowers, lots of rich wood, exquisite antique furniture, and leafy plants.

"Not really." Nate stuck the coded card in the slot and pressed the button for the third floor. "You just remind me of someone I used to know, so I just think about what he would have done in a similar circumstance."

The elevator doors opened onto a luxurious suite that would not have been out of place in the Beverly Wilshire.

"I need some time alone with the detective," Nate told the kid. "We need to talk."

"Yeah, right. That's what everyone does in a hotel room."

Nate heaved an exaggerated sigh. "You know, you really can be one pain in the ass." He opened the mini-bar and pulled out a Coke, a can of peanuts, and a Snickers bar. "This doesn't concern you, so why don't you go into one of the bedrooms and play some video games on the TV?"

Mumbling beneath his breath, he snatched the snack food out of Nate's hands, disappeared into the adjoining room, and shut the door behind him.

"He's going to have junk-food overload," she warned.

"Probably won't be the worst thing that happened to him."

She couldn't argue with that. She skimmed a finger over the glossy top of a Queen Anne desk. "You didn't have to upgrade my room to this suite."

"It wasn't any big deal." Nate was bent down, perusing the contents of the mini-bar. "It was jus' sitting here vacant."

"So, how did you end up owning a third of a hotel?"

"The hotel was built in the 1800s but burned down last year. When the owners rebuilt, they figured they'd get more tourist business if it was redone to look more like Tara, so they hired me to do the job, but they couldn't afford what it was going to cost to do it right. So I took some draws to cover the subcontractor and material bills, then agreed to take a piece of the place as my cut."

"Blue Bayou doesn't exactly seem like a tourist mecca. Won't it take an awfully long time to get your money back?"

"Probably. But I've always had this perverse feeling that it was more important to be happy than rich."

She could identify with that. "And restoring this hotel made you happy."

"As a crawfish in mud."

"You did a very good job." She studied the crown molding, surprised that such an outwardly easygoing man would pay such strict attention to detail.

"Thanks."

"Though, to be perfectly honest, it reminds me more of Twelve Oaks than Tara."

"Sounds like you've got a nodding acquaintance with a certain movie."

"I've seen it a few times." She didn't feel any need to mention that a few translated to a dozen. Her mother once accused her of having hidden southern blood, to be so taken by a mere movie. Regan sighed. She'd never realized at the time how true that might be.

"How about a little Bailey's nightcap?"

"At mini-bar prices?" The TV came on in the other room, the low bass sound of the video game thrumming through the wall. "Who's buying?"

"It's on the house. Besides, even if it wasn't, you're a rich lady now. You can afford to indulge yourself."

"We still don't know, for sure, that I am actually Linda Dale's daughter."

"You wouldn't have come all this way if you didn't think there was a damn good chance." He took down two glasses from the overhead rack, poured the Irish Cream, and handed her one.

"Thanks." She took a sip and felt the liquid warmth begin to flow through her veins. "And no, I wouldn't have come here if I hadn't thought there was a possibility."

Regan wasn't yet prepared to share the story of the Mardi Gras elephant. She sank down on the couch, tilted her head back, and looked out at the flickering gas lights of the town's main street. The Irish Cream was going straight to her head, conspiring with a lack of sleep last night and the long flight, followed by the adrenaline rush of the rescue wearing off.

"I really hate to admit this, but I think I'm afraid to discover the truth."

"You're a detective," he reminded her. "Digging out the truth is your job."

"Yeah, it seems I've done a bang-up job of that." Her head had begun to feel light, but she took another sip anyway. "If the woman who died in that garage is my mother, I've been lied to my entire life and never had a clue."

If there was one thing Nate had always had a handle on, it was knowing precisely what to say in the getting-to-know-you stage of an affair. He let out a deep breath and wondered why he couldn't think of a single word to make this right.

"She probably had a good reason for not telling you the truth."

"Sure she did. Being honest would have brought up a lot of questions she probably didn't want to answer." Regan's strangled laugh held not a hint of humor. "I don't know why I should be surprised. Everyone lies."

She'd told him that the first day. She'd also told him to get lost, but there'd already been too much passed between them to walk away now.

"You'll figure it out, *chère*." He sat down next to her. "Put all the pieces together."

"Yeah." She jerked a shoulder. "You're damn right I will." Nate found the renewed spark of pride encouraging. It was good that she was beginning to convince herself. "There was this detective I worked with when I first got promoted into homicide, who'd drive everyone crazy because he was so slow and methodical." She ran her finger around the edge of the glass. Nate was finding it disconcerting to imagine those smooth lady hands holding a gun, those long slender fingers tipped with their tidy, unlacquered nails pulling a trigger. Especially when he was experiencing this low, thrumming need to have them on him.

"Watching him work a crime scene was like watching a glacier flow," she continued, unaware of the hot, uncensored direction of his thoughts. "Whenever anyone'd rag him about it, or a new partner would complain, he'd just shrug and say that he'd solve no crime before its time."

"It's been thirty-one years. Seems about time, to me."

"Cold cases are the hardest."

"Which is why you should be gettin' some rest." As he'd done at the airport, he skimmed a finger beneath her eyes. "I'll get the kid, take him home and get him settled, and be back in the morning."

"Don't you have to work?" Video game explosions were coming from the bedroom; his outwardly casual touch had ignited other ones inside her.

"Nothin' that can't be put off."

"What about the boy?"

"That's the nice thing about having family. I'll drop him off at Jack's."

"What makes you think your brother can handle a delinquent, runaway teenager?"

"After our dad was killed, Jack became a wannabe delinquent. This kid reminds me a lot of him back then. He's angry and a whole lot lost. 'Sides, I figure any guy who can hold his own with Colombian drug lords should be able to take care of one teenage kid for a few hours."

He went over to the table, where a ballpoint pen inscribed with the inn's name and a notepad were sitting, scrawled some lines onto the paper, and handed it to her. His handwriting was as illegible as hers was neat.

"Is there a codebook that goes with this?" she asked

Regan knew she was in trouble when his deep laugh pulled sexual chords. What she'd told Van was true: all her parts definitely were in working order.

"It's how to get to the library. Not that you wouldn't have found it yourself—this town's pretty easy to get around, bein' that it's all laid out in squares like Savannah, but this might save you some time. The local paper's the *Cajun Chronicle*. Dani—she's Blue Bayou's librarian—can help you dig into the archives."

"How did you know I was going to go digging in the archives?" She'd already tried to do that online, but the thirty-year-old newspaper issues she'd needed hadn't been uploaded to the Internet.

"That's what Jack or Finn'd do."

He had her there. "I'm also going to pay a call on Mrs. Melancon."

"The old one, or the young?"

"Old. Since she was running the company back then, she might know something about how Linda Dale got those stock certificates."

"I doubt that visiting the old lady will do much good, bein' how she's turned pretty reclusive and rumors have her mind going south, but . . . Jesus," he said on an exasperated breath when she shot him a sharp, suspicious look. "You really don't trust anyone, do you?"

"Would you, if you were in my situation?"

"I don't know. Maybe. Maybe not."

His smile turned a little distant as he gave her a considering look.

"What?" she asked, growing uneasy when he didn't look away for a very long time.

He slowly shook his head. "Damned if I know," he said, more to himself than to her. Vivid blue eyes, fringed by lashes most women would kill for, blinked slowly. The air between them grew thick and far too steamy.

Just when Regan's nerves were feeling stretched to the breaking point, he broke the silence. "Guess I'd better interrupt the intergalactic wars."

He retrieved the teenager, who, not surprisingly, wasn't all that wild about leaving the video game. "Two more levels, and I would've been emperor of the universe," he complained.

"Next time," Nate said easily. He paused in the open doorway and skimmed a finger down Regan's nose. "See you tomorrow, *chère*."

After they left the suite, she listened to the footfalls on the hallway carpeting, the *ding* of the elevator, the *whoosh* as it opened, then closed.

Regan leaned back against the door, closed her eyes, and let out a long breath. "*Detective chère* to you, Callahan."

*The two-year-old girl lay in her trundle bed, huddled beneath her sheets, hiding from the full moon that her baby-sitter, Enola, had told her would make her eyes go crossed. She heard her mother's high heels tapping on the wood floor. The voices grew harsher. Louder. Angrier. A sound like a glass breaking had her peeking out from beneath the sheet; the moonlight streaming in through the window cast a silver light over the bedroom, but the corners were draped in deep shadows.*

*Regan shivered, fearful that the loud voices would wake the* cauchemar. *Whenever her mama went out and Enola stayed with her, the sitter would sprinkle holy water from a little bottle over Regan's pillow to protect her from the witch who crept around in the dark, looking for little girls to eat.*

*They were shouting now. Regan had never heard her mother shout and wondered if she was fighting with the* cauchemar *just on the other side of the door. She tried to climb out of bed, but her legs wouldn't move. She tried to call for her mama, but the witch had wrapped its bony crawfish claws around her throat, so no sound came from her lips. Huddling beneath the sheets at the bottom of the bed, she hid from those shining red eyes Enola had told her could set children on fire.*

*She heard a scream; then a crash, then silence.*

Regan jerked awake, bathed in sweat, her mouth open in a silent scream she'd never been able to make heard, her heart beating triphammer hard, triphammer fast.

"It was just a dream," she told herself with a mental shake as she retrieved the pillow that had fallen onto the floor. The nightmare was an old one, going back as far as she could remember.

She took a deep breath, looked over at the clock radio, and saw it was not even three A.M. yet. Groaning, she climbed out of bed and retrieved the journal from her carry-on bag. There'd be no more sleep tonight.

# 13

*The kid had slept like the dead,* revealing that it had been a long time since he'd had any real rest. He also had the appetite of a horse. A Clydesdale. He was single-handedly burning through breakfast as if he hadn't eaten for weeks. Which, Nate considered, just might be the case, seeing as how he was mostly skin and bones.

"What's this stuff?" he asked, poking at the milk-drenched hot cereal Nate had gone to the trouble of fixing.

"*Couche-couche*."

"That doesn't tell me a frigging thing."

"It's cornmeal, salt, baking powder, milk, and oil." A lot of oil. "My *maman* used to make it just about every morning for my brothers and me when we were kids. But she used to serve it with *sucre brule*, which is kind of a syrup." Thinking back on the ultrasweet, golden brown syrup made by cooking water and sugar together, Nate was surprised any of them had any teeth left.

Food had always been an intrinsic part of the Acadian culture; his mother had turned it into a celebration.

"It's not bad." The kid pushed aside the empty bowl. "But I like these better," he said, biting into a sugar-powdered Cajun doughnut.

"They're beignets." Nate wasn't that good a cook—never had to learn since, on the occasions when there wasn't a woman willing to feed him, there was always takeout from Cajun Cal's Country Café. But any idiot could fry up a bunch of dough in a skillet of hot oil. "I don't suppose that, having slept on it, you remember where home is?"

"Nope." He used his third piece of raisin toast to wipe up some yolk from the fried eggs.

"You do realize that DSS will probably end up putting you in some sort of facility if they don't get an answer soon."

His faced closed up. "I thought I was staying here with you."

"Temporarily. Talking Ms. Welch into letting you come home with me for a couple days was one thing, since we're old friends from our school days. But I don't exactly fit a foster family profile. 'Sides, they don't have any way of knowing that you're not a regular Jesse James, running from robbin' a bank or something."

"I didn't rob any bank. And the damn social services assholes can put me anywhere they want, but that doesn't mean I'm gonna stay there."

Nate sighed. The kid reminded him a bit of Turnip, the raggedy old stray yellow dog that had shown up at Beau Soleil last spring. The difference was that the dog had deftly insinuated herself into Jack's life with her unrelentingly cheerful personality. But thinking about Turnip gave him an idea.

"You like dogs?"

"They're okay, I guess. I had me a puppy when I was a kid."

"What kind?"

"I don't know. Some kinda black-and-brown mutt. Someone dumped it in a field by our house. I brought it home and kept it hidden in my room, but the guy my mother was livin' with drowned it."

"Damn." This picture the boy was painting was getting worse and worse. "He still around?" he asked casually.

"I guess." He shrugged and wiped the white powdered sugar off his mouth with the back of his hand. "He'd moved into the apartment, anyway."

"Which is why you're not there?"

"I guess you could say that."

"You realize, don't you, that if you'd be a little bit more open and come clean about your situation, there's a very good chance I might be able to help."

The kid rolled his eyes.

"I guess that's a no." Nate stood up. "Come on."

"Where?"

The unrelenting suspicion was beginning to drive him nuts. "My brother's house."

"Why?"

"Because it's a cool place. With a dog who's always happy to meet new folks who'll throw her a Frisbee to catch."

"You gonna stick around?"

"Well, now, that's the thing. I promised the detective—"

"Yeah, yeah. I get it. Why spend time with a kid when you can be doin' a hot chick?"

"Okay, dammit, that's it." Nate turned on him, the flare of temper catching them both off guard. "I've been trying my best to give you the benefit of the doubt, since you look like you've been rope-drug from the tailgate of a pickup down a long patch of bad road. And if you're not lyin' about that drowned puppy—"

"I'm not."

"—then I've gotta figure that whatever you're running from has got to be a helluva lot worse than what you've gone through on the road, which sure doesn't look like it's been a picnic."

"It hasn't," he mumbled.

"Shut the hell up." It worked. The kid dropped his eyes to the heart-of-pine floor. "Like I said, I'm willing to cut you some slack, but if you don't stop talking such trash—"

"Yeah, yeah, you'll dump me back with the cops."

Nate saw the fear beneath the tough veneer and, though it wasn't easy, held firm. "If you'd quit finishing my sentences when you don't know what the hell you're talking about, you'd discover that you're not the only one with problems."

"Cops don't have problems. They make problems."

"Like when the detective crawled under that electrical wire to save your life?"

"I don't remember asking her to do that."

Damn, what he wouldn't give to have Jack or Finn here right now. Or both of them. They could double-team the kid, who probably wouldn't hold up two minutes when being played by experts.

Nate dragged a hand down his face, wondering what the hell he'd done in a previous life to deserve all this crap dumped on him at one time. Peter Pan was sounding real good about now. Flying off to the island of lost boys had to be a lot more fun than dealing with this runaway kid. If that wasn't bad enough, thanks to him, Detective Delectable's entire life, as she'd known it for thirty-three years, had just come crumbling down around her. How the hell was he supposed to make up for that?

"Like I said, the detective's got some private, personal problems. And I promised to help her solve them."

"What are you, a priest or something?"

Nate laughed at that and put his arm around the kid's shoulder. When he felt the sudden rigidity he lightened up a bit, but did not take his arm away. "Son, I am about as far away from a priest as you can get."

They were on their way to Beau Soleil, the Porchdogs singing "Hello Josephine" on the SUV's CD player, when Nate turned toward his passenger.

"You know, it'd be a helluva lot easier to carry on a conversation if I at least knew your first name. 'Hey, kid' is a little limiting."

He could see the wheels turning behind those pale blue eyes, then the kid blew out a long breath of surrender. "Josh."

It wasn't much. But it was a start.

Regan had to say this about Nate Callahan. He was true to his word. The rental car was waiting for her at the front of the inn when she returned from her early morning run. It had even been washed, she noticed immediately. Since according to Nate's scrawled directions the library was only two blocks away, Regan decided to walk.

The rain had moved on; the day had dawned bright and sunny and as warm as she'd been expecting when she'd left L.A. The library was located on Magnolia Avenue, next door to the Acadian Butcher Shop, which boasted displays of plump chickens and sausages beneath green-and-white-striped awnings, and across the street from a small park ablaze with naturalized daffodils. The interior of the building was brightly lit, and dust covers of upcoming releases were displayed on a wall covered in green, purple, and gold burlap (which she'd read in the hotel's visitor guide were Mardi Gras colors). The windows sparkled like crystal, and old-fashioned oak catalog cases gleamed with lemon oil, which added a fresh scent to the air.

"Good morning." The blond woman's smile, which was echoed in her eyes, was as warm and welcoming as her library. "You must be Regan." She held out a hand. "I'm Dani Callahan, Jack's wife. Nate called this morning and told me you'd be coming."

"It's good to meet you." Regan was momentarily put off by Dani's outgoing attitude; cops weren't accustomed to people being happy to see them.

"Oh, it's wonderful to meet you." Moss green eyes moved from

Regan's face to her wrists. "Though I am a bit disappointed you're not wearing your bracelets."

"Bracelets?"

"Wonder Woman's magic bracelets. You and Nate ended up on the front page of the paper." She held up a copy of the *Cajun Chronicle*. In color, above the fold, was a photo of her ducking beneath the wires to hand Nate the blanket. There was another of Nate pulling the boy from the truck.

"That was a brave thing he did, for a civilian." Or idiotic.

"I doubt if, in his mind, he had much of a choice," Dani said. "Though the fact that there was a child in the truck undoubtedly added to the urgency. Nate's terrific with kids."

"Probably because his emotional growth stopped about twelve himself," Regan murmured.

"You may have a point, since that's how old he was when his father was killed. He told me that he'd told you about that," she said. "It's not something he talks about often, so it's interesting that he chose to share it with you."

"It was just part of the general conversation. He insisted on helping me into my coat because, as he put it, his daddy taught him to, and I suggested his father might want to join the twenty-first century." She still felt a twinge of guilt about that. "He seems all right with it."

"Yes, he does, doesn't he?" Dani braced her elbows onto the glossy surface of her desk, linked her fingers together, and rested her chin atop her hands. "You know, that was a dreadful time, but looking back and seeing all three Callahans from an adult perspective, I think it ended up being hardest on Nate."

"Why?"

"Jack and Finn were older, so they latched onto their roles right away. Finn became the man of the family, something he did very well."

"I'm not surprised."

"No, I expect you're not, having worked with him."

"Seems Nate's been talking about me."

"He's like my brother. We share everything." Her eyes momentarily sparkled. "Well, almost everything. Anyway, Finn just got more adult and serious, and Jack became Blue Bayou's James Dean. He calls it his rebel-without-a-clue period.

"Nate was closest of the three to his mother, which I suppose isn't surprising for the youngest child in a family. They lived out at Beau Soleil, the house I grew up in, so I had a front-row seat after the tragedy. I don't think he left her side from the time she got the terrible news to days after the funeral. Wherever she was, he was, holding her hand, talking her into eating something, telling her jokes."

A small, reminiscent smile teased at the corners of her mouth. "I remember him making her laugh at some silly story the night of the viewing. Mrs. Cassidy, from the market, was scandalized a woman could laugh when her husband was lying in a casket in the same room. I was the same age, and watched him all during that time and wished, just a little, that I could fall in love with him."

"You don't seem to be alone, there."

"Women like Nate," Dani agreed mildly.

"I figured that out for myself."

"You don't have to be a detective to see it." Dani's expression turned a little serious. "He's certainly sexy enough, and charming, but what attracts women is that he's one of those special men who genuinely admires all aspects of us. Which is why most of us like him right back."

"I'll admit he's difficult to dislike." Regan wasn't quite ready to make the leap into Nate Callahan's female fan club.

"I can't think of anyone who's ever had a reason to. As I said, there were a lot of times when I thought how much easier it would be if I'd just fall in love with Nate. Or Finn."

"But you didn't."

"No." She twisted a gold ring as her eyes warmed with private thoughts. "My heart's always belonged to Jack."

Regan wanted to get on with her reason for coming to the library, but there was one thought that had been running through her mind since she'd been jerked from a restless sleep by that nightmare. "I met this woman volunteer at the hospital—"

"Orèlia." Dani nodded. "She's definitely one-of-a-kind, isn't she? My father lives with her during the week."

"So Nate said. He seems like a nice man. Your father, that is."

"He's a good man." Regan, who was used to listening for what people *didn't* say, caught the qualification in that statement. "It's no secret that we've had some rough patches, but fortunately we had a chance to straighten them out before we lost the opportunity." She shut her eyes briefly as she realized what she'd said. "I'm sorry. I didn't mean—"

"I know." Regan sighed. "I guess Nate told you everything."

"He filled me in on what he knows of your situation. If it's any consolation, he was unusually reticent. Except for a brief synopsis of your possible family situation, all he'd tell us was that you reminded him of Finn, were very pretty, and smelled good."

Regan wasn't at all pleased to hear he'd compared her to Finn. Okay, maybe they were both cops, but surely she didn't come off as remote, cool, and rigid as the eldest Callahan. She shook off the momentary pique.

"It's not easy to have to consider that the woman I always thought of as my mother may be my aunt," she allowed. "Orèlia mentioned something about Nate's mother dying, as well." She was not trying to pump Danielle Callahan, but she couldn't help but be curious.

"Oh, that was a terribly sad time. She was diagnosed with breast cancer when Nate was a freshman at Tulane. She tried to keep him in school—he was planning to become an architect—"

"I thought he was going to be a baseball player."

"Oh, I think he could have been a very good one. All the Callahan men are naturally athletic, but Nate enjoyed the game-playing aspect of sports more than the other two. But he was smart enough to realize that even if he did make it to the majors, he wouldn't be playing all his life, so he decided it'd be good to have a backup occupation."

"That's more planning than I would have expected."

Dani smiled at that. "Every once in a while, just when you think you've got Nate figured out, he surprises you. I think he probably has more layers than either of his brothers."

"Finn certainly always seemed straightforward."

"With Finn, what you see is pretty much what you get," Dani agreed. "Though I have to admit that it was fun watching Julia Summers pull the rug out from beneath his tidy, orderly world."

Regan definitely could identify with that feeling.

"Nate's always loved construction. When they were kids playing cowboys and Indians, while Jack and Finn were practicing their fast draws, Nate was dragging home boards he'd find in the swamp to build the jail."

Regan laughed at the idea of Finn Callahan in a cowboy hat, having cap pistol shootouts. "So Nate's an architect?" Her admittedly sketchy investigation of him hadn't revealed that.

"No. He dropped out of school the day he heard the news of his mother's cancer and came home to be with her. I've always thought that he was somehow convinced he could single-handedly save her with love and determination. I firmly believe he's the reason she lived two years longer than the doctors predicted. It was a difficult three years, but he was always there for her.

"Jack was working for the DEA somewhere in Central America when she died, but Finn and Nate were with her at the end. Finn said she died smiling at a joke Nate had told her."

"That's nice." Regan didn't run into all that many people who died smiling in her line of work.

"There was a time when I don't know what I would have done without him to talk to. He was the only person during some hard times who could make me forget my troubles for a little while. And if part of him is still twelve years old, well, perhaps that's what makes him able to slough off his own problems while taking on everyone else's."

Regan didn't want to consider that possibility. It was easier to believe that Nate Callahan was just some immature, hormone-driven southern charmer.

"That's all very interesting," she said, her smile a bit forced. "Could you tell me where you keep your newspaper archives?"

"The newer ones have been scanned into the computer. The ones you're looking for are still on microfiche. I've pulled up the reels for you." She gestured toward a chair and a reader across the room. "If there's anything else you need—"

"No, thanks. That'll do it."

"Great. Do you know how long you'll be staying?"

"I suppose it all depends on what I find and how soon I find it."

"Hopefully you'll be here for the Fat Tuesday party out at Beau Soleil."

Regan hadn't come to Blue Bayou to party. "That's very nice of you, but—"

"Please come, Regan. How else can we live up to our reputation for southern hospitality? Nate and Jack have done wonders with Beau Soleil, and I do so love to show it off. Have you ever visited a plantation house?"

"No."

"Beau Soleil was the model for Tara," Dani said, sweetening the pot. "Margaret Mitchell was a visitor before she wrote the book."

"That's quite an endorsement."

"It's really worth the trip to see what Nate's done with the house. He's more than just a contractor, he's a master craftsman. His millwork is phenomenal. There was a time when I felt sorry for him, dropping out of school and all, but it's obvious that he never belonged building skyscrapers; he's really found his niche."

"That's important."

Regan had once been certain she'd found hers. She was no longer quite so sure. It's not burnout, she assured herself. You just need a break. Like a month in Tahiti. Or maybe in bed. Sleeping.

"If I'm in town, I'll try to come by."

"I'm so pleased. Jack will be, too." Dani's smile suggested she hadn't expected any other outcome, making Regan wonder if all southerners had velvet-bulldozer personalities. Had Linda Dale? "Jack lived in Los Angeles for several years, so you'll be able to share stories."

Regan liked Dani Callahan. If Dani lived in Los Angeles, the two of them might have been friends. Other than Van, whose life these days revolved around Rhasheed and her unborn son, Regan didn't have many women friends. Her job didn't allow time for socializing. If she did take time from work, she was likely to be found sharing a pitcher of beer with a group of cops at the Code Ten.

She realized Dani had asked her a question. "I'm sorry. What did you say?"

"Nate told me he'd asked you to take the sheriff's job?" Her voice went up a little on the end of the sentence, turning it into a question.

"He did. And I turned him down."

"Having met you, I'm doubly sorry you didn't accept." Her slight frown turned into a smile. "Well, perhaps you'll change your mind. My brother-in-law can be very persuasive."

That was an understatement. But Regan had no interest in leaving L.A. for such a small, isolated town. Pigs would be spouting gossamer wings and flying over Blue Bayou before she pinned on that badge again.

As if to prove how different the town was from Los Angeles, the story of Linda Dale's death, which would have been buried in the back pages of the local section in the *Los Angeles Times*, had captured nearly the entire front page. There was also a picture of Dale captioned "In Happier Days"—the New Orleans Mardi Gras photograph.

Inside were more photographs, including the red car in which her body had been discovered by her employer. Another picture showed a woman carrying a toddler out of a tidy, narrow white frame house. Regan recognized her as the woman she'd always thought was her mother, and a chill skimmed up her spine as she realized she was, indeed, that toddler.

Josh was trying his best not to be impressed, which was frigging hard when the house Nate pulled up in front of reminded him a lot of the White House.

"Your brother lives here?"

"Yeah. Jack."

"He must be rich."

"I think he probably does okay for himself. He writes books."

"Yeah?" Josh liked to read; books had often proven an escape from his life. But he'd never actually given any thought to people writing them. "What kind of books?"

"Thrillers, I guess they're called."

The name clicked. "Your brother is Jack Callahan?"

"Yeah, I guess you heard of him."

"Heard of him? Shit, I just finished reading *The Death Dealer*! It's in my backpack." He'd swiped it from a CVS in Tallahassee, along with a can of Vienna sausages and a Milky Way bar. "He rocks."

"He sure does. And I'd say that even if he wasn't my brother. But there's a lot of sex, drugs, and violence in those stories."

"Like there's not a lot of sex, drugs, and violence in life."

"Not in everyone's life." A cold, lethal anger uncurled in Nate's gut. It wasn't often he understood the passion that drove people to do murder. This was one of those rare times. "Look, let's get something straight, right now, okay?"

"What?"

"The folks at DSS are eventually going to find out who you are. But when that happens, you're not going back."

"You're damn right I'm not."

"That's not what I mean. You've got to promise me you won't take off again."

"What kind of chump do you think I am?" Josh sneered.

"I don't think you're a chump. I think you're a kid who got dealt a lousy hand. But you're not going back to an abusive home."

"Says you."

"Yeah." Nate tamped his rare but formidable temper. He was murderously furious at anyone who'd hurt a child.

"What are you going to do to stop them?"

Murder, while surprisingly appealing, wasn't the answer. "I don't know." Nate figured after all he'd been through, Josh deserved the truth. "But I will. Scout's honor."

"It figures," Josh muttered.

"What?"

"That you'd be a friggin' Boy Scout."

Nate threw back his head and laughed at that. Even Josh's lips quirked into a hint of a smile.

"Come on, *cher*," he said as a huge yellow ball of fur the size of a compact car came barreling out the front door of Beau Soleil. "You can meet the family, and Jack can autograph your book for you."

The dog, which Jack claimed to be a Great Dane–yellow Lab–Buick mix, leaped up, put her huge paws on Josh's shoulders, and began licking his scrunched-up face in long, welcoming slurps. When the kid fell to the ground and began wrestling with Turnip, he looked like any normal teenage boy. Which, Nate figured, somewhere, deep down inside, past all that hurt and teenage bravado, he was.

"Uncle Nate!" The nine-year-old wearing a Baltimore Orioles cap and a shirt declaring him to be a member of the Blue Bayou Panthers, sponsored by Callahan Construction, tore out of the house behind the dog. "Guess what?"

Nate pulled off the cap and ruffled his nephew's hair. "You just got called up for the Orioles' spring training camp."

"I'm too young to play in the majors," he said with a third-grader's literalness.

"Well, I already know you're gonna have a baby brother or sister. And I can't think of anything else, so I guess you're just gonna have to tell me."

"Mrs. Chauvet and Ben moved into the guest house last night."

"Yeah, seems to me I heard about you havin' company." He reached down, grasped Josh's arm, and pulled the teenager to his feet. "Josh, this is my favorite nephew, Matt—"

"I'm your only nephew," the boy reminded him. "At least for now."

"Well, there is that. Matt, this is Josh. He's visiting me for a while."

"Cool." The grin was quick and revealed a missing tooth. "Want to see my Hot Wheels collection?"

Josh shrugged in that uncaring way Nate was getting used to. "Hot Wheels are for little kids."

"They're for collectors, too. My uncle Finn found me a deep purple Nomad with Real Rider tires in California. It's really cool." Matt turned and raced back toward the house, Josh with him and Turnip happily nipping at their heels, just as Jack came ambling out.

"Does that kid walk anywhere?" Nate asked.

"Not if he can help it. So, Dani says that she invited your new lady friend to the Fat Tuesday party, and while she didn't exactly agree to show up, she didn't out-and-out refuse, either."

"Terrific." Nate smiled. As much as he'd always liked having brothers, there was something handy and decidedly cool about gaining a sister. "You realize, don't you, that marrying that woman was the smartest thing you ever did."

"Won't get any argument from me on that one," Jack agreed cheerfully.

Nate caught up with Regan as she left the library. She glanced past him toward the SUV he'd parked across the street. "Where's the boy?"

"I took him out to Beau Soleil so Jack could keep an eye on him. And his name, by the way, is Josh."

"Josh what?"

"He wasn't willing to share that yet."

"Well, at least it's a start." As she crossed the street with him, Regan could almost imagine the sound of horses' hooves on the rounded gray cobblestones. "So did you take along a whip and a chair to your brother's?"

"Hey, Jack used to hunt down international drug dealers." He opened the passenger door, put his hand on her elbow, and gave her a little boost up into the front seat. "I figured he could take care of one runaway for a few hours," he said after he'd come around the front of the SUV and joined her. "Besides, he's got himself this big friendly mutt I thought might loosen Josh up a bit."

"Animals have a way of making a connection when people can't. The canine corps is one of the more popular groups in the police department, and using a mounted patrol at concerts is effective because most people like the horses . . . And why are you looking at me that way?"

"I was just wondering about something."

"What?"

"If you taste as good as you look."

"In case you've forgotten, this is a public place."

"The windows are tinted. 'Sides, I don't see anyone watching."

He could tell she was tempted. Having wanted her the first time he saw her in that prim no-nonsense gray suit that showcased a magnificent pair of legs, he opted for giving in to temptation.

"Dammit, Callahan."

"It's Nate," he said absently, not about to apologize for the desire he knew she was reading in his gaze. "I'd say we've worked our way up to first names, wouldn't you, Regan?"

"We've only known each other two days."

"True. But you've got to admit that a helluva lot has happened in those two days."

"Granted. But I definitely don't want to get involved with you."

"I know," he said.

There was a part of him that didn't, either. With the exception of the two women his brothers had married, Nate wasn't used to complex women. Didn't want to get used to them. He preferred easygoing belles who understood that shared desire was a game, a game both parties, if they kept things simple, could win. He doubted there was a single simple thing about this woman.

"Then my suggestion would be to stop before things get out of hand."

"I don't think I can do that, *chère*." He ran his thumb along the tightly set seam of her lips. What was a man to do but take a taste when her lips were so close? So tempting?

"Tell me to take my hands off you," he said, "and I will."

She drew in a breath.

When her golden brown eyes softened, giving him his answer, he lowered his mouth to hers.

# 14

*Oh, he was good!* He didn't ravish, which would have made it too easy to push him away. He beguiled. He took his time, gently, so unbelievably gently, his mouth brushing against hers in a touch as delicate as a dream.

No one had ever kissed her like this. Not ever. How could such a slow, gentle kiss rock her to the bone?

Regan was unaware she was holding her breath until it shuddered out when her lips parted. Rather than invading with his tongue, as so many other men would have automatically done, he surprised her yet again by scattering light kisses at the corners of her mouth, up her cheek.

Her cheek. She tensed, wishing she were perfect. Or, at least not so imperfect.

"Nate—" It was the first time she'd said his name. But the voice couldn't be hers. It was too low. Too ragged. Too needy.

She felt his smile at her temple. "Shhh," he whispered. "Just a little bit more."

Her brain was shutting down. He was muddling her thoughts, stirring up unruly needs she'd always managed to keep tightly reined in.

His lips returned to hers, once, twice, a third time until they finally—thank you, God!—lingered. Even then he was patient. So amazingly, achingly patient.

He drank slowly, savoring her as he might a fine wine. He drank deeply, stealing her breath, along with whatever ragged bits were left of her resolve. One of them trembled. Because she feared it was her, Regan drew away now, while she still could.

Not that he let her completely escape. He pressed his forehead against hers, even as his fingers continued to stroke the back of her neck in a way that was far from comforting. "Kissing you could become a habit, Detective *Chère*."

"A bad habit."

His grin was slow and carelessly charming. "Sometimes those are the most fun."

"You're not my type."

"Well, now, I sure wouldn't want you to take this the wrong way, but you're not exactly mine, either." His eyes lit with easy humor. "But sometimes that doesn't have a damn thing to do with chemistry."

"I suppose you'd know more about that than I would." Hell, she sounded petulant. Pouty.

"Since we don't know each other real well, I couldn't be the judge of that. But if you'd like, I can kiss you again. See if maybe it was a fluke."

"It was. My life's gotten dicey since you charged into it. I suppose I shouldn't be all that surprised that I respond inappropriately to events."

"Inappropriately," he said mildly, as if trying out the word on his tongue. "Now, see, darlin', that's where we're going to have to agree to disagree. Because it seems to me that when a man and a woman have electricity together, it only makes sense to enjoy the sparks." He bent his head again and nipped lightly at her bottom lip. "I've been wanting to behave inappropriately with you since I watched you testify."

"Sure you have." She could feel whatever little control she'd managed to hang onto slipping away. Regan didn't like losing control. She didn't know how to function without it.

"It's God's own truth." He lifted his right hand like a man swearing an oath. "When you first got up on that stand, I started wondering what you were wearing beneath that prim, tidy little suit, then that thought led to another, and another, and pretty soon I was imagining getting you out of it and making passionate love to you in that big black leather chair the judge kept swiveling back and forth in."

"That behavior would have gotten you thrown in a cell for public indecency."

"But I'll bet we would have had ourselves one helluva ride. And I know it would have been worth it."

His easy arrogance irked her. All right, so he was the most gorgeous man she'd ever seen who wasn't up on some movie screen. So he moved with a natural, lazy grace that suggested he was immensely comfortable in his skin. So he was really, really built. That didn't mean he had any right to act as if he were God's gift to women.

"I should have just shot you back in L.A."

"And I should have gotten that kiss over with in L.A. Then we'd have already moved to the next step."

"And that would be?"

He rubbed his jaw. Studied her silently. Then, just when her nerves had begun to screech like the brakes on her crappy cop car, he shook his head. "I think I'll just let you figure that out for yourself when we get there."

She was *not* going to let him get to her. She was a cop, dammit. And not just any cop, she was the cream of the cream, the best of the best. She ate gangbangers for breakfast and sent bad guys up the river for life plus ten, without parole. She could handle Nate Callahan.

"We have this little thing in law enforcement," she said. "Perhaps you've heard of it."

"What's that, *chérie?*"

Her smile was sweet and false. "Excessive force."

"Well, now, I've never been one who got off on rough play, but if you want to drag out some handcuffs, I'm willing to give it the old college try.

"There's this stripper down on Bourbon Street in N'Awlins. Calls herself Officer Lola Law. She starts out wearing police blues, then eventually works her way down to a G-string, some pasties that look like badges, and some shiny black vinyl boots with ice-pick heels that go up to mid-thigh. I don't suppose you'd have an outfit like that?"

She wasn't about to dignify that with a response. "Don't you take anything seriously?"

"I try not to. Life's too short for getting bogged down in details."

"You make details sound like a bad thing."

"Didn't someone once say the devil was in the details?"

"It's a bit hard to solve a crime without details. And while I've never restored a building before, I'd suspect it's probably a good idea to measure before you cut a piece of wood."

"Got me," he said easily. "But since there's no way of knowing when you get up in the morning if you're going to be around by nightfall, it only makes sense to enjoy the moment. Drift with the currents."

"Drifting with the currents can land you into the doldrums. If everyone shared that philosophy, we'd all still be living in caves, hunting woolly mammoths and cooking our meals over a fire."

"Doesn't sound that bad to me." When he tugged on a strand of hair, his knuckles brushed the nape of her neck again and made her skin sizzle. "I like the idea of ravishing you in the firelight."

"How do you like the idea of getting whacked in the groin by your woolly mammoth hunting club?"

"Ouch." He winced. "Some people might think you were a difficult woman, *chère*."

"I work at it. And some other people might think you were a Neanderthal southern male."

"Now, see, that's where we're different. 'Cause I don't work at it at all."

It was hard not to be charmed by his smile. "Look, Callahan, this partnership, or whatever you want to call it, isn't working. Unless you can get me into Mrs. Melancon's house." Regan had called this morning and had been brusquely told that Mrs. Melancon was not entertaining visitors. Not today, nor tomorrow, nor anytime in the near future.

"As it happens, I've been doin' some pondering on that, and have a couple ideas. But since I haven't quite worked them out yet, I figured you might like to take a little drive out into the country."

She arched an exaggerated brow and looked around. "This isn't the country?"

"Cute. Who would have guessed the cop had a sense of humor?"

"I have my moments. And where did you have in mind?"

"The actual destination wouldn't mean anything to you anyway, you not being all that familiar with Blue Bayou," he pointed out. "I just thought you might like to have a little chat with the man who owned Lafitte's Landing thirty years ago."

She remembered something from the newspaper report. "The man who found her body?"

"That's him. He just also happens to be the guy who hired Linda Dale. As well as the guy rumored to be having an affair with her."

"How do you know that?"

"I stopped by Orèlia's on the way here. Between her and the judge, there aren't any bodies buried in town they don't know about." He inwardly flinched when he realized what he'd said. "I'm sorry. I didn't mean that literally."

"I know." She sighed.

"Anyway, the judge proved a regular font of information. Seems Boyce's wife was suing Dale for alienation of affection, then for some reason changed her mind."

"He was married?" It had started to sprinkle, the drops of rain dimpling the dark water on either side of the road.

"Yeah."

"She mentioned my father was married," Regan murmured. "In the journal." She was looking at him again in that hard, deep way that made him feel as if he were undergoing an interrogation. "That's his name? Boyce?"

"It's his family name. His first name's Jarrett."

He wondered if she even realized that she'd reached out and grabbed his arm.

"She called the man she was in love with 'J.' What happened with the lawsuit?"

"Marybeth Boyce dropped her case."

"Maybe he killed her to keep from losing his business in a divorce division of property."

"I suppose that's always a possibility," Nate acknowledged.

"There are probably more cold-blooded murders done over money than passion. Or perhaps his wife dropped the lawsuit because she decided to save the legal fees and take care of the problem herself."

"By dragging Dale out to the garage, stuffing her in her car, and turning on the engine?"

"People can do a lot of things when they're angry that they wouldn't be able to do otherwise. Women have been known to lift cars off their children under the force of an adrenaline rush," Regan said.

"I always wondered if that's true. I've spent most of my life carrying 'round lumber, and I'm not real sure I could lift up a car, even if I had buckets of adrenaline pumping through my veins. Personally, I think all those stories about women lifting cars may be urban legend."

"Do you do that on purpose?"

"What's that, *chère?*"

"Take a conversation all the way around the block before you get back to the topic."

"Oh, that." He considered it for a long moment that had her grinding her teeth. "No," he finally decided.

"No, what?"

"No, I don't do it on purpose." He smiled at her. "I guess it's like my charm—it just comes naturally. And since you want to get back to the topic, murder by carbon monoxide poisoning seems an awfully iffy way to kill someone. Why wouldn't Dale have just gotten out of the car and opened the garage door to let in some fresh air?"

"Maybe she'd been tied up," Regan considered.

"Dad would have put that in his report. And even if whoever'd killed her had stuck around to untie her after she was dead, she would have been left with rope burns. The medical examiner back then might not have been the sharpest tack in the box, but I think even he would have spotted them."

"The wife could have knocked her out. That would explain the contusion on her skull."

"I'm no expert, but could a woman actually slug a person that hard?"

"That depends upon the woman. I could."

He slanted her a look. "I'll keep that in mind."

Regan tapped her fingers on her knee. "She could have used a weapon."

"Sure. She could have gone in with a baseball bat and started swinging. She could have hit her with a lamp. Or a telephone. Anything's possible."

"But you don't think so."

"Doesn't matter much what I think. You're the detective."

"True. But I never in a million years could have imagined I'd be investigating a murder in my own family." The idea was still incomprehensible. Even more than the fact that her life had been a sham. Which brought up another thought. "When your dad died, did people make fun of you?"

He thought about that a minute. "No," he decided. "But they did treat me a lot like some folks treat Homer Fouchet when they first meet him. He's this guy who takes the classified ads down at the paper. He lost both his legs in 'Nam and came home with really bad burns on his face and hands. He doesn't have any facial hair or eyebrows or lashes, and although he's a nice enough guy, there are still people who have trouble looking at him, because he makes them uncomfortable, you know?"

"There but for the grace of God go I," she murmured, having experienced the same behavior from some of the well-meaning cops who'd visited her at the hospital.

"I think that's probably it," he agreed. "Anyway, that's how they treated me. Nobody at school knew what to say, and that made them uncomfortable, so they mostly stayed their distance. And couldn't look me in the eye."

"At least you had your brothers."

"Yeah. Life was pretty rocky then for all of us, but it would have been a helluva lot harder without Jack and Finn."

"Kids can be so mean."

"You won't get any argument there." He thought some more. "There was this girl in school, Luanne Jackson, who had an alcoholic mother and a no-good father. Jack found out later that her father had been raping her and nearly killed the guy, but none of the kids even knew about stuff like that back in grade school, and if any adults knew, they sure as hell didn't tell Dad.

"Anyway, her mama used to spend a lot of time down at the No Name whenever her husband was out shrimpin', which was most of the time, and she'd leave with men she'd pick up there. Kids would hear their parents talking about her at home and rag Luanne somethin' awful. She got suspended a lot for fighting." He smiled at a memory. "If we were anywhere in the vicinity, Jack and I tended to get into it with her. Which usually ended up with us gettin' grounded."

"But you stood up for her."

"*Mais* yeah." He made it sound as if there'd been no other choice. Which, she was beginning to suspect, there hadn't been.

"Sounds like you were close friends."

"We were. Not as close as Jack, though."

"Let me guess. Luanne and Jack had a 'thing.' "

"Now, I wouldn't be one to spread tales, but they were close for a while. But that was before Dani."

"Sounds as if your brother's life is divided into two periods. Before Dani and after."

"I guess it pretty much is. I never would have thought it possible, but she's got him downright domesticated."

"You make it sound as if he's been neutered."

Nate laughed at that. "When you meet Jack, you'll realize that there's not a woman on earth who could do that. But he's pretty much settled down these days and seems real satisfied with his life."

She guessed, from his slightly incredulous tone, that he wouldn't be satisfied to settle into domestic bliss. Which she honestly doubted she would be, either. Having had no role model of husband-and-wife behavior to observe while growing up, she wouldn't have the faintest idea how to be a wife.

"Other than the accusation that Linda Dale was having an affair with Jarrett Boyce, did the judge have any other information about them?"

"Not much. Like I said, the case was dropped. Shortly after that, Dale was found dead, so I guess they just sort of faded back into a normal life that kept them out of courtrooms."

They fell silent for a time. Clouds rolled across the sky as they drove past flooded stands of leafless trees the color of elephant hide. Under ordinary circumstances, Regan would have enjoyed the drive. But these were far from ordinary circumstances.

The house was small and narrow with a deep front porch. The white paint had faded, but an explosion of orange honeysuckle covered a white trellis at one side of the porch. A red-and-white Caddy with fins harkening back to Detroit's 1960s glory days was parked on a white crushed-shell driveway. A brown-and-black hound dozed in a sunbeam on the porch amid a green array of houseplants.

"It looks cozy," Regan murmured, wondering if this was her father's house. And if so, how her life would have been different if she'd grown up here in Blue Bayou, rather than L.A.

"It's a shotgun house," Nate said. "There are literally thousands of them scattered all over south Louisiana. Freed blacks brought the style here from Haiti. They're called shotgun because all the rooms are lined up behind one another, so if you fired a gun from the front door, it'd go right out the back door."

"Not a shotgun, unless you were shooting a slug. When a shotgun's fired using a multiple-pellet shotshell, the pellets spread out into a pattern that increases in diameter as the distance increases between the pellets and the barrel. Depending on the size of the shot, the mass starts to break up somewhere between five and ten feet."

"Anyone ever tell you that you're damn sexy when you're talking like a cop?"

"No." She shot him a warning look that would have had most men cowering in their boots. The problem was, Nate Callahan wasn't most men.

"What's the matter with the men in L.A., anyway? They all must be either blind or gay."

"Perhaps they know enough not to hit on a police officer."

"Maybe someone who met you while you're armed and investigating a murder might want to be a bit cautious about bein' too forward," he allowed. "But you can't spend all your time chasing down bad guys."

"There's where you're wrong. Being a cop isn't just what I do. It's what I am. My life pretty much *is* my work, and the only men in it tend to fit into three categories." She held up a finger. "Suspects." A second finger. "Cops." A third. "And lawyers."

"Maybe you need to expand your circle of acquaintances." He brushed his thumb along her jaw.

She shoved his hand away. "What I need," she said as she unfastened her seat belt, "is for you to back off and give me some space."

He climbed out of the SUV and caught up with her on the way to the porch. The rain had lightened to mist. "Okay."

"Okay, what?"

"Okay, I'll give you all the space you need."

That stopped her. "Why don't I believe you?"

"Maybe 'cause you're a skeptic all the way to the bone. But that's okay. It's sort of an interesting change for me. I can just see you, a sober-eyed, serious four-year-old, sitting on St. Nick's knee in some glitzy L.A. department store, giving him the third degree."

He made her sound grim and humorless. Worse yet was the realization that she actually cared what he thought.

"I never sat on Santa's knee." She started walking toward the house again. "My mother never encouraged me to buy into the myth." Or the tooth fairy or Easter bunny, for that matter.

"Now that's about the most pitiful thing I've ever heard."

"Then you've been blissfully sheltered." Despite the car parked outside, no one seemed to be home. The dog obviously hadn't been bought for his watchdog skills, since he was snoring, blithely unaware of their presence. "Let's check around back."

They found Boyce in a small cemetery surrounded by a low cast-iron fence. Some of the standing stones were so old the carving had been worn down, making it impossible to know who'd been buried there. He was planting roses into a raised bed beside a small stone angel.

When Nate called his name, he turned, then dropped the shovel. "Hey, Nate. I figured you'd be showin' up sooner or later." His rugged face, with its lines and furrows, suggested years of hard living. His age could have been anywhere from fifty-five to seventy.

He pulled off a pair of canvas gardening gloves as he studied Regan's face. "The judge was right," he said, revealing that Judge Dupree had called ahead. "You do take after Linda some, around the eyes." He skimmed a look over her. "I predicted her little girl was going to be a heartbreaker when she grew up, and it looks like I was right."

He glanced toward Nate, who'd leaned down and was scratching the hound, who'd belatedly awakened and ambled over, behind his ear. "It's also going 'round that you hired this little lady to take on the job of sheriff."

"That's a misunderstanding," Regan said, one she was getting weary of correcting. "The mayor only gave me the badge so I could help out at an accident scene."

"Heard about that, too. Sounds like you two did a bang-up job. Maybe you might want to stay on."

"I'm afraid that's not possible. I already have a job in Los Angeles."

"Too bad. The town really needs a sheriff. Last one we had was purely pitiful and a crook besides." He cocked his head and gave her another long look. "Damned if you don't remind me of Linda when you talk."

"She didn't have a local accent?"

"No, which wasn't real surprising, since she wasn't a local girl."

"Do you know where she was from?"

"She didn't talk much about her past. I got the feeling that she wasn't really happy growing up, but it seems she was from someplace in California." He rubbed a stubbled chin. "Modesto, maybe Fresno, somethin' like that. Not the places you usually think of, like Los Angeles or San Francisco."

"Could it have been Bakersfield?" The woman she'd always believed to be her mother had been born in the San Joaquin Valley city.

His eyes brightened as if she'd just given him the answer to the million-dollar question. "That was it. I remember because she said the Mandrell sisters were from there, and she'd always wanted to grow up to be rich and famous like them." The light faded from his gaze. "She could have made it, too, if things had worked out differently. Your mama was a real pretty woman. Talented, too."

"I haven't yet determined that Linda Dale was my mother." Her tone was cool and professional and gave nothing away.

"Regan here's a detective," Nate volunteered. "She likes to get all the evidence in before she makes a decision."

"A detective." His tone was gravelly from years of smoking too many of those cigarettes she could see in his plaid shirt pocket. "Don't that beat all. Never met a lady detective before."

A little silence fell over them.

"Roses are lookin' real nice, Jarrett," Nate said.

The man swept the raised beds with a satisfied look. "They're comin' along. I got some antique bushes from a plantation down in Houma that's crumbling away. The new owner's razing the place to build some weekend getaway, and when I went over there with the idea of buying them off him, he just told me to take the lot."

"That sure is a lot, all right," Nate said, looking at all the burlap-wrapped bushes. Bees were buzzing from flower to flower.

"Marybeth has always liked her roses," he said. "This autumn damask is her new favorite. She's been hankerin' for one 'cause it's supposed to be real good for making oil. Me, I'm sorta partial to the color of this General Jack. You don't get many old garden roses that are such a dark red."

"Your garden's lovely." Having found herself in a discussion about flowers when she just wanted to solve the mystery of her birth, Regan was beginning to understand Finn's impatience with detours. "Marybeth's your wife?"

"Yes, ma'am. We'll have been hitched forty years this March."

"That's a long time." And obviously not all of it had been married bliss, according to Judge Dupree. Regan decided to take a different tack. "How did you meet her? Linda Dale, not Marybeth."

He narrowed his eyes. "You're here about that alienation-of-affection suit Marybeth filed against her," he guessed.

"I am interested in the circumstances behind that, yes."

He let out a long, slow breath.

"Thought I'd put that foolishness behind me a long time ago." He stretched, took a red-checked handkerchief from the pocket of his overalls, and wiped his brow. "Digging holes is thirsty business. Marybeth made a pitcher of sweet tea this morning. Let's go sit on the porch, and I'll fetch you some."

# 15

*We're not going to* get out of here anytime soon, are we?" Regan asked Nate as they sat on the porch in rocking chairs, while Jarrett Boyce went inside to get the tea.

"Nope. But the truth, whatever it is, has been waiting this long to come out. Won't hurt to sip a little sweet tea, chat a bit about some roses. You'll find out what you need to know."

"Eventually."

"Things move a little slower down here," he said, telling her nothing she didn't already know. "You gotta learn to go with the flow."

She'd never gone with the flow in her life. As she watched a hummingbird dipping its long beak into the red bloom of a potted plant by the porch steps, Regan wasn't sure she knew how.

"Here you go." The screen door opened, and Boyce came out carrying three canning jars filled with a dark liquid.

Nate took a long drink. "That just hits the spot, Jarrett," he said with a flash of that smile that seemed to disarm everyone. She watched Boyce's shoulders relax ever so slightly, and decided that she'd love to have Nate Callahan in an interrogation room playing good cop.

She murmured her thanks and studied the opaque liquid, which didn't look like any iced tea she'd ever seen. It was as dark and murky as the brown bayou water, and there were little black specks floating around in it that she dearly hoped were tea leaves. A green sprig of mint floated on top.

She took a tentative sip. Surprise nearly had her spitting it back out. "It's certainly sweet," she managed as she felt her tooth enamel being eaten away.

"Lots of folks don't take the time to do it right, these days. Marybeth boils the five cups of sugar right into the water she brews the tea into."

"Five cups," she murmured. She could feel Nate looking at her with amusement and refused to look back. "That much." She imagined dentists must have a thriving practice here in the South.

"That's why they call it sweet tea." He leaned back in the rocker, crossed his legs, and said, "It wasn't true. Those stories about me and Linda."

"Your wife seemed to think so," Regan said carefully.

"Marybeth wasn't quite right in the head back then." He frowned and stared down into the canning jar as if he were viewing the past in the murky brown depths. "On account of what happened to Little J."

"Your son?"

"Yeah." He reached into his pocket, pulled out the pack of cigarettes, shook one loose, and lighted it with a kitchen match he scraped on the bottom of his boot. "He was two when we lost him." It still hurt—Regan could see it in his eyes, hear it in the roughened tone of his voice. "He drowned."

"I'm sorry." She'd seen it more times than she cared to think about when she'd been a patrol cop.

"So were we." He sighed, and suddenly looked a hundred years old. "Marybeth was hanging laundry, right over there." He pointed to a clothesline about ten yards away. "Little J was playing with his toy trucks right here on the porch. She heard the phone and went into the house to answer it. It was her mama, checking on some detail for the church supper."

He paused. The silence lengthened.

"Mr. Boyce?" she prompted quietly.

He shook off the thought that had seemed to fixate him. "Sorry. I jus' realized that I never knew exactly what the detail was that was so damned important it couldn't wait for some other time." She sensed the obviously repressed anger was directed more toward whatever fate had caused his mother-in-law to call at exactly that moment than at either of the two women. "Carla, that's Marybeth's mama, can talk the ears off a deaf man. Marybeth used to be the same way." The pain in his gaze was, even after three decades, almost too terrible to bear. "She never would talk on the phone again after that day. In fact, she made me rip out the line the day of the funeral."

A funeral for a toddler. Could there be anything more tragic? "You don't have to talk about it," she said.

"You wanted to know what was goin' on between me and your mama, you got to know the circumstances behind it." He squared his shoulders, blinked away the moisture that had begun to sheen his gaze. "We had a puppy back then. A blue-tick hound name of Elvis. I'd bought it the month before, 'cause every kid needs a dog, right?"

"Right," she agreed. She'd never had one; whenever she'd asked, her mother had said they'd shed and bring fleas and ticks into the house.

"The sheriff—your daddy"—he said to Nate, who nodded—"figured that Little J must've gotten bored with playing cars and decided to play fetch with Elvis. 'Course he couldn't toss real good, and this old tennis ball was floating on the water, so it seems that's what happened." He squeezed his eyes shut, as if to block off the memory. Then he swallowed the tea in long gulps, looking like a man who wished it was something stronger.

"Marybeth just fell all to pieces. She got the deep blues and couldn't do much but just lie in bed all day. Talking to her was like talking to one of them stumps." Ashes fell off the burning end of the cigarette as he gestured toward the cypress stumps out in the still, dark water. "She wouldn't eat, wouldn't let me touch her. Never did cry. Not even when they were lowering Little J's tiny blue casket into the grave.

"Everyone else—her ma, my ma, all the aunts, cousins—was sobbing. Even my dad teared up some, and her daddy looked to be about to have a heart attack. I'm not ashamed to admit that I had tears pourin' down my face, too. But folks who say it's good to get things out must not have ever lost themselves a baby, because crying sure didn't help me none that day."

He exhaled another long, slow breath, then drew in on the cigarette. "Marybeth's eyes stayed as dry as that little stone guardian angel I'd got to mark his grave."

The small angel in the cemetery. Nate reached over and laced his fingers with hers; Regan didn't pull her hand away.

"Marybeth didn't want the angel. I found out later that she'd thought it was too damn late for Little J to have himself a guardian angel, but since he'd always been afraid of the dark, the idea of him having an angel nearby comforted me some. So I might have stood up to her about that, if she'd even said anything at the time, which she didn't."

Like during the conversation about roses, Regan was wishing he'd cut to the bottom line. She hadn't realized it fully until now, but she'd just about reached her capacity for human tragedy. Understanding that he had to tell his story his way, though, she held her tongue and looked for signs of herself in the lined face that appeared to be a road map of his life.

"After a while, Doc Vallois decided that she wasn't going to get better here, so he sent her up to this sanitarium in Baton Rouge, where they knew how to treat people who were suffering depression by sending electricity through their brains."

"Electroshock treatment." Regan exchanged a brief look with Nate.

"That's what they called it. She was there six months."

Another silence settled over them like a wet gray blanket.

"Leaving you to grieve all alone," Nate prompted quietly.

Boyce gave him a grateful glance. "Yeah." He took one last long drag on the cigarette, dropped it onto the porch, and crushed it beneath his boot heel. Then he looked back at Regan. "Your mama wasn't stuck-up like some good-looking women are. She was a lot of fun to be around. Had a heart big as all outdoors, and when she smiled at you, it was like the sun came out from behind a cloud. Everybody round these parts loved her."

"That doesn't sound like a woman who'd commit suicide."

"No, it don't," he said thoughtfully. "Didn't know anyone who wasn't real surprised by that. I sure as hell was." He shook his head. "But I guess you never really do know a person, deep down inside."

"I suppose not." She certainly hadn't known the woman she'd grown up believing to be her mother.

"Before she came to Blue Bayou, she was workin' in N'Awlins. Even tried to break into country-and-western music in Nashville, but the way she told it, she was playing in this little club way off Music Row one night when this guy came in and offered her a job singing in some place he owned in the Vieux Carré. That's the French Quarter."

"I know. What made her leave New Orleans?"

"Well, now, she never did say, but I was sure glad when she showed up at the Lounge lookin' for a job. Lord, that girl could sing like a warbler. First week she was there, I brought home an extra ten percent.

After six months the profits doubled, and the place was packed every Friday and Saturday night."

"As nice as Blue Bayou appears to be, it seems she could have had more chance to land a record deal if she'd stayed in New Orleans."

"That thought crossed my mind, too. A lot, but I never asked, and like I said, she never did tell me. I always figured it had something to do with a man. Mebee your daddy."

Regan felt every nerve in her body tense. "Did you know him?"

"Nope. She never did talk about him, neither. But I guess that's 'cause she didn't have real happy memories, and besides, whenever we were alone, she was too busy trying to cheer me up. I was pretty much of a mess in those days." Pale gray eyes narrowed as he studied her. "I guess little girls grow up to be like their mamas even if they don't live under the same roof. She was a fixer, too."

"A fixer?"

"One of those people who always want to help other people out. Cheer them up, get rid of their problems for them. That's what Linda was. Isn't it what a police officer does, too?"

"I suppose." How strange to think she might take after her mother, rather than her father. "It sounds as if you had a close relationship with Linda."

"Not as close as some of the old gossips around these parts seemed to think. I never went to bed with her. Never even kissed her. Not that I didn't think about how it'd be, from time to time," he admitted.

"Day a man stops thinking about kissing a pretty woman is the day he's just lost any reason to keep on livin'," Nate said.

Boyce surprised her by laughing at that. A rich, bold laugh that gave a hint of the man who appeared to have been close friends with her mother. Unfortunately, not close enough to know what Regan had come out here to learn.

"Did she have any other men friends?"

"Just about every man in town. Like I said, she was real popular." The smile Nate had tugged out of him lightened the dark conversation. "Even with most of the women who'd show up at the Lounge. Most nights she'd bring you along, and I never met a woman yet who didn't like playing with a pretty baby."

"She took a baby to a nightclub?"

"Wasn't like the nightclubs you're probably used to in California,"

Nate explained. “Lafitte’s Landing was a family sort of place, where everyone in town got together on the weekends to pass a good time. The supper crowd would range from great-grandmère, who didn’t speak a word of English, to mamas with their newborns, to teenagers showing up to flirt with one another.”

“ ’Sides, it was a good deal for Linda,” Boyce said. “She didn’t have to pay for a sitter. And since I knew she could be earnin’ a lot more in the city, but couldn’t afford to give her a raise, I’d toss in dinner on the house. She even worked a little duet into the routine.”

“A duet?” Regan asked. Once again he’d surprised her.

“Yeah. You couldn’t string a whole sentence together, but you sure knew all the words to ‘You Are My Sunshine.’ ”

Regan drew in a quick, sharp breath of shock.

“It’s a favorite ’round here, since it’s the state song and was written by Jimmie Davis, a sharecropper from up north in Jackson Parish who grew up to be governor. It was a real cute act, especially since even when you were in diapers, ’cepting for the color of your hair, you took after Linda. It was kind of like looking at the little girl and seeing the woman she’d grow up to be, both at the same time.”

“You said the other men in town liked her.” It was her cop voice; controlled and impassive, revealing none of the emotions churning inside her. She felt Nate looking at her again and wouldn’t—couldn’t—look at him.

“Yes, ma’am, they sure did.”

“So she dated a lot, did she?”

“Now, I didn’t say that. I said she had a lot of men friends. She was a friendly girl, but she wasn’t fast. Whenever she went out, she was always in a crowd of folks. Didn’t seem like she had any one fella she was sweet on. She used to read you fairy tales all the time, and I guess she sort of bought into the stories, because she told me her prince was going to show up on a big white horse to take you away from Blue Bayou, and the three of you were going to live happily ever after.” He shook his head. “Guess it didn’t work out that way.”

“No. Apparently not.”

Perhaps that’s why Karen Hart hadn’t encouraged Regan to believe in myths or fairy tales. Perhaps that’s why she’d stressed duty and discipline. Perhaps, believing that her sister’s freewheeling temperament had led to Linda’s death, she’d been trying to save her niece from a similar fate.

"I'd just gotten the Fleetwood then, and started picking her up at her little house and driving her to the club," he said. "Bein' how her own junker was so undependable."

Regan glanced over at the red-and-white Cadillac. "You don't see cars like that on the road much anymore."

"More's the pity," he said. "I'd bought her off a helicopter pilot over in Port Fourchon. She'd been in an accident, and the hood looked like an accordion. The interior was shot to hell, and the paint was primer, but I could see the possibilities. Linda used to help me sand the primer down on Sunday afternoons."

"It sounds as if you were very good friends."

"We both had a lot in common, bein' alone, but not being free to be with anyone else. Oh, we never talked about her man, and I only told her about Marybeth once, on a really dark day when I got drunk and broke down and bawled like a baby, but it was always there between us, and created a bond. But it was always an innocent friendship. Despite, like I said, what some busybodies liked to say."

"People talked."

"Sure. It's a small town," he said with a resigned shrug of his shoulders. "There's not a lot to do, so talking about your neighbor is sorta the local recreation."

Although Regan suspected living in such an environment could prove stifling, there might be advantages to being a cop here—unlike L.A., where you could arrive at a club that had broken fire regulations by packing people in like sardines, have someone get shot in the head at point-blank range, and not a single person in the place would have seen a damn thing. Of course, she doubted there were all that many homicides in Blue Bayou, which made it a moot point.

"Marybeth was a lot better when she got back from the sanatorium, but she was still about as fragile as glass. I used to walk around on tiptoe, not knowing what might set her off."

"Did you keep driving Linda to the club after your wife returned home?"

"Oh, no, ma'am. Not because anything had been going on," he stressed again. "But because I didn't want to be responsible for sending Marybeth back to that place. Her being away was hard on both of us, though it did seem to help with her blues, so I still think it was probably a good thing."

"But someone shared the gossip with her."

"Oh, there were a few women who were jealous of Linda and real eager to let Marybeth know what her husband had been doin' while she'd been gettin' electricity shot through her head." If the sparks glittering in his eyes were any indication, it still made him angry as hell. "Meddling old biddies who, since they don't have any real lives of their own, spend their time sticking their pointy noses into other people's business."

"That's when MaryBeth filed the alienation-of-affection complaint."

"Yeah." He took off his billed cap and dragged his hand through his still-thick white hair. "She didn't mean nothin' by it, though. She was just hurt and went on a tear. By the time I got over to the judge's house, he'd pretty much talked her out of the idea.

"She and I spent all that night talking, and the next day she withdrew the complaint. I thought everything was going to be okay. Then, when Linda didn't show up for work, I went to check on her, and found her in the garage."

Dead. While a two-year-old child was left to fend for herself. Regan had witnessed similar things, and while she'd always felt terrible for the children, never had their loss and the confusion they must have been feeling hit home as it did now.

"You said you and your wife talked all night," she said, carefully wading into deeper conversational waters. "Was that a figure of speech? Or were you literally with her all night long?"

His eyes narrowed as he read the underlying meaning in the question. "We were together all night. So, if you're here on police business, I guess you could say I'm her alibi. And she's mine."

"I wasn't—" Hell, Regan thought, there was no point in lying. "I didn't mean to imply that either you or your wife had anything to do with her death, Mr. Boyce." It wasn't an out-and-out lie. "I'm just trying to get at the truth. If you were as close friends as you say—"

"I don't lie, ma'am." His tone had turned from gravel to flint.

"Yessir. I understand that. And for what it's worth, I believe you. But surely you, as a friend, would want to know what happened to her."

"Killed herself. It said so right on the front page of the *Chronicle*."

"Sometimes newspapers get it wrong, Jarrett," Nate said.

"I read about there bein' an autopsy."

"Sometimes medical examiners get it wrong, too," Regan said. Even knowing that it might tell Nate more about herself than she would have wished, she took the old photograph of her father from her billfold and held it out to Boyce. "Have you ever seen this man before?"

He gnawed on his lower lip as he studied it for a long, silent time. "His face doesn't ring a bell," he said finally.

"Perhaps you never met him," she suggested, not quite willing to give up. "Could you have perhaps seen this photo at Linda's house?"

"No, ma'am." This time his answer was quick, decisive. "The only pictures Linda had around were ones she'd taken of you." He began thoughtfully turning his cap around and around in his hands. "You were the cutest little thing. There were times when I used to hold you on my lap and wonder if things might have been different if I hadn't met Marybeth first, and Linda wasn't hung up over some guy who sure wasn't actin' much like a prince, if you want my opinion. I would've liked bein' your daddy. I told your mama once that if I ever had a daughter, I would've liked her to be like you."

He put the hat back on his head and stood up, declaring the conversation closed. "I still would."

Regan was deeply, honestly moved. "Thank you, Mr. Boyce. That's a lovely compliment."

"It's the truth," he said gruffly. The sound of a car engine a ways down the road captured his attention, and he cursed softly under his breath. "That'd be Marybeth, coming home from the market."

Regan wondered if his wife had entirely recovered. There were certainly drugs available to treat depression these days, but did a mother ever truly get over the death of a child?

Not wanting to inflict another wound on the possibly still fragile Marybeth when there was no hard evidence pointing at any guilt, she turned to Nate. "We'd better be going."

"Thank you, ma'am." The older man's relief was obvious. They were nearly to the SUV when he called out to her.

"Yes?" Regan asked.

"If someone did kill Linda, I sure hope you find him. Lynchin's too good for any sumbitch who'd snuff out such a special life."

# 16

*They backed out of the driveway* just as a late-model Honda pulled in. "That was a nice thing to do," Nate said.

"I didn't want to waste time. After all, we got what we needed. There was no point in questioning his wife."

"And you believed him? About not sleeping with her?"

"I got the impression he was being truthful. Didn't you?"

"Sure. But I'm the civilian here."

She glanced back, watching as Boyce took the groceries out of the car. He literally towered over his wife, who appeared to be about four-eleven and probably wouldn't weigh a hundred pounds soaking wet. "You could have told me Marybeth is so small."

"Seems to me I mentioned my doubts about her dragging Linda out to the car, and you mentioning adrenaline. Since I knew you'd want to check out all the loose ends, it made more sense to let you talk to Jarrett and make your own decision about the involvement of either one."

"Of course, there's always the chance that he was lying to me about their relationship," Regan mused. "Which could give him a motive for killing Dale himself. It certainly wouldn't be the first time the person who reported finding a body turned out to be the one responsible. It's obvious he loves his wife, or they wouldn't have survived the loss of a child and her depression and still be together thirty years later. If he'd wanted to protect his marriage, he'd have a motive for wanting to stop her from telling Marybeth the truth about an affair."

"Thus risking the chance of sending her back into a depression, which in turn would have her returning to the hospital," Nate said. "Do you believe that's a possibility?"

"Anything's possible. But no, I don't believe that's what happened."

"Then I guess we keep looking."

*We*. Strange, how having Nate Callahan as a partner in this investigation didn't seem quite as impossible as it did yesterday.

"Do me a favor?" she asked.

"Sure." She didn't know anyone who'd agree without first finding out what she was asking. "What do you need?"

"Pull over. I need to get out of this car."

He shot a concerned look. "You feelin' sick, *chère?*"

"No." She took a deep breath. "Frustrated. And when I'm frustrated, I need to walk."

"Makes sense to me."

He pulled the SUV over to the side of the road. Regan jumped out before he could open her door and headed off down the road with no goal but to try to clear her head and sort things through.

The energy was radiating from her like sparks from a fire as she marched along the bank of the bayou. Leaving her to her thoughts, Nate kept quiet and just fit his stride to hers.

"I just keep going over and over it," she ground out after they'd gone about two hundred yards. "And I still can't figure out why she never told me the truth."

"Maybe to protect your feelings?"

"Lies always come out."

Sister Augustine had always said the same thing. The nun had warned her often unruly second graders, who'd technically reached what the church considered the age of reason, that lies of omission were no different from those spoken out loud, which meant the transgressor was required to confess to the priest on those long Saturday-afternoon penance sessions Nate had spent on his knees, reciting Our Fathers and Hail Marys when he'd rather be outside playing ball.

"Maybe she kept putting it off until she thought you were older and could handle the news better."

She spun toward him. "I was an adult when she died. How long was she planning to wait?"

"I guess that's something you'll never know."

"I wonder what else she didn't intend me to know." She shook her head and began walking again, then stopped again and looked out over the bayou. "Damn. I sound so damn pathetic."

She didn't look anything like the woman he'd first seen as an island of calm in the midst of a chaotic police station. Nor that intelligent, capable detective who'd testified so calmly and succinctly at that gangbanger's murder trial, sticking to the facts no matter how often the defense attorney had tried to draw her off-track by attacking not just the L.A. police force in general, but her own investigation.

She looked small. Feminine. And strangely vulnerable.

"You don't sound pathetic at all, you." Unable to watch any woman in such distress, he smoothed her too tense shoulders with his palms. "You jus' sound like a woman who's had her world turned upside down. Suddenly the sky's green." He ran his hands down her arms, linked their fingers together. "The grass is blue. The sun's spinning in that green sky, and you're figuring how to handle this new way of seein' things." He drew her closer; not to seduce, but to soothe.

She slapped a hand against the front of his shirt. "I realize this will come as a terrible shock, but not every woman on the planet is panting to fall into bed with you."

"Well, now, that suits me just fine, since I'm not interested in falling into bed with every woman on the planet."

"Dammit, Callahan, if you don't quit hitting on me—"

"*Non, chère.*" He caught hold of the hand pushing against his chest, lifted it, touched his lips to the soft, warm skin of her palm, then folded her fingers again, holding the kiss in. "This isn't hitting."

"People must use a different dictionary in Louisiana. What would you call it?"

"Fixing." He moved a little closer, so they were touching, thigh to thigh, chest to chest, her slender curves to his angles. They fit well. He'd thought they would, back when she'd been on the witness stand and he'd been fantasizing taking her to bed.

"Fixing?"

"That's what I do." He pressed a kiss against her hair and drew in the scent of herbal shampoo. "I'll never make as much money as Jack. Or be as driven as Finn. But I've always been pretty good at fixin' things."

Having accepted early on that a person couldn't change nature, Nate had been happy in his role as a handyman of sorts, fixing houses, people, lives. But until now, until Detective Regan Hart, the only time he'd tried to fix a broken heart had been that horrific day that his *maman* had been widowed.

"I think you and I just might have that in common, Detective *Chère*." He felt the stiffness easing out of her as she slipped her arms around his waist. "So why don't you let me fix you? Just a little?"

"I suppose your method of fixing up will involve getting naked?"

"No. Well, not right this minute," he amended, wondering if Sister Augustine was looking down from some fluffy cloud and admiring the deft way he'd avoided committing a sin of omission. "Maybe later, when you get to know me a little bit better and are more comfortable with the idea."

He was rewarded by something that sounded a bit like a smothered laugh, then felt the moisture when she pressed her face into his neck.

"I am not crying."

"Of course you're not." He slid a hand through her hair, sifting the silky strands like sand between his fingers.

"I never cry." Her voice was muffled. "Not even when my mother died."

He felt her stiffen again as she realized the woman she'd always thought of as her mother probably wasn't.

"Don't think about that right now." He cupped her face between his hands. Her eyes, underscored by shadows revealing too many sleepless nights, were dark with pain.

"That's easy for you to say."

"You know what you need?"

"What?"

"Somethin' to take your mind of all your problems. Jus' for a little while."

Unlike that earlier kiss, when he'd slowly, tantalizingly led her into the mists, this time he dragged her, head spinning, heart hammering, into a storm. Thunder rumbled inside her, lightning sparked every raw nerve ending, and she could have sworn the ground beneath her feet quaked.

It shook Regan to the core. She'd never realized she could feel so much. Never imagined she could want so much more.

Too soon, he drew his head back. "I want you."

"Now there's a surprise." The surprise was that she could actually speak when she was so close to begging. "Have you ever met a woman you didn't want?"

"From time to time." He smiled a bit at that, but his eyes were thoughtful. "This isn't one of those times."

"Then you're going to be disappointed. Because I'm not into casual sex."

"I'd be disappointed if you were."

She arched a brow. "Ah, the double standard lifts its ugly head. Why is it okay for a man to be a player, but if a woman enjoys variety, she's a slut?"

"I have no idea, never having subscribed to that belief, myself." He slipped a hand beneath the hem of her white T-shirt; roughened fingers skimmed over the unreasonably sensitive skin of her abdomen. "I'm going to touch you, Detective Darlin'. All over." The sound of those callus-tipped fingers rasping against the lace of her bra was one of the sexiest things she'd ever heard. "Then I'm going to taste you." He dipped his head again and touched his lips to the nape of her neck. "Every last inch of your delectable female body."

Who could have suspected there was a direct link from that surprisingly sensitive spot behind her ear to her legs, which were turning to water?

"And then, just to prove I'm no chauvinist, I'm going to let you do the same thing to me. But not yet."

His quiet declaration took the wind right out of her sails.

"What?"

"Although I'm surprising the hell out of myself, I'm thinking we should step back a little. Take our time. Slow things down. Get to know one another better. It'll be all the more satisfying in the end."

"You make it sound like a foregone conclusion."

"Isn't it? You say you don't go in for casual sex, which fits, since from what I've seen, you don't take anything lightly. Including that kiss we just shared."

"It was only a kiss. No different from any other."

"You just keep tellin' yourself that, *chère*. I promise not to rub it in too badly when you realize how wrong you were."

She blew out a frustrated breath. "I'm amazed, given your supposed way with the opposite sex, that it's never sunk in that you can be annoyingly, insufferably arrogant."

"You know, if you keep talking like that, you're going to have me falling head over heart in love with you." His smile warmed and widened. "I've always been a sucker for flattery."

They returned to the car, and after a brief drive Nate pulled up in front of a building.

"What are we doing?"

"I thought we'd pick up some lunch to eat while we plan our next move," he said. "You haven't eaten till you've tasted one of Cajun Cal's po' boys."

Two seconds after they walked into the café, conversation dropped off like a stone falling into a well.

"Small towns," Nate murmured.

"Doesn't it get old?" she asked, pretending not to notice that everyone was staring at her. Since at least half the people in the place were too young to have even known Linda Dale's name, Regan could only assume that the news of her arrival in town had preceded her. "Not being at all anonymous?"

He thought about that for a minute. "Not anymore. I guess you get used to it. It was hard when I was in my teens and was trying to get away with anything. One time Jack and I were cruisin' home from school in his GTO, and by the time we arrived at Beau Soleil, at least a dozen folks had already called *maman* to tell her we'd been speeding."

Regan couldn't help smiling at that idea.

He smiled back, then sobered. "I think it was also worse because we were just about the only kids in school whose daddy had died."

"The dead dad's club," she murmured.

"Yeah. Guess you and I are both charter members."

"I guess we are."

The restaurant seemed to be made up of a connecting series of small rooms, each of which had an inordinate number of tables crowded into it. The tables were covered in newspaper, the chairs were a jumble of different styles and colors, and the front counter was red Formica. Daily specials had been printed in white chalk on a standing blackboard beside the counter. The walls, which she supposed had once been white but had become smoke-darkened over the decades, were covered with huge stuffed fish, photographs that, from the outlandish costumes, she assumed had been taken during many Mardi Gras over the decades, and old metal signs advertising various beers—Jax seemed the most popular—soft drinks, and White Lily flour.

The smells emanating from the kitchen made Regan's mouth water.

Cajun Cal was the oldest man Regan had ever seen who was still alive. Nearly black eyes, as bright as a parrot's, looked out at her from a face as dark and wrinkled as a raisin.

"So, you're Linda Dale's little girl all grown up."

She forced a smile, as much for the audience as for the man behind the counter. It was clearly going to be impossible to keep the purpose of her trip from becoming common knowledge. "That's what I'm in Blue Bayou to find out."

"Yeah. That's what I heard." The unlit cigarette in his mouth bobbed up and down as he spooned dark coffee grounds from a bright red bag of Community Coffee into a huge urn. "Your face isn't exactly the same, and your hair isn't the same, but lookin' at your eyes, it'd be my guess you are." He studied her some more. "I also heard you're a big-city cop."

"I'm a detective, yes."

"Detective, cop, G-man, they're all the same thing. I got my start in this business when I was still a kid and my uncle hired me to deliver jugs of white lightnin' around the parish during Prohibition. Best customers we had were the cops." If there was a challenge there, and Regan suspected from his tone that there was, she refused to rise to it.

"That's the trouble with passing a law the majority of the people in the country don't agree with," she said mildly.

"Sure as hell is. Nobody down here paid much attention to Prohibition. Hell, my uncle didn't even bother to hide the stuff. Kept it right behind the counter, servin' it up by the glass to whoever wanted a snort. He brewed the best hootch in south Louisiana."

"Well, good for him." She smiled. "But if it's all the same to you, I'll just have a glass of iced tea. No," she corrected, having already tasted what appeared to pass for tea down here, "on second thought, water will be fine."

"Why don't you make that two lemonades," Nate suggested. "Regan got to sample sweet tea out at Jarrett's place."

The old man cackled. "Marybeth's sweet tea does take some gettin' used to, even if you're not a Yankee. You sing, *chère?*"

Regan didn't so much as blink at the question that had come from left field. She could also feel everyone in the restaurant who was over fifty years old waiting for her answer.

"Not really." She decided belting out Aretha Franklin in the shower didn't count.

"Now, that's a crying shame. Linda had a real pretty voice. As pure a soprano as you'd ever want to hear. But I guess genes are an iffy thing. Lord knows, I'm the best cook in the South, and my daughter Lilah can't even boil water without burning the bottom out of the pot. As for my son, well, I've been pulling dinner from the Gulf since God was a pup, but he's a piss-poor fisherman."

"Maybe there's something your wife never got around to tellin' you, Cal," offered a man the color of coal, wearing a stained white apron and shelling shrimp. "I hear the mailman y'all had fifty years ago couldn't fish worth beans, either."

"Hardy har har," the old man scoffed, then turned piercing dark eyes back to Regan. "I also heard tell you're gonna be our new sheriff."

"I'm afraid the grapevine has it wrong."

"Wouldn't be the first time," he said equably. "We sure could use ourselves one."

"I'm sure Mayor Callahan's doing everything in his power to find the perfect candidate."

"Seems to me any cop who'll crawl under hot wires to save a kid is real close to perfect herself." He lifted a basket of golden fried fish from a deep fryer and dumped it onto a platter.

"We'll have two po' boys," Nate ordered, saving Regan from having to respond. "You want shrimp, fried fish, or roast beef, sugar?"

Not only was there something unnerving about eating fish with all those glass eyes looking down at her, the roast beef in the display case was so heavily marbled she could feel her arteries clogging just looking at it.

"I guess the shrimp."

"Good choice," Nate said. "I'll have the same as the lady, dress 'em both, and throw in a couple cartons of slaw and some hush puppies."

"Why is it called a po' boy?" Regan asked.

" 'Cause it used to only cost a nickel, so poor boys could afford it."

She watched the sandwich being made and decided that a family of six could probably eat quite well on it for a week. She also wondered if she should just call ahead and make an appointment at the hospital for bypass surgery rather than wait for the heart attack.

"Do you eat here often?" she asked Nate quietly.

"Jus' about every day. Why?"

"I was wondering why you don't weigh a thousand pounds."

"I work it off." He paused a wicked beat. "Want to know how?"

"No." Her smile was as sweet as Marybeth Boyce's tea. "I don't."

Nate had been teasing, mostly. Enjoying a little flirtation. Then he made the mistake of looking at her mouth and remembered, with vivid clarity, the taste of those full, inviting lips. The blood suddenly rushed from his head to other, more vital regions, making him feel as dizzy as he had that day Jack had swiped a case of Dixie out of a beer truck delivering out back, and the two of them had taken the pirogue out to their daddy's old camp and gotten drunk by the light of a summer bayou moon.

*Easy, boy*, he warned himself as he felt an almost overwhelming urge to kiss her, right here in Cajun Cal's Country Café, in front of just about everyone in town. He wanted to taste that delectable mouth again, wanted to feel it roaming all over his hot, naked body.

His hunger must have shown in his expression, because her eyes suddenly widened, and he was caught in that gleaming amber, frozen in it, which didn't make much sense, since the air between them had turned about as sizzling hot as a steamy dog-day August afternoon. Yet he couldn't have moved if someone shouted out a hurricane was blowing in from the Gulf and they were standing right atop the levee.

# 17

*Leave this be,* the angel perched on Nate's shoulder warned. *She isn't like Charlene, or Suzanne.* Or any other of the women he'd tumbled happily, easily into bed with over the years since that memorable day when he'd lost his virginity in the backseat of Jack's borrowed GTO with Misty Montgomery.

*Don't listen to him,* the devil on the other shoulder said. *She's a grown woman.* Nate had already determined that for himself, but what he hadn't noticed, until now, was how tight those low-slung jeans were. He wondered if she'd had to lie on the bed at the inn to zip them.

That idea led to another, of knocking all those salt and pepper shakers, metal napkin holders, and bottles of hot sauce off the chipped red counter, lifting her up onto it, unzipping those jeans, and dragging them down those smooth thighs he'd wanted to bite when she'd been up on that witness stand back in L.A.

He imagined her wearing a pair of skimpy red panties that barely covered the essentials, and although she'd beg him, "Please, Nate, rip them off, please, please, darling," he'd torture them both by taking his time, enjoying the way her eyes glazed with lust when he slipped his fingers beneath the silk, jangling her senses, causing every nerve ending in her body to sizzle.

And when he'd tormented them both to the point of no return, when he had her exactly where he wanted her, hot, needy, ravenous, he'd peel those panties down her long legs, inch by erotic inch, and as she cried out his name, he'd—

"Hey, Nate." The voice was deep, way too deep to be hers.

Nate slowly, painfully, dragged his mind back from the sensual fantasy, crashing headfirst into reality when he viewed the fifty-something man standing beside her.

"Hey, Charles," he answered on a voice roughened with lingering lust. "How's it goin'?" Like he cared.

"Fine, just fine." Charles Melancon turned his smile from Nate to Regan, who also appeared to be shell-shocked as she returned from wherever the hell they'd both been. "Hello. You must be the new sheriff I've been hearing all about."

"She ain't the sheriff," Cal said around his unlit cigarette as he wrapped the enormous sandwiches in waxed white paper. "Was just filling in during the accident out at the crossing 'tween that freight and the eighteen-wheeler."

"What a terrible, terrible thing." Melancon shook his silver head. "It was a miracle no one was seriously hurt."

"It sure could've been a lot worse," Nate agreed. His head was beginning to clear, and he was no longer in immediate danger of bustin' the zipper out of his jeans. "Detective, this is Charles Melancon. Charles, Detective Regan Hart, from Los Angeles."

"It's a pleasure meeting you, detective." He shook her hand with the robust action of a small-town politician, which he was. Along with being CEO of Melancon Petroleum, Charles Melancon was head of several redevelopment committees, president of the Blue Bayou Rotary Club, and past president of the Chamber of Commerce. "I was very impressed by your bravery. Did the mayor happen to mention we're in the market for a new sheriff?" he asked.

"As a matter of fact, he did. But I already have a job. I'm an LAPD homicide detective."

"Are you now?" His silver brows shot up. "That must be exciting work."

"Actually, homicide's pretty much society's clean-up crew. We're like the guys with the wheelbarrows who follow the elephants in the parade and shovel up the shit."

Behind the counter, Cal gave a bark of a laugh.

"Still, it must be interesting," Melancon said. "The closest thing to excitement here in Blue Bayou is watching paint dry."

"Oh, I wouldn't think running an international oil company could possibly be dull."

Interest turned to surprise. "You know about Melancon Oil?"

"It would be hard not to, since I see the blue sign every time I fill up my car. Though I never realized the home offices were located in southern Louisiana."

That was, Nate knew, a lie. He suspected that after having learned about the stock certificates, she could probably quote the company's latest balance sheet.

"We're not the biggest fish in the pond, but we make a right nice splash." Charles Melancon might not be the type of guy Nate would swap stories and go fishing with, but he'd always seemed fairly down-to-earth for someone whose father had probably owned half of southern Louisiana at one time. "What brings you to Blue Bayou, detective?"

"Oh, this and that." Despite seeming half the town knowing what she was up to, and the other half undoubtedly finding out by Mardi Gras, she wasn't one to give anything away. Her smile turned as vague as her tone. "Partly I'm here for a little R&R."

"Most folks go to N'Awlins for that."

"I've been there and done all the touristy, French Quarter things. This trip I decided to see the real Louisiana."

"Well, you've certainly come to the right place."

"I don't suppose you conduct tours of your facilities?" she asked.

He frowned. "Not as a rule. Refineries can be dangerous to those not familiar with the work, and our insurance company likes us to keep our liability risk down."

"Well, it never hurts to ask." She sighed heavily in a very undetective-like way. "I suppose I'll just sign up for the alligator swamp tour instead."

"You'd pretty much be wastin' your money," Nate volunteered. "Seein' as how the gators are hibernating right now."

"Oh." Her mouth turned down in a little moue that was far more woman than cop. "Well, I'm sure I can find something to occupy my time. I seem to recall reading that Exxon Mobile has a refinery in Baton Rouge. Perhaps—"

"I suppose," Melancon interrupted her, "it would be all right to show you around, just this once." His eyes swept over her in what Nate decided was an unnecessarily intimate way for a guy who had a wife at home. "After all, what Louisiana Liability and Trust doesn't know won't hurt them."

"It'll be our secret." Her smile would have done a Miss Cajun Days queen proud. "Why don't I drop by Monday morning?"

"I'm afraid I'm going to be out of town on Monday. A meeting in Houston."

"Oh. Well, Tuesday will be fine."

"That's Fat Tuesday," Cal volunteered.

"He's right," Charles Melancon said with what appeared to be a bit of honest reluctance. "Which means that while a skeleton crew will be working, I'm afraid the offices won't be open."

"How about Wednesday?" she pressed on. "Say, about eight o'clock?"

"I'm afraid the office isn't open quite that early."

"Especially on Ash Wednesday, when everyone in the parish is going to be hung over," Cal said.

"Not everyone," Melancon corrected. "Why don't we have lunch together in the company dining room at one on Wednesday?"

Her smile could have lit up Blue Bayou for a month. "That sounds fab."

Fab? Nate stared down at the surprising metamorphosis from cop to belle.

"I'm staying at the Plantation Inn, in case something opens up before then," she said.

"Good choice," he said.

Only choice, Nate thought.

"The inn's a famous historical landmark," Melancon continued.

"So Mr. Callahan tells me. I'll be waiting for your call." She held out her hand like a princess to some duke she was considering marrying. "It was lovely meeting you, Mr. Melancon."

"The pleasure was all mine, Ms. Hart." He flashed his Chamber of Commerce meet-and-greet grin and returned to his table across the room.

"Isn't he a charming man?" Regan said.

"An absolute gem," Nate agreed dryly.

"Order's up," Cal announced.

Nate took the brown bags. "It's on me," he said when Regan began to take some money from her billfold. She looked inclined to argue, then merely shrugged.

"What the hell was that all about?" Nate asked Regan when they were back in the SUV.

"What was what all about?"

"That Scarlett O'Hara act you pulled with Charles Melancon."

"I've no idea what you mean."

"You're not the type of woman who normally goes around batting your eyelashes."

"Too bad you missed my days in vice, when I did undercover prostitution stings." She pulled her seat belt across and clicked it. "I'll have you know, some men found me very appealing."

"Of course you're appealing, dammit. But not in that way."

"And what way is that?"

"You know." Feeling as if he'd somehow landed in verbal quicksand, he skimmed a hand over his hair. "That over-the-top come-and-get-me-big-boy way. You were sending off signals that you were open for a lot more than a damn oil refinery tour."

"That's quite a comment from the man who's claimed he wants to take me to bed, and was undressing me with his eyes when Melancon interrupted."

"I didn't hear you complaining." He jerked his own seat belt closed.

"We were in a public place. I didn't feel the need to embarrass you by telling you to knock it off."

"What a bunch of bullshit." He twisted the key in the ignition with more strength than necessary and pulled away from the curb with an angry squeal of tires.

The heat that had sizzled between them in the restaurant shifted into a low, seething anger. Regan was tempted to tell him to take her back to the inn; she didn't need his help. After all, if she couldn't handle one cold case committed in a town where everyone knew everyone else, which meant someone had to hold the key to solving the murder, she might as well turn in her shield and go sell Avon products door to door.

The problem was, if she stomped back to the inn, she'd risk letting him know how affected she'd been by that suspended moment in the restaurant, when she'd been fantasizing about Nate dragging her down to the black-and-white-checked floor and making mad, passionate love to her.

"I wasn't flirting with him," she said into the heavy silence. "I need to talk to him about the stock certificates. Since I don't have any police powers down here to force the issue, and since he's undoubtedly used to calling the shots, I figured he might be more amenable to charm."

"You couldn't just come right out and ask?"

"With everyone in the place watching us and listening to every word?"

"Yeah, I can see how you'd rather them think you were coming on to a married guy twice your age than have them overhearing you ask a basic business question."

"It's not basic when a woman got killed over it."

He shot her a surprised look. "You think Linda Dale was murdered for her Melancon Petroleum stock?"

"She wouldn't have been the first person to be killed over money."

"And wouldn't be the last," he allowed. "But if that was the motive, then why were the stocks left behind?"

"Maybe the murderer got interrupted and had to leave before he could retrieve them. Maybe she had them hidden." Regan shrugged. "There could be any number of answers. Which is why I want privacy when I talk with Melancon. Not that he sounded real eager for a meeting." She frowned. "I wonder why that was?"

"Are you suspicious of everyone? Never mind," he said before she could answer the rhetorical question; "I know the answer to that. But just because he's CEO of the company doesn't mean he'll be able to tell you anything. His mother was running the place thirty years ago."

"From what you said about Mrs. Melancon, the chances are she wouldn't recall details. But not only would he have access to the records, this is a small town. It seems implausible that anyone living here—especially a nightclub singer—would own that much stock without the family being aware of it."

"Good point."

"Thank you. That's why L.A. pays me the big bucks." Which barely covered the rent on her closet-sized apartment in Westwood and insurance on a five-year-old tomato red Neon. "I wonder if he knew her?"

"Like you said, it's a small town, and it sounds like she was a local celebrity."

"I got that impression from the newspaper even before we talked with Jarrett Boyce." She chewed thoughtfully on a buffed fingernail. "Do you suppose they could have been lovers?"

"That's unlikely."

"Why?"

" 'Cause I already checked it out. Charles got married two years before Linda Dale's death."

"That doesn't mean anything. They could have been having an affair."

"That's also unlikely. Not only does the guy consider himself a pillar of morality, the conventional wisdom around these parts says that he married into money to keep his family in the style to which they'd become accustomed back when oil was king."

"You'd think being CEO of a family petroleum company would pay very well."

"Not well enough. There was a time when his daddy probably had more power than the governor. He'd had more than one governor and several congressmen in his pocket. Regulation slowed the money flow, then the bust tightened things even more. The family's richer than most around these parts, but if it wasn't for Charles's wife's money, they'd probably have to give up the plane, the yacht, the ski chalet in Aspen, and the villa in Tuscany."

"I didn't find any villa when I did my search."

"The title's in his mother-in-law's name. But she lives in one of those retirement communities in Baton Rouge and hasn't been out of the country in a decade."

"I suppose you got that from Finn."

"He did a little digging."

"I don't even want to know," Regan muttered. "I'm beginning to feel as if I'm dealing with the Hardy boys. Maybe Melancon gave Linda Dale the stock to pay her off."

"To get rid of her once he tired of the affair?"

"That's always possible."

"Sure it is. But if that was the case, then why would he kill her?"

"Maybe she refused the offer."

"She had the certificates."

"Okay, maybe she changed her mind. Maybe she took them, then threatened to go to his wife."

"Because she wanted more money?"

"Or because she was in love and decided that she couldn't live without him."

"So he killed her to shut her up."

"That's one scenario."

"You realize, of course, that if you're right, Melancon could be your father?"

"We can't all have heroes for fathers." It was looking more and more likely that she probably didn't. "But the name's wrong. Dale referred to the man she was going to run off with as J," she reminded him. Then paused. "There's something I haven't wanted to bring up. But I don't think we can overlook it."

"What?"

"You do realize that there's someone else who could have been involved with Dale."

"More than one someone. There are a helluva lot of names in this parish that begin with *J*."

"Like Jake."

She'd expected him to swear. Maybe even rage. At least snap back a denial. He did none of that. He threw back his sun-gilded head and roared with laughter.

"It's not that funny."

"If you'd known my dad, you'd think it was. There's no way he would have looked at another woman. He and *maman* used to embarrass the hell out of us kids, the way they used to neck like teenagers. They renewed their vows on their twentieth wedding anniversary, right here at Holy Assumption.

"The very next weekend, on the night before he was killed, they were partying at his fortieth birthday party. I remember groaning with Jack when they were dancing to this slow Cajun song about love goin' wrong and they kissed, right there, in front of God and everyone in Blue Bayou. And not just a friendly little husband-and-wife public peck on the cheek. They were really gettin' into it." His expression turned reminiscent and understandably sad. "Everyone in the parish knew Jake Callahan flat-out adored my mother. And she adored him back."

"I believe that." It wouldn't be that hard to fall in love with a Callahan man, if a woman was looking to fall in love. Which she definitely was not. "But nobody's perfect. People make mistakes. Get themselves in messy situations they never could have imagined."

"Even if he had slipped, and I'm not saying he did, since I don' believe it for a damn minute, if he'd gotten a woman pregnant, he would have done right by her."

"*Done right*. Does that mean marry?"

"Hell, I don't know." He was no longer laughing. In fact, he was as sober as she'd ever seen him. Even more serious than when he was crawling beneath those electrical wires to rescue the trucker and a runaway teenager.

He blew out a long ragged breath. "Maybe. Maybe not. I told you, he took his marriage vows seriously, so I can't see him signing up for a lifetime sentence if he wasn't in love."

"Sentence. Well, that certainly reveals how you think about marriage."

"Actually, I try *not* to think about it. I'm also not real wild about the way you're analyzing every damn word I use, like this is some kind of interrogation. However, as I was about to point out, even if Dad were to go plantin' his seed somewhere, he would have insisted on contributing to his child's support.

"I watched him chase down men who didn't pay their child support and toss them in jail until they decided it'd be better to write the checks, long before it got politically popular to crack down on deadbeat dads. Dad was big on birthdays and holidays, and just taking us boys out to the camp for a lazy summer day of fishing, or even tossin' a ball around the backyard before supper. He'd never desert his own flesh and blood." His hand had curled into an unconscious fist. "He wouldn't have let your mother live in the same town and never acknowledged you."

"I understand why you'd want to stand up for him. I also understand why you'd find it hard to believe that he might possibly commit adultery, since it's obvious you respect him—"

"There's not a man, woman, or child who knew Jake Callahan who didn't respect him."

"I'm also willing to accept that. But we can't ever really know our parents, Nate, because they try their best never to let us see their flaws. I'm proof that an otherwise honest parent might think it's in everyone's best interest to keep a secret from their children."

"Not my dad, dammit. Look, you've met Finn."

"Of course."

"Let me put it this way: our father would make Finn look downright flexible."

"You're joking." She'd never met a more rigid, black-and-white person than Finn Callahan. And living in the world of cops, that was really saying something.

"This is not exactly a joking matter. It's also a moot point, because Dad was working in Chicago when your mother got pregnant."

"He was sheriff of Blue Bayou when she lived here."

"When she died," Nate corrected. "But you're the same age as Jack, and he and Finn were both born in Chicago. We moved here when I was six weeks old."

"Oh. Well, I guess that does take him out of the picture, since there's no indication Dale ever lived in Illinois."

"Not unless you want to concoct some theory about them meeting on some plane trip and becoming members of the mile-high club over Kansas, then going their separate ways after it landed."

The uncharacteristic sarcasm in his tone was sharp enough to cut crystal. "I suppose I deserved that."

"No." He sighed and shook his head. "You didn't. I understand this is tough on you, and you're only doin' what comes naturally. Detecting."

"I'm sure as hell not doing very well at it so far," she muttered.

"Like you said, it's a cold case. You've only been in town two days."

"I know. I just get impatient."

"That's not good for you. Raises your blood pressure and all sorts of bad stuff. Move here, and you're bound to slow down. Live longer."

"Maybe it just seems longer."

He chuckled at that.

"Do you know Melancon's wife?"

"Sure. She's on just about every charitable committee in town. As mayor, I have a lot of dealings with her. She tends to keep busy, and her fingers are in most of the pies around town. She does a lot of charity work, but it's seldom the hands-on kind of stuff. She's more likely to donate a wing to the hospital than drive around in her Jag delivering Meals on Wheels.

"She can be so condescending your teeth hurt from being clenched, and she's a snob, along with being Blue Bayou's self-appointed morality czarina. But I can't see her killing anyone, if that's where you were going. Especially if it'd involve anything that might involve chipping a fingernail."

"There's one thing I learned early on in homicide."

"What's that?"

"Everyone's a suspect."

"You're a hard woman, Detective *Chère*."

"I'm a realist." She had to be. "I'm going to want to meet her."

"Mrs. Melancon?"

"Yeah. The way I see it, I can do it three ways. I can find out her daily activity pattern and just happen to run into her by chance and get to chatting, but that's iffy, and if she's in a hurry, it doesn't give me a real good opportunity to talk with her.

"Or I can just go to her house, knock on the door, tell her that her husband may be a suspect in a thirty-year-old murder case, and could we have a little chat about whether or not he used to sleep around on her back when she was a young bride.

"Or," she said as he pulled up to a four-way stop, "I can have you arrange things."

He braked and briefly shut his eyes. "Why did I know you were going to say that?"

"Because you've spent all your life surrounded by cops. Some of it's got to have rubbed off onto you."

"I use that soap with pumice in it so it doesn't stick."

"You might not want to admit it, Callahan, but on occasions, you, too, can think like a cop."

He frowned. "I don't know if I've been complimented or insulted."

She laughed for the first time, and Nate was struck by how much he enjoyed the rich, full sound. She reached over and patted his cheek. "Why don't you think on it."

# 18

*They stopped for a while* in a peaceful spot next to the bayou for lunch. The sandwich was the richest she'd ever tasted. She'd only been able to finish half of it and still didn't think she'd be able to eat again for a week. They'd parked beside a metal marker memorializing the victory of a battle against the British.

"Isn't that the pirate you were going to tell me about?" She remembered him mentioning that when they'd first entered the ER.

"That's him. Jean Lafitte. Actually, there were three of them—Alexander, Pierre, and Jean—but Jean was the most infamous. Alexander, who, I guess you could say was most respectable, was Napoleon's artillery officer. Jean and Pierre were privateers who earned their living attacking the trading ships comin' and goin' between the Gulf and the river cities."

"I imagine there was a fairly good profit in piracy."

"*Mais* yeah. Jean and Pierre had thirty-two armed warships under their command, they, which was more than the entire American navy at the start of the War of 1812. Both the British and the Americans recruited them, but Andrew Jackson was the one who promised them amnesty if they'd fight in the Battle of New Orleans."

"Which they did," she guessed.

"They did. After they won the battle and sent the Redcoats packing, they went right back to raiding. Tales about his final restin' place flow as freely as Voodoo beer at Mardi Gras, but folks here in Blue Bayou prefer the one where he was buried in an unmarked grave after bein' on the losing end of a duel with one of his lover's husbands. His ghost is real popular, showin' up all over the bayou, sometimes at the wheel of his warship."

"Have you ever seen him?"

"Now, I can't say that I have. But I think I did hear him one night in Holy Assumption's cemetery, back when I was in high school."

"What were you doing in a cemetery at night? Never mind," she said an instant later as the answer came to her.

"I don't expect you'd believe I was studying the stars?"

"Only if you happened to be studying them with a girl."

He rubbed his chin. "Studying was always more fun when you had someone to do it with. I have to admit, the sound of those chains rattlin' nearly scared the pants off me."

"I have the feeling they wouldn't have stayed on long anyway."

He put a hand against his chest. "You wound me, Detective *Chère*."

"I strongly doubt that's possible," she said lightly, enjoying sparring with him. As she'd sat in the SUV and drank in the absolute silence surrounding them, Regan had found herself beginning to relax. It had been an odd sensation; she had actually taken a few moments to recognize the feeling.

Unfortunately, they couldn't suspend time forever. After driving another ten minutes, Nate turned off the main road again and headed through a cane break.

"Where are we going, now?" she asked.

"Beau Soleil."

"Jack and Dani's plantation house?"

"Yeah. I've got some work to do there, and it'll let me check up on the kid."

"Construction work?"

"Sorta. Blue Bayou usually has the Mardi Gras party in the park, but this year Dani decided it'd be fun to host it at Beau Soleil, like back in the old days when her daddy pretty much ran the town. The party's free, of course, but for an extra five bucks you get a tour of the house and some autographed books Jack's donating. Between the home's history and my brother's fame, the tickets have been sellin' like popcorn shrimp. The money goes into the parish's community chest."

"That's nice."

"It's more of a necessity. The parish still hasn't fully recovered from the oil bust, when a lot of folks had to leave land that had been in their families for generations and move into the cities. Those who stayed behind have to work harder to keep things together."

"You really do fit here, don't you?"

He didn't have to think about that for a moment. "Yeah. I do."

"There are a lot of things I like about L.A. The beach, my friends, my work. The fact that I may be making a difference. But I've never actually felt as if it was home."

"Must be hard for roots to settle in concrete and asphalt."

Part of Nate had decided long ago that perhaps not reaching his youthful dream of playing third base for the Yankees hadn't been such a bad thing, after all. He'd have hated to get to New York and discover that the fantasy hadn't been anywhere near the reality. He wasn't, after all, a hustle-bustle kind of guy.

"Maybe you never felt like you belonged in California because Blue Bayou's your true home," he suggested.

"Even if I do turn out to be Regan Dale, I didn't live here long enough to have a connection. I certainly haven't recognized anything, or had any feeling of déjà vu."

"Maybe you're tryin' too hard. Sometimes the answer comes when you're not looking for it."

"Is that something else you've read in one of Jack's books?"

"Nope. That's mine. From when I'll be wrestling a set of blueprints all night, trying to make something work, and later, while I'm having morning beignets and coffee at Cal's and arguing sports scores, the solution will just come right out of the blue."

She'd experienced the same thing, when she'd been working a case that seemed a dead end, and suddenly the answer would occur to her.

"Stay around a while, and Blue Bayou will start to grow on you," he suggested. "Maybe I will, too." He skimmed a hand over her hair.

"Like that Spanish moss hanging from all these trees."

He chuckled, unwounded.

Nate turned onto another unmarked road, which took them down a narrow lane lined with oaks that appeared centuries old. When he turned a corner and the white Greek Revival antebellum plantation house suddenly appeared, gleaming like alabaster in the sunshine, she drew in a sharp breath.

"It really is Tara."

"Pretty damn close," he agreed. "There are those around here who swear Margaret Mitchell used Beau Soleil for the model in her book."

"That's what Dani said, but I'm not sure I took her seriously. Wow.

It's stunning. It's also hard to believe that anyone—any normal person, that is—actually lives here."

"Dani and Jack are as normal as you get, basically. Her family first got the deed to the place in the mid-1800s. Her ancestor, André Dupree, won it in a bouree game on a riverboat. Her daddy, the judge, nearly lost it to taxes a while back when he had himself some personal problems, but Jack came to the rescue and bailed him out."

"That was certainly a grand gesture."

"He said at the time he liked the idea of bein' a man of property, and wanted to stop this New Orleans mob family from turning it into a casino, but personally, I think he bought it for Dani's sake, since he still had strong feelings for her. When they got married, it landed back in the Dupree family again."

"Well, that's certainly convenient."

"Neither one of them married for the house. When you see 'em together, you'll realize they could be just as happy living in a one-bedroom trailer."

"This is certainly not a trailer." Her gaze swept over the white-pillared facade. "I'd feel as if I were living in some Civil War tourist attraction. Did you say you grew up here?"

"Not in the big house. We moved into one of the smaller ones after Dad was killed." He pointed toward a small white house on the outskirts of the compound. "After *maman* died, it sat vacant for a lot of years. Dani's turned it into a guest house. It's real cozy, even bein' haunted like it is."

"Of course. What would an old antebellum home be without a ghost?"

"There you go, bein' skeptical again," he said easily. "He's a Confederate officer who got lost here in the bayou after the Battle of New Orleans. Since the Union Army had taken over Beau Soleil, one of Dani's ancestors hid him in the little house. According to the story, she sent her own personal maid to take care of him during the day, then every night, she'd be real liberal when it came to pouring the port. After all the Yankees would pass out, she'd sneak out of the house and take the night shift trying to nurse that poor Confederate boy back to health, which was a pretty gutsy thing to do, since harboring the enemy was a hangin' offense. Even for a woman."

"That couldn't have been an easy decision." Easier, perhaps, if the southern soldier had resembled the man sitting beside her. She could see a woman taking foolish risks for Nate Callahan. "I take it she failed?"

"Yeah. The poor guy's leg had been blown off, and he ended up dying, probably of sepsis. When we were growing up we heard stories about the lady, who lived to a ripe old age, tellin' folks that he used to come visit her at night, but people figured she'd just gotten a little touched in the head."

"But you believe the stories," Regan guessed.

"I like the idea of them findin' happiness together. I've never seen him, though Jack claims to have heard music in the ballroom, where they're supposed to dance."

"I'll bet Finn never saw the ghost, either."

He rubbed his jaw. "Now, see, that's what you get for stereotyping. Finn's the only one of the three of us who actually has seen him."

"I don't believe that." Finn Callahan was the last person, other than herself, she'd expect to believe in such fantasy.

"My hand to God." He lifted his right hand. "Though I suppose, in the interest of full disclosure, I oughta add that he was feverish with flu at the time, and once he got better he tried to back away from his story about seeing the two of them waltzing."

"It seems as if it'd be hard to waltz with one leg."

"Oh, I don't know," Nate argued. "People can do a lot of things when they're in love that they might not do otherwise. Or so I hear."

She wasn't surprised he referred to hearsay. Nate Callahan did not strike her as a man who'd fall in love. Lust, sure. But the forever-after kind of love? No way. Another thing they had in common

The front door opened, and a huge yellow ball of fur came barreling toward them. "Brace yourself," Nate warned as she tensed. Every cop who'd ever worked the rough parts of town, and a lot who were assigned the cozier suburbs, had learned the hard way that it was best to be wary of strange dogs. "She's not dangerous, 'less you consider gettin' licked to death a problem."

What appeared to be a mix between a yellow lab and a school bus came skidding to a halt in front of them. Her tail was wagging like an out-of-control metronome. "Hey, Turnip." Nate took a Milk-Bone from his jeans pocket and tossed it to her. The treat disappeared in a single gulp.

The dog turned to Regan, who did usually carry dog treats with her, partly because she liked dogs and partly to make friends with the territorial ones. "Sorry, doggie. I'm all out." Wishing she'd saved the other half of the sandwich from lunch, she rubbed the huge head thrust toward her. "Her name's Turnip?"

"Yeah." He grinned as the enormous pink tongue slurped the back of Regan's hand. " 'Cause she just turned up one day." He glanced up as Josh appeared on the front *gallerie*. "She was a stray. Just like some kid I know."

"You just missed her," Josh announced as they approached.

"Missed who?" Nate asked.

"That social worker. Isn't that what you're doing out here?"

"Actually, I came to do some carpentry work. Didn't even know Judi was coming out today. So, I don't suppose your memory happened to make a comeback?"

"Nope."

Nate shook his head. "Terrible thing, amnesia. Who knows, you might turn out to be a spy, just like that Matt Damon character in *The Bourne Identity*. Sure would hate for Blue Bayou to be overrun with international assassins."

"Like that's goin' to happen." He smirked.

"Never know," Nate said mildly. "You have any talents you don't remember learning? Like maybe some martial arts or driving a getaway car?"

"No, but if I did have any, I wouldn't have time to notice, since the famous author's been making me sand woodwork ever since you dumped me here."

"Well, then, we'll just have to keep thinkin' on it and keep alert for any clues. Meanwhile, sanding is an important job. Can't stain without getting the wood all smooth first."

"It's boring."

"I suppose it can be if you do too much of it for too long. So, how'd you like to switch to something a little larger?"

"Like what?"

"I've got to build a stage for the band and could always use an extra hand."

"Shit, this is turning out to be like prison."

"The detective here might know better than me about jailhouse fashion, but I've driven past prisoners workin' the fields up at Angola, and can't recall ever seein' anyone wearing an OutKast shirt. They all seem to favor stripes. So, what do you say?"

"What's in it for me?"

"I'm not real sure. But it's always good to learn a new skill, just in case it turns out you're not a secret agent. Plus, it could just look good on your juvie report in case you've got some police problem that's slipped your mind."

Nate glanced over as another teenager appeared in the doorway. This one was a girl, tall and willowy, with pale hair down to her waist and thickly fringed green eyes. Looking at her, Regan had a very good idea what Dani had looked like at thirteen.

"Hi, Uncle Nate." When she went up on her toes and gave him a peck on the cheek, Regan noticed a flash of something that looked like old-fashioned envy in Josh's eyes. "Guess what? Ben and his mom moved into the guest house last night."

"Good for them, Holly.

"Ben's Misty's boy," Nate explained to Regan. He glanced over at Josh, who was staring at the girl as if she were a gilt angel atop a Christmas tree. "Guess you and Ben'd be about the same age."

The only answer was a shrug.

"They both play ball, too." Holly Callahan's revelation drew a sharp warning look from Josh, but she appeared unaware that she'd just given away something he hadn't wanted them to know.

"Is that so?" Nate said casually. "I played a bit in my day."

"I told him that you played third base for the Buccaneers and went to Tulane. Josh plays shortstop."

"Must have some fast moves."

"I get by," Josh mumbled. Regan was amused when he began rubbing the worn toe of his sneaker in the dirt like a shy six-year-old.

"We usually end up playing a softball game while the Mardi Gras supper's cooking. I don' suppose I could talk you into bein' on my team," Nate said.

Josh was tempted. Regan could see it. But once again trust didn't come easily, and she knew he was looking for the catch.

"You gonna be the cheerleader?" he asked Holly.

"No." Her eyes flashed in a way that suggested a bit of steel beneath that cotton-candy blond exterior. "I play first base. When I'm not pitching, that is." Her smile was sweet and utterly false. "If you don't want to be on Uncle Nate's team, we could always use a mascot. Maybe you could dress up like a pirate. Or a chicken."

The gauntlet had been thrown down.

Josh narrowed his eyes. His cheeks flushed with anger, embarrassment, or both. "I'll play," he told Nate with all the enthusiasm of a death-row inmate on the way to the electric chair.

"Great." Nate threw an arm around both Josh and Holly's shoulders in that easy way he had. Regan saw the boy stiffen again, but Nate ignored it. "Let's keep the fact that you played back home our little secret," he suggested. "No point in helping the other team with the point spread."

"You fixin' softball games again, *cher?*" a deep voice rumbled from inside the house.

Jack Callahan emerged from the shadows, looking even more rakish than he appeared on the back of his books. With his dark hair tied with a leather thong at the nape of his darkly tanned neck and that gold earring, Regan thought he could easily be a buccaneer in the flesh.

"Wouldn't be any challenge if there wasn't money on the line," Nate said.

"With that attitude, it's a good thing you didn' make the pros, since last I heard, gamblin' on games was illegal." Jack turned toward Regan. "Hi. You must be the lady I've been hearing about. Regan Hart."

"Yes." She smiled, truly appreciative he'd used the name she'd always known. "At least that's always been my name."

"We've got ourselves a little family experience with long-lost kids comin' to Blue Bayou to find their roots," he said, flashing a grin at Holly. The way she beamed back told Regan there was another story there. "Even if you find out some stuff about your past you didn't know, it doesn't negate all those other years."

He glanced up as a tall, lanky, dark-haired boy came around the corner from the direction of the guest house. "Looks like the lunch break's over," he said. "I'll drive you and Ben back to school," he told Holly. "If you're going to be here for a while," he said to Nate.

"Yeah. Josh's gonna help with the stage."

"Good idea." He bestowed another warm smile on Regan and walked toward the classic cherry red GTO parked beside the house. Regan watched Josh watching the trio get in the car.

"You just want to make sure I don't run away," Josh said.

"You thinkin' of running, *cher?*"

"None of your business if I am."

"Well, now, you know that's not 'xactly true, since I signed a paper taking responsibility for you."

"I can take care of myself."

"Maybe on a good day. But I get the impression there haven't been many of those lately."

Josh's only answer was to spit into the dirt. Then his gaze drifted to the departing car. He looked like a starving child staring into a bakery window.

"Holly sure is a pretty *fille*," Nate observed.

He didn't respond.

"Smart, too. Gets straight As."

Again no answer.

"She and Ben are really close friends, having as much in common as they do."

"Big freakin' deal."

*Bull's-eye*. "Having a friend is sure enough a big deal. And, not that you asked, because you're probably not real interested in pretty blond girls who smell like gardens, but they're not boyfriend and girlfriend.

"Ben's goin' with Kendra Longworth, whose *maman* teaches third grade at Holy Assumption school. Holly was seein' Trey Gaffney for a time when she first got to town last spring, but they broke up after Christmas, so she's pretty much available. Not that I'd be all that fond of the idea of my favorite niece spendin' Mardi Gras with an amnesiac secret agent," he said.

"I'm not any damn spy."

"That's good to hear. Seems she might jus' have somethin' in common with a ballplayer. Bein' how she's on the girls' varsity team."

"Big deal. It's still just a girls' team."

"You keep that in mind when she strikes you out with her slider," Nate said. "Now, why don't you go get my toolbox out of the back of my truck and we'll get to work."

"I'm not sure your brother would be real happy with you playing matchmaker with his daughter and a runaway juvenile delinquent," Regan said as they watched Josh make his way in unenthusiastic slow motion toward the SUV.

"I wasn't matchmaking; jus' suggesting a couple kids play ball together. After all, there's nothing more American than baseball. Besides, like I said, Jack spent some time in juvie himself. He's not one to pass judgment."

"And Dani?"

He laughed at that. "If there's anyone who knows both the appeal and the downside of bad boys, it's Dani. I figure she can give her little girl the appropriate motherly advice. Besides, it's not like they're going to be alone. The entire town'll be here chaperoning them. Meanwhile, it gives the kid a reason to stick around at least one more day, so maybe we can find out who he is. And what he's running away from."

Seeing how they all seemed to watch out for each other somehow made small-town life not quite so suffocating to Regan.

The outside of Beau Soleil was gorgeous. The inside quite literally took her breath away. She stared up at the mural that covered the wall of the two-story entry hall, rose to the plaster ceiling medallions, then swept up the wide curving stairway she recognized from more than one movie.

"It's stunning. Is it original to the house?" she asked.

"No, but it's real old. André Dupree had the mural painted in memory of the Grand Dérangement, when the English kicked his people out of eastern Canada, where they'd ended up after fleeing for religious freedom even before the Pilgrims landed at Plymouth Rock."

He was telling the story as if it'd happened yesterday. Which, in some people's minds, probably wasn't that far off.

"The Acadians, which is what we Cajuns were officially called, were pretty much left alone to do their own thing for the next hundred years, but after the French and Indian War, the British weren't really happy about these French-speaking people livin' halfway between New England and New France. They demanded the Acadians renounce their Catholic religion and pledge allegiance to England. Well, now, they were a pretty stubborn people—"

"Were?" She arched a brow.

He grinned. "Things don't change much down here in the bayou. Anyway, when they refused, they were rounded up and deported. Some were sold as indentured servants to the American colonies, others were sent back to France, some ended up in concentration camps in England, and a few managed to evade deportation by hiding out in Nova Scotia.

"Things were looking pretty bleak for them when the Spaniards entered into the situation. Since the Acadians were staunch enemies of the British by now and Catholic to boot, the Spanish decided they'd be dandy people to populate their Louisiana settlements. The

Acadians, happy for a chance to reunite their families—families have always been real important in the Cajun culture—liked the beauty of the land, not to mention all the bountiful fresh foods, which tasted pretty good after their years in exile. So they dug into the swamp like crawfish."

"Sounds like a happy ending." She wondered what it would be like to grow up in a place where everyone seemed to be related, if not by blood then by common experience.

"I guess it pretty much is. There's about a quarter million descendants of those original Acadians living around here, though the economy's taken a hit from time to time and caused a lot to move to the cities. But wherever a Cajun goes, he always takes a bit of this place away with him. And his heart always stays here in the swamp."

"Is that why you stay?"

"I don' know." He shrugged. "When I was a kid, I had big dreams and left for a while, but I ended up coming back and stayed for family reasons."

"Dani told me about your mother. I'm sorry."

Another shrug. "It was a bad time I wouldn't want to relive. But there's not much a person can do but keep on keeping on, is there?"

"No." Regan sighed, thinking about her own mother's death. Karen Hart's death, she amended.

"Gotta be hard, losing *two* mothers."

"It's not easy." She no longer doubted that Linda Dale had been her birth mother. "Which is why I'm going to find out the truth of what happened, and make certain that whoever was to blame for her death pays."

"Why if the autopsy report turns out to be true?"

"Those entries in her journal weren't written by a woman about to commit suicide."

"Something could have happened. Maybe your father didn't show up. Or maybe he did, and told her that he wasn't going to leave his wife."

"Eliminating maybes is what I do. I need to know about her life."

"So you'll have a better handle on your own."

Regan wasn't as surprised as she might have been even yesterday at his understanding so well how his news had packed an emotional punch.

"Yeah."

He led her to the huge ballroom, with high ceilings that had been painted a pale lemon yellow and lots of tall windows designed to bring the outdoor gardens inside. It took no imagination at all to envision beautiful women dressed in formal satin, hoop skirts skimming along the polished floor as they danced in the arms of their handsome, formally clad partners. The sconces circling the room were electric, but she could easily picture the warm glow of candlelight.

"It just keeps getting better and better," she said on a deep, appreciative sigh, surprised to discover a romantic lurking inside her.

"You should have seen it back around Thanksgiving. Since it's the biggest room in the house, we've been using it as an indoor workshop for winter and rainy days. You couldn't go more than a couple feet without bumping into a sawhorse. Plaster and sawdust were all over everything, and the floor was covered with paint cans. After Dani decided to hold the Mardi Gras festivities here, about every carpenter, painter, and electrician in the parish has been pulling overtime."

"Well, they definitely earned it." She ran her fingers over a chair rail that had been sanded as smooth as an infant's bottom. "I wouldn't have expected to find such craftsmanship in such a small, out-of-the-way place."

"Actually, towns like Blue Bayou probably hold the last remaining old-time craftsmen. Since we're not in a real dire need for more parking spaces, we tend to hang onto our old buildings. Which means that people who know how to do restoration will probably always be able to find work, even if the annual income probably isn't what they could make in the city."

"The city's more expensive to live in, though." She looked up at the glorious ceiling fresco someone had painstakingly restored. "And I'd imagine this sort of work is more artistically satisfying."

"I've always thought so." He smiled easily, then opened his arms. "*Viens ici*, sugar."

"I thought we'd agreed you were taking a moratorium on trying to seduce me."

"I am. We just finished the floor last week and I figured we should try it out. See if it's smooth enough for dancing, in case it rains tomorrow and we have to bring the party indoors."

Dammit, she was tempted. Too tempted. "There isn't any music."

"No problem." When she didn't go to him, he closed the small distance between them. "We'll make our own."

"Good try, but I think I'll pass."

He tucked her hair behind her ear. "Afraid?"

"Of you?" Her laugh was quick. "No, Callahan, I am definitely not afraid of you."

His fingers curved around the nape of her neck. As she watched his eyes turn from calm to stormy, she felt another one of those inner pulls that both intrigued her and ticked her off. "Maybe you should be." He slowly lowered his head. "Maybe we should both be."

It would be an easy thing to back away, but just as she was about to do so, he shifted gears and dropped a quick kiss on her forehead.

"We'd best go see what's holdin' up the kid, before he steals all my hand tools and heads off to the nearest pawnshop."

Feeling shaky, Regan followed him outside. "You're a strange man, Callahan. I can't get a handle on you."

"Me?" His laugh woke up Turnip, who'd been dozing happily in the shade of a weeping willow. Brown eyes turned limpid, as if hoping for another Milk-Bone. "I'm an open book."

"And I'm the queen of the Mardi Gras. That good-old-boy routine may work with your hometown belles, but I'm not buying it."

He grinned. "Maybe I'm one of a kind, me."

As irritated as she was with him for being so damn appealing, and herself for being attracted, Regan could not dispute that.

# 19

*While Nate and Josh worked on the stage,* Regan took her laptop into the book-lined library and began writing up her notes before the details began to slip her mind. She'd finished with the Boyce interview and her impression of Marybeth when she made the mistake of looking out the window, and her mind went as clear as glass.

The sun had burned off all the morning fog, warming the day. She watched Nate wipe his brow with the back of his hand. He said something to Josh, who shook his head in characteristically negative response. Nate shrugged, then pulled the black T-shirt over his head, revealing a rock-hard chest that looked gilded in the golden afternoon light. A light sheen of sweat glistened on tanned flesh, drawing her attention to the arrowing of gilt hair that disappeared below the waist of his faded jeans.

He took a long drink from a canteen; when some of the water ran down his body, he casually wiped it off his belly, then returned to work, the long muscles in his back flexing and releasing, again and again, as he pounded the nails with that large, wooden-handled hammer.

Determined to avoid the sensual pull of that hard mahogany body, Regan sighed and returned to work.

After turning down dinner invitations from both Dani and Nate—after so many sexual jolts to her system today, she didn't want to risk being alone with him—Regan spent the evening alone in her suite, trying to create a time-flow chart of Linda Dale's life in Louisiana.

Outside the French doors leading out onto a cast-iron-railed balcony, the citizens of Blue Bayou began to get an early start on Mardi Gras celebrations. Music poured from the bar downstairs, people were literally dancing in the street, and the sound of firecrackers being set off all over town—sounding like random gunshots—made her edgy. Edgy enough that she jumped when the phone rang.

She picked up the receiver.

"There's nothing for you here in Blue Bayou." The voice was muffled, and so low she couldn't tell the gender. "You should go back to California where you belong. Before you ruin good people's lives."

"Who is this?" Regan reached for the phone pad, but the dial tone revealed that her caller had hung up.

"Damn." She went over to the window and stared down onto the street and the park beyond. Looking for . . . what? Who?

The phone rang again. This time, when she grabbed it, she didn't immediately speak, hoping her caller would say something that would allow her to recognize his voice.

"*Chère?*"

"It's you." She let out a deep breath she'd been unaware of holding. "What do you want?"

"It'll wait." Nate's voice was rich and deep and concerned. It was also not the voice of whoever had called her earlier. "What's wrong?"

Her laugh held no humor. "How about what's right?" She dragged a hand through her hair. "Someone just called me and warned me off the Dale case."

"You were threatened?" The sharp tone could have been Finn's.

"Not in so many words."

"Give me thirty minutes to drop Josh with Jack, and I'll be there."

"That's not necessary." That was also so Finn, determined to take control of a situation. "Besides, the boy's not a puppy. You can't just keep dumping him on your family."

"That's what family's for. Not for dumping, but for taking care of one another."

She thought about pointing out that Josh no-last-name wasn't family, then didn't. "Well, I'm capable of taking care of myself. Besides, I'm exhausted, and I'm going to bed. I'll be asleep by the time you'd get here." Actually, she was so revved up from the call, she wasn't sure she'd get any sleep tonight.

"I'll call the state cops." The fact that he didn't suggest spending the night in bed with her showed how seriously he was taking the anonymous phone call.

"You will not. The only way anyone can get up here is with a coded key, which probably makes this suite the safest place in the state, other than the governor's mansion. I'll be fine. Besides, I have a gun, remember?"

"It's hard to forget when a woman threatens to shoot you." The edge to his tone was softening. "Maybe we should call Finn. Get a tap on the phone."

"You've been watching too much television. Even if Finn was still FBI, getting a judge to sign off on a wiretap isn't that easy."

"I wasn't thinking about going through a judge."

"That's illegal."

"And your point is? I don't want anything happening to you, *chère*."

"That's very sweet, but—"

"There's nothin' sweet about it. You and I have some unfinished business, detective. I want to make sure you stay alive long enough to experience my world-class, mind-blowing, bone-melting lovemaking."

She snorted a laugh, her tension finally loosening. "You really are shameless."

"You just wait and see," he promised on a low, sexy rumble. "Dwayne's on duty tonight, to make sure people don't start gettin' a jump on passing too good a time. I'll have him keep an eye on the inn. Meanwhile, have yourself a nice sleep, and I'll see you in the morning."

"What's happening in the morning?"

"There's a final meeting of the Mardi Gras dance committee at the courthouse at eleven-thirty. I thought you might want to attend."

"Why would I want to do that?" She'd planned to use the time to track down the doctor who'd signed Linda Dale's death certificate.

"Maybe 'cause the head of that committee is Toni Melancon?"

"Charles Melancon's wife?"

"Got it in one. She and Charles live with the old lady up at the Melancon plantation. I figured if anything just happened to go wrong with her Jag—"

"You're going to screw up her engine?"

"I wouldn't even know how to do such a thing, me."

"But you're not above having someone else do it," she guessed.

"I think I'm going to have to take the Fifth on that one, detective. But let's just say that maybe something *was* to go wrong with that tricky, hand-built British engine, it'd only be gentlemanly for me to offer her a ride home. Havin' been brought up to be a southern lady with manners, she's bound to feel obliged to invite me in for a refreshing beverage after that long drive, and bein' how you just happen to be with me—"

"She'd have to invite me in, too."

His low whistle caused her lips to curl and something in her stomach to tug. "Hot damn, you are a clever woman. I'll wonder if that L.A. mayor knows how lucky he is to have you fighting crime in his city."

"He hasn't mentioned it lately."

"Well, now, there's another reason for you to think about comin' to work here. As mayor, it'd be my civic duty to make sure you felt duly appreciated."

"Dammit, Callahan, I really am beginning to like you."

"That's the idea," he said easily. "So, here's the plan. I've got to enroll Josh in school tomorrow morning—"

"I don't envy you that."

"Strangely, he didn't seem down on the idea. If I didn't know better, I'd say he was actually looking forward to it."

"He's probably scamming you. Pretending to go along with the idea, then tomorrow morning you'll wake up to find him and all your silver gone."

"Lucky for me I've only got stainless steel. Though there was this woman, a while back, who tried to get me interested in flatware. Which would you pick out if you were gettin' married? Chrysanthemum or Buttercup?"

"It's a moot point, since I'm not getting married. And I don't even know what you're talking about. I assume these are sterling patterns and not flowers?"

"Yeah."

"Gee, Callahan, is this a proposal?"

There was nearly a full minute of dead air on the phone line. "I'm sorry, *chère*, if I gave you that impression." His earlier light tone was regretful. "I thought we were just talking, fooling around to lighten the situation up a bit."

"That's exactly what I thought. And it was going along pretty well until you decided to get domestic."

He chuckled at that. "There are those who'd tell you that my name doesn't belong in the same sentence as anything resembling domesticity."

"I've not a single doubt they're right. So why bring up that question in the first place?"

"It just sorta popped into my head. Suzanne—that was her name—always said you could tell the kind of person a woman was by her flatware pattern."

"You're kidding."

"That's pretty much what I said, thinking that she was just bein' a little precious, but no, she had this book that had it all laid out, sorta like horoscopes. Apparently Buttercup girls are always cheerful and upbeat, and Chrysanthemum girls are more flamboyant. She liked to think of herself as being cheerfully flamboyant."

"Apparently there was a limit to her cheerfulness. Since you're not married, one of you obviously broke the engagement."

"Oh, we weren't engaged. She sort of got it into her mind that we were engaged to be engaged, but I never made her any promises about a ring, or anything."

"Or brought up registering for silver."

"Not a word."

Regan had begun to relax again. She twined the telephone cord around her fingers. "So does this story have a happy ending, other than you escaping the institution of marriage? Should I feel sorry for poor Suzanne, living alone with felt-lined drawers full of flatware she never gets to use?"

"Oh, she got hitched to an old boyfriend she met at an Ole Miss reunion, so it worked out well for everyone. She finally decided on Chantilly, which hadn't even been in the early running." When she had no response to that, he added, "I went and looked the book up in Dani's library after I heard. Seems Chantilly girls can be a bit prissy. And though they may seem real sweet, they were often fast in high school. Not that I'm sayin' that about Suzanne."

"Of course not. Being a gentleman and all." She was starting to get a handle on how this southern thing worked. A man might roll in the hay with every female in town, but reputations stayed more or less intact, since a southern gentleman didn't roll and tell. "I realize the only reason you're telling me about all this is to calm me down so I can sleep. But since you brought it up, want to know what kind of girl I am?"

"I already know."

"Oh?"

"You're a mismatched stainless-steel person, just like me, when you're not using the plastic fork and knife from the takeout package."

Nailed that one, she admitted.

"But if you did ever decide to go all out, you'd be an Acorn."

"I'm almost afraid to ask why. Is Acorn for belles who swear and pack heat?"

"No, but you're close. Brides who choose Acorn have a rebellious streak. They've been known to drink beer straight from the bottle, venture north of the Mason-Dixon line to college, and some of them even marry Yankees."

"Horrors." Regan smiled. "They sound downright dangerous."

"That's part of their appeal. My *maman* had Acorn. And the only other person I've ever met who's as out-and-out spunky as her is you, Detective *Chère*, which is how I know you'd be an Acorn."

"Well." What do you say when a man just compares you to his mother, whom he obviously adored, during a conversation where he's reminding you that he's not interested in any serious relationship? "Thank you."

"*C'est rien*. Now it's your turn."

"My turn?"

"To pay me a compliment."

Fair was fair. "All right. You may be frustrating and annoying at times, but you're also very sweet."

"Sweet?" She heard the wince in his voice. "And here I was hoping for something more along the lines of the sexiest man you've ever met, who can turn you into a puddle of hot need with just a single dark and dangerous look."

"Your brother Jack got dark and dangerous. You got cute and sweet."

"Hell. Well, we're jus' going to have to work on that." He paused. "If I asked you to do something for me, would you?"

"I suppose that would depend on what it is."

"Tell me what you're wearing. Right now."

"Is this going to be one of those dirty phone calls, Callahan?"

"One can hope. What are you wearing, Regan?"

"Why?"

"Because I'd really like to be there, but since I can't, I'm trying to picture you."

"Well, you're going to be disappointed if you're looking for sexy, because I'm wearing a navy blue T-shirt that says 'Property of the LAPD Athletic Department.' " She looked down at the oversize cotton shirt that covered her from shoulders to thighs. "I suppose you would have preferred me to lie and say I was barely wearing some skimpy lace number from Victoria's Secret."

"Lace is nice. Skimpy's even better, most of the time. Sometimes, though, contrast can be real intriguing. How long is it? To your knees?"

"Not that long. And you're just going to have to use your imagination from there, because I'm not having phone sex with you."

"Too bad, because if you want to moan lots of sweet nothings in my ear, I sure wouldn't object. But since I'm enjoying just talking with you, how about I tell you a little Cajun bedtime story?"

"Could I stop you?"

"Sure. Anytime you want, you can just hang up."

"I will."

"*Bien*. Now, there was this Cajun who called himself Antoine Robicheaux, and he had himself this camp, which you'd call a cabin, way back in the bayou, miles from civilization. He was a handsome devil, he. Tall, real strong from swinging a hammer all day—"

"He was in construction?"

"General contractor." A vision of Nate as he'd looked this afternoon—shirtless, tool belt slung low on his hips like a gunfighter—flashed through her mind, bringing with it a hot, reckless, sexual need.

"Same as you."

"Now that you mention it, I guess we both do have that in common."

"Life's full of coincidences," Regan said dryly.

"Isn't that the truth? Well now, one night he was coming back from checkin' his traps when he came across this *jolie blon*. She was on her knees on the bank of the bayou, tears flowing down her cheeks, mingling with the falling rain, leaves and moss tangled in her hair. And for a moment, seeing her in the moonlight, he thought he might have stumbled across a wood nymph.

"But then he looked a little closer, he, and saw she was really just a pretty *fille* in trouble. He didn't recognize her, and she didn't seem able to speak, which made it harder for him to figure out how he was going to find out where she belonged. But having been raised up by his *maman* to be a gentleman, he decided she could spend the night at his place, then he'd decide what to do with her in the morning."

"And they say chivalry is dead."

"Like I said, he was a gentleman. Though he did have a bit of misgiving, since he'd heard tales of a witch living out in the swamp. But since she sure didn't look like your stereotypical wicked witch, like the one he'd seen when he was a kid in *The Wizard of Oz*, he helped her into his pirogue and took her back to his camp.

"Dark clouds drifted over the moon. As the boat wound through the darkness, lit only by the lantern at the bow, Antoine felt as if they were being watched. Occasionally, he'd see gleaming points of yellow amid the moss-draped trees, but he reminded himself that these waters were filled with animals and he was being overfanciful. Bein' with a beautiful woman tended to do that to him, 'specially after he'd been working away from civilization for a while.

"Even though the night was warm, the earlier rain had drenched the woman, and her cotton dress was still clinging to her like a second skin when he got her into the little camp. Now, he was a big man, and knew that his clothes would swim on her, but he gave her one of his shirts, pointed her to the bathroom, and went to put on some coffee, since she still seemed a bit in shock.

"After some time, when she still hadn't come out, he began to worry, so he knocked on the door. Since she hadn't latched it, there she stood, still standing there in that same wet dress, staring out the window into the darkness. She was trembling badly, and he was afraid she might be chilled from the rain."

Regan could see where he was going with this. Still, she plumped up the goosedown pillows, leaned back, and prepared to enjoy the journey. "So, Antoine, being a gentleman, decided to help her out of her wet clothes."

"That's 'xactly what he did. But he could tell she was a real nice girl, and shy, and he didn't want to give her the wrong idea about his intentions—"

"Which were only honorable."

"*Mais* yeah. He decided the best thing to do, so he wouldn't scare her, would be to take things real slow."

"Sort of like this story."

"Want me to fast-forward to the good parts?"

"No. It's your story; go ahead and tell it your own way."

"Like I said, she was a real nice girl, and even though it was a hot and steamy evening, she'd fastened that dress all the way up to her pretty throat. So, he began talking to her, real quietly, like you might if you wanted to get close to a skittish fawn. When he flicked the first button open, his knuckles brushed against that little hollow where her pulse took a jump. But not nearly as big a jump as his own."

His voice was deep and vibrantly masculine, without any overt sexuality. But that didn't stop her from lifting her own hand to the base of her throat, where it seemed her own blood had begun to beat a little faster. It had gotten warm in the room, so she threw off the comforter. Then the sheet.

"He moved down, button by button," Nate continued, "opening up that flowered cotton as if he was unwrapping a precious present."

Regan's fingers unconsciously stroked her warming flesh along a similar path.

"Her bra was a teensy bit of lace that looked real pretty against the curve of her breasts, which were rosy pink, like the inside of a summer rose, because she was blushing a little bit, due to the fact, he figured, that she wasn't used to getting undressed in front of a total stranger."

"Even if he was a gentleman." Regan could hardly recognize her voice. It was deep, throaty, undeniably aroused.

"Even if," he agreed, his own voice sounding more rough itself, as if her reaction might be turning him on.

"Of course the bra had to go, too, but since he knew his way around women's underwear, he didn't have any trouble unfastening the front hook. '*Mon Dieu,*' he breathed as her lovely breasts spilled into his hands, 'you are the most beautiful woman I've ever seen.' He wasn't lying and found the way she blushed even deeper unbearably appealing. And erotic.

"He asked if he could kiss her breasts. Her white teeth worried her full bottom lip as she considered the request, but he could see the answer in her eyes before she managed a shy little nod. Her skin was the color of pink marble, and just as smooth. But a lot softer. And warmer. As he took one of those little ruby nipples into his mouth and drank in the warm womanly scent of her, Antoine knew that one taste would never be enough."

Regan slid a hand down the front of the T-shirt and began touching herself as Antoine was caressing the mystery woman: shoulders, chest, then breasts. She rolled a taut nipple between her thumb and her index finger and felt a corresponding tug between her legs. The soft moan escaped from between her parted lips before she could stop it.

"Tell me what you're thinking. Right now," he demanded softly.

"About how Antoine's hands felt on her." Regan licked her lips, which had gone unbearably dry. *And how your hands would feel on me*. She braced the receiver against one shoulder. Both of her hands moved beneath the shirt, caressing, squeezing, stroking breasts sensitized by that deep seductive voice and her own erotic imagination. "What are *you* thinking?"

His answering laugh was quick and rough. "That I'm going to have to get bigger briefs."

"Maybe you should take them off." Had she really said that?

"I will, if you will."

She had never been a woman to play sexual games. In bed, as in all other parts of her life, she was straightforward and to the point. But there was something about being alone in the dark, with just that deep voice touching her all over, that allowed her to imagine she was the naked wood nymph in his story. "I'm already one step ahead of you."

There was a pause. Then a groan. "Wait just a sec, sugar." A longer pause, during which time her hands stilled, waiting for him to make the next move. And then he was back. "I wanted to make sure the door was locked."

"You're not used to talking about sex on the phone with a teenager in the house."

"No. But if Josh wasn't here, I wouldn't be talking to you on the phone right now. I'd be in the truck on my way over there, so we could be doing this in person. In the flesh, so to speak."

His flesh against hers was an arousing prospect. It also wasn't going to happen tonight. "You were telling me about Antoine."

"Yeah, wouldn't want to leave the poor guy hanging out there," he said. "Well, as luscious as her breasts were, Antoine reminded himself that the goal was to get her undressed so he could get her into a hot shower. So he forced his mind back to the task and finished unbuttoning the dress, then let it drop to the floor. She was wearing little bikini panties that matched the bra, and he hooked his thumbs in the elastic and pulled them down. Over the swell of her hips, past the lush blond curls between her thighs, down each long, tanned leg to her ankles.

"She stepped out of them without being asked. Crouched on the floor, looking up at her, he saw tiny beads of moisture glistening like dewdrops in those soft blond curls, and it took all the restraint Antoine possessed not to lick them off."

Moisture was flowing from her; Regan lifted the T-shirt above her waist and let her legs fall open a little bit more, to allow the breeze from the air conditioning to cool her heated flesh.

"Antoine, he stood up, put his hands on her shoulders, turned her around, and walked her into the little tin shower, which barely had room for one person, and turned on the water. Then he stripped off his own clothes.

"Her eyes widened a little at the amazing size of his erection, whether from fear or anticipation, Antoine could not tell. Wanting to reassure her that he'd never do anythin' to hurt her, he touched his mouth against hers in their very first kiss and felt her sigh against his lips.

"He drew her into the shower and lathered the soap between his palms, and as the water pelted down on them and the stall filled with fragrant steam, he smoothed the lather all over her, his slippery hands sliding over her body from her shoulders to her feet, and everywhere in between. When he began washing his way down one smooth firm thigh and up the other, she closed her eyes and leaned back against the wall, her fingers linked together.

"She was shivering, but not from the cold; it was as hot as a sauna in the shower. But not as hot as the thoughts scorching their way through his brain. Seems he wasn't the only one aroused by their situation. '*S'il vous plaît,*' she said on a soft little moan, which is French for please. So she *could* talk, Antoine thought. 'I want . . . I need . . . Touch me . . . There.'

"Antoine smiled. *Mais* yeah, he smiled at this request, since it was just what he'd been wanting to do himself, but had been afraid of pushing her."

"Being a gentleman and all," Regan said as her own wandering hands fluttered down her rib cage and over her bare stomach. Then lower still.

" 'Xactly. So he carefully, with his softest touch, parted those slick folds. Now, you have to understand that Antoine considered himself a bit of a connoisseur of women, and there was nothing he found more beautiful than the female sex. It brought to mind a flower, with soft pink petals on the outside, and a deep rosy color inside. The little nub hidden in there was as hard and gleaming as a perfect pink pearl. She jumped a little when he brushed his thumb over it."

Regan did the same, imagining Nate's clever, callused fingertip.

"He stroked it again, then again, changing the pressure, sometimes hard, sometimes light, fast, then slow. Her back was against the stall, but her hips were thrust out at him, offering, begging for more."

The muscles in her legs contracted. Regan was breathing quickly now, and no longer cared if he could hear her. The world narrowed to his voice, the story of Antoine and his mystery woman, her tingling, burning clitoris.

"He knelt at her feet like a man worshiping a goddess, which to him, she was, and put his mouth on her. She climaxed instantly, cried out, and tried to jerk away, but the stall was so small there wasn' any room to move. And besides, his hands were on the backs of her legs, and he wasn't quite finished with her yet.

"He feasted on her like she was the sweetest, ripest fruit, loving the way he could make her come again and again, and when he felt her body going limp, he stood up again and lifted her onto him."

Oh, God! Regan bit her lip to keep from crying out herself as the orgasm ripped through her.

"Well, when Antoine felt her hot body tighten around him, it was like nothin' he'd ever felt before, like Mardi Gras fireworks goin' off inside him. Her lips pressed against his throat while the water streamed over them, and that's when he found out he'd been right about her not bein' a witch.

"His blood turned hot and thick as her sharp white teeth sank into him, and his own explosion, as he came into her, was like nothing he'd ever felt before. As they sank to the floor, arms and legs entwined, Antoine found himself looking forward to the idea of spending eternity with this sexy vampire."

"I should have seen that one coming," Regan managed to say. "Seeing how we're not that far from Anne Rice country."

She also belatedly realized that he'd never broken stride in the narration. "Did you . . . ?" Regan, who never blushed, felt the blood flow into her face, making her doubly glad he couldn't see her right now. "Never mind."

"The story was for you, *chère*," he said simply, gently. "A bedtime tale to help you get to sleep."

Amazingly, it had worked, she realized. The sexual release had left her more relaxed than she'd been in ages. Certainly since Nate Callahan had arrived in Los Angeles and turned her life upside down.

"It seems I keep having to thank you."

His deep chuckle rumbled in her ear. "Believe me, sugar, it was my pleasure. Sweet dreams."

She hung up the phone, pulled the crisp sheet back over her body, and instantly fell into a deep, nightmare-free sleep.

"I don't see why we're bothering to do this," Josh grumbled the next morning as they drove from Nate's West Indies–style home into town.

"It's not that complicated. You're a kid. The state of Louisiana, in one of its rare acts of wisdom, decreed kids need to go to school. Ergo, you're going to school."

"My name isn't Ergo. Besides, what's the point of enrolling in school if I'm just going to be gone in a few days?"

"You still planning on leaving?"

"I may be."

"Well, I'd just as soon you didn't go taking off without any word."

"Yeah, your life dream has always been to have a delinquent kid around to screw up your sex life."

"Did I say you're screwing up anything?"

"No." He'd give him that. "But you probably would have been with that cop last night if you hadn't had to stay home and play prison guard to me."

"Should I be offended that you called my home, which I built with my own two hands, a prison?" Nate asked mildly. "And yeah, I might have driven over to the inn to be with Regan last night. But not for the reason you think."

"You saying you don't want to fuck her?"

"There are a great many things I'd love to do with Detective Delectable. But when you get older and have some experience, you'll discover that there's a huge difference between fucking someone and making love."

"So you're in love with her?"

"I'm not saying that. I'm jus' stating that there's more to being with a woman than what fits where. That's just plumbing. What two people do together should be more special than that."

"Sex is sex," Josh said stubbornly. Hell, he'd probably listened to more sex in his life than this guy, as cool as he seemed to be, had ever experienced.

"We'll have to continue this discussion later, when we have more time," Nate said as they pulled up in front of a redbrick building.

Students were headed up the wide front steps in groups, talking, laughing, seeming to have a high old time. Josh felt the familiar new-school clench in his gut and, although he'd chain cement around his ankles and throw himself in the bayou before admitting it, he was glad he'd allowed himself to be convinced to take off his Dead Rap Stars T-shirt and change into a plain old black one Nate had pulled from his own closet. Apparently the guy wasn't lying when he said there was a no-message-shirts dress code.

Not that he cared about fitting in. Since he wasn't going to be staying in Blue Bayou all that long.

# 20

*Things were definitely going downhill.* Not only hadn't she been able to find a California marriage license for Karen Dale, or a divorce decree for a Karen Hart, the death certificate was proving yet another dead end. Regan had been working her way through neighboring state licensing files and had found several doctors with the same name, but calls placed to their offices turned up a big fat zero.

The stocks were obviously the way to go. Surely either the mother or the son knew something. Twenty-five thousand dollars might not be a lot of money to a family who owned an oil company. But it wasn't chicken feed, either.

She *was* going to solve this crime. Linda Dale deserved to have her murder solved and the perpetrator put behind bars. Then Regan would donate the stocks to a local charity, return to Los Angeles, and get on with her life.

She had just gone off-line when the phone rang. She paused for a moment, wondering if it was Nate, calling to tell her he was on his way. Or perhaps it was last night's first caller, wanting to make certain she'd gotten the message. The lady or the tiger. Wishing hotel phones had caller ID, Regan picked up the receiver.

"Hey, partner," Van said, "I was thinking about you last night. Rhasheed and I rented *The Big Easy*, and I was wondering if you'd met up with one of those sexy Cajun men."

"There are a lot of Cajun men down here. Some, I suppose, are sexy."

"I hope you're passing yourself a helluva good time."

"Of course." Regan forced a smile she hoped would be echoed in her voice. She told Van about Cajun Cal and Beau Soleil, and meeting Jack Callahan, whose books Van enjoyed as well. She did not mention Nate or her real reason for being in Blue Bayou.

"I'd better run," Van said after about twenty minutes. "My sister's throwing me this baby shower. Can you picture me sitting in a room decorated with paper storks, nibbling on cookies with blue frosting and crustless sandwiches?"

"Just keep focused on all the loot you're going to get." Regan's contribution, which she'd sent to Van's sister before leaving L.A., was a music-box mobile from the registry list at Babies R Us.

"Easy for you to say," Van grumbled. "You're not the one playing name-the-baby games."

"Seems a small price to pay for a feng shui miracle."

Van laughed. "I'll keep that in mind when I'm huffing and puffing through delivery."

"That's what you get for being one with nature. If I ever find myself about to give birth, I'm calling for heavy drugs at the first contraction."

They joked a bit longer, sharing cop stories about babies born in patrol cars, on the beach, in jail. After Van had hung up, as happy as she was for her partner, Regan felt a little tug of regret at how much she was going to miss their daily bantering. The problem with life, she thought as she went downstairs to wait for Nate, was that it just kept moving on, taking you right along with it.

Regan was vastly grateful when Nate didn't mention last night's phone conversation, other than to ask if she'd received any other threats. In the bright light of morning, she was uncomfortable with her behavior. She would have been even more embarrassed if he'd had any idea of the dream she had of him just before dawn. A dream that had involved a steamy shower and a bar of soap.

Blue Bayou might not make much of a mark on the map, but Regan certainly couldn't fault its architecture. The mayor's office was housed in a majestic Italianate building with wide stone steps, gracefully arched windows, and lacy pilasters. A red, white, and blue Acadian flag hung on a towering brass pole below the U.S. and Louisiana flags. There was a life-size statue of a soldier astride a prancing horse. The carving at the base of the bronze statue identified the soldier as Captain Jackson Callahan.

"Is he an ancestor?" she asked.

"A bunch of greats grandfather."

"I thought your father moved here from Chicago."

"He did. But his grandfather was originally from the area. Great-grandpère Callahan moved north looking for work during the Depression, found it, and stayed. When *Maman* met Dad at a fraternity party, they started talking and it turned into one of those 'small world' kind of things. Dad always said that they were destined to find each other, and though he didn't buy into a lot of the voodoo stuff that coexists with Catholicism down here, he also believed that he and *Maman* had shared previous lives and kept finding each other over and over again."

"That's sweet."

"I always kind of thought so. Even though I'm not so sure I buy into the concept, myself."

"Now, why doesn't that surprise me?"

He laughed at that, then sobered a bit. "I think, along with wanting a safer place to raise his kids and knowing *Maman* was homesick, he wanted to get back to his roots.

"Old Captain Jack was one of our local success stories. He'd been orphaned on the boat coming to America from Ireland, and had pretty much grown up wild and barefoot here in the swamp. When they started recruiting for people to fight against the Yankees in the War between the States, he figured this might be his chance to make something of himself. Being Irish, he could identify with the little guy fighting against an oppressive government, so he signed up with the Irish Sixth Volunteer Infantry, which got the nickname the Confederate Tigers."

"Because they fought so hard?"

"Like tigers," he agreed. "Jack, he entered the army as a private and ended up fighting in every eastern-front battle, beginning with the Shenandoah Valley campaign in 1862 under Stonewall Jackson. Since those battlegrounds were pretty much killing fields, the men who managed to survive to fight another day won a lot of battlefield promotions. When Jackson returned home as a captain, folks around here considered it pretty much of a miracle. A lot of people still believe that touching his horse's nose brings good luck."

Regan was not as surprised as she might have been only days ago at the way he spoke about hundred-year-old events as if they'd just happened yesterday. And even though it made her feel a little as if she'd just landed in Brigadoon, a very strong part of her admired his connection with the past.

* * *

Antoinette Melancon had strawberry blond hair, a pink Chanel suit, very good pearls, and an attitude.

"I understand the concept of Mardi Gras," she said for the umpteenth time. "After all, my husband is not only a member of the Knights of Columbus but a deacon at Holy Assumption, and the women in my family have belonged to the Altar Guild for decades. I understand that it's an opportunity to party before we begin preparing during Lent for Easter. I merely do not understand why Blue Bayou can't set the standard as a community who celebrates with grace and style."

"It's Fat Tuesday," Emile Mercier, owner of the Acadian Butcher Shop, pointed out. "Not Lean Tuesday. People are supposed to have a good time."

"It's unseemly." Her pink lips, color-matched to her suit, turned down in a disapproving frown. Regan suspected the Puritans had probably passed a better time at their Sabbath meetings than Charles Melancon's wife did on Fat Tuesday. "However, I suppose I should not expect anything different from a man who makes a very good living supplying sausage for the cookout."

He folded massive arms across his chest and glared at her from beneath beetled gray brows. "Maybe in my next life I can come back as an oil king," he shot back. "And make a fortune dumping poison into the bayous and rivers."

She lifted a chin Regan suspected had been sculpted a bit. "I take offense at that remark."

"Well, some of us take offense at ending up with bags of three-legged, three-eyed bullfrogs when we go out gigging," a bearded man in the back of the room growled.

"Melancon does not pollute."

"Tell that to the EPA," a woman who Regan remembered was an assistant DA for the parish shot back.

"That complaint is in error. My husband is working with the government to correct the misunderstanding."

"Meaning he's lining some congressman's pockets," Cal, who'd winked a welcome to Regan when she'd first arrived, suggested.

Nate was leaning against a wall map of the parish, legs crossed at the ankles, watching the meeting with patient resignation. Now he pushed away from the wall and entered into the fray.

"We're here to discuss the band situation," he reminded everyone in the same easygoing tone he might use to order a po' boy from Cal's. "Now, the Dixie Darlings pulling out at the last minute put us in a bit of a bind, but I played ball with Steve Broussard at Tulane, and since I read he and his group have given up touring for six months to work on their new CD, I thought, What the hell, tracked him down in Houma, and invited him to come play for us."

"Like Broussard and his Swamp Dogs are going to play for us," the attorney scoffed. "Their last CD went platinum after they did the sound track for that movie."

"Said he'd be glad to," Nate said calmly. "And the best part is that the band agreed to donate their fee to the boys' and girls' club."

"Awright," Cal said as nearly everyone in the room broke out in spontaneous applause. Even the ADA looked impressed. Toni Melancon did not, but Regan had already gotten the feeling there was little about this parish that she would find to her liking.

That the woman was a snob was obvious. That she was probably as cold-blooded as those hibernating alligators was also apparent. All of which had Regan wondering, yet again, if her husband might have been sleeping with Linda Dale. Although she certainly didn't condone adultery, she could imagine why a man married to such a woman might stray. And now that she'd gotten an opportunity to see Toni Melancon in action, it didn't take a huge mental leap to imagine her killing a rival. Not for love; Regan suspected she didn't have a romantic or passionate bone in her body. But money was always a prime motive. Granted, the name was still all wrong, but there was still an outside chance that the murder didn't have anything to do with the mysterious J.

Which didn't, she mused, explain why, if Linda's lover hadn't killed her, he seemingly hadn't said a word to anyone when she'd died.

The meeting drew to an end. Toni Melancon was the first to leave, Nate and Regan the last. As they walked from the steps to the sidewalk, Nate reached out and touched the horse's nose.

"Are we going to need luck?" Regan asked.

"A little luck never hurt, sugar."

Of course, sometimes luck just needed a little help.

Toni Melancon was standing beside her racing-green Jaguar, the toe of her Bruno Magli pump tapping furiously on the sidewalk.

"Got a problem?" Nate asked.

"This stupid car won't run." She looked as if she was considering kicking the tire. "I told Gerald we should buy German. But no, he wanted this piece of British trash."

"It's a classic," Nate said. "When it came out back in '68, it was called the most beautiful car in the world."

"It's classic trash." So much for grace and style. Her petulant behavior reminded Regan of Josh, who probably had an excuse for his bad attitude.

"Why don't I take a look at the engine, see if I can spot anything?"

"All right." She sighed heavily, seeming more put out than grateful for his assistance.

Regan watched as he opened the hood and began fiddling with wires as if he knew what he was doing.

"Well, the good news is that it doesn't look like it's going to be a real big problem to fix."

"What's the bad news?"

"I'm not going to be able to get it running."

"Why not?" she said, seeming to take it personally.

"See this red-and-white wire?"

She sighed again and humored him by glancing in the direction of the engine, but she clearly wasn't willing to risk dirtying her suit by getting too close. "What about it?"

"It leads to the solenoid on the starter motor. It's loose, which we could fix, but if you look here"—he pointed to a spot about three inches from the dangling end of the wire—"it's also stripped. It'll have to be replaced."

"I knew we should have bought that BMW," she huffed.

Regan wondered who he'd gotten to take a pocketknife to that wire.

"No problem. I'll just call Earl on my cell phone, have him pick it up and tow it over to Dix Automotive, and I'll drive you out to the house."

His quick, boyish grin appeared to charm even this gorgon. "I suppose that's the best solution."

"It'll be my pleasure," he assured her. "You don't mind if Ms. Hart comes along, do you? I've been showin' her around the parish."

The older woman looked at Regan as if noticing her for the first time. "You must be the new sheriff I've been hearing about."

"People are mistaken. I'm just visiting."

"Well, that's too bad, because we could certainly use one. I still don't know what you were thinking of, hiring Dwayne," she complained to Nate.

"He's a little green. But he's catching on real fast."

"But he's—" Her lips curved downward in what appeared to be her usual expression. "You know."

"A college graduate?" Nate asked blandly.

"Don't be cute with me, Nathaniel Callahan. You know very well what I mean."

"I believe I do, ma'am, and the way I saw it, not only is Dwayne qualified, having earned a degree in criminal justice, he's overly so. We were lucky he even considered coming to work for the force. Along with his qualifications, he's local, so he's got a real proprietary feeling about the parish, a bonus in someone hired to keep the peace. Then there's the little fact that we haven't had an African-American officer since Dad hired Dwayne's uncle back in the seventies. It seemed about time. Past time."

"I realize Jake Callahan has been raised to hero status in Blue Bayou, and I'm truly sorry about the tragic way he died, but as I told him back then, change for change's sake is not always a good thing. Since the subject's come up, I feel the need to say that it's important that Blue Bayou maintain the traditions that have kept it above the decline of so much of the rest of our state."

"Maybe some traditions deserve to die," he said evenly as he opened the passenger door of his SUV, which was parked behind the disabled sedan. "Like slavery. Or were you referring to lynchings?"

"That's precisely what your father said. I made allowances, since he was, after all, a Yankee. But I would have hoped your mother would have taught you more about your heritage."

"Oh, *Maman* sure enough did do that."

Seeming not to notice the way his jaw had gone rigid and the steely cast to his eyes, Toni Melancon allowed him to help her up with a hand to the elbow, and settled into the seat like Queen Elizabeth settling into her gilt coach for a ride from Buckingham Palace to Westminster. It had to be obvious to anyone less egocentric than Gerald Melancon's wife that she'd pushed his patience and charm to the limits.

Regan knew Nate had only held his tongue for her sake, and when his eyes caught hers in the rearview mirror, she mouthed a silent thank-you.

# 21

*The private driveway* to the Melancon house was at least three miles long, flanked by an oak alley created to build anticipation in visitors approaching the plantation. Small one-room buildings Regan suspected were former slave cabins were scattered across abandoned fields, crumbling relics of another time. Untidy formal gardens that at one time must have been magnificent were now in need of a guiding hand.

The house was large as Beau Soleil, but lacked its grace. Unlike the soaring white pillars at Jack and Dani's house, four massive Doric columns squatted thickly on the thick slabs of granite making up the four front steps. Green mold tinged red brick that had faded to a dull rose over the centuries. Although Regan had never been fanciful, St. Elmo's Plantation—named, Nate told her, for the phosphorous green swamp gas that glowed at night—and its surroundings seemed to give off a desolate aura, as if it was inhabited by the Addams family's southern cousins.

Nate pulled up beneath the crumbling portico. "Well, thank you, Nate," Toni said, as if realizing such manners were required, if not honestly felt.

"Anytime," he said as he helped her down from the high seat.

There was a lengthy pause.

"Well, good day," she said. So much for inviting them in for a cool drink.

"You know," he said, "it's been a long time since I've visited with Miz Bethany. I think I'll just pop in and say *bonjour*. Wouldn't want her to hear the SUV and fret that I've come all this way out here without payin' my respects."

Regan watched as his trademark slow, easy smile appeared to do its magic.

"All right." Toni breathed out another of those deep sighs suggesting she found the world so very tiresome. "But don't expect her to recognize you. The old woman's gone absolutely batty."

"Now, that's a real shame," he said as they walked up to the huge front door, carved with what Regan suspected was the Melancon family crest, surrounded by an unwelcoming quartet of gargoyle faces. "Maybe we'll get lucky, and she'll be having a good day."

They were met in the great hall by a nearly six-foot-tall woman who could have been anywhere from sixty to a hundred. Her black dress was relieved only by a heavy chain loaded down with various charms. "Mrs. Melancon is not receiving visitors," she informed them in a deep voice that rumbled like thunder.

"Now, Miz Caledonia, you know I'm not just any ole visitor, me," Nate said, turning up the wattage on his natural charm. "I come bearing gifts." He held out two small gilt boxes he'd retrieved from the glove compartment of the SUV. "Brought you and Miss Bethany some of those candies you like so well from Pauline's Pralines."

She shook her head and clucked her tongue but took the boxes. "You shameless, Nate Callahan."

"Now, you know, Miz Caledonia," he said with a quick wink Regan's way, "you're not the first person to tell me that."

" 'Xpect not," she huffed, then caved. "You can only stay jus' a minute. It's time for Miz Bethany's nap."

"I'll be in and out in a flash," he promised, making an X across the front of his denim shirt.

She shook her head again, then turned and began walking away.

"You probably never read *Rebecca,* did you?" Regan murmured as they walked down a long hallway lined with busts of what she suspected were former Melancons.

"No. But that *fille* I told you about, the Chantilly flatware one, liked to watch the Romance Channel, so I saw the movie."

"Caledonia makes Mrs. Danvers look like Mary Poppins."

"She's a tough old bird," he allowed. "But she's devoted to Mrs. Melancon. Apparently she was her nurse, then just sort of graduated through the household ranks over the years, until she pretty much runs the place."

"Toni didn't appear to like her overly much." The woman had walked past the housekeeper without so much as a word.

"It's my guess she's afraid of her, since rumor has it that when she first married Charles, she wanted to move the old lady out of the house so she could be queen of the manor. Caledonia threatened her with a voodoo curse, and that was pretty much the end of that discussion."

They were led into a parlor filled with plants. Framed photographs of yet more Melancon ancestors frowned down from water-stained, red-silk-covered walls. The atmosphere in the room was so steamy Regan was moderately surprised that the oriental carpet hadn't sprouted mushrooms. The scent of all those flowers hit the minute she entered the room, giving her an instant headache.

Almost hidden by a towering philodendron, an elderly woman, as fragile appearing as a small bird, was swallowed up by a wheelchair. Despite the sweltering heat, she was draped in a trio of colorful shawls.

"*Bonjour*, Miz Bethany," Nate greeted her. "Aren't you looking as lovely as a spring garden today?"

Her gaze remained directed out the floor-to-ceiling windows, where a trio of stone nymphs danced around a green algae-clogged fountain.

"Mr. Nate brought you some of those pralines you like so much." Caledonia's stern voice had turned surprisingly gentle. She opened one of the boxes, selected a pecan candy, and held it in front of the old woman's face.

A beringed, age-spotted hand, laden down with diamonds, snatched it from the outstretched hand like a greedy toddler, and it disappeared between lips painted a garish crimson. She thrust out the hand again, palm up.

"After your nap," Caledonia said, putting the box high up on an ornately carved black teak shelf. She could have been talking to a child.

A heated string of what appeared to be French babbling, interspersed with curses Regan was surprised any southern lady of Mrs. Melancon's generation ever would have allowed herself to think, let alone say, turned the air blue.

"You know you can't sleep when you've had too much sugar," Caledonia said matter-of-factly. "The box will still be here when you get up." She adjusted the shawls. "You gonna say good afternoon to Mr. Nate and his friend?" She put dark fingers beneath the sagging chin and lifted the woman's gaze.

"Miz Bethany." Nate tried again, but he'd finally found a female impervious to that winning smile. She was looking straight through them, her pale brown eyes unfocused. They might as well have been ghosts. Regan's heart sank a little as she realized that her long shot wasn't going to pay off.

"It's time for her nap," the other woman said, announcing that the brief visit had come to an end.

"Thank you, Miz Caledonia." If Nate was disappointed, he didn't show it. "I appreciate your hospitality."

They'd made their way down the hallway, past the busts, across the slate floor of the great hall, and had just left the house when Caledonia caught up with them.

"I've got something for the *fille*," she said. Reaching into a skirt pocket, she pulled out a dime that had been drilled through and strung on a narrow black cord.

Regan exchanged a glance with Nate, then took the necklace. "Thank you."

"You make sure you wear it." Vivid turquoise eyes burned in her burnished copper complexion. "You've stirred up the spirits, you. This gris-gris will protect you."

The ancient woman's intensity, coupled with their brief meeting with the old woman who could have been Norman Bates's mother, sent a chill up Regan's spine.

"We appreciate that a bunch, Miz Caledonia," Nate said, jumping in to rescue her. He took the cord from Regan's nerveless fingers and slipped it over her head. It had to be her imagination, but she could have sworn the coin warmed her skin as it settled at the base of her throat. He bestowed his most reassuring smile on Regan. "No one in the bayou makes better gris-gris than Miz Caledonia. She's a descendant of the Marie Laveaus," he said.

"He speaks the truth, he," the woman said, taking on a queenly bearing as she rose to her full height.

"Isn't that interesting." Regan forced a smile. "*Merci*." It was one of the few French words she knew.

The woman didn't answer, just shut the tall heavy door in their faces.

"Well." Regan let out a long breath. "That was certainly an experience."

"Caledonia is a little colorful even for southern Louisiana," he said. "I'm sorry about Mrs. Melancon bein' so out of it."

"You said she would be."

"I said I'd heard talk. I didn't realize she'd gone so far downhill since the last time I'd seen her, about a month ago."

"Is it Alzheimer's?"

"That'd be my guess, since the old girl used to be sharp as a tack. She inherited the chairman's chair at Melancon after her husband died making love to the mistress he kept in New Orleans's Faubourg Marigny historical district."

"Why does that not surprise me?" Regan said dryly as she climbed into the SUV.

"It was a pretty good scandal, even for down here. Turns out that the woman and Charles senior had three kids together. The fight for inheritance rights took three very litigious years."

"Obviously the family won."

"Mostly, but the mistress and the kids did end up getting to keep the house and the stock he'd put in each of their names before he died."

"There seems to be a lot of Melancon stock floating around down here."

"That's not so unusual, since they're the biggest employer. It'd be like living in Atlanta and ownin' Coca-Cola stock."

"Who are the Marie Laveaus?"

"Oh, now they were an interestin' pair. The first Maria was a hairdresser to wealthy New Orleans Creoles back in the 1820s. Technically she was a practicing Catholic, but she was also the spiritual adviser to slaves and their masters. And, of course, the master's wives, whose hair she fixed. She earned a reputation as a voodoo queen, but she must've had a good heart, since she was also the first to go out and tend to sick folks whenever the fever epidemics swept through the city.

"She still has her cult of believers who mark her tomb with red *X*'s and leave coins to pay for spells. Her daughter, Marie II, took the fame thing one step further and put on elaborately staged voodoo rites that became real popular among New Orleans society. It's been said that she grew so influential, even some of the priests and bishops would go to her for advice."

"And Caledonia's descended from them?"

"So they say."

"Voodoo's just a myth." Regan touched the dime at her throat and wondered which of them she was trying to convince. "She couldn't really know anything about me possibly being in danger."

"Of course not." He shot her a smile designed to lift any lingering dark mood. " 'Less you're talkin' about falling under the spell of my expert lovemaking."

She laughed and began to relax. But there was still the niggling problem of the stock certificates. "I'm really going to have to talk with Melancon."

"Won't have much of a chance to do that till after Fat Tuesday," he said. "So you may as well just plan on enjoying Mardi Gras."

"I suppose you're right."

"Don' worry, Detective *Chère*." He skimmed his right hand over her shoulder and down her arm, took hold of her hand, and lifted it to his lips, brushing a light kiss against her knuckles. "I'll be makin' sure you enjoy yourself, you."

As much as he regretted the unproductiveness of the visit to the Melancon house, Nate couldn't deny that he was grateful for anything that kept Regan in Blue Bayou a little longer. It was strange, the way time was beginning to blur. They'd only known each other a handful of days, but he was beginning to forget how his life had been before she'd come into it.

It was lucky that with the exception of the ongoing work at Beau Soleil and finishing up the sheriff's office remodel, he didn't have any jobs demanding his attention at the moment. He wasn't sure he could have paid enough attention to do them justice. It was as if he'd begun looking at life through the wrong end of a telescope: nearly his entire focus—except what the hell he was going to do about Josh—had narrowed down to Regan Hart.

He thought about her too much and too often. Hell, all of the time. He pictured her intelligent golden brown eyes when he was brushing his teeth in the morning, and visions of her long, lean body were the last thing to pass through his mind before he'd finally fall asleep.

She'd pop into his mind during the day when he'd be fiddling with a set of blueprints, and suddenly, instead of looking at a bearing wall, he'd picture her as she'd looked out on the Santa Monica pier, her smooth sleek hair ruffled by the sea breeze, her fresh clean scent more enticing than the gardens of Xanadu.

During the time he'd been waiting for her to show up in Blue Bayou, she'd filled his mind. So much so that he hadn't even noticed that he was painting the wainscoting in Beau Soleil's dining room French Vanilla, instead of the Swiss Coffee Dani had picked out, until she'd pointed it out to him. Hell, he hadn't made a mistake like that since those summers during high school, when he'd begun learning the construction trade.

It had been bad enough before she'd arrived with big eyes, wrap-around legs, and problems any sensible man would stay clear of. And he'd always considered himself an eminently sensible man when it came to women. But now, it was as if she'd put a voodoo love spell on him, fevering his mind and tormenting his body.

Which was, of course, the problem, Nate told himself as he turned onto Bienville Boulevard, two blocks away from the inn. While his reputation for romancing the Blue Bayou belles might be a bit exaggerated, he couldn't remember ever being this sexually frustrated. Not since he'd made the grand discovery that women liked sex as much as men did. Once he got the delectable detective into his bed and satiated his lust, while giving her a damn good time, too, of course, he'd be free of what was rapidly becoming an obsession.

"Oh, my God."

"What?" The mental image of kissing his way down her slender torso popped like a soap bubble. She grabbed his arm so hard they nearly ran off the road.

"You need to stop."

The stress in her voice made him immediately pull over and cut the engine. "What's wrong?" She looked as pale as Beau Soleil's Confederate ghost.

"It's that house." Her hand trembled in a very un-Reganlike way as she pointed toward a bright cottage, built Creole-style against the front sidewalk. The stucco-covered brick had been painted in historically correct shades of putty and Egyptian blue, and a For Sale sign was tacked to the French red door.

"What about it?"

"It's Linda Dale's."

Obviously the unsuccessful meeting with the old lady and Caledonia's spooky voodoo shit had taken its toll on her.

"Linda Dale's house got wiped out by a hurricane, *chère*," he soothed. His palms stroked shoulders as stiff as the Melancons' granite steps. "Remember? I already checked the real estate records before you came to town."

"They've got to be wrong. Dammit, that's the house." Her eyes were huge and earnest.

"I know the realtor," he said, deciding no good would come from arguing. Best she discover she'd gotten confused on her own. "Let me give her a call and we'll get her out here to let us in."

He knew how serious this was when Regan didn't even make a crack about him knowing a woman named Scarlett O'Hara.

"The key's under the mat," he said after he ended his cell phone call to the real estate office. "She leaves it there in case people want to take a look for themselves without a salesperson hovering over them."

"The living room is to the left when you walk in," she murmured as he retrieved the key from beneath the green mat. "The dining room to the right."

"That's pretty much the way Creole cottages are laid out," he said carefully, not wanting to upset her any more than she already was. "Four rooms, two back to back on either side of the door."

"How would I know that? I tell you, this is the house." She walked into a back bedroom that had been painted black. Nate figured Josh would feel right at home here. "This was my bedroom. It was yellow with a pale blue sky. The sky had white clouds painted on it."

"That's a nice memory," he allowed, still certain she was confused.

She didn't respond. "She was killed in the living room. My bed was there, against that wall." He was losing her; she was looking at things he couldn't see. "It was covered with stuffed toys, but my favorite was a purple, yellow, and green elephant I got for my birthday."

"Mardi Gras colors."

"Yes. I still have him," she surprised him by revealing. "Back in L.A. His name is Gabriel." Regan's brow furrowed. "I have no idea why I named him that."

"It'd be my guess your *maman* helped you name him after Longfellow's poem about the lovers separated during the Grand Dérangement."

"I've never read it."

"It's one of those typically tragic love stories. We had to memorize it practically every year in school. Evangeline Bellefontaine is an Acadian maiden who's torn from her beloved, Gabriel Lajeunesse, on their wedding day. They're separated, and she finds her way here to Louisiana with a group of exiles, only to discover that he's already been here but has moved on. So, she keeps searching and years later, when they're both old and gray, runs across him dying in an almshouse in Philadelphia. They embrace, he dies in her arms, she dies of a broken heart, and they're buried together."

"That is tragic." She sighed heavily. Wearily. "So many love stories seem to be."

"And a lot aren't. One of these days, I'll tell you about Jack and Dani. *Dieu*, they had a hard time, in some ways harder than Evangeline and Gabriel, but look how great things worked out for them."

"That's nice," she said a little absently. "That it worked out." She was looking back at the door to the bedroom. "She died in the living room. I heard shouting and hid under my sheets because I was afraid the *cauchemar* had come to eat me."

"That's an old Cajun folktale people used to tell kids to get them to behave. Be good, or the *cauchemar* will get you."

"It had crawfish claws for hands." She shook her head. "Do you know, as many times as I had that nightmare, it never seemed odd to me that I'd know anything about a witch like that." It had merely been part of her subconscious, a part of her. "There was a terrible crash."

She'd faded away again, into the past, leaving Nate feeling helpless. "I was too afraid to come out of my room. After a while I did, but Mama was gone. I went from room to room. I was so hungry."

He followed her out of the bedroom to the cheery leaf-green kitchen. "I climbed up on a chair and got some cookies out of the cupboard. And some bread." She ran her fingertips over the door of one of the pine cupboards. "I think I slept. I must have."

She went out the back door, stood on the loggia beneath the gabled roof, and looked out at the small cottage that was now the garage. "I don't know how long I waited for her to come back, but I just kept thinking what Mama had told me about never going outside onto the street by myself, or I'd get run over by a car. So I just stayed. For what seemed like forever."

He no longer doubted she'd lived here. Watching her face, he suspected she was reliving every moment. Not caring whether or not she came up with any clues, but understanding that she probably needed to get the memories out, Nate looped his arms around her waist as she continued to stare toward the garage. She leaned back against him, in what he took as an encouraging sign that she'd come to trust him.

"A nice doctor gave me a lollipop. It was cherry, my favorite. And then another nice man with dark hair and kind eyes picked me up and took me home with him."

"That'd be my dad." He learned that from his father's notebook, but hadn't wanted to tell her earlier; hadn't wanted her to think he was trying to somehow take advantage of an act of kindness that would have been second nature for Jake Callahan.

"I'm not at all surprised by that." She turned within his loose embrace and looked up at him, her moist eyes shining. "Finn's not the only Callahan brother who takes after his father."

When she lifted a hand to his face, Nate was lost.

"I don't want you to take this the wrong way, Regan." He covered her hand with his own, turned his head, and pressed his lips against her palm. "And I'm honestly not trying to take advantage of your emotional situation here, and I've been tryin' to do the gentlemanly thing and give you time—but I don't know how much longer I can wait." He skimmed his hand over her hair, down her neck, her spine, settling at the small of her back. Then he drew her to him, letting her feel his need. "I want you to come home with me."

Her remarkable eyes gave him her answer first. Then her sweet-as-sugarcane lips curved, just a little. "Yes."

# 22

*Regan had accepted the idea* that Linda Dale had been her mother. She'd even begun to suspect that the terrifying events that had haunted her sleep for years were more memory than nightmare. But being in the house had triggered images long buried.

"It was pink," she said as they drove down the two-lane road along the bayou. "The house," she explained when he glanced over at her. "It was painted pink. Mama said it was a house just right for two girls to live in." She pressed her fingertips against her forehead, where a killer headache threatened. "At least I think it was pink. I can't separate real life from the nightmares."

"Seems in your case, they'd be pretty much the same thing, *chère*. It could have been pink. Creoles tended to like their colors, and a lot of people replicate the original look."

"If I can remember the color of the house, and the clouds on the ceiling, you'd think I could picture who my mother was having an affair with."

"The trick is probably not to push it."

"I suppose not." Her laugh was short and humorless. "Boy, Callahan, what is it with you and amnesiacs?"

He was wearing sunglasses to block out the bright midday sun, but she could sense the smile in his eyes as he glanced over at her again. "I guess I'm just lucky."

He returned to his driving, and a strangely soothing silence settled over them. He was a man comfortable with silence, which she suspected was partly due to having grown up in a land as hushed as a cathedral. They passed a cemetery, built aboveground as she remembered them in New Orleans, to prevent the bodies from floating to the surface during floods. Sunlight glinted off a broken angel's wing.

"This is like another world," she said as a pair of giant herons took flight from the bayou in a flurry of blue-gray wings.

"I'll bet, before you came to Blue Bayou, if anyone had mentioned the word *swamp*, you'd think of snakes, mosquitoes, and gators."

"You'd be right."

"Tourists come down here from New Orleans and go out on the commercial boats—which I'm not knockin', since everyone's gotta make a living, and it's better than not seeing the swamp at all—but they watch the guide toss some chicken to a gator from a fishing line, down some boiled crawfish and oysters with hot sauce, hear a little canned zydeco, and think they've been to the bayou.

"But they've got it all wrong. You can't roar down here from the Quarter, snap a few pictures, then go racing off on a plantation tour. It's a wandering kind of place. It takes time to soak in."

They came around a bend onto what seemed to be a small, secret lake. On the bank of the lake, perched on stilts, was a single-story house with a low, overhanging roof and a wide porch that appeared to go all the way around it.

"It looks as if it just sprang naturally to life from the bayou."

"It's a West Indies–style planter's house. It's designed for hot climates. The roof line and the porch allow air to flow from open windows through all the rooms." He flashed a grin. "I can also fish from bed, which is a plus."

She smiled at that, as he'd intended.

"Did you build it yourself? Or refurbish it?"

"From scratch. I was hoping to keep the original, but carpenter ants and termites had been using it for a smorgasbord, so it'd been condemned. I mostly kept to the original footprint and tried to replicate it as close as possible, including pegging the timbers instead of nailing them."

"I'm impressed." But not surprised, having seen the work he'd done at Beau Soleil.

He shrugged. "I told you, bein' mayor is pretty much a part-time thing. Building's what pays the bills."

"You didn't choose to restore old houses for the money," she said, remembering his saying he'd rather be happy than rich. Though he could probably make a fortune if he moved to a wealthier area. "It's important to you. And this house was undoubtedly a labor of love."

"There are still a lot of things I want to do to it. It's taken me the last five years, workin' on it part-time between other jobs, but I figure if there's one thing I've got plenty of, it's time."

"Now I *really* envy you." She sighed as she thought of her never-ending stack of murder books, then decided that she wasn't going to dwell on them. Not here. Not now.

The inside of the house was rustic, but warm and inviting and surprisingly neat. The wood furniture was sturdy enough for generations of children to climb on, the upholstered pieces oversize and overstuffed, obviously chosen more for comfort than style. The floor was wide planks, and the open ceiling beams appeared hand-hewn.

Another of those little silences settled over them, this one not nearly as comfortable as the last.

Regan had always thought of herself as a courageous woman. Now that the moment they'd been leading up to since Nate Callahan had appeared in her squad room had arrived, she was beginning to lose her nerve.

Nate was backlit by the sun, making him appear to be cast in gleaming bronze. She remembered how he'd looked with his shirt off, his muscled arm swinging that hammer. He'd been as close to physical perfection as she'd ever seen. She was not.

"You're going to hate me."

"Impossible."

She dragged a hand through her hair, appalled at the way it was trembling. She had the steadiest hands of anyone she knew; she always made the top score in marksmanship. "This is impossible."

His lips curved slightly at that. "Nothing's impossible, *chère*."

"It can't go anywhere."

"It already has."

He didn't exactly sound any more thrilled about that idea than she was. "You don't understand."

"Then tell me."

"I have these scars."

"No one can get through life without a few scars, *chère*. Jack has 'em, so does Finn, and even me, as perfect as I am," he said with a slight smile that turned what could have been arrogance into humor, "have picked up a few over the years."

"No." She pulled away. Turned away. Unreasonably nervous, she went over to a window looking out over the water and wrapped her arms around herself. "I mean real ones." She closed her eyes to shut off the image of the flawed body she'd taught herself not to study in the mirror. "Physical ones."

Nate knew that if he was going to stop this from becoming emotionally heavy, the time to move away had come. If he wanted to prevent himself from falling into a relationship he hadn't asked for, hadn't wanted, all he had to do was to back off. Now.

A very strong part of him wanted to do exactly that, to prove to himself, and to her, that he still could. He hadn't wanted the responsibility of a woman whose life was turning out to be more complicated than even she could have imagined. But he wanted Regan.

Whatever was happening to him—to his mind, his body, and his heart—was beyond his power to stop. Which was why, instead of retreating to safer emotional ground, he crossed the room. "Where?"

"All over."

He took hold of her shoulders and turned her around to face him. "Here?" He skimmed his fingertips over the crest of her breasts. They fit so perfectly into his hands, Nate could almost imagine she'd been created solely for him and him alone.

With her eyes on his, she nodded.

Every other woman he'd ever been with had approached this moment with a casual air of experience, expectancy. Regan, who was proving to be the strongest of them all, trembled when his thumbs brushed her nipples, which hardened beneath the light touch.

Need hammered at him, along with a previously unfelt fear that he wouldn't be—couldn't be—gentle enough. His body urged him to ravish; his mind counseled restraint. His heart, which was expanding in his chest, opted for a middle ground.

"How about here?" His caressing hand moved downward, fingers splayed over her torso.

"Yes." As if not wanting to see what he might be thinking, she closed her eyes. Her usually clear voice was barely a whisper.

Her stomach. "How about here?"

"Yes. Dammit, Nate . . ."

"And here?" Down her thigh.

"Everywhere. And they're ugly."

"Now, I wouldn't want to be accusing you of stretching the truth, sugar, but my *maman* used to have this saying, about pretty is as pretty does."

"I've heard it."

"I 'magine you have. So I'm having a hard time believing that there's anything about you that isn't downright, drop-dead gorgeous." She didn't resist as he drew her closer. When she sighed and rested her head against his shoulder, he brushed a kiss atop her shiny cap of hair.

They remained that way for a long silent time. Outside the house, clouds gathering for an afternoon rain shower moved across the sun, casting the room in deep shadows. As he felt her trembling cease, Nate thought how good she felt in his arms. How perfect.

"I'm afraid," she admitted.

He drew back his head. "Of me?"

"I could never be afraid of you." She trailed a fingernail along the top of his lips. "I'm afraid of what we're getting into."

"Don't feel like the Lone Ranger. Since this seems to be a day for surprises and sharing secrets, want to know what I'm most afraid of?"

"What?"

"That I'm not going to be able to make love to you as well as a woman like you should be made love to."

She surprised—and pleased—him by laughing a little at that. "Now, that may be the only thing in my life I'm *not* worried about." She went up on her toes. Her lips brushed tantalizingly against his, then clung. "Take me to bed, Nate," she said, her words thrumming against his mouth.

He didn't need a second invitation. He swept her into his arms, feeling a lot like Rhett carrying Scarlett up that staircase, but wanting to pleasure more than ravish. Ravishment, he thought with a flare of hot anticipation, could come later.

"Oh, it's like sinking into a cloud," she murmured as he laid her with care atop the mattress of the roomy bed he'd made with leftover pieces of cypress from the house. "I smell flowers."

He lay down beside her. She turned toward him, her eyes shining like a pair of the pirate Lafitte's gold doubloons. "It's stuffed with Spanish moss and herbs."

Her rich, throaty laugh started a thousand pulses humming beneath his skin. "I'm never buying an innerspring mattress again."

Nate knew he was in big trouble when he almost suggested she stay here with him. In Blue Bayou. In his house. His bed. He wasn't prepared to share those thoughts with her yet, not when he hadn't figured them out for himself, but there was one thing he wanted, needed, to get straight before they moved on.

He framed her face between his palms. "You're different from any other woman I've ever known." He could hear a sense of the wonder he'd tried to ignore in his tone, and suspected she could hear it, too. "*This* is different."

"I know." When her gorgeous eyes grew suspiciously bright, Nate felt something inside him move that had nothing to do with sympathy, or lust. "It's the same for me."

Because he'd been raised to be a gentleman, Nate felt obliged to give her one last chance. "We can still stop this. Before things get out of hand."

"Is that what you want?"

"Hell, no."

"Me, neither."

What was the matter with him? Taking a woman to bed had never been this complicated. This important. Frustrated with the situation, even more frustrated with himself for giving in to these sudden self-doubts, Nate decided if he was going to be this lost, he damn well wasn't about to take the long fatal fall alone, and took her lips.

She tensed again when he pulled the T-shirt over her head, and instinctively covered her breast with her hand.

"It's okay." He kissed her again, his tongue dipping in to seduce hers into a slow, sensual dance. "I want to see you, *chérie*." He caught her lower lip between his teeth. "All of you."

Her body softened in a silent, submissive way he knew was deceptive as he undressed her slowly, deliberately, taking time to kiss each bit of uncovered flesh, just as Antoine had done in the erotic story he'd told her on the phone. He smiled when he got down to her panties, which were practical cotton woven into a barely there red bikini, just like the one he'd imagined in his fantasy at Cal's. Contrasts, he thought, as he drew them slowly down long legs, firm and sleek as a Thoroughbred's from daily running.

"I told you," she said, as he cupped the weight of her breast in his hand and pressed his mouth against a long jagged line snaking from her dusky pink nipple to the wall of her chest. What in the hell had happened to her?

"The plastic surgeon was the best in L.A. You can't go to a movie or watch television without seeing his work. He couldn't exactly make me look the way I had before the accident, but he used tiny stitches on my face, and special dressings, and hid the stitches beneath my hair as much as possible. But with all the surgeries to put me back together again, I just got tired of operations, so my body—"

"Is beautiful." He kissed her wounded breast, then proceeded to move his hands, his lips, over her in a sure, leisurely way, feeling the pleasure seep through her.

"You don't have to lie."

"I'm not. Perfection is boring." His tongue glided lower, over her stomach, then lower still. She sucked in a quick, sharp breath when he scraped his teeth along the pink ridge at the inside of her thigh, then laved the flesh with his tongue. He was telling the absolute truth. He found her wonderful. "Whatever marks you might have are merely points of interest on a fascinating tour, *mon ange*."

Nate felt her going lax with pleasure, and even as he enjoyed the absolute control he knew she did not surrender easily, he reined in his own rampant need, keeping his caresses slow and gentle as he moved over every graceful curve and sensual hollow. He touched her everywhere, watching her face. Where his hands played, she burned; where his mouth warmed, she trembled and arched in utter abandonment.

And still, even as the deep, painfully sexual ache went all the way to the bone, he waited.

His fingers sketched slow, tantalizing circles in the dark curls between her legs, then tugged lightly, drawing forth a moan. He did it again, this time covering her parted lips with his, so he could feel the ragged sound as well as hear it.

"*Mon Dieu*, I love you like this." Hot. Hungry. His. He trailed his hand down the soft, silky, smooth flesh of one inner thigh, then back up another. "Open for me, *chère*," he coaxed. "Let me see all of you."

She couldn't believe what was happening to her. She'd known Nate Callahan would be a good lover, skilled in knowing how to please a woman. But what he was doing to her went far beyond pleasure. Although his caresses were achingly slow, his clever hands were everywhere as he discovered erogenous zones she'd never known existed.

Regan had never—ever—ceded control to any man. She'd always preferred being on top, physically and emotionally. But that was before Nate. Lying naked on his moss-filled mattress while he was still fully dressed was strangely erotic, and for the first time in her life she understood that absolute surrender to the right man, a man you could trust absolutely, could be glorious. There was nothing, she thought with a stunning sense of wonder, that he could ask for that she would not give. When he pressed his palms against the inside of her trembling thighs, she opened her legs, offering the most feminine part of herself to his view. Despite the rain, there was enough daylight for him to see her imperfections. But it didn't matter. He still wanted her. Still found her desirable. Even beautiful.

She smiled, unable to remember when any man had called her anything beyond pretty.

"Lovely," he murmured. She moaned as those wickedly clever fingers skimmed over flesh heated from the blood rushing from her heart. She was as exposed, as helpless as she'd ever been, but felt no embarrassment as he parted the tingling flesh.

"Like petals, smooth and soft and glistening with early morning dew."

Her senses swam. Her mind was shutting down. She reached for him, needing to touch him as he was touching her. She wanted to yank down that zipper on his jeans and take him into her mouth, deeper than she'd ever taken a man; she wanted to burrow her face into the crisp male hair around his penis, she wanted to torment him as he was tormenting her.

"Please, Nate." Another thing that was so, so different. She'd never begged any man for anything, least of all sex. "I want you." *Need* you.

"Soon, *chère*." He braceleted both her wrists in his hands. "There's no hurry."

"Easy for you to say," she complained as he lifted her imprisoned hands above her head. Never in her life had she been so helpless. Helpless to resist Nate. Helpless to resist her own escalating desire.

"Easier to say than to do," he agreed in a deep, rumbling voice roughened with sex. "But like I said, down here in the South, we take things a little slower than in the rest of the world."

Just when she thought for certain that she'd die from the wanting, the waiting, his free hand cupped the source of heat and sent her soaring. She peaked instantly, sharply, and as she did, he pressed his mouth between her legs.

He was feasting on her, as a man might devour ripe passion fruit. Drowning in emotions, Regan writhed beneath his ruthless tongue and hungry mouth, the line between pain and pleasure blurring as he drove her up again. Even as this second climax shuddered through her, all Regan could think was *More*.

As if possessing the ability to read her thoughts, he left her only long enough to rip off his clothes. When he took the extra time to protect her, something that had somehow recklessly escaped her sex-fogged mind, she felt something powerful move inside her heart.

His long fingers splayed on her hips, lifting her to him as he slid into her with silky ease. Had anything ever felt so glorious? So right?

As he began to move with a deep, age-old stroke, slowly at first, then faster, harder, deeper, driving them both into the fragrant mattress, she scissored her legs around him and met him thrust for thrust, matching his pace. They came together, catapulting them both into oblivion. And into a relationship neither had planned, or been prepared to accept.

# 23

*Nate had collapsed on her,* loath to move, not sure if he could even if he'd wanted to. He could feel her heart beating against his chest, synchronized with the rhythm of his own as they both slowly returned to normal. He listened to the rain tapping on the roof and knew he'd never hear the sound again without thinking of Regan. He could cheerfully spend the rest of his life in this bed, he decided. So long as he could keep his delectable detective right here with him.

"Incredible." He threaded his hands through her dampened hair, brushing it back from her face, which was flushed from her orgasms. Her eyes were closed, her long, thick lashes looking like dark silk against her cheeks. "Absolutely incredible."

"Mmmm." She ran a limp hand down his sweat-slick back. "I honestly never experienced anything like that."

"Neither did I."

That had her opening her eyes.

"It's the truth." Realizing that he was probably crushing her, he rolled over onto his side, taking her with him. Her lips were deep rose and swollen from kisses. Unable to resist, he nipped at them lightly, savoring her taste. "This changes things."

What had just happened between them was no ordinary event. They'd connected in a way that would have scared the hell out of him if he hadn't been feeling so satisfied.

"It doesn't have to." He felt a pang of loss as she put a bit of distance between them. "We're both adults. It was amazing, hot, mind-blowing sex. But there's no irate father waiting in the wings with a shotgun."

"Well now, I'll have to admit, that comes as a relief," he drawled.

"Seeing as how the idea of gettin' peppered with buckshot doesn't sound all that appealing." Speaking of appealing . . . Unable to resist the lure of her silken flesh, even after what they'd just shared, he skimmed a slow caress down her throat and over a pert breast.

"I told you," he said, when she stiffened again, ever so slightly, "they don't matter."

"I don't want to talk about it."

"I want to know, *chère*."

"You do realize that you can't always get everything you want."

"Believe me, I'm well aware of that," he said, thinking about the murder of his father, the agonizingly slow death of his *maman*.

As if sensing his thoughts, she sighed and hitched up a little in the bed as the postsex languor disintegrated. "It's no big secret. Finn could easily have found the story. Probably even Dani, since I learned later that it not only made all the local papers but got picked up nationally. I was even asked to sit next to the First Lady at the State of the Union address, but I turned the offer down."

"Why?" He knew a lot of women who'd sell their collection of tiaras for such an opportunity to be in the national spotlight.

"Partly because I'm not a real fan of politicians. But mostly because I don't think stupidity deserves a reward."

"You couldn't be stupid if you tried."

"Thank you. That's a very nice thing to say. But unfortunately, it's not accurate." She breathed a resigned sigh. "It was several years ago, back when I was still a patrol cop. I wasn't real popular in the 'hood, because I'd been working with a community policing group and the narcotics guys, doing a lot of drug busts. I was working the graveyard shift and went to pull this vehicle over for expired tags, when it took off. I took off after it."

Her lips curved in an oddly regretful smile Nate suspected was directed inward. "I'd never taken part in a high-speed chase before, and I have to admit, I was enjoying the hell out of it. The adrenaline was jangling in my veins, and everything was intensified—the sound of the siren, the squeal of the tires, and the smell of burning rubber as we kept tearing around the corners."

He thought he could see this coming.

He was wrong.

"I must have been going eighty when we went into the projects." Her voice, her eyes, turned flat and distant. "The car headed down this alley, with me right on its bumper. The minute it got back onto the street, a moving van blocked the exit. I slammed the patrol car into the side of it."

"Christ." His blood went cold as the mental image seared itself into his mind.

"That would have been bad enough, of course," she continued with what he thought was amazing matter-of-factness. "But an accident's chancy, what with airbags and seat belts, and such. The dealers came up with a plan to shift the odds in their favor.

"Right after I wrecked the cruiser, they pulled out the automatic weapons and began firing away. I don't remember anything after the windshield shattered, but I saw the pictures afterward, and the car looked like one of those tin cans people use for target practice. There were more holes than metal left. A lot of that metal and glass ended up in me." She sighed and unconsciously touched her hand to her breast. "End of story."

Rage came instantly, steamrolling over sympathy. He'd always thought what had happened to his father had been tragic. But the horrific thing she'd been through was nothing short of evil. "And you went back to those streets?"

Even Jack, after being ambushed by drug dealers down in South America, had resigned his DEA job, cashed in his pension, and returned to Blue Bayou, where he'd spent several months trying to drink himself into oblivion.

"Not right away. There was a lot of recovery time and rehab." Her slender shoulders lifted and dropped on a long, exhaled breath. "But I'm a cop. There was no way I was going to let those gangsters scare me away from doing what I'd always wanted to do."

"Always?"

"Dani told me how you used to drag wood in from the swamp while Jack and Finn were practicing their quick draws."

"Someone had to build the jail."

She attempted a faint smile she couldn't quite pull off. "Well, when I was a little girl, I used to have Police Officer Barbie arrest Ken."

For the first time in his life, Nate understand how someone could do cold-blooded murder. A very strong part of him wanted to get on a plane, fly to Los Angeles, find those lowlifes who'd done this to her, and kill them with his own hands. Slowly. Painfully. Thoroughly.

"You've no idea," he said, "how much I admire you."

"Why?"

"For surviving such a horrific thing. For being who you are. What you are." Words usually came trippingly off his tongue. But Nate couldn't think of any that even began to express the emotions battering at him. "I can't even begin to tell you."

"Well, then." The light had returned to her remarkable eyes, and her lips curved in a slow, seductive smile. "Why don't you show me?"

Outside, the rain continued to fall.

Inside, with slow hands and warm lips, they lost themselves in a shimmering, misty world of their own making.

Afterward Regan lay snuggled in his arms, listening to the sound of the rain on the roof, and knew that from this day forward, every time it rained, she'd think of Nate.

"What are you thinking?" he asked, skimming down her side with those fingertips that had stimulated every inch of her with a touch like the finest-grade sandpaper.

"How much I used to hate the rain." She caught his hand as it slid ever lower and lifted it to her lips. "And how I'm never going to be able to think of it the same way again."

"Great minds." He pulled her tight against his body. His kiss was slow, deep, and possessive. "I was thinking earlier how nice it'd be if I could just spend the rest of my life right here in bed with you."

That sounded wonderful. Too wonderful. If she wasn't in such a blissful mood, she might have been unnerved by how perfect a scenario he'd just painted.

"Unfortunately," he continued on a long deep sigh, "we're going to have company."

"Company?" She touched her mouth to a small scar on his knuckles.

He glanced over at the watch he'd taken off and put on the bedside table. "I figure we've got about ten minutes before Josh gets home from school."

"Oh, my God, how could I have forgotten about him?" Regan leaped up and raced around the room, gathering up discarded clothing where it had landed on the wide plank floor and furniture. Making love with Nate had wiped her mind as clear as glass. She shot him a frustrated look. "Would you please get out of bed?"

"You don't have to be in such a tizzy, *chère*." He unfolded himself from tangled sheets that had slid mostly to the floor. "There's still plenty of time."

"Don't you have any other speed but slow?" Where the hell were her panties?

"You weren't complaining a little bit ago."

"Actually, I was." There they were. How on earth had they gotten on top of that floor lamp across the room?

"Next time we'll try for a slam-bam-thank-you-ma'am session," he said obligingly.

Regan suspected he'd turned her into a sex addict, since even that sounded appealing.

"What are you doing now?"

"Opening the windows." Thank God for the overhanging roof and wide porch that allowed her to do so while the rain poured down. "It smells like sex in here."

"Well, I'd say we'd probably have had a pretty disappointing time if it didn't. He won't have any reason to come in here, Regan."

"You never know. I don't want him to know that we were having hot, wild sex in the middle of the day." She couldn't remember the last time she'd had afternoon sex. Years, perhaps. She'd always been careful to arrange for dark rooms brightened only, if her partner insisted on light, by the soft glow of a single flickering candle.

"I think he knows men and women have sex. Sometimes even in the daytime."

"It appears he knows a great many things he shouldn't. I don't want to set a bad example for him." She turned to see how much progress he was making and discovered he was still as naked as the day he was born, leaning against an old bureau, with the strangest smile on his face. "What?"

"I don't want to scare you, *chère*. But I think there's something you should know."

"What?" she repeated impatiently.

"Now, you've got to understand, I may be wrong. I'm not real familiar with the feeling, having never experienced it before—"

"Nate, you're a wonderful man—kind, caring, talented, and a marvelous lovemaker—but time is running out here. Could you please, this one time, just cut to the chase?"

"I think I could, just maybe, fall in love with you."

The bra she'd retrieved from the bedpost dropped to the floor from nerveless fingers. Stunned speechless, she could only stare at him. A yellow school bus lumbered to a stop outside the house. Jesus, did she need any more complications in her life? "*Don't*."

She scooped up her bra and disappeared into the bathroom, slamming the door behind her.

"Well." Nate pulled on his briefs and, since he had no idea where his shirt had landed, pulled another from the cypress chest. "She certainly took that well."

# 24

*After a long, hot shower* intended not only to wash off the scent of their lovemaking but to clear her mind so she could deal with this latest problem, Regan took the time to blow-dry her hair so she wouldn't look like a drowned spaniel.

Before getting dressed again, she unwrapped the fluffy white towel from her body and studied herself in the bathroom mirror, running her fingertips over the curved raised lines that truly hadn't seemed to distract him from his goal of making sure that she'd never be able to enjoy sex with any other man ever again.

When she finally came out of the bedroom, she found Josh standing at the old soapstone sink, husking corn. He glanced up. "Hi," he said almost cheerfully. "Nate's outside. He said you're invited to dinner, and he'll be right back in."

She wasn't at all eager to stay after Nate's out-of-the-blue declaration, and Josh's matter-of-fact attitude about her being there made her feel even more uncomfortable. And what had Nate done with the foul-mouthed delinquent when he'd replaced him with this Stepford teen? "How was school?"

"Okay." He shrugged shoulders clad in a normal denim shirt. "I thought I might be behind, but all except for geometry, I'm pretty much ahead of a lot of the class. The counselor's thinking of putting me in the accelerated program. If I'm going to be staying around, that is."

"That's terrific." Her heart tugged as she realized that the chances of that were slim unless Judi Welch could find a family for him to stay with here in Blue Bayou. "I always had trouble with geometry. The teacher said if you just memorized the theorems you'd be able to solve any of the problems. But even though I could recite them all, it never helped me know what to do with them."

"Yeah." He pulled some pale silk off a fat yellow ear of corn and rinsed the corn beneath the tap. "Same with me. I hate those effing sines and cosines. I mean, why the hell do I have to learn that stuff anyway?"

She was almost relieved to see a flash of the Josh of two days ago. "I suppose it comes in handy for something." She glanced up at the intricate placement of the pegged wooden beams. "I'd think Nate would need to know it, to build houses like this."

"Yeah, that's what he said. He also said he'd help me figure it out." His gaze scanned the homey, if decidedly masculine room that, as wonderful as it was, could use a bit of a woman's touch. "This is a cool place, isn't it?"

"It certainly is."

"It'd be way radical to live here."

"Yes," she heard herself saying. "It would."

The door opened, and Nate came in, carrying a handful of the purple-and-yellow irises she'd seen growing wild around the house when they'd first driven up. "I figured," he said, "since Josh and I are having a lady to dinner, I ought to get some flowers for the table."

"They're lovely." And definitely a woman's touch. Now he was reading her mind even before she had the thoughts. Fortunately, there was nothing in his casual manner to suggest that a mere thirty minutes ago, he'd dropped a bombshell on her.

"Trouble is, while I'm a man of many talents, I'm not real good at flower arranging."

"I'll do it." Their fingers brushed as she took the irises from his hand, creating a spark that shot right down to her toes. She looked up into his face to see if he'd felt it as well, but his expression remained absolutely smooth.

Perhaps, she thought, as she arranged the flowers in a hammered pewter pitcher, he'd only been speaking off the top of his head. Perhaps he'd been carried away by great sex and mistaken it for the start of something deeper. Or perhaps he was going to do exactly what she'd told him to do. Not fall in love with her.

As she set the pitcher in the center of the old pine farm table, Regan told herself she should be vastly relieved.

He might not be the cook his brothers were, but Nate thought the dinner of spicy grilled shrimp, dirty rice, and salad turned out pretty damn good for a guy more used to having females cook for him. The conversation flowed surprisingly easily, considering all the undercurrents. Josh was amazingly well behaved, watching his language for the most part. He seemed to respond to Regan, who appeared honestly interested in his desire about maybe being a writer when he grew up, which led to a discussion about Jack's books, which in turn led to a discussion of drugs, which the kid swore he'd never done and never had any intention of doing.

"Drugs are for chumps," he'd muttered as he'd polished off his third plate of dirty rice.

Then, as if to prove that miracles did, indeed, exist, he offered to wash the dishes while Nate took Regan back to the inn.

They were almost down the steps when he called out to Nate, who returned to the porch. "Thanks, man."

"For dinner? Hey, I may not be Emeril, but any idiot can stick some shrimp on the grill."

"No. Well, that was okay, too. I liked the rice stuff."

"Yeah, I could tell."

"I was talking about today. About letting me come home on the bus instead of making it look like I was living with my probation officer."

"You're not," Nate said mildly. "If you decide to take off, there's not much I can do about it." He squeezed Josh's shoulder. "Why don't you get started on that homework after you finish the dishes? I'll be back in a while, and we'll tackle the geometry."

"That's okay." He glanced over at the SUV, where Regan was sitting in the passenger seat in the dark. "I know you've got better things to do."

"I said I was going to help you, and I will." Nate was proud of the firm, paternal tone that sounded a little bit like Jake Callahan's had when he'd been dealing with his sons.

As he drove away from the house, he could see Josh standing in the open doorway, watching the taillights until they'd turned the corner.

"I don't know what you're putting in his RC," Regan murmured, "but I'd never know that was the same kid who was mouthing off at everyone at the hospital the other night."

"He's a good kid. He just needs a little encouragement. Besides, right now he's on his extra good behavior, trying to find himself a home."

"I noticed that. It's a little sad. He reminded me of a stray dog trying to infiltrate itself into whatever family feeds him."

"Yeah. Turnip was the same way. But she's settled in with Jack and Dani and the kids like she's been there since she was a pup."

"There are a lot more people in the world willing to take on a stray dog than a teenage kid with issues."

"You're probably right about that," he agreed, thinking of how hungry the kid looked when he'd been driving away. And not for food.

"About earlier," she said tentatively, obviously feeling her way. "What you said."

"Don' worry about it. It was jus' something that came off the top of my head."

She combed her hand through her silky dark hair. "I wasn't very nice about it."

"A lot happened today. I didn't mean to make you feel pressured or anything."

"It's just that my life is so confusing right now."

"I know, sugar." He reached out and laced their fingers together and rested them on his thigh. "Like I said, it was just a random thought." He squeezed her hand. "You were right about that mind-blowing sex. It was probably leftover hormones speaking."

"Now *that* I can identify with," she said in what sounded like relief.

When they arrived at the inn he accompanied her up to her suite but forced himself not to coax her into inviting him in, which, he suspected from the renewed desire he felt swirling between them in the closed confines of the elevator, wouldn't take that much effort. He kissed her good night, a brief flare of heat that ended too soon for both of them, then walked back to the SUV, absently whistling "You Are My Sunshine."

She was being ridiculous, Regan told herself the next morning. It wasn't like they were going steady. She'd gotten along for thirty-three years of her life just fine without Nate Callahan. Certainly she could survive one morning alone without him around to stir up her hormones and tangle her mind.

He was only out at his cabin with his brothers for a day of fishing that she suspected was mostly a rite of male bonding, which would involve a lot of swearing, spitting, and belching. She wondered what

Nate was telling Jack and Finn, who'd come home for Mardi Gras, about her, if anything. Wondered what they were telling him back.

She'd decided to spend the morning at the courthouse, searching through old parish real estate records for the names of people who'd been in the neighborhood when Linda Dale had been living here. So far she'd found ten names, made ten phone calls, and come up with nine dead ends and a man who seemed to erroneously remember Linda as a go-go dancer at the Mud Dog.

"Here's another one," Shannon Chauvet said, bringing a third thick green leather-bound book from a back room.

Regan had immediately recognized the woman as the one Nate had comforted at the hospital the night of the train wreck. The scrape on her cheek was healing, and her black eye had faded to a sickly yellow-green hue that couldn't quite be concealed by makeup. Her surprised expression when Regan walked into the courthouse suggested she'd recognized her as well, and while their conversation had revolved around the records, Regan decided that before she left the office, she was somehow going to bring up the subject of Shannon's abusive husband and assure her that she was doing the right thing by staying away from him.

"Hey, Regan." She glanced up and saw Josh standing in front of the table. She'd been so absorbed in her thoughts, she hadn't even heard him enter the courthouse.

"Shouldn't you be in school?"

"The sewer line broke, and since tomorrow's Fat Tuesday, the principal decided she might as well let us out of school early."

She'd had a hard time believing Nate could have turned the kid around so quickly. If he was determined to become a juvenile delinquent, he was going to have to become a better liar.

"Well, that's a lucky thing for you. If you need a ride to Nate's, I can drive you out there."

"Nah. It's not that far. I could've walked, or hitched—"

"Hitching isn't safe."

"Life isn't all that safe. But I'm not hitching," he pointed out.

She began moving her pen from one hand to the other. "So what are you doing? Other than ditching school and risking being thrown back to Social Services?"

A red stain filled his cheeks. "Jesus H. Christ, a guy can't get away with anything around here."

"You might keep that in mind next time you try. And don't cuss."

"Like you don't?"

"I'm a cop. It occasionally comes with the territory."

He looked as skeptical as a fourteen-year-old-boy could look. "Shit, that's a real good excuse."

"Seems to me you're the one who needs an excuse. What *are* you doing here?"

"Okay. I saw your car parked outside when the bus went by, and thought maybe you could use a little help finding out about your mother."

She lifted a brow. "You know what I'm doing?"

"Sure." He shrugged. "Just about everyone at school knows. Except a few Columbine wannabes and some nerds who haven't looked up from a computer screen since they got their first Game Boy."

"You have a group of Trenchcoat Mafia kids at the school?" Blue Bayou looked like a place where the Brady bunch would be out playing the Partridge family on the softball diamond in the park.

"Nah. They just try to act that way to be cool. The school board voted in a dress code that got rid of their stupid coats, like that's going to turn them into human beings. It's also why I'm stuck wearing these geek clothes of Nate's."

"I think you look very nice. Besides, white T-shirts are classic. James Dean wore them."

"Who's James Dean?"

She sighed. Somehow, when she hadn't been looking, she'd landed on the wrong side of a generation gap. "Just an actor who died tragically young. Well, since you're here, why don't you sit down?" The way he was shifting from foot to foot reminded her of a bail jumper about to split town. "You can help me go through a few more pages, then we'll head over to Cajun Cal's for lunch."

"Okay." He dumped the books he was carrying onto the table and sat down.

Suspecting she hadn't heard the real reason for him showing up here, Regan handed him one of the ledger pages and waited for the other shoe to drop.

She did not have to wait long.

He watched Shannon Chauvet filing some papers. "She's a nice lady," he said.

"She's certainly been very helpful."

"She invited me to spend the night at the guest cottage with Ben and her. If Nate says yes."

"I guess you'll have to ask him for permission." No way was she going to start interfering in disciplinary matters.

"Yeah. . . . Her husband hit her."

"So I heard."

"He hit Ben, too."

"I didn't know that." But she wasn't surprised.

"Yeah, he tried to get in between them last summer, and the son of a bitch broke his arm."

"Domestic violence sucks."

"Now who's cussing?"

"That isn't cussing. But you're right, I could have chosen a better word."

"Nicer one, maybe. But not better. If I ever have a kid, I'm never going to hit him."

"I'm glad to hear that." Warning sirens were blaring in her mind. She turned the pen around and around, treading softly. "Did someone hit you, Josh?"

He couldn't quite meet her eyes. "It's no big deal. It's what adults do."

"Not all adults."

"Cops can't go around arrestin' everyone who spanks a kid."

"Flat-handed spankings are allowed in every jurisdiction I know of." Though just because it was legal, that didn't make it right.

"How 'bout fists?"

"I suppose again, you're talking jurisdictional differences. But that would be unacceptable to me, and I certainly wouldn't let it slide."

"How 'bout pimping?"

The question had been asked so matter-of-factly, and she'd been so distracted by the way he seemed to be picking up Nate's Cajun patois, that it didn't immediately sink in. "What did you say?"

He still wasn't looking at her. "I figure you wouldn't let a guy pimp a kid, either."

"Shit." She dragged a hand through her hair when he arched a sardonic brow. "Okay, you caught me. That's definitely cussing." Out of the corner of her eye, she saw Shannon headed toward them with another thick record book. "Come on." She pushed back from the desk and stood up.

"Where are we going?"

"For a drive."

"You're not going to call the cops, are you?"

"Of course I am."

"You can't."

"Dammit, Josh—is that even your name?"

"Yeah."

"Well, you've done a real good job of stonewalling so far, but you're not going to be able to get away with it forever. Mrs. Welch is going to find out who you are and where you're from, and she's going to try to send you back." She put one of his icy hands between both of hers and held his tortured gaze with a solemn, determined one of her own. "I'm not going to let that happen. He's never going to hurt you again." Regan would not allow this to turn out any other way.

"He can't."

"That's what I said."

"No." Josh shook his head. Bit his lip. Tears were swimming in his eyes. "You don't get it. He can't hurt me because I killed him."

When she heard the heavy book crash to the floor, Regan thought Shannon must have heard Josh's heated declaration and dropped it in her shock.

"Oh, shit," Josh muttered.

Regan followed his bleak gaze to the doorway and felt exactly like a deer in the crosshairs. The man standing there had a fully loaded ammo belt strapped across his chest, and a Remington deer rifle pointed directly at them.

# 25

*It had been planned as a guy's day out,* a chance to get together out at the camp that had been in their family for generations, shoot the bull, drink some beers, catch some fish, and talk about women, which admittedly wasn't as raunchy a topic since his brothers had gotten themselves married. Nevertheless, Nate had been looking forward to this day. He had not planned to get ragged to death.

"You actually came right out and told her you loved her?" Finn asked in disbelief.

"I said I thought I might, just maybe, be able to fall in love with her," Nate responded as he dug through his tackle box and came up with a silver and copper spinner that had worked real well for him last week.

"That's pretty much the same thing," Jack said. "Once you start thinking the *L* word, you're pretty much hooked."

"Not like you to be so stupid." Finn was looking at him the same way he had back when Nate was fourteen and had filched a pack of cigarettes from the market. "You're supposed to be the Callahan who knows his way around women. Even I would have known better than to just blurt out something that important."

Nate cast from the porch, landing the lure precisely where he'd wanted it. Of the three brothers, he was the only one who actually used this camp a lot for its original purpose.

"You're a fine one to criticize, you," he drawled. "I seem to recall, not that many months ago, you screwin' things up so bad you went on a bender, leaving Jack and me to sober you up and send you off to Kathmandu to grovel. After you broke my nose."

"I was going to go to Nepal, dammit," Finn grumbled. "I was just giving Julia time to adjust to the idea of us being together."

"You're lucky she didn't use some of that time to fall for another guy," Jack said.

"Wouldn't have happened." Nate gave Finn grudging credit for that. "I was there at the beginning. From the time our big brother met her plane in N'Awlins, she never looked at another man. And God knows, I tried to get her to notice me," he said with a wicked grin.

He'd taken to Julia Summers the first time he'd met her at the reception the parish council had held for the visiting TV cast of that prime-time soap, *River Road*. Unsurprisingly, ratings had taken a nosedive after she'd left the show to go to Kathmandu for her role as Bond girl Carmen Sutra, and there were rumors the show was about to be canceled.

"It was only two weeks," Finn shot back, ignoring Nate's fraternal dig to reply to Jack's accusation. "You took thirteen years to get back with Danielle."

"Most of which she happened to be married," Jack pointed out.

"She only married that politician creep because you didn't stay around to make an honest woman of her. You're just lucky that piano dropped on the guy's cheatin' head, or you still might be hanging around here mooning after her like a lovesick pup."

"Goddammit." Jack shot to his feet, ready to rumble. "How was I supposed to know she was pregnant when the judge ran me out of town? If anyone had bothered to tell me—" He shot a blistering accusatory look Nate's way.

"That's bygones," Nate said quickly, hoping to defuse things before they got out of hand and he got his nose broken again. He reeled in the line, cast once more. "Water under the bridge."

"Yesterday's ball score," Finn quoted their father.

"Yeah." Jack blew out a long, calming breath, sat down, leaned back in the rocker, and put his booted feet up on the railing again. "You're right. So," he asked Nate, "what are your plans regarding the lady?"

"If you're talking about my intentions, I don't know."

"What a screwup," Finn muttered. "You take her to bed, have some hot sex—"

"World-class sex," Nate clarified.

"You have sex," Finn forged on in that doggedly determined way that had made him such a good serial killer hunter, "blurt out you love her—"

"Maybe. Possibly. Down the road." He wasn't about to admit it, but Nate was beginning to agree with them. He had screwed up by letting his mouth run away with his brain.

"Same thing," Finn echoed Jack's assertion. "And you bring the subject up when there's no time to talk about it, because a teenage runaway kid has just arrived home from school. You ever think of coming up with a plan beforehand?"

"If I'd had a damn plan, I wouldn't have said anything. I've always been up-front with women; it seemed like the thing to do at the time." He wasn't about to admit the woman had scrambled his brains. "Not all of us live our lives in rigid, controlled, planned-out A to Z fashion. Some of us like to go with the flow."

"Meaning," Jack suggested as he popped the tops on two bottles of Voodoo beer and handed one to Nate, "you don't have any idea what you're going to do next, you."

Nate threw back his head and took a long swallow. "Not a clue."

"It's going to be okay," Regan quietly assured Josh as they faced the gunman.

"Oh, dear Lord, he's going to kill us," Shannon, who was standing beside them, whispered back.

"No, he's not." Regan certainly hoped she could stop that from happening. "I've been in this situation before." Her psychology degree had made her a natural for being called out during similar situations over the years.

"You moved out on me, bitch!" the man shouted at Shannon. His throat, his face, even the tips of his ears, were a brilliant, furious scarlet.

Shannon's hand lifted unconsciously to her face. "I didn't have any choice. You hit me."

"Because you wouldn't shut the hell up!"

Regan thought she heard more pain than anger in his harsh voice. Which could be a good thing, so long as he didn't start feeling so sorry for himself that he became suicidal, and decided to take his wife with him.

"I was only suggesting that maybe we move to town. Just for a little while." Shannon Chauvet's voice was little more than a whisper.

"I'd suffocate in the city. I'd rather die right here. Right now."

*Oh, shit.*

"It's not exactly the city, Mike." Regan suspected he'd heard those coaxing words before. "Breaux Bridge only has about seven thousand people."

"That's ten times the number who live here. How the hell am I supposed to trap there?"

It sounded like they'd had this argument many times before. Regan decided it was time to inject herself into the conversation. "What do you trap?"

He looked toward her as if noticing her for the first time, then moved massive shoulders that would not have looked out of place on a pro linebacker. "Nutria. Gators. Crawfish."

"This must be a good place for that line of work."

"Not this year. Hell, if the crawfish get any scarcer, I'll have to start trapping for cockroaches."

"That's why I thought you could work for my uncle," Shannon said.

"I already told you, goddammit," he said through gritted teeth. "I'd rather shoot myself atop the Huey P. Long Bridge than sell used cars."

"He happens to make a very good living."

"Selling junkers on the weekly pay plan, then repossessing them every Monday, ain't living. It's dyin'. Jus' slower than most ways."

He'd begun cradling the rifle like a security blanket, his fingers absently stroking the barrel. If they slid downward to the trigger, they were in real trouble.

Regan had learned in her negotiation training that all hostage takers had a reason for going off that went beyond just holding some innocent person at gunpoint. It was up to the negotiator to figure out what that reason was.

Mike Chauvet's, she suspected, was about regaining control.

She vowed to make sure he didn't.

They'd had a good time. Hadn't caught any fish, but then again, Nate thought as he drove back to Beau Soleil, the morning hadn't been about fishing. They were about five miles from the house when his cell phone rang.

He viewed the caller screen and flipped it open. "Hey, Dwayne. What's up?" The deputy was talking so fast, Nate could only catch about one word out of four. "Slow down. Take a deep breath. And start again, okay?"

There was a deep gulping breath on the other end of the line as Dwayne did as instructed.

"It's that lady, Ms. Hart."

Nate felt his blood turn to ice when he learned that Regan was locked inside the library with Shannon, Josh, and a drunk, angry, and armed Mike Chauvet.

Telling himself that there'd be time to be terrified later, once she was safe, Nate punched the gas.

Regan heard the squeal of brakes outside.

"Don't move," Mike warned them. "Or you're toast." Still aiming the lethal rifle at them, he went over to the window. "Shit. It's the state cops."

Regan had been wondering if anyone knew they were in there; someone must have seen Chauvet coming into the courthouse with a rifle. So much for Blue Bayou being a peaceful little town. She'd been in town less than a week and had already unearthed one murder and landed in a hostage situation.

Domestic situations could be particularly volatile; the last thing Regan needed was a SWAT team arriving on the scene like a bunch of road warriors.

"We haven't been formally introduced," she said. "I'm Regan Hart."

"Yeah. I heard about you. You're the cop from California who's going to be the new sheriff."

"I'm a detective. And that's a mistaken rumor goin' around, about me becomin' sheriff." Strange, now she was dropping her own g's. Nerves, Regan told herself.

"What kinda detective?"

There was no way she was going to give him any ideas he might not have already thought of himself by telling him she worked homicide. "I've handled all sorts of cases over the years. Sometimes I've helped out guys who have found themselves in your situation."

"I don't need any friggin' help from a woman."

"Well, now, Mike—that is your name, right? Mike?"

"Yeah. So what?"

"I was just asking. That's one of my favorite names."

"Yeah. Sure." His response dripped with acid sarcasm. "I know what you're doing. You're playing me, trying to get on my good side."

"No fooling you, Mike," Regan said easily. "That's pretty much what I'm trying to do, but you know, I really am on your side."

His response was brief and vulgar.

"The thing is," she continued on an even tone meant to calm him, "we've got ourselves a little situation here. Right now, it's not too bad. Everyone gets frustrated from time to time, and we all need to let off a little steam. I can understand that. But the one thing we don't want is for things to get out of hand."

His laugh held no humor. "Just my luck there'd be a cop in here today. Cop killing's probably a one-way ticket to death row. Do not pass Go; do not collect your fucking two hundred dollars." His eyes crawled over her in an asexual way that nevertheless made her flesh crawl. "You carrying?"

"No." She certainly hadn't expected to need her pistol when she'd left the inn this morning.

"Lift up your arms, turn around, and put your hands on the wall so I can frisk you and make sure."

At the moment, Regan had a wide wooden table between them. There was no way she was going to give that up. And while he might put down the rifle to frisk her, she wasn't prepared to take the chance.

"It's got to be difficult, frisking someone with one hand. I don't think I could do it."

"Good try, but I'm not putting this down. I got another idea. Take off your top."

"What?"

"Are you deaf, lady? Take off the shirt!"

She opened her mouth to try to shift his thoughts to something else when there was an earsplitting squawk from outside.

"Mike Chauvet," the voice shouted. "Throw out your weapon and come out with your hands up."

Terrific. That's all she needed, some guy on an electronic bullhorn entering the picture. Hostage negotiation was all about personalizing the situation. There was nothing personal about a bullhorn.

"Take it off." He shifted the gun a few inches. "Or the kid's gonna be one knee short."

"Go ahead, sucker," Josh sneered. "Make my day."

Damn! That's all she needed, for Josh to recover his stupid teen attitude.

"You don't have to do that, Mike." She'd been taught to speak calmly and empathetically to hostage takers. Unfortunately, the guy standing behind the white cruiser continued to shout out orders.

Some cops, she thought darkly, watched way too much television.

Nate slammed on the brakes when he came around the corner and saw the phalanx of state cops and cars. Tires squealed but didn't skid on the damp cobblestones. Jack and Finn were out of the SUV before he'd fully stopped; he caught up with them seconds later, frustrated when some giant cop wouldn't let him pass.

"Hey, Nate." A trooper ambled up to him as if it was just another rainy afternoon.

He looked familiar, and reading the name tag pinned to his uniform shirt, Nate recognized him: Steve Tandau had played third base for the South Terrebonne Gators the year the Blue Bayou Buccaneers had won the state 4-A finals. He'd been a long ball hitter, and a helluva defensive player who'd gone on to play for LSU, spending two years in the Atlanta farm system before a bad knee from Little League days had caught up with him.

"What the hell's going on?" Nate demanded.

"We've got a domestic situation going on. Remember Mike Chauvet?"

"Sure. He was arrested for domestic abuse the other day."

"Well, he's out now."

"Shannon withdrew the charges?" He'd been so sure he'd gotten through to her. If either Regan or Josh were hurt because he'd been arrogant enough to think he could talk her into doing what her therapist couldn't, he'd never forgive himself.

"Naw. The way I heard it, he's out on bail."

"Shit." He listened to the cop yelling on the electronic bullhorn. Though he didn't have any police experience, he didn't believe that shouting out orders like some marine drill sergeant was a good idea.

"Have you tried just calling him?"

"Yep. Phones aren't working. It's my guess he either tore them out of the wall or cut the wire."

"How about tear gas?"

"That's too dangerous." Finn, who knew about such things firsthand, entered the conversation. "Tear gas doesn't work all that well on drunks, and it'd be my guess the guy's been drinking."

"Bobby, down at the Mud Dog, said Mike's been drinking Dixie and Johnny Walker boilermakers all morning," Dwayne Johnson said. The deputy's expression managed to be both serious and excited all at the same time. It was obvious this was a helluva lot more adventure than he'd been expecting when he'd joined the force. Personally, Nate would rather have him dealing with mailbox bashing.

"Besides," Jack said, "the stronger stuff is pyrotechnic. You don't want to risk setting the place on fire with Regan and Josh in there."

If Mike did one thing to harm one hair on either Regan's or Josh's head, he'd damn well better kill himself, or Nate would do it for him. "So, what do we do now?"

"He's not going anywhere," the former third baseman said. "So, what we do is wait. Try to get him to listen to us. Hope that cop inside can convince him to surrender."

If anyone could, it'd be Regan. But Nate wasn't in a waiting mood. "And if he doesn't?"

"Then we'll just have to hope he wanders into the kill range."

Nate followed his gaze to the roof of the building next door and felt his heart stop when he saw the sniper rifle.

"Most often they come out, though," Tandau assured him.

"How long do you wait?"

"As long as it takes."

Well, that told him a helluva lot. Nate glanced at Finn.

"It all depends," Finn said with a reluctant shrug. "I've seen guys cave after thirty minutes."

"We're already past that. What's the longest you've ever seen?"

There was a significant pause. "Ever hear of Ruby Ridge? Waco?"

"Screw that." Before either of his brothers or the cops could stop him, Nate started walking toward the courthouse. He paused to touch Jackson Callahan's horse's nose, then headed up the steps.

# 26

*Regan believed she was getting to him.* Chauvet may not have put the gun down yet, but he was no longer pointing it directly at them.

She was about to suggest again that he allow his wife to leave, when the courthouse door opened. Mike spun around, pinning the newcomer in his sights.

"What the hell are you doing here? And how did you get in? I locked that sumbitch door."

"I'm the mayor. This is the courthouse, where the mayor's official office is. I may not show up in it all that often, but I do have a key. As for what I'm doing here—"

Nate held out his arms, revealing he had nothing up his short sleeves. "I come offering a trade. Let the women and kid go, Mike. I'll stay. We'll talk."

"I got nothin' to say to you."

"Well, that's too bad, because I've got something to say to you, and you better damn well listen. I like you, Mike." Okay, so it was a lie. "I want to help you out here, but you've got to understand that there are a lot of guys with guns outside, who won't be real eager to cut you any slack while you've got these hostages in here."

Mike shot a nervous look out the window. Hopefully he couldn't see the sniper, but there was no way he could have missed all those State Police cars.

"Let 'em go, Mike. If nothing else, it'll be easier on you, not having to worry about keeping an eye on three people. You'll only have me to focus on."

"Why should I listen to anything you have to say?"

"Because Brittany Callais is the presiding family court judge."

"So?"

"So, she and I went steady back in high school, and I dated her some when I first got back from Tulane. Now, I wouldn't want to brag, but when we were working on the food committee for tomorrow's Fat Tuesday festivities, I got the impression she's still sweet on me."

Mike's wide brow furrowed. He reminded Nate of a slow-witted mastodon as he tried to process this piece of information. "You saying you can get her to cut a deal?"

Nate didn't dare look at Regan. "That's exactly what I'm saying."

There was more slow, rusty grinding of mental gears. "Okay," Mike said finally. "The cop and the kid can go." He pressed the barrel of the rifle against Nate's chest. "But you and Shannon are stayin' put."

Nate saw Regan sit down on the table and cross those long legs he'd spent a great deal of time fantasizing about. "I'm not going anywhere."

Josh, damn the crazy kid, stood next to her and crossed his arms. "Me neither."

Terrific. Just goddamn terrific.

Nate was trying to come up with an alternative game plan when the door behind him opened.

"Shit," Mike groaned when Jack and Finn came in, deflating like a balloon with a slow leak. "One Callahan is bad enough. No way I need three in my life." He held the rifle out, the wooden stock toward Regan. "I effin' give up."

"I still can't believe you did that," Regan complained later that afternoon. They'd all gathered in the kitchen at Beau Soleil, where Jack, who was the cook in the Callahan family, had fixed platters of baked stuffed oysters and smothered chicken over rice.

Dani had broken out the coconut pralines she'd baked for tomorrow's festivities. Matt, Dani and Jack's eight- year-old, was upstairs watching *The Lord of the Rings* for what Dani swore was the hundredth time; and Holly, Ben, and Josh, who seemed to be no worse off for his threatening experience, were engaged in a noisy game of horse on the basketball court Jack had built out back. "You had no business just walking into the courthouse like that."

"I'm mayor. What happens in Blue Bayou is my business."

"You could have been killed, you idiot."

He grinned and leaned over and gave her a quick kiss. "Would you have missed me, *chère?*"

"It was irresponsible," she repeated for the umpteenth time.

"It worked," Nate repeated, as he had every time she'd brought it up. "Besides, I had backup."

Jack and Finn returned his satisfied grin, as if what had happened earlier was no more serious than the shootouts they used to have when they were kids.

"At least now the mystery of where Josh came from and why he left is solved." Considering all he'd been through, she was not overly surprised that he appeared to have survived today's excitement with no ill effects.

"Helluva thing, what his mother's boyfriend did," Jack said. "Snatching the kid on his way home from school."

Between their conversation with Josh, and calls to the Florida State Police and the Department of Children and Families, they'd determined that the teen had been placed in a foster home after his mother had died of an overdose. Her boyfriend, angry at having lost the income she'd made hooking, had decided if he didn't have the mother, he might as well make some bucks off her kid.

"He must have been terrified all this time," Dani murmured, shaking her head. "Believing that he could be arrested for having killed that monster."

"I can't say I'm not relieved, for Josh's sake, that the guy ended up with only a concussion from being knocked out," Nate said. "But I sure wouldn't mind if he ended up being some burly lifer's girlfriend for the next fifty years."

"I still can't understand why no one was looking for him," Julia said. Finn and his new wife had returned home for Mardi Gras, and when she'd first met the actress this afternoon, Regan had been a little intimidated by her beauty and lush, natural sensuality. But Julia had turned out to be warm and caring, and had lightened the conversation over dinner by entertaining them with tales of her recent adventures on location in Kathmandu.

"Child welfare agencies across the country lose hundreds of kids every year," Finn said. "Florida's DFC is the poster child for what's wrong with the system. If these kids had anyone watching out for them, they wouldn't have ended up in residential care in the first place. Once they do, it's real easy for a kid to fall through the cracks."

"Especially when they want to disappear," Regan said. She'd seen it too many times to count. When she'd been on patrol, she'd done her best to coax as many street children as possible into nonprofit agencies who knew best how to help them, and she'd always carried phone cards paid for out of her own pocket so the kids could call home.

"We can't let him go back," fretted Shannon, who'd not only filed charges against her husband but also made an appointment with an attorney to begin divorce proceedings.

"The boy won't be going back to Florida," the judge said, speaking with such authority not a single person in the kitchen doubted him.

"Are you sure you should have left Josh at Beau Soleil?" Regan asked later that evening, as Nate drove away from the house.

"He wanted to spend the night. He seems okay, and after all he's been through, it's probably good to be with kids his own age."

"I suppose so." She reached over and put a hand on his thigh.

He covered it with his own and squeezed her fingers. "You want to go to the inn? Or my place?"

"The inn," she decided. "It's closer."

What was it about this woman that kept putting him at a loss for words? As they entered the suite, just the idea of taking her to bed again had him burning from the inside out. It was as intense a feeling as when he'd been wracked by chills at the idea of Mike Chauvet deciding to play shooting gallery. If it wasn't love, it had to be one helluva case of flu.

"You're awfully quiet," she murmured.

"Just enjoying the company." He forced a smile he still wasn't quite feeling. "And thinking how funny life can be."

"Yeah, today was a real barrel of laughs."

"Not that kind of funny. If I hadn't been remodeling the office, I never would have been cleaning out those old files. And if I hadn't been cleaning them out, I never would've found that journal."

"And if you'd never found that journal, you wouldn't have come to L.A., I wouldn't have come here, and we wouldn't be about to spend the rest of the night making each other crazy."

"I'm already crazy, *mon ange*." His hands settled on her waist. "Crazy about you."

She looked up at him from beneath her lashes, the way belles seemed to know how to do from the cradle. It seemed a little out of character, but he couldn't see a bit of guile in her warm gaze. "I'm almost beginning to believe you, Callahan."

"You should." He pulled her closer. " 'Cause it's the truth."

He pressed her against him and kissed her. When her tongue stroked his, it was all he could do not to throw her over his shoulder and carry her to bed.

"I think I made a mistake," he groaned.

"What mistake is that?" She dipped her tongue into the space between his lip and his chin he'd never realized was directly connected to his groin.

"I shouldn't have upgraded you to this suite."

"Why not?" She brushed her mouth against his, retreated, then came back for seconds. "Aren't I worth a suite?"

"Sugar, you are worth the entire inn." He skimmed a hand through her hair and splayed his fingers on the back of her head as he kissed her again. Harder, deeper, longer. "It's just that there's somethin' to be said for a room where the bed's closer to the door."

"Well, then, I guess we'll just have to start here." She tugged the T-shirt from his jeans. "And work our way across the room." Her fingers played with the hair on his chest, skimmed beneath the waist of his jeans. "Anyone ever tell you that five buttons might be considered overkill?"

"They're classic. Traditional."

"Granted." She flicked open the first metal button with a skill he'd admire later. Much, much later, when his skin didn't feel as if she'd just set a match to it. A second button opened. "They also make it harder to seduce you."

"Is that what you're plannin' to do?"

"Absolutely." The blood that had been pounding in his head surged straight down to his cock as she moved on to the third. And fourth. He sucked in a quick, painful breath when she skimmed those short fingernails over his belly. "And you are going to love it."

The final button gave way, allowing his erection to jut out of his jeans. When she curled her fingers around it, lust tightened into a painful knot.

"It must be hard," she murmured, moving her hand up and down in a long stroking motion.

"I'd say that's self-evident," he managed.

Her laugh was rich and throaty and sexy as hell. "That's what I meant." She continued to torment him with her fingers and her nails, tracing the shape, the length, breadth, and heft of him. "There's nothing subtle about you men." She followed a throbbing vein from root to tip, causing his penis to jerk in her hand when she flicked a thumb over the hood. "There's no way to hide the fact that you want a woman."

"Women get wet."

"Well, there is that." She smiled, a slow, breath-stealing smile. "In fact, my panties are drenched right now."

He groaned at the idea of sliding his fingers into that hot moist flesh.

"Not yet," she murmured, backing away as he moved to do precisely that. She undressed him as he had her, driving him to the brink again and again, teasing, tasting, tormenting. Every time he tried to caress her, she'd slip deftly away and find new regions to explore.

Somehow they made it to the bedroom, and as he lay on the antique bed, watching her undress in the silvery moonlight streaming in through the window, it crossed Nate's mind that this was the first time that he wasn't expected to do anything but to take.

She returned to the bed, wearing nothing but a wicked smile. "I love the way you feel." She ran her palms down his chest. "And taste." Her tongue swirled around his nipple, dampening the puckered flesh, nipping at it gently before moving on to plant a lingering kiss against his navel.

Even knowing what was coming, Nate was not prepared for the slap of lust when she took him into her mouth, her tongue and teeth following the same scorching trail her devastatingly clever fingers had blazed earlier. He was about to warn her that she'd pushed him to the very brink when she went up on her knees and reached over his aching supine body.

"I have a surprise for you."

"You went shopping this morning," he guessed as she took out the foil package.

"I did." She tore it open. "But that's not the surprise." Took out the condom. "Watch."

How could he not, Nate thought as he watched her put it between her luscious lips. Surely she wasn't going to . . . No, he told himself—his detective was sexy as hell, but she was not the kind of woman who'd—*mon Dieu*. She lowered her mouth to him again and without touching him with her silky lady's hands, smoothed the thin latex all the way down.

The last thin thread of Nate's control snapped.

"That's it." He dug his fingers into her waist, lifted her up, and thrust his hips off the mattress as he lowered her onto him. They both froze for a moment, body and eyes locked together, Nate buried deep inside her, looking up at her as she stared down at him.

Then they began to move. She pressed her knees against his legs, riding him hard and fast as they both raced over that dark edge together.

"How the hell did you learn to do that?" he asked when he could speak again.

She was curled up against him like a kitten, but her smile was that of a sleek, satisfied cat who'd just polished off a bowl of rich cream. "Back when I was working vice, we raided this place that had hookers working upstairs while the owner had a thriving porno studio on the first floor. Part of the evidence was this so-called instruction video with an obviously phony nurse showing women how to get men to use a condom."

"If I didn't already practice safe sex, that little trick would certainly change my mind." He skimmed a hand down her slick body. "I'll bet it took a lot of practice." He wasn't all that fond of the idea of his detective tangling the sheets with a string of California males, but since he couldn't claim to be a monk, he decided the stab of jealousy was unfair.

"Not that much." Her quick grin pulled a thousand unnamed chords. "Though the room service waiter did look at me a little funny this morning, after my third fruit bowl."

"Are you saying—"

"I don't think I'll ever be able to eat another banana again."

He chuckled and kissed her, enjoying her taste, the feel of her in his arms. "That's quite a sacrifice. Perhaps we can come up with some way to make it up to you."

"Well, now that you mention it." She flicked a finger down the center of his chest. "I've always fantasized about making love in one of those old-fashioned lion-footed tubs."

Amazed by the surge of renewed energy that shot through him at the prospect, he scooped her from the cooling sheets. Regan laughed with throaty pleasure as he flung her over his shoulder and carried her into the adjoining bathroom.

# 27

*Blue Bayou's Fat Tuesday* festivities demonstrated yet again that this part of southern Louisiana was a world apart. Beginning with the fact that they left the inn just as sunlight had begun to spread gilt-tipped fingers of lavender and shimmering pink over the bayou.

"What kind of party begins before dawn?" Regan doubted she'd gotten more than two hours sleep. Not that she was complaining about the way they'd spent the nonsleeping hours.

"A good party," he assured her. "I promise you'll pass the best time you've ever had."

"I'm not sure that's possible. If I'd passed a better time last night, I wouldn't be able to move this morning."

He laughed, leaned over, and with his eyes still on the narrow cause-way, gave her a quick hard kiss. "The *courir* is somethin' special," he explained. "No one's real sure when exactly it started, but we do know our Acadian ancestors were doing it before the War between the States. It's fashioned after a French medieval holiday called the *fête de qué-mande*. It was the one time a year peasants were allowed to mock roy-alty without fear of the consequences.

"They'd dress up in outlandish costumes and roam the countryside, singing and begging for alms. Our *coureurs* do the same sort of thing, but these days we dance and sing for *une 'tite poule grasse*, which is a little fat hen, and the ingredients for tonight's gumbo pot."

"Like singing for your supper," she said.

"That's pretty much it. These days it's just part of the tradition, but I suspect that in medieval times the people really did need help from the farmers to get enough food together for the feast."

A crowd had already begun to gather when they arrived at Beau

Soleil. There were a great many men and women on horseback and others in the back of pickups. Two tractors had been hooked up to flatbed trailers outfitted with benches and festooned in traditional Mardi Gras colors of green, purple, and gold, as well as bright yellow and red.

The mood was already festive; more than half the people were in costumes reminiscent of the colorful scraps of cloth the long-ago peasants might have sewn together. Many wore tall conical hats, much the same as medieval women once favored, and several had donned animal masks adorned with hair or feathers. Neighbors were milling around, catching up on any gossip they might have missed, including, Regan guessed, stories of yesterday's adventure at the courthouse. There was already singing and dancing, and more than a few celebrants had begun drinking their breakfast.

"It's part of cuttin' loose," Nate said when he saw Regan's slightly furrowed brow. "But it's the *capitaine*'s job to maintain control so things don't get out of hand."

Her gaze moved from Josh, dressed in a Harlequin costume and laughing with Holly and Ben and some other kids she hadn't met, to Judge Dupree, who was seated astride a gray stallion, wearing a bishop's miter and looking very much in control of things.

"I doubt the town could have chosen better."

"He's been *capitaine* since before I was born, 'cept for those years he spent in Angola Prison after bein' framed by a bunch of wise guys who were trying to get their hands on Beau Soleil to turn it into a casino. It's good to have him back again." He waved to the judge, who gave a regal nod in return.

"He doesn't look as if he's having that good a time." His expression was stern as his gaze swept the crowd.

"Since it's his first *courir* in seven years, I'll bet he's having a dandy time. He's just sorta like Finn." Nate waved to his older brother, who, while not in costume, at least had arrived wearing not his old standby FBI suit but a pair of neatly pressed jeans and a black T-shirt. "Dancin' on the inside."

Given the choice between riding a horse and riding on the flatbed, Regan opted for the flatbed. Although she suspected that Nate would have preferred being out front with the others, he stayed with her, explaining events as they unfolded.

"*Capitaine*, *Capitaine*, *voyage ton flag*," the throng sang out in unison. "*Allons se mettre dessus le chemin.*"

"Captain, Captain, wave your flag," Nate translated. "Let's take to the road."

They continued to sing as they traveled through the countryside. A great many of the songs were in French, and a few sounded as if they might actually date back to the Middle Ages. When they broke into "The Battle of New Orleans," Regan was able to sing along.

They reached a small wooden house set in a grove of oak trees. "Everyone has to stay here," Nate explained as the judge rode toward the house, carrying a white flag that symbolized the chase. "While the *capitaine* asks the folks if they'll accept us."

A man and woman came out, and there was a brief discussion, after which the judge turned back to the group and waved his flag.

"Now we have to go start earnin' the feast."

The tractor rumbled into the front yard and everyone piled off. Musicians with fiddles and accordions began playing, while the others danced and sang and begged for a contribution to the gumbo pot. After receiving a bag of onions and several links of sausage, they were off again.

*"Capitaine, Capitaine, voyage ton flag. Allons aller chez l'autre voisin."*

"Captain, Captain, wave your flag," Nate translated again. "Let's go to the neighbors."

And so it continued for the next four hours, each stop an opportunity for a party that managed to be spontaneous without losing any of its tradition. Every so often someone would throw a live chicken into the air for the Mardi Gras celebrants to chase, like football players trying to recover a fumble. Often when they'd stop, several young men would climb trees.

"I don't know why," Nate said, when she asked him about it. "I read a book once that said it's some ancient fertility ritual, like symbolically associating with the tree of life. Or maybe they're just fooling around. The one thing that professor never mentioned is that Mardi Gras's supposed to be the last blowout before Lent, and it's hard to have a bad time when you're climbing a tree."

That explanation, Regan thought as she watched Josh and Ben scramble up an ancient oak, was as good as any. Swept up in the timeless event, as the brightly costumed *courir* advanced across the drab late-winter countryside, Regan knew if she lived to be a hundred, she'd never forget this day.

When they finally arrived back at Beau Soleil, they were welcomed back by those who'd chosen to get up at a more sensible time. The food they'd gathered was dumped into huge gumbo pots cooking on open fires. Outdoor tables groaned with more food brought by neighbors.

The sun that had been rising when Regan had dragged herself out of bed eventually sank with a brilliant flare of red-and-purple light into the water. Campfires had been lit to ward off the night chill; sparks danced upward like orange fireflies; smoke billowed from the many barbecues; dust rose from dancing feet. The mood was joyous, the food lavish, seasoned with enough Tabasco to clear Regan's sinuses for the rest of her life.

"I am never going to eat again," she groaned as she swayed in Nate's arms to the slow ballads that were beginning to replace the jauntier dance tunes. Although she'd never considered herself much of a dancer, she was able to follow him smoothly as he twirled her with fluid ease.

"That's the trouble with Cajun food." He pressed his lips against the top of her head. "Four days after you eat it, you're hungry again."

She laughed lightly, nuzzling against him. She'd tried to put away thoughts of Linda Dale for this one special day, wanting it free of any unpleasant memories. But now, as the celebration began winding down toward its midnight conclusion, Regan couldn't help wondering how her life might have been different if her mother hadn't been killed.

She knew from the journal that Dale and her lover were planning to leave Blue Bayou. But would they have stayed in Louisiana?

"A *dix* for your thoughts," he murmured as he nibbled on her earlobe.

"What's a *dix*? And if it's anything more to eat or drink—"

*"Non."* She could feel his chuckle rumbling in his chest. "A *dix* was the French currency. It's where the word *Dixie* comes from."

Regan truly doubted that there was any other place in America, with the possible exception of New England, that clung to its past the way Blue Bayou did.

"I was just wondering, if things had turned out differently, if we would have met earlier."

"Probably not."

Having expected him to spin a long, colorfully creative scenario, Regan was surprised by his uncharacteristic bluntness.

"If there's one thing watchin' Jack and Finn, and bein' with you, has taught me, it's that people can't fool around with destiny. We were fated to meet this way, *chère*. In this time." He skimmed his lips along her cheekbone. "If I'd met you earlier, me, I might not have appreciated you." He tilted his head back a bit. His eyes gleamed a deep, warm blue in the glow from the campfires as he smiled down at her. "It's been suggested that I might have been a bit shallow."

"Never." She twined her arms tighter around his neck and fit her body closer to his. "That's just what you wanted people to think, so it wouldn't screw up your role in your family."

"Which was?"

"The jester."

"Jester?" Hell, Nate figured, that was even worse than Peter Pan. "You mean one of those guys with the funny hat and bells on his curly toed shoes?"

"No. I mean the wise man of the court who was clever enough to tell the absolute truth, no matter how unappealing, in a way that left people smiling. When anyone else who tried to be that frank might have had his head cut off."

He thought about that for a moment. "How do you see Jack and Finn?"

"Oh, they're a lot easier, because what you see is precisely what you get. Jack's the half-reformed bad boy with the heart of gold. Finn's the rock." Her fingers were stroking his neck in a way that made him want to make love to her. Then again, listening to her read a suspect his Miranda rights would probably have him wanting to jump her lovely bones.

"No foolin' a woman with a psych degree," he said easily, deciding he'd best shift his train of thought before giving the town something else to talk about. He scanned the crowd. "Sure was a good turnout. Even more than last year."

Although Nate obviously hadn't been real happy about sharing her, he'd stayed typically good-natured as she'd danced with seemingly every male in Blue Bayou, including Cal, whose moves had been surprisingly fast for a man of his years.

"I suppose getting to see what you've done inside Beau Soleil was a draw for everyone," she suggested.

"I imagine so. Toni cornered me while you were inside frosting the

King cake with Dani. Seems the old lady has most of the family money in company stock, but Toni's planning ahead for the day she's no longer with us, and wants to talk about me givin' St. Elmo's a facelift."

"That house doesn't need a facelift. It needs a heart transplant." Regan glanced over at the *gallerie*, where a stone-faced Caledonia stood guard over her frail charge. "I'm surprised Mrs. Melancon's here tonight."

"She's never missed a Mardi Gras that I know of. And she seems more lucid this evening."

"I thought so, too, when I saw her singing along to some French song a while ago. Music has a way of making connections with people when other things can't get through." Up on the bandstand, the Swamp Dogs had broken into a rousing rendition of "You Are My Sunshine," which made Regan think of her mother.

"I 'spose so." He cupped her butt in his hands, pressing her closer. "What would you say to sneakin' off for a while? I just remembered that I need to measure for the crown molding in one of the guest bedrooms."

The molding had actually been installed last week, but it was the best excuse Nate could come up with, while his body was bombarded with sexual needs like he hadn't even experienced when he'd been thirteen and learning all about sex by reading Finn's *Playboy* magazines out at the camp.

Regan laughed. "I love a man who takes his work seriously."

He led her through the throng of people, and just before they reached the *gallerie*, Charles Melancon stepped in front of them.

"May I have the honor of a dance, Ms. Hart?"

Regan instinctively glanced up at Nate and read the resignation in his eyes as he shrugged. Stifling a sigh, she returned the older man's friendly smile. It was, after all, only one dance. She and Nate still had the rest of the night.

"So," he asked as he moved her through a complex series of steps, "are you enjoying yourself?"

"I'm having a wonderful time. Sorry," she murmured as she stepped on his toes. He was clearly a better dancer; then again, he'd probably had a lot more practice.

"My fault. It's too crowded here to try to impress you with fancy moves." He slowed the pace. "A lot of people think of Mardi Gras and they tend to think of Rio, or N'Awlins. But I've always felt that Blue Bayou's is special."

"You won't get any argument from me about that."

She'd just returned his smile when Bethany Melancon popped up from her wheelchair like some wild-eyed jack-in-the box, wispy hair flying around her face.

"*Putain!*" she screeched, pointing her scrawny finger at Regan. She spat, then reeled down the steps, leaping on Regan, fists in her hair. "You have no business here. I won't allow you to ruin my family!"

"It's okay, Miz Bethany. Nate grabbed hold of her from behind, lifted her off the ground, and pulled her away. "You're just a little confused right now."

Finn and Jack cut through the crowd, putting themselves between Regan and the old woman, who was screaming incoherently in French. Ragged nails clawed impotently in the air. If she hadn't been concerned about breaking her in half, Regan would have just taken her down.

"It's okay," Nate repeated soothingly.

"I'm not letting you take my son away from Blue Bayou, Linda Dale!" Mrs. Melancon screamed, switching to English.

It took a moment for Nate to realize what he'd just heard. He knew he wasn't alone when the quiet began to slowly extend outward from the *gallerie*. A spooky hush came over the crowd as everyone turned toward a stricken, white-faced Charles Melancon.

By unspoken consent, Mardi Gras came to an abrupt halt. People began to leave, the low level of excited conversation echoing over the swamp.

Eve Ancelet appeared from somewhere in the crowd. "My bag's in my car," she said. "Try to calm her while I get a sedative."

"Take her upstairs," Dani suggested. "You can put her to bed in the guest room."

"I'll go with my mother," Charles said. He did not look all that eager.

A typically stoic Caledonia took the woman from Nate's arms. "Mo' better you stay down here, Mr. Charles," she instructed. "You caused enough trouble as it is."

She lifted the frail woman into her arms as if she weighed no more than a rag doll, walked into the house, and followed Dani up the stairs.

Regan's heart was still pounding in her ears as the rest of them gathered in the library.

"You want to explain what just happened?" Nate asked Charles, who'd gone from ghost white to a sickly shade of gray.

"The past caught up with me." He looked a thousand years old.

"The past, meaning me," Regan suggested.

He sighed heavily. Wearily. "You probably won't believe this, but in a way I'm relieved the truth has finally come out."

Regan still didn't know what, exactly, the truth was. "Perhaps if you began at the beginning," she suggested.

"I fell in love," he said slowly, painfully. The fifty-something man was far from the congenial Rotarian she'd met at Cajun Cal's; he looked drained and grim. He also had not looked once at his wife, whom, Regan noted, didn't appear that surprised by the revelation. "For the first time in my life, I was truly, deeply, in love."

"With Linda Dale," Regan said.

"Yes." He dragged both his hands down his haggard face. "I fell in love with her the first time I ever met her at a nightclub in New Orleans. I was entertaining clients. She wasn't a star yet, but every man in the place wanted to be the one to take her home at the end of her set."

"But you were the lucky one who did," Nate said.

"Yes."

"Even though you were married," Regan, who usually was able to keep her mouth shut during questioning, said.

"The marriage was a business arrangement I entered into at my mother's insistence. Love had nothing to do with my arrangement with my wife." He finally glanced over at Toni. "It still doesn't."

"The deal was that you wouldn't embarrass me, Charles. I believe you're doing a very good job of that tonight." Toni Melancon rose from her chair with a lithe grace learned in finishing school. "I'll be calling my attorney first thing in the morning."

A little silence settled over the library as she left the room. Regan took a deep breath and dove back into the dangerous conversational waters. "The man Linda Dale wrote about had a name beginning with the initial *J*."

"My father was Charles Melancon, senior. I was called Junior while I was growing up, and it wasn't until he'd been dead for two decades that I began to finally put that name behind me."

Regan thought about what Nate had told her about the elder Melancon being so influential. It must have been hard growing up in his shadow, especially at a time when the family had begun to lose their power and influence.

"What happened after you took Linda Dale home from the club that night?"

"We made love. All night long." Both his expression and his eyes softened at that long-ago memory.

Regan had figured that part out for herself. "And afterward?"

"I explained to her about my situation. My responsibilities to my mother and the stockholders. There was no way I'd ever be free to marry her."

"I can't imagine she was thrilled with the idea of being your mistress."

"To be honest, I believe the idea of not being able to make a life with her bothered me more than it did Linda. She was an amazingly generous person and understood responsibility, more than most. She was willing to accept whatever life we could manage to carve out for each other."

"Which is why she moved to Blue Bayou from New Orleans."

"Yes. I thought it would be easier, having her here close by, where I could see her more often. But it proved harder. Because the more time we spent together, the more I wanted to be with her. It became frustrating, and after a time, my regret and bitterness at my marital situation threatened to ruin what we had together. That's when I knew I had to do something drastic."

"So you killed her?" Nate asked, slipping a protective arm around Regan's shoulders.

"Of course I didn't!" Charles leaped to his feet. "I loved her, dammit. I wanted to spend the rest of my life with her. I decided to leave Blue Bayou and start a new life with Linda. Mother did not take to the idea."

"Because if you ran off with your mistress, your wife would file for divorce and take her money with her."

"Yes. We argued. She told me I was no better than my father. I'd promised Linda I'd come over after my talk with Mother, but I was so angry, I drove to New Orleans and drank my way through the Quarter."

Regan found it hard to feel sorry for him. He was, after all, still alive.

"What happened to Linda?" she asked. The fury that had twisted Bethany Melancon's face flashed in her head. "Did your mother kill her?"

"Yes." He raked his fingers through his pewter hair. Shook his head. "No."

"Which is it?" Regan asked, reining in her impatience.

"Both." He huffed out a deep breath. "My mother never drove. Never needed to. There was always a chauffeur to take her wherever she wanted to go. But of course servants talk, and that night she didn't want the staff to know where she'd been, so—"

"She had Caledonia drive her," Nate guessed.

"Yes. She hadn't believed me when I'd told her that Linda loved me as much, if not more, than I loved her. She was so sure this 'white-trash golddigger,' as she'd called her, was only after my money. So she took along twenty-five thousand dollars in stock certificates to buy her off."

"But Linda didn't want the money." Regan had learned enough about her mother to know this. She'd also dealt with enough homicides to envision the scene. The old woman, who would have been about the age her son was now, would have started out cold. Regal. Like a duchess talking down to a peasant. But she was about to discover she'd met the one individual Melancon money couldn't buy.

Frustrated, she would have argued. Probably even started screaming, as she did tonight. Screaming, Regan thought, like the *cauchemar* in her nightmare.

Her mother would have stayed calmer. After all, she had a child asleep in the bedroom. She might have even tried to get past her to open the door, perhaps to call Caledonia for help. There would have been pushing. Shoving. The room was small; although Regan couldn't recall the furnishings, there must have been tables in it.

"It was an accident," she decided.

"That's what Mother said," Charles confirmed flatly. "Apparently Linda fell and hit her head on the corner of the coffee table. Caledonia would lie through her teeth to protect my mother, but I believed her story then." He sighed heavily. "I still do. Mother was apparently distraught, and together they decided to make it look like a suicide. Caledonia helped her carry Linda's body out to the garage. They put her in her car, turned on the engine, then left."

"Did it occur to either one of them that they left a two-year-old child alone in the house to fend for herself?" Nate asked, furious on Regan's behalf.

"That was"—Charles paused, as if searching for the right word—"one of the worst parts of the tragedy."

Nate felt guilty he'd even brought this mess into Regan's life. If it hadn't been for him, she'd have gone on thinking that her father was a war hero, rather than this man who'd chosen to remain quiet and allow his daughter to be taken from him.

Regan thrust her hand through her hair. "Let's get one thing straight, Melancon. You don't have to worry about suddenly having to turn paternal. I've gotten along thirty-three years without a father, and—"

"What?" His surprise was too genuine to be faked. "I'm not your father, Ms. Hart. You were an infant when I met Linda."

Nate could tell Regan was as surprised as he was by this revelation, but she managed to hang onto that inner strength he admired.

"Then she obviously had another relationship," Regan said.

"I'm sure she had several before she met me. I never held that against her."

"That was goddamn big of you," Nate muttered.

Charles shot Nate a look. "I loved her," he repeated. "I was willing to give up everything for her." He turned back to Regan. "And you." Despite the seriousness of the conversation, his lips curved slightly. "I'd never thought I'd have children—Toni made it very clear from the start that she wasn't the maternal type—but I came to care for you as if you were my own daughter."

"Do you happen to have any idea who she'd been with before you?"

"No. But even if I did, it wouldn't tell you who your father was."

"Why not?"

His eyes gentled, revealing a caring side of the businessman Nate had never seen. "Because, detective, Linda Dale wasn't your birth mother."

# 28

*I don't understand."* Regan felt the blood drain from her face, and she was distantly aware of Nate tightening his hold on her.

While she had learned to expect the unexpected during investigations, she felt as if she'd landed in one of those Halloween haunted houses, where goblins and ghouls kept leaping out at you as you wandered through twisting hallways in the dark.

"It's obvious that I'm the toddler the police discovered in the house after Mr. Boyce found her body." The image of Linda Dale lying in the front seat of that car would stay in her mind for a very long time, and she hated that it wasn't softened with happier memories. "I have the elephant."

"Gabriel." He closed his eyes and exhaled a long breath. When he opened them again, he smiled faintly. "It was from a little store in the Quarter. You dragged it around with you everywhere. It was the first—and last—child's toy I ever bought.

"When I first returned home from my weekend binge and heard Linda was dead, my first thought was that Toni had killed her. She might not have any love for me, but she definitely enjoyed being Mrs. Charles Melancon. Her people had made their fortune in the slave trade, which even down here was considered unseemly. Marrying into my family bought the respectability she craved."

"And made her queen of the parish, once your mother couldn't hold the crown," Regan guessed.

"Exactly." His look was one of respect. "That's a very good analysis, considering you haven't been in Blue Bayou very long."

"I'm a quick study." It helped in the murder business. "When did you realize your mother killed Linda?"

"Decades later. She and Caledonia kept their secret well; it was only when her mind began to go and she'd have these flashbacks to the past that I discovered the truth."

"That must have been rough," Nate said. "Realizing that your mother was responsible for the death of the woman you loved."

"Yes. But it wasn't as difficult as believing Linda had committed suicide because she thought I'd betrayed her."

"How do you know she wasn't my mother?" Regan asked.

"Because she told me, of course. We shared everything."

Regan's mind spun as she tried to think why on earth an unmarried woman with a career not conducive to motherhood would take on the responsibility of an infant. The answer, when it hit, was staggering.

"She was my aunt, wasn't she?"

He nodded. "Karen Hart was your birth mother. She'd married your father while they were both in law school, and they had plans to go into practice together. He drew a bad lottery number, so since it was obvious he was going to get drafted, he enlisted in the marines. While he was in Vietnam, he discovered he liked being military police and decided he'd go into law enforcement when he got out, which wasn't what he and Karen had agreed upon.

"Shortly after she'd filed for divorce, she discovered she was pregnant. She was going to get an abortion when Linda talked her into going through with the pregnancy and giving the baby—you—to her." This time his faint, reminiscent smile touched his eyes. "Karen wasn't the only tough-minded sister. In her own way, Linda could be very persuasive. And she knew what she wanted—which was you. She was also a natural-born mother. I don't think she was ever happier than during those years with you."

That was something, at least, Regan thought, trying to find some silver lining.

"I called Karen to tell her what had happened," he continued, answering a question that had been niggling at Regan: how Karen Hart could have known about her sister's death when Nate's father hadn't been able to locate her. "She came to get you. I asked if I could stay in touch, since we'd gotten close and I knew you'd miss the woman who'd been the only mother you knew. I never knew if Karen didn't believe the story of Linda's suicide and perhaps didn't trust me, but she said she didn't want to confuse you about who you were. She also warned me that if I ever tried to contact you, she'd do everything she could legally to ruin not just my reputation and my business, but my life as well. I believed her."

As did Regan.

"But the real reason I allowed her to have her way was because I thought perhaps she was right about it being better if you never knew about the circumstances surrounding the first two years of your life."

He heaved out a long breath, as if relieved to finally get the secret out in the open. "I realize this has all come as a shock," he said, proving himself the master of the understatement. "But I'm going to say the same thing to you I did to Karen. I'd like to stay in touch. If you think that might be possible."

"I don't know." Regan was not going to lie. "I have to sort things out in my own mind."

He nodded gravely. "I can understand that." He stood up. "I'd better go retrieve Mother and take her home."

There was no statute of limitation on murder, and while it might have been an accident, the woman lying upstairs had taken a life. Even knowing that, Regan didn't make a move to stop him as he left the room.

Regan was extremely grateful when Nate didn't talk on the drive back to the inn. She felt too drained for conversation.

A little more than an hour after Bethany Melancon's attack, they were back in the suite.

"Well," she said on a long sigh. "I was thinking earlier that I'd never forget this day. Charles Melancon and his mother certainly made sure of that."

"Helluva story," he said.

"No kidding."

"What are you going to do next?"

"I can't see that there is much to do. There's no point in trying to open an investigation. Mrs. Melancon's obviously not capable of presenting a defense, and Caledonia's an old woman who doesn't need to be hit with an accessory murder charge."

"Linda must've been a really special person," Nate offered. "Taking on her sister's baby that way."

"Yes." Regan sighed again, weary from the strange emotional roller coaster. "She must have been. I suppose I have to give my mother credit for having carried me, when she certainly didn't have to."

"I am certainly grateful for that." Regan seemed to be doing remarkably well with all this. Then again, his detective was a remarkable woman. "I feel guilty about having opened this can of worms," he said carefully, trying to find a way to say the words he'd never thought he'd want to say to any woman.

"I'm fine."

He doubted that was precisely the case yet, but she would be. He knew that.

"It occurred to me," he said with as much casualness as he could muster, "sometime between when you were being held hostage and tonight's party, that the thing to do would be to spend the rest of my life making it up to you."

He felt her stiffen in his arms. Not a good sign.

"Oh, Nate." She dragged a hand through her hair.

Damn. Definitely not a good sign.

"I love you, Regan."

"You can't."

That was certainly definitive. "Of course I can. I was going to tell you earlier this evening, but then things got a little crazy."

"That's certainly an understatement." She shook her head and looked out over the moon-gilded bayou. "There's a full moon."

"It's real pretty."

"It is. But everyone knows people behave differently during full moons. I've learned never to schedule weekends off then, because homicides always increase, and heaven knows, when I was a patrol cop—"

"What I'm feeling isn't related to any full moon." Wishing she seemed a little happier about his declaration, he took her distressed face between his hands. "I love you, Regan. And I want to marry you." There. He'd said the M word and survived. In fact, hearing it out loud sounded amazingly cool.

"It's too soon."

"Okay." He could live with that. "I understand that women like long engagements so they have enough time to plan a big blowout wedding, and while I'm really looking forward to our honeymoon—Jack recommends Kauai, by the way, since he and Dani had such a good time there—I'm open to anything your little heart desires—"

"Nate." It was her turn to interrupt him. "I'm not talking about needing time to make wedding plans. It's too soon to fall in love."

"Well, now, I would have thought the same thing myself, once upon a time. But since meeting you, I've decided that love sort of makes its own time. When it's right, it's right." He brushed his knuckles up her cheek. Threaded his fingers through her hair. "And this is right."

"It's lust."

"That, too," he allowed. "But I think that's a plus, don't you? That I know I'll still want you when we're old and gray, and we're watching our grandbabies—"

"Grandbabies?"

"I sorta like the idea. But if you don't want kids, Regan, I'm okay with that." The idea of a houseful of little girls who looked just like Regan and who'd dress up their Barbie dolls in police blues and have them arrest Ken was surprisingly appealing, but Nate figured he'd have plenty of time to convince her.

"It's too soon to be talking about this," she insisted. "We haven't known each other long enough to even be thinking about marriage. We both have our own lives, our own work—"

"They don't need contractors in California?"

"What?"

"Relocating for the woman you love is kind of a family tradition." He was winging it here, but surprisingly, he figured he could handle Los Angeles if he had to. For Regan. "My dad moved here from Chicago for *Maman*. Finn moved to California for Julia. And I'm willing to relocate if you want to keep detectin' in L.A."

She was staring at him as if he'd just suggested they become a modern-day Bonnie and Clyde and start robbing banks for a living.

"Besides," he said, realizing that he ought to let her know what other changes he was planning to make to his life, "Josh might get a kick out of surfing in the Pacific Ocean."

"You're going to adopt him?"

"Yeah, I thought I would. But I'm not askin' you to marry me to find him a mother, if that's what you're thinking."

"No." She waved away his suggestion. "Of course I wouldn't think that." Things were definitely on a downhill slide here. "I think you're making a good decision, where Josh is concerned."

"Thank you," he said dryly.

"Even if it is a bit impetuous."

"That's me. Mr. Impetuosity."

He figured it sounded better than Peter Pan, and while there were a lot of things he was willing to try to change for Regan, Nate knew it'd be useless to attempt to change his nature. Which had him belatedly realizing that he never should have expected her to fall into his arms and tearfully accept his out-of-the-blue proposal. She'd already told him she wasn't a go-with-the-flow type of person. The gods, who obviously had one helluva sense of humor, must be laughing their heads off at having fixed things so he'd fall in love with a female version of Finn Callahan.

"I don't even know who I am," she murmured, looking away again.

"Of course you do. You're the same person you've always been. Your family situation might have been a little screwed up, but if you want an old-fashioned kind of family, you've got one waiting for you." He held out his arms. "The Callahan clan might seem big to someone who grew up pretty much all alone, but we've always got room for one more.

"Look, *chère*." When he saw a sheen of moisture that hadn't been in her eyes the entire time she'd been learning the truth about her past, Nate was sorely tempted to pull her into his arms and kiss her doubts away. "I'm glad to give you some time to make up your mind, but there's something you need to know. When I found out you were in that courthouse with Mike, and realized I could lose you, it dawned on me that part of the reason I've spent my entire life dodging serious relationships is because I lost two of the people I loved most, and I didn't want to take the risk of getting emotionally hammered again.

"Now, I'm not going to beat myself up about that, since I've never—ever—met a woman I wanted to spend all that much time with, anyway. Until you. I love you, Regan. Enough to risk someday goin' through the pain of losing you, because the alternative is not having you in my life at all. And that flat-out isn't acceptable."

"Dammit, Callahan." A tear escaped to trail down her cheek. He brushed it away with the pad of his thumb. "When you said I was an Acorn kind of silverware woman, you said I was like your mother. But that's wishful thinking. To hear Dani tell it, she was a cross between Donna Reed and Mother Teresa. I'm nothing like either one of them."

"I think you may be a bit off the mark about that, but I don't want Donna Reed or Mother Teresa. I want you. What you have in common with *Maman* is that you're willing to take risks, that you're brave enough to trust your instincts, even when they might go against the norm. I can't imagine it was easy for her to go to college, back in a time when folks around here tended to think people who went to college were lazy and just didn't want to work, since an education wasn't going to help you on the farm or in the sugar refinery. Or help you raise up your babies, which is pretty much what women were expected to do.

"But she did go to college. Not only that, she broke family tradition and ventured north across the Mason-Dixon line. Then to top it all off, she up and married herself a Yankee, which certainly set tongues a-buzzin'. But you know what?"

"What?"

"She didn't care. Because she trusted herself. And she trusted my dad. And never, not once, tried to change him."

"That's just as well. Since it's impossible to really change a person."

"True. Which is another reason why I know we belong together. You've never once mentioned changin' me."

"Why would I?"

"I have no idea. Bein' how I'm pretty damn close to perfect." He grinned to lighten the mood a bit. "But every woman I've ever met starts gettin' the urge to change me."

"Which isn't going to happen." She'd never met a man more comfortable in his own skin. "And I'd never want to change you."

"See? We're perfect for each other. You're smart, and strong, and brave, and honest—"

"Now you're making me sound like a Boy Scout."

"You interrupted me before I got to the good parts." He laced his fingers through her hair, pushing it back from her face. "You're also gorgeous, sexy as all get-out, and I can't get within twenty feet of you without wanting to do this."

Partly because he couldn't resist those tempting, sweet lips another moment, partly because he wanted to leave her with something to remember, Nate bent his head and gave her a long, deep kiss that left them both breathless.

"I don't supposed you'd be willing to run off and marry me right now?"

"Of course not."

He hadn't thought so, but it'd been worth a shot. "Okay. See you around, sugar." If he didn't leave now, he never would, and Nate knew it'd be a huge mistake to risk her someday feeling that he'd pressured her into spending the next sixty years with him. "Give me a call when you make a decision."

Ignoring the shock on her lovely face was the second hardest thing he'd ever done. Getting up and walking out of the suite was the hardest.

"Nate?"

He paused in the doorway. Closed his eyes. Braced himself. Then slowly turned around. "Change your mind already?" he asked pleasantly.

"I want to donate the proceeds from the petroleum stock to charity. I thought you might be able to suggest some local ones."

Stifling a sigh, Nate reminded himself that he shouldn't have expected an instantaneous one-hundred-and-eighty-degree turnaround. "I'll send you a list. In L.A."

"Thank you." She did not, he noted, reject the notion of returning to California.

"*C'est rien*. Speaking as the mayor, I can assure you that the town'll be real grateful."

He left without looking back. And reluctantly prepared himself for a long, lonely wait.

Nothing was the same. Her job, which she'd already begun to find frustrating, grew more so every day. There was nothing wrong with her new partner, who'd transferred in from Narcotics, but he wasn't Van.

She'd always liked California, but the view of the swimming pool from her apartment window couldn't live up to herons nesting on the bayou, and the constant sun, which was such a part of the Los Angeles lifestyle, now seemed too predictable.

She'd received a letter from Charles Melancon, and on impulse called him back. She wasn't certain that she'd ever think of him as a surrogate father, but she thought they might be able to become friends one day.

Other than a polite official letter written on Office of the Mayor stationery, thanking her for her generous contribution to various local charities, she hadn't heard from Nate. She might have thought he'd written her off and moved on had she not received a pager message from Dani a week after her return to L.A., suggesting she might want to call Nate.

The cop in her instantly feared for the worst, and she immediately called, only to get his answering machine.

*"Hi. Josh and I are at baseball practice. If you're calling about a booth at the Cajun Days festival, call Jewel Breaux at 504-555-1112, and she'll be glad to take your reservation. If you're calling about the upcoming parish council meeting, it's Monday night at seven-thirty. Give or take a few minutes. We'll be voting on what color to repaint the bleachers at the Buccaneer baseball park. If you want some construction work done, leave a message and I'll get back to you as soon as possible. And if this is Regan calling . . . I still love you,* chère."

Regan's heart was thrumming a thousand miles an hour with anticipation as the pirogue wove through mist-draped black waters.

"I really appreciate this," she told Jack. It was a month since Mardi Gras. After having discovered a recent storm had temporarily turned the road to Nate's house back to water, she'd been afraid she wouldn't be able to pull off her surprise.

Jack's grin flashed white in the moon-spangled darkness. "It's easy enough for someone who's lived their entire life in this bayou to get lost at night. If you got lost, it could take the search-and-rescue squad until morning to find you. Which would give you the chance to change your mind 'bout marrying my little brother."

"I'm not going to change my mind."

"I'm real pleased to here that, *chère*. Since Nate isn't, either."

"I know." She'd been calling him every day, choosing times she guessed he'd be working. While the answering machine message changed every day, the closing line had remained the same. The idea still amazed her—delighted her. She finally realized that he'd been right. She'd been falling in love with him from the beginning—if not when he'd shown up at the station, at least from that night they'd rescued Josh together.

Time didn't really matter at all. Except for the fact she'd already wasted thirty long days and nights they could have been together. It was past time to put her heart before her head.

"It's also very nice of you and Dani to take Josh for the weekend."

"The three of you have a real good start on a nice little family." The house came into view as they came around a corner. Jack cut the electric engine and drifted toward the dock. "But sometimes a man and woman just gotta have themselves some privacy."

A welcoming yellow light shone from the windows. For the first time in her life, Regan understood the concept of coming home.

"I don't 'magine you've ever been to a Cajun wedding?" Jack asked as he tied up the boat.

"No, I haven't." The idea of any wedding was still more terrifying than facing down an urban riot. "I was thinking of something quiet. Maybe just for family and a few close friends."

His rich, bold laugh startled a trio of herons nesting in the reeds. They took to the night sky, wings silhouetted against the full white moon. "There's no such thing as a quiet Cajun wedding. The womenfolk have been planning the festivities for weeks."

"They were that sure I'd cave in?"

"We were all that sure the two of you belonged together." He retrieved her spruce green canvas carry-on from the bottom of the pirogue. "You sure you don't need me to carry that for you?"

"It's not that heavy." She smiled up at him. "Thank you. For everything."

"It is truly my pleasure." He bent his head and brushed a kiss against her cheek. "Welcome to the Callahan family, *chère*."

She waited until he'd climbed back into the boat and disappeared around the corner. She was definitely on her own now. There'd be no turning back.

She took the cell phone from her purse and dialed the number she knew by heart.

"Hi," she said when Nate's familiar deep voice answered on the first ring. "I'm calling about the sheriff's job. If it's still open, I've just arrived in town—well, actually, I'm here at the dock—and I'd like to schedule a personal interview."

The door flew open. Regan thought her heart was going to sprout wings and fly when she saw Nate standing there, illuminated in the moonlight.

"I'm also looking for a place to live," she continued into the phone, "so I'd appreciate any suggestions Blue Bayou's mayor and best contractor might have."

He was coming toward her on long, purposeful strides as she walked toward him. "Of course, since I've given away all my inheritance and the parish budget can't afford to pay me nearly what I was making back in L.A., I'm willing to take a signing bonus. I was thinking along the lines of season tickets to the Buccaneers' home games—

I hear the team has a new sophomore player this year who's a phenom."

They were only a few feet apart.

"This is Regan calling."

She flipped the phone closed and wondered how on earth she could she have stayed away from this man for so long. A wealth of love was gleaming in his eyes as she went up on her toes, twined her arms around his neck, and lifted her lips to his.

"And I'll always love you."

Two great books—
one great price!

Each book features two classics
by your favorite authors together
in one collectible volume!

*Coast Road • Three Wishes*
Barbara Delinsky

*The Taming • The Conquest*
Jude Deveraux

*Twin of Ice • Twin of Fire*
Jude Deveraux

*Velvet Song • Velvet Angel*
Jude Deveraux

*Angel Creek • A Lady of the West*
Linda Howard

*Shades of Twilight • Son of the Morning*
Linda Howard

*Guardian Angel • The Gift*
Julie Garwood

*Castles • The Lion's Lady*
Julie Garwood

*Honey Moon • Hot Shot*
Susan Elizabeth Phillips

*Scandalous • Irresistible*
Karen Robards

*Homeplace • Far Harbor*
JoAnn Ross

*The Callahan Brothers Trilogy*
JoAnn Ross

sit **www.simonsays.com**

13361